MIND OUT OF TIME

Cassidy immediately made a priority judgment. As she sped toward the two men, her mouth dry with fear, she realized that Shad wasn't just trying to pull the loathsome creature off Kevin. In one sinewy hand, Shad clutched the blunt haft of a skinning knife, its long blade buried to the hilt in the all-too-substantial tissue of the monster's coiled body.

Cassidy flung herself to her knees on the ground beside Kevin, her own knife poised to plunge. She reached out, both to brace herself and to secure the creature's winding thickness before she stabbed it. But the instant her fingers closed around the tough, gleaming skin—*the world simply stopped.*

Too startled to realize what had happened, Cassidy thought she'd had some kind of seizure or blackout. But she was still conscious. At the periphery of her vision, she could still see Shad, frozen in time with his knife embedded in the creature's flesh. She was alive and she could see; she could even feel the odd, cool texture of the monster's smooth, leathery skin. She just couldn't move. *Nothing moved.*

by Karen Ripley
Published by Ballantine Books:

PRISONER OF DREAMS
THE TENTH CLASS

The Slow World
Book One: THE PERSISTENCE OF MEMORY
Book Two: THE WARDEN OF HORSES
Book Three: THE ALCHEMIST OF TIME

THE ALCHEMIST OF TIME

Book Three of *The Slow World*

Karen Ripley

A Del Rey® Book
BALLANTINE BOOKS • NEW YORK

A Del Rey® Book
Published by Ballantine Books

Library of Congress Catalog Card Number: 94-94413

ISBN 0-345-38118-1

Manufactured in the United States of America

First Edition: December 1994

10 9 8 7 6 5 4 3 2 1

To my friends—
Who make this not only possible, but worth it.

PART ONE ◀▉▉▉

Chapter 1 ◀▥

"Do you feel better—or do you think you're going to puke again?"

Kevin's arm around her waist and the grip of his hand around her upper arm were the only things keeping Cassidy from summarily toppling over the side of the boat and into the darkness of the heaving sea. Considering the fathomless depths of her nausea, and the utter misery and indignity of her propulsive and repeated vomiting, she wasn't entirely certain that it wouldn't have been an attractive solution to her spectacular seasickness. But Kevin had been so kind and sympathetic toward her that she didn't want to rebuke the young man.

Cassidy spat down into the churning crest of an exuberant wave as it broadsided the hull, its force causing the deck beneath her feet to lurch sharply. "I don't think so," she said, as Kevin's arm tightened around her.

The blond boy's long hair whipped around his head in wet, darkened strings, lashing the side of Cassidy's face. He blinked into the driving rain. "You don't think you're feeling any better?" he asked. "Or you don't think you're going to puke again?"

"Either one," Cassidy muttered. But she allowed Kevin to pull her back from the rail, and to hold onto her until she could get a good grip on one of the wooden struts along the boat's side.

Lightning exploded across the boiling night sky, turning the sheeting rain into streamers of silver and the turbulent surface of the sea into a series of glistening furrows. Not more than six feet away on the slippery deck another pair of people had been playing out a nearly identical scenario. But in that instance the aid and comfort had been offered by Valerie, the captain of the Troopers, and helplessly accepted by an extraordinarily seasick warden of Horses. Glancing sideways through the dimness and the pounding rain at their two drenched and leather-clad companions, Cassidy felt a certain perverse sense of satisfaction that the one person she held responsible for both her greatest advances and her greatest disappointments since she'd first found herself in that bizarre world was as profoundly miserable as she was, riding out the furious storm on the great Gray Sea.

From his position at the helm, Webb, the owner and pilot of the vessel, shouted something unintelligible at them. Despite the fury of the storm, Cassidy could have sworn the bastard was enjoying himself! Even though she didn't understand what he had called out, she automatically dropped down onto her knees on the slick deck, just as the creaking boom of the boat's mainsail swung over them, slicing through the downpour where only seconds earlier her head would have been. Beside her, Kevin's fingers locked onto the wet leather of Cassidy's filthy tunic to prevent her from sliding sideways any farther, as the boat plowed down into another black trough of water.

Next to them on the slippery planking, the tall female Trooper anchored her warden in much the same fashion. The young man accepted the necessary assistance with characteristic good grace, throwing Valerie a wry nod of thanks before turning to look across at Cassidy and Kevin. Not even the ravages of his nausea or the chill drenching of the cold rain could obliterate the classic clarity of the familiar planes of his face, or completely extinguish the spark of self-deprecating humor that lurked behind those chocolate-brown eyes.

"Just who was it," the warden said above the lashing roar of the wind, "who said it would be a good idea to take a little sea cruise?"

The automatic reflex to respond with some tart retort was at least partially tempered by Cassidy's continuing sense of guilt. None of those people, she realized as she braced herself on hands and knees on the wet and pitching deck, had asked for the dangerous turn of fate that had been dealt them. *Not that I asked for it, either,* she reminded herself with some asperity, *but at least they all think they belong here in this world.*

From his post at the helm, the seaman, Webb, called out again. "Coming 'round!" he shouted; Cassidy swore it was almost gleefully.

Already down on the deck's planking, Cassidy only glanced up as the swift shadow of the swinging boom again passed over their heads. She glared toward the stern of the boat, where the silhouette of Webb's drenched body was thrown into sharp relief by another flash of lightning. The bastard *was* enjoying himself, even though his vessel was plunging and wallowing like a cow caught in a bog hole and every fierce gust of wind and pounding hammer of wave threatened to tear the pilot loose from his position at the wheel. The idiot had probably never been seasick a day in his life.

Cassidy, on the other hand, had never before had the chance to find out just how susceptible she was. Where she had grown up and lived back in the Slow World—*the real world*—she had been hundreds of miles from the nearest ocean. Since coming to that world she hadn't been on water any rougher than the rapids of the Long River, the route she had so recently taken on her raft trip to the warden's Iron City. And already that experience almost seemed as if it had happened to someone else.

Distracted by the recollection, it took Cassidy a moment to re-alize that Kevin had spoken. Fortunately, he had been speaking to the warden, so she didn't have to scramble to make an appropriate response. Still holding on to the back of Cassidy's tunic, the pale-haired young man had turned to face the warden, who was only a few feet away across the soaking deck. And whatever Kevin had said, the warden reacted by nodding ruefully as he reached out and clapped Kevin on the arm.

"Not a bad idea," the warden said. "It seems that not only don't I have the stomach for the sea, I don't exactly have sea legs, ei-ther!"

Cassidy surmised that Kevin had proposed they all remain down on the planks, rather than trying to stand up again. She had no problems with that idea, although from the grimace on Valerie's face it appeared that the captain resented having to yield to anything, even the power of the storm-whipped sea. The woman kept one hand clamped around her warden's wrist, much as Kevin automatically kept Cassidy secured. But there was a dif-ference in the way the curly-haired Trooper held her charge. Kevin helped Cassidy because he was her friend and because he was able to; Valerie's grip on the warden was a fiercely proprie-tary mixture of duty and devotion.

A cold sluice of water from a high swell swept over the boat's rail, briefly inundating them all. The chill wash jolted Cassidy's mind away from the train of thought that it was inevitably pursu-ing, not particularly to her regret. Valerie's possessiveness toward the young man at her side had reminded Cassidy of the woman's brisk efficiency among her Troopers, of her matter-of-fact physi-cal courage, and then of her oddly arch and bitter contempt for

Click, the leader of the local Tinkers. And Cassidy did not want to be reminded of Click or of anything to do with him.

In the next shattering explosion of lightning, Cassidy could see that Webb was regarding his hapless passengers with outright amusement. The tough and lanky seaman shouted, "You could always go below, you know!" As the rain streamed across his face, he showed his teeth in a grin. "Hell of a night to be on deck!"

Hell of a night for anything, Cassidy thought; but she didn't need to say as much. Somehow the thought of being belowdeck with the way the boat was being pitched and tossed about seemed even less appealing than continuing to cling topside in the rain. She was relieved when the warden echoed that sentiment.

"Thank you for the courtesy, seaman," the warden said, shaking back the dripping strands of hair from his eyes, "but for the sake of your boat, I'd prefer to stay topside until either this storm or my stomach settles."

Webb laughed appreciatively, the muscles in his arms cording as he wrestled with another wave for the control of his helm. "Suit yourselves, warden," he replied. "But I feel it's only fair to point out that in either case you're most likely in for a long—"

The pilot's words were bitten off as the boat suddenly dropped into a deep trough of water. To her distinct unease, Cassidy realized that had she still been trying to stand up on the deck, the precipitous shift in the vessel would have sent her right over the rail and into the sea. She looked out through the rain and spray beating against her face, to see a solid dark wall of water rising alongside the boat, the broad side of the tremendous wave that had just dumped them into its trough.

Cassidy hadn't even been aware of how Kevin's grip on her leather tunic had tightened until she realized that the young man was actually pulling her backward a few inches across the slippery deck, away from the rail. In the dim and flashing light of the boat's wildly swinging lanterns, she could see that Kevin's mismatched eyes were wide with fear and apprehension, and for the first time since they'd fled from the burning city, Cassidy was forced to consider just why he had come with them. She had conveniently overlooked the fact that although Kevin was doggedly loyal, at least as much to the warden as to herself, he was not particularly given to bravado. By her role in the events that had necessitated the warden's flight from the Iron City, Cassidy had unwittingly but inexorably condemned Kevin to the same fate.

Cassidy forced the corners of her mouth to turn up in a small smile as she quipped, "You're a good swimmer, right?"

But the pale-haired boy's face remained grimly set as the next big wave lifted the deck beneath them. "I've never seen a storm like this," he murmured.

Cassidy threw a look over her shoulder toward the stern of the boat, where Webb was braced at his helm. She immediately noted that the seaman no longer looked particularly amused. He didn't look frightened, or even worried; but it seemed to Cassidy an ominous portent that the rugged pilot didn't seem to be enjoying himself anymore.

As the boat dropped into the trench of another trough between the massive waves, the drenched planks beneath Cassidy's hands and knees were abruptly jolted. If they hadn't been out in the middle of an ocean, she would have sworn that the keel of the boat had just lightly struck bottom. But as her eyes swept the dark fluid wall of the next wave, which rose up alongside the rail before her, Cassidy realized that would have been impossible. Not only were they well out into the Gray Sea, they were being borne still farther out, away from the shore and the mouth of the Long River. The driving force of the galelike storm was relentlessly forcing them out to sea, and Webb had been complying with that impulsion, keeping the prow of his vessel turned so that she was swept along with the powerful gusts of wind.

He knows where to take you, Click had said of the pilot in those last moments before Cassidy and the Tinker had parted in the Iron City. Cassidy did not doubt the truth of that, but she also was fully aware that the ferocity of the storm was going to make reaching their original heading along the southern coast secondary to just staying afloat long enough to outrun the heavy seas. Webb may have known where to take them, but actually getting them there was going to be another matter. And as the oncoming swell of the next giant wave propelled the boat upward again, Cassidy conceded that for the moment she was more than willing to settle for just surviving her first ocean voyage.

Kevin's actions in tugging her back from the rail had brought both Cassidy and the odd-eyed boy closer to Valerie and the Warden, all of them still sprawled on the slick deck. Cassidy saw that the curly-haired Trooper still kept a firm grip around one of the warden's wrists, and that with the other hand she kept the pair of them anchored by grasping one of the rail's uprights. Her short dark hair was crazed by the wind and water into a frenzied mop of tangled tendrils, but there was nothing equivocal in the stubborn set of that finely chiseled face. The captain was glaring out balefully over the rail at the rain-lashed ocean, as if she were

holding all of nature personally responsible for the danger and inconvenience of their unruly sea journey. The posture and the attitude that it implied were both so characteristic for the tall proud
woman that Cassidy nearly smiled. But then the ocean dropped
the boat back into another trough, and Cassidy lost even the
slightest inclination to smile at anything.

That time, as the boat suddenly descended into the waiting
trench of water, the concussion on her hull was firmer, and unde-
niable. It wasn't like hitting a reef; or at least not what Cassidy,
with her admittedly meager nautical experience, assumed that hitting a reef would feel like. The object that they struck wasn't anything that hard, although it was firm enough to send a sharp jolt
through the hull's timbers to the planking beneath their crouched
bodies. It felt more like—

Oh, God, no!

The boat's hull impacted again with the submerged object—or
rather, the submerged object impacted again with the hull; for in
a chilling rush of unwanted insight, Cassidy realized that was
more precisely what was occurring in the water beneath them.
The boat had not yet even begun to lift up out of the trough between the two waves when the second hard thump shook the deck
planks. Then the concussion was repeated several more times in
rapid succession; a lighter, more tentative, almost playful sort of
bumping.

It was the warden with whom Cassidy almost involuntarily
locked gazes then, for in those wide-set brown eyes she could see
the same unwilling knowledge that she also possessed. And for a
few rueful seconds, she almost wished for the warden that same
blissful state of unawareness which the young man exhibited in
her own world, the real world, where she knew him as Andy
Greene. Andy wouldn't have had to deal with all of the disasters
that Cassidy seemed to have visited upon the warden and his parallel world: riots, rebellion, and the seemingly endless threat of
the hideous creatures that followed her. But on his wet, filthy, and
yet indelibly handsome face, Cassidy saw none of the recrimina-
tion that she was so ready to heap upon herself. In the brief look
that the warden exchanged with her, she found only what she had
come to expect: courage, determination, and honest concern.

"It's them, isn't it," Kevin whispered from beside Cassidy.
"The monsters . . ."

Kevin had not phrased it as a question; he needed no confirma-
tion. Oddly enough, Cassidy understood just what it was that the
young Finder did require. She just wasn't sure if she was capable

of providing it for him. She was a pretty good liar, especially after her experiences in that world; but it was a situation where a lie would have sufficed only if Kevin had been willing to accept it. Not to her surprise, it was the warden who innately understood the response the situation called for and who had the capacity to supply it.

With his free hand, the arm not being held in Valerie's grasp, the warden reached out across the few feet that separated him from Kevin and gently gripped the younger man by the forearm. "They haven't hurt us yet, Kev," he pointed out. "If they'd wanted to kill us, they could have done that when we were still in the water."

Pretty much the same thought had occurred to Cassidy more than once since the four of them had been driven from the city docks, forced to jump with their horses into the harbor's roiling waters. She wasn't sure if the water monsters' behavior in that regard was reassuring or just baffling; but, as the warden had noted, so far that particular form of the nightmarish creatures they called monsters had never directly threatened Cassidy's life. That didn't necessarily mean that the massive creatures were harmless, however, but it hardly seemed timely or productive to point that out to Kevin then.

At the warden's touch as much as at his words, the long-haired boy relaxed fractionally. There was more than just loyalty on that dripping face; there was also trust.

Then another huge wave lifted them, tilting the slippery deck like some sort of bizarre carnival ride. Cassidy felt herself sliding into Kevin as the boat rode out the furious surge of water. Suddenly the vessel was dipping again, dropping down into the trough between the waves. And again something large and powerful that had been waiting submerged beneath the surface of the sea thumped forcefully against the hull.

The guttering light from the boat's swaying lanterns provided poor illumination, and the most intense of the storm's lightning had already passed over them. But Cassidy didn't need to get a good look at Webb to be able to interpret the seaman's mood; the tone of his voice alone did that quite nicely.

"I'll be damned!" the pilot exclaimed, in his voice a perfect mixture of irritation and bafflement. "What the hell *is* that?"

Even as Webb spoke, the hull reverberated again with another sound thump. That time the whole boat actually lifted, buoyed up from beneath for a few moments by a strong, surging push. The vessel met the next wave halfway, caught it broadside, and jerked upwards with teeth-snapping abruptness. Cassidy felt as if the wet planks beneath her knees were going to rise up and toss her right over the rail, and she was grateful for the dogged tug on her soaked tunic as Kevin hauled her backward again.

Even as they rode out the tossing rock of the wave's crest, Cassidy exchanged another look with the warden. There was no way to avoid telling the seaman exactly what they were dealing with; in all probability the creatures would put in a personal appearance anyway, and she'd far rather have him hear about them before he actually had to see them for himself. Valerie's mouth was set in a disapproving crimp, but Cassidy ignored the captain and addressed Webb directly.

"How strong is this boat?" she called out to the man at the helm.

But before Webb could respond, the vessel was dropping again, diving like a loon into the next trench of water as another solid blow shook her hull. The pilot slung his head sideways, flinging off the wet strings of hair that had escaped from beneath his saturated woolen cap. His fingers were locked around the polished wood of the wheel. "Damn!" he exclaimed, as a second thump jolted them, although to Cassidy he still sounded more mystified than alarmed. "Why, how strong does she need to be?" he shouted back then in reply.

"There are creatures in the water," the warden said, loudly enough to be heard over the sounds of the storm and the waves, and yet with an odd calm. "Large creatures," he added, somewhat superfluously.

To Cassidy's surprise, Webb took in that statement with seeming equanimity. His next comment surprised her even more. "The things that tore up the piers," he surmised, grunting as another blow shook his boat.

"You knew about them?" Cassidy couldn't keep from asking.

Once again she did not need to be able to see the seaman's face clearly to judge what expression she would have found there; Webb's mildly sardonic tone told it all. "With what's been going on in the city, I could make a good guess," he pointed out. "What the hell do these things look like? And why are they attacking my boat?"

Since Cassidy was, by default, the resident expert on monsters of all sorts, it was left to her to try to explain. "I'm not sure what they look like," she temporized. "I've never seen one out of the water." *Yet!* she added grimly to herself. "But from what I've seen of them, they're like great big—"

She had to break off abruptly as the boat shot upward again, propelled by both the next wave and the capricious impulsion of one or more of the water creatures. She wondered anew how the hell Webb could stay standing at the helm; it was all she could do to just stay on deck, and she was practically lying flat out on the planks.

Sputtering as a wind-driven sluice of rain buffeted her face, Cassidy tried to continue with her explanation. "They drove us into the harbor and followed us in the water when we were on our horses. The one we saw then had a head the size—"

Two things made Cassidy break off again. One was the boat abruptly topping the crest of the wave and beginning another descent, a plunging movement that caused her to slide sideways on the deck again, into Kevin. She ended up with one elbow wedged between the young man's thighs, but she was too glad for the temporary anchor even to consider the social dynamics of the position. The second thing that made her break off was that she had been about to say that the creature had a head the size of a Buick. While she was grappling for a more useful comparison, however, further description became unnecessary.

As the boat bottomed out in the wave trough, the hull shuddered with another submerged thrust. In the frenetic light of the crazily swinging lanterns, Cassidy watched as the intimidating wall of dark water from another wave rose alongside the rail. Then suddenly, smoothly, something else was just *there*, interposed between the frothing climb of the wave and the side of the vessel. A massive head, skin gleaming as the sea water streamed from it, arced up high over the rail, momentarily blocking the stormy night sky above them.

Kevin made a whimpering sound, so softly that only her immediate proximity made it audible to Cassidy. From its underside, the water monster's long neck and head bore an unsettling resemblance to a horse's neck and head seen from the same perspective, a recognition that for a few moments so totally occupied Cassidy that she failed to notice Webb had finally moved from his post at the helm. If Valerie hadn't shouted, Cassidy might not have realized what the pilot intended to do until it had been too late to stop him.

"No, wait!" the captain commanded.

As the boat shot upward on the breast of another wave, the huge dark curve of the monster's neck rose with it. Cassidy had to clutch at Kevin with both hands to keep from slipping as she spun around to locate the cause for Valerie's call. How Webb had managed to make his way so swiftly from the helm to the small cannon mounted at the boat's prow was beyond Cassidy; how the hell he had made it that far at all across the slick and pitching deck was beyond her. But the pilot was crouched against the cannon's mount, pivoting the weapon's barrel around to take aim at the monster's looming and sinuous form.

"No!" Cassidy echoed, lunging free of Kevin's protective grip. She shot across the slippery planks like a stone skating across ice. It was only blind luck that her scrabbling fingers managed to snag hold of the sopping-wet leg of the seaman's cotton trousers, and only sheer desperation that made it possible for her to cling there. As the momentum of her sliding body impelled her past Webb, her grip on his leg twisted the seaman sideways. The roar of the boat's small cannon sounded like a crack of thunder in Cassidy's ears.

"No!" Cassidy gasped, pulling so hard at his pants that she felt the fabric begin to tear between her fingers. "No—don't shoot at it!"

Grunting something loud but unintelligible, Webb swayed above her, nearly falling to his knees atop Cassidy. She felt her fingernails biting into the hard flesh of his calf, but she hung on tenaciously. And when she was finally able to turn her face up into the driving rain, she was relieved to find that the great form of the water monster's giant head and arched neck were gone.

Webb was shaking his leg, not with enough purpose to dislodge Cassidy deliberately, but with enough vigor to express graphically his feelings about her highhanded maneuver. "You made me miss!" he growled at her. "Damn! That thing could have crushed this boat like an eggshell!"

Still panting for breath, Cassidy was more stunned by just how close she had come to being washed overboard than she was by any potential threat from the monster. "No" was all she could repeat breathlessly, doggedly shaking her dripping head.

Anchoring himself with one arm to the cannon's support brackets, the pilot bent and used his other hand to scoop Cassidy up onto her knees beside him on the deck. She crouched there, unabashedly clinging to the gutsy seaman's legs. "What the hell do you mean, *no*?" Webb persisted, sounding more puzzled than angry.

The boat had already completed another cycle of drop and climb, into a trough and then up onto the crest of another wave, all without even the slightest concussion against her hull. Cassidy didn't understand why the creatures had fled suddenly, but she was not surprised by it. Remembering what Click had told her earlier in that endless night, when he had saved her from the repulsive carrion-eating monsters along the road into the city, she tried to explain.

"Click told me that if you shoot them, they explode," she told Webb. In all truth, Cassidy had no idea if that proscription applied only to the carrion eaters, or if it was true of all of the monsters, and she really didn't care. There was another reason, one she could not have explained and didn't want to examine further, why she hadn't wanted Webb to shoot at the water monster.

Webb took in her explanation with a patently skeptical grunt; but Cassidy didn't have the sense that the canny seaman was angry with her, any more than she had the sense that they had ever really been in any danger from the huge creatures. "That son of a bitch," Webb said without malice, obviously referring to Click, "has a hell of a lot of explaining to do, in my opinion!"

Casually riding out another precipitous rise on an oncoming wave, Webb used the brief lull when they dropped into its trench to gesture to the warden, Valerie, and Kevin. "Come on then, the lot of you," he said with a quick show of his teeth. "Seasick or not, I want you all belowdecks." He tugged Cassidy to her feet, holding her like a sack of wet sand as she helplessly staggered against him. "We've got a good ways to go yet before we'll ride out this bastard storm, and anyone who takes a notion to go over the side is likely going to have to stay there."

As he yanked open the cabin's low hatch for them, he gave Cassidy one last quick grin, the rain streaming across the tough and tanned skin of his face. "Don't worry," he promised her with mock gravity. "I'll let you know if any of your little pets show up again!"

Then, as the four of them stumbled down into the dim and smoky warmth of the boat's tiny cabin, the hatch dropped shut behind them with a sodden thump.

Chapter 2 ◄▥

She was riding on her horse, the gray mare's big body rocking along between her knees, the long strands of iron-colored mane whipping and curling against her bare forearms. In an oddly comforting sort of nonspecificity, she was not riding to or from anywhere; she was just riding. And she was neither Cassidy nor Cathy Delaney. She just was.

Cassidy awoke with a start, vaguely surprised to have been so rudely jerked out of sleep from what had been a singularly harmless set of imagery. And as she awakened, she was surprised afresh to be momentarily unable to recognize just where she was. It was murkily dark, and she was scrunched up uncomfortably on her side on some firm flat surface. Her clammy clothing clung to her like a second skin.

Lifting her head, Cassidy winced at the stiffness in her neck. Inches from her face, someone murmured softly in sleep, and then her mind immediately filled in the gaps. She was on a narrow ledgelike shelf that ran the length of the boat's small cabin, covering some kind of storage compartments. The surface apparently doubled as bunk space, but if the positions into which they'd all been forced were any indication, it obviously had never been intended to accommodate four people at the same time. Kevin was lying beside her, curled around the warden's legs. Beyond the interlocked forms of the two young men, Valerie slumped half sitting against the wall, her arms folded across her chest. Even in her sleep the captain appeared to keep a protective position over her leader.

Awkwardly unfolding her limbs, Cassidy carefully slid off the edge of their rude and narrow communal bed. Her legs and back ached stupendously, and she could feel anew every physical indignity to which her battered body had been subjected over the past

14

twenty-four hours. The little cabin was warm enough, but it reeked of damp leather, damp hair, and damp bodies. She shuffled cautiously forward in the near darkness, trying to remember where the hatch was located, and if there was anything free-standing in the small space over which she might stumble. The boat was still rocking, but it was rolling gently then, the slow and familiar rhythm of her dream.

Finding the outline of the hatch, Cassidy fumbled with its catches. Fortunately it pushed outward, so that when she tripped over the high sill and fell through the opening, at least she was still able to get past. Outside on the deck, the fresh salty air and the pinkish glow of dawn hit her with equal alacrity. Blinking her gritty eyes, she scanned an uninterrupted dome of sky that stretched to 360 degrees of horizon, hung with the tatters of old storm clouds and rosy with the promise of a clear day.

"You the only survivor?"

The ironic comment jerked Cassidy back from her muzzy contemplation of the early-morning sky. Across the short expanse of shadowy deck, Webb still stood at the helm of his vessel; but he was no longer clinging there or wrestling with the wheel. All things considered, Cassidy realized that he looked far less the worse for wear than any of the rest of them.

"Everyone else is still asleep," she said, stepping with exaggerated care toward him across the fairly steady deck. As weary as she felt, Cassidy remembered that Kevin, Valerie, and the warden all had had even less sleep recently than she had had. At least she had been able to doze in the warden's front room, while she waited for him and the Troopers to return to his compound the night before. And when she thought of everything that had happened to them in the last twenty-four hours, it seemed incredible that any of them had survived, even before the fierce storm that had swept them out to sea.

Webb was beckoning to Cassidy, holding out something to her. As she crossed the short distance remaining between them, Cassidy could see that it was a Tinker-made canvas water bottle. The pilot offered it to her with a wordless nod of encouragement. After clumsily uncapping it, she tilted back her head and drank deeply.

Not for the first time, Cassidy thought it was one of the supreme ironies of her situation that this world was a place without intoxicants. *This would be a great morning for a stiff shot of Irish whiskey!* she observed to herself, as the cold water sluiced down her dry and scratchy throat.

When she lowered the bottle again, she saw that Webb was proffering something else with equal casualness. "You look like shit," the seaman said with an almost cheerful candor, as Cassidy took the torn-off chunk of soft bread from his hand.

Eyeing him as she bit into the bread, Cassidy was forced to admit that Webb looked relatively unscathed by his grueling duel with the storm and the water monsters. At that proximity and in the gathering light, she could see that he was even a rather attractive man. He had discarded the dark woolen cap that he had worn pulled down over his head the night before, and his shoulder-length hair was a sun-streaked shade of brown, bleached nearly to blond at its tips. That ready grin sat comfortably on his angular face, abetted by a pair of light-brown eyes, which were both good-natured and shrewd in their frank scrutiny. The loosely-fitted seaman's clothing he wore had already dried in the brisk breeze, unlike Cassidy's own soggy Trooper's leathers, and beneath it his body was trim and well muscled. He was obviously a man used to hard work, and not easily intimidated. Cassidy found herself relieved and grateful that Webb was the man to whom Click had entrusted them.

Cassidy realized that she had been wolfing down the bread; but when she glanced up in embarrassment at Webb's face, the pilot just showed his teeth in another hearty grin. "Long time between meals, I take it," he said, reaching down to the small parcel at his feet to offer her more bread. "Sorry that I don't have more variety," he added, "but this wasn't supposed to be a long cruise."

Gazing out over the rail to where the rising sun was beginning to gild the long rolling swells in tints of pink and gold, Cassidy tried to chew more slowly. As the aching cavern in her belly began to fill, her mind was already searching for the implications of what had happened to them, and to plumb automatically those implications for further useful knowledge. Even the abrupt return of her memory of her own world had not dulled that survival reflex; she still viewed everything and everyone as a potential source of whatever crucial information it would take to enable her finally to return home. And Webb seemed like a smart and friendly sort, the type of man who might know things. What Cassidy had failed to reckon with was that the seaman might have some questions of his own.

"So tell me about these monsters of yours," Webb said, the question just as casual as the small adjustments he kept making to the set of his tiller.

Cassidy's head snapped around so quickly that she almost

choked on the piece of bread she was just swallowing. Webb actually started to reach forward, as if to pound her helpfully on the back, before she was able to catch her breath and sputter out, "The monsters?"

"Yeah," he said, "the big things in the water." One of his brows arched quizzically at the patently startled expression on Cassidy's face. His broad shoulders traced a slight shrug. "You think I'm being overly curious?" he asked. "Those things could have turned my boat into kindling wood!"

Nodding ruefully, Cassidy was forced to agree. "I know they could have, but they didn't."

Studying her with a sharp interest, Webb was silent for a few moments. When Cassidy didn't go on, he said, "Click told me about you—the things you remember, the Slow World."

Further embarrassed and surprised, Cassidy just murmured, "So you think I'm crazy, right?"

Not precisely answering the question, Webb merely said, "I know that you've seen those creatures before; hell, half the city knows that."

"By now half the city's probably seen the damned things for themselves," she pointed out dryly.

"And they're what's been tearing up the city?" the seaman asked.

"Ever since I got here," Cassidy amended. Slowly yet precisely she began to recount the history of her experiences with the incredible creatures everyone she met called monsters, beginning with the very first night she had found herself in that world. Repeated performances of the recitation had honed her delivery but had done nothing to blunt its startling details. If anything, with every repetition of the story she seemed to have gained new episodes to add. Just as being able to remember the real world had only made the one she was in seem all the more implausible, each additional confrontation with the gallery of monsters—the stinking carrion eaters, the huge and terrifying air monsters and their attendant little demons, and even the serpentlike water monsters—only made the retelling seem less believable.

Webb listened without comment, his only movements the smooth, almost continuous motion of his tanned hands over the polished wood of the boat's wheel. His stubbled face was calm and thoughtful as Cassidy finished explaining how she and the others had been driven from the burning, riot-torn city by the creatures destroying the wharves.

"Then they're the things that've been killing people around the harbor the past few nights," the seaman said.

Feeling an uncomfortable sense of guilt, Cassidy nodded. "Yeah, I'm sure they are."

"Yet they've never hurt you?"

For some reason that fact only made her feel more guilty. "No," she admitted, "not so far, anyway."

"Well, don't look so disappointed," Webb said, bending over easily to offer her his water bottle again. "If you hadn't been aboard, those damned things probably would have smashed this boat last night. As it was, all they really did was push us a little farther out to sea, and the storm was taking us out anyway."

If she hadn't been aboard, the monsters probably never would have come anywhere near Webb's boat, but Cassidy didn't see any advantage in pointing that out. Eager to shift the focus of the conversation, she gestured with the water bottle at the seemingly featureless expanse of sea surrounding them. "Do you know how far out we've come?"

"No idea," Webb said with cheerful candor. "But there's the sun; we put her at our backs and at least we'll be headed in the right direction again."

If my little buddies don't show up again, Cassidy thought morosely; but she did not voice that disturbing possibility. With a man like Webb, she doubted that it would be necessary to belabor the obvious. Instead she glanced out over the rolling sea, its surface glittering then with the low oblique rays of the rising sun. "Have you ever been out in a storm like that before?" she asked curiously.

"Hell no!" Webb shot back, with an utterly guileless lack of bravado. "You'd have to be an idiot to take a boat out in a storm like that."

An idiot or a friend of Click's, she thought; and Cassidy was beginning to wonder if they were one and the same thing. Still curious, and cautiously encouraged by the pilot's easy forthrightness, she asked him, "If you knew who I was, and the storm was so bad, then why did you do it? Why did you agree to take us?"

Webb grinned again, his big white teeth dazzling in the stubbled tan of his weathered face. "Click, that son of a bitch," he said, but without rancor. "I owed him." He made another minute adjustment to the wheel, glancing up at the healthy billow of the mainsail. Then he looked down directly into Cassidy's face. She could only imagine what he might have read there, or just what else Click might have told the seaman. But Webb just grinned again, his amusement softer and more gentle. "Don't worry," he said, "the bastard's still alive. He has to be, because now *he* owes *me*!"

A faint smile found its way onto Cassidy's mouth, only moments before an unexpected yawn.

"Go on, get below," Webb advised her, his tone of voice almost affectionately teasing. "Might as well sleep; there's not a hell of a lot else to do out here in the middle of nowhere."

And Cassidy had neither the argument nor the desire to debate that point with him.

When Cassidy awoke again it was to the oddly familiar sensation of someone vigorously shaking her by the shoulder. The rude interruption of her slumber was as urgent as the voice that accompanied it.

"Cassidy, wake up! Wake up—he's doing it again!"

Sitting up, Cassidy blinked groggily into Kevin's anxious face. Almost instantly she was aware of exactly where she was and how she had come to be there. When she had returned belowdeck after her early-dawn conversation with Webb, she had elected not to try to squeeze back onto the narrow bunk with her three companions. Instead she had appropriated a slightly musty-smelling long coat from a hook beside the hatch and had stretched out with it on the floor of the little cabin. There she had fallen asleep almost immediately again, a deep and dreamless slumber that had remained uninterrupted until Kevin's sudden intervention.

Fully awake, Cassidy glanced hastily around the small room. Other than Kevin and herself, it was empty. She didn't need any explanation of who "he" was, or just what he was "doing" again; but she was a little confused about one thing. "Where the hell is he?" she asked Kevin as he impatiently tugged her to her feet.

"Outside, on the deck," the blond boy said, pulling her toward the hatch. "Valerie is with him. Hurry!"

Outside the cabin the sun's midmorning brilliance hit Cassidy full in the face, making her squint. Both the vast cap of sky and the featureless expanse of ocean around them were an almost painfully bright blue, and the brisk breeze stung her face. A few yards away she saw Valerie crouched at the rail, bent over the supine body of the warden. Webb stood at the downed man's feet, and he and the captain were having a loud exchange of words.

"You should have told me he was prone to the fits," the pilot said vehemently. "Hell, he almost went right over the rail! If I hadn't been standing practically right next to him—"

Valerie glared up at Webb. "It's not a fit!" She looked down again at the warden, her hands locked protectively around his upper arms. "He's been driving himself right to the edge for days—damn it! Can't you see that he—"

Cassidy dropped down on her knees at the warden's side, interrupting them and effectively forcing Valerie to release her hold and move back. "What happened this time?" she asked.

Throwing Webb a final brief glare, the captain said, "When we woke up he went up on deck. He must have gone to the rail to relieve himself when he—" The curly-haired woman broke off, pausing as if defying Webb to contradict her explanation. "—when he collapsed," she concluded.

Cassidy figured that Valerie's account was a reasonable deduction, because as she knelt by his side she could see that the fly on the young man's leather trousers was indeed unfastened. Studiously ignoring that little distraction, she studied his slack and grimy face. Just as the previous episode in his own bedroom, the warden's eyes were open, unfixed and unseeing. With an utter and unnerving accuracy of detail, the warden of Horses had once again been transformed into Cassidy's autistic pupil from the real world, Andy Greene.

Cassidy reached for one of his wrists. The moment she touched him there was a small jolt, almost like a crack of static electricity, except that it was something more seen than felt. In a second it was gone, and yet it had startled her enough that she had almost dropped his hand. Concentrating on the strong, regular pulse beneath her fingers, she asked, "How long has he been down?"

Webb spoke up more quickly than Valerie. "A couple of minutes." He gestured at the boat's wooden rail. "I'd seen him come out on deck, but I wasn't exactly watching him, if you understand my meaning." Cassidy understood, and the pilot went on. "I just caught him out of the corner of my eye. Damned if he didn't drop like a stone—he almost went over the rail!" He fixed Cassidy with a direct stare. "What the hell is this?"

Cassidy knew that Valerie was giving her a furious and forbidding look, but she ignored it as she slid down into a sitting position beside the warden, lacing her fingers with his limp ones. "I don't know," she said. She studied the smooth, soot-smudged face, still astonished by the pure Andy-ness of it. "But it has something to do with the Memories, something to do with me."

Resentment stiffened Valerie's posture as she hovered protectively over her warden. "You weren't anywhere near him the first few times it happened," she said tautly.

Cassidy threw the woman a glance. So Valerie had known about the previous episodes, just as Kevin had. Was Cassidy the only one who had been kept in the dark? That was ironic, since she was the one person most directly connected with the warden's bizarre "lapses."

"Leave me alone with him for a few minutes," she said.

Kevin gave her an anxious look but took an automatic step backward. Valerie, however, was less tractable. "Why?" the captain said, her eyes narrowed suspiciously. "What are you going to do?"

Webb still seemed to view the whole incident as just one more nuisance to add to the debit side of Click's ledger. "If he's passed out, how come his eyes are still open?" the seaman said.

Cassidy was prepared to ignore Webb's question, but before she could advance her argument with Valerie, the warden stirred beside her. Cassidy felt his fingers tighten slightly on hers; then those blank and unfocused eyes blinked.

"Cathy?" the warden said.

For a few seconds Cassidy was literally too astonished to reply. Even as she was looking directly into that incredibly familiar face, she saw a glimmer of cognizance come over it. It was not the keen, wry cognition of the warden of Horses. The young man who lay on the deck's sun-warmed planks was still Andy Greene; but he was a strangely self-aware Andy Greene.

Webb, Kevin, and Valerie were all staring at Cassidy with varying degrees of surprise and expectation. Giving his fingers a light squeeze, Cassidy said softly, "Andy? I'm right here."

Those chocolate-brown eyes blinked, then focused. He licked his lips, which were trembling slightly as he looked up at her with anxiety and confusion. "You were hurt," he said, his voice a low croak. "They took you away."

Cassidy leaned in a little closer over him, her second hand joining the first to sandwich his between them. As she bent over him, looking down into that wrenchingly vulnerable face, her heart began to thud.

"I'm right here, Andy," she repeated. "I'm okay."

The young man blinked again, his expression both uneasy and bewildered. "I saw them take you away," he insisted, his voice grown a little more steady.

Oh, God—he knows!

The drumming of her pulse pushed the adrenaline through Cassidy's veins, leaving her arms and legs feeling shaky and making her vaguely light-headed. She blocked out everything else around them—Valerie, Kevin, Webb, even the brightness of the sun and the sharp smell of the sea—and focused completely on the man who lay before her, this Andy-who-was-not-Andy.

"Who took me away, Andy?" she asked quietly.

"Men with a truck," he said promptly. His hand rested between hers, warm and trusting. When he looked up into her face, his expression was somewhat baffled but entirely without guile.

Cassidy had to fight to keep her voice calm and reassuring. "Who were the men, Andy? Who took me away in the truck?"

Frowning, the young man hitched his shoulders in a slight shrug. If he realized that he was lying flat on his back, if he was in fact aware of anything else other than Cassidy's presence, he gave no indication of it. "I don't know," he said unhappily.

Forcing the impatience from her tone, Cassidy redirected her approach. "Where did these men take me?"

His whole demeanor seemed to ease up a bit again, his confidence returning. "To a big house," he said.

Momentarily stymied, Cassidy remembered that he had given the identical answer the last time she had seen him in one of the bizarre dissociative states, when she had asked him to tell her where they were. "A big house," he had said then. In her frustration at the time, she had assumed that he was referring to the building they had been in, the warden's big brick house outside the Iron City. But Cassidy was no longer so sure.

Gently squeezing his hand again, she asked him, "Where is this big house?"

"The city," he said. He blinked, his expression growing more anxious again. "Lots of lights, white halls," he said, his voice escalating into a rapid singsong. "Cathy needs help!"

Cassidy was temporarily jolted out of her intense state of concentration by someone bumping into her. It was Kevin, automatically leaning in closer, concerned as his warden became visibly agitated. Trying to refocus on the young man lying on the deck, Cassidy said reassuringly, "But I'm right here now, Andy. Why do you think that I need help?"

But suddenly, irrevocably, the moment was broken. Just as swiftly and yet as absolutely as it had the first time, a complete and obvious change came over the chestnut-haired man. And just as before, Cassidy knew immediately that she was no longer dealing with Andy Greene, even the uncharacteristically cognizant Andy Greene. For the puzzled face that looked up at her as she quickly dropped his hand belonged to one person, and that person was again the warden of Horses.

"Ca-Cassidy?" he said uncertainly, his darting glance taking in both his position and his surroundings. As soon as he tried to sit up, Valerie was there, lifting him by the shoulders. Interpreting the expressions on Webb's and Kevin's faces, probably far more easily than the one on Cassidy's, his tone turned rueful. "I did it again, didn't I?" he said.

Once the warden was sitting up, Kevin dropped down beside him, his anxiety palpable. "Are you all right?" the blond boy blurted out.

Valerie released the warden the moment he was sitting on his own. Giving his captain a quick, grateful look, he reached out and lightly clapped Kevin on the arm. "I'm fine, Kev—or at least as well as I was when we woke up this morning."

Barely placated, Kevin nevertheless dropped back onto his heels.

The warden eyed Webb for a few seconds before quickly refocusing his attention on Cassidy. "What did I do?" he asked her bluntly.

Cassidy's face was deliberately neutral. "What do you remember?" she countered.

The young man glanced down into his lap and, with self-effacing candor, replied, "Going to the rail to relieve myself." Calmly refastening the fly on his leather trousers, he added wryly, "Apparently it happened before I had the opportunity."

"You nearly went over the rail," Webb said, making a graphic gesture.

"You were talking to me," Cassidy said. "You called me by my real name, and you responded as Andy Greene."

Brushing back the tangled forelock of his dirty hair, the warden gave her a curious look. "I thought you said that Andy Greene couldn't speak," he said.

But Cassidy refused to be put off, however genuine his puzzlement. Something had been different about the whole incident, from the very moment she had first touched his hand. She knew it, and she suspected that the warden knew it, as well. But she also realized that he might be understandably reluctant to discuss it in front of the others, especially Webb. And so when Valerie pointedly offered the warden a hand up, Cassidy moved back out of the way and did not try to press on with any further questions.

"Nothing you said made any sense anyway," the captain assured the warden as he gained his feet. "I still think you need to get more rest."

But the warden was studying Webb, a candid mutual inspection passing between the two men. "I think our pilot here is the one who needs some rest," he said. "All I need is a chance to get cleaned up and get something to eat, and I'll be fine, Val."

Webb grunted in agreement. "I'll have to get some sleep," he said, "and I'd best do it while we have calm seas and full daylight. I can give you towels and soap; even extra clothing, if you want to get out of that stinking wet leather. There's nothing but bread and dried food on board, but you're welcome to whatever you need. And when you've finished, I'll give you all a quick lesson in how to keep this boat running on course."

Cassidy joined the others in thanking Webb and accepting his hospitality. He was able to provide them with a couple of wooden buckets for washing, plus several lumps of sweet Tinker soap and some worn but clean towels. Then he left them on deck to wash up while he went to sort through his stores for a suitable breakfast.

For all of her experiences in that world, and all of her careful rationalizations about the situation, Cassidy was still disturbed by the people's casual nudity. Regaining her memory of sex and the real world had only made remaining unaffected in that world a more difficult act to pull off. And the fact that she knew the warden—really *knew* him, as Andy Greene—made it doubly taxing just to ignore him when he calmly began to shuck off his damp leather clothing.

While Valerie lowered one of the buckets over the side by a rope, Cassidy reluctantly tugged off her wet boots. She had to struggle to assume if not a clinical sense of detachment, then at least a passable semblance of disinterest in the two good-looking young men who were stripping off their trousers on the deck beside her. As she reached for the waistband of her own pants, she froze for a second, but modesty had nothing to do with it. She had totally forgotten that she still had the small pistol Click had given her; it had been snugged up against the small of her back for so long that she no longer even felt its presence. Fortunately, no one was paying her any particular attention, and she rapidly pulled down her trousers so she could conceal the weapon beneath them.

As she finished undressing and joined the others in dipping into the bucket of sea water, Cassidy found that two things helped alleviate some of her distress. Ironically, one was Valerie's presence. Not only was Cassidy determined not to act suspiciously in front of the self-assured captain, but somehow the sight of another woman, so nonchalantly naked in front of the nude men, helped blunt the impact. And the second thing, more surprisingly, was that once Cassidy had actually removed her own clothing, being naked as well made the others' nudity seem less sexual.

Cassidy hadn't realized just how filthy she was until she had the chance to wash up again. Beyond the reek of the wet leather clothing that she'd appropriated from the woman Trooper back at the warden's compound, she was still crusted with sooty stains from the burning city and with the foul residue of monster slime. Even the pounding rain from the storm and her subsequent soaking in the ocean hadn't done much to dispel the greasy excrescence. Standing there on the deck wearing nothing but the Ford key that hung from her neck, Cassidy began to scrub herself vigorously with a lump of the herbal-scented soap. She wondered how Webb had been able to stand the smell of them; it was slightly amazing he hadn't gotten one good whiff of them and just sailed on, leaving her stranded in the harbor's turbulent waters.

Even before Valerie would bathe herself, she insisted on inspecting the warden's bite wounds from their ill-fated encounter with the little monsters they had dubbed demons. The warden endured her critical scrutiny in good-natured silence for a time, before he finally wryly pointed out that she also had been bitten in that attack, and far more severely. What surprised Cassidy was that neither of them seemed to have any serious aftereffects from the network of shallow but sharp little wounds. In fact, the Warden's leg and chest and Valerie's hands and forearms seemed remarkably well healed for injuries sustained less than twenty-four hours earlier.

Ultimately it was Kevin who settled the matter by simply moving in with a soapy rag and beginning to scrub down the warden's bare back. That led the warden to make a conciliatory little gesture to Val, who in turn permitted him to wash her back, as well.

Cassidy stayed pretty much off to one side, observing the social dynamics of her three companions without interfering with them. She was so relieved just to be able to get clean again that she was able to temporarily push the image of so many lithe naked limbs and the almost playful camaraderie between them from the forefront of her mind. She had become so absorbed in trying to ease the mass of snarls from her freshly washed hair that she jumped abruptly when she felt the sudden touch of a wet rag between her shoulder blades. Her head snapped around in mild surprise to meet Kevin's wide, mismatched eyes.

"Sorry," he said, "I was just going to do your back for you."

Relaxing, Cassidy gave him a quick smile. "Thanks," she said, and went ahead and enjoyed the scrubbing.

By the time Webb reappeared on deck, they were all toweling off. Cassidy managed to keep her towel strategically placed as the pilot eyed the piles of their old clothing with a certain amused distaste. "Whew, that wet leather stinks!" he said. "Like I said, I could probably find enough extra clothes to fit all of you if you want."

The warden, Kevin, and Valerie all declined. "If we spread them out on the deck, they'll dry quickly enough in the sunshine," the captain said.

But Cassidy was more than willing to take Webb up on his offer. She had no sentimental attachment to her Trooper's leathers; not only were they stolen, they were ill-fitting to boot. In fact, she felt considerably more comfortable being rid of them, even if the cotton tunic and trousers the pilot gave her were laughably large, requiring much rolling up and tucking in. The only part of her old outfit she wanted to keep was her boots, which she laid out on the sunny deck to dry. Once she had surreptitiously transferred the small pistol to her new outfit, she unceremoniously tossed the ragged leathers over the rail.

Webb brought them food and instructed them while they ate. He explained in simple terms the basics of keeping the rugged little wooden boat on course and how to avoid hopelessly tangling the sails or braining themselves on the main boom. He conducted this little discourse as if he fully expected any one of those mishaps might occur while he slept; but he concluded his instructions with the reminder that he would always be only a few yards away—and that he would be far less upset over being awakened for help than he would be if they managed to destroy his vessel.

Despite the bread she'd eaten at dawn, Cassidy felt as ravenous as if she'd had nothing that day. As she greedily chewed on the beef jerky and dried fruit Webb had provided, she again marveled at the pilot's equanimity in the face of what could only be considered a monumental inconvenience. She could not have imagined any tradesman, even the farming Villagers, who would have gone so far out of their way as to give that kind of carte blanche assistance to someone in need, not even to the warden. She didn't know where Webb got his calm and good-humored willingness to help them; no debt to Click, however extensive, seemed equal to the amount of trouble they had already caused the seaman. Sitting there on the sun-washed deck of his boat, eating his food, she was freshly grateful for whatever sense of obligation Webb felt he was discharging.

Once they had finished eating, Webb returned to the cabin to sleep. Despite Valerie's urging, or perhaps because of it, the Warden declined to join him. Cassidy noticed, however, that once the captain was devoting her attention to her turn at the helm, the young man stretched out prone on the pile of damp towels they had left near the rail. There, with Kevin casually sitting nearby like a loyal watchdog, the exhausted warden finally gave himself back over to sleep.

For a time Cassidy occupied herself on the opposite side of the boat, keeping the vessel's squat cabin between herself and the two naked young men. The sea's swells were long and low, gently rocking the boat with a hypnotically repetitive rhythm. Looking out over the deep blue-gray water, it seemed hard to believe just how recently and how furiously the storm had carried them there. There was an odd silence on the ocean. The only sounds seemed to come from the boat herself: the soughing of the wind in her sails, the creaking of her rigging, the soft sucking slap of each wave against her hull. Struck by a stab of philosophic melancholy, Cassidy found herself wondering if there would have been any sounds out there at all, had they not been there to cause them.

The clean cotton clothing Webb had provided was comfortable and dry, if not particularly stylish, and both the breeze and the sunlight felt kind upon Cassidy's arms and face. She was clean and fed and not in any immediate danger. It could have been a time for some contentment, had not her mind been so crowded with unanswered questions and unresolved conflicts. She missed her gray mare more than she thought possible and was desperately worried about her; she could no longer feel the presence of Dragonfly in her mind. She was equally concerned about the friends she had had to leave behind when they had fled the burning city, Rowena, Allen, and Becky. And then there was Click . . .

Tossing her head as if to evade that thought, Cassidy turned instead to trying to focus on what had happened earlier that morning. The second episode with the warden had convinced her beyond a doubt that those lapses were definitely related to her presence there in his world. Somehow during those brief periods of altered consciousness, the warden was reconnecting with the person he had been in the real world; however fleetingly, he was becoming Andy Greene. But he was not the Andy Greene that Cathy Delaney had known; he was an Andy Greene who seemed every bit as lucid as a normal person. And after the episode that morning, Cassidy was convinced of something else: Whether the warden knew or believed it or not, Andy Greene knew how Cathy Delaney had come to be brought to the warden's world. He had

seen the men who had taken her from her own world. And that
meant that he might also know how she could return to it.

Near dusk, Webb reemerged from the cabin, yawning and
stretching, to resume command of his vessel. He inspected every
foot of the boat, deftly checking ropes and rigging, and consulting
several archaic-looking instruments that he took from the watch
box at the helm.

Cassidy watched the ritual with a genuine respect. "Any idea
how far we are from land?" she asked, as the pilot restowed his
equipment.

Webb had been eyeing her oversized seaman's clothing with
overt amusement. "More than a few miles, at least," he said, "or
we'd see gulls." He made a broad, nonspecific gesture toward the
boat's prow. "Our heading is south-southwest; I reckon we'll get
there sooner or later." He paused a moment, studying the angle of
the setting sun. "Of course, losing this damned headwind would
help."

More bread and jerky and dried fruit made up their supper.
Dressed once again in their leather clothing, the warden, Kevin,
and Valerie looked a little more normal to Cassidy, although she
suspected that none of the three had minded their afternoon of
nude voyaging. Their tunics and trousers were still far from clean,
although superior tanning had rendered them supple despite the
conditions to which they'd been subjected.

As the sun sank below the horizon, Webb returned to his helm.
There had been very little to see from the boat even during the
day, and once it grew dark there was even less. Webb lit the lanterns, but their illumination was more for the purpose of safely ne-
gotiating the deck than anything else. The little cabin was better
lit, but barren of amusements. As the evening progressed, sleep
became an increasingly attractive choice.

Webb had produced another thin pad, much like the one that
covered the narrow shelf that served as his bunk. Spread on the
cabin's floor, it offered additional room for them to stretch out
more comfortably. Cassidy enjoyed a brief and covert moment of
amusement over the bit of silent wrangling that went on between
Valerie and Kevin for the space next to the warden. The young
man seemed oblivious to the duel of loyalties being fought over
his favor, and in Cassidy's opinion the captain ultimately pulled
rank and essentially bullied Kevin by the sheer force of her stern
will into settling for bunking on the floor. Cassidy was just as
willing to share her space on the floor mat with him. She didn't

even give it a second thought when Kevin curled up companionably against her, his one arm flung loosely over her waist.

But Cassidy could not sleep. She was warm and dry and comfortable enough; certainly she should have been tired enough. Both the dimness and the rocking motion of the boat were soothing and safe. But her mind simply would not let go. She kept thinking about what had happened with the warden, and she kept thinking about Click. Even when she tried to derail her thoughts of him by forcing herself to plan what they were going to do once they reached the coastline, and began in earnest their search for the elusive Alchemist, she could not keep the other two men out of her mind. One of those men was there with her, and she was more certain than ever that he was at the root of the solution she'd been trying to find. The other man was separated from her—*maybe even dead*, she could not keep from thinking—and far from being part of the solution, she could not help wondering if Click was not instead the antithesis of her hopes of escaping that world.

In his final moments with her in the chaos of the Iron City, Click had neatly negated what Cassidy had long come to accept as a basic truth about that world. She had discovered that Click remembered sex.

A quiet movement in the darkness of the cabin temporarily sidetracked Cassidy from her unsettling memories. Beside her, Kevin still slumbered on, his arm a comforting weight across her side. The sound had come from the bunk above them. Cassidy waited motionlessly, feigning sleep, as someone slowly and carefully rose from the narrow shelf and stepped lightly around their recumbent forms. Even in the darkness she could not have mistaken the particular grace of that oddly familiar body. It was the warden.

After he had slipped from the cabin, Cassidy waited a moment longer to make sure that he had not awakened Valerie. When the captain didn't stir, Cassidy cautiously slid out from beneath Kevin's arm. She was only a few feet from the hatch, so it was a simple matter to push it open and step out over the high threshold. Outside, the air was cooler and faintly aglow from the boat's lanterns. She saw Webb leaning back against the rail at the helm, but she did not immediately see the warden.

Belatedly realizing that the young man had very likely come out onto the deck to relieve himself, Cassidy experienced a brief moment of embarrassed indecision. Much as she wanted to be able to talk alone with the warden, she doubted that disturbing his privacy would get any discussion off to a good start. While she hesitated just outside the hatch, Webb took notice of her. The pilot didn't speak, but she could tell from the subtle alteration of his posture that not only was he watching her, he was curious about and amused by her circumspection. With a little tilt of his head, he seemed to be urging her to proceed. When Cassidy remained right outside the hatch, staring quizzically at him, Webb repeated the gesture.

Slowly and soundlessly Cassidy edged around the side of the cabin and along the narrow strip of deck between it and the rail. Ahead of her at the prow of the boat she could see the warden, a dark form silhouetted against the dim silver of the sea. He stood at the capstan, gazing out over the ocean. Once she was out there in plain sight, Cassidy didn't want to appear to have been sneaking up on him, so she tried to move as casually as possible. Even then, when he spoke and Cassidy was still several feet away from him, it startled her, since he had seemed too preoccupied to have noticed her approach.

"Do you think they're still out there?" he asked quietly.

Stepping up alongside him at the rail, Cassidy glanced out over the moon-lit waves. "The monsters?"

The warden's hands rested on the smooth rounded wood of the capstan. He nodded. "Do you think they're still following you?"

"Probably," Cassidy admitted. She had no reason to assume otherwise, and she was somewhat perplexed by his question, since she seriously doubted that thoughts of monsters were keeping him from sleep that night. But before she could come up with a tactfully phrased comment to that effect, the young man turned toward her.

"It was different this last time, wasn't it?" The tone of the warden's voice suggested his expression in the darkness: open, calm, speculative. "Afterward, I could tell that it had been." He paused. "I'm sorry that I couldn't say anything then, but I thought it would be best if we could discuss this alone."

Since she understood his reluctance, Cassidy merely asked, "How was it different? Do you remember anything about it?"

Standing that close to him, Cassidy could still smell the faint odor of smoke on his leather clothing, although there was also another, more subtle scent about him. It took her a few moments more to recognize the fragrance as the Tinkers' herbal soap. He was looking back out over the water again, his fingers lightly stroking the capstan. "I was frightened," he said.

It was not what Cassidy had expected. She cocked her head. "Afraid of what?"

He turned his head again, the dim oval of his face meeting hers. "I don't know," he confessed. "Not of anything, I think. I was afraid for you."

Cassidy had been touched by the warden often enough, casual and spontaneous gestures, that it ought not to have surprised her to feel his hand land lightly on her shoulder. And yet it did surprise her. She remembered what had happened that morning on the deck when she had reached for his hand. But it was not like that; there was no abrupt flash of light, no startling brilliance. There was just the warm weight of his reassuring hand.

"Why were you afraid for me?" she said.

"I felt like you were in some kind of danger, like you needed my help."

His words were an eerie echo of what Andy Greene had said during the episode. Something definitely had been different that time: The warden had remembered something of Andy's experience. Cassidy hesitated a moment, looking up into the shadowy outline of his face.

"I think you saw the men who took me away, and that's what's troubling you," she said quietly. "You think I'm in danger because you saw them—I think you know how I got here."

The warden was silent for a long moment, and in that interval Cassidy became unnaturally aware of the soft suck of the water along the boat's hull. He did not look away, and he did not remove his hand from her shoulder. When he did speak, it was obvious that he had been putting serious thought into what she had said.

"You're still convinced that I'm this person you know, this Andy Greene," he said.

Cassidy simply nodded.

"I don't know how that could be." But his words did not carry the same innocent conviction they once had, and in that moment Cassidy sensed that he was, as never before, desperately searching for the explanation for what had been happening to him. The lapses were beginning to blur the line between all that he thought he knew and the chaotic morass of impossibility that lay right beyond it. Just as Click's kiss had destroyed that boundary for Cassidy, the warden was also seeing the barrier between his world and the Slow World becoming distorted, fragmented, ineffectual.

"And I don't know how it *couldn't* be," she replied. "I *know* you—and when you slip across to the other side, you know me, too." She reached up and gripped his wrist, holding his hand against her shoulder. His bare skin was warm, his pulse strong and regular beneath her fingers. "I don't know why I was brought here," she went on. "I don't know what those monsters are, or what the hell they have to do with me. All I know is that I want to go home again." She tightened her grip. "You may not understand what's happening, you may not even want it; but somehow you're a part of all this."

The warden did not resist her hold on his arm; he didn't even resist her logic. That desperation to understand that Cassidy had sensed in him earlier seemed to guide his response. "I want to help you, Cassidy," he said, softly and intently. "I swear it on my blood. I only want to find out the truth."

"Then *tell me* the truth!" Her voice was scarcely louder than a whisper, but for all its intensity and their close proximity it could just as well have been a shout. She squeezed his wrist harder, her nails digging into his skin. "We've left the city now, we're going south—tell me the truth about the Alchemist."

For a few moments the warden was so utterly still that Cassidy wondered if he was beginning to fall into one of his bizarre lapses again. When she realized that he wasn't, she then wondered instead if he was trying to compose some sort of evasive reply. But neither possibility was the case. He was merely searching for a satisfactory approach to a most difficult topic.

"I've already told you what little I know, Cassidy," he finally said, his voice soft and without reproach. "And I've never lied to you."

"Then tell me what you *think*," she persisted. "Do you think this Alchemist really exists? Have you ever sent anyone to search for him?"

But the warden was already shaking his head before she had even finished speaking. In the faint glow of the moonlight and Webb's lanterns, the dark wisps of his tousled hair were like a shaggy corona around his shadowed face. "I wish there was such a person, Cassidy, someone with such knowledge. But I have no reason to believe there is. No one who has gone south has ever returned with any evidence of his existence, and the stories about him have spanned the lifetimes of dozens of men."

Something in his statement spurred a chilled recognition in Cassidy's mind. "You said Click had been sent south by his Warden," she said quietly, looking up into that dimly lit face. "Was he sent to look for the Alchemist?"

Again there was a significant pause before he answered her, a palpable air of searching for the best form of response. In the end the warden employed a question of his own. "He's never told you?"

"No, he never even told me that he was a Trooper—had once been a Trooper, I mean," she amended, quickly adding, "What happened to him? Why did he ever leave the Troop?"

Cassidy should have been able to predict the warden's response on the basis of past experience alone. He just shook his head again, slowly but gently. "I think that's for Click himself to tell you, Cassidy."

"Yeah, if we ever see him again," she muttered, suddenly dropping her hand from the warden's wrist.

To her surprise, he slid his own hand down from her shoulder, capturing her fingers. "I wouldn't give up on him yet," he said. "Click is a very resourceful man; he's survived far worse than this."

Cassidy looked up into the shadowy oval of the warden's face. "Like going south to look for the Alchemist?" She shook her head in frustration. "We're looking for a man that you doubt even exists, and you won't even tell me what Click found down there?"

"I can't tell you," the warden said simply, "because I don't know. He's never spoken to me of it. I thought that he'd mentioned it to you." He gave her fingers a reassuring squeeze. "Perhaps when we find him again, he'll tell you what he knows."

Unaccountably uncomfortable with that calm assumption, Cassidy tried to slip her hand from his grasp; but the warden didn't permit it. "You're right when you say that I don't understand all of this, Cassidy," he said. "But I also believe you're right when you say that I'm a part of it, as well." His fingers tightened fractionally on hers, his face bending lower, closer. "I'll do everything in my power to help you find out if this Alchemist does exist; I swear that you will have your answers."

Chapter 3 ⬅||||

It was early afternoon, during Cassidy's turn at the helm, when they first saw the gulls.

Actually, Cassidy was not the first to see them. Webb had spent not only the entire night but also a good portion of the morning at the wheel, making occasional calculations with his arcane instruments and humming contentedly to himself. It was midmorning before he relinquished control of the boat to Valerie, and then only after explaining to her at some length how to keep constantly correcting for the rising northwest wind that they had encountered. By the time Cassidy took over after lunch, she had become mildly paranoid about mucking up their navigation. It had seemed simple enough the day before, when they had been out in the middle of nowhere, but she had grown more anxious about keeping the correct heading as they sailed nearer to land.

Because of her vague anxiety, and because she genuinely enjoyed his company, Cassidy had been pleased when Kevin had joined her at the helm. She was secretly amused to have gotten him away from the warden; sometimes they seemed like twins separated at birth, even if they bore no physical resemblance to each other, other than both being attractive young men. The blond-haired boy had stripped off his tunic and stretched out on his stomach on the warm deck planks, pillowing his head on his crossed forearms. He reminded Cassidy of a young cat taking a little sun in a barnyard doorway.

The warden and Valerie were at the opposite end of the boat, wedged into the angle of the prow like two mismatched figureheads. They appeared to be arguing about something, although they were too far away and speaking too quietly for Cassidy to overhear. But there was little mistaking the tension in their postures as they faced each other, and more than once Cassidy saw the captain shake her curly head.

Recalling his words of the night before, Cassidy found it increasingly difficult to view the warden with dispassion. If he and Valerie were having some kind of disagreement, she was concerned, as well. After all, she told herself, her fate was connected to that of the warden. That was the reason she suddenly felt so protective of him.

"What's going on with those two?" Cassidy asked Kevin casually.

The young man didn't need to look up to know what she was asking about. Nor did he feign misunderstanding; Kevin was not given to dissembling. "They're arguing about the Alchemist," he said.

Cassidy was hardly surprised, but she did wonder just how much Kevin knew. "What about him?"

Kevin sighed and rubbed his cheek against his forearm. Not for the first time, Cassidy was struck by the sleek symmetry of his tanned and naked back. She was alternately relieved and disappointed that he hadn't decided to shed his trousers, as well. "Val wants to go back to the city," he said.

Cassidy had to stifle her surprise to keep her voice from becoming an audible exclamation. "Back? She was the one who insisted that he leave in the first place!"

Kevin shifted slightly, finding a more comfortable arrangement for his chest and hips on the bare deck. "She thinks it's crazy to look for the Alchemist; says it's too dangerous. When we reach the coast, she wants to drop you off and then go back north again with Webb. She figures that by the time we get back to the city, the worst of the trouble will be over."

"Well, at least she doesn't plan on just dropping me overboard," Cassidy muttered under her breath, her fingers tightening on the wheel. But silently she had to admit that Valerie was probably right. And regardless of any residual hostility left in the Iron City, with Cassidy and the monsters gone the warden would undoubtedly be far safer there than he would be mucking around in the trackless southern swamps.

"She says she has a duty," Kevin added.

Cassidy couldn't argue with that; in fact, she found the captain's loyalty admirable. But what she said was "What do you think, Kev?"

The question was open to interpretation; Kevin had a guileless way about him that made him consider it in its broadest sense. "I think the warden will try to do what's best for everyone," he said seriously. "This whole thing with the Memories and the Slow World is really important to him. If the monsters are connected to that, and he has to find the Alchemist to get the answers, then I know he's going to try to find the Alchemist."

Cassidy marveled at Kevin's simple faith. He may not have understood all of the forces pulling at his warden, but he was convinced that the young leader would do the right thing. In spite of what had happened the night before, Cassidy had to admit that her own trust was not quite so absolute.

For a few moments Cassidy remained silent, confirming their heading on her instruments. Then she looked back down at the browned expanse of Kevin's bare back, which slowly rose and fell with his breathing. Had he fallen asleep? The pale cap of his long hair, only loosely confined in a ponytail at the nape of his neck, shone like spun gold in the sunshine. With an almost wistful sort of irony, she realized that she'd known Kevin longer than she'd known anyone else in that world; and yet she felt as if she hardly knew him at all.

"Kevin?" she said. "Can I ask you something—about the monsters?"

His golden head lifted from his crossed forearms; there was a faint imprint, like an odd wrinkle, across his otherwise smooth cheek, and his mismatched eyes widened quizzically. "Sure," he said.

"Have you ever seen them before? Before the other night, I mean, when they attacked the warden and your party outside the city?"

Cassidy's question had made him uncomfortable; she could see a sudden bunching of the long muscles along his spine. At first she assumed it was because he didn't want to have to tell her about his experiences, and so she was taken aback by his candid reply.

"I'm not sure," Kevin said.

Cassidy considered that for a moment. Then she asked, "Kevin, do you remember when you first got here?"

His response to that was prompter and far more detailed. "No, not really; but I know that I used to remember it." He drew up one knee, rolling over onto his side so that he was facing Cassidy as she stood at the helm. There was a calm, pensive look on his face as he continued. "Rafe and I were in a little village in Edmund's Territory when Yolanda found us. She was the one who taught us to be Horsemen." The memory seemed to evoke feelings more pleasant than melancholic for him. "The people back there might still remember when I got here, but I don't remember it anymore."

Much as she valued tact, Cassidy found it much easier just to be forthright with Kevin. "When I first met you, you seemed really concerned about being left in the dark after sunset. What were you afraid of, Kevin? Was it monsters?"

He shrugged, his tanned shoulder hitching. "It was something that happened to me when I first got here," he said. "I don't remember any more what it was. I just knew that there were other things out there that could be . . . dangerous."

"Do you remember what I said about the first time I saw one of them?" Cassidy asked him. She knew she had Kevin's total attention by that point. His odd-colored eyes widened when she reminded him of her own experience along the riverbank her first night in that world, when she had seen a monster in the water. "I thought I must be going crazy," she told him. "Even once I realized there was something that you were afraid of, too, I still kept thinking that I must have imagined what I saw that night."

Kevin's voice was so soft and low that it was barely above a whisper. "I once thought that, too—I know I saw something, and I thought it must have been—" He broke off, visibly struggling for a word. When his eyes locked with Cassidy's, his expression was one of both wonder and relief. "When I first came here, I must have seen a monster, too!"

"That would explain a lot," Cassidy said, oddly relieved by Kevin's revelation. "But you tried to convince yourself that you couldn't have seen anything like that, because it didn't make any sense; and as time went on, you began to forget."

Drawing up his other leg, Kevin deftly gained his feet. Face to face with Cassidy then, he looked at her with a mixture of excitement and expectation. "What do you think they are, Cassidy? Where have they come from?"

But to her frustration, Cassidy still had no real idea. "I don't know, Kevin. They're like something out of a nightmare. But I still think they must have something to do with the Memories, because—"

"Wait, look!" Kevin interrupted her, suddenly pointing out across the deck to the other side of the boat. "Gulls!"

Momentarily disappointed by the abrupt truncation of their conversation, Cassidy needed a few seconds to realize the significance of gulls. She swung around at the helm, squinting off into the flat brilliance of the afternoon sun. But she could see nothing but the washed-out blue of the sky and the harsh reflection of the sunlight off the bluish-gray waves.

"Where are they? I don't see anything."

Glancing to her, Kevin shook his head and pointed again. "No, not that high. They're dipping along right over the tops of the swells."

Cassidy had to concede that the young Finder had better eyes than she did; even after she repeated directions to the birds' location, it took her a full minute before she was able to see them. By that time the warden and Valerie had come back from the prow of the boat to find out what all the excitement was about.

"We're nearing land then," the captain said. "We'd better wake the seaman."

But the warden reached out and touched Val on the sleeve, restraining her. "Not yet, Val." He gestured at the distant, nearly colorless ellipses of the swooping gulls. "We still must be miles from the coast. As soon as we actually sight land will be soon enough to wake him."

The curly-haired woman certainly had other expressions, but the one most indelibly associated with Valerie in Cassidy's mind was a look of fixed determination. Whether she was commanding Troopers or accepting a command from her warden, the expression was much the same. The woman had a way of adopting a position and then sticking to it.

"But if we're nearing land, we could already begin to turn north," she said pragmatically.

Although Cassidy understood and appreciated the woman's strengths well enough to realize why the warden had chosen her to be his captain, she sometimes wondered if he had had any idea just what he had been setting himself up for with Valerie. His manner with her was calm but firm. "Webb has told me he was instructed to set us all ashore at a particular place, a cove known to the seamen." He looked Valerie directly in the eye. "After he has discharged that obligation, if you wish to go north again with him, you will have my leave to go."

From the corner of her eye Cassidy could see Kevin shift anxiously, taking a fractional step away from the rail and toward the warden. The blond boy had more courage than Cassidy; the captain's dark eyes were literally gleaming with suppressed fury. The only question in Cassidy's mind was whether Valerie would break her years of discipline and directly contradict her warden in front of them. But Val's voice was surprisingly even and contained when she responded to the warden's sardonic suggestion.

"How much do we know about where this seaman is taking us?" she asked. "And who gave him these instructions—a Tinker?"

She pronounced the last word like an epithet, and Cassidy felt her own spine automatically stiffen with anger. "Click saved our lives," she reminded the other woman.

"The seaman saved our lives," Valerie said, with a scornful shake of her head. "Your Tinker friend has had far more experience with losing lives than saving them."

"Val," the warden cautioned.

By further small movements, Kevin had reached the warden's side. Cassidy doubted the young man had even been aware of his automatic defensive gesture, he was so absorbed in the incipient conflict between his warden and the two women. Kevin's glance kept darting up to the warden's face, and his stance was almost protective in nature. But it didn't seem to Cassidy that the warden was the man who was in need of defense there.

"Click saved my life at least twice in one night," Cassidy said stiffly. "And without him we never would have been able to—"

Valerie shocked Cassidy by actually spitting on the deck only inches from Cassidy's boots. "Then courage has come late to your Tinker," the captain said coldly.

The warden reached out again for Valerie's arm, this time with the obvious intention of retraining her; but she ignored him, continuing harshly, "Or has he never told you about his last trip to the southern swamps—and of the Troop he abandoned there, left to die in the very place all of you now seem so determined to let him lead—"

"Val, enough," the warden said more sternly, actually pulling on her arm.

But Cassidy faced the angry woman's accusation squarely. "I know that Click was once a Trooper," she said calmly, "and I also know that he was sent by his warden to find the Alchemist."

"A Trooper?" Valerie echoed mockingly. "He was the *captain* of the Troopers, sworn to lead and protect them! And he left them all there to die while he—"

The warden jerked so hard on Valerie's arm that the slender woman had to stagger sideways to keep her footing. She glared angrily at him, but he would not release her, while Cassidy was left to try to make some sense of the captain's shocking revelation.

"Click was the captain of the Troopers?" Cassidy repeated stupidly. What could have ever happened to him to have made him

renounce not only that title, but also his entire life as a Horseman?
Too stunned to speak, Cassidy could only stand there looking
mutely into Valerie's face as the woman spat out her final recrim-
ination.

"He would have been the next warden, as well," Valerie continued, her voice honed as hard and sharp as steel, "if he'd had the
courage to face what he had done. Instead he chose to turn away
from us, to spend the rest of his life wandering around the hills
peddling pots and pans with that bunch of—"

Cassidy was certain that the warden would have interrupted
Valerie's harsh tirade if he had been able; but it was through no
effort of his that the angry woman was suddenly forced to break
off. Later, Cassidy would not be sure which thing happened first,
the dull impact thudding against the boat's wooden hull or the odd
change she saw come over the warden's face. The whole vessel
shuddered, but it was only by the most automatic and distracted
sort of effort that Cassidy kept her balance. Her real attention was
focused on the warden's strangely vacant expression.

It's happening again, she thought, just as another hard thump
reverberated through the vessel's timbers. She stumbled sideways
and had to catch herself on the wheel. *He's—*

But as Cassidy's other arm shot out, swiftly and reflexively, to
grab hold of the suddenly vacuous-looking young man before he
toppled over the rail, something startling happened. As her fingers
closed over the soft leather covering his arm, she was consumed
in a brilliant flash of light. Just as the previous morning's episode
on the deck, the galvanizing flood of radiance was not exactly
electric in nature; it was almost like diving into sunshine. But unlike the last time, she did not immediately release her hold on the
warden.

Cassidy was vaguely aware that both Valerie and Kevin were
shouting something at them, trying to coax her and the warden
farther from the rail. But at that moment their interference was totally extraneous; she was completely taken up in the rushing
stream of light. She was aware of the solidity of the warden's
flesh beneath the grip of her fingers and of a rhythmic pulse that
seemed to thrum like a heartbeat between the two of them. With
an almost painful clarity, she felt a sense of the fragile tenuous-
ness of her life—of all life—as the overwhelming brilliance
washed over her.

Then, just as suddenly, it was gone. It took Cassidy a few seconds to realize that another blow to the hull had succeeded in tearing the young man from her grasp. Valerie had caught him by the

arm, but the contact was broken, the fierce light and the incredible sensation of connection vanished. Cassidy abruptly found herself lurching sideways across the tilting deck; only Kevin's intervention kept her from going right over the rail.

"It's the monsters again!" Kevin shouted, his fingers locked in the loose material of her cotton shirt, his other hand anchoring them to the helm. A few yards from them, Valerie secured the warden by looping one arm around his shoulders, while she used her free hand to hold onto the frame of the hatch. But the man she was holding was no longer her warden, even if Valerie had yet to realize it.

Jolted by another hard thud to the hull, Cassidy stared across the deck at the man who had again become Andy Greene. Although he looked mildly confused, he was cognizant, and it was that particular awareness which she had found so remarkable when displayed on Andy's face. Despite the strength of Valerie's hold on him, he seemed oblivious of the captain's presence and was instead looking anxiously toward Cassidy.

"Cathy?" he said plaintively.

Just then another, even more emphatic thump hit the bottom of the boat. The hatch flung open, nearly dislodging Valerie, and Webb thrust himself out through the narrow aperture. Valerie staggered back out of his way, battling both the lurching of the deck and the recalcitrance of her charge as she struggled to keep her feet.

"It's the monsters again!" Kevin repeated unnecessarily, as if for the seaman's benefit.

Ignoring Kevin's wide-eyed alarm, Webb made a vehement gesture. "Come on, we're taking on water," he said tersely. "I need two of you in the hold to work the pumps."

Cassidy would have been willing to wrest Andy away from Valerie if she'd had to; but that didn't prove necessary. As the captain threw a quick, measuring look from the grim expression on Webb's face to the anxious, obviously unfamiliar expression on the warden's, he began to struggle to disengage himself from her hold. Another sound thud against the hull seemed to decide Valerie for sure; she firmly pushed the warden in Cassidy's direction and commanded, "Come on, Kevin—let's go!"

Kevin's reluctance was palpable, but he obeyed. As the young man released Cassidy, Andy came staggering toward Cassidy. She reached out and caught him by the elbow as he nearly stumbled right past her.

Andy's face was filled with dismay, and his voice quavered unsteadily. "Cathy?" he repeated anxiously. But Cassidy realized that his distress had nothing to do with monsters, or the way the boat was jolting beneath their feet. Wherever he was, he was no longer in that world.

"It's okay, Andy," she said, reaching out for his other arm just as another concussion shook the deck planks. "I'm right here."

That time when she had touched him there had been no brilliant flash of light, no overwhelming sense of intimacy. Instead, something equally remarkable happened. Andy literally launched himself into her arms, clinging to Cassidy like a frightened child. "Cathy!" He sobbed, embracing her with an almost crushing intensity.

Automatically she succored him, bolstering his frantic hug by wrapping her own arms around his larger form and murmuring wordlessly soothing things to him as he wept noisily. The spontaneous display of strong emotion was one of the most startling things that had happened during the bizarre episodes. She had never seen Andy Greene evince even the slightest capacity for such feeling. In that regard the young man who clung so trustingly to her could have been a total stranger; yet in every other way, from the breadth of his shoulders, to the warmth of his skin, to the sweet smell of his hair, he was utterly familiar to her.

"It's okay, Andy," Cassidy repeated, gently patting his back. "I'm right here; you're all right now."

Exhausted by his weeping, Andy snuffled loudly and gasped to regain his breath. "Cathy, I thought you were *dead*!" he exclaimed into the dampened cotton shoulder of her seaman's tunic.

The deck danced beneath them again, a staccato burst of sharp blows to the submerged portion of the hull. But for all that it mattered to Cassidy then, the attack could have been taking place on some other planet. A chill and fragmentary feeling of déjà vu swept through her, and her fingers slipped up to gently pry Andy's face back off her shoulder. "Why, Andy?" she asked him quietly. "Why did you think that I was dead?"

His face lifted. Tearstained and distorted by fear and anxiety, it was still a face that sent an unaccountable throb of emotion through Cassidy, the naked vulnerability in those swollen eyes only deepening the pang. "A truck hit you," he said. "And you just laid there—you didn't talk or move or anything, and they took you away." There was a tremor in his voice again. "I thought you were dead!"

A particularly vigorous impact against the hull caused the boat to lurch forward through the water, surging like a vessel caught in a sudden tide. The motion caused both of them to slew sideways, tripping along the deck until they were caught against the rail. Despite the involuntary change of position, Cassidy was stunned by what she had just heard. Just as she had suspected, Andy knew what had happened to her. But the whole platform of supposition upon which Cassidy had been so carefully building her theory had suddenly given way beneath her feet like the trapdoor on a gallows, plunging her into a fresh abyss of the unknown.

"Andy, where am I now?" she asked him, her mouth gone dry, her words scarcely more than a whisper.

"The big house," he said promptly. He paused to sniffle loudly. "The house with the white walls and the bright lights."

It was the same description he'd given her before, most recently just the previous morning. And the worst part about it was that Cassidy was utterly certain that he was sincere. Even as she looked into those deep brown eyes, the deck jolted sharply beneath them again, nearly knocking her to her knees. Had she not still been holding Andy's arms, they both would have fallen from the force of the impact. But for Cassidy their current situation— asea in a wooden boat not much bigger than the average RV, under attack by creatures that were easily that size themselves— was simply wiped from her mind.

He's not here, she thought in numb amazement. *He's there— and he thinks I'm there, too.* All of Cassidy's earnest speculation, her building excitement at the certainty that she had somehow been kidnapped and that Andy Greene had seen it happen, fell away from beneath her. Andy had not just been describing what had happened to Cassidy before she had been taken from her own world; he was describing her present condition there in that world. And that was impossible.

I'm here, Cassidy thought dazedly, barely aware of the bite of Andy's fingers into her shoulders as the boat lurched upward again. *No one can be in two places at the same time.*

Then Rowena's words came back to haunt her: But maybe they can be in the same place at two different times.

"Cathy?" Andy asked anxiously.

Forcing herself to focus again on the uneasy young man who was still so desperately gripping her, Cassidy tried to keep her voice as calm as she could. "Andy, this big house where I am, what am I . . . ?"

The boat spun sharply in the water, the deck beneath their feet rotating a full 90 degrees or more. The unexpected torque slewed Cassidy and Andy sideways, and they stumbled into the wall of the cabin, breaking their grip on one another. Cassidy felt her elbow impact painfully with the weathered planks, and she dropped to her knees. A shout came from belowdeck, and for the first time Cassidy noticed that there was water streaming from a hose in the hatch, flowing toward the scuppers from the pump below. Then someone bellowed again, loud enough that the voice could easily be identified as Webb's.

"Out! Damn them, we're going down! Out—*now*!"

Moments later the pilot appeared in the hatchway, dragging a drenched and panting Kevin from the cabin like a mother cat rescuing a drowning kitten. Valerie staggered out behind them, her wet leathers sticking to her like a dark skin.

"Get the dinghy!" Webb shouted with a broad gesture. "On the starboard side, lashed to the cabin!"

The captain hesitated a moment, obviously torn by concern for her warden. But even as Cassidy felt a steadying arm help draw her to her feet again, she looked up into a face that was both familiar and concerned. But it was not the face of Andy Greene; once more he was the warden of Horses, present in his own world.

As Cassidy awkwardly bumped into him, the warden quickly took in the chaos around them. "What's happening?" he asked, genuinely confused.

Webb's white teeth showed in a virtual snarl. "We're *sinking*, that's what's happening!" he shouted above the sudden screech of rending wood. "Those damned creatures just punched a hole the size of a cow in the hull!"

Cassidy still viewed the uproar around her with remarkable detachment. She was having some difficulty making the transition from her incredible conversation with Andy to the present and very formidable attack by the water monsters. She noted Kevin lurching forward almost as if he were moving in slow motion, like someone swimming through the air. As the blond boy reached for the warden's hand and their fingers connected, the deck surged up beneath them and suddenly the whole axis of the boat tilted.

The vessel practically flew forward across the surface of the water, obviously propelled by one or more of the giant creatures. Cassidy remembered the sinuous power of the great coiled body that had lifted her up out of the river the day the Tinkers' rafts had come down the rapids. Then suddenly the boat was hanging crookedly in the air, and anything on her not fastened down was scuttling across the deck toward the rail. That would have included Cassidy herself, had not the warden still been gripping her arm. The warden's other arm was locked with Kevin's, and his leg was hooked around the base of the main mast, tenuously anchoring all three of them on the steeply pitched deck.

Valerie had been in the process of unfastening the dinghy when the boat had lurched up out of the water. She had managed to secure herself by hanging on to one of the metal cleats from which the small skiff hung. From her vantage point there, right at the rail, the dark-haired woman peered over the side of the boat; her eyes widened.

At the edge of the rail, a sleek and gleaming serpentine projection appeared, easily the thickness of a man's thigh. It seemed to hover there, casually undulating like a Hindu's trained cobra. It couldn't have been one of the creature's necks because it bore no head. It was more like a tentacle of some kind; the impression enhanced when the questing appendage began to wind its way among the rail's posts, snapping the wooden spindles like matchsticks.

"Damn their blood!" Webb exploded. He was still braced in the hatchway, and he glared at Cassidy. "I thought you said they've never tried to hurt you!" he accused.

Still gripping the cleat in one hand, Valerie let her body swing free, away from the cabin wall. With one boot she kicked forcefully against the tentacle's glittering but unyielding surface. Cassidy feared that the creature would immediately abandon its leisurely demolition of the rail to turn on Valerie; but to her surprise, quite the opposite happened. After the captain had delivered five or six good sound kicks to the sinuous coil, it suddenly went limp and dropped back over the edge of the deck, vanishing from sight. Then, swiftly but with deliberate care, the boat was lowered back down until it was again level in the water.

The moment the boat settled into the water, Valerie released her hold on the cleat and spun to face the others across the deck. "This is because of *her*!" she said angrily. "The damned things are here only because they're following *her*! If we put her over the side, they'd go!"

With the hull submersed again, water had resumed pouring in through the breach into the hold, causing the deck to tilt drunkenly. But Webb had excellent sea legs, and he crossed the planks with a swift and catlike grace. Placing himself between Valerie and the trio that still clung to the mast, he turned on the captain.

"No one goes over the side on my boat unless I've put them over myself—and don't tempt me! Now unlash that damned dinghy, or we're all going to be swimming in about two minutes!"

Valerie probably would have willingly argued with the pilot, no matter that they were standing on the deck of a sinking ship. But when the warden spoke up, it caused her to hesitate.

"Quickly, Val," he urged her, with an uneasy glance for the sea's suddenly empty and gently rolling surface. "I'd just as soon not have to share the water with those things if we can avoid it."

Webb grasped Cassidy by the arm, relieving the warden of his increasingly tenuous grip on her. "I thought you said they've never attacked you," the seaman said again, his aggrieved tone suggesting that he took the creatures' unseemly behavior as a personal breach of naval etiquette.

"They never did—not before this," Cassidy said breathlessly, wincing at the bite of his fingers. "I don't know why they'd want to sink the boat."

"Well, they're certainly succeeding," Webb said grimly, casting a glance over the rail, where the water was already lapping alarmingly close to the level of the deck. Muttering some obscure seaman's oath, he pulled Cassidy after him across the planks.

Still clutching Kevin's hand, the warden began to follow, although their progress was considerably less steady on the listing deck. The blond boy's eyes were huge with fear as he registered the size of the dinghy that Valerie had released from the side of the cabin.

"We're going out in *that*?" he asked. "They'll kill us!"

Webb let go of Cassidy's arm to help Valerie maneuver the little skiff. Without glancing back, he reminded Kevin, "Well, you can stay here if you want, boy—but you'll be riding her to the bottom in a few minutes."

"It'll be all right, Kev," the warden said, with more conviction than actual credence. "The dinghy is seaworthy, and we're not that far from shore now."

Webb spared a moment to throw the warden a look of patent skepticism, but Cassidy quickly added her own reassurances. "They're probably gone for now, Kevin," she said, waving a hand at the surrounding sea. "See? The surface is quiet again. And I still don't think they meant to hurt us."

That last remark earned Cassidy looks of utter disbelief from both Webb and the captain, but her logic had worked a temporary salve on Kevin's terror. Urged on by her and the warden, the young Finder moved forward toward the shattered section of rail, where the pilot and Val were lowering the dinghy into the water. Webb hopped down into the little wooden skiff, settling in her stern where he could unfasten the stowed oars. Valerie controlled the dinghy with the rope tied to the prow, urging the warden, Kevin, and Cassidy over the rail. Only when everyone else had boarded did the lithe woman spring down off the deck of the sinking boat.

After dropping the oar pins into their brackets, Webb pushed past Cassidy to take the center seat. As Val shoved them off from the wallowing boat, the pilot took one last look at his pride and joy. "That son of a bitch," he muttered darkly, plunging the blades of the oars into the water and drawing back on them with such a furious jerk that the little dinghy shot forward across the swells like a spooked horse. And Cassidy had no doubt to just what son of a bitch Webb was referring; when the two men met again, Click was going to have some explaining to do.

If they ever meet again, Cassidy couldn't help reminding herself. But she stolidly pushed the thought away and turned toward Kevin, who sat huddled beside the warden on the seat in front of Webb's. "I think they're gone now, Kev," she repeated hopefully. "At least there doesn't seem to be any more sign of them."

Less than a minute of Webb's powerful rowing had already taken them a good hundred feet from the floundering hull of his boat, so that when the wooden vessel finally took on enough water to overcome her buoyancy, they were in no danger from her backwash. Swiftly but almost gently, with barely a gurgle of protest, the sinking craft slipped beneath the blue-gray surface of the sea. But Webb never paused; he didn't even look up as she sunk from view. He just bent even more stolidly over the oars, the muscles in his back and forearms cording as he plied the blades.

Alone on the narrow stern seat of the dinghy, Cassidy glanced aft past the others to the captain. The woman's handsomely chiseled face was set with a grim frown, her eyes methodically sweeping the surface of the rolling swells around them. In the second seat Kevin sat hunched, huddled against the warden. The boy's leather trousers were soaked from pumping out the hold, and he still looked anxious and miserable. Only the warden seemed calm and approachable; and when his gaze happened to catch hers, Cassidy found herself blurting out something in self-defense.

"I know those things are . . . connected to me somehow," she said uneasily. "But I swear, I don't know what's making them do this. I don't have any control over them."

Ignoring Valerie's stabbing glare of disapproval, Cassidy concentrated instead on the warden's kind and understanding face.

"No one blames you for this, Cassidy," he said, a reassuring sentiment though hardly a universal one. He had one arm slung over Kevin's shoulders, and he gave the younger man a little squeeze. "At least we can be grateful that no one's been injured."

That brought a rude grunt from Webb, who obviously considered his boat a casualty worthy of note.

Kevin glanced sideways at the warden. "How far is it to land?" he asked, his hands knotted nervously in his lap. "We saw gulls, so—"

Because Cassidy was facing aft, and Valerie, Kevin, and the warden were all facing toward the stern, none of them realized why her eyes had suddenly widened. But something in Cassidy's speechless expression of alarm must have given them a pretty good idea. Before Webb could notice the abrupt silence and look up from his task, Cassidy said with low urgency, "Row faster!"

Not more than a dozen yards off the prow of the little skiff, the huge head and long columnar neck of one of the sea creatures had silently risen from the depths of the grayish water. Its vast mouth was partially open, and for the first time Cassidy realized that the monsters didn't really have teeth. The fleshless lips bordered directly on a hard, chitinous ridge, much like the beak of a bird. In the creature's jaws it daintily held a circular object that Cassidy recognized as the wheel from the helm of Webb's boat. The spoked wooden device appeared almost comically small in that giant maw, a mouth that looked large enough to easily accommodate a horse—sideways.

In spite of Cassidy's command, or perhaps because of it, Webb paused long enough to look up. His expression seemed caught between outrage and amazement. "That's my wheel—the damned things are *eating* my boat!" he exclaimed.

Better than eating us, Cassidy thought; but what she said was "Just keep rowing; we can go around it."

Not that the pilot had much choice, but he put forth a renewed effort and cut the dinghy sideways, veering away from the towering monster. The creature just watched them calmly, its huge head bobbing slightly with the roll of the waves. Then with an almost playful little flip of its dripping snout, it spit out the wheel, tossing it across the water toward their skiff. The discarded rim skipped across the surface of the water for a good twenty feet before coming to rest near the prow of the dinghy. With astonishing grace and speed, the long sinuous neck slid back down into the sea, disappearing without so much as a ripple to betray that it had ever been there at all.

Literally shuddering in terror, Kevin twisted around on the seat beside the warden, his eyes rolling. "W-where did it go?" he stammered, his hands clutching the side of the skiff with white-knuckled force.

Cassidy shook her head helplessly. "I don't know, Kev. Maybe it—"

With a silent fluidity entirely disproportionate to its massive size, the creature's broad head breached the surface of the water directly alongside the dinghy. Towering over the skiff's hapless occupants, water streaming from its coarsely gleaming hide, the monstrous head seemed to nod gently, almost thoughtfully. Its small dark eye was like an oval jewel set into the bony ridge of its brow as it regarded them.

Cassidy thought that she was going to scream; but her throat closed in a spasm of fear, her tongue too frozen to form any sound. Blocking out the blue sky above her, the creature's head was easily the length of the fragile skiff.

If Cassidy was too frightened to move, then Kevin was absolutely catatonic. The blond boy sat beside the warden, his face gone bloodless. The warden seemed to be trying to shield him from the sight of the menacing creature by crossing his forearms over Kevin's bowed head.

Although Webb and Valerie had initially frozen in surprise, each of them quickly reacted in their own typical fashion. The pilot lifted his oars, slicing the blades down to take a tremendous bite out of the water and shooting the dinghy forward again. And the captain lurched to her feet, swinging something on a length of rope over her head. It wasn't until she'd let fly with her makeshift weapon that Cassidy realized Valerie was trying to pelt the giant creature with the dinghy's puny little anchor.

Easily, as casually as a horse cropping twigs, the water monster's massive head dipped toward the dinghy. With a delicate precision those huge blunt jaws closed on Kevin's shoulders, tearing the petrified boy from the warden's grasp seemingly without even having touched the other man. Then the long neck reared back, rapidly lifting Kevin far over their heads.

"Oh, God!" Cassidy gasped.

"Kevin!" the warden shouted, shooting to his feet so rapidly that he nearly fell over Webb, his lurching movement making the dinghy rock wildly.

The seaman leaned back, splaying his oars to steady the pitching craft. In that moment he must have realized what the warden intended to do, for Cassidy could see Webb's hands leave the oars, an oath erupting from his lips as he grappled futilely for the younger man. But it was too late. With a clumsy trajectory born of pure desperation, the warden was over the side and into the rolling water.

"No!" Valerie commanded, leaping over his empty seat as her warden began swimming furiously toward the gigantic creature. But before the captain could follow him over the side, Webb's hands caught her in a viselike grip and he shook her, angrily, hard enough to make her head snap back.

By that time the warden had reached the thick column of the creature's protruding neck and was groping to get a hold on the coarse hide. To Cassidy's amazement, he wrapped his arms and legs around the trunklike appendage as if he intended to scale it. But before he could lift himself out of the water, the monster began to glide away across the water, towing the warden with it.

Without even realizing that she had moved, Cassidy found herself poised at the side of the skiff, about to go over. Dropping Valerie, Webb rounded on her with another angry bellow. "Damn you, stay put!" he fumed. "We don't need any more people in the water—I can *row* faster than either of you can *swim!*"

Valerie probably would have disputed that had she been able, but the pilot's sound shaking had temporarily incapacitated her. She slumped back onto the seat as Webb wielded his oars. Cassidy's head spun as the skiff swung around in a 180-degree arc and took off in pursuit of the two men and the monster.

As Kevin dangled from the creature's jaws, easily twenty feet above the surface of the water, Cassidy was terrified that the young man was already dead. His body lolled limply, as lifeless as the man-shaped stuffed creations the Woodsmen had left hanging from the big trees along the Long River. But the warden's fierce determination to free his friend and companion was undaunted. The moment the monster slowed its pace, he began whacking furiously against the tough wet hide of the huge upraised neck.

"Don't!" Valerie shouted impotently from the prow of the approaching skiff. "Wait!"

As if the warden would—as if he could have. The creature still held Kevin's boneless body casually in its mouth, one glittering eye narrowing to peer at the warden's insignificant attack.

They never hurt me, Cassidy reminded herself, a numb mantra of desperate hope as the dinghy raced closer. *If they wanted to kill us, they could have done that back in the harbor . . .*

But the fact remained that there was nothing harmless in the harrowing sight of Kevin hanging from that huge chitinous mouth. The creature could easily crush him with one indifferent twitch of those massive jaws; and it could simply drown the warden with a bob of its serpentine neck. All of which made the warden's feckless rescue effort all the more amazing to Cassidy. As horrified as she had been by Kevin's abduction, the warden had reacted before she could even force her frozen limbs to move.

As they neared the water monster, the warden was still pounding at its neck with his fist. "Get back!" Valerie shouted at him; but he was like a man possessed, and Cassidy doubted that he had even heard his captain's furious command. He was determined not to let the creature take Kevin.

Cassidy wasn't sure just what to expect as Webb's powerful rowing brought them closer to the scene of the conflict. Just as back on the boat when Valerie had kicked at the invading tentacle, she feared that the monster would somehow retaliate, both for their proximity and for the warden's continuing attack. But that was not exactly what happened.

Smoothly and swiftly, the monster started to pull away from the approaching dinghy, Kevin still held high above the water in its jaws. Once again wrapping his arms and legs around the thick neck, the warden was towed along, like a leech clinging to a fish. Cassidy held her breath as the monster's speed increased. It was so huge; in just minutes it easily could swim miles from them—or it simply could dive beneath the surface again, drowning both men.

"Damn you, let it go!" Valerie shouted vehemently, but to no effect.

The creature slowed and paused again, some two hundred feet from the dinghy, its sleek head dipping lower. The moment he could gain his balance, the warden resumed his angry pounding on the monster's glittering hide. Its deep-set eye, gleaming like a diamond in the dark skull, seemed to regard the puny effort with bemused annoyance. Then suddenly the mighty head dropped lower, and Cassidy cringed, certain she was about to witness the death of both of her friends.

For a moment the only sounds were the frenzied creak of Webb's oars in their sockets as the pilot continued to row across the swells and the dull thud of the warden's ineffectual fists on the creature's powerful neck. Then, to Cassidy's breathless astonishment, the water monster gently opened its jaws. Kevin's limp body rolled out, practically right into the warden's arms.

The creature pulled back, its huge head poised like a rattlesnake about to strike. But all the monster did was draw farther away, the sinuous column of its neck slicing so neatly through the water that it barely even raised a wake. When it was about twenty feet from the two men, suddenly it was just gone, dropping like a stone back into the depths of the sea. The grayish-blue water rolled so silently over it that the massive creature might never have been there at all.

Chapter 4 ◀▥▥▥

While Webb used the oars to steady the little craft, Cassidy helped Valerie haul first Kevin and then the warden over the side of the dinghy. In their waterlogged leathers, the two men looked like drowned animals. As Cassidy pulled him forward between the seats, Kevin was so limp and motionless that for one painful moment she wondered if he was still alive. But as the warden clambered in after him, he was quick to reassure them.

"He's just fainted," the warden said breathlessly, automatically smoothing back the darkened strands of Kevin's long wet hair. "He's got a few bruises and scrapes, but I don't think it really hurt him."

Webb had already swung the skiff around and was leaning into the oars again, propelling them toward the distant shore. Whatever the pilot thought, he made no comment. But the captain of the Troopers was still visibly seething over what had just happened, her anger fueled in a large part by her own impotence in the situation.

"What did you think you were doing, going over the side after him?" she railed at the warden, her dark eyes blazing. "You could have been killed by that thing!"

The warden sat at the bottom of the dinghy, Kevin's slumped torso pulled across his lap. He looked up at Valerie with a characteristic mixture of tolerance and irony. "Kevin is the one who could have been killed, Val. I had to protect him."

Real fury sparked in the woman's eyes, an emotion echoed in the coiled lines of her taut leonine body. "And *I* am sworn to protect *you*, damn your blood! You aren't supposed to have to protect your own Troopers!"

The warden's head bowed, his wet and tangled hair falling across his face. The posture almost suggested penitence, but

53

Cassidy doubted that the effect was calculated; he was merely studying Kevin's slack and pallid face. "He's not a Trooper, Val," he reminded her quietly. "He's just a boy."

Valerie's jaw was clenched, as if she were biting back some more vitriolic response. "A boy who nearly got you killed," she finally said, her voice low but unmistakably bitter.

The warden chose not to take it any further, and his captain would not continue to rail on without his response. She subsided back onto the small seat at the prow of the dinghy, where she sat glaring out across the empty sea.

And Cassidy kept her own counsel. Watching the warden cradle Kevin's limp body in the bottom of the skiff, she remembered the way he had shot over the side of the craft after him and the way he had attacked the water monster. Was it possible that less than half an hour earlier the same man had been huddled in her arms, crying Andy Greene's tears? Once she had thought that she had known the warden simply because she remembered Andy Greene. But the man who sat before her, holding his unconscious friend, was a constant surprise to her. When she had discovered that the warden of Horses was Andy Greene, she had been convinced that it was Andy who would be able to help her go home again. There on the calmly rolling sea, Cassidy finally realized that it was going to take both of the extraordinary men who inhabited that familiar body to make that return possible.

Cassidy had no idea how far they traveled before Valerie finally sighted land, but it seemed to her that Webb had been rowing for hours. The seaman had not complained, and he shook off with a wry look her offer to spell him at the oars. But the sun was sliding low in the western sky as they came in across the big breakers that raced over the shoals.

Cassidy felt an enervating weariness that had less to do with actual physical exhaustion than it did with the sheer stress of what they had been through. She was relieved at Webb's steady skill in piloting the flighty little dinghy in over the rolling waves. Her back and limbs ached as she joined Valerie in going over the side into the knee-deep foaming water to help beach the skiff. Even the warden left Kevin and climbed out to help them drag the flat-bottomed vessel ashore, several yards up over the wet stones.

The captain looked up and down the rocky beach, its features already half obscured in the deep shadows of the adjacent trees. "You have any idea where we are?" she asked Webb.

The seaman looked up from lashing the anchor rope to a particularly large stone. He glanced around. "No," he admitted easily, "but that's hardly our first priority right now."

"He's right, Val," the warden said from beside the dinghy. "We need to get a fire going and see if we can find something to eat." He looked down into the skiff at Kevin. "I want to get him out of those wet leathers before he takes a chill."

For a moment Cassidy thought that the warden's solicitous concern for Kevin was going to inspire another tirade from Valerie, but there was no perceptible hesitation before the woman nodded in agreement.

"I'll look for firewood," Cassidy quickly offered, anxious to do something useful.

The warden gave her a grateful smile. "Thank you, Cassidy."

Secretly embarrassed by how his approval warmed her, Cassidy added, "Maybe I can find some berries or something, too, while I'm looking."

Valerie had been studying the stony strand, its pebbled surface rapidly purpling in the gathering dusk. "Don't go into the woods," she warned. "Stay out in the open and stay in sight."

Cassidy questioned the need for that restriction, but she held her tongue. The last thing she wanted to do was start an argument with a woman who was demonstrably a master of the verbal barb. Besides, she figured that once she had moved away from the dinghy, Valerie probably wouldn't try to keep track of where she went anyway. As Cassidy started off across the uneven rocky beach, Webb was helping the warden lift a still-unconscious Kevin from the skiff.

As she bent to snag her first piece of weathered driftwood from the beach, Cassidy automatically reached out for her innate sense of the gray mare's presence. She was freshly disappointed and discouraged when she found no trace of the horse. It had been bad enough when they'd been asea, but at least there she could console herself with the fact that miles of water separated her from the shore. Somehow once they were back on land again, Cassidy found the absence of the horse's familiar presence even more depressing. Glancing up from the ragged shoreline, she stared into the dark bank of trees. How far away must the mare still be, if she couldn't even detect any trace of her?

Would I even know if she was dead?

Shaking away the morbid thought, Cassidy redevoted herself to the task of gathering firewood. Although the beach was bare of vegetation and littered with small drifts and ridges of washed stones, there was a surprising amount of sticks, branches, seaweed, and other flotsam along the tideline. Then again, Cassidy realized as she bent to snag another chunk of wood, there was no one else around there to have scavenged it.

When the foul odor first hit her nostrils, Cassidy was several hundred feet up the beach from where they had come ashore with the dinghy. For a moment she just froze, motionless in the deepening gloom. *Oh, God, not again—not now!* she prayed. After everything that had already happened that afternoon, she didn't know if she could have coped with the stinking hanging monsters. But as she forced herself to scan the surrounding area slowly, she grew more puzzled than alarmed. She was a good twenty yards from the nearest trees, too far for the creatures' stench to be that strong. And the beach itself was nearly flat, with no feature more prominent than a few shallow shelves of stone. Even in the growing darkness there certainly wasn't enough cover to hide something the size of the fetid carrion eaters.

Cautiously stepping forward, Cassidy studied the stretch of rocky ground ahead of her. She sniffed again. Then she almost laughed aloud. "Dead fish!" she proclaimed, feeling both foolish and relieved. She kicked with the toe of her boot at a waterlogged tangle of seaweed, uncovering a pale flash of rotting flesh, gone furry with mold and decay.

Moving farther, Cassidy used the tip of one of the branches she'd picked up to prod at the stringy sludge. Some of the fish looked a little fresher. Curious, she explored the next drift of flotsam. Beyond the seaweed, on the jagged washline of the beach where the rolling waves ceaselessly broke and pulled back, lay several perfectly intact fish, their dead eyes still shining and clear.

By the time Cassidy returned to the dinghy, it was almost dark. She was surprised to see that Valerie already had a small fire going and was feeding it bits of twigs and dried seaweed that she had found in the immediate area. The captain looked up impatiently at Cassidy. "About time," she said, holding out her arms for the wood.

Once Valerie had taken the firewood, Cassidy went over to the warden, who was kneeling beside a recumbent Kevin, gently chafing the unconscious boy's hands. Kevin had been stripped of his soaked leathers and was dressed in Webb's shirt. The loose cotton garment was so big on him that it looked like a nightgown, and came halfway to his knees. The blond boy's face was slack but untroubled; he looked particularly childlike and vulnerable in the oversize shirt.

"How is he?" Cassidy asked quietly.

The warden glanced up at her with a reassuring smile. "He was conscious for a few moments when we were dressing him."

"Is he going to be all right?"

The warden was gently arranging Kevin's long bare legs; he didn't look up as he replied. "He was a little upset; I don't think he exactly remembered what had happened. But his color is better now. He has a few bruises on his chest, but I don't think there's been any serious damage done."

Cassidy stared down helplessly at Kevin, unable to erase the image of that limp body lolling from the massive creature's jaws. If there had been no serious damage done to him, it was only because the monster had spared him deliberately.

Cassidy finally realized that the warden was looking up at her again, his nose wrinkling. "What is it you have there?" he asked.

Suddenly remembering her find, Cassidy reached into the capacious pockets of her seaman's shirt and produced a handful of fish. "They're dead," she explained, "but they still look pretty fresh, and I couldn't find anything else out there that we could eat."

Webb had come up directly behind Cassidy, startling her when he spoke from right over her shoulder. "Alewives," he said. He shrugged with equanimity. "They're rough fish, and no treat even fresh, but I've eaten worse."

The warden gave Cassidy a tired but encouraging smile. "They'll do just fine," he said. "And I'd rather not have to do any more foraging until daylight."

Valerie had set an efficient fire by then, its warmth and light painting the immediate area with a cheery glow. Against her will, Cassidy thought of other camps, other fires. It seemed that her whole history in that world could be recorded in a trail of campfires, always on her way to somewhere else. Abruptly discarding the memories, Cassidy turned toward Webb as the bare-chested man reached for some of the fish she held. "Do you think that in daylight you'll be able to tell where we are?" she asked him.

"Maybe," he said mildly.

Valerie looked up from arranging a semicircle of flat rocks around the perimeter of the fire. In the flickering light, the aquiline planes of her smooth face stood out in bold relief. "We know which way north is," she said. "In the morning we could start back toward the city."

Involuntarily Cassidy winced. But the warden seemed entirely unperturbed by his captain's persistent insubordination. Lightly brushing back a damp strand of Kevin's pale hair from that peaceful face, the warden ignored Valerie's comment and instead addressed the pilot. "How far do you think we are from the cove where you were to take us?"

Webb threw Valerie a quick glance before he replied. "It would have been a day's travel, maybe less, by boat. Now—" He shrugged, indicating the dinghy with a tip of his shaggy head. "—with that thing, maybe two or three days. No more."

The warden nodded. "Then with your help, seaman, we'll leave in the morning." As if to intercept her imminent protest, his eyes moved to Val, pinning her as he concluded, "For that is what I have sworn to do."

The captain bit back whatever she had been about to say, and Cassidy found that she could not begrudge the woman her reservations. She was sworn to protect her warden, not to lead him into danger. In her place, Cassidy would have done no less. But she also could not help feeling relieved by the warden reiterating his determination to keep his promise to her, despite the setbacks they had suffered.

Immersed in thought, at first Cassidy missed what Valerie had said to her. It wasn't until the woman impatiently repeated her request that Cassidy jerked into action. "I said, are you going to give me those fish—or did you intend to eat them raw?"

There had been no question about the need to set watches, and Cassidy offered to take the first one. For a time she thought that either Valerie or the warden could just as easily have taken over, since neither of them seemed prone to sleep. The captain sat at the edge of the fire, idly arranging the coals and occasionally feeding in a new chunk of driftwood. And the warden kept his silent vigil over Kevin's limp form, moving only now and then to slightly rearrange the unconscious man's position.

As for Webb, he uncomplainingly settled in right after they'd finished eating. Despite the rough scrapple of rock on the beach, the pilot managed to scoop out a small, smooth depression for himself, in which he curled up like a dog. Within minutes he was snoring softly.

The night air off the Gray Sea was cool and damp. Cassidy crossed her arms over her chest and hugged the baggy shirt to herself as she slowly paced the perimeter of their little camp. Overhead, the black and cloudless sky was strewn with countless gleaming stars, their cold brilliance as glittering as the remorseless eyes of the sea creatures. Shivering, Cassidy looked out across the water, where the long waves ceaselessly rolled in over the shoals, their foaming tops effervescent in the starlight. Was it the same sky, the same stars, the same ocean as the real world? she wondered.

With that thought came a whole host of unwanted memories, both of her own world and of the friends she had made in that one. Cassidy found that not only did she deeply miss her mare, she also missed Rowena. Forced for the first time to travel without the plucky brunette, Cassidy longed for Rowena's loyal companionship and her ready humor. And Rowena was the only other person who remembered the real world; Cassidy wished she could tell her about the bizarre things Andy had revealed during the warden's lapses. Perhaps Rowena would have some insight into the episodes, not to mention the objectivity that Cassidy herself so sorely lacked.

That thought led Cassidy to another uncomfortable realization. It was becoming increasingly unsettling for her to be so close to the warden, since she had come to see him as a person distinctly separate from Andy Greene. And then there was Valerie to deal with; the captain's fierce protectiveness and her vociferous opposition to searching for the Alchemist made Cassidy wary of the dark-haired woman.

Absently kicking at a rounded stone, Cassidy admitted that Rowena was not the only person she missed. They could use Allen's steadfast calm; and even a little of Becky's unfettered determination would be helpful. And Click . . . well, perhaps it was better not to think about Click at all.

Cassidy started at a small sound behind her and whirled around to see Valerie's slim form less than a dozen feet from her. *Boy, you're really alert!* she chided herself. An entire Troop could have stormed the beach while she had stood there reminiscing.

"Can't sleep?" she said to Valerie. It sounded inane even to her own ears, but she felt awkward around the captain even under the best of circumstances.

Cassidy thought that the captain was going to reproach her for her obvious lack of vigilance, but the woman merely nodded. She stopped a few feet from Cassidy and stood with her hands clasped behind her back, gazing out over the breakers. If Cassidy had known Valerie well, she would have surmised that the captain was uncomfortable about something; but Valerie had always seemed so self-contained, so in control, that Cassidy thought that couldn't be possible.

Just when the silence between them had stretched out to the point where Cassidy felt she would either have to say something or just move away, Valerie finally spoke. "I want to apologize for what I said to you back on Webb's boat," the captain said without turning.

Cassidy had to do some rapid mental backpedaling to search for what comment could have sparked so remarkable a gesture from the warden's captain. Her confusion was so evident that Valerie finally turned to face her.

"I wasn't serious about throwing you overboard," she said by way of explanation. "I was just angry and frustrated. I realize that even if those creatures are following you, you aren't responsible for them."

Still mildly stunned, Cassidy tried to diminish the importance of the incident. "That's all right," she said. "I knew you didn't mean it." She further attempted to leaven the moment with a bit of self-deprecating humor. "Besides, if you'd tossed me overboard, the warden would've just had to jump in after me."

Even in the faint starlight, Cassidy could detect the small rueful smile that lifted Valerie's delicate lips. Briefly shaking her head, the captain conceded the point to Cassidy. Then her expression turned more serious again. "Earlier on the deck, before the monsters attacked us . . ." She paused, making a slight but oddly evocative gesture. "Was it like the other spells he's had?"

Cassidy wanted to trust Valerie, and maybe there was no reason not to; but she'd grown too well conditioned in dissembling to just be able to blurt out everything she had learned. "More or less," she temporized. "Luckily, he snapped out of it before the boat started to go under."

The captain gazed into Cassidy's face, her expression a thoughtful frown. "You still think he's someone else, though? This person you know from the Slow World?"

"I'm not sure," Cassidy said honestly. "It's almost like he's two different people." She shrugged artlessly. "I believe that most of the time he's exactly who he thinks he is, your warden. But when he has these spells, it's like he becomes the person I know."

"Because he recognizes you then?"

Cassidy nodded. "Not only that, but he even acts differently, more like the person I know. He acts like he's still in the Slow World." She hesitated, debating the wisdom of revealing any more to this strong-willed woman. But Valerie's expression was calm, interested, expectant. "And when he acts like he's in the Slow World," she concluded, "there's something going on there that's scaring the hell out of him."

The captain considered that in silence for a few moments.

Cassidy was surprised when the leather-clad woman reached out then and lightly squeezed her shoulder. "I don't pretend to understand what's been happening to him," Valerie said, "and I don't doubt that your coming here has been responsible for it. But regardless of that, I'm glad that you're here with him. I don't know how anyone else could get him through this."

Staring into that serene and finely chiseled face, Cassidy caught a glimmer of the deeper purpose that drove the warden's captain. Yes, she was sworn to protect him; but it was more than that, as well. What Valerie felt toward her warden was far more than mere allegiance or duty. She may have lived in a world without romance or sex; but it was not, Cassidy had learned, a world without devotion.

Cassidy fumbled awkwardly to make some response. But before she could speak, Valerie dropped her hand from her shoulder and said matter-of-factly, "Why don't you turn in now? I'm wide awake anyway, so I may as well stand watch."

"Are you sure?" Cassidy asked. "I'm not sleepy, either." *You aren't very alert, either,* her little inner voice added; but fortunately Valerie was more tactful.

"I'm used to night duty," she said. She studied Cassidy for a moment, then added, "If you really can't sleep, maybe you could offer to sit with Kevin for a while. I'd like to see the warden get some rest."

"Okay," Cassidy readily agreed. She tried to read in Valerie's faintly illuminated face the woman's true feelings about the protective affection the warden lavished upon the blond boy; but the captain's brief moment of self-revelation seemed to have passed, and her returning gaze was a study in neutrality. "I'm not sure how much luck I'll have," Cassidy said, "but I'll give it a try."

Slowly making her way back across the rocky beach toward their fire, Cassidy glanced back once toward the shore. She could barely make out Valerie's silhouette, a dark sylph against the pale phosphorescence of the foaming waves. But Cassidy still felt a strange satisfaction from her encounter with the captain. She had always admired the woman and wanted to like her, as well. Their conversation had gone some distance toward making that possible.

In the muted glow of the banked fire, Cassidy could see the curled form of Webb's body, peacefully sleeping on. But the warden still sat vigilantly at Kevin's side, watching the recumbent boy with a simple and uncomplaining attentiveness. Cassidy came around from behind them and squatted down on the other side of

Kevin, gently touching his pale brow. The warden looked up at
her with a small, tired smile.

"Why don't you try to get some sleep?" Cassidy said. "I can sit
with him for a while." Seeing the incipient protest pass across that
handsome but worn face, she quickly added, "Kevin knows me
and trusts me, too. If he would wake up and be frightened, I know
I can reassure him."

The warden's mouth quirked ruefully at his own transparency.
"I feel responsible for him," he said needlessly. "But if you could
watch him for just a few minutes?" He smiled again, an expression of utter and devastating ingenuousness. "I need to relieve
myself."

"Go," Cassidy urged, motioning briskly at him. "He won't even
know you've been gone."

When she saw how stiffly the usually graceful young man rose,
and how his creased and rumpled damp leathers hung from his
body, Cassidy became determined to extend the warden's little
respite. "You won't be of any use to him or to anyone else, yourself included, if you exhaust yourself," she pointed out as he
stretched to take the kinks out of his limbs.

"I'm aware of that, Cassidy," he reminded her. "And why
aren't *you* sleeping?"

"Touché," Cassidy replied; the gist of the word seemed to
translate, even if the specific idiom didn't. She gestured a dismissal. "Just go piss, would you?"

"Yes, sir," he teased, starting away from the campfire.

Cassidy sat down on the little cleared spot of beach alongside
Kevin. The packed sand was cool and firm beneath her. She
lightly rested one hand on the loose cotton fabric that covered the
blond boy's chest, but her gaze wandered, automatically tracking
in the direction in which the warden had disappeared. She was relieved just to have things ride easily between them for then. The
bizarre emergence of Andy Greene had forced her to admit how
much more easily she could relate to that man, even as silent and
unreachable as he had been. It was the warden of Horses who stymied her, and she wasn't sure just how to respond to him anymore. Once their uneasy alliance based on mutual self-interest had
collapsed under the weight of the siege on the Iron City and their
traumatic escape, she had been left with a confusing confliction of
feelings. But she could not escape the irony of one brutally honest
realization: *You always wanted Andy Greene, even though you
could never have him. And now here you are with the very man
he essentially would have been, had Andy been born normal . . .*

And in some way she still refused to examine, that idea scared the hell out of her.

Cassidy was jolted out of her introspective musings by a movement beneath her hand. Kevin groaned softly and tried to push up. Leaning over him, she saw his eyelids flutter open and his eyes darted blearily around.

"C-Cassidy?" he croaked unsteadily.

"Shh, you're all right, Kevin." She gently held him down. "Don't try to sit up yet."

Kevin squinted, frowning distractedly in the dim light of the fire. "Where are we?" he asked her.

"On the beach," she said. "We're safe now, Kev; everything's okay."

Kevin made another attempt to sit up, wincing at the effort and easily thwarted by even Cassidy's light restraint. "Hurts!" he complained.

"I know, but you'll be fine," she reassured him. Cassidy hesitated a moment, then asked, "Do you remember what happened, Kev?"

His odd-colored eyes looked luminous, almost ethereal as they widened in the faint light. "The boat sank," he said. But then, before Cassidy could probe any further, Kevin yawned widely and announced, "I've got to pee."

"Okay," Cassidy said, trying not to smile. "Can you wait just a minute?" She paused. "Kev?"

But the blond boy's head had lolled back against the inviting ground, his eyelids dropped closed. Once again Kevin slept.

Moments later the warden reappeared in the unsteady circle of firelight, his gait considerably more limber and his leathers more neatly arranged. He looked quizzically at Cassidy's expression as he sank down again on the other side of Kevin.

"He was awake again for a minute," she explained.

Concern creased that youthful face as he glanced down at the sleeping boy. "Was he frightened?" he asked.

But Cassidy shook her head. "A little sore, a little confused," she said, "but he wasn't agitated. I'm not sure that he remembers anything past the boat sinking." She automatically swept back a few errant strands of Kevin's long pale hair and smiled. "He said that he had to pee—and then he fell right to sleep again."

Smiling as well, an expression that could be utterly devastating on that boyishly handsome face, the warden said, "That usually isn't the way it works!"

For a few moments neither of them spoke, each caught up in

his own thoughts and feelings about the friend they shared in common. Then Cassidy said, "Are you sure you won't try to sleep, too? I'll stay right here beside him."

But the warden shook his head. "I don't feel sleepy," he said.

Cassidy didn't really feel sleepy, either, but she was willing to make a try at it. Just as she was about to get to her feet, the warden spoke again.

"This afternoon on the boat," he said quietly, as if by way of introduction. "These . . . spells I'm having are changing."

Few topics could have held Cassidy there beside him more effectively. She looked at him across Kevin's recumbent form, forcing herself to stifle the obvious question in order to find out just what the warden would say unprompted. He was gazing past her and Kevin, toward the campfire, his classic profile rimmed by its pale honeyed light. When he went on, his voice was reflective and subdued.

"Whatever it is that happens to me when I have one of these episodes, it's getting harder and harder for me to separate myself from it when it's over." His eyes suddenly shifted, looking directly into Cassidy's face. "This last time on the boat, when I came around again, for a few moments I didn't even know where I was." He paused significantly, then added, "I didn't even know *who* I was."

At that time, Cassidy had been too concerned with the basic matter of survival to have noticed; but when she thought back on what had happened, she remembered that the warden had seemed briefly disoriented. Luckily that confusion hadn't lasted long, and the matter had been lost in the harrowing events that had followed. Although she itched to question him more specifically about what he had experienced, she still held back, waiting to see where he would take the subject.

"I think I'm remembering more of what happened during the episodes, too," he said. He glanced down at Kevin's slumbering form, absently smoothing a fold of the seaman's loose shirt along the slender young man's side. "I know that something happened to you and that I was very frightened for you." He looked directly into Cassidy's face again. "I know that seeing you again and speaking with you was all that reassured me that you were still alive."

Cassidy felt a shiver run through her, a chill that had nothing to do with the cool sea air. She automatically pulled up her knees, locking her arms around them and hugging her thighs. The warden had remembered at least the essence of everything that Andy

Greene had described to her from the Slow World: her presumed injury, seeing her lifeless body, fearing that she was dead. Even if he didn't seem to remember the details, how long would it be before Andy's life became as indelibly real to him as his own?

Cassidy wasn't certain how the warden had interpreted her continued silence, but when he spoke again his voice seemed to project both curiosity and frustration in equal measure. "If I'm somehow slipping into the life of this other person, this Andy Greene, then why is it that he doesn't understand what he sees in his own world? Why don't *I* understand it?"

The truth, or at least what Cassidy then suspected to be the truth, seemed too ruthless a response. Hedging for a moment, she decided to take a more oblique tack. Looking down at Kevin's chest, where the warden's hand still rested lightly, she said, "Do you think it's possible for a person to be in the same place at two different times?"

Frankly puzzled, the warden just stared at her for a moment, his brow furrowed in thought. "You mean like you sitting here when I just came back a few minutes ago," he asked, "and you still sitting here now?"

"Not exactly," Cassidy said carefully. Her hands lifted, describing imaginary brackets a few inches apart in the air. "Closer than that—like maybe almost at the same time, but not quite." She searched his face for signs of comprehension. "Like maybe just a split second apart."

His eyes narrowed and his voice fell slightly. "You think that's what the Slow World is?" he asked intently. "Not a place in the past, but something—" He visibly grappled for a term. "—almost superimposed upon our world?"

Cassidy leaned forward, her own voice automatically matching the warden's quiet intensity. "How else could you be both Andy Greene and the warden of Horses?" she said. "How else could you exist in two places—how else could *I*?"

The young man considered that remarkable proposal in silence for a few moments, his chocolate-brown eyes unwavering on her face. "Let's assume that you're correct," he said then. His hand rose swiftly, cutting off her incipient interruption. "No, let's just assume it, Cassidy," he reiterated. "Then why am I the only one who seems to be able to—to flash back into the Slow World? Why can't you?" He gave a vague little wave. "Why can't anyone here?" Then he paused, frowning. "Or am I the only one here who has an alternate identity in the Slow World?"

Taking a deep, calming breath, Cassidy plunged onward,

scarcely able to believe what they were so evenly discussing and afraid that at any moment she might blink and the whole conversation would just dissolve into the kind of evasion and apathetic double-talk to which that world had accustomed her. "I'm there, too, remember? Andy sees me when you—when he—speaks to me." Her voice dropped even lower, a husky whisper given conspiratorily across the slumbering body that lay between them. "I think that everyone in this world also exists in the Slow World, in some way. I'm just not sure exactly how."

The warden sat back a bit, rubbing his chin in an unconscious gesture of deep thought. "And you think that this Alchemist—if he exists—can reach these other people in the Slow World," he surmised.

Cassidy's arms tightened around her raised knees. "I think it's more than that," she said quietly. "If you can become Andy Greene, then I think that anyone here can become who they are there. And if that's possible, then there's no reason why they can't become that person and stay that person. I think the Alchemist can help me get back home."

The warden appeared to digest that for a long, wordless moment, while he gazed past Cassidy's shoulder and out over the darkened strand of beach. She found that she could not interpret the particular look of sober rumination on that deceptively familiar face. She had no idea that she might have in any way hurt his feelings until he spoke again.

"Do you find this world so wretched then, Cassidy?" he said, his soft voice treading so fine a line between rueful teasing and genuine sadness that she could not tell on which side it fell. "So unbearable that you would do anything you could to leave us?"

Squeezing her knees together, Cassidy deliberately closed her heart to the implications of his question. "I don't belong here," she said doggedly. "I belong in the real world, the world I remember. I just want to go home again."

But as she sat there on that rocky beach, it was not the first time Cassidy found her fixed sense of resolve being compromised by feelings that she was desperate to avoid examining further.

Rude awakenings had seemingly become the natural order of things, and Cassidy was less than surprised when she was catapulted from an exhausted if troubled sleep by a loud commotion. Jerking upright in her crude bed in the small hollow she had scooped out between the larger rocks, she blinked grittily into the pale light of early dawn. The warden was already on his feet but still standing beside Kevin, who had sat up and was looking around groggily. The shouting had come from farther out on the beach, near the shoreline, where Webb and Valerie stood beside the dinghy, swearing at each other and wildly gesticulating.

After exchanging a quizzical glance with the warden, Cassidy yawned and lurched to her feet. She began stumbling after him over the stony ground. From that distance she couldn't figure out what all the fuss was about; neither the pilot nor the captain nor the little skiff appeared to be in any danger. But as she drew nearer to the wave line and could make out some of the loud words Webb and Valerie were exchanging, Cassidy felt a sudden chill spread through her.

"Damn it, it was *your* watch—it's *your* boat!" the captain was berating the seaman. "How the hell could you let this happen?"

By that time Cassidy was close enough to see the huge effort Webb was expending just to keep himself from slugging the infuriated Trooper. But she still couldn't see any problem with the dinghy.

"I told you, I was awake the whole time!" Webb growled through gritted teeth. "And I didn't see anything!"

The warden's voice from right behind her caused Cassidy to start. "What's going on here?" he asked calmly. "Val?"

Cassidy glanced over as the warden stepped forward, looking from his captain to the grimly frowning pilot. "What's the problem?" he repeated with authority.

"The problem is that he was supposed to be watching the damned boat!" Valerie railed.

"I *was* watching it!" Webb snapped back.

Valerie turned her full glare back on the big brown-haired man. "Then how did *this* happen?" she demanded furiously.

Kevin ambled up beside Cassidy, yawning widely. "What's going on?" he asked sleepily.

Warily skirting Webb and Valerie, Cassidy edged close enough to inspect the dinghy. Even from only a few yards away, the craft had appeared completely normal, resting on the rocky beach in exactly the same place where they had dragged it the night before, still tethered by its anchor line to one of the larger stones. It wasn't until she actually peered over the side of the skiff that Cassidy finally understood the problem.

"What the hell happened?" she blurted out in surprise. "It's full of *holes*!"

The entire bottom of the dinghy, from bow to stern, was pocked with dozens of neat round holes, their diameters varying from the size of a quarter to nearly six inches across. Several had even cut right through the heavier timber ribs of the vessel's framework.

As Cassidy stepped back from the little skiff, her gaze moved out unwillingly across the relentlessly rolling waves. She couldn't think of a single rational explanation for the destruction of the dinghy, although she thought she knew the cause of the damage. But there was one thing she knew for certain: They wouldn't be sailing anywhere again in that craft.

Chapter 5 ←|||||

Absently popping another crisply cooked alewife into her mouth, Cassidy watched Webb's actions with an avid curiosity. The pilot's shoreline ritual was obviously some form of navigational plotting, but he was performing the feat with no instrumentation more sophisticated than a couple of sticks and a length of string. Squatting near the water's edge, the shaggy-haired man used the piece of string carefully to remeasure the long shadow of one of the sticks, which he had stuck upright in the wet sand. Then he inserted the second stick in a direct line with the shadow of the first and stretched out the string again.

Munching the last of her fishy breakfast, Cassidy decided that the alewives actually weren't so bad once you got used to them. Gutted and baked by the fire, they tasted something like slightly rancid potato chips. Which was probably a good thing, since so far the fish had been the only edible thing any of them had found near the beach. Continuing to study Webb's calculations, she wished that she'd paid more attention to basic geometry when she'd been in school. A lack of written language and numbers notwithstanding, what the pilot was doing definitely was some sort of reckoning based on the measurement of the angle of the sun and some other geometric variables. She had no idea how he was doing it, but he seemed satisfied with the results.

Alerted by the sound of footfalls on the shifting rocks, Cassidy turned to find Kevin at her shoulder, proffering her a few more fish. The young man looked entirely normal again, dressed in his dried leathers and with his long hair pulled neatly back into his customary ponytail. Cassidy smiled at him and shook her head in polite refusal.

Some fifty feet away, around the remains of their campfire, the warden and his captain were engaged in terse conversation. The explosion Cassidy had expected between Valerie and Webb had never occurred; the warden had seen to that. But it seemed that the warden and Val had been locked in a quiet battle of wills ever since the irreparable damage to the dinghy had been discovered.

Cassidy noticed that Kevin had glanced back toward the fire; she gave him a sympathetic look. "Still at it, huh?" she asked.

"She wants to go back north, to the city," Kevin confided to Cassidy. "She wants all of us to go back, I mean."

Cassidy didn't need to comment. Things would have been far simpler if they'd still had a skiff. Traveling on foot was an unattractive prospect at best, and a dangerous one at worst. But the little craft couldn't be repaired, even if they'd had something to caulk her with.

Despite Webb's indignant protestations, and the warden's direct command that she drop her accusations, Valerie still blamed the seaman for what had happened. The captain continued to insist that the only logical explanation for the damage having been done undetected was Webb's negligence at watch. But Cassidy knew that in that world, logic was an optional quality, and she was certain that there was no way the seaman could have prevented what had happened. Undoubtedly it had been monsters, she thought; probably the little ones, which they had dubbed demons. The neatly incised holes in the dinghy were eerily similar to the type of wounds they had inflicted upon their human victims.

Kevin was still standing companionably beside Cassidy when Webb gained his feet again and dusted the damp sand from his hands. The pilot glanced briefly out over the waves and then said, "This would have been a hell of a lot easier if we still had a boat."

"Do you know where we are?" Cassidy asked him.

The seaman met her eyes. "Yeah," he said, "and I know where we're going—I'm just not sure how the hell we're going to get there if we have to walk!"

Noticing that Webb had completed his calculations, the warden approached them across the beach. Although Cassidy was certain he had still been arguing with Valerie, his expression was calm and expectant. "Were you able to calculate our position?" he asked Webb.

The pilot kicked at a loose stone. "We've come farther south than I originally thought. The storm must've carried us more southeast than east." Cassidy noted that he didn't even mention the intervention of the water monsters. "The cove where I was going to take you would be less than a day's journey from here—by sea." Webb frowned, throwing a look across the rugged beach to the edge of the tree line, where the morning sun colored the vegetation a brilliant green. "Walking, I don't know how long it'll take. I don't even know if it can be done."

Cassidy lifted her jaw determinedly. All of her journeys in that world had held their own particular difficulties, their own inherent perils, even traveling with the Tinkers down the Long River. "If it's less than a day's trip by water," she said reasonably, "it can't be more than a few days on foot. And I'm sure we'll be able to find something better than alewives to eat once we—"

Webb cocked a sardonic brow at her as he interrupted. "It wouldn't be more than a few days' trip *if* we can walk it. But unless you know how to walk across water, it's going to be a bit more complicated than that."

Valerie had finally come up behind them, her curiosity overcoming her resentment. "What are you saying?" she asked him.

Webb turned to her with an expression that bordered on grim satisfaction. Valerie's unjust accusations had managed to rankle the usually even-tempered man, and he seemed to welcome the opportunity to be the one to break the bad news to the captain. "We could walk it in a few days if there was nothing between here and the cove but beach and woods," he said. "But there are rivers and their estuaries—two or maybe three of them, if my reckoning is right. And they're going to be a problem."

Kevin looked puzzled. "Can't we just cross them?" he asked ingenuously.

The pilot favored the blond boy with a mild and tolerant look. "If they aren't too wide; but just finding a place we can ford them might take us pretty far inland. And with this wet season—" Webb spread his big hands, a gesture that managed to convey both the potential width of the rivers and the magnitude of the challenge that faced them. "—if they've flooded the lowlands all the way back into the swamp, there's no way we'll get across them."

Webb's glum pronouncement hung over them for a few moments, like a dark cloud. Cassidy found that she could not bring herself to meet the warden's eyes, even though she was anxious to gauge his reaction to the seaman's bad news. She already knew that she had to go on, alone if that became necessary. If she didn't reach the cove that had been their original destination, there would be no hope of rendezvousing with Click and the others. And if she didn't find them again . . .

Then I could be trapped here forever . . .

Cassidy refused even to consider that possibility.

She felt her heart drop in her chest when the warden calmly asked Webb, "What about going north again, then? How far are we from the city, and is the way passable by foot?"

Valerie straightened subtly, looking with an expression of deliberate impassiveness at the warden rather than at Webb as the pilot replied.

"You could probably walk it in two or three days, if your luck held and none of the rivers between here and there was too high to be easily forded." Webb stroked his broad, stubbled jaw. "There aren't any estuaries between here and the city, but this time of the year you might have to cut pretty far inland to be able to cross a couple of the rivers."

Kevin's expression was openly stricken as he faced his warden. "We aren't turning back, are we?" he asked plaintively.

To Cassidy's surprise, the warden broke into a smile. "Not exactly, Kev," he reassured the younger man. Turning to Webb, the warden continued, "You have more than discharged your duty to us, seaman; and I'll still consider myself in your debt. I want you to give us the directions we'll need to find this cove we seek. Then you are more than free to return to the city."

"No," Valerie and Webb both said, nearly at the same time. The shock of their unprecedented agreement struck both of them momentarily speechless, and they eyed each other with surprise and mutual suspicion. It was Webb who spoke first.

"While I appreciate your intentions, warden, my agreement wasn't with you," he reminded the younger man. "I vowed to Click—damn his skin!—that I would see you safely to Clam Cove." His white teeth showed in a brief and humorless little smile. "Besides, along with all the other supplies there's another skiff stowed at the cove, and I'm not real fond of the idea of walking back to the city. So unless all of you want to go back, I'm afraid I'll be going on south with whoever else does."

Cassidy wasn't sure what Valerie originally had intended to say. Webb's backhanded loyalty to his oath seemed to have deflated some of the captain's wrath. And so what she said was "It's foolish enough to go on, but it would be even more foolish to split up. If we're going on, then we'll all go."

Favoring her with an expression of wry irony, the warden merely shrugged. "You've said it yourself, Val," he told her. "Then we all will go on."

* * *

None of them could have known it at the time, but that first day of travel afoot turned out to be the last good day they would have for a while. Had Cassidy known it, it might have tempered some of her resolve to go on, since the entire day was hardly a pleasant experience.

After salvaging everything possible from the ruined dinghy, including the anchor rope and a few pieces of the metal hardware that could be used as crude knives, they finished the last of their crisped alewives and started south. Walking on the beach itself for any distance would have been difficult, since the dunes, ridges, and piles of wave-washed loose rocks made the footing extremely unstable. But the forest, which came down nearly to the tideline in some places, was nearly impassable, trackless and tangled with brushy growth and vines. They ended up straddling the line between the beach and the trees, crossing over onto one or the other as needed to get past. Cassidy couldn't help but acknowledge that the terrain would have been impossible to negotiate on horseback. As much as she missed Dragonfly, it was one time she was glad the gray mare wasn't with her.

In spite of the occasional cool breeze off the sea, the air quickly grew hot and humid as the morning wore on. Even Cassidy's loose cotton clothing became soaked with perspiration. The only wildlife they encountered were birds, but clouds of gnats and blackflies swarmed out from the woods to bedevil them. By the time the sun was straight overhead, Cassidy's legs ached, her arms and neck itched, and she found herself wondering how she was going to endure such conditions for several more days.

What a wimp! she silently berated herself. Living in the warden's compound must have softened her. She and Rowena had put up with far worse discomforts after they had fled from Double Creek, at least before they'd taken up with Click and the other Tinkers. But her mind shied away from those memories. She missed Rowena terribly, and Click—well, Click was still something she didn't want to have to deal with.

Cassidy was relieved when the warden called a halt for lunch. Then she remembered that they didn't *have* lunch; they were going to have to go out and forage for something before they'd be able to eat. When they split up to search for food, Kevin followed the warden along the beach in one direction, and Valerie silently started out in the opposite direction. Cassidy automatically glanced at Webb and saw that the pilot was regarding her with some of his old bonhomie.

"Come on," he said, gesturing toward the trees, "let's see if we can find some blackberries or crabapples."

Cassidy hesitated. "Do you think it's a good idea to go into the woods?" she asked dubiously.

Webb grinned, transforming his stubbled, sunburned face into something boyishly mischievous. "Do you think it's a good idea to eat nothing but alewives?" he replied.

Grinning back at him, Cassidy quickly followed as he pushed his way through the heavy tangle of creeper vines that festooned most of the trees at the forest's edge. For a few moments she could see little but the cotton-covered wedge of the seaman's broad back as he plowed through the clutter of vines. Disturbed from their resting place amid the thick leaves, irate mosquitoes whined around her ears. Then they were through the worst of it and stumbling out onto the relative clearness of the forest floor.

"Lots of old growth," Webb noted, scanning the huge boles of the nearest trees. "But there still might be some wild apples or even a hazelnut tree." He pointed. "You go that way and I'll go this way. Yell if you find something."

Cassidy hated to argue, but she felt distinctly uneasy about his plan. "I don't think we should split up," she said. "It might not be safe."

Webb just shook his head. "We made enough noise coming through those vines to scare off anything bigger than a gnat." He gestured again. "Go on; I'll watch your back for you if you're worried."

It was difficult to continue to protest in the face of the pilot's breezy assurances, so Cassidy swallowed her trepidation and began to move off through the trees, carefully winding her way around exposed roots and clumps of suckers. It was noticeably cooler in the woods than it had been out along the edge of the trees, where the sun had beaten down on them; and the insects, while annoying, were hardly any worse than they had been out on the beach. The circuitous route Cassidy had to take to move amid the big tree trunks convinced her that they would have made terrible time had they tried to travel south in the woods, but the ground was softer and covered with dead leaves, and the filtered light was pleasantly subdued.

Cassidy had searched for only about five minutes before she recognized a thorn apple tree. She didn't see any fruit on its gnarled and barbed branches, but by this time of year it might have already fallen to the ground. She glanced back over her shoulder, but she couldn't see Webb. She was about to call out to him when she hesitated. Before she brought him running, she decided she better make certain there actually was something there to eat.

Cassidy's stomach rumbled in anticipation as she crouched down in the leafy detritus beneath the big tree, and for the first time she realized just how hungry she really was. The baked fish had been nutritious enough, but it had been a long time and a rough hike since breakfast. Her fingers winnowed through a stretch of fallen leaves before they encountered a thorn apple, but it was a large one, still plump and firm-fleshed with a shiny rosy skin. Pleased, Cassidy dropped onto her knees in the soft humus and crawled forward, her hands fanning in searching arcs on either side of her. It was a good piece of luck, she thought; thorn apples were very tasty when cooked. She and Rowena had made many a meal of the ruddy little fruit.

Gathering several more of the apples, Cassidy thought again of calling for Webb. But it seemed a shame to disturb him if he had been equally successful in finding something, she rationalized, and she really didn't need his help. After dropping the apples into one of her shirt's wide pockets, she crawled farther under the tree, her head intently bent to her task.

When the first hint of the distinctive odor hit her nostrils, Cassidy was so preoccupied with the happy thought of producing something edible for lunch that the smell didn't register immediately as anything but an unpleasant annoyance. Unconsciously frowning, she crawled forward another step before memory came hurling in. The stench, like rotted flesh, like fetid death, was faint but terrifyingly familiar.

Oh, Jesus!

Cassidy set a new personal best for speedily launching herself to her feet. Without so much as a backward glance, she bolted in the direction from which she'd come, not even noticing the way the thorn apple's lower branches rudely clawed at her, tearing several small rents in her shirt, or the fact that her carefully collected apples were bouncing out of her pockets as she fled. Less than twenty feet from the apple tree, she tripped headlong over an exposed root and went flying face first to the ground. As she frantically regained her feet, she chanced a glance back over her shoulder—and lurched right into Webb.

"Whoa!" the pilot commanded, his powerful arms easily containing even Cassidy's adrenaline-fueled flight. As she reflexively struggled to free herself, he looked down at her in bemusement.

"Where the hell are you going in such a hurry?" He noticed her bulging pockets. "What have you got there?"

"Thorn apples!" Cassidy exclaimed, still squirming to get away.

"Well, you're spilling them all over the place," Webb pointed out mildly.

Still panting, Cassidy twisted around again to look back the way she had just come. "Let's get out of here!" she urged.

"Easy now—trim your sails a bit, will you?" Webb counseled. He extended his arms, holding Cassidy away from himself so that he could study her anxious face. "What the hell are you running from?"

Temporarily ceasing her struggles, Cassidy saw no reason for circumspection. "There's a *monster* in that tree!" she retorted. "One of the stinking hanging ones, a carrion eater. I can smell it!"

But Webb seemed singularly unimpressed. "A monster?" he repeated. "Did you actually *see* this monster?"

Freshly irritated by the pilot's skepticism, Cassidy threw him a withering look. "No, I didn't have to *see* it," she snapped, "I could *smell* it!"

To her astonishment, not only did Webb appear disinterested in fleeing, he actually began to move back toward the thorn apple tree, pulling her along after him. She sharply twisted her arm, breaking his hold on it, and staggered back, gaping incredulously at the seaman. "You're going back there? I told you, there's a *monster* in that tree!"

"No, what you told me was that you *smelled* a monster in that tree," Webb corrected. While Cassidy just stood there, trying to decide if he could actually be that amazingly stupid, or if he just had a remarkably suicidal side she'd had yet to see, Webb held out his hand, waving her on. "Come on, let's go see for sure," he said reasonably.

Taking another automatic step backward, Cassidy doggedly shook her head. "Uh-uh!" she said with finality. "I've already seen the damned things, thank you very much. I'm not that big a fan of stinking slime!"

Webb's upper lip lifted slightly, baring the neat white edge of his teeth. He cocked his shaggy head at her. "If you didn't actually see anything, how can you be so sure what's in that tree?" he posed. He made another gesture. "Look, we're only a dozen paces from the tree. Don't you think if one of those creatures were up there, we could smell it from here?"

Reluctantly Cassidy considered that. She was loath to concede that the pilot had a valid point. Although frighteningly familiar, the rotted stench that she had smelled was hardly the exclusive property of the carrion-eating monsters. And she had to admit that even when she'd been right under the tree, the odor had still been faint, unusually subtle for the hanging monsters.

Easily reading her wary acquiescence on Cassidy's face, Webb said calmly, "Let's go look. I think I know what you might've smelled."

Allowing him to take her by the hand and lead her, much like a small child, Cassidy cautiously followed Webb back to the gnarled branches of the big thorn apple tree. He ducked and pulled her under the uneven canopy of the barbed limbs. Then Cassidy tugged her hand free and slowly tilted back her head.

At first she could see nothing but the irregular patchwork of branches and leaves above them, stretching high overhead to the old tree's crown. Still apprehensive, she barely noticed that the pilot had moved past her and skirted around to the other side of the trunk. She had not imagined the smell; it fouled the cool, shady air with the sharp pungence of decay. But she had to admit that the odor was not overwhelming or cloying, as it had been the other times she'd encountered the fetid creatures. She began to grow embarrassed to think that she had gone running like an idiot from some harmless dead bird or half-rotted mouse buried in the leaves.

From a few yards away, Webb gave a throaty little chuckle. "Come here," he urged, beckoning Cassidy with one hand. As she sheepishly approached him, he pointed upward, directing her gaze toward something high in the leafy crown branches of the old thorn apple tree. "There's your monster," he said genially.

It took Cassidy a few moments to focus against the shifting background of green and the brief flashes of blue sky, but then she picked out what Webb had been pointing to. Hanging from the tree's highest limbs, tethered by bits of vine and sinew, was a bizarre collection of skulls and bones, intricately arranged to dangle like some kind of giant ghoulish mobile. Immediately certain that none of the bones was human, Cassidy was able to catalog several other distinct species—fox, raccoon, rabbit, and even those of some sort of large raptor, like a hawk. Although nearly picked clean of flesh, the skulls and bones still retained a faint aura of corruption, like the dark shreds of matter that still clung to their thews and crevices. That was the slight stench that Cassidy had first detected when she'd been on the ground beneath the tree.

Too intrigued then even to be embarrassed any more by her

hasty panic, Cassidy couldn't even take her eyes from the suspended display as she asked Webb, "What on earth *is* it?"

While the seaman was openly amused by her reaction, Cassidy didn't get the sense that the big man was in any way mocking her for her earlier fear. He shrugged eloquently. "I don't know what you'd call it, but I know who did it. A Woo—"

"A Woodsman," Cassidy finished for him, giving a self-deprecating little snort. "I should have known." She finally pulled her gaze away from the grisly collection and looked at Webb. "We saw some of their handiwork along the Long River on the way to the city."

"Clothes stuffed with dead grass, hanging from the trees?" Webb surmised. He shook his head in cheerful bafflement. "The Woodsmen love their little jokes." He gestured at the overhead arrangement. "I'll admit it stinks a bit, but I figure it's hardly a danger to anyone."

Taking the subtle tweaking with good nature, Cassidy gave him a rueful grin. Then she tilted her head back again and studied the strangely ornamented treetop. "What do you suppose it means?" she mused.

"What makes you think it means anything?" the pilot said.

Looking at him again, Cassidy said, "It took a lot of time and work to hang all that stuff up there like that; there must be some reason for it."

Webb chuckled again. "Try thinking like a Woodsman," he suggested.

"No thanks," she muttered, remembering the humiliating treatment she and Rowena had suffered at the hands of one of those unwashed denizens of the forest.

Easily dropping down into a squat to begin searching the leafy ground for more thorn apples, the seaman merely offered over his shoulder, "They're harmless-enough fellows."

Cassidy made another snorting sound, one more deprecating than self-deprecating, as she knelt down beside him. "Click called them the wild ones; said they just liked their solitude." Recalling the Tinker's words caused an unwitting pang of pain to stab through Cassidy, and to prevent the conversation from turning to their mutual friend, she quickly asked Webb, "Just who are the Woodsmen anyway? Where do they come from?"

Scooping up another fallen apple, Webb threw her a wry look. "Where does anyone come from?" he replied. But before she could become annoyed at the seemingly flip answer, the pilot went on. "They're just people who don't fit in," he said. "That's why they live in the woods, because they prefer solitude."

Temporarily abandoning any pretense of continuing to glean for apples, Cassidy paused to study Webb's face. "What do you mean, they don't fit in? How don't they fit in?"

"They don't have the Memories, if that's what you're thinking," the pilot said. "If anything, they're probably as far from people like you as anyone could be." He threw a glance back over his shoulder, up toward the bizarre creation that hung high above them. "They don't have a problem adjusting here because they remember some other life. They just don't want anything to do with other people."

Following Webb's gaze up to the dangling collection of skulls and bones gently twisting in the breeze, Cassidy said, "Do you think they're crazy then?"

"Maybe," Webb replied with equanimity, "but that's not for me to say." His attention seemed to return to his search for fallen apples, but a moment later he added, "Then again, people might think you're crazy, too."

Cassidy knew the seaman's sense of humor well enough by then to realize that he was just teasing her, and so she responded by flipping a handful of the leafy forest humus in his direction. She liked Webb, and she had grown increasingly grateful for his presence. Perhaps that natural fondness was part of the reason it proved so easy for him to blindside her, as he did when he suddenly spoke again.

"I know you're worried about him, but don't be. He'll be all right, and he'll protect your friends." Webb's tanned face was thoughtful and open, framed by his long, sun-bleached brown hair. It was almost impossible not to believe such a face, even if his incisive candor had made Cassidy acutely uncomfortable. He flashed her a quick grin. "Besides, considering everything that's happened to us already, I'd say that bastard's had the luck of the draw again!"

"I was just worried about my friends," Cassidy lied, and badly.

"Of course," Webb said blandly, resuming his search through the fallen leaves.

Cassidy felt relieved that even though the pilot could obviously see right through her, he was apparently willing to let the painful subject drop. Therefore she was surprised when he spoke again, adding as if as an afterthought "You know, Click has always liked his solitude, as well. It's been odd to see him break it."

Deliberately misunderstanding, Cassidy said, "Leading the Tinkers hardly seems like a life of solitude to me."

"There's more than one kind of solitude," Webb replied sagely. And then he really did let the subject drop.

After a few more minutes of silent work, they both had filled their shirt pockets with the small plump thorn apples. After rising to his feet, Webb offered Cassidy a hand and easily pulled her up. "At least these should help cut the taste of fish," he said wryly. "Let's hope the captain has managed to run down some poor rabbit and strangle it with her bare hands."

Cassidy couldn't help herself; the mental image of Valerie doing just that made her chuckle aloud. And she was freshly appreciative of the pilot's perceptiveness as he continued.

"Much as I think that woman could use a good laugh," he said, "let's not tell her about your little adventure, eh?"

"Let's not tell anyone," Cassidy said fervently. She was still embarrassed by how easily she had been spooked.

Webb clapped her heartily on the back. "Agreed," he said. "Now let's get back out onto the beach before they've already eaten everything they've found and started on without us."

Smiling at the seaman's inveterate hyperbole, Cassidy followed him out from under the canopy of the thorn apple tree and back toward the crude little trail they had thrashed through the wild creeper vines.

To Cassidy's relief, the rest of the day passed fairly uneventfully. Despite Webb's hopeful comment, neither Valerie nor either of the young men had managed to bag a rabbit. They had to settle for a lunch of cooked thorn apples, a few handsful of half-ripe blackberries, and the ever-present alewives before they resumed walking.

By midway through the long, humid summer afternoon, Cassidy noticed just how exhausted the warden was becoming. He never would have said anything; it was not in his nature to complain, and he never would have conscienced slowing them down in any way. Cassidy was certain that Valerie also could see all of the signs of her warden's weariness, but the captain would never have mentioned anything in front of them. And as for Kevin, the young Finder saw what he wanted to see in his hero, and his devotion blinded him to the warden's human frailty. But Cassidy watched the warden's occasional stumble and the growing slump of those usually erect shoulders with increasing concern. She was as anxious as any of them to reach Clam Cove, but she gladly would have sacrificed a little time to give the warden a breather.

The terrain only compounded the problem. At several points they had to choose between clambering over stretches of huge boulders and eroded gullies along the beach, or else fighting the trackless brush and tough vines to make their way through the trees. Scratched, hot, dirty, and tired, Cassidy was almost grateful when they finally rounded a stony peninsulalike projection of the beach and saw spread out before them in the late-afternoon sunlight the sedge grass–choked mouth of the first estuary.

"Already a river," the warden murmured, genuinely disappointed by the obstacle that would most certainly call a halt to the day's travel.

Webb shielded his eyes from the sun with one hand while he scanned across the broad body of algae-tinted water to the estuary's far side. "Aye, not a very wide one," the pilot said, "but still far more trouble than I'd care to take on this late in the day."

"Are we stopping then?" Kevin asked—hopefully, Cassidy thought.

"All of us except for you, Kev," the warden teased, lightly punching the blond boy's shoulder. "You're going to look for firewood!"

"Come on, Kevin," Cassidy said quickly, "I'll help you. There should be lots of wood caught along the edges of the marsh."

Valerie had been studying the immediate area with an eye toward the best, and probably the most defensible, campsite. She threw both Kevin and Cassidy a brief but significant look. "Stay out in the open," she said, "and watch out for sinkholes."

"Well, that's certainly going to take all of the fun out of this," Cassidy said under her breath, just loudly enough for Kevin to hear it. She was immediately rewarded by one of his sunny smiles as he followed her toward the edge of the estuary.

Although sunset was still some hours away, the local contingent of gnats and mosquitoes stirred into action as the two of them disturbed the tall vegetation along the water. "Val should have warned us to watch out for the bugs!" Kevin complained, swatting the back of his neck.

Wishing she still had some of the Tinkers' insect repellent, no matter how smelly it had been, Cassidy slapped her bare arm. But fortunately she had been right about the plenitude of wood. Old branches and other woody debris, carried along by the river that had formed the estuary, had gravitated downstream until they had eventually come to rest along the murky edges of the slough.

Much of the wood was half submerged in the sludgy water, but enough of it was dry that Cassidy knew it would all burn. She and Kevin were able to fill their arms quickly, with no more mishap than getting their boots wet.

Glancing back toward the campsite, Kevin suddenly confided to Cassidy, "I'm glad that we had to stop early. After what happened yesterday, I don't think the warden's quite got back his full strength yet."

Surprised, Cassidy looked across directly into Kevin's boyish face. "Do you remember what happened yesterday?"

"Sure," he said, promptly and without hesitation. "The boat sank, and one of the monsters grabbed me in its mouth." Unconsciously Kevin rubbed his side, where Cassidy had seen the faint bruising from the creature's chitinous jaws. His sudden smile was shy but filled with warmth. "The warden saved my life," he said simply.

Cassidy hesitated a moment, then said, "I don't think the monster really intended to kill you, Kev. If it had, no one would have been able to stop it."

To Cassidy's surprise, Kevin nodded in agreement. "They don't scare me so much anymore," he told her. He glanced back in the direction from which they had come, toward the beach and beyond, where the low rays of the sun danced off the rolling breakers. "That sounds stupid, doesn't it?" he said with a small shrug.

But Cassidy found herself shaking her head. "Not really," she said. "Look at everything we've been through already. Sometimes in order to be able to keep going on, you just have to stop being afraid."

Kevin shifted his armload of wood. "Well, I think we'd better get this firewood back to Val and try to find something else to eat—or I'm afraid we'll be eating alewives for supper again!"

Cassidy had been deeply immersed in a dream when she was rudely awakened.

In the dream, she was lying beneath the old thorn apple tree, cushioned on the thick leafy humus. Far above her, the tree's spreading branches were filled with the Woodsman's grotesque piece of mobile sculpture. The little skulls and bits of bones spun lazily on their tethers, each seeming to move independently, as if to their own individual breaths of breeze.

Someone was kneeling beside her, bending over her, his big warm hands running over the sides of her face and down her bare arms. His touch stirred something deep within her, the entirely pleasant liquid heat of desire. Then the larger body covered hers, pressing and sliding.

Her eyes tightly closed, she lifted her chin, reaching for a kiss. But it was not her dream lover's lips that met hers; instead, some-thing cold and hard and dry was pressed against her face. Her eyes snapped open and she automatically recoiled, for the object touching her mouth was the grinning white skull of a fox.

Jolted into wakefulness by someone urgently shaking her shoul-ders, Cassidy spontaneously blurted out, "Click!"

But if Valerie had heard or understood the name, she gave no sign of it. "Come on, Cassidy, wake up," the captain repeated, pulling her up into a sitting position. "He needs you."

Even in her state of disorientation, Cassidy immediately real-ized who "he" was and why he would need her. *This always seems to happen at the worst possible times,* she thought groggily. Not that there would have been any particularly good times for it. Blinking grittily, she allowed Valerie to haul her to her feet. "How long?" she asked, trying not to yawn or trip over any rocks while crossing their crude campsite.

"I think it just started," Valerie said, guiding Cassidy around the remains of the fire and toward the three men on the opposite side. "He woke us all up with his crying."

As they neared the warden, Cassidy was surprised to find that the captain had meant literal crying—weeping, and not just crying out. The warden was huddled on the bare ground with his knees drawn up nearly to his chin, sobbing loudly while Kevin help-lessly tried to soothe him. Webb hovered nearby, his dimly lit face concerned. The seaman threw Cassidy a look of patent relief as she approached. Even Kevin quickly got to his feet, willingly sur-rendering his place to her.

As Cassidy dropped down onto her knees before the man who had once again become Andy Greene, his tear-streaked face lifted to hers with an almost beatific look of joy. "Cathy!" he ex-claimed, flinging his arms around her.

And Cassidy felt herself being shot through with light.

The desperate young man embraced her with such zeal that she was nearly pulled right into his lap. Not that she would have no-ticed if she had been, because for those next few moments all Cassidy was aware of was the stunning flare of incandescence that burned through every cell in her body, illuminating her from within like a flood of molten fire. It was a cool fire—light without heat, brilliance without burning. And yet in that shockingly direct surge of contact, she felt as if she had not just fallen into the young man's embrace, but actually *into his body*, so that the achingly bright light that shone through her had come from somewhere within his center and had then spread out into her.

Like some slippery residue of her erotic dream, the sensation was disconcertingly intimate, if not precisely sexual. Alarmed by its intensity, and dismayed to think that Valerie and the others must be able to see what she was feeling, Cassidy struggled briefly but fiercely to free herself from Andy's grip. The moment she succeeded in pulling back from him, wrenching free of his touch, the consuming brilliance vanished. She found herself sitting before him on the gritty sand, and Andy was reaching for her again, his eyes huge with tears.

When Cassidy allowed Andy to crawl into her arms again, nothing so overwhelming happened. She devoted herself to trying to calm him by patting his leather-clad back and murmuring softly to him. "I'm here, Andy; you're okay now."

At last he snuffled loudly and whimpered something unintelligible into her shirt. "What?" she asked gently, trying to lift his head. "Tell me, Andy."

His wet face drew back from her shoulder. His eyes were puffy from weeping, and yet so filled with pain and fear that Cassidy felt a powerful visceral reaction arc through her, a sensation independent of that initial mysterious cold fire. The strength of her feelings for him caught her by surprise as she gazed into his face. He had dangerous eyes, she thought, her excitation tinged with a certain rueful resignation. Eyes like that could make a woman do anything.

"They—they were going to *kill* you!" he whispered rawly.

Automatically stroking his hair, soothing him the way she would calm a spooky horse, Cassidy said quietly, "You know I'm okay now, Andy. You may have thought that I was dead, but remember? I'm still alive. I'm right here."

But Andy vehemently shook his head. The tears that had run down his cheeks created glittering trails; a drop of moisture, gleaming like a jewel, trembled on his upper lip. "You're alive, but you can't move," he insisted. "If you can't move, they're going to kill you!"

Cassidy tried to place Andy's agitated declaration within the admittedly shaky context of his previous statements. It seemed to take an extraordinary effort just to think. Cassidy felt as if she had been suffering from some kind of hangover from the startling illumination she had experienced, because everything about him then—the solid warmth of his body against hers, the boyish disarray of his hair, even the faint horsey smell of his leathers—all seemed to conspire to distract her from logical thought. Retreating to more familiar terrain, she asked him, "Andy, where am I?"

"In the big house," he replied immediately.

"The big house with the white halls and the bright lights?"

"Yes," he said, seemingly impatient at the pointless review. "In a white bed. But you won't wake up, so they're going to kill you!"

"I'm in a bed?"

"Yes, but you aren't just sleeping because you won't wake up." His voice rose precipitously. "If you don't wake up, they'll kill you!"

Cassidy shifted slightly on the sand, her bent legs aching, a blunt rock digging into one thigh. "Andy," she said calmly, "who's going to kill me?"

The tone of his prompt answer suggested that surely she must have already known the answer. "The white men," he said.

Stifling her natural impatience, Cassidy persisted, "Who are the white men, Andy?"

But the young man stirred anxiously in her arms. "You have to wake up now, Cathy," he said plaintively. "You have to get up so they won't kill you!"

Concerned by his growing agitation, Cassidy tried to divert the conversation slightly again. "It's okay, Andy," she repeated soothingly. "I'm here now with you; no one's going to hurt me here."

Although to Cassidy's way of thinking, her statement had only set up a massive contradiction, it seemed to have worked the desired effect in calming him. He sagged in her arms again, sniffling softly, and she gently stroked back his tousled hair.

"Okay," he said, almost as if he was speaking to himself, "you're with him now."

Cassidy's hand froze at his temple, and for a few seconds she held her breath, willing herself not to betray the astonishment that had suddenly seized her. "Who am I with now, Andy?" she asked him softly.

He lifted his head slightly, his expression that same transparent pane of simple innocence that suggested the answer was self-evident. "With the warden," he said mildly.

Stunned by what was happening, Cassidy found herself frantically flailing about for a calm and rational response. *He's here!* she thought, dizzy with amazement. *He's here—or at least he realizes that there* is *a here, and that* I'm *here . . .*

The realization took her bizarre contact with Andy Greene to an entirely new level. "Andy," she said slowly and distinctly, "do you know who the warden is?"

The young man's expression both softened and brightened at the same time, and a small smile shaped that voluble mouth. "I love horses!" he declared happily.

Reaching up to frame his jaw in the spread fingers of one hand, Cassidy directed his face toward hers. "Andy, do you know who the warden is?" she repeated intently.

A rapid panorama of expressions passed over his face: a slight furrowing of that smooth forehead, a quizzical lilt to one brow, and then a rush of pleased warmth, like melted chocolate, unfurling in his eyes and lifting his lips. One of his hands rose to cover hers, to squeeze her fingers where they still touched his cheek. "I am, Cathy," he said softly. "I'm the warden of Horses."

Someone made a small sound; Kevin, Cassidy thought, although it could have been Valerie. The sound was genderless in its shocked recognition. Fiercely and deliberately tuning out everything but the man in her grip, Cassidy asked the next inevitable question.

"Andy, do you know who Cassidy is?"

For a moment there was no reply, and Cassidy held her breath, her chest aching, afraid that she had unwittingly miscalculated. But when she looked more closely at him, the young man's expression explained his delay. His brows tented and he cocked his head, his genial mouth assembling a smile. "You're kidding, right?" he said. "You're Cassidy."

Her exhalation nearly a gasp, Cassidy quickly recovered, concealing her incredulity with a ragged little laugh. "Yeah, just joking around," she told him, "but humor me, Andy. Do you know who Valerie is?"

His smile mutating into a puzzled frown. "No," he said.

Although his denial was entirely without pretense, Cassidy found it difficult to accept immediately. She leaned in a little closer to him again, her voice dropping. "Are you sure? What about Kevin? Do you know who Kevin is?"

Open anxiety seeped back onto that vulnerable face, his brown eyes blinking rapidly. "No," he repeated, a slight quiver in his voice again. Beneath her hands the sleek body shuddered. "Cathy, just wake up. Wake up or they—"

And then the transformation came over the young man, swiftly and totally, and suddenly he was no longer Andy Greene. Cassidy had only to look into his face to see that he was again the warden of Horses, back in his own world, with no trace of his other identity remaining. Simultaneously disappointed and relieved, Cassidy sat back onto her heels, her hands dropping from him.

The warden stared at her in obvious confusion, studying Cassidy's face as if for some clue to what had happened to him. Just as the last time, when they had clung to the deck of the sinking boat, he did not seem immediately certain of where he was—or perhaps even *who* he was. It was not until he had glanced up and taken in the shadowy figures of Val and the others, standing nearby, that he resumed the full appearance of normalcy.

Looking back to Cassidy, the warden said somewhat ruefully, "Cathy, what the hell did I just do?"

A monumental weariness had descended over Cassidy, as if a dark curtain of utter exhaustion had just been dropped down upon her from the very night sky itself. She felt almost unbearably achy and fatigued as she reached out to pat the warden's shoulder. "Let's talk about it in the morning." She yawned.

To her immense relief, the warden accepted that. Within minutes the camp had settled down again, Kevin curled up on one side of the young man and Valerie on the other, with Webb returning to his watch. Cassidy tried without success to reposition herself comfortably in the little hollow she'd made in the rocky sand. In the end she decided that comfort was relative and that any recumbent position would do.

It was only as she lay groggily tottering on the cusp of sleep that she realized that after his spell had ended, the warden had not called her Cassidy; he had called her Cathy.

Chapter 6 ◄▬▬

The next morning no one, not even the warden, mentioned what had happened during the night. Cassidy found herself suspiciously willing to go along with the conspiracy of silence, gamely bowing to the simple expedients of the new day as she bent to gather more wood for a cook fire, with Kevin working uncomplainingly at her side.

Webb managed to surprise three crows along the tree line and relieved them of the picked-over but still relatively fresh carcass of a rabbit, over which they had been loudly squabbling. "Something's eaten the best parts," the pilot said philosophically, holding up what some fox or weasel had left behind, "but at least it's not fish, and I've eaten worse."

Watching Valerie deftly skin the animal's remains, Cassidy thought whimsically that they would have made great slogans for some fast food place: "At least it's not fish," and "You've eaten worse."

The warden's demeanor seemed entirely normal, as he sat cross-legged by the fire with his portion of the cooked rabbit and a handful of alewives, discussing with Webb the logistics of getting past the estuary. Surreptitiously watching him, Cassidy half wondered if he could have somehow forgotten what had happened the night before. She certainly had been unable to forget it.

Every time Cassidy had begun to delude herself into thinking that she understood just what the hell was going on, the warden or his alter ego managed to throw her another curve. Just when she had convinced herself that Andy Greene knew nothing of the existence of the warden's world, he had shot that neat little hypothesis to hell. He wasn't only *there*, as Andy Greene in the Slow World; it appeared that he was also *here*, as the warden of Horses—and he *knew* it. What's more, he knew Cassidy as two distinct people in the two different worlds, a prospect that literally made her head ache. But then why didn't Andy know who Valerie and Kevin were?

It took her a conscious effort of will to wrench her mind away from the confusing and unproductive line of thought. She tried instead to concentrate on what Webb and the warden were discussing, and intersected their conversation just in time to hear Kevin say "But it could take hours to go inland. Why can't we just cross the estuary right here?"

Looking up from herding the last of the coals together with a half-burned stick, Valerie made a disparaging sound. "Too hazardous, Kev," she said tersely.

Far more tolerant of the young man's innocent questions, the warden leaned forward and tried to explain. Cassidy realized that she could just as easily have been the one to have asked the same thing, had she not been naturally more wary of ridicule than was Kevin; and so she listened for the answer with an interest that was just as keen, even if better concealed.

"The mouth of the estuary is the widest part of the river," the warden said, graphically spreading his hands. "The farther upstream we go, the narrower it becomes. Besides, down here where the fresh water from the river mingles with the salt water from the sea, the bottom is especially unstable. The action of the tides, and the reaction between the waters, often creates sinkholes and other nasty surprises."

"It might take longer to hike upstream to cross," the pilot concurred, "but conditions will be a little more predictable. Just remember, it's always easier to ford a river than it is to cross an estuary."

If nothing else, her extensive travels in that world had convinced Cassidy to heed the advice of the locals. The time she and Rowena had spent traveling alone after they had fled Double Creek had proven dangerous enough, and they hadn't even encountered any particularly harrowing natural hazards. *We couldn't even get through the woods without falling into a Woodsman's pit!* she reminded herself dourly. So when they broke camp that morning, she was more than willing to follow the seaman's lead.

As the low morning sun began to climb over the Gray Sea, the day promised more heat. That would have been unpleasant enough even had they been able to continue along the shoreline, as they had the day before. But the heat was even more enervating when they had to hike inland, following the irregular contours of the marshy banks of the vast estuary. In most places there was enough of an apron of solid land, choked with tough waist-high sedge grass and various other wetland plants, that they didn't actually have to force a path through the adjacent trees and brush. But the going was still arduously slow, the ground uneven and boggy, and the tall vegetation a constant obstacle. By the time they'd been walking for less than an hour, Cassidy's face and arms were scratched and itching, and her shirt was soaked with perspiration. The clouds of insects were an irritating reminder that they were right on the edge of a swamp. The mosquitoes were particularly merciless, and Cassidy was grateful when Webb showed her how to help repel them by rubbing her exposed skin with the sap of one of the marsh plants.

"Jewelweed," the pilot said, anointing the back of her neck for her. "Stinks, but it does the trick."

"I don't mind the smell if you don't," Cassidy assured him with asperity.

Webb and the warden were the most efficient at breaking a path through the fibrous, broad-bladed sedge grass, and Cassidy was happy to allow the men to lead the way. As she stumbled along after them, she thought longingly of her mare. The horse could have made short work of the miles, even in that rough footing. She wondered what kind of terrain the mare had already negotiated on her journey south. Cassidy refused to think in terms much beyond the treasured image of the horse coming on her way to them. That image was like a talisman that Cassidy could cling to, a surety that gave her hope. And without that hope of reunion, there would not have been much reason for her to go on.

When Webb finally called a halt, it caught Cassidy by surprise. She hadn't really been paying attention to how much change there had been in the waterway they had been paralleling. The broad stagnant slough of the estuary had long since disappeared, replaced by a body of water that, although sluggish and reed-clogged, was definitely a river. In fact, when she shaded her eyes with one hand and squinted across its opaque and sun-gilded surface, she could even see the trees that marked the other bank, several hundred feet away.

"Are we going to have to swim across that?" she asked skeptically.

"I hope not," Webb replied. "I'm not that good of a swimmer."

The warden touched Cassidy reassuringly on the shoulder. "The rivers in this area are very shallow," he said. "We probably won't get in over our heads, even in the middle of it."

"Unless you step in a sinkhole," Webb couldn't seem to resist adding, but Cassidy took the comment as it was intended, a good-natured jibe. The pilot was unfastening the coil of the dinghy's anchor rope from around his waist as he gazed out over the river with a calculating eye. "All we need is a volunteer to be our point man."

"I'll do it," Valerie said immediately. She had been standing knee deep in the turbid water, testing the muddy bottom with the toe of one of her boots. The humidity had frizzled her hair to an umber tangle, and her once-elegant leathers were stained and torn, but Cassidy thought the captain still looked as composed and regal as a queen.

"No, I'll do it," Kevin quickly offered. He turned to the warden, his voice earnest and persuasive. "I'm good on my feet and a strong swimmer. I can do it."

For a moment Cassidy thought the situation might deteriorate into one of those odd little battles over the warden's favor, those weird little conflicts of which the object himself seemed so oblivious. But the warden simply smiled at the blond boy and said, "All right, Kevin, if you wish." He threw the captain a quick glance. "I'm sure Val will get her chance soon enough."

As Webb handed Kevin the end of the rope, and said, "Come on, Cassidy, you're the lightest," the seaman said. "You go next."

When Cassidy looked up she saw that Kevin had already waded out several yards into the river, the rope tied around his waist. Grasping hold of the line at the river's edge, she began to slog out into the cloudy, tepid water. The mucky bottom was soft but surprisingly even, and the water's temperature was just cool enough to provide a pleasant respite from the muggy air. Maybe crossing the river wouldn't be such an ordeal after all, Cassidy thought hopefully, as the rope between her and Kevin gently tugged her forward.

Valerie entered the water behind Cassidy, followed by the warden, with Webb bringing up the rear. They spaced themselves out along the rope about ten feet apart, like a train of pack mules.

About a hundred feet out into the river, where the murky water was chest deep, Kevin suddenly hesitated. "I just stepped on something," he said. "I think it was a stump."

"Might well be," Webb replied. "The channels of these rivers are always changing, so there's a lot of old rotted trees submerged on the bottom. Watch your footing, or you could twist an ankle."

When Kevin moved on, Cassidy stepped with some trepidation past the area where he had hesitated. She felt nothing beneath her boots but the yielding muck of decayed vegetation.

Cassidy had no doubt that all of them were entertaining the same thought, even if none of them would speak it: monsters. The water creatures had already proven themselves quite adaptable to inland waterways; Cassidy had seen her first one in a stream only a fraction the size of the one they were crossing. But she firmly clamped the lid on her riotous imagination, because that was the only way she could go on. The monsters could be anywhere; but if you believed that they were everywhere, then you might just as well give up.

Fording the river was slow going, but in many ways it was no more difficult than trekking along the bank had been. Yet when they had reached what appeared to be approximately the midpoint in the wide body of water, Cassidy was struck by the unnerving realization that they were very far out in the middle of nowhere, hundreds of feet from dry land and up to their shoulders in scummy water. The sudden sense of helplessness dismayed her, but fortunately her hold on the rope made it impossible to do anything but go on. Kevin was steadily forging on, creating a small cloudy wake in the sluggish water.

Cassidy was vastly relieved when she saw that they were definitely drawing nearer to the far bank of the river and that the water level was beginning to recede. She was slogging along in water that was hardly waist deep when the rope between her and Valerie abruptly tightened as the captain paused.

"What the hell was that?" Valerie said.

"Don't touch it," Webb told her. "Just keep moving."

Cassidy automatically turned to look and nearly stumbled in the thick muck. Several yards downstream from Valerie the opaque surface of the water was broken by a spiraling corkscrewlike trail of ripples, heading rapidly away from them. Certainly not a monster, Cassidy realized gratefully, for the wake was far too small.

Forced by the rope to stop, as well, Kevin also looked back, his head cocked quizzically.

The pilot just grunted dismissively and gestured them on. "Water snake," he said. "Just keep moving."

"Are they poisonous?" Cassidy asked, slowly resuming her pace as she reluctantly pulled her gaze away from the reptile's distinctive wake.

"Some are," Webb replied.

"I doubt that they'll bother us if we don't bother them," the warden said.

"Yeah, just like the Woodsmen!" Cassidy muttered under her breath. Suddenly the last hundred feet of the river looked as wide as an ocean, the turbid thigh-high water concealing a host of potential hazards. She clutched the wet rope in both hands and focused on following the dark leather of Kevin's back. But she still imagined that every sucking footstep was something clutching at her boots, and the greenish water seemed filled with hidden peril.

Then Cassidy was sloshing clumsily through the reed-dotted shallows, tugging after Kevin as fresh clouds of gnats boiled up around their ears. The rude swath of coarse sedge grass had never looked so welcome to her, and she stepped faster, tightening the slack between herself and Valerie, and then finally abandoning the rope entirely as her soaked boots scythed through the rough grass. The wet seaman's cottons clung to Cassidy's body like a second skin, but she had no false sense of modesty about her appearance. She was just too relieved to be out of the river. How many more of them were they going to have to cross? she wondered, convinced that nothing could have persuaded her to go back into the water again that day.

Cassidy was just straightening up from pouring the river water out of her boots when she happened to glance over at Kevin. The blond boy was casually wringing out the end of his ponytail, which had trailed in the water and which, wet, was several shades darker than the rest of his hair. Taking a step forward to come up behind him, she touched him on the shoulder and said, "Just a minute, Kev; I thought I saw something on your neck."

Obligingly pulling his ponytail off to one side and stooping, Kevin canted his neck. "What is it?" he asked curiously.

One moment Cassidy was leaning in closer, her fingers reaching to flick off whatever bit of dead leaf or slime she had seen there; and the next moment she was sharply recoiling, jumping back with a little squeal of surprise. "Jesus!" she exclaimed. "It's a—"

"It's just a leech," Webb finished, moving past Cassidy to pry the creature gently free from the untanned portion of the boy's neck. The pilot held it out for Cassidy's inspection. The parasite was flattened and ribbon-shaped, gleaming a lush velvet black and easily the length of her thumb. Webb flipped it over so that Cassidy could see the sucker disk of its mouth. Then, laughing at her expression, he flicked the leech back into the river.

"Hey! You let it get away!" Cassidy said indignantly.

Webb grinned in amusement. "What, you think I should have killed it?" He jerked his stubbled chin toward the water. "There must be millions of them in there." Then his grin widened. "Although I'll wager there're a few dozen less right now."

Suddenly understanding, Cassidy's eyes widened in horrified comprehension. "You mean . . . we all . . . ?"

Webb's amusement remained unabated. "Yeah," he said, "so we'd better check each other over before they have a chance to dig in and have lunch."

With absolutely no thoughts of modesty, Cassidy was the first one to shuck off all of her wet clothing. She did, however, have the foresight to move closer to Valerie in the process, so that it was the other woman who performed the obligatory leech hunt on her dripping body, and not one of the men. In turn, she was also more comfortable searching the captain's body for her than she would have been going over every inch of the naked skin of any of the male members of their group. To her surprise, Cassidy was actually quite at ease inspecting Val for the unctuous black creatures, hooting in triumph when she found one.

Cassidy tried to keep her eyes averted from the trio of naked men, acutely aware of her own curiosity about Webb's physique. She turned to Valerie with a smile on her face, but the captain's expression was something of a cipher. After shaking out her wet cotton shirt, Cassidy pulled the garment on over her head. Glancing over to where the warden and Kevin were laughing at a shared joke, she remarked to Valerie, "They're really good friends, aren't they? He's lucky to have someone like Kevin."

Valerie's deep umber eyes met Cassidy's. There was nothing malicious or reproving in the look; and yet there was something that made Cassidy reluctant to explore what lay behind the expression. The captain's curly head nodded. "Yes," she said, "he's a man who needs all the friends he has."

Cassidy finished dressing in silence, glancing only fleetingly over to the warden and Kevin. But when she did, the niggling half memory of some elusive emotion kept tugging at the edges of her mind.

It took the rest of the morning and the early part of the afternoon to retrace their route back downstream to the sea on the other side of the estuary. The going was a little easier on the southern side of the river, but it still was a wearying trek in the muggy heat. They had all agreed not to stop for lunch until they'd reached the beach again; but long before they got there, Cassidy was yearning for the breath of a cool breeze off the Gray Sea. Her wet clothing had never dried properly, and her damp socks and boots chafed her feet as she plowed on resolutely through the sedge grass and weeds. She already found herself thinking fondly of the day before, when their biggest worry seemed to have been whether they would be able to find anything besides alewives to eat.

When they finally skirted the last of the marshy ground and trudged out onto the stony beach, Cassidy was relieved to feel the refreshing brush of a temperate sea breeze. She felt like walking right out into the waves, but Valerie was already organizing the search for food. Unconsciously and automatically falling into her role as captain of the Troopers, Val quickly assigned everyone a task and an area.

"The warden and Kevin can go down the beach and look for fish," Valerie said briskly. "Cassidy can gather wood. Webb and I'll go back along the tree line. Pick up anything that's edible, but don't go out of sight of each other."

The warden gave her a little bow, his thinly veiled amusement at her martial approach entirely lost on Valerie, and then he and Kevin started away across the rocks. But before the captain could commandeer Webb, the pilot's sharp eyes caught sight of something down by the outlet of the estuary, where the long breakers were rolling into the slough and being swallowed by the shallow, sluggish water.

"Look at that," he said, pointing.

Cassidy imitated Valerie, shading her eyes with one hand and squinting against the glint of the sun on the scummy water. But Valerie was quicker at picking out what the seaman had seen.

Valerie gave Webb a sidelong glance; Cassidy was surprised by the glint of humor in her eyes. "Are you thinking what I'm thinking?" she asked.

Cassidy finally saw what they'd both been looking at. At the edge of the estuary, near the last of the clumps of reeds, a half-dozen sea gulls were noisily bickering over something pale and bloated and only vaguely fish-shaped. "You're kidding," Cassidy said in disbelief. "That thing must be putrid!"

"Not the fish," Webb assured her, "the gulls!"

As Val and the pilot started across the beach, Cassidy just shook her head and dutifully began searching for firewood. She kept half an eye on the unlikely pair of hunters as they cautiously neared their quarry. At their initial approach, the gulls scattered into the air, their mewling cries creaking like rusty gate hinges. But gulls being gulls, and the perceived threat receding once they became airborne, the birds quickly began to resettle on their rotting feast. That was when Webb and Val both let fly with a barrage of fist-size stones.

One of the gulls flopped sideways, but it rapidly righted itself and joined its fellows in flight, crawking and squawking self-righteously. The graceful gray-and-white birds milled overhead for a time, never veering far from their interrupted meal. Eventually once again they appeared to forget what had happened, and began to return to the bloated carcass of the big fish. Armed with more rocks, Valerie and Webb resumed their bombardment.

Two of the birds tumbled onto their sides. As the others took noisy flight, Val darted up and pummeled the two dazed gulls with another rock. Seizing them by their necks, the captain turned and triumphantly held up the dead birds with a flourish. She and Webb were actually joking together like old comrades by the time they'd returned to where Cassidy was working.

"Not exactly the world's smartest creatures," the pilot said, "and they're likely tough as boot leather, but—"

"But you've eaten worse," Cassidy finished for him.

Webb merely laughed at her deadpan comment. "Better to eat the gulls that eat the garbage," he said, "than to eat the garbage the gulls eat."

Unfortunately, they didn't have the gulls for lunch. Valerie decided that it would take too long to cook them then, and no one else wanted to spend time that they could use traveling. They settled for more cooked alewives and a few sour grapes and black-berries, and Webb slung the gutted gulls over his shoulder to be cooked later.

"It'll give you something to look forward to for supper to-night," he consoled Cassidy. "Now, if we would just come upon a few sacks of rice or milled barley along the way, we could really make something of these stringy old biddies."

Yeah, Cassidy thought sardonically, *and if we would just come upon a boat, we wouldn't be tramping around in the wilderness all day, looking forward to eating sea gulls!*

"Who knows?" the seaman continued as they started back along the beach. "Maybe we'll find a few mushrooms, or some more thorn apples."

Scarcely cheered, it took all of Cassidy's will to refrain from making a sarcastic comeback. After all, Webb was hardly the cause of any of their troubles; all he had done was made the best of a bad situation. "Yeah, maybe," she dutifully replied. But she seriously doubted it.

In spite of Cassidy's jaundiced outlook, the terrain improved significantly for the rest of the afternoon. Within an hour's hike from the south side of the estuary, the beach grew broader and clearer. Rather than a jumble of rocks, it was covered with a coarse but level bed of dark sand. They were able to walk along the beach, even right along the waterline. It was also much cooler along the shore, and for the first time since they'd been forced to abandon the dinghy, conditions seemed almost pleasant.

Walking in the lead for a time, Cassidy gazed ahead along the long sweep of smooth-washed sand and thought wistfully what a great place it would be for a gallop on the gray mare. For a brief period, she could almost feel the wide, warm body between her knees, the powerful muscles bunching and surging beneath the horse's silky hide, and the long iron-colored mane whipping against her bare forearms as she leaned over the horse's withers. The conjuration of those sensations was so real, so immediate, that Cassidy felt tears welling up in her eyes. *Dragonfly* . . . God, she missed the horse. It was almost as if—

Even though the sand was smooth and level, Cassidy stumbled, and for an instant her normal sense of balance nearly failed her. It was as if her feet had momentarily forgotten that they were on the ground, and her legs briefly failed to propel her forward. Still disoriented from the sensation, she started when she felt a hand land on her shoulder.

"Cassidy? Are you all right?" Valerie had been walking right behind her, and, seeing Cassidy stumble, she had naturally reached for her.

"Yeah, sure," Cassidy automatically responded; and by the time she had spoken, it was true. The sand was again solid beneath her feet, and the odd sensation was rapidly fading. She turned and looked into the captain's concerned face. "I was just thinking what a great place this would be to ride my mare, and I just—"

To Cassidy's surprise, Valerie actually smiled. "And you felt for a moment as if you were actually riding her," she finished. "She must be getting closer then; you're starting to pick up her presence."

Trying to control her sudden rush of hope, Cassidy said, "You really think so? But I can't really sense her—not like I usually can."

Clapping Cassidy lightly on the arm, Valerie nodded encouragingly. "You're developing a more refined sort of bond with her," she said. "It's making you more sensitive to her presence than you've been, but it's not as direct."

"But I don't even feel it anymore," Cassidy admitted. "It only seemed to last for a few seconds."

The warden had caught up with them, and even though he had not noticed Cassidy stumble, it was obvious that he had overheard enough of their conversation to surmise what had happened. "It will come again, Cassidy," he said. "Your bond with your mare is very powerful, but it's never had to be tested over so great a distance."

"I've known Horsemen who could sense their horse's presence a full territory away—days of travel—their bond was that strong," Valerie asserted.

As they continued to walk along the packed sand, the warden and Valerie discussed other Horsemen and horses, reminiscing in an almost jovial vein. Only half listening, Cassidy was struck by one poignant thought. Both of them were Horsemen, as well, bonded to horses that they had left to come south with her. If she missed Dragonfly that badly, even though she expected to be reunited with the mare soon, how must Valerie and the warden feel? Their journey was taking them farther and farther from the cedar-chestnut gelding and the coffee-colored mare, with no promise of seeing either horse again in the near future.

Dogged by guilt, Cassidy did not recognize the most significant aspect of her odd experience until several minutes later. If she could sense Dragonfly's presence, then the mare definitely was still alive. And the thought coming hard on the heels of that was: *And if she's still alive, then maybe they all are.*

Their good luck lasted only as long as the afternoon sun. A couple of hours before sunset, Kevin called everyone's attention to the eastern sky. Turning to put the sinking sun at her back, Cassidy scanned out across the monotonously rolling breakers. About a hundred yards from the shoreline, soaring along effortlessly right above the water, were two large white birds, sailing with their long legs trailing out behind them.

Cassidy smiled at their beauty. "Cranes?" she asked.

But Webb was frowning. "Yeah, egrets," he said.

As the warden exchanged a telling look with the pilot, Cassidy asked, "Why, what's the matter? They certainly aren't dangerous!"

Webb's sunbrowned face was turned toward the horizon again, tracking the egrets' graceful flight. "They nest in estuaries," he said dourly.

"Oh," Cassidy said in a small voice. But she still thought the birds were beautiful.

In less than half an hour they saw the distant green haze of sedge grass and reeds spilling out toward where yet another river had mated with the sea. Another half hour brought them to the edge of the second estuary.

"It's not as wide as the last one," the warden said confidently. "We shouldn't have to go so far upstream to be able to cross this one."

Much to Cassidy's relief, Webb added, "Well, it's too late to do anything more about it today anyway. We can start fresh again in the morning."

Valerie stood studying the broad marsh for a few moments. Then she turned to the pilot, her expression an eloquent mixture of irritation and skepticism. "Are you sure there are only two more rivers between here and this cove of yours?"

Lowering the gutted carcasses of the two sea gulls to the sand, Webb merely shrugged. "No, I'm not sure. I've never had to travel there overland like this, and by sea you tend to overlook little details like rivers. For all I know, this could be the last one," he added.

Valerie made a disparaging little sound and announced, "I'm going to look for firewood. Maybe the rest of you can find something more appealing than dead fish to go with those two birds."

Thorn apples or mushrooms had been too much to hope for, but Kevin found a veritable treasure trove of clams along the tideline; and Webb used his pocketknife to unearth some sort of fleshy roots from along the edge of the estuary, which he insisted were edible if baked. It was an eclectic combination, but Cassidy had to admit the meal was better than anything they had had since they had been forced to leave Webb's boat.

The sandy beach itself was also a better campsite than what they had had to endure the past two nights. After fording the river that morning, and weary from the afternoon's long trek, Cassidy was looking forward to the simple pleasure of being able to stretch out on a patch of relatively soft ground to sleep. And so when the warden approached her after supper, as she sat half drowsing in the dimness beside the waning cook fire, mild annoyance was as much a spontaneous part of her reaction as was simple surprise.

The young man squatted down beside her, with the kind of artless agility of a natural athlete. "Come walk with me awhile, Cassidy."

Cassidy was mildly embarrassed to realize just how obvious her reluctance must have been to him, her awkward hesitation incriminating her even if the poor light hid most of her expression. He just smiled and held out one hand, easily pulling her to her feet.

"I promise we won't go far," he assured her. "I realize you've already walked quite enough today."

Kevin looked up from where he sat toying with a few discarded clam shells. Ordinarily he was the warden's shadow, and for a moment Cassidy was certain the blond boy automatically would try to follow them. But something made Kevin remain sitting where he was, even if his eyes followed them until they were swallowed by the darkness.

A few yards from the campfire, the beach was as black as pitch. Even the faint starlight that barely delineated both the tops of the incoming breakers and the inky silhouette of the tree line seemed to be absorbed by the coarse and nonrefractive sand. Cassidy let the warden lead, able to pick out the dim outline of his body as he walked ahead of her. The starlight lightly touched the tousled crown of his hair and the gently swaying fringes on his leathers. Cassidy found her muscles and joints entertaining a cacophony of aches, and she was grateful for the soft level surface of the sand beneath her feet and for the casual pace the warden set.

As she followed him, Cassidy was puzzled by her own reluctance to discuss what had happened the night before. Or maybe she did understand it, she just didn't want to have to confront it or examine her reasons. Every other time he had had one of his lapses, she had been eager, even impatient, afterward to discuss the incident with him. But that night she felt more of a vague sense of apprehension. Was it because of what had happened during the lapse, or because of what she thought he might have remembered about it? And why did the possibility that the warden might be beginning to remember more of what had happened during his interludes as Andy Greene disturb Cassidy rather than excite her?

Cassidy was so self-absorbed that she nearly collided with the warden's back when he finally came to a halt. Trying to cover her inattentiveness, she then found herself standing uncomfortably close to him. She took a clumsy step sideways and pretended to be scanning the pale silvery waves. The cool breeze off the sea lifted the edges of her hair, but her face still felt flushed with heat.

For a few moments the warden colluded with her, allowing her some time and breathing room. The only sound on the beach was the soft rhythmic *shussh* of the waves breaking against the sand. But when he spoke, his words frankly surprised Cassidy.

"I feel that I owe you a very extensive apology, Cassidy," he said.

She turned sharply, trying fruitlessly in the darkness to read the details of his expression. "What do you mean?" she asked.

His response was oblique. "It's becoming so real to me now. Last night, even after it was over, I *knew* that I had been Andy Greene." His voice dropped to a velvety hush. "I could *remember* it."

Reminded of how he had called her Cathy, even after the spell had been over, Cassidy felt her hunger to know beginning to overcome her previous wariness. "Do you remember what you—what Andy—told me?"

She could see the dim shape of his dark head shake. "Not specifically," he admitted, seemingly frustrated by that fact. "But I could still feel his anxiety, his fear." He took a half step closer to her, standing only inches away. "He's extremely worried about you, Cassidy. Something in his world has made him greatly fear for your life."

Trying not to look directly at him, fixing her gaze instead at some point just off the dim outline of his shoulder, where she could see the cold and distant canopy of stars, she tried to explain what little she had learned during the episode. "Andy keeps saying that I'm just lying there and not moving. I'm in some kind of bed. Now that he realizes I'm not dead, he seems to think that I'm sleeping." She paused, then concluded, "He keeps repeating that they're going to kill me if I don't move, if I don't wake up."

Lightly taking her by the shoulders, the warden forced Cassidy to look up into the shadowy oval of his face. "No wonder he's frightened," he said earnestly. "What could it mean? Who's going to kill you?" His voice grew taut with frustration. "If only I could *remember* more! But it's all like trying to see something through a fog. Everything seems somehow fuzzy and muffled."

Cassidy shook her head helplessly. How could she begin to explain to that vital and intelligent young man that his other identity was so disconnected from the world in which he lived that he might as well be living in a fog? And although the touch of the warden's hands did not carry with it the same sort of stunning illumination she had experienced when they first touched during one of his lapses, she still was finding his nearness discomfiting. It had been far easier to distance herself from him when she had been able to think of the warden and Andy Greene as two distinct and remote entities. Knowing what was beginning to happen to him, his growing cognizance of Andy's presence, made Cassidy feel distressingly vulnerable when she was alone with him.

She knew that he was studying her face. Even though she could not imagine what he could hope to see in the near darkness, she felt a flush climb from her neck and spill across her cheeks. Her pulse had begun to thump, and the sensation of his hands resting so lightly on her shoulders suddenly burned like something incendiary.

"Cassidy, there's more," the warden said.

Befuddled by her own churning emotions toward him, she blurted out, "More what?"

To her alarm, he actually moved in slightly closer to her, so close that she could finally see the liquid gleam of his brown eyes in the symmetrical shadows of his face. "You were right all along, Cassidy," he said. "I know that now." He paused briefly, as if searching for words. "I *know* you," he whispered then, disconcertingly close to her ear. "At least when I'm Andy, I know you. And I *am* Andy Greene, just as you said from the very beginning."

Finally beginning to understand the source of the warden's initial contrition, Cassidy quickly attempted to leaven the moment and at the same time put some distance between herself and the alarming intimacy he was fostering. She took a half step backward on the packed sand. "That's okay," she said. "Even I had started to think I must be nuts. So I can hardly blame you for thinking I wasn't making any sense."

She could not clearly see his lips, but she heard the charmingly rueful smile in his voice. "I'm still not saying that you make sense, Cassidy," he pointed out, giving her shoulders a gentle, playful shake. Then his tone grew serious again. "How can I be two people—how can you?" He shook his head, a gross enough movement that she could easily see it. "I've been told that I came here as an infant; I've lived here my whole life. And yet you've only been here a short time. How then can we both be these other two people, existing in the Slow World?"

Cassidy didn't know how to begin to explain that massive paradox to him. Sidestepping it, she focused on something simpler and more concrete. "You said that you've lived here your whole life?" she asked.

His dark head cocked quizzically. "Yes, they found me as a baby."

Cassidy hesitated a moment, still distracted by his nearness. She could detect the faint scent of him, leather and soap and skin. "I'm sure you can't remember that," she said, "so are you sure that it's true; or is it just what you've been told?"

Understanding her point, the warden gently tugged her closer. "Do you remember what I told you about the babies?" he asked over the crown of her head. "When you had become so upset by what you had seen down at the docks?"

She just nodded mutely. His body was so close against hers that she would have sworn she could feel the slow and steady thump of his heart against her side.

"I told you that most of the infants who come here end up dying, usually very young," he went on quietly. "But I was strong and healthy when I was found by Troopers. I was raised in the warden's house." He paused, absently pushing back an unruly lock of Cassidy's hair that hung over her forehead. "That's why I have always decreed that no one kill an infant."

Cassidy's mind raced to come up with some sort of coherent comment or question. But luckily for her, no response was needed as the warden continued to speak.

"And yet now I know that I have also always been Andy Greene, even though I didn't even know he existed until I met you." His warm fingers brushed her face again, smoothing back her hair. Even though she didn't dare look up to meet those dangerous eyes, she knew that he was regarding her with a fond and bemused expression. "Nothing in my life has ever been more important to me than this, Cassidy," he said earnestly. "If you hadn't come to me, if you hadn't persisted in the face of everyone's ridicule . . ."

Flushing afresh, Cassidy tried to avert her face, but found her cheek turning into the smoky, chamoislike leather of his tunic, its fringes brushing her lips. From the very beginning, all of her reasons for persisting in her quest had been venal and self-serving. His admiration and praise only exacerbated the guilt she felt at having involved so many innocent others in her crusade to find her way home again. But to her dismay, she found that even that guilt had a way of heightening her physical awareness of him, the smooth tanned skin of his neck only inches from her mouth. She shivered, and to cover the reaction she blurted out, "But we still don't even know how all of this fits together—or if it even does."

"We still have the Alchemist," the warden said encouragingly. "He may be the key to everything."

"If he even exists," Cassidy quickly reminded him, amazed in some small part of her mind to find herself playing devil's advocate.

She shivered again, so obviously that she could not conceal the shudder from him. Automatically pulling her even closer and putting his other arm around her, as well, the warden looked out over the top of her head to the vast expanse of sea, where the thin starlight glittered like quicksilver on the foaming crests of the breakers. "Well, if we didn't look for him, we'd never know for certain, would we?" he said quietly. His face lowered, his cheeks resting lightly on her temple, while Cassidy's traitorous knees liquefied beneath her.

It's not *sex!* she told herself fiercely, even as her thighs trembled and her nipples ached. Hell, she had seen the warden show the same simple affection for Kevin. He was just . . . fond of her. But the logic rang hollow, as unconvincing to her as the practiced detachment she had tried to employ to deny what she had felt for Andy Greene.

"I just want you to know," he said, "that no matter what has happened to us, Cassidy—no matter what might yet happen—I'm grateful that you convinced me to do this." He paused, giving her a little squeeze before adding "Please feel free to remind me of that as often as needed in the future!"

Her voice incriminatingly unsteady, Cassidy just managed to croak "Okay." And when she tried to pull free of his embrace, another shiver ran through her, making her shoulders quiver.

The warden released her but clasped one of her hands, keeping it. He gently tugged her forward, starting back up the beach toward their camp. "You're chilled," he said, chiding her out of genuine concern for her. "Sleep with Kev and me tonight, at least until your watch."

The suggestion was both enticing and deadly, but in the end she agreed to it. She was surprised to find herself not only comfortable lying with them, bracketed by their warmth, but also able to fall asleep almost immediately, untroubled by all of the disturbing questions that the warden had raised.

Chapter 7 ◀▥

The morning dawned cool and damp, and even before they had finished breakfast it had begun to drizzle. The gray weather only added to the unpleasantness of having to cross another river. Cassidy hoped that the warden's optimism hadn't been misplaced when he had said that one wouldn't be as wide as the last one. But as she scanned the dull, pewter-colored sky, with the rain from her already-saturated hair trickling down the back of her neck, she wasn't seriously counting on it.

They started inland along the soggy banks of the estuary. The miserable weather reminded Cassidy of the conditions she and Rowena had endured on their way from Double Creek to the Iron City, especially before they had encountered the Tinkers and such amenities as tents and hooded cloaks. With an unexpected stab of melancholy, she thought of the wonderful gray woolen cloak that Mitz had made for her—the cloak she had used the night of the monster attack outside of Pointed Rock, to staunch the flow of blood from Allen's wounds and save the sheriff's life. She wasn't even sure anymore just what had happened to that cloak. Had one of the Tinkers salvaged it for her? Was it still back at the warden's compound, along with the other personal possessions Click had brought to her?

Click . . . Cassidy hadn't wanted to think about him again, but in a veritable orgy of brooding, she allowed the image of the dark-haired Tinker to linger in her mind. Click, who had from the very beginning both attracted and frightened her. Click, who had protected her without fail, without ever once taking her into his confidence; who had risked his own life to save hers and had called it nothing more than common courtesy. Click, whose sardonic amusement had always safely obscured his own agenda. Click, who remembered sex . . .

Startled out of her deep reverie by someone calling her name, Cassidy was embarrassed to discover that she hadn't even realized the others had come to a halt. She had no idea how long they had been hiking along the bank of the river. She looked around to see her four companions regarding her with varying degrees of quizzical bemusement.

"Combing the clouds?" Webb asked.

Translating the expression as another term for wool-gathering or daydreaming, Cassidy quickly nodded. "I guess I was," she admitted. "Where are we? Why are we stopping?"

The pilot was already uncoiling the anchor rope. "We were just about to ford this river," he teased, "if you'd care to join us." He tossed the free end of the rope at her and Cassidy reflexively snatched at it, fumbling but catching it.

"I'll walk point this time," Valerie declared.

Cassidy passed the captain the end of the rope, playing out enough line so that she would be in second place. When she took her first good look at the river, she was happily surprised to see that it was indeed considerably narrower than the last one had been. At that point it was only a few hundred feet to the opposite shore, and the sluggish mud-colored water suggested that the channel wasn't particularly deep.

Kevin came up alongside Cassidy, his blond hair darkened and stringy in the cool drizzle. "You want me to go next?" he asked her.

She shook her head. "No, that's okay, Kev. You can follow me." She gave him a friendly smile. "Just pull me out if you see me sinking, huh?"

The warden came forward, uncoiling the rest of the rope. "I don't think we have to worry about that this time," he said. "The river should be pretty shallow here."

As the warden shook his wet hair back out of his eyes, Cassidy tried not to remember what it had felt like to have had him hold her in his arms the night before. She told herself that he smelled like perspiration and damp leather and stale smoke; but then again, her little voice pointed out, so did she. Quickly looking away again before he noticed the strange expression on her face or the sudden color rising on her cheeks, Cassidy stepped into the river behind Valerie, the calm, rain-pocked water closing around her legs.

Since she was already soaked to the skin, Cassidy didn't care about getting wet. Even the sensation of water running into her boots was only a minor annoyance. The mucky bottom of the river was soft and cloying, like walking in deeply tilled earth; but the turbid green water came up only to her knees, and it was easy to step forward. Focusing on the back of Valerie's damp curly head and the darkened leather of her tunic, Cassidy determinedly thought of nothing but reaching the other bank.

They were midway across the river before Cassidy noticed that Webb was whistling, some low and almost tuneless little ditty. Slogging through water that was then thigh deep, she was a little embarrassed about the way she had continued to take the pilot's steady good nature for granted. She realized that there would never be a way she could repay him for everything he had done on their behalf; and debt to Click or not, she still felt deeply beholden to Webb. The very least she could do, she thought then, was try to match his stolid equanimity about the unexpected overland trek and try to show him her appreciation by not making the situation any worse. *And someone definitely owes him a new boat!* she thought emphatically.

Cassidy was about to start whistling herself, when directly in front of her, Valerie abruptly dropped in the water. The captain hadn't tripped, and she didn't fall forward; she just suddenly went from being hip deep in the river to being in water up to her neck. In the split second it took for Cassidy to react and pull back, she felt the oozy muck beneath her feet pitch off sharply. And if Kevin hadn't hauled her back by pulling on the rope, she might have plunged in right behind Valerie.

"Valerie!" Kevin cried out. He pulled even harder on the rope, forcibly reminding Cassidy that she held the woman's lifeline in her own hands.

Valerie's head, the only part of her body that remained above water, tossed back like that of an unbroken colt. "Shit!" she swore, hauling back on the rope between her and Cassidy. "It's a sinkhole! Back up—pull me out of here before I go under!"

Tightening her grip on the wet rope, Cassidy found herself being hauled backward, as well, her boots sliding on the slippery mud of the river bottom as the three men behind her applied themselves to the line. The segment of rope that separated her from Valerie slapped tautly across the surface of the scummy water. For a few moments Cassidy thought that the captain was going to go completely under or lose hold of the rope. But then Valerie suddenly surged toward her, her shoulders breaching the brackish water. Staggering backward, Cassidy allowed herself to be towed along.

By the time Valerie had regained her footing, they were nearly thirty feet from where she had been caught in the mud. Righting herself, Cassidy panted, "What happened?"

"A sinkhole," Valerie repeated, spitting out some river water. "It was like stepping down a damned well!"

Kevin, the warden, and Webb came up to the two women, still gripping their portions of the line. But Valerie didn't look as if she needed any assistance, and she was hardly a person who tolerated casual touching. In fact, as she slapped at the wet leather of her trousers, sending clots of mud swirling into the already opaque water, she seemed more peeved than anything else.

"Sinkholes are common on these rivers," Webb explained for Cassidy's benefit. "Sometimes the current causes a pit to form on the bottom. The silt washes into it in layers, with water trapped between them. It's like quicksand if you step into it. It sucks you right down."

"It's a damned nuisance is what it is," Valerie muttered, making a final futile effort to wash the muck out of her leathers. "Come on, let's get moving again."

"We'd better head upstream a bit then," the pilot said. "Sinkholes tend to be elliptical with the long axis of the river; we want to be sure we've gone well around it."

Momentarily flummoxed by the terminology Webb was so casually slinging around, Cassidy had to scramble to keep up. *Elliptical with the long axis of the river*—who was this guy? she thought. A seaman by way of MIT?

Strung out again along the rope, they crossed the rest of the river without incident. And on the boggy ground on the opposite bank, a quick strip-down in the cool drizzle showed no sign of unwelcome leeches.

"First good piece of luck we've had today," Valerie grumbled as she struggled back into her clammy wet trousers. And, Cassidy added silently, the river had been shallow and narrow enough for them to have crossed it in less than fifteen minutes, even with detouring around the sinkhole.

As they trekked back toward the beach along the southern bank of the river, they saw several more pair of egrets. The big white birds looked like ghosts in the fine gray veil of rain, perched on the blackened skeletons of long-dead trees in the estuary. When the travelers drew close, the cranes silently took wing, their S-shape necks folding back against their snowy breasts, their long dark legs trailing out behind them like rudders.

Considerably more aware of her surroundings on the trip back downriver, Cassidy was surprised to find that they had hiked only about half a mile inland to ford the river. Despite the rain and the sinkhole, perhaps the day's travel would go better than the day before. Her wet clothing and the constant drizzle didn't really bother Cassidy so much as long as they kept moving and seemed to be making some progress. Surreptitiously trying to avoid being too close to the warden, after a time she found herself walking alongside Webb. Remembering the way the pilot had whistled while they slogged through the river, she glanced sideways at him, studying his tanned and angular face.

Catching her looking his way, Webb flashed Cassidy a little grin. "Lovely weather, eh?" he said, teasingly but not sarcastically. Without his woolen cap, his soaked hair lay lank against his head, little runnels of water dripping from its lighter-colored tips.

Curious, and emboldened by Webb's affable nature, Cassidy asked him, "Where did you learn to navigate?"

He laughed, a short little burst of good humor. "You mean the sinkhole? I've done my share of scut duty on the rivers before I was fit to sail the Gray Sea."

"Not just that," Cassidy said. "I mean all of it—the stuff you do with the sticks and string. How did you learn that?"

"Had a good teacher," Webb said somewhat more seriously. "An old pilot who'd been up and down this coast a hundred times. He taught me how to navigate by the sun and the stars." He shrugged. "Amazing what you can learn when it's important to you." His eyes narrowed shrewdly. "Like you and horses, I suspect."

Cassidy was silent for a few moments. Since that episode on the beach the afternoon before, she had not been able to sense any presence of Dragonfly, and it troubled her. If they were growing closer to her horse and her friends, why wasn't she able to sense the mare again? She glanced over to see that Webb had been watching her, and when he spoke, she realized how transparent she had been to him.

"I wouldn't worry about the horse," the pilot said evenly. "If he said he'd bring her, he'll bring her."

Trying to change the subject, and only partially succeeding, Cassidy asked, "Do you think they're already at the cove?"

Webb spread his callused hands. "They could be by now," he said, "or at least close to it. If things had gone according to plan, we would have been there a couple of days ahead of them. It's a pretty rough journey overland—" He caught himself, grinned wryly, and amended, "Well, not as rough as this has been, but it's unsettled land with little more than deer paths for trails. They

might have been able to ride for a day or two, but then after
that—"

Surprise caused Cassidy to look directly at the seaman. "You
mean they won't be coming on horseback?" she asked, almost
plaintively.

Webb chuckled sympathetically at her stricken expression. "It's
not like the Eastern Territories, where you've got trails," he said.
"I'm not saying that it's impassable for horses, but you'd make
better time on foot once you reach the boggy land." He paused
and gave Cassidy another incisive look. "He'll bring your horse
because he promised on his blood that he would; but I wouldn't
count on doing much riding if you're planning on going into the
Great Swamp."

Trying to conceal her dismay, Cassidy trudged alongside Webb
in silence. Once again her lack of knowledge about that world had
led her to make the wrong assumptions and to be disappointed.
Searching for the Alchemist was proving a daunting enough task;
the idea of having to do it on foot just made it that much less appealing to her.

Another unpleasant surprise was waiting for all of them when
they reached the shoreline again. Unlike the flat coarse sand on
the other side of the estuary, the beach on that side quickly became a narrow rocky strand. As bad as that was, the edge of the
woods soon became even worse. A bank appeared along the juncture of the forest and the stony beach, at first only a few feet high,
but craggy and crumbling. During the course of the rest of the
rainy morning, as they scrabbled along over the wet rocks, the
bank grew steadily higher and steeper. By the time the warden
called a midday halt, the cliff rose nearly twenty feet above sea
level, the dark and dripping ranks of trees hanging down from its
rim like leafy green towers.

They stopped near a small ravine that split the shaley wall of
the cliff face. A creek poured out from the narrow and overgrown
floor of the little gully; but rather than emptying into the sea, the
stream appeared just to vanish into the rugged stones on the
beach.

"It runs underground from here," Webb explained. He pointed
out across the cold gray waves. "If you look real close, you can
see where the outlet is. See where the water is a little different
color out there? Right out past where the waves are breaking."

"At least we won't have to cross it," Valerie muttered, less than
impressed by Webb's knowledge of the terrain. The captain

moved past Cassidy and began to search along the beach for firewood.

Ignoring Valerie's sarcasm, the pilot continued, "We're getting close to the cove now, because there's this same kind of rocky face there. It's what forms the caves and grottoes where seamen have found shelter and stored their supplies."

Heartened by that thought, Cassidy made another quick but deliberate effort to reach out for her mare's presence. Her eyes half closed in the chill drizzle, she tried to concentrate on the essence of the gray horse: her short, in-curved ears, her long patrician nose, her mane and tail the color of spun steel, the sweet silky feel of her skin . . . And for a few moments Cassidy thought she felt—something. Perhaps it was just her memory playing tricks on her, but for a fleeting bit of time she thought she could sense the gray mare again.

When Kevin came up behind her and touched her on the shoulder, she was startled not only out of her reverie, but also nearly out of her skin, as well. "Cassidy, do you want to help me look for food?" he asked.

"Yeah, sure, Kev," she said. She pushed her dripping hair back off her forehead and looked around. Both the warden and Valerie were already fifty yards down the beach, looking for firewood. Cassidy glanced at the creek. "Let's try going a little way into the ravine. Maybe there'll be some berry canes or something in there."

Since he was the only one left nearby to do it, Webb reminded them, "Be careful." Except that the pilot did it with good humor.

Taking her by the hand, Kevin began leading Cassidy across the rocks. She was a little nonplussed by the gesture, but Kevin's friendship was so simple and spontaneous that she allowed the touch. In a few moments she discovered that his handhold was also helpful, because the balancing effect of his grip made it easier for her to clamber over the slippery stones.

The mouth of the ravine was choked with brush and brambles, but none of the briars had fruit on them. Kevin soon needed both hands to clear a path through the dripping vegetation, and Cassidy kept right behind him to avoid getting slapped with the wet branches. She didn't think that she could have gotten any more soaked than she already was, but somehow the fresh drenching made her feel cold and uncomfortable all over again, and the tough briars tore at her soggy cotton clothing. As they moved deeper into the narrow gully, under the overhanging boughs of the trees, the sound of the creek grew louder, until it finally drowned out the distant hiss of the waves. The ground underfoot was rocky and uneven, and several times Cassidy tripped over stones and roots.

Just when she was becoming fast convinced that it had been a bad idea to go into the ravine looking for food, Kevin gave a triumphant little yip. "Look, Cassidy, blackberries! And they're even ripe!"

Her mouth watering at the thought of fresh ripe berries, Cassidy pushed in behind the blond boy. After forcing aside the branches, she was rewarded by the sight of the thorny stalks of the blackberry canes, their plump and lobular fruit gleaming blue-black in the rain.

Grinning conspiratorily at each other, Cassidy and Kevin greedily filled their mouths with the first of the berries. There was plenty of fruit on the canes, she rationalized, and it just made sense for them to fill up first, rather than carry more berries out to the beach to eat them there. She and Kevin could eat most of their lunch right there, and the others could have what they would carry out.

Besides, Cassidy was hungry. She ate ravenously and without shame.

When they both were finally sated, their lips and fingers stained a bruised purple, Cassidy and Kevin pushed farther into the patch of canes. Since her cotton shirt had the biggest pockets, Kevin stayed beside her and dumped his pickings into them, as well. It began to rain harder again as they were picking, but Cassidy just shook her hair back out of her eyes and forged ahead, her stained fingers nimbly searching over the canes. It took them only a few minutes to fill her pockets to capacity; slightly beyond capacity, if you counted the juicy berries that had been squashed, but she doubted that anyone would quibble over that detail. Popping a few more berries into her mouth, Cassidy adjusted the wet fabric of the sagging shirt so that it didn't cut into her shoulders.

"I guess that's enough," Kevin said, stifling a soft, contented belch.

"At least it's all I can carry," Cassidy agreed. "But maybe after lunch we can—"

Kevin had been stripping another handful of berries off the nearest cane when Cassidy suddenly broke off. When she didn't go on, he turned to look quizzically at her. Her head was cocked at an odd angle, as if she were listening to something of extreme interest. "What is it?" he asked, his voice hushed.

But Cassidy didn't seem to be making any effort to keep her voice down. "Do you smell that?" she asked him.

Kevin turned his head farther, sniffing audibly. "What?" he repeated, puzzled.

The breeze, heavy with chill humidity off the sea, was at their backs. Cassidy tugged Kevin forward a couple of yards through the soggy tangle of berry canes. Then she paused, pointing farther into the depths of the ravine. "That rotting smell," she said, "like spoiled meat."

Kevin's puzzlement changed to disgust. "We can't eat anything that's rotten," he said. Then suddenly his expression changed again, his odd-colored eyes going wide with alarm. "You don't think it's one of those . . . ?"

But Cassidy was shaking her head. "Naw, the stink's not bad enough for monsters," she assured him. "But I think I know what it is. Come on." She tugged on Kevin's arm. "I saw one of these the other day when I was with Webb."

"One of what?" Kevin persisted, hanging back a bit initially, but then allowing himself to be led along. He seemed frankly curious, his wariness stifled by Cassidy's calm demeanor.

"You'll see," she said mysteriously.

Beyond the blackberry canes, the brush finally thinned slightly, and it became possible to walk without having to thrust forcibly through a barricade of briars. Still following the faint fetid scent, Cassidy began to look for the nearest large tree. The rain was like a falling mist there beneath the canopy of leaves, but the putrid odor grew steadily stronger. The narrow but deep cataract of the creek churned busily among the rocks, drowning out all other sounds. The rushing water was as clear as crystal, marred only by the occasional floating leaf or twig.

"What are we looking for?" Kevin repeated. He was still interested, but he seemed somewhat confused why they were going to such lengths to pursue something that couldn't even be eaten.

Cassidy towed Kevin after her as she ducked past some dripping saplings and under the low boughs of a large larch tree. "I bet it's up in this tree," she said. The larch stood only a few yards from the bank of the creek, its gnarled roots sprawling out across the rocky ground.

"I don't think we should go this far away from the beach," Kevin said uncomfortably.

Standing upright near the trunk of the big tree, Cassidy tilted her head back, blinking into the feathery mist, and began to scan the shadowy undersides of the high limbs. The stink was strong enough that she knew they must be right under the bizarre hanging collection of—

Cassidy took a sudden involuntary step backward, nearly falling over Kevin's feet. He made a sound of protest, but then he was struck speechless. Just inches from Cassidy's startled face, a long glistening streamer of fetid slime slowly spun down like a rope of phlegm. The exudate almost seemed like a living thing as it twisted and spiraled toward the damp earth at their feet.

Unwillingly but inexorably, Cassidy looked up again, her vision sharpened by the sickening certainty of what she would find high in the larch's branches. There amid the deep shadows of the massive tree's thick foliage, she could see the big black shapes of two—no, three—of the hideous carrion eaters, their grotesquely everted torsos pulsing and roiling with gelatinous gleaming slime, as if all of the wretched worms of corruption were barely contained there beneath their throbbing, pustular skins. Frozen in horror, Cassidy's eyes locked on their foul and filthy forms as another long candle of rotting residue oozed toward the ground.

It took Kevin to break the terrified impasse. "Monsters!" the blond boy yelped, tearing free of Cassidy's hand with no need for discussion or rational thought. And then he took off, crashing heedlessly through the brush and briars toward the beach.

In that moment, only one thought solidified in Cassidy's madly whirling mind: *Dragonfly!* Automatically, for the first time since she had left the warden's compound, she found herself desperately Calling the gray mare. Then the grim reality of her situation reasserted itself. The gray mare was not there. Cassidy's muscles exploded into action and she ran after Kevin.

Slapping branches and blackberry thorns tore at her bare arms and her clothing, but Cassidy was oblivious to their hindrance. Several times she tripped and would have fallen, had not her furious momentum kept her on her feet. By the time Kevin plunged through the thick brush at the mouth of the ravine and pelted out onto the rocky beach, Cassidy was practically on his heels.

Valerie was bent over a small pyramid of driftwood, striking with her flint to ignite the tinder at its base. The warden and Webb squatted a few feet away, gutting alewives. All three of them stood immediately as Cassidy and Kevin burst out of the gully and scrambled across the slippery stones.

"What the hell?" the captain began. But Kevin ran right past her. He ran right past the warden and Webb, as well, and Cassidy thought he was going to run right out into the ocean before he was finished. She was half convinced he could have stayed atop the waves, the way he was moving.

Recovering from his initial surprise, the warden executed a swift sprint and intercepted the young Finder, catching him by the sleeve and whipping him around so hard that both of them nearly tumbled onto the rough stones of the beach. Wild-eyed and panting, Kevin struggled blindly but ineffectually in the warden's grasp. The warden finally had to pull him into a bear hug to calm his frantic efforts to free himself.

"Kevin! Kevin, what is it?" the warden demanded, his arms locked around the smaller man.

Cassidy staggered to a halt, aware that both Valerie and Webb were eyeing her with wonder and wariness. Gasping to catch her breath, she managed to choke out "Monsters! There're hanging monsters in there!"

Valerie crossed the few steps that separated them, holding out one hand reassuringly, as if she were approaching an unfamiliar and spooky horse. "Easy," the captain said. "In where? The ravine?"

"What the hell is that all over your shirt?" Webb put in, sounding more confused than alarmed.

Glancing down the front of her shirt, Cassidy saw that whatever blackberries hadn't bounced out of her pockets during her mad dash from the ravine had been turned into an impromptu sort of blackberry jam. The unbleached cotton fabric was stained with huge hemorrhages of purple juice, her pockets sagging with lumps of mashed pulp and seeds. "Blackberries," Cassidy said inanely, making a futile brush at the mess on her shirt. "We found a big patch of blackberries, and we picked a bunch of them, and then I smelled something rotten and I thought it was just one of those Woodsman's things, and we saw *monsters*!—hanging monsters in the tree!"

"Whoa, slow down," Valerie said calmly, still holding out her hand. "Exactly where did you see them? And how many?"

Darting a sideways glance at Kevin, who then was clinging to the warden like a frightened child clutching his mother, Cassidy said, "Three, I think; maybe more." She pointed toward the ravine. "In there, in a big larch tree."

Throwing the warden a look, Valerie said evenly, "I'm going to go take a look."

"I'm going with you," the warden responded—which immediately struck Cassidy as absurd, since Kevin was stuck on him like a leech. He wouldn't be going anywhere without the blond boy, and Cassidy seriously doubted that any power in that world, even his beloved warden, could have made Kevin return back up that gully.

"No," Valerie said, stating the obvious. "You stay here with Kevin."

"I'll go," Webb said evenly.

The captain's expression flirted with dissent and then assumed a casual sort of agreement. It was plain that she considered the warden preeminently valuable and the pilot distinctly expendable. It would have been amusing to be able to read so easily the judgment on the captain's face, had not Cassidy's heart been banging in her chest and her limbs still trembling with adrenaline. "Okay," Valerie said to Webb, "come on then."

For a moment Cassidy wondered if she was expected to guide them; but she didn't think she could have forced herself to go back into that ravine, even if she had been commanded to. But Valerie and Webb strode off without a single backward glance, quickly disappearing through the thick tangle of wet brush alongside the creek's outlet and into the misty shadows of the gully. The last thing Cassidy saw of them was the broad cotton-covered wedge of Webb's shoulders, twisting to duck between the dripping branches.

The warden murmured softly to Kevin, allowing the younger man to remain tightly pressed against him, all the while gently encouraging Kevin to compose himself. Somehow Cassidy did not find Kevin's fear extreme or disproportionate. Even though she had seen the hideous carrion-eaters several times before, she was still terrified of the damned things. She shuddered to think of how close the putrid slime had come to hitting her right in the face. She was grimacing in remembrance when the warden looked across to her, his expression concerned and sympathetic.

"They're just scavengers, Kev," he said quietly, one palm rubbing between the boy's trembling shoulder blades. "I don't think they'd hurt you; they just eat dead things."

"Oh, y-yeah?" Kevin hiccoughed, not lifting his head. "W-what if they get t-tired of w-waiting?"

The warden laughed softly and gave Kevin a light shake. But Cassidy didn't find the boy's comment very amusing. She could not forget her own encounter with the repulsive creatures on the road outside the Iron City the night of the fires, and what Click had done to kill the one that had draped itself over her. Enfolded in that malignant mass of reeking flesh, she had been certain that the monster had meant her harm. If it hadn't been for Click . . .

Seeing Cassidy shudder again, the warden freed one arm from Kevin to reach out to her, beckoning her to join in the soothing reassurance of his embrace. But Cassidy stood back, her chin lifting in stubborn stoicism. Some things were more frightening to her than even the wretched hanging monsters, and the comfort of the warden's arms was only one of them.

Only a few minutes later Cassidy heard the brush noisily part and saw Valerie and Webb pushing their way back out onto the beach. Both of them were slightly scratched from the briars and stained by blackberry juice, but neither looked out of breath or in any way alarmed. Slapping the wet leaves off the darkened fringes of her wet leathers, the captain walked directly to the warden to make her report.

"There's nothing there now," she said. "The tree is empty."

Cassidy felt her spine stiffen. "Are you saying that we were seeing things?" she demanded of Valerie. She gestured toward Kevin, who had lifted his head from the warden's shoulder and was blinking in confusion. "That both of us imagined it?"

"No," Webb said, stepping forward around Valerie. "We found this." He held up a short piece of stick, its surface liberally coated with the foul dark slime exuded by the hanging creatures. "This muck was all over the lower branches and the ground under the tree."

"They'd been there," Valerie concluded, "but they're gone now." She looked at Cassidy, her elegantly arched brows rising. "Maybe you scared them off."

Cassidy wasn't certain if the curly-haired woman was mocking her or, more likely, merely stating an opinion. For the moment she didn't really care either way; she was just relieved that the monsters were gone.

The warden had Kevin standing on his own again, however shakily. He gave both the blond boy and Cassidy a sympathetic look. "I don't suppose either one of you wants to go back into the ravine to pick more blackberries," he said wryly, "so I suggest that we make do with what's left in Cassidy's pockets and these fish. And then we'll get moving again."

All afternoon they trudged along the rocky beach in silence. The skies remained gray, and a cold drizzle continued to fall. The embankment along the beach kept gradually climbing, while the shoreline seemed to grow even more rugged. Once they had left the ravine behind. Kevin's anxiety receded; and although his mood could hardly have been described as cheerful, at least he relaxed again and took a curious interest in his surroundings. He even walked with Webb for a time, plying the pilot with all sorts of questions about the Gray Sea and the various bits of flotsam and jetsam he found washed up on the beach.

Much of the afternoon passed in a haze for Cassidy. She kept thinking about the gray mare and the way she had automatically Called the horse when she was in danger. It was the first time she had done so since she had been separated from Dragonfly, and yet it certainly wasn't the first time Cassidy had felt that her life had been in danger. What was it that had made the experience in the ravine different? Had she instinctively sensed the horse's growing nearness? Her earlier feeling of momentary unity with the mare seemed to suggest it. And could the horse have possibly heard her Call?

Cassidy had no answers to the insistent questions, but at least they kept her mind occupied as she clambered over the endless wet and slippery rocks, barely aware of the continuing discomforts of the long trek along the shore.

Late in the afternoon, when Valerie sighted the mouth of the third river, Cassidy almost felt a sense of relief. It was as if another purely physical challenge—something that could be confronted bluntly and overcome—was a welcome respite from all of the unsolved turmoil in her mind. And she reminded herself that every river brought them closer to the cove. If Webb's reckoning had been correct, it might be the last one they would have to cross.

Because of the rocky cliff along the edge of the land, the outlet of the third river was not a vast and brackish estuary. The river didn't appear very large, but over time its waters had carved out a wide notch in the steep face of the sea bank. From the top of that notch, water poured down in a thick, churning waterfall, roiling across the slablike rocks and then out over the narrow beach into the sea. From down at sea level, it was impossible to tell what the river looked like on top of the cliff, whether its channel was narrow or if it had spread out into an upland bog.

Once they were within a few dozen yards of the waterfall, the roar of its gushing water was loud enough to drown out the rumble of the waves and most other natural sounds. Shielding her eyes against the drizzle, Valerie scanned up the face of the cliff. She had to raise her voice to be heard over the noise. "If the river bed's not too wide," she said matter-of-factly, "we could cross it and still be able to travel for a few hours today."

"If there's not just one big mucking swamp up there," Webb agreed mildly, also studying the stark rocky face of the bank.

"But first we'll have to get up that cliff," the warden reminded them both, "and it's going to be especially slick going in this rain."

"That's no problem," the captain said with simple self-assurance. She still scrutinized the steep embankment. "We just need one person to free-climb with the rope. Then the rest of us will have a good handhold."

"I can do that," Kevin said immediately. As all eyes turned to him, the blond boy resolutely stuck out his chin. "I'm a good climber," he insisted. "I could always beat Rafe to the top of any cliff."

Bestowing a fond smile on his faithful follower, the warden glanced quickly at the others. "I take it there are no objections to continuing on yet today?" he asked. As everyone voiced agreement, the warden gave Kevin a nod. "All right then, Kev, the job is yours. Just be careful—and don't lose the rope."

It made Cassidy's arms and legs ache in sympathy just to watch Kevin scramble up the rough, almost barren face of the rocky cliff. He had not been exaggerating his skills as a climber; he was as agile as a monkey, and quite fearless as he crawled up the crumbling surface, boldly reaching from one nearly nonexistent handhold to another. As Kevin ascended, Webb played out the rope. Cassidy began to wonder if the line would be long enough to reach to the top of the bank. There were plenty of solid anchors at the lip of the cliff where Kevin could secure the rope. The prows of outcropping boulders and the thick protruding stubs of nearby tree roots would all be solid enough to hold their weight.

At the very top the angle of the bank was slightly undercut, forming a harrowing stretch of perfectly vertical drop. But Cassidy was both impressed and relieved when Kevin squirmed up the nearly featureless surface like a fly on a wall. Then the boy was standing at the top of the cliff, his soaked leathers smeared with muddy clay.

"Anchor the rope, Kev!" the warden called up to him.

"What about the river?" Valerie added. "What does it look like up there?"

Kevin turned ninety degrees, his profile clearly cut against the gray backdrop of the dreary, rain-washed sky. He briefly scanned the area. "It's not real wide," he shouted down, "but there's a lot of old fallen trees and stuff. I don't know if we can cross it here."

"We can worry about that once we're all up there," the warden pointed out. He gestured to Valerie. "Why don't you go next?"

Kevin tied the end of the rope around the base of one of the largest rocks at the top of the cliff. Valerie automatically tested the integrity of his workmanship by tugging hard on the line. When the rope held, she began scrambling up the rugged surface, using an overhand technique to pull herself along as she climbed. Watching the captain's assent, Cassidy felt badly outclassed. On a horse she could have given any of them, even the curly-haired woman, a run for their money. But on the ground she knew she lacked Valerie's innate agility.

As Valerie crested the cliff and joined Kevin, the warden offered the end of the rope to Cassidy. He gave her a quizzical look when she shook her head and said, "That's okay, you go next." But Cassidy felt especially sensitive about having him in particular see her fumble awkwardly up the face of the bank. The warden just shrugged agreeably, grasped the line, and began to climb.

As the two of them stood on the rainy beach watching the young man make his way up the steep surface, Webb threw Cassidy a conspiratorial look and said, "You'd better go next. I climb like a cow, and with our luck, I'll probably break the damned rope, too."

Cassidy had seen the pilot's considerable strength and physical dexterity before, but she still was grateful for his thoughtful self-deprecation.

The climb was not as difficult as Cassidy had anticipated, although the trampled clay subsoil of the cliff was becoming slippier with every boot track. The bank wasn't quite as high or as steep as it had appeared from the beach; and even though she was pretty out of breath, and her arms and legs were protesting by the time Kevin and the warden helped her over the top, she had managed the distance without disgracing herself in any way. And much as she had expected, Webb quickly scrambled up the cliff without any noticeable difficulty.

From the top of the cliff, Cassidy looked inland beyond the head of the waterfall with dismay. Kevin had been right about one thing; the river wasn't particularly wide. But the channel had obviously made numerous alterations in course over the years, and the treacherous black stumps of flooded-out trees dotted much of its width. Amid the stumps were a multitude of old snags, trashy catch-alls where seasons' worth of logs, branches, and other woody debris had lodged, creating whirlpools. From the volume of the flow over the falls, the water must have been well over their heads, and the current was strong.

Hands on hips, Valerie surveyed the cluttered and turbulent river with patent disgust. "I wouldn't even take a raft across this," she grumbled, "much less try to ford it on foot."

Glancing overhead at the drizzly sky, the warden frowned thoughtfully. "With this weather, we've only got a few more hours of traveling light left," he said. "We'll go upstream; but if we don't find a place where we can ford soon, we'll have to come back and make camp on the beach. I don't favor spending the night inland in this country."

No one disagreed with his assessment, but Cassidy had to wonder if they were actually any safer on the beach. Theoretically the beach may have been more defensible, with the sea on one side. But the existence of the water monsters seemed to make traditional tactics obsolete.

Once Webb had retrieved and recoiled the rope, they started upstream. The ground along the river was boggy, thick with clumps of coarse reeds and the rotting remains of logs and stumps. Cassidy found herself constantly tripping over half-buried snags, and the tangled sedges snared her boots. In spite of the cool rain, she was perspiring from the effort within ten minutes. Several times they had to wade out into the river to make their way around fallen trees or impassably thick brush on the bank; once when they had to do so, the water came nearly to their chins. Tired, wet, and discouraged, Cassidy grew certain they would have to return to the beach before nightfall. And what was worse, that idea actually had begun to seem more attractive than its alternative of crossing the river, even though returning would mean renegotiating the rugged course they'd just traveled.

Her mind was becoming fuzzy with fatigue, and she was caught off guard when Valerie suddenly called a halt. Studying the river, Cassidy was surprised to find that although it had grown wider, it also appeared more shallow, and it definitely was far clearer of debris. For a group of riders on horseback, the stream would have been easy to ford. Perhaps it was only her weariness then that filled Cassidy with a vague foreboding.

Valerie looked at the warden. "Well, what do you think?" she asked.

The warden was silent for a few moments, and as he studied the river, Webb offered, "I expect it keeps getting wider upstream, at least for a few more miles. But it probably gets shallower, too."

Kevin was gazing out across the opaque gliding water, his expression anxious. Cassidy suspected he might be thinking what she was: There could be almost anything in that water. "Are we going to cross here?" he asked uneasily.

"If we don't cross here, we'll go back to the beach for the night," the warden said. Cassidy realized that although the young leader didn't rule by consensus, he'd always shown a marked sensitivity to input from the people who followed him. "Are we agreed to go across then?" he asked. "If not, we'll wait until morning to try."

Although Kevin had been the one to voice his concern, suddenly Cassidy felt as if all eyes were upon her, at least once Valerie and Webb expressed their willingness to proceed. Despite her misgivings about crossing the river, Cassidy doubted that she would have grown any more enthusiastic about it by morning, and a mounting desire was growing in her to just see the crossing done.

"Let's go now," she said stoically.

The warden cocked a brow at Kevin, but the blond boy's consent seemed a forgone conclusion.

As Webb unfastened the rope from his waist and began uncoiling it again, Cassidy surprised herself as much as anyone else by stepping forward and taking the end of it. "It's my turn to take point," she said resolutely, keeping her face averted. She didn't want to examine the particular speculative look on Valerie's face further, nor did she want to see what she might find on the warden's. Tightening the rope around her waist, she stepped into the greenish water, determinedly telling herself, *First one in is the first one across and out.*

As the water swirled around her knees, Cassidy's only thought was that it felt almost refreshingly cool after their sweaty tramp along the marshy bank. The surface of the river was almost identical in color to the washed-out gray of the sky, and perfectly opaque. It was rather alarming to feel the water grow deeper with every cautious step she took, but the bottom was relatively solid compared with the other two rivers they had crossed, and the increasing depth was gradual enough not to come as a surprise. Glancing over her shoulder, Cassidy saw Kevin right behind her, followed by the warden and then Valerie, with Webb bringing up the rear. Ever mindful of water snakes and sinkholes, she redevoted her attention to the river, placing each footstep with deliberate care.

Cassidy had initially estimated that the river was about a hundred yards across. The terrain on the other bank looked pretty much like what they had just left, a strip of boggy ground, littered with deadfalls and reeds, backed by the dark wall of the trackless forest. As Cassidy neared the midpoint of the river, the water came nearly to her shoulders. If it grew deeper, could she swim if she'd have to? Exhaling levelly, she tried to tell herself that from there on, she was on her way *out* of the river, rather than into it.

A tug on the line around her waist caused Cassidy to hesitate. She heard the warden say, "Kevin?" When she looked back, the blond boy was standing with his head cocked, his expression oddly tentative.

"I—I thought I felt something hit my foot," Kevin said uncertainly.

"Probably a submerged branch," Webb said from the rear of the line. Because the pilot was considerably taller than Cassidy, the dull-colored river water only came up to midchest on him. "There's a lot of waterlogged wood rolling along in this river."

Cassidy liked that explanation a lot better than the ones racing through her own mind; it was logical, calming, and best of all had nothing to do with monsters. When she slowly started forward again, she found that her pulse rate had doubled, her heart thumping soundly against her ribs. She had to fight to keep from pushing herself incautiously through the sluggish water, desperate to be on dry land again.

To Cassidy's immense relief, within a minute the water level began to recede again. Instead of washing around her shoulders, the river then barely came to her nipples. The water also no longer felt particularly refreshing; it was chilling, almost uncomfortably so, causing her nipples to rise into painfully tight little nubs beneath the soaked cotton of her seaman's shirt. Fixing her eyes on the dark skeleton of a dead tree on the far bank, Cassidy moved steadily through the water, willing the distance between herself and that old snag to evaporate.

Cassidy's concentration was so intense that for the first few seconds after her feet began to sink, she had real difficulty recognizing exactly what was happening to impede her progress. Fortunately for her, Kevin was more alert. The moment he saw Cassidy begin to drop into the water, he threw himself back against the rope that linked them.

"Sinkhole!" Valerie cursed.

Cassidy said nothing. She unexpectedly found her mouth and

nostrils filling with water, and in her struggle to clear her face, she could barely keep her head above water.

"Hang on, Cassidy!" the warden shouted at her. The rope cut more tightly into her waist as all four of them began to haul back on it. "Try to pull your feet free—let yourself float if you can!"

Filling her lungs with air, Cassidy struggled to comply. But her boots only seemed to sink deeper into the suddenly insubstantial bottom of the river. She felt the turbid water closing over her head. The rope dragged at her, but it was only pulling her body sideways, forcing her even farther beneath the water.

Get your boots off! she commanded herself, with remarkable logic for a woman only a minute or two away from drowning. *If you can get your boots off, you can get your feet free of the mud!* Grasping the rope in one hand and using it as a lever, she bent to reach for her ankles. Much as she hated to lose her boots, she didn't want to be buried in them, especially not at the bottom of some godforsaken river. But just as she dug her fingernails into the soggy leather of one boot top, something shifted radically beneath her feet, and suddenly she was free, shooting toward the surface, propelled by the tension on the rope. She coughed, spitting out water.

Her astonishment at finding herself on the surface again was rivaled only by her surprise at finding all four of her companions also beginning to mire down in the muck. Since she had just crossed that portion of the river without incident, she was incredulous to see them floundering and beginning to sink. Even Webb, who was at least fifty feet back from where Cassidy had originally gotten stuck, was almost up to his neck in water. Then to her horror she saw the top of Kevin's head abruptly slip beneath the surface.

The rope between Cassidy and Kevin slacked for a moment, then immediately snapped taut again as the warden hauled back hard on it. But there was nothing impeding the rope between Cassidy and the warden then; Kevin was no longer holding onto the line.

"Kevin!" the warden shouted, furiously trying to wrench his feet free from the imprisoning hold of the river bottom.

"No, wait!" Valerie commanded from behind him. As far as Cassidy could tell, the captain was just as bogged down as the warden, yet she was ordering him not to try to go to Kevin's aid. And both of them were hauling back so hard on the line in their efforts to kick loose of the muck that they were towing Cassidy backward toward the area where Kevin had just disappeared.

What the hell? Cassidy thought fatalistically. She was free, at least for the moment, and as long as she kept swimming and didn't try to touch bottom, she wouldn't become entrapped again. She was really the only one in a position to help the boy. And so when her kicking foot struck something firm but yielding beneath the opaque surface of the water, she sucked in a huge breath and dived into the river.

Underwater, visibility was nonexistent; in the grayish-green murk, everything was defined by touch alone. Her groping fingers first found Kevin's head, then one of his flailing arms. Just as Cassidy had, he was trying to wriggle free of his boots; but he was already buried to his knees in the muck. Her lungs began to burn, demanding air. She could only imagine what Kevin must have been feeling.

Squeezing his shoulder, she shot to the surface again. Gasping for air, she panted, "He's really stuck! I'm going to try to get the rope around him so we can pull!" Cassidy filled her lungs with several heaving breaths. Then she dove under the water once more.

For a moment she couldn't find Kevin, and she nearly panicked. Could he have already been sucked completely under? Then her sweeping fingers touched the streaming strands of his long pale hair, and she clasped her hands around his head. Tipping headdown, she pulled herself down to him, until she felt her face bump against his. *Please don't freak out on me, Kev!* she pleaded silently as she slid the fingers of one hand across his cheek. She found his nose and pinched shut his nostrils. As her mouth fastened upon his, she felt one of his arms come up around her shoulders, steadying her, and with a rush of relief she knew that he understood. His lips felt as cold as ice, but when she exhaled into his mouth he greedily took in the air, barely a bubble escaping around their joined mouths. With her lungs nearly emptied, Cassidy pulled back from him and then dove deeper.

It took precious seconds to work the wet knot free from the rope, and several more to secure the rope around Kevin's waist. Cassidy winced when she thought of the old bruises she had seen across his chest and belly from his encounter with the water monster. But she doubted that he even felt the injuries, given the situation.

With the rope fastened around Kevin's waist, Cassidy forced herself even deeper, trying to pry his legs free of the sediment without trapping herself. She could feel his muscles cording as he struggled to pull himself loose. She had no illusions about how long the shot of secondhand air she gave him would last, and her own chest was aching desperately again. Just when she was about to unwillingly abandon him again, driven by the age-old imperative for oxygen, one of Kevin's legs suddenly kicked free. Then the two of them were rushing to the surface together, their ascent accelerated by the tension on the rope around his waist.

Cassidy's first moments on the surface were totally consumed by coughing out water and gasping in air. She trod water, oblivious to Kevin's arm around her as she choked and wheezed.

"Cassidy! Are you all right?" she heard Webb call from across the water.

"Yeah," Kevin answered for both of them, his voice several octaves deeper than usual and hoarse with aspirated water.

When she had finally caught her breath, Cassidy was relieved to see that the pilot had hauled himself free of the muck and was swimming toward Valerie and the warden. Even as she watched, Webb helped the warden, who had also just gotten free, pull Valerie from the sucking mire.

"Keep on swimming!" Webb shouted, still holding Valerie by the back of the neck of her leather tunic. "Cassidy, get a grip on the rope again! I don't care how big this damned sinkhole is—just keep swimming!"

Cassidy fumbled for the rope, her arms and legs alarmingly weary. The bank was only about a hundred feet away, but it was a distance that then looked immeasurably vast. Her lungs still stung, and she was trembling from exhaustion and half-spent adrenaline. Then Kevin was swimming alongside her, encouraging her.

"Go ahead, Cassidy," he said huskily, "I'll be right beside you."

Feeling a powerful rush of emotions, Cassidy forced herself to swim in short, economic strokes, fighting the drag on her oversize cotton clothing. She had saved Kevin's life, and yet in some odd way she felt overwhelmingly grateful to the boy. The rope played out behind them and, arrayed along it, like fish on a stringer, swam the warden, Valerie, and Webb. *I never want to see another damned river as long as I live!* she thought vehemently, lifting her face from the cool greenish-gray water.

Later Cassidy would have time to reflect on how it always seemed that catastrophes tended to dull her senses to the anticipation of further disaster. Her harrowing experience in that world should have honed her already well stropped cynicism to a new edge. But the relentless pace of calamity there wearied her, having the effect of causing her to cling to any letup, letting her guard slip out of sheer exhaustion.

One moment she was doggedly swimming along in the turbid water, and the next thing she knew, the rope was being jerked from her hand. She heard a wordless shout of surprise from the warden. When she spun around, she saw that directly behind her and Kevin the surface of the river had been ruptured by what she could, in her amazement, only describe as some kind of whirlpool. Then the force of the swirling current caught hold of Kevin, sending him tumbling back toward the others.

The warden caught the younger man as he came rushing toward them, while the sudden violent current buffeted them, like twigs captured in strong rapids. Whirling around in a circular pattern, Webb rode out the watery melee, crashing into Valerie and nearly riding right over her body as they both struggled to keep their heads above the roiling surface of the water.

Cassidy's astonishment quickly gave way to genuine terror as she realized that the suction of the building whirlpool was beginning to pull her back into it, as well. Automatically she did the one thing she had so determinedly been trying to avoid since she'd gotten free of the sinkhole: She plunged her feet to the bottom of the river and tried to brace herself against the inexorable draw of the current.

The river was only waist deep—or at least it was for the few seconds Cassidy managed to stay standing on its spongy bottom. Then, to her dismay, she began to sink deeply into the soft muck. The entrapment temporarily prevented her being drawn into the whirlpool, but as she looked out across the water, her heart sank when she saw that the others were beginning to become mired down, as well. As they had tried to prevent themselves from being swept under by the surging current, they had unwittingly become foundered again in the treacherous sinkhole.

Even though she had already sunk to the point where the churning water was up to her chest, and her feet felt as if they were encased in well-set cement, Cassidy realized that she was the only person who had any hope of acting. She was closest to the bank, and she wasn't actually caught in the suction of the whirlpool. She also had lost hold of the rope, and she couldn't move her feet, she reminded herself ruthlessly; but she was damned if she'd give up. *I didn't come all this way just to drown!* she thought fiercely, as she wrenched her torso forward, trying to twist her legs free.

The warden had slid down the rope to Kevin, leaving a long

gap between them and Valerie. Cassidy realized that her only hope
of helping them lay in getting a hold on the rope again, but there
didn't seem to be any way she could reach it. She tried to shout
to them, but no one could respond. Coughing and choking, they
all were just trying to keep their heads above the turbulent surface
of the water, as they sank deeper and deeper into the boggy bottom.

Cassidy's arms thrashed uselessly, raising a greenish foam.
They weren't that far away from her, and if she just had the rope
maybe she could—

And then beneath her, something *moved*. It was as if the entire
bottom of the river buckled, throwing up a sudden backwash of
murky water that drenched Cassidy's face and lifted her feet so
unexpectedly that she felt her knees crumple.

In a strobe of memory she was reminded of the first time she'd
been mired in the sinkhole. She had suddenly broken free—but
had she actually pulled loose, or had something *pushed* her up?
Like a dizzying echo of that experience, Cassidy felt the sucking
mud beneath her boots rapidly solidify into something firm but
slightly yielding; something that shuddered delicately, like the
skin of a horse throwing off flies; something that then rose in the
water, dropping her to her knees as she rode out its astonishing ascent.

As her hips breached the surface of the water, the shifting force
beneath her rippled, and Cassidy fully expected to see the elongated head and sinuous neck of a water monster rise from the turbulent river. In the growing maelstrom of turbid water, she could
see both Kevin's and Valerie's heads repeatedly dipping beneath
the surface. The warden and Webb were still sinking, as well, and
frantically trying to help their companions. If Cassidy could just
reach the rope; it was still the only hope.

The massive thing beneath her shuddered harder, whipping up
great slapping waves of water and abruptly tumbling Cassidy
backward into the roiling river. Spewing out water, she came
gasping to the surface just in time to see the trailing segment of
rope between Valerie and the warden wash past her. Lurching forward, she seized it and hung on.

The wet rope felt as slippery as an eel in her numbed hands,
and its fraying hemp cut into the waterlogged skin of her palms
as she desperately began to pull. As she gathered in the line, she
started to be drawn forward into the whirlpool again. Ignoring her
past experience, Cassidy dropped her feet down and dug in her
boot heels. But when she did, there was nothing but mud beneath

her feet, soft but firm enough to support her weight. Cassidy twisted the rope around her hands and pulled back with all her strength as the taut hemp cut into her fingers.

The frothing current spun around her four trapped companions, a disturbance far more turbulent than just the whirlpool's course. The thing was out there with them, Cassidy realized in dismay. But would it set them free—or kill them? If she could draw them in the moment their feet came loose of the muck . . .

Cassidy's soaked clothing dragged at her as she staggered back, leaning into the rope with what was left of her considerably diminished strength. And even though her face was twisted in a grimace of pain, and the muscles in her arms and back and shoulders were trembling with fatigue, she really didn't feel any of it. She had so narrowly focused her concentration on the impossible task she had set for herself, she had deliberately blocked out everything else.

That was why when the large creature bounded up behind her in the river, splashing through the churning water and coming so close to Cassidy that it bumped right into her back, she actually didn't notice at first. It was not until the powerful grip of two sinewy hands clamped around her upper arms that she started in fresh alarm. And then a voice from above her—harsh, familiar, like some archangel calling her out of that hell—further astonished her.

"Cassidy, give me the rope!" Click commanded her. "Hang onto me and give me the rope!"

Chapter 8 ◀▥

Afterward, much of what happened then would become a numbing blur to Cassidy. When she swung around, staggering in the thrashing water, and saw Click mounted on the gray mare, her first thought was totally mundane: *Christ, he looks as bad as the last time I saw him!* So did she, she supposed, as Click leaned over the horse's side to keep his viselike grip on her arms. Rain-drenched and haggard, his clothing torn and dirty, the leader of the Tinkers looked entirely the worse for wear.

"Cassidy!" Click repeated, giving her a sharp shake. "Give me the rope! Grab onto my leg and give me the rope—*quickly*!"

Finally jolted from her daze, Cassidy numbly fumbled to comply. "Dragonfly," she whispered hoarsely, reaching up for the long iron-colored mane as an excited nicker rumbled deep in the mare's chest. Cassidy tried to bury herself in the horse's warm neck, clinging to that slippery hide, her throat painfully closing in an aching spasm of purest relief.

But Click was forced to pry her arms away from around the horse. "Climb up behind me! I have to fasten the rope around the horse—*now*, Cassidy! There isn't much time!"

Like one of those frustration dreams executed in excruciating slow motion, Cassidy felt herself being pulled free of her embrace around the gray mare. Loose in the water again, she was help-lessly clumsy, and Click had to expedite matters by hauling her up bodily behind him on the gray's broad wet back. She clutched awkwardly to anchor herself, her arms grappling around his waist, her fingers digging in. Then the mare swung around in the river, greenish water churning around her belly as she leaned into the rope Click had knotted over her withers and around the base of her shoulders. Slowly and steadily at first, like a draft horse get-ting a heavy load rolling, the mare moved forward, her hindquarters bunching beneath her as she plowed a course toward the bank. Within a few moments she was splashing along at an even pace, her long neck arched, her head bent. In the shallows just before the bank, her big hooves sent up swooping arcs of spray. And when Dragonfly lurched up out of the river, Cassidy had to lock her arms around Click to keep from sliding right off over her rump.

Once they were up on the bank, Click dropped with Cassidy from the horse. Her legs buckled as her feet hit the boggy ground, and she swayed in the grip of his hands. Then, breathless and still numb, she looked up directly into that lean face. Click's dark eyes were like two umber pits suspended in deeply etched nets of lines; water dripped from the silver tips of his mustache, and his hair was a tangled mat hanging over his collar.

"Are you all right?" he asked her.

Unable to speak, Cassidy just nodded. And when she did so, Click's hands slid from her arms and she slumped down onto the clumpy sedge grass.

Cassidy didn't pass out, but for a few moments she would have been hard pressed to have kept her eyes open, or to have moved, or even to have formed a single rational thought. And when her mind began to work again, her first thoughts had nothing to do with Click or his summary abandonment. *Dragonfly!* she Called, and suddenly the damp velvety muzzle was there, whiskering over Cassidy's hair, exhaling soft, grass-sweet breath over her face. Hot tears carved clean tracks down Cassidy's cheeks as she rose to her knees and flung her arms around the mare's lowered neck.

Cassidy had no idea how long she knelt there beside the river in the chill drizzle, hugging the gray's neck, weeping soundless tears of exhaustion and relief. But she was jerked back to reality by the prosaic sound of someone gagging and retching nearby. She lifted her head from the mare to see a bedraggled Kevin, down on all fours on the riverbank, bringing up some of the swampy water he had swallowed.

Cassidy staggered to her feet, pulling herself up by the horse's mane. In the marshy shallows right off the bank, she saw Click helping the warden pull Valerie from the water. The captain hung between the two men like a sack of wet sand; but as they lay her down in the sedge grass, Cassidy could hear her coughing raggedly. Click thumped Valerie between the shoulder blades a few times and then left her to the warden's care while he waded back out into the shallow water. That was the first time Cassidy noticed the surface of the river appeared perfectly calm again, with no trace left of the violent whirlpool except for a diffuse and frothy greenish foam.

As Cassidy began to walk unsteadily toward Kevin, she saw Webb lurch up from where he had been wallowing in the murky shallows. Click reached for the pilot's arm, and when Webb heaved himself out of the water, he practically launched himself right into the Tinker. The two men collided, staggering sideways like two drunken comrades across the soggy ground, until Webb threw his arms around Click in a crushing bear hug. The two of them spun around in a half circle, the seaman pounding Click on the back.

"You son of a bitch!" Webb barked hoarsely; but despite the epithet, Cassidy could see that he was not angry. "Here for days I've been looking forward to filleting you and feeding your guts to the fish! But now that you've saved our damned lives, I suppose I'll have to give up that plan!"

Click gave Webb a hearty shake, heedless of the muck covering the pilot's sopping clothing. "Cassidy was already saving your lives," he said. "Although in your case, I can't see why she went through the trouble."

The two of them slogged up onto the bank just as Valerie vomited onto the grass. Click skirted around her and the warden and instead gave Kevin a hand in gaining his feet. As the blond boy swayed, Cassidy reached out to steady him, and Click stepped back.

"What the hell are you doing here in this river?" Click asked Webb, without further preamble.

But before the pilot could reply, Kevin rasped loudly, "Sea monsters sunk the boat!"

"Three days ago," Webb elaborated. His blunt fingers raked back through his dripping hair, dislodging bits of chartreuse scum. "We were damned lucky to make it ashore in the dinghy."

At Click's expectant pause and the inquisitive rise of his brows, the warden continued. "Our first night ashore," he said, from his position kneeling beside Valerie, "something destroyed the dinghy." He gave the captain's shoulders a sympathetic squeeze. "We've had to travel overland ever since."

Valerie coughed explosively; then, spitting to clear her mouth, she glared up at Click. "How did you find us?" she demanded of him.

Given her ragged condition and her undignified position, Valerie's acerbity would have been amusing in light of the past antagonism between her and the Tinker. But Click's response was entirely devoid of deprecation. "The mare," he said simply. "She'd been especially restless since late yesterday. Then earlier this afternoon she became nearly unmanageable." He spread his muddy hands with equanimity. "I decided if I couldn't keep the horse from going, then I had better go with her. What I couldn't understand was her insistence on going in this direction, because I thought—"

"You thought we'd be at the cove by now," Webb supplied with a rueful grunt, "and not here mucking around in some damned river!"

"Exactly," Click concluded.

Earlier that afternoon, Cassidy and Kevin had encountered the hanging monsters in the larch tree; earlier that afternoon, Cassidy had Called the mare.

Interrupting her reverie, Click pushed doggedly onward. "Can all of you travel?" he asked. Forestalling any questions or protests, he went on. "I'd prefer not to have to push you like this, but we're not that far from the cove. The others should already be there by now, and there'll be food and blankets and dry shelter." He made a small, almost apologetic gesture. "I'm afraid if we rest here much longer, it'll grow dark before we can get there. We wouldn't be able to find our way again until morning."

Cassidy glanced around at the others. They were all as wet and filthy and exhausted as she was. But Click had a compelling point, and the promise of the reunion with her friends and the comforts of the cove were both powerful incentives. "I can travel," she said stoically.

With the warden's aid, Valerie rose unsteadily to her feet. She fixed Click with a steely gaze, unbowed in spite of the tremor in her limbs. "We all can travel," she said tightly, "provided that you know where you're going."

Once again declining to be baited, Click merely nodded. "The most direct route is back the way I came," he said. "There are some rough spots, and we won't be able to ride. But then again, I doubt that the horse could travel well in the boggy ground along this river; and the beach would be impassable for her." For the first time since they slid down together from the horse, Click looked directly at Cassidy. "But at least you can hang onto her tail. She'll help you along." Faint amusement lifted the bedraggled tips of his mustache. "She's taken me over many a bad spot in just the same way during the past few hours!"

For the first time Cassidy noticed the gray mare's tail had a large loop braided into the end. She recognized the style, and had utilized it herself when trail riding in areas where the ground was too rugged or wet or steep to ride safely. By hanging onto a horse's tail, a person afoot could gain some badly needed propulsion. And suddenly in her mind's eye, Cassidy could envision the big gray dragging Click along after her, relentless in her quest to answer Cassidy's Call.

"Are Becky and everyone else all right?" Kevin asked as they started to trudge forward through the sedge grass. Cassidy was embarrassed to realize she had never even thought to inquire about Rowena and the rest of her friends.

"A bit footsore and tired of eating rabbit," Click said, "but otherwise well." He touched the blond boy's arm reassuringly. "We can trade tales later, Kevin, once we're all fed and dry again."

Cassidy hooked her aching arm through the loop in the mare's tail, and the horse fell into line behind the others as Click began to lead them away from the river. The dark and dripping tangle of the forest loomed before them. But despite her fatigue, it felt like nothing, a mere mindless task, for Cassidy to just keep setting one foot down after another, allowing the pull of the gray's tail to tow her along. The uneven ground, the clawing branches, the shaley inclines, the incessant drizzle—all of it meant nothing to Cassidy then.

She had numbed her mind to all but one thing: They all were alive, and more or less well; and Click had brought her mare, just as he had sworn. Nothing else seemed to matter.

That last leg of their long journey to Clam Cove seemed comparatively brief to Cassidy; but she realized that her self-induced state of stupor had distorted her sense of time. It was almost dark by the time they slid down one last steep wooded hill, to find themselves atop the sheer cliff face by the sea. From the lip of that precipice, a narrow footpath led down the rocky bank in a series of cutbacks. And at the bottom of the cliff, in the mouth of a low, oblong cave, a large fire blazed. As they made their way down the winding trail, several shadowy figures detached themselves from beside that fire and came forward to meet the weary travelers.

Cassidy stumbled to a halt, freeing her cramped arm from the loop in the mare's tail just as the familiar bulk of a warm, substantial body captured her in a crushing embrace. "Cassidy!" Rowena exclaimed, squeezing from her what little breath seemed to be left in her aching lungs. "God, I thought I'd never see you again!"

Then Cassidy, who had sworn to herself that she would not cry, began to sob incoherently, burying her dirty face in the comforting solidity of Rowena's shoulder. And the stalwart brunette just held her even more tightly, like a mother succoring a tearful child, murmuring continuous reassurances. When Cassidy finally came up for air, wet-faced and sniffling, she felt herself being gently pulled back and turned around. Then she was looking up into the shaggy silhouette of Allen's head, his hair and beard bronzed by the backlighting of the fire. The big sheriff hesitated only a moment; then he, too, drew Cassidy into his arms and hugged her.

"You look like a shipwrecked seaman," he told her, setting Cassidy back at arm's length again, his voice both soft and gruff. "What the hell is that you're wearing? And where have you been?"

Looking from one welcomed face to another as she tried to choke back further tears, Cassidy just croaked hoarsely, "We're going to have some damned good stories to exchange!"

As Rowena pulled her in for one last quick squeeze, Cassidy saw the shadowy shape of a familiar diminutive woman approaching them. Becky stood back for a moment, eyeing Cassidy with elaborate skepticism. Then the black woman gave a little shake of her head, her dreadlocks bobbing. "Damn, just look at you!" she said fondly. "I should of known it'd take more than a riot to stop you!"

Cassidy managed to surprise and mildly discomfit the independent little woman by capturing her in a quick, hard hug. Then Cassidy stepped back, shaking back her dirty, wet hair, and gave them all an expectant look. "I hear you've got blankets and food here," she said hopefully.

Laughing, Rowena led her toward the generous fire that crackled at the opening of the large cave.

Although the seamen seldom sailed that far south, Clam Cove's warren of caves were stocked with a varied cache of supplies for use in an emergency. Becky and Rowena had found a basic array of cooking utensils such as pots and pans and dishes, and a large store of preserved staples such as beans, rice, oatmeal, coffee, flour, and even jerked beef. There were also blankets, wax-coated matches, several knives, and another coil of rope. There was even a limited selection of herbs, spices, and tea.

"All the comforts of home," Rowena teased, urging a blanket on Cassidy.

With her wet clothing spread out to dry inside the cave, Cassidy was soon wrapped in the blanket, sitting by the fire and gratefully

sipping at a mug of hot tea. Light-headed from hunger, she greedily inhaled the scent of cooking food. An odd contentment quickly
seeped through her weary bones, just as the heat of the fire seeped
into her body through the folds of the blanket, and she felt her
eyes growing heavy. She watched with detached bemusement as
Kevin and the warden teased each other, jockeying for places to
prop their soaked leathers near the fire. She happily endured
Rowena's solicitous mothering as the buxom woman alternated
her attention between the cooking and checking on Cassidy. And
she was moved to see that Allen had gone out and climbed to the
top of the cliff again, and cut a big armful of ash and alder
branches for the gray mare. The horse stood placidly hip-shot in
the shelter of one of the nearby rocky outcroppings, munching
on the browse.

As the meal was prepared, the entire group gathered in around
the big fire. And by the time the food was ready to eat, Cassidy
could hardly keep her eyes open. It was plain fare, but after several days of scavenging off the land, the simple staples tasted like
a feast to her. She thought that if she never had to eat another alewife in her life, it would barely be compensation enough. And
while Cassidy half drowsed over her tin plate, with Rowena sitting beside her and leaning companionably against her, the exchange of stories began.

At the others' urging, Click spoke first, although his tone
suggested that there was not that much to tell. When he and Rafe
had left the burning city, they returned on the road to the warden's compound. They had encountered unruly mobs of people
who were fleeing the city as well as scattered squads of hard-
pressed Troopers. It was Rafe, Click said, who had been able to
persuade a small group of Troopers to go with them rather than
go on into the city. When they finally found Rowena, Allen, and
Becky in all of the chaos, their gig cart was being besieged by an
angry mob with aspirations of holding an impromptu lynching.

The Troopers helped forcibly disperse the threatening mob.
Then they had been further convinced to lend the group several
horses and to escort them as far as the river. The cart had been irreparably damaged in the melee, and there would have been no
way to have driven it across the river anyway.

"Shit, you should have seen how fast I learned to ride!" Becky
muttered over the rim of her mug.

"We'll make a Horseman out of you yet," Click told her wryly.

Surreptitiously studying Click from across the fire, Cassidy was
certain that in his smooth and matter-of-fact narration, he was be-

ing deliberately glib about the difficulties they had faced. And, Valerie's antipathy notwithstanding, Cassidy was sure that his success in escaping the Iron City was because the Tinker still commanded a certain following among his erstwhile comrades.

Crossing the Long River, Click explained, had been rough but without incident. On its southern bank, he had dismissed Rafe with the directive that the black youth return with the other Troopers. Cassidy knew Rafe well enough to suspect that he had resisted, but she also knew the kind of logic Click would have used to prevail. The city had needed every Trooper that night, and Rafe's duty to his warden was best served by going back with the others.

Afoot, it had taken them nearly a day to reach the Slough River. As a Horseman and a Trooper, Click innately understood the importance of keeping a close eye on a horse in rough country, and Cassidy knew without a word being said that he had taken extraordinary care of her mare. The Tinker's description of their overland journey across the rugged forest between the Slough and the cove was economic and typically understated; he did not embellish, nor did he complain. He didn't have to, because Becky and Rowena chimed in to remind everyone of the mosquitoes, the monotonous food, and the cold wet nights.

By the time Click's calm recitation was winding to a close, Cassidy found herself staring quite openly at him, studying him thoughtfully across the width of the big cook fire. Fed and relatively dry again, sitting casually cross-legged with a mug of steaming coffee cradled in his lean browned hands, Click looked much as he had in those first days Cassidy had known him, as she traveled with the Tinker band down to the Long River. But if she looked closely enough, she could see the scrapes and bruises on Click's face and wrists and on the tanned skin beneath the ragged fabric of his tattered shirt collar. She could also see the real depth of the lines that bracketed his deep-set eyes and the twin furrows of fatigue that framed his mustache. And even in the firelight, she could tell that the darkened stains on his battered trousers were actually blood.

Then Click's umber eyes suddenly lifted, catching her watching him. Cassidy swiftly looked away, her hands locking defensively around her mug of tea. But what little she had seen of the expression on that familiar face had been a cipher, composed and unreadable.

Webb began the story of the stormy start of their journey to the cove. Unlike Click, the pilot relished a bit of embellishment, particularly when it came to the sea monsters and the wanton destruction of his boat. He seemed especially diligent in detailing to Click the precise value of his vessel and exactly whom he held responsible for her loss! But after he reached the point of the incident with the dinghy during their first night ashore, Webb seemed content to let the warden take over the narration, with the pilot merely adding occasional grunted comments.

The warden seemed intent on rivaling Click's sparse style for describing their own harrowing journey once they had been cast ashore. Cassidy was relieved that she was not called upon to elaborate on her and Kevin's discovery of the hanging monsters in the ravine. The warden simply mentioned the incident and then moved on to the rest of that exhausting afternoon's events. It was only at the end, in describing what had happened to them during that final river crossing, when the young man was forced to solicit input from the others.

Staring unblinkingly into the flickering flames of the cook fire, the warden said flatly, "It was no ordinary sinkhole, no ordinary whirlpool. I'm certain of that."

"I've navigated all sorts of rivers in all kinds of conditions," Webb said, "and I've seen a lot of crazy things. But I've never seen anything like that. It was like the bottom of the river was—"

"Alive," Cassidy said quietly, her fingers whitening on her mug. "There was something down there that pushed me out of the mud, or I never would have gotten out."

For a few moments there was an uneasy silence around the fire; the only sounds were the dripping of water, the distant hiss of the waves, and the soft sizzle of the burning wood. Then, beside the warden, Kevin shifted uncomfortably.

"I—I felt something, too," Kevin said reluctantly. "Something big, beneath my feet."

Webb shook back the damp, tangled locks of his sun-bleached hair, his brow furrowed. Bathed in the flickering firelight, the pilot looked somehow softened, almost boyish, despite his disheveled attire. "Not those things that sunk my boat," he said. "The water was much too shallow for anything that size."

"Something else then," Cassidy said implacably, "something different." *Something we haven't seen—yet.*

"Well, there's no way of knowing anymore," Valerie pointed out briskly, dumping the dregs of her coffee into the sand. "And whatever it was, we've left it behind us."

Much as Cassidy welcomed the captain's logic, she still felt a shiver go through her when she remembered the vast sunken force that had risen beneath her from the quagmire of the river's bottom. It had been alive; and it had been so large that it had been capable of radically transforming the entire surface of the river. Thinking that they had left it behind was unconvincing to Cassidy, and seemed to her a fool's comfort at best, as she settled down in her blanket and plummeted into an exhausted sleep.

She lay adrift in comfortable warmth, a cocoon of floating silence and darkness. Something rolled over her, something nearly smothering in the intimacy with which it covered the contours of her body; and yet the presence was distinctly pleasant at first, almost sensual in nature. She murmured and reached up to pull the thing even closer; but as she did so, it was suddenly transformed into a cold, crushing layer of choking mud. She tried to scream then, but as she opened her mouth the chill sludge poured into it, suffocating her until she—

Sitting bolt upright, Cassidy nearly banged heads with the warden, who had been crouched beside her, trying to waken her. Looking up into the dim outline of that familiar face, faintly painted by the thin light from the banked embers of the fire, she had the oddest sensation that she had been the one who had just awakened him, rather than the other way around. She had to study his expression closely to be sure that the warden hadn't had another lapse and that she wasn't dealing with Andy Greene again.

"Cassidy, are you all right?" the warden whispered softly, his brown eyes wide with concern. "You were gasping and thrashing . . ."

Beside Cassidy, Rowena's blanket-wrapped shape slumbered on, oblivious. Cassidy had long since become convinced that the brunette could have slept through almost anything short of an earthquake. The warden had been sleeping on the other side of Rowena, and when Cassidy looked further, she could see that he was not the only one she'd wakened with her noisy nightmare. Kevin's head was poking out from beneath the edge of his blanket, just beyond where the warden had been lying; and beyond Kevin, Valerie rolled over, grumbling softly at the disturbance.

"I'm sorry," she whispered, feeling foolish. His hand still rested on her bare shoulder, distracting her. "I just had a bad dream, but I'm okay now."

For a moment Cassidy was afraid that the warden might want to pursue the subject, especially considering how many times she had held such little middle-of-the-night tête-à-têtes with him, pulling from him all the details of whatever Andy Greene could tell her. But to her relief, he merely nodded and gave her shoulder a reassuring little squeeze. Within a minute he was resettled in his own blanket, with Kevin again scrunched up companionably against him. Then the dimly lit cavern returned to silence.

But Cassidy found that she could not return as easily to sleep. The residue of the nightmare seemed to cling to her, as persistently as the caul of cold mud had clung to her body, leaving in her a confusing mixture of both longing and loathing. Even the sand beneath her blanket then felt lumpy and unwelcoming.

Cassidy lay there for a time, listening to the soft, safe sounds of the breathing and the minute movements of the other people within the shelter of the cave; but her restlessness remained. Finally relenting, she rose soundlessly to her feet and groped at the edge of the fire for her clothing. Except for her boots, everything was nearly dry, and she swiftly and methodically dressed. Then she stepped out across her blanket and slipped out the mouth of the cavern.

Outside on the sand of the cove's beach, Cassidy tilted her head back and scanned the night sky. The cloud cover was still absolute, but the rain had finally stopped, and the damp air felt more bracing than chilling. Rendered cautious by the unfamiliar terrain, she made her way toward the ghostly shape of the gray mare. Sometime during the night, after the drizzle had stopped, the horse had left the shallow cave where she had originally bedded down and had moved out onto the beach. Scattered stubs of cut branches still littered the area where the mare had munched on the last of the fodder before, her hunger satisfied, she had settled to sleep, standing hip-shot on the wet sand.

At Cassidy's approach, the horse swung her head around, a low nicker rumbling in her throat. Cassidy plowed her fingers into the thick mane, gently pulling the long head down to her chest. The mere physical presence of the mare still seemed like a miracle to her, and she was reminded of Webb's simple declaration regarding Click's promise to her: *"If he said he'd bring her, he'll bring her."* And Click certainly had. Inhaling the horse's sweet smell, Cassidy wished that everything about the Tinker could be that honest and plain.

Actually, Cassidy could not think of a time when her whole situation had been less simple. Her profound relief at being safely reunited with her friends had raised in her mind some disquieting questions about the basic validity of her quest. Whatever their motives, she had a group of people who had remained loyal to her, in spite of the obvious hazards of that loyalty. Having seen them all brought back together had served as a painful reminder of the kind of chaos that had originally torn them apart—chaos for which Cassidy had to accept most of the responsibility. And when she thought of the terrifying events in the river that afternoon, it grew increasingly difficult to justify the kind of jeopardy in which she was placing so many lives.

The mare's ears swiveled, and Cassidy automatically looked up, scanning the faint black-on-near-black outline of the cliff top high above the beach. When she detected the vague suggestion of movement along that rim, she froze, peering even harder into the darkness. It was Click. She did not have to be able to pick out the shape of his body to recognize that catlike gait, the sure and soundless way he moved in the almost complete blackness, a lone sentinel gliding along that line where the faceless rock met the endless sky.

For a moment Cassidy was afraid that the mare would nicker at Click, betraying her presence there. The idea of having to confront the Tinker then, in the cloaking secrecy of the darkness, suddenly seemed an even more frightening prospect than facing down some unknown danger. Cassidy's pulse had kicked up, her heart thumping rebelliously in her chest, and the joints in her fingers burned. In her dream, the pressure and warmth of the embracing presence that had covered her had at first been pleasant—sensual, even sexual. As she stood there on the beach in the shadow of the gray mare, the fear that drummed through her with her racing heartbeat was something that seemed to offer both pleasure and nameless peril. And as she silently watched Click's faint silhouette disappear beyond the range of her limited sight, she felt a relief leavened with an odd disappointment.

After giving the horse a final caress, Cassidy carefully made her way back across the beach to the mouth of the cavern. But when she was rolled again in her blanket, her uneasy thoughts preoccupied her for a long time before sleep finally reclaimed her.

The next time Cassidy awoke, it was naturally. Sitting up in the foggy grayness of the predawn light, she saw that a couple of sleeping places around the ashes of the firepit were empty, the shallow depressions in the sand filled only with discarded blankets. But Click was there, sleeping curled on his side on the opposite side of the cavern. His blanket was rolled around him like a cocoon, with little more than the dark tangle of his hair protruding. Cassidy was bemused to realize that she could not remember having ever seen the Tinker sleeping.

Since she was already dressed, she was able to slip away from the cavern quickly without waking anyone else. As she made her way down to the sea, she was pleasantly surprised to find that she wasn't nearly as stiff or sore as she'd anticipated, considering the physical ordeal she'd been through. It was amazing, she thought, squatting down along the washline of the incoming waves, what some decent food and a little rest could do for you.

As she cupped up a double handful of water, splashing it across her face and scrubbing her wet skin, Cassidy automatically reached for her sense of the gray mare. Some time before dawn, the horse had moved up the narrow trail to the lip of the cliff high above the cove. *Breakfast!* Cassidy thought wryly.

After completing her abbreviated toilet, she stood and slowly surveyed Clam Cove in the thin light of the coming day. A natural bay formed the curve of the shoreline, where the two arms of land and a submerged breakwater served to temper the force of the waves and had fostered the broad sand beach that fronted the rocky face of the cliff. A few large boulders dotted the strand, looking oddly out of place jutting out from the otherwise smooth sand, like huge but shapeless animals slumbering in the early-morning fog. Turning back toward the cliff, Cassidy scanned its uneven surface. The bank was pocked with numerous caves and grottoes, ranging in size from the big one in which they had spent the night, to little indentations not much larger than a man's head.

Movement about a hundred feet down the beach caught Cassidy's eye, where the curve of the bay reached its deepest point. The dim shapes of two men slowly emerged from a narrow cavern in the rock, their backs bent as they carried some long and much larger object between them. She immediately recognized Allen and Webb, but she had to close half the distance between herself and them before she could clearly see what it was that they were dragging from the cave. It was a skiff, one roughly the size of the dinghy in which they had fled the pilot's sinking boat.

The two men had pulled the skiff clear of the cleft in the rock and were conferring quietly when they noticed Cassidy approaching. Webb raised one arm in a friendly little salute and greeted her with a good-humored bit of banter.

"I thought you'd sleep till noon," the seaman teased her, "considering the way you looked last night."

Ruefully tossing back her bedraggled hair, Cassidy accepted the easy jibe and stepped forward to study the small craft. "Is this the boat you were talking about?" she asked somewhat dubiously. The skiff was slightly longer and a little heavier than the ill-fated dinghy, but it still looked like a glorified rowboat to her. In addition to the oarlocks, there was a stout metal socket on the bottom of the skiff for the insertion of a mast pole. And lashed alongside the oars and the tapering shaft of the mast was stowed a neat parcel of canvas, which must have been the small craft's sails.

"It just looks pretty small," Cassidy said.

Webb just laughed. "It's big enough," he assured her. "Besides, I've—"

"Yeah, I know," she interrupted him, "you've sailed in worse!"

The pilot was chuckling as he bent to continue his methodical inspection of the skiff. Cassidy threw Allen a look. The big bearded man still looked a little haggard, but she also had seen him look a hell of a lot worse. The sheriff was studying her with the same sort of speculative candor, so she gave him a small ironic smile. Gesturing to her, Allen stepped back from the skiff.

With one last glance at Webb, who was whistling under his breath as he puttered around with the gear stowed in the vessel, Cassidy fell into step beside Allen as he started back up the beach. It was unexpectedly pleasant to be able to spend some time with him again. Allen had been the first person in that world really to give her a chance, and for that he still held a special place in her heart.

Allen had been scanning the cliff face as they walked, and Cassidy soon saw what had caught his eye. High on the lip of the bank, wreathed in wisps of fog, the gray mare stood watching them, her jaws slowly grinding as she chewed a mouthful of twigs.

"Thanks for cutting her some feed last night," Cassidy said as Allen's gaze moved on past the horse. "It really should have been my job; she's my responsibility."

From the look on Allen's face then, Cassidy was immediately reminded of two things. As a sheriff, Allen was long accustomed to thinking of a horse's welfare before his own; what he had done was not out of any special deference to her, but merely an automatic extension of his lifelong duty. And the other thing was the painful realization of just how dramatically she had changed Allen's life, as well; even though he was not a Horseman like the warden or Valerie, she also had taken him from the animals he loved. But neither of those things made Cassidy any the less grateful to him.

Allen gave her a brief sidelong glance, shrugging. "She's already saved our necks more than once," he said.

Cassidy was certain there were some interesting stories behind

that remark, just as there were behind all of Click's calmly understated narrative of the night before. But for the time being, she
was content to let it pass.

They had reached the point along the shoreline that was opposite the large cavern where they had camped. It was light enough
then that Cassidy could see movement in its shadowy interior, and
she heard the flat clang of metal on rock. But rather than turn and
head up that way, Allen just kept on walking along the wave line.
His keen eyes kept sweeping the surrounding beach and the cliff
face, but it was a practiced vigilance born more of years of ingrained habit than of any assigned guard duty. When they had
moved on beyond the campsite, Allen spoke again, entirely without preface.

"What happened to you yesterday in the river; you think there's
another kind of monster then? Something we haven't seen before?"

Surprised by both the topic and his blunt approach to it,
Cassidy quickly pointed out, "We still haven't actually seen it.
But yeah, I think it's a different kind. None of the other ones
could have been on that river bottom or have done what this thing
did."

Allen just grunted, a sound that could have signified either
skepticism or grudging agreement. "I guess you were right then
about them following you" was all that he said. After a long moment of silence between them, Allen matter-of-factly shifted topics again.

"Has anything more happened with him?"

Startlement sat obviously upon Cassidy's face; she stumbled,
even though the sand was firm and smooth beneath her feet, and
she tried to cover the clumsy movement by pretending to sidestep
a wave. There was no point in pretending she didn't know what
Allen was talking about. But since the sheriff hadn't been witness
to the single episode that had occurred in the warden's house,
Cassidy had to wonder how he knew anything about the lapses.
The answer to that question came to her as he spoke again.

"Rowena and Becky told me what happened the night we left
the city," he said. "They said he had some kind of a spell." He
cocked one brow expectantly, still waiting for her response.
"Well?" he prompted. "Has it happened again?"

"Yeah, a few more times," Cassidy admitted. Neither Rowena
nor Becky knew the full import of what had happened that night
in the warden's bedroom. There had simply been no time to discuss it before they had fled the city. And the disturbing changes

in the warden's "spells" since then—well, Cassidy didn't know where to begin explaining. She wasn't even sure she wanted to talk about the disturbing phenomena at all. But as she glanced back across the deserted beach toward the cavern where a new cook fire was already blazing, Cassidy realized that she might not have another opportunity to speak alone with the sheriff before he left them to return north. And there was no doubt in her mind that Allen deserved to know everything she had discovered; he had more than earned that right.

Just as she was about to go on, however, Allen held up his hand. "You don't have to explain it all right now," he said gruffly. "We can talk later, when Becky and Rowena are around. It'll probably make a lot more sense to them than it will to me anyway."

Fresh surprise held Cassidy speechless, until Allen finally turned his head and looked directly at her, his shaggy head cocked quizzically. "What?" he said then. "You weren't going to tell them?"

"No!" Cassidy blurted out. "I mean yes, I *am* going to tell them—but aren't you going back north again with Webb?" The alternative simply had never occurred to her.

"Back to the city?" Allen shook his head. "I wasn't planning on it."

"But what about the village—your duty?" Cassidy said clumsily, still confused by the implications of his intention to go on with them.

Allen came to a halt, looking down into Cassidy's face. His expression was calm, and there was a distinct tone of patience in his explanation. "I can't go back to Double Creek, Cassidy; Misty would see me hanged."

Comprehension finally came to Cassidy, bringing with it an unwelcomed wash of guilt. "You mean because of me and Rowena?" she asked in a small voice.

Allen nodded. "If I tried to come back without you," he said, "I would have failed in my duty to the village."

"But you could just tell Misty that we were dead," Cassidy said earnestly, appalled by what she had so unwittingly done to him. Her departure from Double Creek had not only forced Allen to follow, but had nearly gotten him killed by monsters outside of Pointed Rock. Then, by giving her his allegiance, the sheriff had effectively exiled himself forever from the only home he had ever known. How many more lives was she going to destroy in that world before she was finally able to return to her own?

"She'd want to see your bodies," Allen said dryly.

"Tell her the monsters killed us!" Cassidy urged him. "Tell her there *weren't* any bodies!"

Bemused, Allen again shook his head. "It wouldn't do any good to lie to Misty," he said. "I told you, she can always tell if someone is lying." He shrugged. "Then I'd be hanged for a coward, as well."

Dismayed, Cassidy looked up into those gold-ringed eyes, helpless in the face of Allen's calm, inexorable logic. "I never meant to take you away from your village," she said unhappily.

"I know. You tried to leave without me."

Unmollified, Cassidy said, "But you don't have to come any farther with us, Allen. This is a dangerous journey; I don't know what else might happen."

Allen shrugged again, a slight hitching of those broad shoulders that seemed to suggest uncertainty and even danger were of little consequence to him. "I swore an oath to help you," he reminded Cassidy.

"Yeah, but not *forever*!" she blurted out. "I can't ask you to—"

One of Allen's big tanned hands lifted, again halting the rush of her words. And Cassidy looked up into that ruddy, bearded face, perplexed afresh at the man: a sheriff who had forsaken his duty to help her, the man who had made her remember sex but who did not remember it himself. "Then don't ask me," he said implacably. "Don't ask me to do anything, least of all to go back now. Whatever happens, Cassidy, I intend to see this through."

Eerily, his words recalled to Cassidy the redevotion of purpose that she herself had made earlier on that same beach, in the small hours of the morning. She knew what was driving her, but she still could not fathom what was driving the big man who stood beside her on the sand. She felt that it probably was finally the time to ask.

Evenly meeting Allen's gaze, Cassidy said, "Why did you take Rowena out of Green Lake?"

If Allen was caught off balance by the question, there was no indication of it in that stoic face. "They had no use for her there," he said simply.

"Me, then," she went on. "Why did you save my life and take me in, even when you knew I'd been riding with Horsemen?"

Allen seemed to consider that even more self-explanatory. "You never would have survived on your own," he said. "Besides, you had a skill that the village could use."

Yeah, and Rowena made a terrific goatherd, Cassidy thought.

But what she said, her voice calm and even, was "You didn't save us in spite of the fact that we were different; I think that you saved us *because* we were different."

A fleeting spasm of unease passed over that otherwise composed face. For a few moments Allen looked out over the sea, where the rising sun was painting the crests of the waves with a rosy gilding and a few ambitious gulls were making early strafing runs. When he looked back at her again, Cassidy thought that he had expected what she asked him.

"Did you have the Memories, Allen?" she said softly.

The russet wings of his mustache lifted, an expression more of irony than amusement. "No," he said, "I wasn't lying to you when I said that I don't remember ever being any other place." He spread his hands. "And I honestly don't understand these things that you and Rowena and people like you know. I don't have the Memories."

But Cassidy merely waited, calm with her expectation. And after another long moment, Allen shrugged in acquiescence. In the low rays of the sun, his hair and beard looked like spun copper, and his eyes were unblinking in their steady study of her face.

"I don't remember another place—but I still remember that there once was a time when I did. I still remember the pain, even if I don't remember anything else. And so when I saw someone like Rowena, like you . . ." His voice trailed off, and for the first time he seemed visibly uncomfortable with what Cassidy had pried from him.

Gently reaching for his arm, Cassidy offered, "You saved us."

Nodding, Allen concluded, "Because you were different. Because I once was different, too; even if I don't remember it anymore."

Cassidy returned to the cavern alone. As soon as she approached the cook fire, she could see that she had missed something. Nothing unusual was happening at the moment; if anything, the activity around the wide mouth of the cave seemed to be totally innocuous and banal. But something had been going on before she had gotten there, something that Rowena's hearty devotion to her pots and pans couldn't conceal and that all of the casual posturing of the cavern's occupants couldn't erase. Voices may not have been raised there, but hackles had been.

Nodding a greeting to the warden and Kevin, who were busily rolling up blankets, Cassidy edged past Becky. The black woman stood with her back to the fire, looking out across the beach, and didn't even acknowledge Cassidy's return. A quick glance was all she received from Valerie, as the captain barely looked up from sorting the packaged foodstuffs. Dropping down beside the fire, Cassidy caught Rowena's eye and mouthed a silent query.

"Don't ask!" Rowena muttered under her breath. The brunette looked about as exasperated as Cassidy had ever seen her, and her usually sunny friend didn't wear the mood well. Rowena used a stick to poke the coffeepot a little farther into the fire. Then she reached for a tubular canvas water bag. "Here," she said, proffering it. "You mind getting me some more water?" Her tone suggested that Cassidy should be grateful to do just that, to be permitted to escape gracefully from the tense atmosphere within the cave. "There's a seepage from a spring along the cliff wall, about a hundred feet south of here."

With one last wordless look around the cavern, Cassidy noticed that Click wasn't there. She took the water bag from Rowena and quickly left. Outside, she looked up and down the faintly foggy beach. She spotted the Tinker about fifty yards to the north, where he stood along the shoreline, conferring with Webb near the skiff. Allen was still some distance down the beach in the opposite direction, approaching the cave. Silently wishing him good luck, Cassidy set out along the cliff face.

A few minutes later, as she stood holding the mouth of the canvas bag up to the gleaming trickle of water that runneled down the slick surface of the rocky bank, Cassidy wondered what the hell was going on. Just how had the exhausted but relieved camaraderie of the night before so quickly mutated into the starchy standoff that she had just witnessed in the cavern? It didn't take a genius to come up with a few probabilities. Valerie had had several days of arguing with the warden to hone her mutinous streak; and once again the captain had Click to contend with. And Becky—well, no matter what side that woman was on, Cassidy never wanted to be on the other.

By the time Cassidy returned to the cook fire, Rowena had breakfast well under way, and Kevin was helping her serve it up. Both Webb and Click had returned to the cave and were engaged in a discussion with Allen about the outlook for the day's weather. The warden was sitting beside them, passing food and offering his own comments. Even Valerie and Becky looked about as placid as Cassidy had ever seen either of them. And yet the taut undercurrent was still there, right beneath the glib surface of domestic tranquility.

As Cassidy gave Rowena the water bag, Click gave her a silent nod of greeting. Feeling herself flush slightly, she quickly sank down onto the sand between Kevin and Allen. When Rowena passed her a mug of coffee, Cassidy shot the buxom woman a quizzical look. But Rowena merely rolled her eyes.

For the next few minutes Cassidy concentrated all of her attention on eating. When she did begin to pick up on some of the conversation around her, it all seemed to be fairly mundane stuff. Webb was offering a convoluted description of the topography of the local shoreline, with Valerie firing off specific questions about the terrain. It took until her plate was nearly empty before Cassidy realized that what was actually being discussed were the plans for their route of travel into the Great Swamp.

On their second mugs of coffee by then, with empty plates set aside, Click and Webb gravitated out onto the damp packed sand just outside the cavern. The pilot picked up a thin stick from among the firewood and was tracing something on the ground as he spoke. Allen, the warden, and Valerie all drifted out to oversee the proceedings. Becky followed a minute later, coffee mug still in hand. By the time Cassidy went out to join them, the beach cartography had already become quite extensive, with Click wielding his own pointed stick to fill in some of the northern inland details. Coming up behind Webb, Cassidy studied the elaborate line drawing from the perspective of the ocean side.

Like some counterculture professor offering a discourse on the geography of a mythical land, Click started at the northern edge of their map. "The Iron City and the Long River," he said, pointing. Then his stick touched a series of wavy lines he had drawn perpendicular to the sea. "The Slough River, the Dandelion, the Bracken, the Teat, and the Deadfall."

Cassidy was still trying to orient herself on the wide tracery when Webb stepped in, using his own stick to touch the shoreline above one of the rivers Click had just named. "This is where we came ashore in the dinghy," he said. "Just above the Bracken River." His stick skipped down over the next three wavy lines. "We crossed the Bracken, the Teat, and the Deadfall."

"If only it had been that easy," Valerie said under her breath, drawing a sympathetic look from the warden. The Trooper's droll comment had surprised Cassidy; but when she looked up, the curly-haired woman seemed entirely engrossed in studying the map.

"Clam Cove," Click went on, sweeping his stick over the short arc Webb had drawn to represent the small bay. Then the tip of his stick made quick touchdowns on half a dozen other perpendicular lines drawn intersecting the shoreline below the cove. "The position and even the number of these rivers is just an estimation," Click said. "As far as I know, none of them is even named."

Webb's representation of the coastline had grown noticeably more sketchy once it extended beyond the cove. The pilot traced a few ambiguous squiggles out in the area of the sea, absently doodling as he explained, "I've sailed farther south a few times; mostly unintentionally, when I've been caught by storms. So what I've drawn of the coast probably isn't very accurate beyond this point."

"Which way did we come?" Becky interjected, peering past Click's shoulder.

"We traveled this route," Click said. He drew a more or less direct line south from where they had forded the Long River just outside the city, extending it across the inland representations of the other five rivers, and finally cutting due easterly to the cove.

"And what about this?" Valerie asked, gesturing at the unmarked area beyond the western edge of their map. "What lies ahead of us?"

Stepping back, Click began to sketch rapidly in the blank sand, where moments before there had been no landmarks save the shallow imprints of his own boots. He worked methodically, the tip of his stick sweeping across the coarse sand in a series of lines, whorls, and circles. From her perspective on the seaward side, Cassidy could not detect any real pattern to the drawing. But it soon became obvious that most of the detail in Click's map was centered on the northern and eastern edges. The farther south and west he sketched, the fewer and vaguer his markings became.

When he finished drawing, Click began to point out and name the salient features of the map he'd created, starting with a mass of concentric whorls directly west of the cove. "These are the margins of the Great Eastern Bog," he said. "This is where it becomes the Great Eastern Swamp. They say this marsh continues more or less all the way down to the Southern Sea." He paused a moment before adding dryly "We will want to avoid it."

There was no "Southern Sea" on Webb's portion of the map because the drawing simply did not extend that far. Cassidy was craning her neck, still trying to picture the relationship of that sea to Click's bog and swamp, when Becky said, "What do you mean, 'they say'? Who the hell's ever been down there?"

Throwing her a brief look, Click said, "No one who's ever drawn a map of it, Becky. This is the Southern Bog," he continued, his stick delineating the area almost immediately southwest of the cove. "Even though it's not called 'Great,' it's probably even more extensive than the Great Eastern Bog." The silvered tips of Click's mustache lifted slightly, his expression ironic. "No one knows for certain how large it is, because no one has ever reached its western limits."

"At least no one who ever drew a map," Becky muttered under her breath.

Click tapped his stick along the narrow segment of land separating the two bogs. "We'll try to avoid the Southern Bog, as well, at least for as long as we can. But eventually—" And there he sketched a quick sweep westward. "—we'll have to enter the bog in order to reach the Great Southern Swamp."

Cassidy heard Allen clear his throat. "I thought that no one has ever gone into the Great Southern Swamp," he pointed out; not querulously but quite matter-of-factly. The sheriff's shaggy head was canted toward Click, calmly awaiting his response. But Valerie was the first to speak, her voice taut and low.

"People have gone in," the captain said, clipping off each word, her tongue as sharp as a sword. "But only one man has lived to return."

Cassidy found that she had automatically curled her hands into fists and that she was holding her breath, her chest uncomfortably tight. But Click merely nodded, as if allowing Valerie's indictment to stand as his answer to Allen's question, and then simply went on.

The tip of his stick sketched a series of short arcs. "Here, here, and here," he said, "are spits of higher ground, where the terrain is more passable. Passable—but not easy to cross. Travel in the bogs is difficult and hazardous. But beyond here—" His stick twirled out over the vast, nearly featureless area he had left so sparsely illustrated. "—we will have very little choice."

There was a short moment of silence before Becky voiced the obvious question. "Just how far into this damned swamp are we going to have to go?"

The question was inherently unanswerable, but Click gave the black woman a totally serious reply. "Right now, Becky, I don't think there's anyone who knows the answer to that." He let the end of his stick trace a delicate curl in the air above the inscribed sand. "I trust we'll find the answer to that question once we get there."

Valerie did not allow any interval of silence to give the weight of legitimacy to Click's response. She turned to the warden with an impatient toss of her curly head. "This is lunacy!" she declared loudly. "Following this madman—this *coward*—into some stinking bog to hunt for something that probably doesn't even exist, when there's so much to be done now!" She spread her hands; but with Valerie, the gesture was somehow more one of command than entreaty. "Come back to the city; let these fools pursue this so-called Alchemist!"

Certain that she was witnessing a replay of at least one of the volatile disagreements enacted earlier that morning in the cavern, Cassidy watched warily as the warden took a step closer to his captain. But to her surprise, he did not appear to be angry at Valerie's loud insubordination, and when he spoke, his voice did not contain even a trace of exasperation.

"We've already discussed this, Val," the warden said quietly, "and you know well my decision." He inclined his head toward Webb, continuing "You also know that you have my leave to go back to the city with this pilot—hell, you have my *blessing* to go back." A small, resigned smile played over his lips. "If I thought you would obey, I would *order* you to return."

Indignation raised Valerie's brows to exaggerated arches, her dark eyes flashing. "I am sworn to protect you," she maintained stiffly.

"You are also sworn to *obey* me, Val," the warden said ruefully. He shook back the dangling forelock of his errant chestnut-colored hair, his expression elevating resignation to a new level, a veritable art form. "You might protect me by restoring some order to my city," he reminded her.

Too irate to acknowledge the warden's subtle admission that she had already bested him, Valerie asserted, "You know that's not where my skill lies. Tag and Walt know far more about civil order than I do. My place is with you—but *your* place is back at the compound, not slogging around in some rotten swamp!" The captain made a sweeping gesture, almost forcing Cassidy to take a step backward. "Let Cassidy and the others seek this Alchemist; they're the ones who have the Memories. This has nothing to do with you."

But the warden just shook his head gently. "That's where you're mistaken, Val," he said quietly. "I'm afraid it has everything to do with me."

Snorting in disgust, Valerie abruptly turned on her heel and strode away, nearly colliding with Kevin as the blond boy came down onto the beach. He had been in the cavern, helping Rowena clean up after breakfast, and he gave Valerie a puzzled look as she dodged around him.

"Well, then," Webb said mildly, just as Kevin arrived at the warden's side, "is there anyone here who'll be coming back to the city with me?" He grinned. "Or will I be eating all of those provisions myself?"

Rowena had followed Kevin from the cave, arriving just in time to hear the pilot's comment. "Hey, I didn't pack you *that* much stuff," she said. Then she began to curiously study the patch of illustrated sand.

Cassidy glanced around at the others, her gaze slipping quickly over Click's impassive face. Once she had thought that Allen would be returning with the pilot; and she could have predicted that the warden would try to dispatch Valerie, and possibly even Kevin, to safety. But it appeared that Webb would be making his way back north alone.

Kevin stood companionably close to the warden, peering at the sand map. But it was Becky who began explaining the drawing to him, while the warden addressed Webb.

"When will you be leaving?" he asked the seaman.

Webb tilted back his head, scanning the low-dragging bellies of the tattered clouds. "We've got fair weather on the way," he said. "It'll take a little time to get the masthead and boom fitted and the sails unfurled; then I'll be away."

"Will you do something for me, Webb?" the warden said.

The pilot's one brow climbed, his expression more bemused than skeptical as he studied the young man in the stained leathers. "Within reason," he agreed candidly.

"Will you take a message for me to Justin, at the compound?" The warden's lips curved in a rueful smile. "He may not realize it yet, but he happens to be first in command back there now. Let him know where we are and that we all are well."

Webb shrugged his broad shoulders. "I can take your message," he said, "but I may not be believed. Your Troopers don't know me from a keg of nails—and I don't much fancy being hanged for my troubles."

The warden shook his head, briefly smiling again. "Justin will know that the message you deliver has come from me," he assured the pilot. "Just tell him that the wind still favors me; he'll know what you mean." At Webb's quizzical look, and to Cassidy's surprise, the younger man actually colored slightly. "An old joke between us," he explained.

Shrugging again, Webb nodded amiably. "Then I'll carry your

message, warden, and see it delivered to your man. And now if you'll all excuse me, I intend to see to my worthy vessel."

"I'll give you a hand," Allen immediately offered.

As the two men turned away from the map drawn in the sand, Cassidy blurted out, "I will, too." Quickly following their longer strides, she caught up to them and walked alongside Webb, looking like a slightly tarnished miniature of the seaman in her soiled and baggy cotton clothing. She swore she could feel Click's eyes watching them, but to her relief he made no move to join them.

Little conversation passed between the two men as Allen and Webb dragged the small skiff the rest of the way down to the shoreline, but their movements were oddly coordinated for two people who had never worked together before that morning. Cassidy scrambled along behind the craft, pushing against the flattened stern, but she didn't delude herself into thinking that she was being of much help. When they hoisted the mast out of the skiff's belly and upended it, she was able to be of some real assistance in guiding the pole's butt into its socket. Allen held the long shaft upright as Webb deftly threw the bolts home and tightened them.

Watching the pilot lay out the crosspiece of the boom, Cassidy was again struck by the odd bonhomie between the two men, as Allen automatically helped him secure the wooden crossmember in place. Allen and Webb had met only the night before, and then hardly under the best of circumstances. At first they seemed to be nothing alike; and yet they had apparently fallen into an immediately comfortable relationship, the basis of which, Cassidy suspected, lay in their mutual tolerance for the endless vagaries of life. Like two soldiers thrown together in battle who had become best friends, Cassidy mused, they had developed a sort of foxhole camaraderie. Perhaps Webb and Allen were more alike than she had first imagined: Webb was much the man that Allen would have been, if the sheriff had had a sense of humor.

Mulling over that thought, Cassidy was startled when she heard Rowena's voice from directly behind her.

"Wow, that looks neat," the brunette said, apparently referring to the mast and rigging. As Rowena came up alongside her, Cassidy could see that she was carrying a rolled blanket and a collection of small wrapped parcels. "You ready to load up?" Rowena asked Webb.

"Just about," the pilot replied, skillfully arranging what looked to Cassidy's eyes to be a hopeless tangle of lines from the sails.

He paused long enough to peer at the brunette. "What have you all got there for me?"

"Not exactly an even split," Rowena said, sounding slightly apologetic. "A blanket, two pots, coffee, some dried beans and rice—"

Interrupting her inventory with a hearty laugh, Webb said, "More than enough! Hell, I could sail home from here with nothing more than a good knife, if it came to that."

Literal-minded, Rowena hastily added, "Oh, I gave you a knife, too."

"Then I'll travel in luxury," Webb assured her with a wink. "And you all will hardly be getting more than your share; you'll need the rest far more than I will."

Although his tone was bantering, Webb's words carried a certain sober burden of truth. His reminder of the enormity of what they proposed to do hung there for a moment, until a new voice swept it aside.

"You must be getting homesick in your old age, Webb" came the familiarly wry drawl. "I've never seen you hoist canvas so swiftly."

Cassidy edged over a few steps without even glancing sideways at Click as the Tinker approached the skiff. In the full light of day, he looked even more ragged than Cassidy had noticed earlier outside the cave. But although his clothing was tattered and dirty, she could see that Click had made the effort to wash up and tame his hair; he had even shaved. And despite the condition of his clothing, its familiarity, his fitted trousers and shirt and the conchaed vest, lent him a certain reassuring air of normalcy.

Looking the craft up and down, Click watched Allen assist Webb with the final securing of the neatly furled sails. "You have everything you need?" Click asked then, his tone far more serious.

Climbing over the side of the beached skiff, Webb favored Click with a crooked grin. "Come to see me off, have you? Or have you regained your senses and come looking for a safe ride home?"

Shaking his dark head in amusement, Click began to unburden Rowena of her armful of parcels, passing them to the seaman. As Webb was methodically arranging the supplies, Cassidy saw Becky, the warden, Kevin, and Valerie all coming down across the sand to bid their farewells.

Webb took their good wishes and thanks with his usual equanimity, but beneath his seemingly nonchalant manner, Cassidy could sense in the pilot a definite eagerness to be off, back on the sea and headed toward home. He was the only one with any sense, she thought with a touch of melancholy. And as she watched Webb clap Allen on the shoulder and thank the sheriff for his help, Cassidy suddenly realized just how much she would miss the stalwart seaman with the amazingly good heart.

She was struggling to hold back tears as Webb moved on to the warden, pausing to reiterate his agreement to carry the warden's message. His farewells to Kevin and Valerie were candidly affable. Then, to her surprise, Cassidy found herself being engulfed in a generous bear hug, her feet suddenly lifting from the sand as Webb swung her around in an embrace.

"Good luck to you, Cassidy," he whispered over the top of her head; then, more loudly, he added, "And I hope to hell you'll be taking your little pet creatures along with you!"

Released again, Cassidy stumbled to regain her footing as Webb nodded his acknowledgments to Becky and Rowena. Then he was standing toe to toe with Click, locked in a piercing staring contest with the Tinker. But Webb was the first one to break the mock confrontation, pounding Click affectionately on the back hard enough to have made a lesser man stagger.

"Well, debt or no debt, you've certainly gotten the best of me on this one, you smooth-tongued bastard!" the pilot declared fondly. "But damned if I don't hope you live long enough to do it again."

With one swift looping motion of his fingers, Click slipped the leather thong from around his neck and pulled out the little brass key from beneath his shirt. He held it out to Webb and, at the seaman's puzzled look, said, "When you return, take this to Bonnie and Tad in the enclave, and tell them about your boat." He dangled the little bit of metal before Webb's face. "Have them take you down to the shipyards and the canvas workers. Your new boat and all of her fittings will come from my account, my friend."

Webb looked frankly surprised—although Cassidy noticed that he accepted the proffered key with alacrity. Quickly tugging the thong down over his own head, the pilot covered having been caught off guard by swiftly jibing "And if they think I pulled this off your dead and mangled body, Tinker?"

The silvered tips of Click's mustache lifted ever so slightly, his small smile fleeting and wolfish. "Then you will have an even larger account than you had anticipated, seaman," he said evenly.

With one last thump to Click's back, Webb turned and took his place near the stern of the skiff. With the help of Allen, Click, the warden, and Kevin, the craft was quickly launched into the smooth rolling waves of the bay. As deftly as any Horseman leaping astride his mount, the pilot flipped himself up over her side and into the bottom of the skiff. Balanced there on his knees, he began to play out the fresh canvas, his big tanned hands moving skillfully over the lines. The skiff bobbed rhythmically over the waves, slowly propelled forward as Webb set her sails. When all of the canvas was unfurled, she was already a good hundred feet from the shore. Then Webb turned to toss them all a quick salute in farewell.

A man in his element, Cassidy thought, trying to tamp down the sudden surge of sadness and loss she felt as the little skiff nosed out into the wind and the sails bellied, shooting her forward. But it took every bit of will she possessed to keep the tears dammed deep inside, as she watched the graceful scull sweep out toward the distant arm of the bay, carrying Webb away.

Chapter 9 ⬅▥

As the group of people who had been assembled at the shore-line began to break up, the warden cut across the beach to intersect Click. Walking alongside the Tinker, he said, "If no one has any objections, I'd like to leave as soon as possible." He glanced around at the others. "I realize the past few days have been difficult for everyone; but I would rather get under way again, even if we have to shorten our pace at first."

Cassidy felt that several people there, herself and Rowena included, fell into a rather nebulous area of not being directly under either the warden's or the Tinker's jurisdiction. She would have put Allen into the same category, despite his nominal allegiance as a sheriff. But she was not surprised when the big bearded man merely shrugged.

"I've got no objections," Allen said, "but I'm only speaking for myself."

Click came to a sudden halt, causing the warden nearly to overshoot him before the young man could correct his pace. Click's thoughtful gaze rested on the warden for a moment before panning over Allen and the others. Cassidy met the look squarely, too curious about Click's intentions to be discomfitted, and alert to the powerful undercurrent of conflicting purpose being played out there on the barren strand of beach.

"Before we go any farther," the Tinker said levelly, "we'd better get some matters settled among us."

The warden proved a quick study, instantly atuned to the implications of what Click was advising. "An excellent point," the warden said. "A Troop can have only one leader, or there is chaos. And where we're going, discipline might mean the difference between life and death."

"Wait a minute." Valerie spoke up irately, making an obviously dismissive gesture toward Click. "This man is no Trooper! Why should we take orders from him?"

Click's face was so composed that it was almost without expression. Only something in the unmined depths of his dark eyes betrayed any hint of emotion at the captain's harsh words. "I'm merely suggesting that only one person can be in charge," he pointed out. "I'm not suggesting that I be that person."

"Well, then I'm suggesting it," Allen said, one big hand rising to forestall Valerie's predictable objection. "Click has led the Tinkers, so he knows how to pull people together." The blunt appraisal in those gold-ringed eyes held Click without wavering, but the Tinker seemed not in the least uncomfortable with the close assessment. "And no offense to the warden, but the past few days have convinced me that Click knows how to get by in a scrape— whether with other people or with the terrain. And all else aside, he's the only one who's traveled in this area before."

"Well said, Sheriff Allen," the warden agreed quietly. "To survive where we're going, we're going to need to be united under one person; and I see no better candidate than Click."

Valerie's sculpted cheekbones were bright with high color, her indignation plain even though she had held her tongue as long as possible. "You can't be serious!" she exclaimed to the warden. Her dark eyes raked over the calm and silent Tinker. "This man is a traitor, a failure—a *coward*! Do you really expect me to take orders from him?"

"No, Val," the warden said simply, "I expect you to take your orders from *me*. And I will be taking my orders from the Tinker."

The captain fumed like an explosive with a faulty fuse. And Cassidy realized that, like that short-circuited munition, the ultimate display of Valerie's temper was only being delayed, not extinguished. The explosion could come at any time, probably when it was least expected and most inconvenient. But for the moment the curly-haired woman managed to hold her tongue.

Since Valerie had been coerced into temporarily acceding, and Kevin obviously would do anything his warden asked of him, from the warden's household that left only the matter of Becky's allegiance. But Cassidy was not surprised by the black woman's pragmatic approach to the situation.

"Hell, I've got no problem with letting Click lead," she said promptly. "I'm no Woodsman—I'll follow anyone who can get us through this shit! And so far he's done just fine by me."

Although she should have expected it, Cassidy still was disarmed by the directness of Click's gaze as he turned his attention to her. One of his dark brows rose, its set both quizzical and sardonic. And if the flush on Valerie's face had come from barely checked outrage, the warmth that Cassidy felt spreading up across her neck and ears had an entirely different source.

"Uh, it's fine with me, too," she said awkwardly, throwing Rowena a quick look.

The brunette, entirely unruffled, was nodding agreeably. "We've already traveled a long way with Click," she reminded everyone, "and he's always done a good job of taking care of us."

"Then it's decided," the warden said evenly. "Click, if you are willing, we would be grateful if you would assume the leadership of this group for the rest of our journey."

The Tinker nodded shortly, finally looking away from Cassidy. Instead he looked directly at Valerie as he replied, "I will accept—on one condition. If at any point the majority of you wish to replace me, I would ask to be relieved of my duty."

The choice of his last words was calculated, Cassidy was certain. Valerie's body visibly tightened, but she held her silence. If the warden noticed her reaction, he chose to ignore it. "Then let me ask you," he said to Click, with a hint of wry humor in his voice, "when would you like to get under way?"

Click's expression remained neutral, but Cassidy knew him well enough to detect the faint tone of amusement in his words. "As soon as we've finished packing up our supplies," the Tinker said, adding, "although for today, at least, we may want to shorten our pace."

From the glint in Allen's eyes, for a moment Cassidy thought the big burly man was actually going to laugh aloud. But instead he just made a grunting sound and said gruffly, "Well then, let's get at it—or come sunset, we'll still be standing here on this beach like a set of rocks."

Just as Webb had predicted, the day brought fair weather, sunny and pleasantly cool. Cassidy was especially appreciative of the dry, temperate air once they had turned their backs on the Gray Sea and began their trek inland. Distributed evenly among all of them, their spartan cache of supplies didn't amount to a burden for anyone. Cassidy found that even carrying her own blanket and dishes was easy; neatly rolled together and slung over her back, the small pack was quickly forgotten. But the terrain they covered was barely passable, a thick growth of trees and rampant brush, unbroken by so much as a rabbit run, and slashed by the occasional steep and shaley ravine.

Dragonfly seemed relatively unhampered by the jungle of bushes and branches, although staying on the horse's back for more than a couple of minutes without having been swept off by the clawing foliage would have been impossible. The mare's sheer bulk and strength allowed her to plow through the dense growth where humans had to wind their way slowly. But the abrupt and crumbly dropoffs in the ravines gave the horse more difficulty, and she often resorted to disappearing for a time, going farther afield to scout out a more amenable route up and down the slopes. Still, even if Cassidy couldn't ride the mare, the horse's mere proximity and the familiar sense of her presence comforted her.

There was another presence that gave Cassidy considerable comfort, and that was Rowena's. In those few harrowing days since they'd separated at the warden's house, Cassidy had missed the cheerful brunette more than she would have thought possible. She was chagrined to consider what her journey would have been like had she abandoned Rowena back in Double Creek, if Valerie and the other Troopers would have been willing to take Cassidy back with them the night of the fire in the village. Reunited with the woman's slightly skewed sense of humor and her seemingly indefatigable optimism and loyalty, Cassidy was profoundly thankful that she would not have to face without Rowena the ordeal that most certainly lay ahead of them. Even as Cassidy struggled to deflect the slapping branches that seemed to mesh shut again immediately in Allen's wake, she was aware of Rowena right behind her, gamely following her on yet another leg of the bizarre journey that had begun with their vow to each other to find their way back to the real world.

Brushing a sticky bit of torn vegetation away from her face, Cassidy considered one aspect of her friendship with Rowena that she had been deliberately avoiding ever since their reunion the night before. So many things had happened during their short separation. Some of it, such as the physical details of her harrowing experiences in the Iron City, on the sea, and traveling down the coast, would make good stories in the retelling; and Cassidy had no problem with that, no matter how distressing the original incidents may have been. Neither of them had ever shied away from such grisly truths between each other. But there were other things that were far less straightforward and would be more difficult to explain.

Cassidy realized then that she was the only person who knew everything that had happened during the warden's lapses. Even the young man himself had only the vaguest sense of what had happened after the episodes were over. So far Cassidy had told no one—not even the warden himself—everything she suspected about the significance of the bizarre dichotomy between Andy Greene and the warden of Horses. If Cassidy felt uneasy with the thought of trying to explain her suspicions to Rowena, how would she ever be able to tell anyone else?

And there was also the last, most secret knowledge, which she still withheld from her friend. Despite the fact that hiking through the brush had made Cassidy perspire, she still felt an odd shiver at the memory of what Click had revealed to her in that moment of extreme stress.

Cassidy knew one thing for certain. Until she could confront Click, alone and to her satisfaction, no one else needed to know exactly what had happened between them.

No one had ever defined what was meant by a "shortened pace" for the day's travel, but by the time they stopped for lunch, Cassidy already felt as if she'd put in a full day's worth of trekking across the rough-scrabble terrain. At the bottom of one of the brush-choked gullies, they found enough of a crudely cleared spot for all of them to be able to sit together to rest and share a meal. They probably had covered only a few miles all morning, and the sun was just directly overhead, but Cassidy's aching muscles and burning feet protested that it was long past time to stop.

Valerie coaxed together just enough dry wood to make Rowena aspire to heat up the cooked food left over from breakfast. While those simple preparations were under way, Cassidy slipped away into the bushes to relieve herself. For the first time in a very long time, she felt uncomfortably aware of just how little privacy there could be when you traveled with a group of people, even when you were out in the middle of nowhere.

That need attended to, Cassidy Called the gray mare. Moments later she heard the snapping and cracking of branches as the horse plowed through the undergrowth. The gray popped out of a thicket of yellow dogwood, incriminating twigs of some unidentified shrub still hanging from her mouth. Her sharply cocked ears suggested a certain interest in Cassidy's Call, even if the horse had been interrupted in the middle of lunch. Then again, all day was "lunch" to a horse at liberty, Cassidy thought dryly as she tugged a few twigs out of the mare's mouth before briefly cradling the big head against her shirt front.

Even though she had thoroughly checked over the mare that morning on the beach, Cassidy began to give her another going over, paying particular attention to her legs and feet. Part of the examination was out of legitimate concern, because of the rough ground they had been covering. But part of it was more self-serving. The methodical routine of examining the horse was somehow soothing to Cassidy, a ritual that transcended time and place, and served seamlessly to connect her with her old life in the real world.

Because she stood bent with the mare's forefoot cradled between her knees, and her back was to Click, Cassidy didn't notice him approaching. And because the Tinker had a way of moving like a cat when he wanted to, she never even heard him. It wasn't until he spoke that she became aware that he was almost beside her; and then she was so startled by him that she nearly lost her hold on the horse's hoof.

"Be sure to check her for woodticks," Click said, from only a few feet away. "Especially up under her mane."

Abruptly setting down the mare's foot, Cassidy straightened and took a quick step sideways, putting another couple of feet between herself and the Tinker. "I did," she said.

Click took the last couple of steps to the mare's shoulder, where he stood, casually rubbing the gray's jugular furrow. "They haven't been too bad yet," he said, "but this is certainly the country for them."

Unaccountably annoyed by how willingly the mare leaned into Click's caress and by the deft familiarity of that touch, Cassidy's voice was a bit testy when she said, "I always check her for ticks, no matter what kind of country we're in."

"Of course you do," he said mildly, still slowly rubbing the horse's neck. "You're as dedicated as any Horseman I've seen, Cassidy."

Something both in his easy tone and the way he said her name suddenly reminded Cassidy just why she had been so studiously avoiding Click for the past twenty-four hours. It would have been the perfect opportunity for her to have thanked him for taking care of the mare and bringing her back just as he had promised. But Cassidy found that all the potential words of gratitude stuck in her throat then. To speak of his vow to her would have brought them dangerously close to another subject that had surfaced on that same night—a subject Cassidy suddenly was strenuously eager to avoid entirely.

Click was still standing beside the mare, his long fingers idly tracing the flat muscle beneath her sleek hide. His expression was benign enough, those dark eyes calm and devoid of any hint of mockery. Cassidy was struck then by just how comfortable she had once felt with him, and how long it had taken her to get to that point—and how far she felt from it again.

"Uh, I think I'll go see if Rowena needs any help," she said awkwardly, her excuse so obviously fabricated that she felt outright foolish as she started to step around Click. From the corner of her eye she saw his arm reach out, and she felt his fingertips just graze the baggy sleeve of her cotton shirt.

"Cassidy, don't," Click said, his voice a soft rasp.

But before she could turn, before she could even decide for certain whether she wanted to jerk away from him or stay and answer that quiet entreaty, she saw someone pushing his way toward them through the thick brush, and a familiar voice rang out.

"Click?" the warden called. As soon as he could see the two of them beside the horse, he added, "Good, I've found both of you." His boyish face was drawn with what had become an increasingly common expression for him, his once-smooth brow furrowed and his wide-set eyes alight with concern. He made a swift beckoning gesture. "Becky has found something. You'd better come look."

For better or worse, the moment between them was irretrievably broken, and Cassidy gave Click only the briefest of glances before starting after the warden. She knew the Tinker was following right behind her.

About a hundred feet down the ravine, well past the site where Valerie had laid a fire and where the meal Rowena had prepared still sat, uneaten, the rest of their group stood silently clustered around something on the ground that was concealed by the thick vegetation. When Becky noticed the three of them approaching, she immediately turned and addressed Click.

"It's like I told the warden," the little black woman proclaimed, her tone a mixture of irritation and disgust. "I just stepped out to take a pee, and then I find *this*!" She looked down balefully at the ground in the center of the circle of onlookers. "A person can't even take a pee around here!" she concluded.

Cassidy let Click overtake her then, so that the Tinker was the first one to follow the warden. As the warden pulled back the dense foliage of a cluster of young alders, Cassidy found that she could see quite enough from her vantage point behind them. In fact, when she automatically jerked back in surprise and alarm, she was glad that she didn't have Click or anyone else standing directly behind her.

Sprawled on its side across the damp earth beneath the branches of the alders was a naked, partially decomposed body.

At first Cassidy couldn't even tell if it had been a man or a woman; neither the position nor the condition of the body revealed its gender. But from the size of the remains, she thought it must have been a man, even though the hair was shoulder length.

Kevin had been edging closer to the warden. When he reached the older man's side, he leaned forward, peering with widened eyes. "Who—who do you think it was?" he stammered in a hushed voice.

Valerie was viewing the corpse with far more clinical detachment than either her warden or the young Finder. She used the toe of one boot to nudge a long, stringy-looking thigh, her face a mask of hard indifference. With precise deliberation, she turned and looked directly at Click. "Perhaps a Trooper—one of yours, Tinker?" she asked icily.

Click did not reply; he didn't even react visibly to the slur. Instead he calmly stepped past the others and dropped down into a crouch beside the body, ducking beneath the branches. Carefully, almost gently, he took hold of the exposed shoulder and hip and turned the corpse onto its back. Cassidy winced and looked away for a moment, for there was almost nothing left of the dead man's face, the empty eye sockets and lipless teeth stark amid the skull's thin shroud of shriveled brown flesh.

The warden's voice was even, utterly without indictment, as he asked Click, "Do you think he was a Trooper?"

Click replied without looking up from his steady study of the body, his own tone equally neutral. "I doubt it," he said, "even if he had, for some reason, been left here, stripped naked." His hand dropped down to the dead man's feet, the tips of his fingers just barely brushing the sunken pads of rotted flesh. "From his calluses, this man must have spent years going barefoot." Click looked up briefly then, just the fleetest of glances, directed at no one in particular. "My guess would be that he was a Woodsman."

Click's pronouncement caused a palpable decrease in the level of tension among the onlookers. Not that a Woodman's life necessarily meant less to them, Cassidy thought, but given the wild ones' crude and solitary lifestyle, any manner of fates could have befallen the poor fellow, and thus his death need not signify anything particularly sinister.

After a long moment of silence, Allen spoke up. "Well, Woodsman or not, I guess the man deserves a decent burial," he said stoically.

Click lithely rose to his feet, absently dusting his hands on the fronts of his trouser thighs. "Woodsmen don't believe in interment," he replied mildly, "but if you're willing to help me, Allen, and we can spare a few feet of rope, we can give him a proper resting place in the style he would have preferred."

After Becky's discovery, lunch was a sober and abbreviated affair. By the time Click and Allen had returned from their task, everyone else had eaten, and the two men took their meal in silence. Even Cassidy, who had once entertained fond hopes of a long rest stop in the ravine, was then quite willing to get under way again.

Finding the corpse seemed like some strange sort of ill omen to Cassidy, and she was eager to leave the site of Becky's grisly discovery. As they climbed up out of the ravine, dog-legging up the shaley slope to wind around the worst of the undergrowth, she looked up into the boughs of a huge, storm-crippled chestnut tree that hung over the lip of the gully. High in its branches, tethered in a crotch like a ghostly parody of a mounted Horseman, the decomposing body of the dead Woodsman seemed to mock Cassidy and her hopeless quest.

The afternoon seemed to pass quickly, even though the rough terrain hampered their pace. But it was at least an hour before sunset when Click first called a halt. They were crossing a thickly wooded ridge of ground between two brush-choked gullies, and he had to wait for everyone to catch up to him before he spoke.

"We've already put in a good day's travel," Click said. "If we stop for the night now, we could clear an area here on high ground."

The warden cocked a brow expectantly. "But?" he prompted.

The Tinker spread his hands, an equanimical gesture that suggested the only reason he was even mentioning any alternative was because the warden had dragged it out of him. "But if we continue southward along this ridge, we may be able to find a storm cut—a clear spot left behind where a large tree has gone down." He shrugged, as if the matter was really of little consequence to him one way or the other; he was, after all, only their dutiful point man. God, he could be smooth! Cassidy thought with reluctant and grudging admiration. "It would make a more comfortable site to camp," he added, "and there'd be no shortage of good dry firewood."

Allen's shaggy head canted, and there was something remarkably akin to amusement glinting behind the steady gaze of those sand-colored eyes. Cassidy had almost forgotten how well the sheriff and the Tinker, two men physically disparate and yet oddly similar, had worked together during their trip to the Iron City. Allen and Click were two leaders who had quickly earned each other's respect. "How far?" he asked Click.

Scanning the western sky, as if to estimate the angle of the waning sunlight, Click considered for a moment. "I would give it another hour," he said then. "If we don't find a cut by then, we'll stop anyway. The terrain won't be any rougher than this."

"Fair enough," the warden agreed, and no one else had any protest.

Most of the trees along the ridge were mature, and their large size choked out some of the undergrowth and made travel a little easier. And the ground, although uneven and shaley, was drier and firmer than that in the ravines. Cassidy figured that even an hour of hiking along the ridge wouldn't be too exhausting, compared to the trek they had already put in that day. And from the chill already creeping into the air, she realized it was going to be a cool night. The thought of having a large and readily accessible supply of firewood was definitely appealing.

Less than half a mile from the point where they had mounted the ridge, they found an irregularly shaped area almost free of brush. Near the center of the clearing stood about six feet of shattered stump from what had once been an impressive oak tree. Torn sideways from that stump, most of its long dark skeleton trailing down the steep incline of the gully, lay the remains of the big tree. Although the oak probably had been downed several years earlier, the ground that had once been shaded beneath its massive branches was still nearly free of encroaching undergrowth. And the thick horizontal bulk of the tree's trunk formed a sturdy windbreak for a campsite.

Cassidy felt a vague guilt about not having been particularly useful lately around camp, so she eagerly joined in the mundane tasks of gathering wood and laying the cook fire. She was sitting beside Rowena in the shadow of the ancient tree trunk, helping the brunette and Becky arrange rocks around the periphery of the fresh blaze, when Click came up and casually squatted down beside her.

Uneasiness rolled through Cassidy, so strongly that she had to fight to keep from visibly flinching away from the Tinker's sudden proximity. Only moments earlier she had been silently mulling over how she would be able to get Rowena, Becky, and Allen alone to talk with them, without being too obvious about it. But with Click's unexpected arrival, the only thing Cassidy could think about was how she could put some distance between herself and him, preferably immediately, and not even necessarily very gracefully.

The dark-haired man lightly chafed his hands, warming his long tanned fingers in the heat from the flames. "The air will be brisk tonight," he said, glancing over at the parcels of staples Rowena was unwrapping. "Your cooking will be especially appreciated, ladies."

While both Rowena's and Becky's moods seemed to flourish under Click's attention, Cassidy just felt increasingly uncomfortable beside him. She had to concede that his choice of positions may have been entirely innocent; but that didn't make his sudden nearness any less unnerving.

Click deftly nudged the butt end of a burning stick farther into the fire and said, "Starting tomorrow, we'll have to make more of an effort to forage for food as we travel, so that we don't deplete the—"

Surprising even herself by her rude abruptness, Cassidy quickly stood and announced, "I'm going to go check my mare yet, before it gets really dark."

Because her attention was focused on the baffled expressions on both Rowena's and Becky's faces, she was caught completely off guard when Click also gained his feet, with all of her speed and considerably more grace. "I'll have a look at her for you, Cassidy," he said evenly. His dark eyes studied her for a moment before he added, "Why don't you sit? You look weary."

Then, before she could even protest, Click was moving away, his lean frame easily winding around the sparse clumps of vegetation even in the dim twilight.

"Cassidy, what *is* it with you?" Rowena hissed at her.

"Woman, you are jumpier than a damned cat around that man!" Becky added candidly.

Dropping back down onto the ground, Cassidy hastily glanced around them; but no one else nearby seemed to have overheard or to be paying any particular attention to the three women. The warden, Kevin, and Val were unpacking the bedrolls, and both Click and Allen were out of sight.

"I thought you and that Tinker were old friends," the black woman went on, her voice somewhat lower. "Why the hell are you—"

"Shh!" Cassidy shushed her, glancing around them again. "Listen, I need to talk to Allen and you two about some stuff—alone."

Rowena shrugged, leaning forward to push the coffeepot farther into the glowing coals at the edge of the fire. "There's not likely to be much privacy around here any time soon," she murmured, sotto voce.

Becky's dark head was cocked, her canny eyes shrewdly pinning Cassidy. "What do you need to talk to the three of us about that you can't just tell everyone here?" she asked suspiciously. "Is this about those other spells the warden's had since he left the city?"

Cassidy shouldn't have been surprised, but she was. Her shoulders jerked back and she quickly leaned in closer to Becky, regarding the smaller woman with wide eyes. "He told you he's been having more lapses?" she said, somewhat stupidly.

"That what you call them?" Becky said. "Yeah, we talked about it some."

For all of the black woman's peckishness, Becky and the warden were friends; Cassidy realized that they probably had known each other far longer than she and Rowena. And until Cassidy's arrival, Becky had been the young man's primary link with the Memories. Cassidy should have realized that the warden naturally would have confided in Becky, especially considering the reason for the difficult journey they were undertaking.

Interpreting Cassidy's silence as either continuing disbelief or just plain old-fashioned confusion, Becky added helpfully, "He told me about it today, while we were whacking our way through this damned jungle." Giving the immediate area of the campsite a quick look, she concluded, "Valerie and Kevin were there, too. And I don't see that there's anything about these spells, or flashes, or whatever you want to call them, that everyone else shouldn't know about."

A faint glimmer of suspicion rose in Cassidy then. She leaned back a bit, her voice still lowered, but her tone and demeanor deliberately more casual. "Just what exactly did he tell you about what's been happening to him?" she asked.

The black woman shrugged. "He said that when he has one of those spells, he acts like he knows you," she said. "That he acts like this Andy guy that you think you know from the Slow World. But afterward, when he comes out of it, he doesn't remember what he's said to you." She made a small, vague gesture. "He said that you know more about what's happened than he does, and that what he was telling us was just pretty much what you've told him."

Her suspicions confirmed, Cassidy chanced a quick glance across the campsite, to where the subject of their covert discussion still knelt beside Kevin and Valerie, stacking the dishes he had removed from their packs. In the waning light, the youthful lines of his profile were classic and clean, convincingly guileless. But just as Cassidy had suspected, the warden had held things back, deliberately deceiving Becky and the others by giving them only a portion of the truth—just as Cassidy herself had chosen to hold back from him the entire truth of what was happening between them during those episodes of increasingly bizarre intimacy.

Suddenly realizing that Becky had just said something to her, Cassidy immediately leaned in closer so that when Becky had to repeat her remark, she wouldn't feel compelled to do so in a raised voice.

"He said that he hasn't had one of those spells for a couple of days, though," Becky repeated. "Not since that first night when you headed inland." Her rounded face wore a thoughtful frown. "You think maybe they're done with?"

"I suppose that's possible."

But somehow, despite the interval since the last episode, Cassidy felt that although almost anything was possible, the probability that the lapses were over seemed quite unlikely.

Kevin approached the fire with an armful of dishes, effectively ending their hushed conversation. But Cassidy did not miss the way Rowena kept throwing telling looks in her direction. The brunette would not be put off as easily as Becky had been on the subject of either the warden's spells or Cassidy's obvious aversion to Click. Cassidy knew that she would soon have to determine just how much of the truth she intended to tell her friend.

The last thing Cassidy thought about that night, as she lay rolled in her blanket, nodding on the cusp of sleep, was a puzzling bit of semantics. That midday in the ravine, beside the gray mare, when she had tried to evade Click, he had entreated her, "Cassidy, don't." Not *"stay,"* not even *"don't go"*—just *"don't."* Don't *what*? she wondered then. She was still fruitlessly mulling over the word when she finally sank into slumber.

In her dream, she was riding the gray mare, galloping along the familiar twists and turns of one of the wooded trails on Joel's Greenlea farm. Riding ahead of her, keeping just out of reach, sped Andy Greene. He was not mounted on any of Joel's school horses, however; he rode the warden's leggy chestnut gelding. Man and horse moved in perfect synchrony, like one mythical organism rather than two separate species. Andy's tall, coltish frame assumed an easy poise, leaning in over the gelding's withers with a seemingly effortless balance.

She called out to Andy to wait for her, but the big chestnut never slowed. Andy never responded, never even turned to look back at her as she urged from the gray mare an even more furious burst of speed. When she drew up closer behind him, she called out again, even more imperatively. But Andy did not acknowledge her.

The mare's powerful body surged between her knees, bringing them nearer, almost to the gelding's haunches. She reached out then, her fingers straining to catch hold of even just the fluttering edge of the back of Andy's shirt. She pleaded with him to wait—

And then suddenly Andy turned and looked back at her, and he was a corpse, *an eyelessly leering skull with slablike rows of yellowing teeth and long fleshless hands reaching for her, their gleaming white bones barely held together by stringy brown shreds of desiccated sinew.*

And she screamed—

Lunging upright, Cassidy didn't know if she was still dreaming or finally awake, because suddenly there were gripping fingers biting into the soft flesh of her shoulders, and as they grasped her—

Light exploded behind Cassidy's eyes—*within* her eyes, within her brain, and for a few moments of utter blindness, she was not the person frozen there, caught by the hold of those strong hands: She was instead the person whose grip had immobilized her. Stunned and dazed, she felt a strength far greater than her own ripple through a body whose form and mass were alarmingly alien to her; and yet—

And yet, she realized, as the molten light rapidly ran back out of her, it was not a body with which she was completely unfamiliar. Blinking dizzily in the aftermath of both her nightmare and the fiery fusion, she recognized that body. It was the same body that still knelt beside her, the body of Andy Greene.

"Cathy! Are you okay?"

Both the sound of his voice and his overriding concern were so much like the warden's that, in her confusion, Cassidy wondered if she had actually dreamed or hallucinated those few seconds of cool, invasive brilliance that had so intimately connected her with the young man. But he had called her Cathy, not Cassidy. And as she sat there, immobilized more by her surprise than by the hold of his hands and desperately grasping for some kind of coherence, she could see that it was not the warden who held her.

"Cathy?" he repeated, his anxiety increasing.

"I—I'm okay, Andy," she stammered, honestly wondering if

she was telling him the truth. But as the terrible immediacy of that bizarre flare of altered perception faded, like the dimming of its radiant light, Cassidy felt that perhaps she was.

She had no idea what hour of the night it was. In the cool darkness, the soft *chirr* of insect song hummed in her ears. She could see faint movement to either side of them, further grounding her in the present reality of their camp on the ridge. In the thin starlight she could identify the vague forms of her companions: Becky, trying to come in closer, but being restrained by Valerie and Kevin; Rowena, silently urging Allen to stillness; and Click, a tall shadow, motionless in the gloom. Then Andy spoke again, his voice almost breaking with distress, and Cassidy redevoted all of her attention to the young man kneeling on the edge of her blanket.

"They wouldn't let me see you, Cathy! I thought maybe they had killed you, because they wouldn't let me see you for so long!"

Cassidy slipped her arms up to bracket his, grasping his forearms and squeezing them gently. "I'm here now, Andy; see? I'm still okay."

For a moment she thought he was going to try to crawl into her arms again, as he had the last time, when he had been equally upset. And she would have permitted him, no matter who was watching them then. His skin was warm and smooth beneath her fingers, and his sweet musk of smoke and leather, horses and perspiration, teased at her nostrils. Disarmingly, she found she actually longed to embrace him. But he was able to regain his composure more quickly than before, and the tautness in his body eased slightly.

"Cathy, you've got to get out of here!" he said.

My thought exactly, Cassidy thought, but she forced herself to keep concentrating on what she could see of that anxious young face in the near darkness. "Andy," she said quietly, "where am I? Am I still in the big house with the bright lights and the white halls?"

"Yes, yes!" he said, nodding impatiently, as if trying to hurry along her needless reiteration of something that was self-evident. "But you've got to get up—get out of bed and get out of here! What if they won't let me come back again?"

Cassidy avidly wished for some of the earlier illumination of that cold fire which had poured through her senses, because she desperately wanted to see the details of his expression then. In the same way, she wished for some enlightenment in deciphering the puzzling conundrum with which he had again presented her. All she could do was stare at the faintly silvered planes of that dangerously attractive face, silently reaching into her memory for some clue to unlock the continuing mystery of Andy Greene's ethereal visitations.

"I don't like coming here," Andy murmured, ducking his head as if to avoid something unpleasant. "I want you to get out of here, Cathy. Then I won't have to come here any more."

"I know, Andy," she reassured him softly, lightly squeezing his forearms again. "But I think I'm going to need your help to get out of here."

"I've tried, Cathy!" he said, his voice rising plaintively. His face twisted in an anxious grimace. "But I can't! I—" He broke off, his breath tearing raggedly, its intake almost a sob. "He's the only one who can see," he whispered hoarsely.

Cassidy abruptly sat back, nearly pulling him off balance. Like a stray shaft of the all-penetrating brilliance of that phantom light, comprehension struck her, and she understood.

"Andy," she said, "the warden is the one who can see, isn't he?"

But the young man seemed to assume that bit of insight was merely a given; he had other, far more urgent concerns. "But he can't reach them, Cathy," he insisted, again as if reminding her of an obvious fact. "He can't get you out of here!"

His long fingers were digging painfully into her shoulders, distress turning that boyish face into a canvas of despair. Ignoring the discomfort of his grip, Cassidy gave his arms a little shake to regain his complete attention.

"Andy, listen to me: *You're* the warden of Horses, aren't you." She made it a statement of fact, not a question.

His growing agitation abruptly stilled, as if there was a freeze-frame button for his anxiety and Cassidy had somehow managed to push it. Even the tone of his voice was perceptibly different, much calmer and deeper, as he replied, "Now I am." He was looking directly at her, the gaze of those chocolate-brown eyes utterly contained, utterly serious. "When this happens, I am."

Goose flesh prickled across Cassidy's arms and chest, stinging her skin, tightening her nipples until they ached. The thunderous quickening of her pulse was an annoying distraction, and she had to squeeze his forearms again to help center herself. "Andy, I need the warden to do something for me; something to help me."

"To help you get out of here?" he said promptly and hopefully.

Cassidy nodded. Then, because his gaze was so unnervingly

level that she couldn't be certain he had seen or understood the movement, she said, "Yes, something to help me get out of here." She lowered her voice, letting it soften as she leaned in closer to that rapt face. "I need to know more about where I am, about the big house. I need the warden to look around very carefully, Andy." Her voice had fallen to a near whisper. "Where am I lying? Is there anything else around me?"

For a few moments Cassidy's breath caught in her throat, as she convinced herself she had somehow overstepped the unseen boundaries of whatever rules circumscribed the warden's spells. The clean, handsome lines of his face were distorted by a frown. It took her a full minute or more of heart-thudding waiting before she realized that what she had originally taken for incomprehension in his expression was merely intense effort—an effort that was taking place a world away.

"It's just a room," he said then, still frowning. "Your bed, narrow, white covers . . . and there's a noise—I don't like that noise, it never stops."

Cassidy was certain that she had not moved or done anything to disrupt him in any way, and yet he suddenly jerked back, his hands flying from her shoulders. Even in the dim light, she could see that his expression was entirely changed. The spell had ended.

It was the warden who looked at her then across the small space separating them, blinking in confusion, his familiar face wearing a puzzled frown. "What did he do?" he asked her.

Becky was again trying to approach them; Cassidy heard the black woman snap irately at Valerie as the captain and Kevin still restrained her. Rowena, Allen, and Click all stayed back, as if awaiting some sign from the principals before they intruded.

Automatically reaching for the warden's hands again, Cassidy leaned in closer to him, studying those wide-set eyes. "What do you remember?" she asked.

His boyish brow furrowed; then an odd excitement came over his features. He squeezed her fingers. "Cassidy, I *saw* Cathy—I saw where she is!" His voice grew hushed with wonder. "She's lying on a tall narrow bed, covered with a white sheet." He hesitated, the shadow of his frown returning. "But she must be asleep, or sick; and there are these—things . . ."

Cassidy's grip tightened on his hands. "What kind of things?" she urged him. "What do they look like?"

The warden shook his head in frustration, the long forelock of his chestnut hair tumbling over his forehead. "I—I don't know," he admitted, disappointed. "There was something on her arm, but—" His expression was earnest, utterly sincere in his desire to be able to describe what he had seen, but he was stymied. "It wasn't anything familiar to me, Cassidy. I thought that I could at least tell you what it looked like, but—" He broke off again, slipping his hands free from hers. "I'm sorry," he said unhappily. "It wasn't anything I recognized, and now I've lost it."

Cassidy almost reached automatically for his hands again, as if by sustaining the contact she could somehow resurrect the image; but she stopped herself. "It's okay," she reassured him, an eerie if unwitting echo of her assurances to Andy only minutes earlier.

The warden raked his fingers back through his tousled hair, pushing it back off his forehead. "They tried to keep him from you," he said, seemingly so puzzled by that fact that he failed to notice how easily he had just fallen into accepting the existence of the two worlds that he was so uneasily straddling. "He thought maybe they had killed you." He paused uncomfortably, then suddenly looked directly into her face again. "He still thinks you're in grave danger, Cassidy; he's convinced of that."

Becky had finally either wrested herself free of Valerie and Kevin, or they had given up and released her. The little black woman strode right up to where Cassidy and the warden still knelt together on Cassidy's rumpled blanket. "Who the hell is 'he'?" Becky demanded of them. "And what do you mean, she's in danger?" She shook her head, her dark dreadlocks bouncing wildly. "Just what the hell is going on here?"

"Legitimate questions" came Click's calm drawl, "especially considering our purpose here." The Tinker had approached, as well, his lanky silhouette opposite Becky, with Cassidy and the warden between them. "And yet in this matter," he went on evenly, "they still are questions whose answers will have to wait on the indulgence of the warden and his Horseman." As if anticipating the inevitable further protest from the black woman, Click added with finality, "And if nothing else, they're questions that are better left to daylight."

His timely intervention seemed to have effectively diverted Becky's ire from Cassidy and the warden and redirected it toward the Tinker himself. Cassidy suspected that had been Click's intention all along. Sidestepping the edge of the blanket, Becky glared up into the shadowed oval of the much taller man's face. "I still want to know what the hell's going on," she repeated doggedly. "After all, we're all risking our necks in that damned crazy swamp. If they've found out something about the Memories or the Slow World, I sure as hell would like to hear about it!"

But Click's steady stance was unflinching. "I'm sure we'll find out everything there is to know," he said agreeably, "in the morning."

While Becky had been squaring off against Click, the warden had gained his feet. He took the few steps over to Becky's side and lightly touched her on the shoulder, his voice quietly reasoning. "The Tinker is right, Becky," he said. "We can talk about this in the morning."

The diminutive woman's baleful stare traveled from one of the two men to the other, and then back again. "Yeah, sure—the Tinker is right," she muttered, quite obviously aware of just how smoothly her demand had been defused. "The Tinker is *slick*, that's what the Tinker is. He must be just about the slickest white man I've ever seen!" Permitting the warden to guide her away from beside Cassidy's blanket and back toward her own side of the campfire, Becky shook her head in grudging capitulation. "We'll talk in the morning, then—but don't think that we won't talk!"

"Are you all right?" Rowena had come up behind Cassidy, touching her lightly on the back.

"Yeah, fine," Cassidy replied with a convincing calm. "Let's go back to sleep."

As Rowena and the others began to settle in again, Cassidy sat back cross-legged on her blanket and slowly let out her breath. Around the periphery of the banked fire, small adjustments were made as bedding was shaken straight and comfortable positions sought. In the dimness, Cassidy found the familiar sights and slight sounds reassuring. It was odd to discover that such mundane matters could somehow seem more immediate and real than the bizarre thing that had just happened between her and the warden.

Cassidy sat there a few moments longer, trying to decide whether she'd be able to sleep through the rest of the night if she didn't get up then and pee. The totally banal decision preoccupied her enough that when Click spoke up directly behind her, she nearly wet her pants in surprise.

"Cassidy?" he said quietly from the darkness. "I would like to speak with you for a few minutes, if I might."

Despite Click's polite phrasing, Cassidy didn't consider it a request; and the thought of suggesting that he wait until morning never even occurred to her. A few hours earlier, even the prospect of just sitting beside him had made her so uneasy that she'd been ready to bolt from him like a spooked horse. With a certain glum fatalism, she realized that like the night itself, Click was an elemental force of nature that could not be denied. Fires could be built against it, lanterns and lamps lit; but ultimately, when the small hours inevitably captured you, there was nothing left between yourself and the darkness but the strength of your own will.

"Just for a few minutes," Click repeated; and Cassidy could see in the dimness that he had extended one hand to help her to her feet.

Ignoring his outstretched hand, Cassidy stood. She shook back her tousled hair and tried to loosen some of the wary tension that knotted her body.

Wordlessly leading the way, Click started across the little clearing, his tread catlike and certain over the uneven ground, despite the darkness. Watching his black shape moving ahead of her, Cassidy found herself unwittingly thinking of Becky's words. *"I thought you and that Tinker were old friends . . ."* Carefully picking her way along after him, Cassidy mused ironically, *Yeah, once I thought that, too.* No matter what Click's intentions were then, she decided with a morose resignation, there was simply no way to avoid him any longer. Maybe it was best to just have it out and over with right there, so that during whatever remained of their arduous journey, at least she would no longer have to deal with the prickly uncertainty she had thrown up as a defensive barrier between the two of them.

One constraint of the location of their campsite was that they couldn't go too far from the fire without stepping off the edge of the ravine or plowing into the brush. And so they had walked barely a dozen yards before Click halted, by a clump of stunted dogwood at the margin of where the heavier undergrowth took over again. Cassidy was so distracted that she almost stumbled right into him when he stopped; but as he turned, she took a half step back, putting if not a comfortable then at least a conversational distance between them.

Click spoke without preface, his voice low and even. "After it had come over him, and he went to where you slept, and yet before he even touched you to waken you, you screamed."

It took Cassidy a few moments of mental scrambling to put Click's words into context and then to realize that it had been meant as a query.

"I was having a nightmare," she replied, "a bad dream. I must have screamed in my sleep, because I know that's what woke me up, not just the warden touching me."

Click was silent for a moment, and she grew increasingly uncomfortable It was stupid, she thought, since he was the one who had wanted to talk to her in the first place; but she was the one who felt compelled to go on, filling in the silence out of sheer uneasiness.

"It didn't have anything to do with his lapse—not my nightmare or my scream. The dream was just . . . frightening. I'm sorry, but at first I didn't even realize that I'd screamed out loud."

Click made some small movement, shifting his weight, and even though he had not moved detectably closer to her, Cassidy was aware then of the particular faint scent of him. It was as distinctive as the warden's scent, but definably different: old smoke and dried perspiration and the persistent herbal balm of Tinker soap. She could not keep from remembering the feel of him as well then, the warm solidity of his chest, the sinewy strength of his arms, and the stubbled roughness of his chin. She even remembered the sensation of his tongue against hers, and the taste of his mouth. There had been times since that night when she thought that what had happened had been nothing more than a dream; the only thing that made her certain it had not been were the physical sensations she could remember. And she could still call them up, in all of their perfect clarity of detail, whenever she needed to know that it had been real.

When Click spoke again, it tore Cassidy from the memory. "From the way you reacted when he first touched you," he said levelly, "I thought that perhaps something about it had been painful."

"No—oh, no, that wasn't it," Cassidy said hastily. What exactly had Click seen? she wondered. Had the stunning brilliance that had consumed her actually been visible? But then why had no one else ever noticed it? Peering fruitlessly at the vague suggestion of his features, she wished then that she could just see what was on Click's face.

"For just a moment," he went on, "perhaps before you realized who it was who had touched you, your whole body seemed to . . . contort." His tone grew more familiar then, dry humor tinged with irony. "Perhaps if that is the effect of dreaming, the rest of us aren't missing that much after all."

"Yeah, maybe you're right," she said warily, still unwilling to believe that he had dragged her out there at that time of the night just to ask her why she had screamed. When she'd followed him away from the campfire, she'd been convinced that Click was either going to ask her more specifically about the warden's flashes, or finally going to confront her about the one particular Memory they both shared—or maybe both things. She figured she could still bullshit her way around the first subject; she'd already had plenty of practice at it. And as for the second subject—well, Click didn't hold the exclusive right to confrontation on that little eye-opener. She had plenty of questions herself for that former captain of the Troopers, that one-time heir apparent to the title of warden, who just happened to remember sex.

But Click was neither confronting nor questioning her then. She saw the outline of his shoulders shift as he made a quarter turn back toward their camp. "We still have several hours until day-light," he said calmly. "We would be wise to get some sleep."

Surprised and inexplicably irritated, Cassidy blurted out, "*That's* all you brought me out here to talk to me about?"

She didn't need to be able to see Click's face to know what expression she would have found there; from the cant of his dark head she knew that one brow would be arched, the argent tips of his mustache lifted slightly in bemusement. "Did you think I intended to interrogate you about what happened tonight?" he asked wryly. "I assure you, if I had wanted to know more, I would have left you to Becky's tender mercies—the woman can be quite ruthless. But I meant what I told her: Whatever you choose to tell us is entirely between you and your warden. And," he added, "it most certainly will keep until morning."

Damn him! Cassidy thought, more nonplussed than angry; he was more than slick. With utter nonculpability, he had deftly maneuvered Cassidy precisely where he had wanted her.

Click took another step forward, lightly touching her shoulder to turn her in the same direction, his hand casually familiar. "Every heart has its secrets, Cassidy," he concluded softly.

When she realized exactly what Click had done, she almost laughed aloud at how skillfully he had managed to position himself, offering her both a challenge and a way out. Every heart had its secrets, indeed! Was he daring her to confront him about his own, or implying that he would not try to pursue any more of hers? And either way she chose to interpret his remark, Click had neatly stepped back beneath a cloak of innocence, leaving the decision entirely up to her.

For a few seconds Cassidy dug in her heels, both literally and figuratively, suddenly sorely tempted to violate that bizarre truce that Click had just so adroitly fashioned. But she had to admit that had she done so, she would have been acting only from anger, a reaction that the Tinker honestly did not deserve. How could she be angry at him for keeping secrets, when she had hoarded so many of her own, not only from him, but also from the warden and even Rowena? And so in the end, Cassidy allowed him to sling his arm over her shoulders in a gesture of simple comradeship and to lead her back to their camp without anything more being said between them.

There she lay awake for a very long time, mulling over the warden's spell and vainly trying to make everything she had learned from those episodes thus far fit into some kind of plausible theory. She was still working at it when the first birds of morning began to stir in the brush.

Chapter 10 ◀▥

A few hours of sleep may have blunted some of Becky's ire, but they had done nothing to lessen her resolve to learn everything she could about the warden's spells. The morning had dawned cool and clear, and the invigorating weather seemed only to have stropped the black woman's interrogatory zeal. As soon as everyone was up and moving in their camp, even before Rowena had finished preparing breakfast, Becky confronted the warden.

The young man accepted Becky's full frontal attack with good humor. Yawning broadly as he held up his arms in mock surrender, he said, "Could this at least wait just a couple of minutes longer, Becky? I'd like to be able to empty my bladder!"

Her wine-colored lips curling in a little smirk, Becky brandished her tin mug. "I don't care if you piss right here in my coffee, boy," she told him. "I just want some answers!"

"And you'll have them," the warden assured her, "just as soon as I've relieved myself."

Once the warden had slipped out of sight, Cassidy became aware of Becky scrutinizing her. She still felt uncertain about how much to reveal to everyone else about what had been happening during the lapses, but she gave the woman a friendly smile. If she was lucky, Becky would confine her inquisition to the warden himself. And not only did the warden seem unaware of the real significance of some of the things that had passed between them, he also had already demonstrated an admirable guile when discussing what he did know.

The usual routine of daybreak in the camp went on, blankets being shaken out, dishes being gathered together, and personal hygiene being attended to, just like any other morning. Accepting a mug of coffee from Rowena, Cassidy tried not to make more than fleeting eye contact with the brunette. Holding out on her best friend was not exactly something of which Cassidy was proud; and yet the more complex the situation had become, and the more people who had become privy to it, the more difficult it became for her to revert to the simple candor of their early days together. There would come a time—a more auspicious time, she told herself, and soon—when she would be able to tell Rowena everything.

Low, thin sunlight was gilding the ground, brush, and surrounding trees as the warden reappeared and approached the campsite. Kevin looked up uneasily from where he knelt rolling up his own, the warden's, and Valerie's blankets. Cassidy felt a stab of sympathy for the blond boy; in his own way, Kevin was at least as protective of the warden as was the more outspoken captain. Neither Kevin nor Valerie could have been feeling particularly comfortable with what had been happening to their leader, any more than they could turn a completely unjaundiced eye toward Becky's aggressive pursuit of the facts regarding it. But when Kevin got to his feet and went to the warden's side, the older man favored him with one of those fond, indulgent smiles he seemed to reserve for the young Finder alone, and he beckoned for Kevin to sit down beside him at the fire.

Allen and Click were seated on the opposite side of the firepit, engaged in a discussion of ways to increase their larder as they traveled. But when the warden returned, they both fell silent. Valerie came around the other side of them, passing a stack of plates to Rowena before sitting down between Cassidy and the warden. Rowena, busily tending to her pots and pans, was the only person who had not fallen into an unnatural and expectant stillness.

For a few moments the only sound was the raucous cawing of several big black crows, which had perched on the shattered stump of the old oak tree and lurked there, probably hoping for food. When they briefly fell silent, Cassidy was relieved that the warden began to speak. She had been afraid he would expect her to share in the narrative duty. But as he sat there cross-legged before their morning fire and calmly took up the first threads of the story, Cassidy realized what must have been apparent to him from the very beginning: To his mind, the lapses were his experiences; he was not only the logical choice to explain them, he was the only choice.

"I began to have these odd spells the very first night Cassidy and her friends came to my compound," the warden said, his long tanned hands loosely dangling between his knees. "But at first the episodes were so brief, so vague, that I didn't relate them in any way to her presence."

Cassidy could have predicted that Becky was not a woman disposed to allow his tale to remain a monologue for long. The black woman had a more confrontational style of discourse. No one, least of all the warden himself, seemed surprised when she interrupted him so early on.

"You didn't even make any connection to Cassidy after she told you she had the Memories?" Becky asked skeptically. "Even after she told you that she thought she knew you from the Slow World?"

"I had no reason to see any connection," the warden said patiently. "All that had happened to me were like momentary little lapses in awareness. I wouldn't even have noticed that anything was amiss, if others hadn't noticed." He glanced to the young man at his side. "Kevin was the one who first realized that I was having some kind of . . . spells."

Abashed by the attention suddenly drawn to him, Kevin ducked his head. "He would just kind of . . . stop moving for a few moments," he said softly. "He still seemed to be conscious—just not conscious of where he was."

"When the spells continued," the warden went on, "I even thought that I might be having dreams." He added, with a self-deprecating little smile, "Obviously, I had no idea of what dreams are really like, or I wouldn't have made that assumption." His hands shifted slightly then, the fingertips lightly touching. "The first real clue I had came the night we had to leave the city."

"In your bedroom," Becky recalled, "right before Valerie came to get you. That was the damnedest thing! It was like you were sleeping, or unconscious, except that your eyes were still wide open."

The warden gave her a rueful nod. "Perhaps I was lucky to have had no idea or memory of what was going on," he said wryly. "But when Cassidy came to me that night, she recognized something about me that no one else could have. During that brief period, I became exactly like Andy Greene, her friend from the Slow World. What's more, during the episode I also recognized her as Cathy, the person she believes she was in the Slow World."

Beside Cassidy, Rowena shifted a steaming pot of cooked cereal grain off from the fire. The thick, moist fragrance rose around them in the cool air. Momentarily distracted, Cassidy was mildly surprised when the next question came not from Becky, but from Valerie.

The captain's voice was neutral, her features without any specific expression. "But you didn't remember anything that happened during that spell," she simply pointed out to the warden. "All you have is Cassidy's word for what happened."

"Yes," the warden easily agreed, "from that time I only know what Cassidy told me. But the next time it happened, we had more witnesses."

"That first morning on the boat, after the storm," Valerie said, "when you almost went over the rail."

That raised a few eyebrows around the fire, but the warden merely nodded. "That second time, even when it was over, I knew that something very odd had happened to me." He threw Cassidy a glance before he elaborated. "Cassidy told me afterward that I told her, speaking as Andy Greene, that I had seen her—or Cathy—suffer some serious injury and be taken away. I was very agitated, very frightened for her safety. I kept telling her that Cathy needed help. Even when the spell was over, I still felt the vestiges of that fear, that profound anxiety for her safety." His fingers lightly meshed together, his youthful face grown pensive. "It was the strangest thing," he said quietly. "I think it was the first time I really understood what Cassidy had been trying to explain to me about my *becoming* Andy Greene, because I knew afterward that I had just experienced someone else's emotions."

While the warden had been speaking, Rowena had begun serving the food. Becky seemed annoyed by the distraction. But before the black woman could ask any more questions, Allen spoke up.

"You think that you actually went back to the Slow World then?" the big bearded man asked the warden. The set of his bushy brows articulated the skepticism that he had managed to keep from his voice.

Cradling his plate of cereal, the warden reflected upon that for a moment. "I realize that sounds crazy," he admitted, "but I believe that during my spell the two worlds somehow . . . connected. Whether I went back to the Slow World, or Andy Greene came into this world, the effect was the same. While it was happening, I *was* this man from the Slow World, the place where Cassidy was a woman named Cathy."

Ignoring her own plate, Becky impatiently shook back her dreadlocks and prodded the warden to continue. "So that was the second time it happened," she said. "But what about after that, after that morning on the boat?"

"When the monsters attacked," Kevin murmured, stirring uneasily at the warden's side.

The warden's casual posture didn't change, but he threw Kevin a brief look of reassurance before responding. "That was the next day, in the afternoon. We'd just sighted gulls for the first time, so we knew we were finally nearing land. Then the sea creatures began to attack the boat again." A small, self-effacing smile crept onto his lips as he recalled what had happened that day. "I guess one of the advantages of these lapses is that they temporarily remove me from everything that's happening around me. I didn't even realize that the boat was sinking until after the episode had ended."

"But was it the same?" Becky persisted. "Did you become this Andy guy again in the Slow World?"

For a few moments the warden just sat silently staring off across the fire, his untouched plate balanced between his knees. To anyone else he might very well have looked as if he were merely trying to remember all the details of some complex experience. But Cassidy suspected that there was another entirely different component to his hesitation, as well. That third episode had been the first time the warden had confirmed for her that the two worlds, his own and the Slow World, coexisted in some fragile framework of time, with the warden of Horses and Cassidy in one world, and Andy Greene and Cathy Delaney in the other. That lapse was when he had discovered that the Slow World was not just some distant relic of the past; it was nearly superimposed upon his own world, and he had somehow been able to cross the temporal border between them. Cassidy knew that the warden was hesitating then because he was undecided how much of that incredible realization that he was willing to reveal.

"I could remember more after that episode had ended," the warden finally resumed, not precisely answering Becky's question. "I described seeing Cathy again, in some building that had white walls and bright lights. And I still was very frightened that she was going to be harmed if she stayed there."

"You were frightened, or Andy Greene was frightened?" Valerie asked him, her tone suggesting more than mere curiosity. The captain was a tough one, Cassidy realized; not only was she intelligent, but she was familiar enough with the warden to see through any evasion on his part more easily.

The warden made a small shrugging movement. "At that time, Val, I think it was pretty much the same thing," he said. "During the flash, I *was* Andy Greene; and I responded as if I were there in his world, not here in this one."

"Then what about last night?" Becky said immediately. "Last night you said you were the warden; are you telling us that this Andy Greene thinks that he's *you*?"

The warden shifted slightly, absently setting aside his plate of untouched food. "I had another spell after that second one on the boat," he temporized, "a couple of days after we'd started inland."

"You woke up crying like a child," Valerie recalled, an abstracted, reflective look on her face. "You were so upset, you practically crawled into Cassidy's lap."

The warden nodded. "*Andy* was very upset. I think that Cathy is the only person he trusts, and he was still very frightened that someone was going to harm her."

"But when the spell ends, you don't know what it is he's so scared about?" Becky asked, frowning.

"No, but that's what Cassidy and I were trying to pursue last night," the warden said, adroitly bypassing the real significance of what had happened during his lapse that night on the beach—the night he realized that he was both Andy Greene and the warden of Horses, and that Cathy and Cassidy were one and the same person.

But Becky was not easily sidetracked. "If you think that you're Andy when you're having one of these spells," she pressed, "then last night why did Cassidy say that you were the warden?" Her forehead furrowed in concentration. "And why did Cassidy say that she needed the warden, not Andy, to do something for her?"

Shrugging again, the warden turned toward Cassidy, handing off the question to her just like lobbing her a hot rock. "I don't remember that part," he said, quite ingenuously and probably with total honesty. She and the warden had not had a chance to discuss further in private the ramifications of his most recent episode. And although the warden had remembered the image of what Andy had allowed him to see in the Slow World, it was also very possible that he had no knowledge or memory of the method Cassidy had employed to obtain that image from him.

Everyone's attention had turned to Cassidy then. She found her mind churning, desperately reaching for that same mixture of partial disclosure and honest confusion that had served the warden so ably thus far.

"The Andy Greene that I know is autistic," she began awkwardly. "Mentally disabled." She was acutely conscious that the physical embodiment of that same young man sat only a few feet from her, calmly listening. "In these lapses, when he becomes Andy, the warden's perceptions seem to be limited by Andy's condition." She searched for an analogy. "It's like asking a blind man to describe what he sees in a room," she said. "So I thought if I could get him to act like the warden rather than like Andy, he might be able to tell me more about whatever is happening to me—to Cathy—that has him so frightened."

It was a credible enough explanation, more plausible perhaps than even the truth would have sounded, and to her relief Cassidy saw that Becky and the others seemed to accept it. All except the warden, of course, she thought with asperity, because he already *knew* that he was also Andy Greene, even if he had not yet admitted it to anyone else but her.

But Becky was still not entirely satisfied. "Then what was he saying last night after this spell had ended again?" she persisted.

"I was trying to describe to Cassidy what she had been able to make Andy see, as the warden," the warden replied. "I could only remember the barest details of it after the flash was over. That's what makes these episodes so crucial," he added earnestly. "Each time I have one, I can remember more about what happened during it."

"You think that you can see back into the Slow World?" Allen said, not quite able to keep the dubious tone out of his gruff voice.

"Yes, Allen, I think I can," the warden said with quiet conviction.

"But what the hell does it *mean*?" Becky said doggedly, still not satisfied. Cassidy was bemused to realize that, very much like herself, the more the black woman learned, the more questions she seemed to have. "What's all this shit about Cathy, and a big house, and a bed?"

"If Cassidy's belief is correct," the warden said, "and she really was a woman named Cathy Delaney who came from the Slow World, then perhaps what Andy sees is what happened to her there."

"Well, she sure as hell isn't there anymore," Becky complained peckishly. "No one can be in two places at the same time. So why does this Andy still have his pants in such a knot over her?"

"That's something I hope we'll learn, Becky," he said, spreading his hands. "That's why the lapses are so important to what we're trying to do."

Oh, he was a slick one, too, Cassidy thought in silent admiration. The warden had deftly managed to lead them all just where he had wanted them, and he had done it so convincingly because he had never precisely lied; he had merely withheld the more incompatible truths. And yet even as Cassidy had watched him doing it, she never had the sense that he was enjoying the subtle misrepresentations he had painted. She suspected that, much like herself, he found the unmitigated truth of everything that had transpired between them both confusing and disturbing, and that he would have gladly shared it with the others if he had thought it could have somehow eased the path they had to follow. Yet like herself, he must have realized that until they could be sure just where the lapses were leading them, it would have been irresponsible and possibly even dangerous to take the others along with the two of them, just for the sake of having some company during the free fall.

There was a brief pause, during which the sound of Allen scraping his fork across his plate sounded unnaturally loud and seemed to trigger a rowdy chorus of caws from the nearby crows. Then the warden leaned forward, resting his elbows on his knees, and went on.

"Neither Cassidy nor I have had any control over these spells," he said. "I realize that they seem to occur at particularly inconvenient times, and so I am especially appreciative of your indulgence." He allowed his gaze to pan across the others, deliberately not singling out Becky for his remarks. "But because of their importance, no one else must interfere when they do occur." A small smile tugged at his lips, unwittingly capitalizing on his boyishly appealing face, and his gaze settled with an equal lack of calculation on Kevin and Valerie. "This is something I must ask of you as your warden, at least from those of you whose obedience I can still command." His eyes continued to move over the others around the fire as he concluded, "And something I must ask from the rest of you as your friend."

When they were passing out slickness, Cassidy thought, the warden must have been standing in line right behind Click. The charming young man should have been a politician.

Rowena had begun to pass the coffeepot, but Cassidy noted that most of them hadn't even touched their first mugful yet. With the discussion of the warden's spells over, she had to wonder just how satisfied Becky was. But the black woman merely dumped out her cold coffee, refilled her mug, and asked Rowena to pass her a little more hot cereal.

Sipping at her own mug of tepid brew, Cassidy was sure that Valerie and Kevin would not have questioned the warden further in public, even if they hadn't been satisfied by his explanation. And as for Allen and Rowena, her two friends probably believed that Cassidy had told or would tell them everything.

Peering covertly over the rim of her mug, Cassidy shot a swift glance in Click's direction. The Tinker was reaching for the coffeepot as it was passed to him, the expression on his lean, tanned face mild and inscrutable. As always, Click was keeping his own counsel.

Cassidy ate the rest of her breakfast without really tasting it, without even really being aware of most of the small talk that easily sprang up around the cook fire, even though she took part in some of it. She kept thinking about the warden and Andy Greene, who were—at least by virtue of the phenomenon of the warden's last lapse—one and the same person. If the warden had been able to blur that line between the two people, to bridge that gap between the two worlds, then what was to say that Cassidy couldn't, as well? If the warden could not only cross from that world into the real one, but also could retain his identity there rather than existing solely as Andy, then there must be a way that Cassidy could do the same.

Only one niggling concern kept intruding to disrupt the solidity of Cassidy's fresh resolve. Andy had told her that Cathy was in terrible danger in the Slow World; even the warden had seen her just lying there immobile. If Cassidy made it across the temporal breach, if she was able to reassume her rightful identity as Cathy Delaney, in just what sort of situation might she find herself there?

All day the weather remained fair and cool, and although the terrain was rough and trackless, they were able to cover a good distance. None of their attempts to hunt for fresh meat along the way had met with much success, but Valerie did manage to surprise and snare a few mourning doves in the thick brush. The birds didn't seem like much; skinned and gutted, Cassidy thought that their pitiful little carcasses looked more like someone's mutilated pets than like supper. But with a nod of wry deference to Webb's credo, she thought she had certainly eaten worse.

Toward dusk they found a good campsite in a slightly sloping little clearing beneath the spreading branches of a huge grove of maple trees. There nothing but the occasional stunted sucker poked its way up among the sprawling network of gnarled and protruding roots, and the ground was thickly covered with a bed of dead leaves. While Kevin and Becky cleared a firepit and gath-

ered wood, and Valerie spitted the doves, Rowena took up their
two canvas water bags and approached Cassidy.

"You want to hike over this ridge with me?" the brunette asked
her. "I think there's water on the bottom of that next ravine."

Cassidy had been examining the gray mare, contentedly fussing
with the big horse. After a day of trekking over hill and dale
through the rank undergrowth, the idea of "hiking" anywhere held
little appeal. But she knew Rowena could use the help as well as
the company. So Cassidy slapped the mare's shoulder dismissively
and said, "Sure." As she reached for one of the water bags, she
added, "Just so we get back here before her gets dark."

"Hey, no problem," Rowena assured her blithely, the other water bag slung over her shoulder like a large and ugly purse. "I've
already had my fill of things that go bump in the night!"

Noticing the two women starting toward the top of the slope,
Allen called out to them, "Need any help?"

Cassidy wouldn't have minded the burly sheriff's company, but
before she could reply, Rowena said, "No, that's okay; it'll only
take us a few minutes."

Allen regarded them for a moment longer. Then he said, "Take
all the time you need; just don't go out of earshot."

Cassidy and Rowena climbed the shallow incline in silence.
Even though the ground was crisscrossed with the twisted runners
of tree roots and littered with dry leaves, the footing was easily
passable if they gave it their attention. The gray mare tagged
along behind them, her hooves digging into the soft earth and releasing the deep musky smell of humus, as she nipped in passing
at saplings and stray bits of brush.

From the crest of the ridge, Cassidy could see that Rowena had
been right. In the ravine below them, the bright splash of a little
rill of water glittered amid the clumps of brush. When she looked
back the way they had come, all she could see of their campsite
was the leafy green canopy of the thick grove of maples.

"I think we're going to be out of earshot," Cassidy remarked as
they started down the steeper slope.

"Don't be so sure," Rowena replied, scooting down the incline
like a goat. "I can yell like a stuck pig if I have to."

And after the night of the fire in Double Creek Cassidy had
learned just how loudly a pig could squeal. Filled with an unexpected pang of nostalgia, she found herself reveling in the simple
camaraderie of being alone again with her best friend, facing un-
explored territory. Close on the heels of that pleasant memory
came a sharp prod of guilt. Not for the first time, Cassidy won-

dered if she was making a mistake by not confiding in Rowena about everything she knew about the warden's lapses into the Slow World. She hated keeping secrets from Rowena, especially after the matter of the monsters; and she wished that she had the benefit of her friend's perspective and memories. But the warden himself had set the unspoken boundaries of what he was willing to reveal. Friendship or not, Cassidy felt that taking the brunette into her confidence would have been a violation of the warden's trust.

They descended the slope along an old wash, a relatively clear but badly eroded stretch of ground where spring flooding had once swept away all of the superficial vegetation and most of the topsoil on its rush down to the creek at the bottom of the ravine.

At the bottom, Rowena shook back her hair and whacked the dust from the back of her trousers. She threw Cassidy a grin and said raffishly, "Express track!" Then she unslung her water bag and pushed through the waist-high bushes that crowded the edge of the small stream.

While Rowena began to fill the water bags, Cassidy pulled off her boots and socks and waded out into the cold, shallow water. She ignored the brunette's exaggerated expression of mock dismay and her loud admonition, "Hey, stay downstream, will you? We have to *drink* this water!"

Dragonfly had reached the bottom of the ravine and had splashed nosily into the creek about a dozen yards downstream. Cassidy watched with amusement as the horse played in the crystalline water as she hobbled on her bare feet over the algae-slicked pebbles that lined the streambed. When she approached Rowena, she startled the brunette by flicking a few spritzes of water at her. Rowena promptly retaliated in kind, and there quickly ensured a brief splashing battle, which dampened their clothing and left them both breathless from laughing.

"Geez, I feel grungy," Rowena complained, running her dripping hands around the collar of her filthy shirt. "It sure would feel great to take a bath."

"Not in here, it wouldn't," Cassidy pointed out with some asperity. "This water is like ice! Besides, with our luck some damned Woodsman would probably come along and steal our clothes."

Rowena did not respond immediately, but from the particular pensive expression on that broad and agreeable face, Cassidy knew that the brunette must have been thinking pretty much the same thing she was. It was inevitable to reminisce about their

early days on the run from Double Creek, back when being out-
witted by some Woodsman was the biggest problem they had.
Cassidy understood exactly what it meant to yearn for the naive
simplicity of those days, before their journey to find their way
home again had grown so incredibly complicated and had sucked
in so many other people.

"Well, at least if it happened to us again," Rowena said, "we
wouldn't have to go far to find a friendly Tinker."

Cassidy had been poised on slippery rock, about to climb out
of the creek. She nearly took a tumble at Rowena's comment.
Moving briskly to obliterate any traces of her initial reaction, she
dropped down onto the bank and reached for her socks.

Rowena merely watched Cassidy in silence for a moment,
toying absently with the straps of the bulging water bags. "Is everything okay again between you and Click?" she finally asked.

"Sure," Cassidy said, too swiftly to be convincing. "It's fine."
Socks on, she was staring at her boots, studiously avoiding looking over at Rowena. Nostalgia or not, Click was one subject she
definitely did not want to discuss with the brunette.

Rowena hesitated again, worrying the worn leather straps between her fingers. When she spoke, her voice was uncharacteristically subdued. "I know why you're mad at him, Cassidy," she
said softly. "And maybe he should have told us . . . but it isn't
like he ever lied about it."

Cassidy's head jerked up and she looked directly at Rowena,
surprised and more than a little flustered. How could the buxom
woman have known about Click?

Interpreting Cassidy's shocked expression, Rowena quickly
went on. "Listen, I know that he was the captain of the Troopers.
But his past has never really had anything to do with his dealings
with us." She spread her plump hands in a placating gesture. "I
don't think that you can hold it against him, Cassidy. He must
have had his reasons for leaving them."

Cassidy realized that she was staring stupidly at Rowena. She
tried to keep the odd relief she felt from her voice, without ameliorating too much of her expression of surprise. "How did you
know that he'd been captain of the Troopers?" she asked, honestly
curious enough to be able to hold just the right tone of voice.
"Did Click tell you?"

Rowena shrugged. "Allen told me."

Cassidy cocked her head. "Allen? How did he . . . ?" She broke
off then, the answer already self-evident. "The other Troopers."

The brunette shrugged again. "I guess all that time he spent hanging around the garrison was good for something," she said. As Rowena continued to study Cassidy's face, her tone grew more sober again. "No matter what might have happened in his past, I know we can trust Click. That night we had to leave the city, he was—" She broke off, her plump hands tightening on the water bags' straps. "I know he made it sound like getting out of the city and the whole trip down here was no big deal, but he saved our lives more than once. That mob would have killed us—hell, for a while there I thought even the *Troopers* were going to kill us." Rowena's voice dropped even lower, gaining intensity. "He *commanded* them to help us, Cassidy, and they listened to him. He risked everything for us."

"I know," Cassidy said. She was unable to shake the persistent image of Click with her on that wet city street, with the flames guttering all around them, and the smoky smell of the gray mare's steaming hide rising like incense in her nostrils. And she was equally unable to shake the memory of his whispered promise, or the shocking touch of his warm mouth on hers.

Like an eerie echo of that bizarre night, Dragonfly's loud snort shook Cassidy from her reverie. Rowena quickly got to her feet and looked downstream at the mare. "What's the matter with her?" she asked, more puzzled than alarmed.

"I don't know." Cassidy tugged on her second boot and stood, fighting the automatic reaction just to Call the mare until she could first see what the horse was going to do.

The gray mare was still standing knee-deep in the cold clear water, but all the playfulness was gone from her. Her long aquiline muzzle lifted, dripping, and surveyed the air, her nostrils bellowing out and fluttering. Her scimitar-shaped ears swiveled restlessly. She whuffed a few times, rapidly inhaling interrogatory breaths, and then snorted again.

Cradling the water bags to her chest, Rowena shot a quick glance around the brushy little ravine. "You don't think it's . . . ?"

"Monsters?" Cassidy easily supplied. "No, I don't think so." She didn't add that the horse had never seemed particularly alarmed by the hideous creatures. Cassidy scanned the surrounding area intently, but she saw nothing amiss. "She smells something, though."

"Maybe a fox or something?" Rowena suggested hopefully.

Maybe something a lot bigger, Cassidy was thinking; but she saw no purpose in saying that aloud. A little jolt of uneasiness jostled its way through her when she thought of the distance between them and the grove of maples on the other side of the ridge.

Suddenly the washed-out slope seemed far too high and steep.
"Let's just head back," Cassidy said, Calling the mare.

Rowena was completely agreeable, but with each of them
weighted down by a full water bag, they found the eroded stretch
of the slope almost impossible to climb.

"Sling that bag over your shoulders and hang on around my
waist," Cassidy instructed Rowena. Dragonfly was still testing the
air suspiciously. Cassidy tied a knot in the end of her long tail and
then sent the horse up the brushier part of the incline, allowing
her to tow them unceremoniously behind her. They had to stumble
over rocks and branches, and the ungainly water bags flopped and
buffeted them, but it was a swift and sure ascent out of the ravine.

At the top of the ridge, Cassidy released the mare's tail. As she
and Rowena both slapped the dirt and dead leaves from their
pants legs, she looked back down toward the creek. The ravine
was deserted and still, purpled in the deepening shadows of the
gathering dusk. And yet Cassidy still felt an abiding uneasiness
when she thought of the way the mare had acted.

By the time they returned to the campsite, Becky had supper
well under way, and Valerie's mourning doves were perfuming the
evening air with the distinctive scent of cooking meat. It made
Cassidy's mouth water, and she was willing to accede that the
scrawny little birds were looking better and better all the time.

"Beginning to think you two got lost," Allen greeted them
gruffly, relieving them of the heavy water bags.

"Do you think there're bears around here?" Rowena asked him
ingenuously.

At Allen's sudden sharp look, Cassidy quickly explained the
gray mare's behavior down in the ravine.

"But you didn't see anything?" Allen asked. When they both
shook their heads, he just gave a low grunt. "We're far enough
south, I suppose it could be swamp cats," he said.

"What are swamp cats?" Rowena asked, her tone more curious
than concerned. Back in camp, with the horse browsing placidly
only a few dozen feet away, the subject must have seemed largely
academic to the brunette.

"They're like a bobcat, but a lot bigger," Allen explained. He
stretched out his arms, the two water bags describing a distance of
five or six feet. "They've got a long tail, like a barn cat. But they
can climb like a squirrel, and they kill like a wolf."

Swell! Cassidy thought. What Allen had just described sounded
very much like a cougar or mountain lion, which could prove to
be another real hazard. Bogs, sinkholes, Woodsmen, and assorted

monsters seemed like trouble enough to her; they hardly needed the local wildlife to add to the danger of their trip.

"Do they attack people?" Rowena asked uneasily, no doubt thinking about just how exposed they had been down in that ravine.

"They usually avoid people," Allen assured her, "but we'd better discuss this with the others. Click might want to post double watches from now on." The big man swung around and had started back toward the fire with the water bags, when he paused and turned back to Cassidy again. "It'd be best to keep your mare in close at night," he said. "Swamp cats supposedly have a taste for horsemeat."

"Great," she said.

They found Click hunkered down with the warden and Kevin, testing the sharpened points of several long sticks. The Tinker had been explaining the strategy for hunting for rabbits with spears by flushing them from their runs at dusk, when they first came out to feed. He greeted the news of what Cassidy and Rowena had experienced in the ravine with thoughtful silence, and then concurred with what Allen had proposed.

"We're a bit far east for swamp cats," Click said, "but a hunting pair often maintains a large territory as their range, so it's possible that a couple have come into these hills. They like to stalk their prey in relays by keeping downwind; so if that's what your mare smelled, they weren't hunting. They also normally shun all contact with humans. Even if there is a pair of them about, it's unlikely they'll bother us." He rubbed his chin then, his callused thumb sliding up to stroke reflectively at the edge of his mustache. "But Allen is right about keeping your mare close to camp, Cassidy. Although their usual catch is small animals like rabbits, or the occasional odd marsh deer if they happen to get lucky, swamp cats do have an affinity for fresh horsemeat."

Cassidy threw an involuntary glance to where the gray mare was still browsing along the periphery of the brush as Click concluded, "We'll begin tonight keeping a double watch. There's no sense in taking needless chances."

The warden gave a small, wry smile. "The cautious man will live to bury a fool," he said.

"Discretion is the better part of valor," Cassidy murmured. As the others turned in unison to look at her, she was somewhat abashed. "It's just a saying we have in the Slow World," she said. "It means the same thing: Better safe than sorry."

"Indeed," Click said, his dark eyes gleaming with ironic humor. "Then starting tonight, we'll begin being doubly discreet."

Swamp cats or not, the next two nights and days passed without significant incident. The weather gradually grew warmer and muggier again, but the sky remained clear, with no threat of rain. The terrain became less hilly, the deep ravines and high spines of land giving way to more gentle inclines that were still choked with trees and brush. Small marshy meadows began to dot the occasional low areas, creating reedy little sloughs where peeper frogs sang and the insects churned up in lazy clouds above the tall, coarse sedge grass. The going was rough, but never impassable, and they covered a good distance both days.

At night they kept watch in pairs. Cassidy teamed up first with Kevin and then with Allen; but everything remained quiet. The mare was unhappy to have her freedom to range limited, but she more than made up for it during the day. While the terrain would have been a nightmare for a mounted rider, the trackless undergrowth didn't seem to deter the horse, and Cassidy was often surprised afresh by just how agile the big gray was.

Over those two days and nights, there was another sort of quiet, as well. The warden didn't have another lapse, and the uneasy truce that Click had conjured up between himself and Cassidy held. Too exhausted by dusk to do more than eat and catch a few hours of sleep until her watch, Cassidy ignored the vague feelings of anticipation and dread that dogged her. She could not help but wonder if the absence of more of the warden's episodes meant that something was keeping Andy Greene from Cathy again. But in a more pragmatic sense, she was relieved for the respite. It was not the best of times, but considering the hazards and arduous travel conditions, she was willing to settle for the interval of peace.

Then during the second night after she and Rowena had gone down into the ravine, their camp was disturbed a good part of the night by the gray mare's restlessness and loud whuffing and snorting. Something was about, and if that something was swamp cats, Cassidy wished the damned things would lose interest and move on. They had camped on a narrow strip of slough grass along the edge of one of the numerous little sumps, but with the dark tangle of forest all around them, there would have been ample cover even for large animals. Even after her watch, Cassidy abandoned the idea of trying to sleep, and stayed with her horse. She hoped to quiet the mare's loud snorts enough so that at least the others could sleep.

At dawn, Kevin returned from his early-morning trip into the trees with an odd expression on his boyish face. He went directly to the warden and said, "There's something out here you'd better have a look at."

Valerie and Allen had overheard and accompanied the two men back into the woods. More than merely curious, Cassidy followed them. About fifty feet from their campfire, less than twenty feet from the edge of the clearing, the blond boy pointed to a young hickory tree whose trunk was about the diameter of a man's thigh. From about a yard off the ground to a height of nearly eight feet up, the tree's bark had been slashed and shredded. The extensive damage involved nearly the entire circumference of the trunk, and looked as if someone had attacked the tree viciously with a machete or a gaffing hook.

As Allen and Valerie examined the destruction, the warden stood before the hickory and lifted his arms high over his head. The mutilation extended far over his head, almost as high as his raised hands could reach. As he ran his palms over the shredded bark, a few small curls of incised wood drifted down to the ground.

"You think it was a swamp cat?" the warden asked Allen.

The sheriff had circled the tree a few times, squatting to study the ground. But there was too much leafy debris to find any clear tracks. "Well, it wasn't a bear," Allen said as he stood again. "I've seen bears tear the hell out of trees, but their claws aren't this sharp." He traced one deep narrow gouge with his fingertip and then glanced up again at the upper limit of the lacerated bark. "All I can say is that if it is a swamp cat, it must be one damned big one."

When Click examined the damaged tree, his demeanor grew sober and his response became laconic and businesslike. He spent a good fifteen minutes or more silently and methodically searching the surrounding area before calling them over to a small pocket of muddy ground, deep in the brush beneath several large trees. Pulling aside the branches, he displayed what he had been searching for. A short series of distinct tracks were pressed into the bare, wet earth.

"Holy cow," Rowena said, kneeling to place her hand into one of the indentations. "How big *is* this thing?" Her hand, with fingers spread, barely spanned the pawprint.

"I suspect it may be a lone cat—a rogue," Click said, dusting some leaves off from his trouser knees. "Which might explain why it seems to be stalking us. Rogues are often too old or too crippled to hunt their normal prey successfully. Cassidy's horse probably looks extremely good to this poor fellow."

"Well, if you expect me to feel sorry for the damned thing, forget it!" Becky said indignantly. "Look what it did to that tree!"

While Cassidy could have agreed with Becky's sentiment, she merely asked, "What are we going to do about it?"

Resting his hands on his thighs, Click briefly surveyed the surrounding forest. "Hunt it down and kill it," he said then. "I doubt it will give up; we don't have much choice."

"Wait a minute," Becky interrupted him. "I don't want to spoil you boys' fun, but just what the hell are we going to kill this thing with? Pots and pans and jackknives?"

Turning to the outspoken woman, Click patiently spread his hands. "We have several good skinning knives, Becky. Lashed to a stout stick, each will make a serviceable spear." He paused, his gaze shifting then to Cassidy. "We also have two pistols."

Cassidy wasn't particularly surprised that the Tinker had admitted that he was still carrying a firearm, but over the past several days she had managed nearly to forget about the gun she still carried in her bedroll. As Becky and the others all looked at her, Cassidy shifted uncomfortably under their scrutiny. "It's gotten wet so many times," she blurted out, "I don't know how good it—"

"Bring it to me, Cassidy," Click said. "Any shells that are still in it are undoubtedly useless, but I have more."

Now why doesn't that surprise me? Cassidy thought dryly. But before she could go retrieve the weapon, Valerie rounded on Click.

"What is she doing with a gun?" the captain asked him tartly, her hands on her hips. "For that matter, what is a *Tinker* doing with munitions, and why—"

The warden effectively cut off Valerie's impromptu interrogation by reaching out with one hand, his fingers closing around her upper arm. As her words choked off, Val's head snapped around and she glowered at the warden; but she did not go on. "What is your plan?" the warden asked Click.

"We'll have to split up," Click replied. "Some of us can circle back around behind him." As he spoke, his fingers had begun to search the inside pockets of his leather vest. "Now is the time to do it, while he's likely holed up for the day and believing himself safely downwind of us."

Valerie didn't have to risk the warden's censure by interrupting again; Becky did it for her. "What do you mean, split up?" the black woman demanded. "If there's some damned cat out there big enough to leave those tracks, and mean enough to do that to a tree, I don't much favor the idea of us splitting up!"

Click paused just long enough to glance over at Becky, his dark eyes hooded beneath the sober cast of his brows. "The cat's been stalking us because of Cassidy's horse," he said mildly, even as he deftly extracted something from inside his vest. "If we split up and circle back around behind him, we can take advantage of the fact that he knows his prey is still ahead of him. He won't think anything is amiss."

But Becky, as usual, was not easily wooed by sheer logic. "Fine," she said. "If that thing's after the horse, I'd just as soon be somewhere else anyway! I'll just come with you."

Under less serious circumstances, Cassidy thought that the exchange between the black woman and the Tinker might have had its amusing aspects. Click's natural sense of irony would have surfaced by then, and he probably would have had some wry retort for Becky. But as it was, Click merely shook his head. "No, the warden and Allen and I will go back."

Becky had a quick tongue and no problem with reticence, but Valerie responded first. "I'm going with the warden," the captain said, easily assuming an attitude of command.

Cassidy had been watching Click's perusal of his pockets with interest, and she recognized the objects he had removed from them. They were bullets, their metal casings dulled by what appeared to be a light coating of wax or paraffin. He slowly rolled them across the palm of his hand as he regarded Valerie. It should not have surprised her, Cassidy thought, that a man like Click would have managed to keep his powder dry, come hell or high water. And watching him then as he calmly faced off against the captain, Cassidy was struck anew by how some of the most mysterious things about the Tinker had nothing to do with the secrets of his past.

"I need you here with the horse, Valerie," Click said. "In my judgment—"

"In *my* judgment your judgment is not to be trusted!" Valerie shot back at him. "And I'll be damned if I'll—"

From the grim expression on the warden's face, Cassidy was certain the young man was poised to intervene; but Click made that unnecessary. He cut Valerie off without even saying a word, silencing her by the simple expedient of taking a step toward her.

When he stood directly in front of the captain, he was a good head taller and although nothing in his posture could have been construed as threatening, everything about the man still commanded attention. He didn't need the leathers to look like a Trooper, and he didn't need the title to command like an officer. The attitude was still a part of him, much as he might have tried to bury it.

"I need you to stay with Cassidy and the horse, Captain," Click said, quietly and succinctly, unblinking in the face of Valerie's barely checked outrage. His free hand, the hand without the bullets, casually slipped inside the hem of his vest again. "If we shake loose this cat but don't succeed in killing him," he continued, "or if he just catches wind of us and bolts, the horse could be in danger." Valerie's eyes widened as Click held out both of his hands to her then, surprised into automatically reaching for whatever he was proffering. "And you're the best shot, Valerie," he said, passing her his pistol and the handful of bullets. Click allowed a small arch to quirk his brows and a barely perceptible twitch to lift the ends of his mustache. "Better than I ever was," he concluded, "and far better than Cassidy."

Outmaneuvered, disarmed figuratively even as she was armed literally by the Tinker, Valerie stepped back from him, her grip tightening on the weapon and its ammunition. The glare was still there in her dark eyes, but it was no longer precisely a look of contempt. "Do you expect to fail then, Tinker?" she said sarcastically; but the edge to her tone was far less convincing than it would have been a few minutes earlier.

Click's dark head inclined slightly toward her; not concession, Cassidy thought, but a sort of ironic accession. "I make it a practice not to expect anything, Captain," he replied.

Then the moment of confrontation between them was broken, as Becky loudly protested, "Wait a minute! You mean we're staying here with this horse—and she's *bait*?"

"You'll be safest here, Becky," the warden assured her. "We'll be the ones out stalking this cat."

Click had been searching his pockets again and had produced a long folding knife. "Just stay together and in the open," he said. "We won't be able to leave you much in the way of weapons, but Valerie can protect you adequately as long as she can see you." He looked to Allen. "We'll need a few good stout sticks to use for spears."

"I want to go with you," Kevin said. The blond boy had spoken so softly that at first Cassidy doubted if anyone else had heard him. There was no question that Kevin's protest fell outside of Click's domain, and he wisely stayed out of it, occupying himself with the contents of his pockets while the warden turned to face his most loyal friend.

"Kevin, I wish that I could have your help in this," the warden said with utter sincerity. He reached up and gently brushed back a few wisps of Kevin's long blond hair, which had escaped from his ponytail to hang like golden threads around the boy's deeply tanned throat. "But only Val and Cassidy have had any experience in defending themselves. Becky and Rowena may need someone skilled in fighting to protect them. I need you to stay here with them and the mare."

To Cassidy's ears, the explanation lacked a certain convincing logic, a lack that was only partially compensated for by its ego-stroking flattery. But then Cassidy was never going to be able to look up into those chocolate-colored eyes with the same innocent devotion as did Kevin. For a moment she thought that Becky, or even Rowena, might take exception to being classified as helpless; but if the reflex to object rose in either of the women, one look at the plaintive disappointment and reluctant acquiescence in Kevin's face must have caused her to choke it down again.

Then Cassidy was jolted from her contemplation of the warden and his young disciple by Click's voice quietly reminding her "Your gun, Cassidy?"

While Cassidy went back to the campfire to get the weapon, Allen and Kevin began to search for suitable saplings to cut for spears. Valerie methodically checked and loaded the pistol Click had given her. Glancing back at them, for the first time Cassidy felt a pang of guilt over her adamance about bringing the horse along with them. It seemed unlikely that swamp cats would have been a problem if they had been traveling without twelve hundred pounds of fresh horsemeat.

When she handed Click the small silver gun, she didn't realize what her frowning expression might have suggested to him. As he took the pistol, Click cocked his head at her and said lightly, "Don't worry, Cassidy; I'll try not to lose it."

Flustered, Cassidy took a quick half step back from him. "I wasn't worried about that," she said hastily, uncomfortable that she was more or less alone there with Click. The discomfort prompted an unwitting frankness in her. "I was just thinking that if I hadn't brought my mare, we probably wouldn't be having this trouble."

To her surprise, the Tinker nodded in agreement. "Quite likely you're right," he said, casually cracking the pistol's barrel open and starting to pry out the waterlogged bullets with his thumbnail. "Without the horse, you, the warden, Valerie, and Kevin all would have drowned in that river, and the rest of us probably would have long since headed back home to properly mourn your untimely deaths."

He was gently teasing her, she realized, not mocking her or making fun of her concern. And so Cassidy knew that the sudden color which had suffused her neck and cheeks owed nothing to righteous indignation. She was standing close enough to him to be able to study his face candidly then, without having to make any pretense of being oblique about it. As Click continued to clean and reload the small pistol, she catalogued every familiar feature of that saturnine face, as well as some things about it she had never noticed there before. Was there more gray in his mustache or did it just seem that way because he had allowed it to grow out a little longer than usual? There was no doubt in her mind that there were more lines bracketing those deep-set umber eyes and channeling down to the corners of his mouth; and what lines had already been there were etched even deeper, testament to the toll of fatigue and stress he had endured of late. And his eyes themselves, still bright with some secret irony, were more deeply hooded, set in a bed of bruiselike shadows that betrayed his long sleepless nights.

Cassidy found herself actually relaxing as she continued her forthright appraisal. Old feelings, feelings that had been deflected and denied ever since that night they had fled the city, overtook her again. She realized that she had never seen Click look so worn, not even after their arduous journey down the Long River, when he had been responsible for not only the whole band of Tinkers but for herself, Rowena, and Allen, as well. One restless night had left Cassidy feeling irritable and tired; yet how much sleep had Click been getting, even on the quiet nights? No matter who had the assigned watch, how many hours had he kept his own patrol, pacing silently in the darkness?

A distinct longing rose in Cassidy then, a yearning nearly as old as her association with Click. She wished that things could just go back to being the way they had been between them, before that kiss. She wanted desperately to give him her friendship and trust again. When he came back from the hunt, she told herself resolutely, watching as his long tanned fingers deftly snapped shut the shining barrel of the gun; when the hunt was finished and that particular danger was over, she would take another, more deliberate risk and try to bridge the rift his shocking secret had opened between them.

"Well, that takes care of my shirt," Rowena said cheerfully, holding the dangling thread from her sewing needle between her lips as she smoothed out the front of the garment. "Or at least as good as it's ever going to get. You sure you don't want me to fix up some of the rips on your stuff?"

She and Cassidy sat side by side in the long slough grass on the small slope that led down to the shallow marsh. Cassidy glanced over at her with a smile. "Thanks, but maybe later," she said.

Rowena ran her fingertips over the neat little stitches with which she had just mended her own tattered clothing and sighed. "Good thing Bonnie and Mitz can't see us now," she said, a trace of wistfulness coloring her humor. "They'd kill us—we look like a couple of tramps!"

Automatically checking for the thousandth time to see that the gray mare had not wandered from the coarse little meadow, Cassidy leaned back with her arms propped behind her and let her gaze run over the marsh's nodding green reeds. Thinking of all of the Tinkers' beautiful clothes just made her morosely nostalgic for the time she and Rowena had spent traveling with the band of itinerant craftsmen. It was a journey that she hadn't properly appreciated at the time, when she had been so impatient, so eager to get on and reach the Iron City and the warden of Horses . . .

"And if Bonnie could see you in that baggy outfit," Rowena went on, nodding to Cassidy's outsize seaman's cottons, "I don't know if she'd laugh or cry." Pausing a moment to study Cassidy's somber expression, the brunette offered again, "You sure you don't want me to patch up some of those rips for you?"

But Cassidy merely shook her head. Rowena had already repaired Becky's ragged clothing as well as she could; and neither Valerie's nor Kevin's leathers had sustained the kind of damage that a simple sewing needle could improve upon. The Troopers' outfits were more durable than cloth, even if they had become stained and had lost some of their fringes and much of their other ornamentation.

It was barely midday, and already Cassidy felt both anxious and bored. She had vainly hoped that the men would have returned by then, preferably dragging the carcass of a dead cougar; but they had seen or heard nothing of the hunting party that had left shortly after breakfast. Up until that morning, Cassidy would have said that she would have welcomed a respite from their travel, some time off to just sit around and rest. But after only a few hours of forced inactivity, she had quickly come to realize that unless you were traveling, there was stunningly little to do out there in the middle of nowhere. Before that morning, boredom had never been a problem. They had stopped only to eat and sleep, and were always too tired and too rushed to worry about anything more than the energy to go on. But being unwillingly stuck there at the campsite was both unnerving and stupefyingly boring.

Glancing over at her horse again, Cassidy realized glumly that she couldn't even go for a ride on the mare. Valerie was constantly surveying the entire clearing from her vantage point at the top of the slope, near the edge of the forest. Even if Cassidy had been able to escape the captain's vigilance, there wasn't more than a few hundred feet in any direction open enough for horseback riding.

Steeped in her melancholy musing, Cassidy started when she heard the slough grass rustle directly behind her and Rowena. Becky and Kevin came around alongside them, both of them looking as much at loose ends as Cassidy was feeling. Cassidy had only to remember Kevin's expression when the warden had left without him that morning to realize that she was not the only one faced with a long and unhappily impotent wait.

"You guys want to go swimming with us?" Becky asked them.

"Swimming?" Cassidy echoed skeptically. "Where? In that bog hole?"

The black woman shrugged in rare concession and said, "Okay, *wallowing* then."

Rowena looked from Becky and Kevin down to the marsh and then back again. "It's all scummy and full of algae," she pointed out somewhat reluctantly. Cassidy could tell that the brunette felt grubby and bored enough to be sorely tempted by the idea.

"It's not any dirtier than we are," Kevin said with a self-effacing grin.

"Yeah," Becky agreed, bumping the much taller blond boy with one sharp elbow, "and I told him if he didn't wash off some of that stink, I wasn't going to stay in the same camp with him another day!"

"Come on," Kevin entreated. "It'll feel good to clean up a little."

Cassidy figured that even "a little" was stretching the cleansing capacity of the reed-choked marsh beyond credulity, but she didn't say so. Instead, with a pointed glance over her shoulder, she said, "Are you sure Valerie will let you go in the water?"

"Yeah, it's okay with her," Becky said. "She just told us to keep in sight."

Rowena chuckled. "Well, you sure aren't going to be able to dive in over your heads in that little puddle!"

"So are you guys coming?" Becky repeated, her voice taking on its more customary tone of impatience.

Cassidy still demurred. "No thanks."

"Maybe later on," Rowena said. "We'll just wait and see how much good it does you two."

As Becky and Kevin resumed their way down to the edge of the bog, Cassidy leaned back again, sinking down so that she was propped on her elbows braced behind her. She tried to assume a no more than casual interest as the two would-be swimmers shucked off their clothes; but from the wry sidelong look Rowena threw her, Cassidy knew that she was not being particularly convincing. So she tried looking up at the cloudless sky instead, feigning a fascination with the featureless blue dome.

"Since I remembered sex," Rowena teased, "some things in this world have gotten a little more . . . interesting."

In spite of herself, Cassidy's gaze dropped back to the marsh, where a completely naked Kevin was playfully chasing an equally nude Becky into the shallow, torpid water that was nearly hidden amid the clumps of cattails and sedge grass. The contrast between the tall, coltishly lanky blond boy and the short, distinctly plump black woman was unavoidably amusing. But there was more than that to draw her eye to Kevin, Cassidy had to admit. He was nearly as uniformly tan as Becky was dark, his lithe body so appealingly proportioned that she was as much disappointed as relieved when the two of them tumbled, tripping over each other, into the greenish water.

"Maybe we should have gone with them," Rowena said jokingly, thoroughly enjoying Cassidy's discomfort, "in case Kev needs someone to wash his back . . . or whatever."

"Rowena!" Cassidy hissed at her, having to struggle not to smile in raunchy complicity. "That's not—"

"Not what?" the brunette said. "Not fair?" She flopped back alongside Cassidy. "In case you haven't noticed, these guys could care less. So we might as well look, because it's all we're going to get."

Both of them were companionably silent for a few moments, letting the sun soak their upturned faces, while the sounds of splashing and frolicsome cries drifted up from the marsh. Cassidy could imagine what Rowena was thinking about, and the brunette probably assumed that Cassidy was thinking about the same things. But Cassidy's thoughts had taken a different, more somber turn. Once again she recalled everything she was keeping from her friend, and again she seriously debated telling Rowena everything she had discovered about Click. But she kept running into the same immutable objection: If she told anyone else about what had happened between her and the Tinker, then it would become impossible for her to keep on pretending that it didn't matter. If she told Rowena the truth, then she would be forced to do something about it.

A particularly loud, playful shriek from Becky pulled Cassidy's attention back to the two bathers sloshing around in the slough. If she hadn't looked up then, she might have been completely blindsided by what happened next. As she watched Becky and Kevin splashing like two overgrown frogs in the knee-deep water, from the corner of her eye Cassidy caught a blur of movement racing over the coarse ocher-colored grass, directly toward the marsh.

Valerie's sharp, imperative shout almost caused Cassidy to look back automatically toward the captain. But when she did force her eyes away from the streaking shape, it was her mare that Cassidy sought. The gray mare was no longer placidly grazing near the trees. Suddenly the horse was in motion, thundering across the narrow meadow hard on the heels of the charging swamp cat, a whinny of challenge trumpeting from her throat as she ran.

Chapter 11 ◄▥

As she sat helplessly frozen on the ground, watching her mare race after the attacking cougar, Cassidy's first thought was both useless and inane: *I thought cats didn't like water!* She also had a split second in which to entertain the thought that since the swamp cat had been stalking the horse, it seemed particularly ironic that the horse was instead pursuing the cat.

The desperate cry of alarm and warning Cassidy had intended to give stuck mutely in a throat gone dry as sand. The first thing to jolt her out of her shocked immobility was the hard bite of Rowena's fingers digging into her arm, roughly dragging her to her feet.

"Down!" Cassidy heard Valerie bellow, and she spun around to see the captain pounding across the open meadow, Click's pistol raised over her head. "Drop down and *stay down!*"

But both Cassidy and Rowena stayed locked in place, unable to take their eyes from the terrifying scene in the marsh. Becky and Kevin had looked up just in time to see the big buff-colored cat hit the shallow water at the edge of the reeds. But to Cassidy's astonishment, neither of them tried to run from the animal. Instead they both dropped down into the slough, sinking like stones beneath the turbid, algae-covered surface. The cougar, temporarily blinded by the spray of water that it had sent up by plunging into the marsh, passed directly over the point where they had been standing only seconds earlier.

Cassidy finally realized that Valerie had not been shouting at her and Rowena; she had been commanding Kevin and Becky to get down. Even as Cassidy watched, the big cat swung around in a circle, its huge paws thrashing the reeds. Then the sharp retort of a gunshot cracked over the marsh.

The gray mare's pace had never slackened, and the horse hit the

water almost simultaneous with the sound of the shot. The wet
and angry cat spun toward the mare, an unearthly cry issuing from
its fanged mouth with a spray of spittle. Had Valerie *missed* the
damned thing? Cassidy wondered numbly. The captain wasn't that
far away, and Click had said she was the best shot.

In a blur of churning water and whipping reeds, the horse
reared, her forelegs darting out to strike at the screaming cat. One
dark hoof connected with the wet fur over the animal's long lean
back, and the angry screech became a howl of outraged pain. Seconds later Becky's and Kevin's algae-spattered heads breached the
surface of the water, both of them coughing and sputtering.
Cassidy realized then that Valerie hadn't missed; she had deliberately fired in the air over the cougar, because she couldn't risk hitting Becky or Kevin.

The gray mare struck again, her ears flattened against her skull,
her eyes narrowed to slits as her nostrils unfurled like bellows. By
then Valerie was almost to the edge of the slough. She slid to a
halt and held the pistol with both hands, braced out in front of her.

"Cassidy!" the captain shouted. "Call her!"

But even as the command was forming in the tumult of her
mind, Cassidy watched in stunned horror as the huge cat launched
itself up out of the murky water. Like some hideous parody of a
Horseman, the cougar landed on the mare's back. Its clawed forefeet slung like grappling hooks around the horse's shoulders, and
its rapierlike rear nails sunk into the silky hide over the mare's
loins. And in that moment, all Cassidy could see was her horse in
danger. All of time and the world was simply reduced to the gut-
wrenching sight of bright crimson blood blooming across that
sleek gray coat, and the glint of yellowed fangs bared to tear
across the mare's throat. And then the horse exploded.

Plunging like a rodeo bronc, the mare shot straight up into the
air, no two parts of her body seeming to agree upon the same direction for the ascent. When she hit the water again, on legs stiffened like pile drivers, she was facing nearly 180 degrees around
from where she had started. Immediately the horse launched herself again, her head and neck whipping down while her rump flew
up and slewed sideways with a vicious kick. No human rider
could have stayed astride her as she thrashed up out of the marsh,
bucking, twisting, sunfishing in a blur of mane and tail and limbs.

Valerie swung around in the knee-high grass. Barely a dozen
feet from the violent dance of horse and cat, the captain pivoted
to keep the pistol aimed on target. Cassidy could see the cougar's
snarling jaws and spread forefeet ripped free from the mare's

shoulders as the horse spun like a top. A splatter of blood and gobbets of saliva sprayed from the cat's head. Then the big cat's coiled body finally lost its grip on the mare's back, and it was abruptly slung loose.

For one discrete moment, every detail of the scene before Cassidy seemed etched in perfect clarity, enhanced by the frenetic goad of the adrenaline that poured through her veins. The angry horse continued bucking across the slough grass meadow, bloodied but not disabled. Then the cougar's piercing scream jerked Cassidy's gaze back to the cat, just as the tawny creature sprang upon Valerie. Suddenly the two bodies, one clad in leather and the other in wet, gore-streaked fur, were rolling across the ground, locked in a deadly embrace.

Kevin and Becky stumbled out of the marsh, soaking wet and clumsy with shock. They seemed to be moving in slow motion. Cassidy felt dazed and shaky; yet when the cat's powerful hind feet came up, slashing viciously at the woman he held captive in its grip, she found herself lurching into action.

Did Val still have the gun? Cassidy wondered with remarkable calm as she raced across the grass. All she could see of the entwined pair was a flying blur of limbs—fur and leather and blood. If the captain had dropped the weapon, Cassidy had no idea how to locate it in the trampled grass. Without the gun, they probably were as good as dead anyway, Cassidy decided with fatalistic detachment. She just did the first thing that came to mind. Running up to the pair entangled on the ground, she began furiously kicking at whatever parts of the cougar's anatomy she could reach.

Within seconds, her booted foot must have connected with some sensitive portion of the creature's body—its balls, she hoped with a fierce vengeance—to cause the cougar to drop Valerie so suddenly. As the animal swung around with a glottal roar, Cassidy stumbled backward. *Oh, shit!* she thought. She didn't have a backup plan. For a moment the cat crouched facing her, its long tail flicking like a whip; its oval eyes were as large and bright as two Krugerrands. Then the deafening crack of a gunshot set Cassidy's ears to ringing painfully.

Still lying supine, her face contorted with pain and the effort it had taken her just to bring up her arms and aim the pistol, Valerie fired off two more shots into the fallen cougar. As the tawny cat jerked for the final time, the captain's head fell back, the gun slipping from her bloodied hands.

Cassidy didn't remember moving, but she found the ground abruptly jumping up to smack her on the knees. Swaying for a moment on all fours, she tried to crawl toward Valerie, but the dead cat lay between them. Then she felt Rowena's hands gathering her under the arms, helping her make an uncertain return to her feet.

"Kevin! Get me my shirt!"

Becky's loud command caused Cassidy to start, for she hadn't even been aware that the black woman was so close by. Cassidy heard a loud groan, and then Becky's voice again, softer and reassuring. "Shh, don't try to move, you damned fool," Becky said to Valerie. "You're bleeding like a stuck pig."

The earth seemed to be wandering distressfully under Cassidy's feet. She leaned heavily against Rowena's solid bulk, murmuring "My horse . . . ?"

"Are you okay?" Rowena's voice sounded oddly filtered, attenuated by the peculiar buzzing in Cassidy's ears. "Your boot and pants leg are covered with blood."

"I'm fine," Cassidy asserted, even as she sagged, her weight pulling her free from Rowena's grip. She landed on her rump in the grass. As long as she was sitting there, she thought she might as well study her bloody trousers and boot. Her head jerked up again at an irritating sound, the high-pitched saw of ripping cloth. The abrupt movement of her head made her vision swim, and she swayed dizzily for a moment before she was able to focus again.

Becky, still naked as a jaybird, was crouched over Valerie's recumbent form, her dripping dreadlocks dangling as she swiftly and surely staunched the bleeding from the captain's wounds with the bindings that Kevin was obediently ripping in strips from what was left of Becky's shirt.

Cassidy looked up stupidly into Rowena's pale, concerned face and blinked owlishly. "It's okay," the brunette reassured her, trying to steady Cassidy by the shoulders. "Everybody's going to be okay—*Jesus!* Cassidy, you could have been killed!"

Cassidy just continued to stare up at her friend. "What is Becky going to use for a shirt?" she asked fatuously. Then, lulled by the dull roaring in her ears, Cassidy slumped sideways and fainted.

When she returned to consciousness again, Cassidy became aware that her head and shoulders were being supported by the firm but comforting presence of someone's lap. The faint scents of horses, leather, and old smoke surrounded her. Levering her eyelids partially open, she blinked with surprise into the full daylight. "Click?" she murmured.

A warm hand gently brushed over her forehead, shading her

eyes, and a soft voice—familiar, even if not the one she had expected—said, "Easy, Cassidy; don't try to sit up too quickly. You still look pale as plaster."

Ignoring both the warden's advice and his unflattering comparison, she reached up for his shoulder and used the leverage to pull herself into a sitting position. Her body protested the maneuver with a symphony of new aches, and her mouth felt cottony and sour, as if she'd been sucking on old socks. "My horse?" she croaked, still clutching the warden's shoulder for support, as she forced her gritty eyes to focus on that handsome, sympathetic face.

His own hands went to Cassidy's arms to restrain her. "She'll be fine, Cassidy," the warden quickly assured her. "Allen and Click are treating her wounds right now."

Reluctantly conceding that she was nowhere near able to leap to her feet and go to the horse then, Cassidy turned her head, scanning the meadow for Dragonfly's reassuring presence.

"Don't Call her," the warden reminded Cassidy, his hands lightly squeezing her arms. "She's right there; see her? Click will poultice her wounds."

Once Cassidy was a little better able to orient herself, she realized that she was still sitting right where she had fainted. But the dead cat no longer lay a few feet from her, and Valerie was no longer sprawled just beyond on the flattened spot of blood-soaked grass. Swallowing dryly, Cassidy croaked, "Valerie?"

"They've just moved her nearer to the fire," the warden said. "Becky needs to suture some of her wounds, and—" He broke off as he realized the exact implication of Cassidy's query. He met her eyes directly, reinforcing his assurances. "She's lost a lot of blood, Cassidy, but she'll be all right." His fingers briefly tightened again on her arms. "They tell me that you probably saved her life."

Looking away from that grave face, Cassidy's gaze skipped over the tawny meadow until she picked out the gray mare. "No, Val's the one who saved us," she said quietly, her voice still raspy. She looked out steadily over the grass, to where Allen stood beside the bloodied horse, and Click was hunkered down amid the coarse stalks, working over something on the ground. "She could have shot sooner—she could have protected herself. But she didn't."

To Cassidy's surprise, the warden drew her in closer to himself, almost into an embrace. He gave her a gentle little shake. "Val would never have risked hitting your horse," he told her, his tone near admonishment. "She had to wait until the cat was clear of the mare."

Uneasily allowing herself to accept the dangerous comfort of his closeness, Cassidy relaxed against the warden's arm. She had finally located Valerie's recumbent form up by the campsite, spread on a cushion of blankets, with a half-naked Becky bent over her. Rowena was tending something in a pot at the freshly kindled fire, with Kevin squatting beside her to feed more wood into the flames.

"They're boiling a few horse tail hairs," the warden said, following her gaze, "so Becky can use them for sutures. No, don't try to get up yet."

The last was said when Cassidy shifted in his arms, automatically preparing to get to her feet and go to offer assistance. "I can help," she said insistently.

But the warden continued to restrain her. "Everything is under control, Cassidy," he soothed. "I want you to rest yet; you really look pretty shaken."

Cassidy irrationally resented the characterization, but she acquiesced nevertheless. She hadn't been aware of just how carefully the warden had been studying her face until he spoke again, his voice low and confidential.

"Cassidy, did something . . . something else happen before you lost consciousness?"

It took her a few moments to comprehend just what he was being so circumspect in asking. Only then did she realize that it had been the first time in that world that she had simply fainted, without it having had anything to do with the Memories. "No," she said quickly, "it wasn't anything else. You mean like when I first saw you?" As he nodded, she felt herself color slightly, a bit embarrassed at having merely been susceptible to exhaustion, stress, and fear—just like everyone else. "No," she reiterated, "I just fainted. I guess it just finally occurred to me how close I came to being killed by that damned cat!"

With genuine affection, he tousled her already disheveled hair. "You're completely worn out," he said with fond but firm concern. "I'm going to roll you up in your blanket, and I want you to sleep for at least a few more hours."

"But—"

"No," he said flatly, in his best commanding tone. "Click and Allen will see to your horse, and Becky has plenty of help with Val. You're going to rest."

Her second attempt at protest was truncated when she found

herself being lifted in his arms, the warden gaining his feet with as little effort as if she weighed no more than a bedroll or an empty kettle. "I can walk!" she objected, but without much conviction. He didn't even bother to validate her assertion with any comment.

Cradled against his leather-clad chest, her arms around his neck, Cassidy gave in and decided that being carried made a lot more sense after all. As the warden walked, their bodies swayed gently together; it was almost like being astride a horse. Later, she would realize that she could not even remember him ever setting her down, for she was asleep before she ever touched the ground again.

When Cassidy awoke again the sun had sunk beyond the marsh, the tips of the cattails and slough grass bathed in ephemeral gold as the surrounding brush and trees were already cloaked in shadow. In the last of the dusk's fading light, she briefly grappled to free her arms from the blanket and then sat up, yawning. She felt stiff but rested.

Valerie lay a couple of yards away, only her head protruding from her blanket. The captain's face was partially averted, her eyes closed, her breathing slow and regular. Becky sat alongside the sleeping woman, her own blanket wrapped around her shoulders like a poncho and a steaming mug cradled in her small hands. When she noticed Cassidy stirring, she looked over at her and said, "Well, well; glad to see you join the living."

The cook fire had been built up to a steady blaze, its warmth detectable even from where Cassidy sat. Rowena was marshaling her pots and pans, well into the preparation of the evening meal. Kevin knelt at her side, moving pots and stirring things for her, his boyish face wreathed in fragrant steam. A few feet away, the warden sat cross-legged on his bedroll, sipping at a mug of something hot. When Becky spoke to Cassidy, the others all looked over and saw that she was awake.

The warden smiled at Cassidy, that utterly innocent smile which unwittingly transformed even his careworn face to such devastating effect. "How do you feel?" he asked her, adding even before she could answer, "You look far better than you did this afternoon."

"That wouldn't take much," Rowena said, pouring a mug of coffee for Cassidy from the pot. "You really looked like shit!"

"Thanks," Cassidy said dryly, reaching over to take the mug.

She settled back on her blanket, looking to Valerie again. "How is she?" she asked Becky.

The black woman shrugged economically but eloquently. "She's not going to feel up to wrestling any swamp cats for a while, and she's going to have some interesting scars to show off back at the garrison, but given some time, she'll heal."

Cassidy gazed silently at the blanket-covered form for a few moments, struck by how even the glow of the firelight seemed to flatter the captain's high cheekbones and elegant features. "She saved our lives," she said softly, to no one in particular.

"As was her duty," a matter-of-fact voice said from over Cassidy's shoulder. She turned to see Click materializing from out of the gathering gloom. He carried a small kettle, which he handed to Rowena before dropping down into a squat between her and Cassidy.

Of all of the myriad of topics that Cassidy was not going to debate with the Tinker, Valerie definitely was high on the list. Instead she set aside her mug of coffee, which still was far too hot to drink anyway, and said, "I want to see my horse."

Squatting there, his forearms resting on his bent knees with his long hands dangling between them, Click looked utterly at ease. Only the light of the fire betrayed him, ruthlessly revealing the haggard cast to his features even as it had flattered Valerie's, magnifying the lines on his face and the dark rings under his eyes. Seeing his exhaustion, Cassidy was immediately reminded of the resolution that she had made only that morning, before Click had gone off to track down the cougar. She had been determined to reclaim her old relationship with him. It had seemed so elementary then; but looking over at him, squatting there beside her, Cassidy suddenly was far less certain.

"Very well," the Tinker said to her. "But don't Call her." He smoothly gained his feet again, straightening out of the deep squat with an easy fluidity that belied his fatigue. "It would be better if she doesn't move around yet tonight," he explained, "so that the poultices stay on her wounds." He extended Cassidy a hand to help her up, cocking a dark brow at her as she failed at first to reach for it. "She doesn't care much for this coarse slough grass," he added. "Allen is cutting her some good browse, so she won't have to forage for herself overnight."

Belatedly gripping his hand, Cassidy stood, briefly unsteadied by the sudden ascent. "Is she lame?" she asked him anxiously.

But Click shook his head. "No, but she'll certainly have some stiffness for a few days. The cat's claws didn't penetrate very deeply, but these kinds of wounds are always nasty."

"What did you poultice her with?" Cassidy persisted, stepping awkwardly over her blanket and only then discovering that Click still held her by the hand.

"Come," he said. "I'll show you and explain everything."

Momentarily distracted by the process of trying to extract her hand unobtrusively from Click's, Cassidy nearly missed the warden's words of concern. "Make this a brief inspection, Cassidy," the young man said from across the fire, his bantering tone a thin disguise for his honest regard for her welfare. "Right now the horse still looks better than you do."

"Yeah, and this food'll be ready in about ten minutes," Rowena added; although Cassidy noticed that the brunette did not make eye contact with her.

Cassidy was well aware of the secret perverse delight Rowena must have been taking in the idea of Cassidy tramping out into the darkness alone with Click. She was damned if she was going to give Rowena the satisfaction of seeing her display any discomfort, so she stopped trying to slip free from Click's hand. And she was genuinely touched by the warden's concern. "Don't worry," she said. "I'll be back before you know it."

Just a few yards from the campfire, even before Cassidy had begun to reassert her struggle for the repossession of her hand, Click simply let go of her. The unexpected action caused Cassidy to fall a step behind him, and she stumbled to catch up again. Away from the fire's light, it was already nearly fully dark; the coarse grass underfoot was only a faintly lighter blur. Fortunately it was only a few dozen yards across the small meadow to where Dragonfly stood, and neither of them felt any need to speak.

The contrasting lightness of the mare's body resolved itself into a large silver shape as they approached; the mare's long pale face turned toward them, a throaty nicker rumbling in greeting. Cassidy was ambushed by emotions so deep and overwhelming that she suddenly felt her throat close and her eyes sting. Moving past Click, she took the last few steps on legs gone rubbery with relief. Then she had the big head clutched to her chest, and her face was pressed into the thick mass of the mare's mane.

For a few long minutes Cassidy just stood there holding the horse, reveling in the feel, the scent, the solidity of her. The tears seeped out from behind her clenched lids and trickled across her cheeks. She wasn't sure she had ever felt happier to see Dragonfly, not even that afternoon when Click had ridden the mare into the Deadfall River to drag them out of the sinkhole. Then again, the mare had not been in any danger then; she had not been wounded and mere seconds from having her throat torn out. After what had happened with the cougar, everything about the horse seemed like a fresh miracle to Cassidy: the broad planes of her skull, pressed against Cassidy's chest; the perfect symmetry of her curved ears; the velvet of her muzzle and the coarse hair of her mane; and the fine sweet smell of her breath against Cassidy's belly.

After a time, when Cassidy had begun to try to snuffle up some of her tears, she became aware that Allen had come around from the other side of the horse and that he was standing there, his arms filled with leafy branches. There had already been a considerable pile of fodder on the grass in front of the mare, but the big bearded man had cut even more, and had obviously been hesitant to disturb Cassidy and the horse by tossing down the last of it. When she released the mare's head and took a small step backward, wiping the back of one hand across her wet eyes, Allen dropped the branches and gave Cassidy a nod.

"You okay?" he asked her gruffly.

"Yeah," she said, disconcerted to find that her voice broke on even that single word.

In the near darkness, Cassidy couldn't see the exact expression on Allen's face; but she knew him well enough to recognize the genuine concern in his blunt query. She was grateful for the care he'd given to Dragonfly, and would have said so, had she been able to trust her voice. But before she could speak up, Click did.

"They have hot food waiting for you," he said to Allen, "and you're long overdue for a chance to just sit for a while."

Click clapped Allen on the arm as the larger man turned away and started back across the meadow. The gray mare had already dropped her head to investigate the fresh fodder. While Cassidy absently stroked the long, lowered neck and tried to compose herself, the horse began to sort deftly through the branches for the youngest leaves and tenderest tips.

Once Cassidy had sniffed up most of her tears and crudely wiped away the rest by rubbing her face against the shoulders of her cotton shirt, she began to take a closer look at the mare's body. What she found first puzzled and then surprised her; for spread across the gray's withers, shoulders, and loins were large, irregular patches of something much darker than the horse's coat and raised lumpily above it.

Throwing a quizzical glance over her shoulder at Click, Cassidy stepped back along the horse's side and gingerly reached out to touch the nearest swatch. Its surface was cool and sticky, but the entire patch felt spongy beneath her exploring fingertips. The mare didn't flinch away, but she did exhale with a loud, rude snort, causing Cassidy to jerk back involuntarily.

Cassidy looked to Click again. "What did you poultice her with?" she asked again, baffled by the dressings.

Click took a step closer; in the dimness, only the silver conchaes on his vest stood out clearly. "Valerian, wintergreen, and cattail root," he said. He paused while he took another step forward, which placed him right next to Cassidy. "The coverings of the poultices are pieces of hide from the dead cat." His shoulders traced a small shrug. "I skinned it and scraped off the hair. The rawhide stays flexible as long as it's wet, and it molds to the shape of her body. The natural tissue adhesives—"

Click broke off then, for Cassidy had begun to make a most peculiar sound. Her torso was jerking in small, regular spasms, and the laughter finally burst from her in a helpless gale. Coming hard on the heels of her episode of weeping, the sudden display of hilarity might have appeared both bizarre and unseemly. And indeed Cassidy felt completely out of control, her loud expression of mirth leaving her weak-kneed, teary-eyed, and in imminent danger of wetting her pants. But perhaps it was that very juxtapositioning of emotions that made the hearty laughter all the more necessary. Her feelings had truly run the gamut that day, from anxiety and longing, to boredom and terror, and then finally to relief and release.

Click did not seem at all disturbed by her odd behavior. If anything, from the cant of his dark head, he seemed more bemused than anything else. And since he was still standing right beside her, it was a simple enough matter for him to reach out when Cassidy swayed, as she gasped to catch her breath, and to support her with a hand around her upper arm.

"God—I'm sorry!" she sputtered, when she was finally able to speak again. "It's just that it struck me, this is the *second* time today that my horse is wearing that damned cat!"

Click made a small sound of amusement, as Cassidy coughed, hiccupped, and brushed the back of one hand over her freshly streaming cheeks. Clearing her throat, Cassidy looked up then to find herself standing directly in front of Click, his face a featureless oval in the darkness of the deserted meadow. He was so close that she imagined she could feel the tiny stirring of the air from his breathing, could even feel the warmth of his body heat across that small gap that barely separated them. The faint scent of old smoke and perspiration and herbal soap seemed to bring him even closer, so close that it was almost no different than if she had been touching him. And as she stared up wordlessly at him, suddenly so sober that the whole world seemed preternaturally silent, Cassidy thought for one amazing moment that he was about to kiss her again.

"What—what happened out there this morning?" Cassidy blurted out, catching her balance by taking a half step back from Click. "When you went after the cat?"

His hand still rested on her arm, and there was a gentle note of self-mocking in his voice. "It took us most of the morning to track him to where he had holed up, beneath a big deadfall in one of the ravines. But whether he'd heard us coming or caught scent of us, he was gone by the time we'd gotten there. All he'd left behind were a few bits of rabbit hide and several piles of scat." Click shifted slightly, not moving closer, yet making Cassidy even more acutely aware of his proximity. "We realized he was probably headed back this way, so we didn't even try to track him. We just came as quickly as we could." He paused before concluding dryly "Unfortunately, even an old swamp cat moves much more quickly than three men."

Cassidy was silent for a moment, uncertain how to respond. It seemed presumptuous of her to offer Click platitudes, to tell him that he and the warden and Allen had done the best they could under the circumstances. She didn't want to infer in any way that she felt he was responsible for the ultimate outcome, because that was absolutely untrue. So she allowed her absence of a reply to his last comment become, by default, her response. Instead she said, "I'm just glad Valerie had your gun."

In the near darkness she saw the dim outline of Click's shoulders rise and fall. "As it turned out, it may have been better if I had left you your gun, as well."

Again Cassidy could not bring herself to agree with him, for to do so seemed like nothing but meritless castigation for events no one could have predicted. She veered away from the topic of what had already happened and voiced what she knew must have been a common concern around their campfire that night, even if no one else had yet broached the subject. "What will we do now?" she asked Click. "Will Valerie be able to travel?"

Cassidy could not read his expression, but she could see the broad movement as Click shook his head. "Her wounds aren't life-threatening, unless infection sets in," he said. "But she's lost a lot of blood, and there's been enough damage to her legs that it will be some time before she's fit to travel."

Cassidy hesitated a moment, then said, "How long do you think it'll take for her to recover?"

Rather than directly answer her question, Click asked one of his own. He shifted again, moving slightly nearer, seeming to study Cassidy's face in the cloaking darkness. "How crucial is time to this quest of yours, Cassidy?" he said, his voice quiet and unexpectedly intent. "How quickly must you find this Alchemist?"

Because she found the intimacy of his closeness discomfitting, Cassidy had to lower her face. "I don't know," she admitted, shaking her head helplessly. She didn't need to add the obvious: *If we ever find him—if he even exists.*

A welcome touch of wry amusement leavened Click's tone then, even if his face was still unnervingly close to hers. "That's one of the problems with not being certain exactly where you're going," he said. "You have no idea how long it might take to get there."

Cassidy started perceptibly as Click's free hand landed on her other arm; his touch was light but distracting.

"In his lapses, the warden senses that you are in great danger in your world," he went on. "I think we must assume that time could be crucial here."

Cassidy was reluctant to concur, but there was no way around it. "Are we going to have to leave Val behind then?" she asked, unable to keep a note of distress from her voice. The captain had saved both her and her horse's lives. She was loath just to abandon the woman as reward for that heroism.

Click's hands tightened gently, reassuringly, on her upper arms. "We'll discuss it in the morning, Cassidy, when we have a better idea how she's doing. I won't endanger her life; it would be foolish, and it's not necessary. But yes, I'm afraid we will have to go on without her."

Temporarily looking beyond her own dismay at the prospect, Cassidy had a moment of insight into the dilemma that was unique to Click. Given the bitterness between him and Valerie, and the supposed betrayal of duty that had led to her emnity, it would be particularly difficult for the Tinker to have to abandon the captain, no matter how valid the reason. Cassidy didn't want him to have to make that decision alone.

"Listen, I know you're in charge," Cassidy said, "but I don't think it's fair for you to have to be the one to make a decision like this on the basis of—"

Click cut off her anxious words by smoothly placing his fingers over her mouth, startling her into silence. He kept his hand against her lips even as he said, "Yes, I'm in charge; but we all will discuss this, Cassidy." His dark head canted slightly, and she could imagine, even without seeing it, the arch of his brows and the lift of that silver-tipped mustache. "It may not be a popular decision, but it will be a fair one." Slowly lowering his hand then, his fingers lingered lightly over her lower lip. "And I think Valerie might surprise you," he said. "She might very well be the one who insists most vehemently that we go on without her."

Somehow Cassidy doubted that, but she was too distracted by the intimacy of Click's touch to say as much. As they stood there, she thought again of that brief moment after her burst of uncontrolled laughter, when he had moved in so close. Had she been afraid that he would kiss her again—or disappointed when he hadn't? Ever since the night they had fled the burning city, Cassidy had thought her crucial question to him would be *Why didn't you tell me?* But now, heady with the sense of his nearness, she wondered if her real question was instead *Why did you ever let me find out?*

Suddenly Click's hand was slipping from her upper arm, sliding down to clasp her hand again, his warm, callused fingers lightly meshing with hers. "Come," he said, gently tugging her after him, "we'd better get back and eat." As Cassidy stumbled after him, Click added, "I wouldn't want the warden to think you'd come to any harm out here."

The easy teasing in his voice made Cassidy realize that perhaps she had at least partially achieved her goal after all. Click seemed entirely comfortable with her again, and she had survived yet another bout of his friendship.

Her dream was one of those intensely explicit erotic ones, even though it seemed to start out benignly enough with her riding Dragonfly. The horse's forequarters, unmarred and powerful, bunched and surged rhythmically between her gripping knees, and the heat of the mare's back seeped through her pants legs and into her thighs. The wind carded through her own hair, even as it tossed the gray's long mane as the horse galloped on.

Then that perfectly synchronized coupling segued seamlessly into a coupling of another sort, the kind of joining that seemed to drain all of the blood from her brain and to pool it, urgent and pulsing, in the core of her body. The other body that fit to hers then was not the gray mare's, and the head that she pulled down

*against her own was not the horse's. She didn't know whose body
and head it was. But perhaps that was the real beauty of erotic
dreams, she thought hazily, even as she pushed back against the
heat of that phantom touch, the utter simplicity that could never
be duplicated in the waking world. The dream lover was always
perfect because he was totally the creation of the dreamer.*

Cassidy was just reaching that transcending crescendo of pleasure that usually presaged a muzzy and sated awakening when she
was rudely snatched from the arms of her ethereal partner. Very
corporeal fingers were gripping her by the shoulders, lightly but
insistently shaking her, as a familiar but distinctly apologetic voice
roused her.

"Cassidy? Come on, Cassidy, you've got to wake up," Rowena
entreated her. "He's having one of those spells again!"

Still groggy, and disoriented from the graphic nature of her
dream, Cassidy muttered, "Andy?"

"Yeah, that's who he thinks he is," the brunette said, still shaking Cassidy.

Opening her eyes into almost total darkness, Cassidy blinked in
confusion. It took her a few moments to realize that she had expected it to have been the warden—or Andy—who was trying to
awaken her. Then she heard a plaintive wail from the other side
of the firepit, and she abruptly sat up.

"When?" she asked Rowena, clumsily kicking free of her blanket. "When did he start?"

"Geez! Just a minute ago," Rowena replied, as the two of them
tripped across the brunette's blanket and nearly fell over Allen,
who had been just about to stand up.

"Hurry up, will you?" Becky's voice shot out from the dimness
on the other side of the fire. Cassidy could barely make out the
black woman's diminutive form, crouched protectively beside
Valerie's supine body. "I don't want all that damned yelling upset-
ting her!"

If Valerie was still asleep, she must have been the only one,
Cassidy thought; for Andy's agitated cries were loud and heart-
rending enough to jolt even a heavy sleeper like Rowena into consciousness. As Cassidy followed the brunette in the near darkness,
tripping over pots and pans and the stack of extra firewood, she
could finally see where the warden had spread his blanket. The
bedding had been flung aside, as if hastily discarded when the episode had overcome him, and he was down on his knees in the
flattened coarse grass, crying out her name. Click held him by one

arm and Kevin by the other; but both men were barely succeeding in preventing his frenzied escape.

Almost running the last few steps, Cassidy dropped down before him. As she did so, Kevin abruptly released the warden's arm. But Click was still holding on as Andy launched himself at Cassidy, sobbing loudly as his free arm caught her around the neck. And so Click was still touching him when Andy touched Cassidy, and that icy incandescence burned through her in a brilliant wave of light.

For a few fiery seconds, everything that was in Andy Greene became a part of Cathy Delaney: the large things, like his thumping fear and his panicky distress, as well as the smaller things, like the trickle of perspiration beneath his leather tunic and the firm pressure of the ground against his knees. For those few incendiary moments, she *was* Andy Greene, living inside his brain and feeling the world through his skin. And there was something else, as well, something that was so shocking and fleet that later she would wonder if she had only imagined it. For the briefest fragment of time, Cassidy thought that she felt *Click*, as well—or at least a burning millisecond distillation of who Click was—a flare of sensation so bright that it almost caused her to pull back. But then the moment passed, and the stunning cold fire was gone again.

Click had released the younger man's arm, freeing him to clasp Cassidy in an almost painfully tight embrace. Over and over again, Andy chanted her name, like a mantra against whatever demon possessed him. She held him closely, convincing him of her presence with repeated assurances, trying all the while to moderate his deathlike grip. By the time Andy had begun to calm, Cassidy could see that both Kevin and Click had moved back, giving them the privacy the warden had previously asked for.

Still somewhat distracted by the power of what had happened when she had first touched Andy, Cassidy kept up an automatic stream of soothing words. She shifted slightly in relief when the force of his bear hug finally eased, and she could gently set him back at arm's length. She could see the features of his grief-stricken face only faintly, but it was hard to miss the shudder that ran through him then, wracking his body.

"I'm here now, Andy," she murmured, one hand cupping the side of his face. "You don't have to be afraid."

"Th-they're t-taking you away!" he stammered urgently.

Cassidy noticed that a glinting bead of moisture hung from the tip of his nose, the natural aftermath of his jag of weeping. Using her shirtsleeve to wipe his nose, like a mother tidying a child after a crying bout, she asked him quietly, "Who's taking me, Andy? Where are they taking me?"

"I—I don't know," he confessed miserably, his eyes huge with distress. "But what if I never see you again?"

Struggling to keep the anxiety from her own voice, Cassidy forced herself to remain calm. "Andy, when you say they're taking me away, do you mean they're going to . . . kill me?"

The taut posture of Andy's body suddenly eased a notch, as if her question had somehow distracted him from his previous fervor. "Oh, no, they can't," he said immediately. "Not yet, anyway."

Momentarily stymied, Cassidy was briefly at a loss for words. "Andy, what do you—"

But he interrupted her abruptly, his arms tightening around her again. "Don't let them take you away, Cathy!" he wailed. "If they do, I'll never see you again!"

Her incipient questions swept away by his renewed agitation, Cassidy again tried to soothe him. "Andy, you'll always be able to find me," she told him. "You're the warden, and the warden will always be able to find me."

But far from having the desired ameliorating effect, her mention of the warden only seemed to increase Andy's dismay further. He hugged her so tightly that her breath left her, and her cheek was pressed hard against the smooth damp skin of his neck. "Not if they take you away!" he cried. "You can't go away, Cathy—you have to get away from them!"

Crushed in his embrace, Cassidy tried ineffectually to give him some reassuring touch. Her lips were nearly at his ear as she said softly, encouragingly, "Andy, the warden—"

"No!" he exclaimed, startling her with his vehemence. His arms bit into her sides. "Cathy, don't you see?" he whispered raggedly. "Without you, I can't be the warden of Horses."

Even without being able to see his face, Cassidy knew the instant that Andy Greene disappeared from the body that so closely embraced her own. Suddenly the aching tension ran out of those tightly muscled arms, and he slumped back, partially pulling away from her. Dazed, as if he'd just been awakened from a particularly vivid bad dream, the warden lifted his head and looked uncertainly into her face.

"Cassidy, are you all right?" he asked her, his voice softly hoarse.

At first blush the question may have seemed like a non sequitur, but Cassidy understood what he meant. The warden still swam in the stormy sea of emotion left to him by Andy Greene. Doubtless he was wondering what sort of things he may have said or done in the throes of that strong fear and desperation.

"I'm okay," she assured him, quickly adding "What do you remember?"

The warden blinked, partially averting his face, almost as if the rawness of Andy's volatile reactions distressed him. "I couldn't find you," he whispered slowly. "Not the big house, the bright lights, the bed—none of it. It was like in the very beginning: All I could feel was Andy's fear for you." He hesitated then, finally looking back directly into her face. His expression was a mixture of confusion and dread. "What's happening, Cassidy?" he asked almost plaintively. "What did he tell you?"

Cassidy felt the cold rush of a deep unease spread through her, like a cruel parody of that all-encompassing brilliance of the incandescent light. "He said that they were taking me away," she said in a low voice. She looked helplessly into those wide-set brown eyes. "He said that if he couldn't find me, he wouldn't . . . he wouldn't be the warden anymore."

The warden considered that, his lips thinning as his expectant expression grew soberly thoughtful. "And if Andy can't find Cathy, then I won't be able to see into the Slow World again," he said quietly. His facial muscles tightened as his comprehension expanded exponentially. "Cassidy, do you think that if Andy can't find Cathy in the Slow World, then he won't be able to come to you in this one?"

Cassidy sat back onto her heels, her lungs suddenly feeling so airless that she had to wait a moment and drag in another breath before she could even speak.

"I think," she said hoarsely, "that if we're going to find this Alchemist, it'd better be pretty damned soon—or else no matter what the hell he knows, it might be too late to help us."

Chapter 12 ◀━━

Clouds had moved in during the night, muting the dawn and thickening the air. Cassidy felt oddly groggy, almost as if she had slept too much, even though she had scarcely closed her eyes once she had returned to her own blanket after the warden's episode. The brief and unsettling event had raised disturbing possibilities that had dogged her even into the new day.

In the first faint gray light, Cassidy checked on Dragonfly. The horse's condition lifted her spirits. Little remained of Click's odd poultices, but the wounds they had covered were clean and scabbed over, with almost no swelling around them. Nickering a greeting, the horse moved a bit stiffly and deliberately as she came over to Cassidy, but she was not lame. Cassidy picked a few pieces of dried fascia and vegetable matter off from the gray's sleek coat, and then began a methodical examination of the horse's entire body, once again soothing herself with the mechanics of the simple routine. Just as Cassidy was finishing with the mare's final hoof, she sensed a familiar presence, and straightened to find Allen standing a few yards behind her.

"She looks pretty good," he said, studying the horse.

"Amazingly good," Cassidy amended, running her hand over the curve of the mare's rump. "You and Click did a great job with her."

"Mostly Click," Allen pointed out; and when Cassidy looked over to him, she noticed that his eyes were on her, not on the horse anymore.

"How's Valerie?" she asked. She had left the camp without disturbing Becky's early-morning ministrations to the injured woman, but she had seen that the captain was awake. She had also caught a glimpse of the network of ugly punctures and sutured lacerations on Val's legs and trunk.

"She's better," the bearded man said, the dry humor in his tone not quite reaching his solemn eyes, "but nowhere near as good as the horse."

"She won't be able to travel yet," Cassidy surmised, glancing down as she tugged her fingers through the long sweep of the mare's tail.

Allen looked at her soberly and said, "The warden told us about what happened last night." His shaggy head tilted, an abbreviated gesture of beckoning to her. "Come on; Click wants to discuss our plans."

In the camp, Rowena had kindled a fresh fire upon the ashes of the old. To Cassidy's surprise and relief, she saw that Valerie was actually sitting up, albeit still looking shaky and pale, swathed in her blanket with both Becky and Kevin fussing over her like a pair of geese with a sick gosling. Click and the warden were a small distance from the cook fire, ostensibly repacking the bedrolls and other supplies. But Cassidy could tell from the two men's demeanor that their thoughts were on topics far more serious.

"Coffee's almost ready," Rowena said to Cassidy as she passed.

As Cassidy approached Valerie, the captain looked up at her with a keen and completely lucid expression. "Your mare?" she asked immediately.

"She's good," Cassidy replied, squatting down. She still felt vaguely guilty, despite Click's brusque comment about Valerie's duty. As she surreptitiously studied that familiar face, Cassidy noted several small abrasions and purpling bruises, all silent badges of the woman's matter-of-fact courage. "How do you feel?" she added quickly.

Valerie grimaced slightly, pointedly ignoring the way Kevin was tugging on and settling the folds of her blanket. "A lot better than I would be feeling if you hadn't gotten that damned cat off me when you did," she said. "I thought that bastard was about to have my entrails for lunch."

Before Cassidy could respond, she saw Click and the warden approaching them. Both men nodded a greeting. Then the warden dropped down before Valerie with his usual artless grace, sitting cross-legged.

Cassidy knew that the warden had already discussed his most recent lapse with the others. She also assumed that in her absence there also had been some talk about the need for haste in pushing on. Still, Cassidy was a little disconcerted by how candidly the warden began the discussion. Looking directly at his captain, he said without further preamble, "How long do you feel it will be before you'll be able to travel?"

But frankness had always suited Valerie, and she was not in the least put off by his blunt question. She shot a swift sidelong glance at Becky, whose stern face wore a no-nonsense expression, and then asserted, "Three days, to get started; four or five to be able to travel all day."

Becky immediately shook her head, her dreadlocks bouncing. "Uh-uh," she contradicted loudly. "Five days before I'd even let you start; and then a good week, if you're lucky, before you'd last all day out there." She cut off any incipient protest from Valerie by adding pointedly "Woman, you've got almost forty stitches in you—I know, because I counted them myself. You're not going *anywhere* in three days!"

The warden struggled to keep from forming an automatic smile at the black woman's fussy but entirely genuine concern. Cassidy thought he was about to speak, but before he could, Valerie did.

"Three days, or five days, or a week," the captain said evenly, "it's all the same. You have to be traveling yet today." She made an economic gesture. "Leave me a gun and enough provisions for a few days, and I'll follow you when I'm able."

Cassidy tried to conceal her surprise. She had to force herself to not look at Click, who stood silently behind the warden. The exact thing the Tinker had suggested to her the night before beside the gray mare had just been proven true. Valerie had not only not put up a fight about being left behind, she actually had been the one to propose it.

"Gun or not," the warden said, "I'm not leaving you out here alone."

"I'll stay with her," Allen said quietly.

That time Cassidy was unable to conceal her surprise. She hadn't even noticed that the sheriff had been standing right behind her until he had spoken. He came forward then, his broad shoulders tracing a brief, noncommittal shrug. "I'm a fair shot with a gun," he continued, "and I'm strong enough to carry her, if it would come to that."

For a few seconds, Cassidy was certain that Valerie was going to erupt in protest at that last remark about being carried; but if that had been the captain's intent, she was promptly superceded by Becky. "I'm staying with her, too," she announced. "The woman still looks like a patchwork quilt. I put a hell of a lot of work into her, and I'm damned if I'll let it all go to waste by letting her drag herself through some bog hole and tear out all my stitches." She met Valerie's direct stare unflinchingly. And lest anyone might think Becky guilty of any glimmer of sentiment, she grumbled, "I'm getting mighty tired of tramping around these woods anyway, so the rest of you can just take that walking piece of horsemeat and go on ahead. I'm taking it easy for a while." Throwing Cassidy a final, if unconvincing, baleful look, she concluded, "And while you're at it, take that noisy white boy and all those damned monsters with you!"

Cassidy could see that the warden was having even less success than she was at concealing his expression, but he made no effort to hide his honest appreciation for what both Allen and Becky were offering. "Are you both certain?" he asked of them.

"Damned right I'm certain!" Becky said. "Besides, you don't really need me—and this woman does." She gave Valerie a challenging stare. "Whether she'll admit it or not."

Allen merely shrugged again. "You don't need me, either, or at least not as much as they will. With the two of us, we can spell each other on watches, and I can do all the heavy work."

Click spoke up for the first time. "Then if the captain has no objections," he said, "it's decided. She and Allen and Becky will remain behind, while the rest of us go on."

Cassidy couldn't see Click's expression without turning obviously to look at him; but Valerie's face was a calm mask, elegantly composed. "We'll follow you as soon as possible," she said pointedly.

The warden rose up onto his knees, leaning forward to touch Valerie gently on one blanket-draped shoulder. Cassidy knew well the look on his face, for she had often seen his captain reduce him to that same state of wry and self-effacing resignation. "I don't suppose," he said, "that it would do any good for me to command you to return to the city?"

"You could command *me*," Becky muttered loudly.

But Valerie's face was set and implacable, and her reply was a paragon of logic. "With all of those steep ravines and thick woods and the rivers? It would be weeks before I'd be fit to undertake a journey like that. It only makes sense to go on."

The warden's mouth crimped in a rueful little smile. "Of course," he said, gracious in defeat. He reached up and lightly brushed Valerie's crown of curls before adding indulgently "And a good Trooper does what's sensible."

Valerie finally yielded slightly, allowing him the irony the same way she had allowed the caress. "A good Trooper," she corrected him, "would never have let you come here in the first place."

* * *

Immediately after breakfast, Cassidy helped Rowena divide their utensils and staples, leaving a selection for Becky, Allen, and Valerie.

"Hey, all I need is two pots," the black woman protested. "I don't want to have to lug around all that iron once we start moving again." She grinned impulsively. "Besides, I'm not that good of a cook, so two pots'll be more than enough. Wait—not so many beans! Hell, I don't want to be stuck in camp the next few days with those two and all those beans."

Leaving Becky and Rowena to squabble amiably over the final disposition of the foodstuffs, Cassidy crossed the camp to where Allen was standing alone. He was methodically checking over the pistol Click had given him, and as she came up alongside him, she could see the gun was the same one Click had given Valerie the morning before. It was the pistol Click had long carried for himself.

Allen grunted a greeting as he balanced the pistol in his big callused hand. "It has a good heft to it," he said, almost grudgingly. Watching him weigh the firearm, Cassidy couldn't help thinking of how much his life had changed since that night in a forest meadow, weeks ago, when Allen had fired his rifle at Rafe and had nearly blown himself up. That had been another gun, a gun Cassidy had been told Allen had taken off a dead Trooper. They stood in a different meadow now, and it was a different gun, and most definitely a different Trooper who had provided it. Cassidy was surprised afresh at how dramatically things had changed in a world in which she originally had been convinced there was absolutely no drama at all.

"I wish you could go on with us," she told Allen, "but I'm also glad that you're willing to stay with Val and Becky."

Allen glanced over at her again, his bearded face set in a familiar stolid expression. "We'll catch up again eventually," he said.

Cassidy realized something else then, but it did not surprise her: She would genuinely miss Allen's reassuring presence on their journey. "You could still go back to the city," she pointed out.

Allen turned toward her, the gun seemingly forgotten as he looked down directly into Cassidy's face. His sand-colored eyes were solemn and unblinking. "Valerie would never go back," he said, "and I'm staying to help her. Besides," he added, "I already told you that I intend to go with you all the way, until you find whatever it is you're looking for."

Cassidy knew that Allen would only be perplexed by the emotional response, but she also knew that he wouldn't evade her, so she tipped up on her toes and gave him a hearty hug. How oddly appropriate it seemed, she thought, as she buried her face in the smoky-smelling solidity of his shoulder, that the first man in that world who had ever tried to protect her and her dangerous secret should still be the only man there whom she would have felt completely comfortable embracing. How ironic that Allen, who had inspired her to remember sex, would then be the one man with whom she could feel so sexlessly safe.

The next three days of their journey were among the quietest and yet most physically taxing of the entire trip. The muggy weather spawned a long spell of rain, which was seldom heavy but which fell without respite. As they began to leave the hill country behind, the raised spine of land they'd been following started to deteriorate. Low-lying bogs and sloughs stretched across wider areas, and the terrain sometimes forced them well out of their way to skirt them.

With the marshy land, mosquitoes became a real nuisance again, rising in humming clouds from every sump hole or bog. Even reeking of crushed jewelweed and mint, every inch of their exposed flesh became a target for the voracious parasites. Cassidy was especially concerned that the combination of the constant drizzle and the insects would infect her horse's healing wounds. But for some reason, perhaps the lingering after-scent of Click's poultices, the mare was bothered by the biting pests far less than were the humans.

Dragonfly also tolerated the constant rain and the long detours around the bogs with relative equanimity. Cassidy realized that she often forgot that the mare didn't have the same perspective on things as the rest of them did. A horse simply looked upon each day as another search for as much good-quality forage as possible. If that involved a certain amount of travel or other inconvenience, the mare merely accepted that as given.

Cassidy also doubted that the gray mare spent any time worrying about the three people they had left behind, or that she even missed them at all. She, on the other hand, found herself both worrying about and missing them even more than she had anticipated. She even missed Becky and the black woman's unique prickly panache. And she had more than enough time, as they thrashed their way through the dripping brush or slogged across the soggy meadows to skirt a marsh, to wonder how well their absent friends were faring. Only at night did she think about nothing. By the time they stopped each night, she was exhausted; and in the drizzle, none of them lingered long around their smoky campfire. After wolfing down whatever food Rowena prepared, usually some staple supplemented by a rabbit or even a few mourning doves, Cassidy didn't even attempt to cadge some private time to talk with the brunette. Like her companions, all Cassidy wanted to do was just roll herself in the dubious shelter of her damp blanket and spend the hours until her watch in weary, dreamless sleep.

As often as Cassidy had replayed in her mind the details of the warden's last contact with the Slow World, and as unsettling as the implications had been of what Andy had told her, she still found herself guiltily relieved that she was not being disturbed nightly by more of the episodes. At times during the long rainy days, she allowed her mind to gnaw uselessly at the warden's worrisome supposition: What if Andy would not be able to come to her in that world if he was not allowed to see Cathy in the real world? And by extension she also tormented herself with the inevitable conclusion: What if the warden never had another lapse, and she had lost Andy forever?

But even in the gloomiest depths of those long, dreary afternoons, with her soaked cotton clothing hanging on her like some clammy second skin, while her sodden boots searched for each step of solid footing in the squishy muck, Cassidy never allowed herself to abdicate all hope completely. She kept reminding herself that she hadn't come all that way just to fail. And every hazard she had survived, every ordeal she had endured, only served to reinforce her resolve. Something would happen, she was convinced of that. Each time before, whenever her situation had seemed the most hopeless, something had always happened.

And no matter how it was still separated from her, by whatever dimension of time or space, the Slow World did exist. The Warden had been able to see into it from his own world, had been able to see Cassidy as who she really was. Armed with that certainty, nothing could have made her give up.

However urgent their quest may have been, when Click called a halt earlier than usual on that third rainy day, Cassidy was unashamedly relieved. They had skirted around two large bogs that day; her legs ached and her feet were chafing in her wet boots. Back on the narrow spit of slightly higher ground, there were groves of trees to provide them with firewood and passable fodder for the mare. And Cassidy was not the only one who was feeling the accumulation of small miseries by then.

"With a little effort," Click said, "we can cut enough poles and fresh branches to make a small shelter." Cassidy watched with morose fascination as a few drops of rain dripped off the ends of his mustache as he spoke. "It won't be completely waterproof, but overnight with the fire we should be able to get both our clothing and our blankets at least partially dry. And even if it's still raining tomorrow . . ." He paused, one dark brow arched sardonically. "Then at least we will have had one night of relative comfort to look back upon during our future suffering."

"It sounds well worth the trouble," the warden agreed heartily. He looked at the others' weary faces. "One dry night and a hot meal would make up for a lot of what we've come through in the past few days."

Cassidy missed Becky complaining that *nothing* would make up for what they had come through in the past few days; but rather than say it herself, she just shrugged off her pack and turned to Rowena. "I'll see if I can find you some halfway decent firewood," she said.

But Rowena had an oddly expectant look on her face. "Let's do that later," she said. "Right now what I'd really like for you to do is come back with me to that last grove of burr oak we passed."

Puzzled, Cassidy cocked her head in the direction from which they had come. "Back there by the edge of the bog?" she asked.

Grinning conspiratorially, Rowena nodded. "I swear I saw grapevines in those trees," she said eagerly. "We haven't had any fresh fruit in two days. I don't know about you, but I sure could go for some grapes tonight!"

Cassidy glanced over in Click's direction. He was several yards away, casually bent over his pack, but she was certain he had been able to overhear what they had been discussing. "Okay," Cassidy agreed, "as long as we don't go too close to the bog."

"Or stay gone too long," Click added without even looking up.

Ignoring Rowena's chuckle, Cassidy dutifully echoed, "Or stay gone too long."

"And take your horse," Click said. He straightened up, his knife in hand, and looked directly at them then. "In this kind of country it's best to rely on the keenest eyes and ears."

Cassidy and Rowena each took a small kettle from among the cooking utensils. The stand of burr oak was only a hundred yards back, a simple enough walk even in the drizzle. It wasn't just the possibility of fresh grapes that lightened Cassidy's mood; she found herself pleasantly content just to spend some time alone with her friend. The foraging expedition not only didn't seem like a chore, it actually was something of a lark, considering the kind of traveling they'd been doing lately.

Wherever conditions made it possible, Cassidy walked alongside Rowena, the light rain all but forgotten. For a long time neither of them felt compelled to say anything, and their silence was comfortable and companionable. Yet Cassidy was not surprised when the brunette finally did speak, because it had been obvious to her that Rowena had had something on her mind.

"This is probably going to sound stupid," Rowena said, her kettle slowly swinging from her hand, "but I really miss Allen."

Cassidy shrugged, ignoring the water which dripped from the ends of her hair. "I miss him, too," she said.

Rowena shot her a wry, sidelong glance. "You know, when we were running away from Double Creek, he would have been the last person I would have wanted to see. But now . . ."

As the brunette's voice trailed off, Cassidy said quietly, "You know he can't go back to the village again."

"Yeah," Rowena said, making the single word as wistful as a heartfelt sigh. "But maybe that's just as well. Maybe he deserves better than having to knuckle under to Misty for the rest of his life."

Cassidy hesitated a moment, then said, "You know why he helped us, don't you?"

"I kind of figured it out," the brunette told her. "But I think maybe it's more than what he says. I think he's just a good man."

Cassidy couldn't argue with that.

They had reached the oak grove, and for a short time neither of them spoke. Cassidy led the way through the apron of brush and saplings that ringed the larger trees, wincing as a wet branch slapped her sharply across the chest.

"Maybe he'll stay on at the garrison," Rowena mused, pushing past the last of the underbrush. She shook herself like a dog, resettling her damp clothing. "He gets along pretty well with the Troopers, and I know the warden really likes him."

"The warden likes everyone," Cassidy muttered. But Rowena's suggestion did have a certain amount of merit. It just struck Cassidy as the ultimate irony that a man like Allen, who had undoubtedly hanged more than one Horseman during his tenure as sheriff of Double Creek, would find himself welcomed into the company of the ranks of Troopers.

"There, look!" Rowena commanded. "Grapevines!" She positively beamed. "What did I tell you?"

Cassidy stepped closer and circled the oak tree, studying the gnarled tangle overhead. "I see plenty of vines," she conceded, "but I don't see any grapes."

"They're higher—up there." Rowena rose on tiptoes to point out the grapes. "They're up in the branches of the trees." She swept over to the next tree, still searching overhead. "Look, here's some I bet we can reach from the ground."

For the next several minutes, the only sounds were the rhythmic patter of the oak leaves as the steady accumulation of rain water dripped down off them and the soft plop of the small clusters of ripe grapes landing in their metal kettles. Once Dragonfly gave a loud, bored exhalation as she stood on the edge of the brush, nibbling on the branches. Cassidy popped a few grapes into her mouth; they were a little sour, but quite edible, and well worth the trouble to pick them. Most of the vines had snaked up far into the limbs of the trees, but there were loops that dangled lower, accessible from the ground. They picked for a time in silence before Rowena spoke up again.

"Cassidy, you know who you are in the real world, right?"

A little nonplussed, Cassidy looked over at her. "Yeah; Cathy Delaney."

"And we know that the warden is really Andy Greene," Rowena went on. She paused a moment to drop a cluster of grapes into her kettle. "Well, what if I'm nobody there?" she said quietly then. "How would I ever be able to go back?"

Cassidy's brief but perceptible hesitation owed nothing to surprise; she had often considered that possibility herself, and from every possible angle. Especially after the night when Andy, during one of the warden's spells, had failed to recognize either Valerie or Kevin, Cassidy had been forced to consider the chilling question: What if not all of them had counterparts in the Slow World? Rowena had gone directly to the crux of the problem with that possibility with her second question. But Cassidy had not hesitated because she was uncertain, either. She merely wanted to select her words very carefully, because she had never spoken aloud of her conviction before.

Letting her kettle hang low against her knee, the grapes temporarily forgotten, Cassidy met her friend's eyes without reservation. "You exist in the Slow World, Rowena," she said firmly. "You might not remember yet who you are there, but that's just because we still haven't discovered anything that's jolted your memory the way that seeing the warden jolted mine. I think all that means is that you haven't met anyone here yet who was also someone you knew in the real world." Cassidy reached out with her free hand, gripping Rowena's shoulder, feeling the warm solid flesh beneath the cool damp fabric of the brunette's shirt. "I'm positive that everyone here also exists in the Slow World. After all, how else could we even be here? Where else would we all have come from?" She flashed a quick, ironic little grin at her friend. "Or should I say, *when* else would we all have come from?"

Spontaneously grinning back at her, Rowena teased, "So, I see you've finally given up your depressing little theory about all of us being dead!"

"Yeah, for the moment at least," Cassidy said. "Although who knows? The way things have been going on this trip, the odds of winding up dead are looking better and better all the time."

Sobering again, Rowena said speculatively, "Then do you think that everyone in the real world has a—a *time twin* here in this place?"

But Cassidy promptly shook her head. She also had thought a lot about that possibility, and had always come to the same conclusion. "No, I don't think that's possible. If that was true, there'd be more people here." She shrugged evocatively. "I still don't know how this world corresponds physically to the real world, or if it even does at all. But if everyone back in the real world also existed here, it'd be a hell of a lot more crowded. And I think it'd be more technologically advanced, too, because I think there'd be more Memories."

Rowena nodded in agreement. "Yeah, you're right. If all the same people from the real world were here, too, you'd think I'd've bumped into at least one person I knew by now!"

"What I want to know is *how* we got here," Cassidy went on, her hand dropping from Rowena's shoulder. "Whether it was something random, or if we're all connected in some way."

Grinning irrepressibly, Rowena reached up to resume picking grapes from the dripping vines overhead. "Geez, what would we have in common with some of these people?" she gently jibed Cassidy. "You and me, maybe; but someone like me and Allen?" She paused briefly for a studied effect. "Or you and . . . Click?"

Refusing to be baited, Cassidy lifted her own kettle again. The connection was another matter to which she had given a lot of thought. "I don't know," she admitted after a moment, as she plopped another bunch of wet, pea-size grapes into the kettle.

"But I keep thinking the stuff about being Horsemen must have . . ."

Cassidy broke off then, her voice trailing away as she turned her head and lifted her chin. "Do you smell something funny?" she asked Rowena.

"You mean like the bog, or—" The brunette had glanced over at Cassidy, and she suddenly cut off as she recognized the particular expression on her friend's face. "Jesus, Cassidy!" she exclaimed, wide-eyed and nearly dropping her kettle. "Do you smell one of those—those *things* again?"

Realizing that Rowena was on the verge of bolting in panic, Cassidy quickly held up a reassuring hand. "No, it's not the hanging monsters," she said calmly. "It's not strong enough for that. But there's something . . ."

Cassidy looked over her shoulder to the edge of the oak grove, where Dragonfly still browsed amid the dripping brush. The horse looked utterly unconcerned. Then again, she reminded herself with some asperity, the damned mare had never seemed especially concerned about the monsters.

About twenty feet from where they stood, a small embankment led down to the bank of the large slough that they had spent the better part of the afternoon hiking around. The burr oaks grew right up to the lip of the incline, but Cassidy could not see over its edge. The embankment itself was overgrown with thick clumps of willow and alder. But whatever she smelled seemed to be coming from that direction.

"I think it's coming from right over that bank," Cassidy said. "I'm going to go take a look."

"We've got enough grapes," Rowena said anxiously. "Let's just go back to camp."

"Wait here. This'll just take a minute."

Still unconvinced, Rowena wrinkled her nose. "You don't think it's another dead body, do you?" she said unhappily.

Cassidy set down her kettle and started forward. "I'm not sure," she admitted. "But I think we—"

Cassidy abruptly broke off and ducked down as something dark and formless swooped over her head. At first she thought she must have startled a bat out of its refuge beneath the sheltering boughs of the big oaks. Then in rapid succession, several more black objects soared out ahead of her and over the edge of the embankment. When she looked down, she was shocked to see a phlegmlike gobbet of foul slime glistening against the damp fabric of her shirtsleeve.

Ignoring Rowena's alarmed plea, Cassidy rushed forward to the lip of the slope, plunging through low boughs and hanging vines. Below her, above the surface of the marsh, five bizarre creatures floated like a small flock of some mutant parody of birds. Cassidy couldn't describe the creatures' movement as flight, because they didn't have anything that resembled wings. Yet they were deliberately gaining altitude, so they couldn't have been gliding. She wasn't particularly frightened by them because they were moving away from her, and they were considerably smaller than the hanging monsters she had seen before; although in almost every other regard, the carrion eaters were what the creatures most closely resembled. Their foul and gleaming bodies pulsed with the same kind of malignant, perverted life that she had seen throbbing in the larger monsters, and while their stench was not as overwhelming, they exuded a constant trail of putrid slime. *Monsterettes!* Cassidy thought, with a touch of sudden whimsy, as she stood atop the embankment and watched the group of black, turkey-size creatures drift higher and farther away, out across the immense expanse of the slough.

Rowena pounded up beside Cassidy, wide-eyed and out of breath. She stared out over the edge of the slope, watching in amazement as the hideous creatures slowly sailed into the distance. "What the hell *are* those things?" she asked, stunned.

"They look like the hanging monsters," Cassidy explained, evincing a surprising calm. "You know, the carrion eaters. Only these are a lot smaller than any of the other ones I've seen."

"Shit!" Rowena breathed. "You don't think they're—*babies*?"

That possibility hadn't occurred to Cassidy; but it would have been deliciously ironic, she thought, if in a world where people had forgotten sex, it was the monsters who had remembered it. But before she could respond to Rowena's horrified question, something else down in the marsh drew her attention.

"Rowena, look down there," she instructed, pointing down past the tangle of brush and grapevines that choked the steep incline. "About a dozen feet out into the bog; what the hell is that?"

Obviously expecting some new horror, Rowena only reluctantly stepped forward to the lip of the embankment and peered down through the gray veil of drizzle to the algae-covered surface of the slough. After a few moments, she said slowly and quite unwillingly, "It looks like a—a *head*."

"Jesus!" Cassidy exclaimed. "There's someone *stuck* down there!" Before Rowena could stop her, she had leapt over the edge of the incline and was plunging and skidding down the muddy, brushy slope.

"Cassidy!" Rowena shouted after her in dismay. "Wait! Let's go get help!" But even as she was shouting, Rowena was following Cassidy down the slippery embankment. If what they had seen from the top of the slope was indeed a human head, and if the person attached to that head was still alive, then he was about two minutes away from being sucked completely under by the cloying muck of the bog.

"Jesus!" Cassidy exclaimed again, tottering on the edge of the slough, the toes of her boots sinking into the opaque water. The object they had seen *was* a person's head: filthy with a heavy crusting of mud, splattered with shocking crimson streaks of fresh blood, and sunk to its chin in the depthless quagmire of the marsh. And whoever it was, he was a good ten feet beyond their reach from the bank.

Skidding up alongside Cassidy, Rowena panted in dismay. "Oh, God—it *is* a head!"

Cassidy looked frantically up and down the reed- and sedge-clogged bank. "How the hell are we going to get him out of there?" she said desperately. "We'll never be able to reach him without getting stuck, too."

Rowena's voice fell to a loud whisper. "Do you think he's still alive?"

Both women started as the muddy, blood-spattered head lifted, weakly trying to stretch farther above the murky surface of the slough. "I'm alive, you damned fools!" the man in the swamp croaked hoarsely. "But I won't be for much longer, if you two don't quit jawing and get me out of here!"

Astonishment quickly gave way to frenetic activity as Cassidy waved hastily at Rowena. "Grapevines! Get some of those vines from up the slope. We can use them like a rope."

But as tough as the vines had seemed when they had had to push their way through them coming down the embankment, the lengths of vine they tugged free broke far too easily when they tested them between clenched hands. "We need something thicker, something stronger," Cassidy commanded. She and Rowena had begun to scramble farther up the slope when they heard a strangled gasp coming from the marsh.

When she spun around, Cassidy saw that the man's head had sunk even deeper; his nose and mouth were just barely above the surface then, held there only by the last of his strength as he lifted his chin as high as possible.

"Oh, shit!" Cassidy said. She flung herself back down the slope, confident that Rowena would be right behind her. There was no longer time for logic, or even for concerns of personal safety. There was only the two of them, the relentless slough, and a man they didn't even know who was about half an inch from drowning.

At the edge of the marsh, Cassidy instructed Rowena, "Get down! Lay flat on your belly and grab me by the ankles—and whatever you do and whatever happens, don't let go of me!"

Automatically obedient, Rowena flopped down onto the coarse wet grass. Cassidy dropped down beside her, grimacing as her shoulders and chest slid forward into the foul water. If it worked on thin ice, she thought determinedly, then maybe it would work in sinkholes, too. She spread her arms and averted her face to one side. Then, with an awkward sort of swimming motion, she propelled herself farther out into the unwelcomed embrace of the shallow, turbid water.

The flat surface of Cassidy's prone body distributed her weight in such a way that, at least initially, her natural buoyancy kept her from sinking too far into the bog. Rowena's grip around her ankles helped move her forward. But when Cassidy was stretched out to her full length across the water, even with her arms fully extended in front of her, the man's head was still several feet beyond her grasp.

"Rowena!" she called, sputtering when her chin dipped into the brackish water. "You're going to have to slide out a little farther, too. Just don't let your legs slide off the bank!"

"I already have slid out," Rowena responded. But almost immediately, Cassidy felt the brunette propel her a little farther out into the marsh, bringing her groping fingers within reach of the mired man's face.

The water was up to his nose then, and his head had dropped forward. Cassidy wasn't even certain if he was still breathing, but she hooked her thumbs under the angles of his jaw and desperately pulled upward. His head suddenly jerked up, spraying her with dirty water and algae. "Ouch!" he howled, struggling anew.

"Give me your hands!" Cassidy commanded him. Her own body was beginning to sink into the thick muck that lay right below the surface of the shallow water, and she was acutely aware of just how precarious her position was.

The man's head jerked back again, rudely dislodging her fingers. "If I could get my arms free," he exclaimed, coughing roughly, "do you think I'd still be stuck out here?"

Cassidy thought that he probably would have been, but she didn't say that. Straining as far forward as she could against the anchor of Rowena's grip, she plunged her hands down alongside the man's neck. His bare shoulders just crested the layer of thick goo imprisoning him. Clawing deeper, she tried to force her fingertips between his arms and his body, hoping to be able to hook her hands under his armpits.

"Ow! Ow!" he protested as Cassidy's desperate efforts to get a grip on him grew less cautious.

"Shut up!" she sputtered at him, having to struggle just to keep her own face from being drawn beneath the surface of the muddy water. An energizing burst of anger at his complaint shot through her limbs, doubling her fervor. "Shut up, you stupid ingrate son of a bitch!" she fumed at him. "Or I swear I'll just let you drown!"

Fueled by indignation, Cassidy made one last lunge forward. She finally felt her fingers dig into the softer flesh beneath the man's arms. She didn't care if she was hurting him; she sunk her nails in as deeply as she could and then pulled back with all of her strength. For a few moments, nothing happened, except for the shooting pains that played like white-hot lightning up and down the overstrained muscles of Cassidy's arms and back and legs. Then ever so slightly and ever so slowly, she felt the man's buried body lift a few inches from the muck.

Her fingers cramped mercilessly, and Cassidy was forced to release her hold on him. It took all of her effort just to keep her own head above the water then, and she gasped for breath while sparkles of light flickered like shooting stars behind her closed lids. When she focused again, she saw to her relief that the water only came up to the man's neck again; and even if he couldn't free his arms yet, at least he didn't begin to sink lower immediately.

Cassidy was still lying there, half floating in the foul water and feverishly thinking of what she could try next, when she felt Rowena's hold on her ankles suddenly tighten. Then she was being drawn abruptly backward, being swiftly and surely pulled on her belly out of the bog.

"Wait!" She panted in surprise. "What the hell are you . . . ?" But her protest was cut off as an entirely familiar and utterly welcome voice spoke soothingly from behind her.

"It's all right, Cassidy," Click said as he crossed his arms under her waist and lifted her onto solid ground again. "We'll get him out now."

Click propped her, wet and filthy and dripping with swamp

muck, into an unsteady sitting position. She leaned sideways, bumping into Rowena's bent knees, and then looked past the seated brunette in confusion. Behind them, the warden and Kevin were sliding down the embankment, dragging two long sections of stripped saplings.

Cassidy felt Rowena's arm come around her waist, and she glanced over at the buxom woman. Rowena's shirt was covered with mud, and there was algae in her hair, but the concern in those hazel eyes was entirely selfless. Rowena was worried about Cassidy and, more amazingly, she was worried about the ill-tempered stranger in the bog. Cassidy found Rowena's hand and clasped it, squeezing reassuringly, still too breathless from her rescue efforts to be able to speak.

Working in concert, the three men quickly dropped the two poles out across the surface of the marsh, parallel to each other. Using the wooden rails as a sort of crude ladder, Click began to crawl out on them as the warden and Kevin steadied the butt ends on the bank. The far ends of the poles were just inches from the trapped man's head. Click knelt balanced on them, both his knees and his crossed ankles submerged beneath the turbid water.

Click bent forward, his arms buried well over the elbows as he methodically scooped out a slurry of mud from around the imprisoned man. He worked swiftly but economically, utterly heedless of his precarious position or anything around him. He didn't even flinch back—as Cassidy and Rowena automatically did—when the trapped man's arms suddenly came free and flew up from beneath the surface of the water, sending twin sluices of greenish water spraying across his lowered face. Then those same dirty naked arms were snaking up around Click's neck in a clinging embrace, endangering the Tinker's risky perch on the narrow rails.

"Easy," Click said, the single word in that tone of command instantly calming the other man's panic, as the muscles in Click's arms and legs and back worked to steady himself again. "Start trying to kick yourself free as I pull back on you."

Other than being slightly out of breath, Click's voice sounded so completely normal that he might just as well have been instructing Kevin to cut more firewood. If he was concerned about his hazardous position, there was no hint of it in his demeanor then. He locked his arms under the other man's and slowly began to draw back. His lean body tightening, Click threw all of his strength against the suction that still trapped the stranger in the viscous mud. Like two bizarrely mismatched lovers locked in a mud-covered embrace, for a few moments they hung bent over the surface of the slough. And then abruptly the man was free, shooting up out of the dark muck with such impulsion that both he and Click nearly toppled off from the poles.

As Click grappled to keep his balance without losing his hold on the other man, Cassidy felt Rowena prod her sharply in the ribs. She immediately knew the reason for the brunette's reaction. Even the thick coating of sticky mud and decaying vegetation that clung to the newly freed man could not conceal the fact that he was naked. They had just risked their lives to save a Woodsman.

The warden and Kevin slid down along the wooden poles, grasping hold of both Click and the man he had rescued and pulling them up onto the trampled sedge grass. Cassidy and Rowena both scrambled back out of the way as the four men crawled up onto solid ground. Click shook back his wet, dirty hair and then nodded to the warden's repeated query if he was all right. And the stranger, the Woodsman, went down on all fours just like a dog, coughing up swamp water and retching loudly.

As soon as Click had regained his breath, he got to his feet. He looked like hell, Cassidy thought: clothing all hanging askew, soaked with filthy water, and splattered with rotting bits of sedge and algae. The warden and Kevin had already gained their feet and stood watching the miserable-looking Woodsman. Click reached down to the stranger, offering him a hand up. But the other man, wearing his coating of muck and filth like a second skin, just shook his head and staggered to his feet on his own.

Swaying slightly, the Woodsman brushed irritably at the crown of mud that still caked his head. Cassidy could see then that the fresh blood splashed across the man's skull had come from a relatively small but messy wound on his temple, and that beneath the cap of mud, the man's head was completely bald. He was not a very imposing specimen in any regard, about Cassidy's height and well into middle age, as skinny and wiry as a jockey. But that was not to say that the grubby little man did not still have the power to surprise.

Drawing himself up to his full height, heedless of the steady streams of muddy water that still dripped from every protruberance on his naked body, the Woodsman fixed Click with a calm and appraising stare. "So, Captain," he said in that oddly harsh and raspy voice, "I see you've come back. But times must be hard indeed in the Eastern Territories if what you wear is what now passes for a Trooper's leathers—and if these rude women are what now passes for a Troop."

Chapter 13 ◀▭▭▭

Having long since accepted the Woodsman's rejection of his proffered hand up, and with far more equanimity than Cassidy knew she would have been able to summon under the circumstances, Click had set himself to straightening his sodden clothing. At the Woodsman's words, the dark-haired man looked up sharply, his eyes narrowing. But Click looked more intrigued than surprised and more bemused than confused.

"Have we met before?" he said, studying the dirty little man with a steady and inoffensive stare.

Wincing slightly as his fingertips connected with the raised lump on his temple where his skin had been split, the Woodsman replied, "Oh, I've seen you before, although it's been some time." His tongue swept around the margins of his muddy lips and abruptly but almost casually he spat a stream of muddy saliva onto the grass at his bare feet. Then he gave Click another direct, penetrating look. "Didn't expect ever to see you again."

From the corner of her eye, Cassidy saw Rowena shift; and for a moment she thought the brunette was going to get to her feet, or speak, or both. But Rowena did neither, and when Click didn't respond to his last remark, the Woodsman went on.

"You had some proper Troopers with you then," he said, "not this ragtag crew."

It was obvious that the Woodsman didn't know who the warden was, Cassidy thought ironically. She glanced over at the leather-clad young man, whose trousers were still soaked with swamp muck from his part in rescuing the filthy little ingrate. But the warden stood silently with a restraining hand on Kevin's arm.

"These two women saved your life," Click pointed out. "If they hadn't seen you when they did, no one would have ever found you. And if they had thought of their own safety and come looking for help first, we would have arrived far too late to have saved you."

The Woodsman showed small, uneven teeth in a humorless smile. "A crack Troop after all," he said sarcastically. "And now I suppose I am indebted to you for my life."

Click merely spread his hands, the dripping tips of his mustache lifting slightly as he responded, "Some things are simply a matter of duty. We serve at the warden's command."

The Woodsman probably missed the dry irony behind Click's remark, but he regarded the Tinker with renewed intensity. "As instruments of the warden, you're a far trek from your own territories, Captain," he said skeptically.

Cassidy would have willingly admitted that her and Rowena's own distasteful experience with the Woodsman who had captured them in his pit trap and had then stolen their clothing and destroyed their supplies had predisposed her to view any of the wild ones with suspicion and mistrust. And thus far she had seen nothing in the behavior of the mettlesome, scratchy-voiced little man to ameliorate that impression. Thus she was both surprised and dismayed by Click's forthright candor with him.

"We're seeking someone," the Tinker said. "Perhaps you might even be able to help us."

Cassidy had already decided that it was more in keeping with the scruffy little bald man's nature to be irritable and cynical than it was to be helpful. It was a deduction she made partially on the basis of the way he had chosen to live and partially because she recognized something of the same tendencies in herself. So it was easy to detect the brief war between sarcasm and grudging acquiescence that was being waged behind that dirt-encrusted face, as the Woodsman considered Click's leading comment.

"As I make it a point to avoid people," the man said, "particularly people like you, it would seem unlikely that I could help you."

Cassidy knew that Rowena was as surprised as she was when Click suddenly changed tacks, because the brunette gave her another sharp but surreptitious nudge in the ribs.

"How did you come to be stuck in that bog?" Click asked him, his tone suggesting nothing more than mild curiosity. "Surely you knew its hazards."

Touché! Cassidy thought, barely managing to keep a smirk off her face. What had Becky called Click? Slick. Click had effortlessly put the Woodsman back on the defensive; slick indeed.

The Woodsman muttered something unintelligible under his

breath and flicked a forefinger in annoyance at a long gluey strand of decaying sedge grass that clung to his hip. Cassidy couldn't help but notice that other than his armpits and his crotch, the man didn't seem to have a single hair on his entire body. She thought that he must have had skin like shoe leather to be able to run around in the brush naked like that.

Cassidy was caught off guard, and more than a little chagrined, when she realized that the Woodsman was looking directly at her and Rowena; she had probably been staring rather impolitely at him. "It was those things," the Woodsman said. "These women saw them, I'm sure."

With the attention directed toward her and Rowena, Cassidy quickly spoke up. "We saw some kind of little monster," she explained, pointing up the embankment toward the dark copse of burr oak. "They were like the carrion eaters, but much smaller; and they sort of—" She made a vague gesture, miming flight. "—floated away when we chased them out of the trees."

"Stinking little things," the Woodsman pronounced, spitting again. He looked at Cassidy and Rowena almost resentfully, perhaps irritated that the two women seemed oddly well versed in the creatures. Then he looked back to Click and went on. "I was up in the trees, getting grapes, when the foul beasts startled me. I . . ." His stare hardened, unblinking, as if daring anyone to find his plight amusing. "I fell out of the tree and started running." He didn't detail the obvious, which was that in his blind panic he had blundered right into the slough. Rather, his hand went again to his abraded temple, automatically probing the sore spot as he concluded, "I must have cracked my head on a branch."

"A bad piece of luck," Click said, smoothly sincere. "But you were most fortunate that these women shared your taste for fresh grapes." Click's umber eyes were solemn and sympathetic. "Out here one can't always count on finding help when it's needed."

Neatly outmaneuvered, and conceding but refusing to be graceful about it, the Woodsman grumbled, "Enough of this jabbering then! Who is it that you seek, Captain?"

Gracious in victory, Click merely inclined his head slightly toward the shorter man and said, "A man they say lives in these bogs, but not a wild one like yourself. A man with strange ways." He paused. "He's been called the Alchemist."

The Woodsman suddenly shook himself, explosively, exactly like a wet dog. Spatters of muck and gobbets of algae and other bits of rotted vegetation flew from him in a messy spray. But when he looked up at Click again, the dark-haired man had never moved or even flinched. "I know of a strange man," the Woodsman said grudgingly, "but I've never heard of that name. I've never seen this man myself, but it's said he lives in the earth, and inhales fire, and knows odd things." He stared even more fiercely at Click, as if daring his ridicule. "I've even heard that this man can leave his body and then come back to it; but that sounds to me like a bit too much for any man, strange or not."

Click favored the Woodsman with a bemused look, his brows quirking. "Strange indeed," he acceded, "but this sounds like the man we seek. Where have you heard that this man can be found?"

Implicit in Click's phrasing was both the acknowledgment of the Woodsman as an important source of information and yet also the tacit understanding that a rational man such as himself might not believe in such odd notions as a man who could inhale fire and return from the dead. Still, the muddy little man visibly debated whether his further cooperation was incumbent upon him as part of his life debt to those annoying people. For a few moments, Cassidy thought that the Woodsman either might refuse to answer or might at least deny that he had any further information for them. To her surprise, however, in the end he did neither.

"You know of the Snake's Spine?" he said testily.

"Yes, I know of it," Click replied.

"Follow the Spine to its end," the Woodsman said. He paused, eyeing Click's face with an almost gleeful expression. "Ah-ah! You think there's nothing there but a great swamp, don't you?" He cackled hoarsely, then spat again. "Troopers! You've never been there yourself, and yet you believe anything that's been said."

Click accepted the reproach without rancor. "Then why don't you tell me something worthy of my belief, Woodsman?" he suggested mildly.

The Woodsman spread his dirty fingers, gesturing expansively. "At the end of the Snake's Spine, there's an island in the swamp. You're only a few days' travel from it. That's where it's said this strange man lives." He showed his uneven teeth in a sudden feral grin. "And now I've repaid you for my life, Captain—and with any luck we'll never see each other again!"

Certain that the Woodsman was about to bolt into the brush, like some crazy wild boar, Cassidy quickly commanded him. "Wait!" The Woodsman was not the only one staring at her as she clumsily lurched to her feet and confronted the naked man. On an equal footing, she was able to stand eye to eye with him. "I'm one of the women who saved your miserable life," she declared loudly, "and there's one more thing I want from you before I'll consider myself adequately repaid."

Irritation and incredulity vied for dominance on the Woodsman's face. He darted a baleful glance at Click before glaring at Cassidy. "What now?" he demanded impatiently, very much as if he were a busy executive being detained from some important business meeting, rather than a grubby little bare-assed hermit about to rabbit off into the woods again.

Taking a page from Click's book, Cassidy fought to keep her expression both implacable and yet mild. "Three days' travel behind us, to the east, are three more of our companions," she said. "One of them is wounded, but all of them are armed—and good shots." She didn't know how easily intimidated Woodsmen were by firearms, but she figured it wouldn't hurt to exaggerate in any case. "I want you to go to them and tell them what you've told us," she concluded, "so that they'll know where we've gone."

The Woodsman rolled his eyes—the only clean thing in his begrimed face—in patent disbelief. "You want me to approach three armed Troopers and convince them that I'm telling them the truth—before they decide to shoot me for sport?"

Cassidy would have been amenable to being bailed out by Click, or by anyone else for that matter; but no one else spoke up, and she was left to face off with the exasperating little man on her own. She realized that what she was asking for would be a far more difficult payment than what Click had just extracted from him. It also would be impossible to determine if he had actually carried out his task until it was far too late to call him on it. She could think of only one way to coerce him into cooperating, and that was by preying upon the one weakness the wiry and self-reliant little man had shown.

"You may wonder," Cassidy said, "why my friend and I weren't frightened by the same creatures that surprised you enough to cause you to flee into the bog." Certain that she had the Woodsman's attention, she shamelessly pressed her advantage. "After all, who knows where those foul things may go, or where they'll turn up next?" After pausing to let him consider her implication, Cassidy continued, "But they've never harmed any of us, because we carry a charm that wards them off." Casually straightening the soggy hem of her seaman's shirt, she added, "Of course I would never ask a man to journey for me—even a man who owed me his life—without protecting him from such creatures."

Eyeing her suspiciously, the Woodsman asked, "You say you're familiar with these creatures?"

"We've seen them many times," Cassidy said honestly, "and yet they've never harmed us."

Convinced against his will, the bald little man persisted, "And you swear that this charm of yours will protect me, as well?"

Cassidy's fingers dipped under her shirt collar, snagging the thong that held her Ford car key. "It'll protect you as well as it's protected us," she said with a perfectly straight face. "I swear it on my blood."

Cassidy studiously avoided meeting Click's eyes as she passed the thong to the wary Woodsman. She didn't want the Tinker to think that she was belittling the importance of the gift he'd given her, or the weight of a Trooper's oath. But she'd known of no other way to convince the Woodsman to agree to what she'd asked. As the wild one quickly snatched the key from her and slipped the thong over his own grubby neck, she fervently hoped that Click would understand why she'd done it.

"Remember," she said firmly, "three companions, three days' travel from here. And when they see this charm, they'll know that you've brought the message from us." She could tell that the Woodsman was on the verge of bolting; his scrawny little body was coiled like a spring. So she tried to give her parting words maximum impact. "And as long as you've done what I've asked for saving your life," she avowed, "the charm will protect you from the stinking black creatures."

The Woodsman's eyes were narrowed, glinting back at her like those of a cornered animal. "Life debt or not," he growled, "this is the last damned thing I'll ever do for any of your Troop!" He threw them all one last glaring look and then he was off, sprinting over the coarse wet sedge grass like a deer.

Watching him, Cassidy found it almost impossible to believe that barely ten minutes earlier, the same man had been near death, neatly entombed in the sludge of a sinkhole, just seconds away from breathing swamp water rather than air. Except for the filth that still covered him, and the faint traces of blood, the man could have been any of the wary wild ones, fleeing for his freedom. He never even slowed when he reached the brush-choked tangle of the embankment; he scrambled straight up, nimbly dodging and slipping through the snarl of branches and vines. In less than thirty seconds he was out of sight, disappearing into the heavy gloom of the burr oak grove, leaving nothing behind but the muddy trampled place were he had stood before them to prove that he had even existed.

Kevin was the first to speak, his tone more curious than skeptical. "You think he'll go and tell them?" he asked, of no one in particular.

"Yes, I think so, Kev," the warden said, giving the younger man a companionable clap on the back. "He was an irascible lout, but such men are often incapable of dishonesty."

Click made an amused sound, as he bent over to pluck a long sticky string of pond weed off the knee of his sodden trousers. "He'll go," he said, "because Cassidy has convinced him that if he reneges on her demand, she'll sic those flying sacks of offal on him!"

Cassidy felt herself beginning to color, but everyone else seemed to have found her strategy amusing; and if Click in particular had taken any offense at the methods she had employed, he was betraying no hint of it.

"Come on, let's get back to camp," the warden said, giving Kevin's arm a little tug. "Now we'll have all the more reason to welcome shelter, a good fire, and a chance to dry off."

But Cassidy hesitated for a moment. With the crisis over, she was more than curious about one thing. "How did you know where to find us?" she asked. "How did you even know that we needed help?"

Click's face was impassive, a mask of utter innocence. "I told you not to be gone for too long," he said enigmatically.

"Your mare," the warden admitted, with a smile for the Tinker's deliberate obtuseness. "When she came back to camp without you, we knew something was wrong. And she led us right to you."

Looking up to the rim of the embankment, Cassidy saw the tall pale shape of her horse, like a silver cut-out against the dark backdrop of the dripping oaks. Dragonfly stood calmly looking back down at her, her jaws working rhythmically on a mouthful of twigs, her expression as studiously bland as was the Tinker's.

Rowena was chuckling as they all started the slippery climb back up the brushy slope. "Just like Lassie!" she teased Cassidy.

The others looked appropriately puzzled at the reference, but Cassidy just thumped the brunette on the back with a conspiratorial laugh. Let them wonder, she thought with satisfaction.

Few things on their arduous journey had appeared as welcome to Cassidy as the sight of the crude little shelter that the three men had erected beneath a copse of cedars. Beneath the large, low-spreading trees, they had built a framework of poles from stripped saplings, which they had then covered with a thick overlapping layer of cedar boughs. Like a little cabin with open walls, the structure provided a covered area large enough to accommodate both a firepit and enough space for all of them to spread their blankets out of the rain.

"We've already gathered wood," the warden said, "so as soon as we get a fire going, we can get out of these muddy clothes and dry off."

Cassidy ignored the smirk Rowena was aiming at her back. She was well aware that the brunette found the idea of a group strip to have great entertainment value. That was because Rowena didn't know about Click, Cassidy thought dryly; but all she said aloud was "Maybe Rowena and I should get some food started first. I'm really hungry."

"You should have eaten more grapes," Rowena taunted her playfully.

"I'll help you, Rowena," Kevin offered. "And we'll probably have to fill the water bags again if we're all going to wash."

"I'll go get the water then," Cassidy said, throwing Rowena a pointed look.

"We can all get out of these wet clothes while the food is cooking," the warden said, ducking under the thatched roof of the shelter. "Right now even a damp blanket would feel better than these soggy leathers."

As the warden dropped down beside his bedroll and began to tug off his saturated boots, Cassidy glanced uneasily at Kevin and Rowena. They were unpacking the cooking utensils and the rest of their larder with a practiced efficiency. Cassidy did not look back over her shoulder at Click, because she did not want to see the barely veiled amusement in those dark eyes. She seriously debated just how odd it might look to the others if she first wrapped herself in her blanket and then undressed undercover, and the hell with even bathing. But Cassidy found her eyes being helplessly drawn to the sight of the warden deftly peeling his wet tunic off over his head, revealing a damp expanse of tanned and leanly muscled torso. She watched in glum fascination as he began working on the fastenings of his trousers.

She was so unwittingly engrossed in watching the warden, without appearing to stare, that when Click first spoke up directly behind her, Cassidy nearly jumped out of her clothing on the spot. "I'm going to take one last look around," he said, "before we lose all light. Then I'll take the first watch." She could hear the hint of humor in his voice as he concluded, "I'm already wet, and I expect this rain to end tonight. This way, perhaps once I get dry, I will stay dry."

Once she was certain the Tinker was out of sight, prowling through the gathering gloom, Cassidy stepped the rest of the way under the shelter roof and squatted down beside her bedroll. Flushing slightly, she deliberately met Rowena's eyes. The brunette was hunkered down over her pots and pans, with Kevin at her side, kindling the fire. Then Cassidy firmly grasped the dirty hem of her seaman's shirt and hauled it off over her head.

By the time the meal was ready, all four of them had had the chance to strip and take a rudimentary bath. Cassidy didn't even blink when Kevin asked if she wanted him to wash her back; even Rowena's constant covert mugging and winking and leering didn't ruffle her composure. Without Click present, Cassidy found that she was able to revert to a simple acceptance of the casual nudity and asexual kind of touching so common in that world. And once they were all seated around the fire, wrapped in their blankets and sipping hot coffee, Cassidy even relaxed and felt more comfortable than she had in days.

Once the food was ready, Click ducked under the thatched roof for a brief time. He dropped down and sat cross-legged at the fire as he ate, looking a little out of place amid the four blanket-clad figures and the draped piles of their damp clothing spread out to dry. Cassidy still found herself avoiding looking at him. She was grateful for his tacit consideration in leaving earlier; but at the same time some part of her was oddly irritated by it, as if by giving her her privacy he had somehow patronized her. But she was determined not to examine that ambiguous feeling, at least not then. She just tucked it away with all of the other dangerous feelings about Click, which she kept safely secreted for some future reference.

As they ate, they discussed what had happened in the bog and what the Woodsman had told them. Growing sleepy over her third cup of coffee, Cassidy allowed herself to nurture the smallest bloom of hope that their hazardous quest had not been in vain.

"Do you think he was telling the truth then?" the warden asked Click, the younger man's soft, chestnut-colored hair hanging in a half-dried forelock across his temples, his expression openly seeking something promising upon which to hang his own hopes.

Click nodded as he stirred his coffee. "The truth as he knew it," he said.

"Geez, we saved his life!" Rowena interjected. "He sure had a good reason to tell us the truth."

Click looked up over the rim of his mug at her. "Perhaps,

Rowena," he said evenly. "But more important, he had no reason to lie."

"This Snake's Spine he spoke of," the warden went on. "You said you know of it?"

Click nodded again, and Cassidy surreptitiously studied that lean, familiar face. She was certain it had been obvious to everyone why the Woodsman had recognized Click; the fact that he'd called him "captain" was explanation enough. The encounter had forced a part of the Tinker's past to the fore again, and she doubted that they had seen the end of it. As he took another swallow of coffee, Cassidy watched a droplet of water form at the ends of his dark hair and slither down his neck to disappear beneath his shirt collar. With a little stab of guilt, she realized that Click was the only one of them who was still soaking wet.

"The Snake's Spine," Click said, "is the terminal reach of this little spit of high ground we've been following. As the Woodsman said, I'd assumed it just ended by disappearing into the bogs of the Great Swamp. But if there's an island at its end, then we are indeed only a few days' travel from it."

"Only a few days from the Alchemist . . ." Kevin said, his voice automatically hushed.

"Or a few days from nothing," the warden said. "So far all we still have to go on are stories people have told."

"Yeah," Rowena muttered, setting aside her coffee mug, "and those stories are starting to sound crazier and crazier!"

"In that case," Click remarked, "perhaps we're getting closer after all."

Cassidy had drifted off into a study of Click's profile, and she started involuntarily when the warden spoke again. It took her a moment to decipher his words in context.

"Do you want me to relieve you now?" the warden asked Click.

"No need," Click said, lithely gaining his feet again. "Let's wait a bit and see if the rain will break." He shrugged with equanimity. "Sleep while you can; I'll wake you later."

Rolled in her blanket by the warmth of the fire, Cassidy drowsed on the edge of sleep for a long time, strangely comfortable with the proximity of the other bodies around her and their small sounds. The little shelter smelled of smoke and wet leather. She no longer even gave a second thought to the way Kevin burrowed up against the warden to sleep, his head pressed into the hollow between the older man's neck and shoulders. With her own head less than two feet from Rowena's, she listened with fond amusement to the brunette's soft snoring. Temporarily dry, temporarily safe, Cassidy declared a moratorium on the ever-increasing list of nagging questions that she seemed to have accumulated over the weeks, like a ring of millstones around her neck, and gratefully gave herself over to sleep.

Cassidy awakened smoothly and swiftly, with absolutely no idea what the reason had been. She also had no idea what time of the night it was, although the banked coals still glowed in the firepit, and the three other shapes lying around it were still those of Rowena, the warden, and Kevin. It must still have been early then, she thought; surely no later than midnight if Click still stood watch. Unless he intended to let the rest of them sleep for most of the night, something he had been known to do in the past.

Suddenly interested in the Tinker's whereabouts, Cassidy silently rolled over under her blanket, turning so that she was facing out of the shelter. Turning so that she was facing Click.

Cassidy sucked in a shallow breath and willed her body to go limp, feigning sleep. Just outside the ragged thatch edge of the structure's roof stood Click's familiar dark lanky form, his torso bent as he wriggled to pull his damp shirt up over his head. His boots and socks were already on the ground beside him, and his leather vest was conveniently draped over one of the prop poles that supported the shelter's framework.

Her eyes religiously scrunched shut, Cassidy reminded herself to keep breathing, slowly and regularly. Click couldn't have seen her roll over, she convinced herself; not with his shirt up over his head. She just hoped that he wouldn't notice that she had suddenly changed positions. But as she heard the soft shucking sound of Click's fitted trousers being peeled down over his hips, her eyelids traitorously cranked open a fraction, and she squinted at the Tinker as he casually stripped off the last of his clothing.

Even though the rain had stopped, there was no light from the overcast sky. There wasn't much more light from the banked fire, but at that proximity its muted glow was enough; more than enough for the particular warm incandescence of that firelight to gild the long planes and lean curves of Click's naked body, throwing into distinct relief every contrasting shade of skin and texture of body hair.

Much as her sudden surprise had become guilt, Cassidy then discovered her momentary flirtation with guilt turning into an unapologetic appreciation and frank interest. Still forced to squint through nearly closed lids, she continued to breathe slowly and evenly, her body rocking lightly as she watched. Click bent to retrieve a scrap of cloth and a small knot of soap from the pot of water at his feet. His movements were smooth and economic, those not only of a man at home in his own skin but of a man in his own environment, who was capable of finding the simple luxury in even a bath taken out of a kettle of cold water in the middle of the wilderness.

Click buried his face in the soapy cloth, scrubbing it over his forehead and cheeks and mustache. Cassidy tried to squeeze shut her eyes. Then again, what harm could it do to just watch? she told herself, even as her little inner voice chuckled at her duplicity. What harm indeed, with her heart beginning to thump like a drum and the hot blood billowing through her veins, leaving her feeling fuzzy with a flush of heat and making the joints in her fingers ache with longing.

Click tilted his head back, the soapy water running down his neck and across his shoulders and collarbones. He swept the cloth lower then, over his chest and belly. He had not changed that much, Cassidy thought, from that summery morning along the Long River, the day he had stripped to wade out and check on the condition of the rapids. His hair was perhaps longer, his mustache shaggier and its tips grayer. He had a few more lines and a lot more old bruises and small, nearly healed wounds, including one across the bottom of his ribs that looked suspiciously like an old knife cut. But he was still essentially the same man who had so bedeviled and baffled and intrigued her that day that she had not been able to look away from him. And since that day he had become so much more: the man who had taken her in his arms and kissed her, the man whose hot tongue had filled her mouth, the man who remembered sex.

Cassidy's chest ached with the effort of maintaining the limp imitation of sleep, yet she kept watching Click. He had finished washing his legs, and his tanned and callused hands moved higher. Then he was scrubbing himself there, the rag moving a bit more slowly but just as casually. Cassidy knew that she had stopped breathing, and she tried to jolt herself out of the odd paralysis that seemed to have seized her. His body was no different from that of the warden or Kevin, she told herself; and only a few hours earlier she had seen those men wash themselves in the same manner. But it *was* different with Click, and Cassidy knew why.

The thunderous pulse of desire that Cassidy felt burning through her was no less painful for its utter lack of purpose. Just the fleetest thought, vigorously torn from her mind before it could

take root, of touching Click there—of touching Click anywhere—
was like trying to swallow a hot coal and then having to smother
its heat inside her belly. In desperation, she finally clenched her
eyes shut again, closing her lids like fists and choking back a long
exhalation of frustration and resignation.

A minute or two passed, Cassidy forcing her heart rate to slow
and her head to clear. When she squinted again through slitted
lids, Click was balanced on one foot, his other leg raised and bent
so that he could scrub at his sole and between his toes. He had
mopped most of the water from the rest of his body, but his skin
still gleamed dully in the dim firelight; moisture accentuated the
long lines of his arched back and highlighted the way his flanks
hollowed as he bent to his task.

Overcome by a potent mixture of guilt and desire and despair,
Cassidy let her eyes drop closed again, trying to refashion a convincing semblance of sleep, so that when the Tinker finally came
over to enter the shelter she would not have to perform any sudden transformation that might then betray her wakefulness. And
that was exactly how she was lying when Click's quiet words
caught her completely by surprise.

"Perhaps I could trouble you, Cassidy," he said, his calm whisper pitched just softly enough not to wake anyone around the fire
who had truly been asleep, "to reach my bedroll for me?"

Too astonished to even make any pretense of not having heard
him, Cassidy sat bolt upright, her eyes flying open as her mouth
dropped. In that moment it didn't matter that he was still standing
there stark naked; she just stared at him with a wide-eyed mixture
of shock and indignation. "You *knew* I was awake!" she hissed in
accusation. "Why didn't you *say* something?"

Utterly still, his posture as composed as his tone, Click merely
replied, "Why didn't you?"

Cassidy could feel the potent heat of a blush flooding up her
neck, pouring across her face until she was almost light-headed
from it. She scrambled furiously to her feet, one hand clenched
into a fist to keep her blanket securely wrapped around her shoulders, as she leaned over to snatch up Click's bedroll. Turning so
abruptly that she nearly tripped over the hem of her blanket, she
ducked out from under the overhang of the shelter's low roof and
crossed the few steps to where Click stood. But by that point her
automatic surge of energizing outrage had run its course, damped
out for lack of fuel, and Cassidy found that she could not even
look up to meet Click's eyes as she held out the bedroll to him.

Her gaze was lowered and her mind was rapidly stuttering

along over thoughts of apology when Click touched her. Because she still held his bedroll in one hand, and clutched her own blanket closed with the other, she was at a certain disadvantage when she felt the rough warmth of his palms lightly bracket her face, the sides of his thumbs gently brushing over the corners of her mouth. She was forced to look up at him then, despite his nakedness, despite her flushed face, despite the tremor that raced through her hands. And when she looked up it was directly into those dark eyes, eyes that suddenly seemed filled with a heat as intense and yet as covered, as protected, as the banked coals of the midnight fire.

Looking mutely at Click's face, Cassidy's gaze slipped lower, studying the curve of his lips beneath the damp sweep of his mustache. As vividly as if it had just happened, she remembered the touch of that mouth. Once again, just as she had on the night after the cougar's attack, Cassidy thought that perhaps he was about to kiss her. Only the possibility did not alarm her then; she *wanted* it.

But Click didn't kiss her. His hands slowly traced lower, coming to rest atop both her shoulders, the old irony kindling tenderly in those umber eyes. "There's no need to feel ashamed, Cassidy," he said softly. "I was not offended. And if I gave you any offense, then you have my deepest apology."

He was not mocking her, she knew; he was not even teasing her. And his utter sincerity was the one thing against which she had no defense. She didn't even have to speak, because he could simply read everything on her unshuttered face. For all of the good it did, she might just as well have dropped the blanket she still clutched around her; she was that naked before him.

But the moment had to come to an end, and Click ended it then. Tugging his bedroll free from her nerveless hand, he deftly flipped it open, unfurling the blanket and shaking his personal belongings into a small stack at his bare feet. As he casually slung the blanket over his shoulders, he turned to gather up his wet clothing. When he did so, Cassidy quietly slipped back to her own place beside the fire. And by the time Click ducked under the edge of the thatched roof's overhang and squatted down beside the warden to wake him for his watch, she was lying next to Rowena again, her back to the fire, her eyes closed.

With nothing more than an exchange of murmurs, the watch was changed. Cassidy heard the warden dress in his leathers, and the soft tread of his boots as he stepped out past her. Then she heard Click settling in, spreading his wet clothing by the fire, and the soft rustling of his blanket as he sank down into the humus.

Before she slept again, she heard over and over in her mind the simple candor the Tinker had offered her. *"I was not offended."* Had Click realized the helpless depth of her desire for him—or was he merely being honest? And considering their situation, she reminded herself glumly, did it really matter?

That night the rainy spell broke, and they enjoyed two days of clear and cooler weather. The terrain was still as rough, but with the fair skies and a brisk breeze, the mosquitoes abated. And even having to wind their way around the sumpy ground and bogs seemed far less of a chore in dry clothing and the sunshine.

The Snake's Spine, the narrow, twisting ridge of higher ground that they followed, proved a deceptive trail. On that first clear day there were relatively long stretches where the ridge was high enough above the sloughs that following its course was fairly easy. But the Spine had a disconcerting habit, much like the body of the animal for which it was named, of suddenly dipping down and just disappearing into the marshy ground. Then they would be forced to fan out and detour around swampy stretches before they found the ridge of firm ground again.

Cassidy was constantly surprised at how well Dragonfly adapted to the unpleasant vagaries of the swampland. Boggy ground was especially hazardous to horses, whose entire body weight was supported by four comparatively small feet. But Cassidy had already taken Dragonfly through some pretty awful footing during their stay in that world, often at the most imprudent of speeds, and the horse's agility had never failed her. Left to pick her own way, the mare usually showed them the quickest way to solid footing and the shortest distance between any two exposed points on the Spine.

The weather was not the only thing that seemed to have cleared after the night they had spent in the cypress grove. Perhaps the sunshine and the cooler air were at least partially responsible for the discernible upswing in everyone's mood; but Cassidy was certain that the better part of their improved spirits was due to finally having a more concrete goal in sight. She had believed that something would happen, and it had. Whatever quirk of fortune had brought the Woodsman to them and then engineered the circumstances that had ensured his indebtedness, she wasn't about to question it. She wasn't even going to question the accuracy of his information—at least not yet. For the first time since they'd left the Iron City, she finally felt that their goal was within reach. There was no point in spoiling that feeling with too much logic.

And if Cassidy had feared that somehow she had altered the balance of things between herself and Click, she didn't need to be concerned. To her surprise, if anything she felt even more comfortable around him. And for his part, Click continued to treat her with a genial ease. If at odd moments throughout the day, or most particularly at night when she lay waiting for sleep, Cassidy found her mind replaying select images from what happened that night—well, no one else, including Click, needed to know that.

The only one whose mood seemed oddly troubled at times was the warden. It was nothing explicit. He was his usual uncomplaining self as they trudged around the bogs or through the brush, and he was as willing as ever to do more than his fair share of the camp chores. He held forth with Click about the terrain, the weather, and foraging for supplemental food. He was consistently good-humored and indulgent with Kevin, treating his young follower as both a lifelong chum and a favored child. But there was still something about the warden that signaled to Cassidy a vague unease she could not pin down.

Cassidy thought that perhaps the problem was his concern for Valerie and regret for having to leave the captain behind. She realized with a twinge of guilt that since they had encountered the Woodsman, she had devoted far less time to worrying about the fate of the trio they had left behind them. But even that reason did not ring completely true for the warden. By the morning of their third day of fair weather, she determined that she would try to speak to him alone, to see if she could discover what had been bothering him.

As they broke camp that morning, Click said, "By my reckoning we've passed now beyond what are known as the Great Bogs."

Kevin's eyes widened. "You mean we're in the Great Swamp?"

The surrounding terrain was marshy lowlands to both sides, broken only by the narrow and wandering low ridge of the Spine, which was dotted with knots of brush and trees.

"It doesn't look any different to me," Rowena said.

The warden threw her a wry look. "Although this little ridge of land we've been following has become a bit more . . . capricious."

Click had been bent over his pack, tightening the straps. He straightened, easily shouldering his burden. "That's the main reason," he noted, "everyone has always just assumed that the Snake's Spine disappeared into the swamp."

As the others lifted their packs, the warden asked, "Then no one has ever followed it to the end?"

The ends of Click's mustache quirked, lifting in self-deprecation. "Woodsmen, obviously," he replied. "But the wild ones tend to keep their own counsel."

"But you think we're close to the end of it?" Cassidy persisted, glancing back to locate her mare.

Ahead of her, Click shrugged, settling his pack more comfortably against his back. The worn fabric of his shirt was just visible beneath the bottom of his leather vest. "A day or two by the Woodsman's count," he said.

For a few moments none of them spoke, each seemingly occupied with the significance of that possibility. Then Rowena said, "All I can say is I hope this Alchemist guy is also a whiz of a cook, because I sure am getting tired of seaman's rations and rabbits!"

That evening the mosquitoes returned with a vengeance. The day had been marked by repeated detours around bogs and a frustrating encounter with an almost impenetrable thicket of swamp alder. They made camp on the clearest spot they could find on the high ground, but the surrounding brush was still filled with clouds of the biting insects. Cassidy had been unable to find any jewelweed all afternoon, but Click showed her another flowering plant that seemed to have similar repellent properties, even if its bitter sap was sticky as well as stinky.

Cassidy helped Kevin gather firewood. The task had become more difficult the farther they traveled into the swamp because there were fewer large, old trees. Then she left Rowena to her pots and pans while she checked on the mare.

Cassidy was particularly relieved that Dragonfly's wounds were scabbed over and well on their way to healing, because as dusk settled the mosquitoes began gathering around the horse like field hands around a communal kitchen. The mare's long tail and mane were in constant motion, swishing and shaking irritably as the gray wedged her way into some low bushes, trying to dislodge as many of the pests as possible. Cassidy had gathered a bundle of ironweed during their last hours of travel, specifically to provide some relief for the horse. As she stood alongside the mare, twisting the wilted stems between her hands to release the pungent sap, Dragonfly sniffed suspiciously at the plants. Then, in that universal expression of disgust common to horses everywhere, the mare stretched out her neck and curled her upper lip in disdain.

"I don't think she cares much for the smell of that," an amused voice said from behind Cassidy.

She turned to see the warden standing by the edge of the bushes, casually swatting the mosquitoes from his own neck. He stepped closer then, reaching to take some of the crushed ironweed from Cassidy as he came up alongside the horse.

As she divided the bundle of twisted stalks with him, Cassidy drawled in a passable deadpan imitation of Webb, "But I've smelled worse."

Laughing appreciatively, the warden began rubbing down the mare's right side while Cassidy worked on the left. "I see you miss our pilot," he said, briskly chafing the gray's sleek coat with the odoriferous herb.

Cassidy glanced at him over the horse's broad back. "He should be back to the city by now," she said. Even as she said it, she realized it was a rather insensitive remark to have made to the erstwhile leader of that same city, a man who for all practical purposes had been forced out of it, and largely because of Cassidy herself. But from what she could see of his face then, lowered as he bent to his task, he seemed undisturbed. If anything, he appeared a bit pensive, absorbed with the rhythm of his hands sweeping over the big mare's body.

Seeing him with the horse, Cassidy was immediately reminded of just how at home the warden was around horses and how much he undoubtedly missed his own. He moved calmly and confidently around the gray, his hands deft and sure, but his attitude one of genuine affection for the mare. And Dragonfly responded to that, just as she responded to Click when the Tinker worked around her. For reasons Cassidy still did not fully understand, Click had given up his position among the Troopers and among all Horsemen. The warden had not abdicated his position by any means, and yet by default his exile was no less complete. There in the swamp the gray mare was the only horse in his custody; he had become a warden of one. Cassidy thought that he was probably as glad as she was for the mare's continued presence.

Shaking off her musing, Cassidy remembered her earlier decision to speak alone with him. She doubted that she would get any better chance. So when he squatted down to rub the crushed ironweed over the horse's lower legs, Cassidy also crouched down on her own side of the mare, looking over at the warden beneath the pale expanse of the gray's belly.

"Are you worried about Valerie?" she asked him without preface.

The warden seemed surprised by her question. His hands paused, wrapped around the mare's knee, and when he looked back across at Cassidy there was a mildly quizzical expression on his face. "Val is a very self-sufficient person," he said. "If anything, I'd worry about the sheriff and Becky, forced to try to keep her down!" As Cassidy smiled appreciatively, he went on. "I regret that we had to leave her behind, because I know how much it disturbs her to be separated from what she considers her overriding duty. But she and I both know that we did what had to be done, and there's been no permanent damage done."

So much for that line of discussion, Cassidy thought, resuming rubbing down the mare's foreleg. She supposed she should have realized that whatever had been troubling the warden could not have been anything as simple as Valerie's injuries or absence. While she pondered other possible inquiries, the warden caught her entirely off guard.

"What do you suppose has happened to Andy in the Slow World," he said quietly, "that he hasn't come to you again?"

So that was it, she thought. Suddenly reluctant to reveal the depth of her own concern on that very subject, Cassidy just shrugged and replied, "I don't know; but from what happened before, I'd guess that he hasn't been allowed to see me—Cathy—again."

The warden's hands remained stilled, caught cupping the bruised stalks of ironweed around the mare's cannon bone. "But this is different," he said soberly. "The last time, he said that they were going to take you away." He paused, then concluded, "What if they've taken you somewhere where he won't be allowed to see you any more? What if he never comes back?"

In Cassidy's opinion, the warden had every right to harbor mixed feelings about his lapses, considering how much they had disrupted his life. She was impressed by how, from the very beginning, he had been far more than merely tolerant of them; he had in fact welcomed them and cooperated with her in every way possible. Not for the first time, she marveled at the young man's resilience and equanimity in the face of such a powerful and potentially destructive force.

Squatting on the opposite side of the horse, equally still then, Cassidy made a mirror-image bookend to his own unmoving figure. "I don't think that'll happen," she said with genuine conviction. "I don't think Andy will let it happen, because I don't think he'll give up that easily."

A small smile, no less dazzling for its measured containment, illuminated that handsome face. "No, he isn't a quitter, is he?" the warden said, with satisfaction. But at his next question, spoken in that same soft, moderated tone, it was Cassidy's turn to feel surprise. "When you look at me, Cassidy, who is it that you see now: the warden of Horses, or Andy Greene?"

Caught momentarily speechless by the unexpected bluntness and unwitting intimacy of the question, Cassidy could only look across beneath the mare's belly at that painfully familiar face, torn by emotions that must have been clearly visible to him.

"When you first saw me," he said softly, "I know you thought that I *was* Andy. Then I tried to convince you that I *wasn't*." His self-effacement was a genial thing, effortless and almost conspiratorial in tone. "And now we both know that I am Andy—or at least that I'm both the warden and Andy."

"Is that—does that upset you?" she blurted out, suddenly assailed by another attack of the same vague guilt that seemed to have accompanied most of her ruminations about the warden of late.

But his smile was gentle, serious without being somber. Not precisely answering her question, he said instead, "You care a great deal about Andy, don't you, Cassidy?"

The mare shifted slightly then, her head whipping around to dislodge a mosquito from her shoulder. But Cassidy squatted there without even flinching. "The Andy you've shown me isn't exactly the same Andy I knew," she admitted. "In our world, there was never a way for me to reach him. So if I cared about him, I don't know if he ever realized it."

The warden's hand crossed the small distance between them, reaching out beneath the mare's belly to lightly clasp Cassidy's forearm. "Of course he realizes it, Cassidy," he said earnestly. "Look at how he trusts you; how concerned he is for you." His voice dropped then, softly intense. "There is no one else in your world who really matters to him."

To her embarrassment, Cassidy felt sudden tears filling her eyes, prickling behind her swollen lids. When she looked at the courageous and compassionate young man before her, she was cruelly reminded of all of the things Andy Greene could have been—would have been, had he been born normal.

But if he had been born normal, you never would have met him, would you? her little voice taunted.

To her further chagrin, she felt the gentle brush of the warden's fingertips across her cheeks, delicately sweeping away the tears that had silently spilled from her burning eyes. "Oh, Cassidy," he said tenderly, his face softened by the intimacy of all that only the two of them had shared, "don't you see? He knows how you feel—*I* know how you feel." He cupped her chin, his touch as ardent as a lover's. "I don't know what's going to happen to us, or how we will find our way. But I swear to you that neither Andy nor I will let you down."

By dawn low and rumpled clouds had replaced the fair skies, just as a certain anxious anticipation had replaced the group's previous hearty sense of purpose. The course of the Snake's Spine grew even more tortuous that morning, winding brokenly through the seemingly endless marshland, its uneven and eroded surface choked even more frequently by thick clumps of rank bushes and copses of stunted trees. Like a highway to nowhere, Cassidy thought morosely, during one of the many times they had had to wade out into the bog to get around a particularly impenetrable mass of undergrowth. It became easier for her to understand why everyone had assumed that the crumbling ridge of ground eventually just deteriorated completely, disappearing into the Great Swamp beyond. How could an island possibly exist in the midst of those vast reaches of unrelenting slough?

All morning Cassidy had noted a sort of edgy watchfulness in Click, even beyond his usual caution. He had said that he'd never been to the end of the Spine, but she knew that he had traveled the bogs before. Valerie had said Click had lost an entire Troop on just such an excursion, pursuing the same phantom. She had to wonder what unpleasant memories the swampland stirred in that dark, taciturn man. It pained Cassidy to consider the kind of cruel burden she may have placed again, however unwittingly, upon the uncomplaining man's shoulders. And it was the kind of pain that kept insistently nibbling around the edges of her heart, wearing at her defenses, daring Cassidy to admit the exact nature of the complex feelings she carried for the Tinker.

At midday they encountered yet another tangled overgrowth of thick brush and scrubby-looking trees, covering the entire width of the narrow ridge of higher ground they had been following. They all came to a halt, everyone scratching at mosquito bites and perspiring freely in the increasing humidity.

With a glance overhead at the cloudy skies, Click gave the others a speculative look.

The warden shrugged. "Let's go on ahead yet, through this," he suggested. "We can stop for lunch on the other side."

"Yeah," Rowena grumbled, "there's probably another sump on

the other side anyway." Even the brunette's cheerfulness was beginning to wear thin.

Whenever possible, they had been pushing their way through such sections of overgrowth, rather than risk wading out into the marsh. Vivid memories of the treacherous nature of the swamp's bottom continued to reinforce their wariness. However tiresome, a struggle through brush and branches usually seemed preferable to the chance of stepping into a sinkhole.

Cassidy encouraged Dragonfly to go on ahead of them. The mare's broad body plowed a crude path through the tangled brush, and she easily avoided the thin boles of the stunted trees. If nothing else, the terrain had grown relatively flat, with no sudden dropoffs or shaley ravines to clamber up and down. The most common hazard was getting smacked in the face by an errant branch or briar, or having to battle the clouds of insects that rose, humming, from the thick foliage.

It took them almost twenty minutes to fight their way through the section of overgrowth. Finally Cassidy tripped over a half-exposed tree root and stumbled after the mare out of the tangled brush. Beyond the last bushes, there were a few yards of relatively clear ground, dotted with short sedge grass and even a few bare spots littered with pebbly scree. It was an unexpectedly good spot for their lunch stop. Or at least it would have been, had it not been for one little detail.

Cassidy didn't have to turn around and look back; she could hear each of the others, as they pushed their way out of the bushes behind her, come to a complete and abrupt halt. For the first long moment not a word was spoken; but what wasn't spoken hung in the air, as thick as the pall of humidity.

Beyond the small clear strand where they stood, tired and scratchy and sweating, the ridge of higher ground they had been following simply disappeared into the reedy green expanse of the Great Swamp.

Chapter 14 ◀▥

Rowena was the first to break the silence, her voice filled with disgust. "That little shit *lied* to us!" she exclaimed.

Just then the gray mare exhaled noisily; she quickly fell to cropping the short tough grass. Cassidy looked from the marsh, which seemed to surround them in almost a 360-degree arc, to the grazing mare, and then back again. She was speechless with disappointment and irrationally irritated at the horse for her indifference. She glanced sideways as Click stepped past her, nearly right to the edge of the slough, where he stood staring out across the swamp.

Kevin turned to the warden, his boyish face utterly crestfallen. "What are we going to do now?" he asked plaintively.

But the warden seemed singularly undaunted. He stepped up alongside Click and joined him in gazing out over the marsh. After a moment the warden said, "We're going to go on."

"What?" Rowena asked in amazement. She gestured. "Out into *that*?"

Click looked back at them then, his dark eyes alight with some secret irony. "The Woodsman didn't lie," he said matter-of-factly. "He merely told the truth as he knew it. You must remember, we've had a very wet summer." His head inclined slightly toward the marsh. "The Spine is still there; it's just been partially submerged."

"Come here," the warden urged, beckoning them forward. "If you look carefully, you can still see the tops of many of the bushes out there in the swamp, sticking up just above the surface of the water, where there aren't any reeds or sedges."

Reluctantly scrutinizing the vast marshland, Rowena muttered skeptically, "You've got to be kidding! If those are the tops of the bushes, how deep do you think that water is?"

266

"Actually, it's probably only a few feet deep in most places," Click said mildly. He shielded his brow with one hand as he slowly scanned the glittering greenish surface of the stagnant water. "This part of the Spine is probably under water at least part of every season, unless it's been an unusually dry year. Trees don't tolerate that kind of constant flooding; but the brush regrows each year when the waters recede. Most of the bushes out there are only about waist high."

Cassidy glanced from the seemingly endless swamp to the Tinker's calm face. "You mean we can just walk out there—right through the marsh?"

The tips of Click's mustache quirked slightly. "Right down the Spine, yes," he said, "if we're careful."

"But where are we going?" Kevin asked uneasily. "There's nothing out there."

"Oh, but there is," the warden assured him. "Come here, Kev." As the blond boy came alongside him, the warden put one arm over Kevin's shoulder and used his other arm to point out across the swamp. "You see out there, right along the horizon? Those darker green clumps?" He patted Kevin encouragingly on the back. "Unless my eyes fail me, those are the tops of trees."

Kevin shot him a quick, excited look. "The island?"

The warden smiled. "Well, technically it's a peninsula, I suppose, since most of the time it's connected to this ridge of land."

"I don't care if it's the lost continent of Atlantis," Rowena muttered under her breath, "I'm not walking out into that swamp!"

Ignoring the brunette, Cassidy looked over at Click. "How far do you think it is to those trees?" she asked.

Click didn't even have to glance out at the marsh again to answer. "About two miles would be my estimate." He met her eyes directly. "A good afternoon's trek, under the circumstances."

"You're kidding," Rowena said. "We're really going to just walk right out into that bog?"

But no one needed to respond. Even Rowena realized that if they failed to go on, they had simply failed.

Shucking his pack, Click easily fell into the basic pragmatism of command. "While lunch is being prepared, the rest of us will cut some saplings and make a small float for our bedrolls and other supplies." At Rowena's continuing frown, he explained, "There's a chance the water will be deep enough in places that we'll have to swim."

"Why don't we just build a raft then?" Rowena asked.

But Click just patiently shook his head. "Even if there were trees here that were large enough, it would take at least a day to construct a raft big enough to carry us." He gestured out over the reed-choked swamp. "And even if we had a raft, we'd never be able to propel it through this marsh. Rafts have a deep draft, Rowena; they're suitable for open water, but not for these kinds of conditions."

"So we have to walk?" Rowena said glumly.

"It shouldn't be too difficult," the warden said sympathetically. "Remember, we'll still be walking along the Spine, so we'll be on firm ground."

"As long as we're careful," Click added, pulling his knife out of his pack.

"Yeah, careful and lucky," Rowena said morosely. But she began to prepare lunch without further objection.

It took Click about twenty minutes to fashion a small, sled-size float; less time than it took Cassidy and Kevin to gather tinder and Rowena to ready the food. Cassidy was impressed by the way the Tinker had managed to weave the entire little craft together out of saplings, without having to use any of their rope or other binding material. While they sat eating, Click cut a short length of the old anchor line to provide a pull strap for the float. After lunch was over, and all of their bedrolls and other supplies were safely stowed, Click uncoiled their other rope, the one they'd taken from Clam Cove.

Although Click had acted nothing but utterly calm, Cassidy could not shake the distinct feeling that some deeply unpleasant memories had been the Tinker's constant companions on their entire journey; and something was stirring them again. "One of us will have to walk point," Click said evenly, "and lead us along the Spine. The rest of us will follow at the end of the rope."

Cassidy frowned at him. "Aren't we going to space ourselves out along the rope?" she asked, thinking of the way they'd crossed the rivers on their way down to the cove. "So the point has some backup?"

Click's tone was simply explanatory, but something darker moved briefly across his expression, betraying some old unnamed pain. "That might provide more backup for the point," he conceded easily, "but it would increase the risk for the rest of us. This way, if something happens to the point, we still have the full length of the rope in which to react. And four of us will be available on the end of it if the need arises."

Just what the hell had happened to Click's Troop? Cassidy found herself wondering, as she watched those tanned and sinewy hands play out the loops of hemp. What secret loss and shameful disgrace were hidden behind those hooded eyes? And how could a man who was both more clever and more courageous than any man she had ever known in either world have been responsible for such a catastrophic failure?

Click nodded at Kevin. "You would be my choice to lead," he said, "if you're willing."

"I want to do it," Kevin said stolidly.

The warden helped Kevin fasten one end of the rope around his waist with a hitching knot. "Just follow the clumps of brush, Kevin," he prompted him, "and keep testing the ground ahead of you to be sure you're still on firm footing." He gave the younger man's shoulder an affectionate squeeze. "And remember, all of us will be on the other end of this rope."

"I'm not afraid," Kevin repeated simply. But Cassidy could see that he basked in the warden's confidence, absorbing the implicit praise like dry earth soaking up water. She thought Kevin probably would have tried to cross the swamp by walking on water, if that was what the warden had asked of him.

Before Kevin stepped into the slough, Click gave them all some further instructions. "I'll take second position," he said, "as I have the greatest strength." There was no self-aggrandizement in his statement; it was merely the truth. If Kevin got into trouble, they would need the strongest person right behind him on the rope. "I want Rowena behind me," Click went on, "then the warden with the float." He gave Cassidy a small nod. "I want you in the rear with your horse, Cassidy. Let her find her own path, but keep her behind us." He paused, his gaze taking in all of them again. "If we are careful, this will just be one more obstacle to cross. But you must understand one thing: If there's trouble, *listen* first to what I tell you to do—don't just react." Click's dark eyes were shuttered then, hard and almost blank in their intensity. "Just listen to me, no matter what happens."

His words sent an unbidden chill through Cassidy, and she felt a slight shiver in spite of the muggy warmth of the overcast day. As she watched Kevin slowly wade into the shallow, opaque water, for the first time since her earliest days of traveling with Click and his band of Tinkers, she found herself needled by the thinnest sliver of doubt about the man who led them. She immediately rejected the thought as unworthy, but the fact that it had occurred to her at all was enough to make her vaguely uneasy.

Click played out the rope evenly as Kevin carefully stepped farther into the slough. The water only came to slightly above the young man's knees, but he moved as deliberately as some ancient arthritic making his way through deep snow. When Kevin was finally almost to the end of the rope, Click waded out into the algae-covered water. Right behind Click, like some dutiful peasant wife following two paces behind her husband, Rowena entered the marsh. The warden took hold of the frame of the loaded float to launch it before he, too, stepped into the water, the tow strap wrapped tightly around his hand.

Cassidy initially had wondered why Click wanted the mare behind all of them as they crossed the flooded ridge. It seemed more sensible to her to allow the horse to go first, since the animal's heightened senses and natural instinct for self-preservation would give her an added edge in dangerous situations. Cassidy had no doubt that Dragonfly would have been able to follow the sunken Spine, no matter how deep the water grew. But she figured that Click must have his reasons. For one thing, she thought, if one or more of them did become mired in the muck, they might need the horse's strength to pull them free again. In that case, it made sense to keep the mare near the end of the rope. And conversely, if the horse did somehow manage to get caught in a sinkhole, it would have been almost impossible for them to get her out of it. Perhaps Click wanted the horse behind them so that she would be the safest.

Once she was actually out in the marsh, walking slowly through the knee-high water, Cassidy tried not to let her mind wander. It seemed especially important to be on the alert there, even if the going was still quite easy, with the unseen ground reassuringly firm beneath her feet. She didn't even think about the fact that she was going to get soaking wet again. She just concentrated on keeping her place behind the steadily moving line of people.

Although the mare obediently trailed Cassidy, she quickly grew bored with their funereal pace. Cassidy could hear the muted slosh of the gray's legs, punctuated by the light flapping sound of the horse lipping at the greenish surface of the water and the occasional nasal gust of her snorts as she amused herself. And in some odd way, Cassidy found the horse's boredom reassuring.

They hadn't traveled very far into the marsh before the unpredictable course of the Spine had become obvious. Just as in its unsubmerged portions, the ridge never took the shortest distance between two points. Fortunately, Kevin was extremely conscientious on point, taking absolutely nothing for granted as he made his way from one nearly covered clump of brush to another. Click meticulously duplicated Kevin's path, as if he had memorized the very footsteps of the young man who waded the rope's length ahead of him.

It also didn't take very long before their goal became more clearly visible. Strung like a green mirage along the western horizon, the trees that marked the proof of higher ground grew more distinct. And what they had been able to see from the last dry point on the Spine was no small patch of forest; as they progressed farther into the marsh, Cassidy could see that the nearest trees covered only the closest spit of land. Beyond that narrow wedge was a much larger body of land, its thickly wooded surface spreading out to either side as far as she could see. The "island" the Woodsman had spoken of was beginning to look more like a continent.

The first time the water grew noticeably deeper, they had traveled nearly a quarter mile into the swamp. Cassidy had been alternating between watching Kevin and watching the few feet of disturbed water that lay between her and the float, when she saw the blond boy hesitate momentarily. Like a blind man finding his way solely by touch, Kevin felt with his boot before proceeding. As he moved forward again, the water level began to climb along his thighs. When it had reached the middle of his chest, he paused again, deliberately studying the lime-green surface of the slough.

"Steady, Kevin," Click said quietly from behind him. "If it gets so deep that you'll have to swim, wait until we all have reached you before proceeding."

"I don't think it's going to get that deep here," Kevin said. He started forward again, his body slicing smoothly through the tepid water, like a solo dancer in some bizarre aquatic display.

Cassidy wished that she could take the increasing depth of the water with Kevin's equanimity. Water that was midchest on him came nearly up to her neck. But there was nothing to do but follow. She ignored the mare's stenorous grunts and groans of boredom from behind her, and instead tried to concentrate on the gentle glide of the baggage float, riding silently behind the Warden. Had she not, in fact, been so focused on the little raft, she might entirely have missed what happened then.

Automatically falling back a step or two, Cassidy stared at the little wooden float. Had she actually just seen it bob up in the water like a sled riding over a bump in the snow? Nothing around the small craft had moved; she was certain of that. There had been no disruption of the surface of the slough, nor of the tips of the

reeds and sedge grass that barely crested the water on either side
of them. Had she just imagined the random movement?

Looking back over her shoulder, Cassidy saw that the mare was
still plodding patiently behind her, bright chartreuse algae sticking
to her chest and flanks, her crescent-shaped ears lolling out at
half-mast to either side of her lowered head as the horse idly
nipped at the tips of brush she passed. No sign of alarm there,
Cassidy thought; although the horse had never seemed afraid of—

A sudden chill raced out along Cassidy's veins, dancing on the
heady swell of adrenaline. *It* can't *be monsters!* she told herself,
painfully and pulse-poundingly aware of being stuck neck deep in
the middle of nowhere, balanced on a narrow high wire of safe
ground in the middle of a vast sea of sucking mud. *Not now—not
like this, when we're so close—*

As if to mock her, directly in front of Cassidy the wooden float
gracefully rose a few inches in the water and then waggled rhythmically on its tether, like the wriggling tail of a happy dog.

Since the float wasn't tugging against its line, the warden
seemed unaware of what was happening behind him. The little
display appeared to have been calculated for Cassidy's benefit
alone; and she could only stare at it with dry-mouthed dread,
waiting for whatever might follow.

But nothing followed. Cassidy was concentrating so hard on
keeping her eyes on the float that for a few moments she almost
forgot to keep walking, until the interval between her and the warden had nearly tripled. Then she hurried forward again, her legs
feeling numb and tingling. Had she imagined what she thought
she had seen?

Within a few minutes, the submerged ridge of land began to
rise again. Kevin's torso reappeared above the surface of the water; then his hips, and finally even his thighs. Soon they were
sloshing along in water barely knee deep. The distant trees were
definitely growing closer, but they still were decidedly too far
away for Cassidy's comfort. Unlike the mare's tolerant boredom,
her own restlessness had been honed with a new sharp edge of
anxiety. The remaining distance, while insignificant compared to
what they had already traveled since leaving the Iron City, suddenly seemed unbearably far.

When the warden spoke to her, he startled Cassidy. "How's
your mare doing?" he asked, without turning back to look.

"She's fine," Cassidy replied promptly, biting back the urge to
start some nervous, inane conversation. "I think she's getting
bored, though."

"Good," he said. "Let's hope she stays that way."

For a long distance, the water remained shallow; so shallow in spots that their greatest problem was not in following the submerged ridge, but in making their way over or around the low scrubby brush that dotted it. The mare cropped at a few branches as they passed, more out of habit than any real hunger. After a time, Cassidy began to relax a bit again and to study the characteristic ways the people ahead of her moved. Even in the water, each of them more or less duplicated the way he or she usually moved on dry land.

Cassidy was more disappointed than surprised when the water grew deeper again. The change was gradual, with Kevin's body slowly resubmersing in the swamp's stagnant embrace. The exposed tops of the brush that he used as guidelines disappeared, and Kevin spent what seemed to Cassidy to be a nerve-wracking length of time testing and retesting the hidden bottom with his feet before he would proceed. When the water had reached his chest again he faced an open expanse of marsh, where all landmarks had vanished.

"What do you think, Kevin?" Click said calmly from behind him. "Is the water still growing deeper?"

Kevin nodded solemnly. "I think it'll go over our heads," he said. "And I'm not sure where the ridge goes from here."

"Stay where you are," Click instructed him evenly. Then he looked back over his shoulder at the others in line behind him and said, "Stay directly behind me." Slowly and steadily, Click closed the gap between himself and Kevin, coiling up the loops of rope as he advanced. By the time they had reached Kevin, the water was once again up to Cassidy's neck.

"I don't like this," Rowena said anxiously, her glance skimming over the flat and motionless expanse of torpid marsh.

"I don't much care for it myself, Rowena," Click agreed easily, "but we're nearly halfway across now." There was irony in his voice, but his tone was more one of sympathy than teasing. "It would be as far now to go back as to go on; and I'd much prefer being in that forest ahead of us than back on that dead-end ridge of land."

"I think we're going to have to swim," Kevin said matter-of-factly. The blond boy's steady pragmatism in the face of adversity made Cassidy especially glad that she hadn't said anything earlier when the incident with the float had made her suspect monsters.

Click looked past Kevin, studying the flat, algae-coated surface of the marsh. "I think you're right, Kevin," he said. He pointed out across the water. "You see that place where there are three clumps of reeds in a row? And the stippling of sedge grass just beyond it?"

Kevin squinted dutifully across the swamp, then nodded. "Just past that long gap after the two patches of reeds?"

"Exactly," Click replied. "Swim directly to that point. Don't worry about trying to follow the ridge, and don't try to touch bottom, even if the water appears shallow enough. Just beyond those three clumps of reeds are the tips of several bushes. Don't try to gain your footing until you've reached that point. Once you're on firm ground again, the rest of us will follow."

Nodding his understanding, Kevin quickly released the hitching knot that bound the end of the rope around his waist.

"Do you think that's a good idea?" Rowena said dubiously. "I thought we were all supposed to stay together, in case someone gets in trouble."

But Kevin turned and gave Rowena a reassuring look. "Don't worry," he said. "I'm a good swimmer, and it's only about a hundred feet."

"Go directly to that point, Kevin," Click repeated as he recoiled the slack in the rope.

Free in the water, Kevin swam like a young otter, slicing so smoothly through the scum of algae and greenish slime that not even his sodden clothing seemed to fetter him. Cassidy couldn't help but remember the first time she'd seen the blond boy swim, on her first morning in that strange world. When he had walked out of the river, totally naked, he'd given her quite a surprise. She was impressed by the tantalizing detail of her recall.

It took Kevin only a couple of minutes to reach the clumps of reeds. He circled a moment before he righted himself. His expression was bemused as he straightened and stood, because the water came only to his waist. Tossing back his soaking ponytail, he called out unnecessarily, "It's a lot shallower here."

Click looped the coil of rope over one shoulder and around his neck. "We'll cross one at a time," he said. "Don't begin until the person ahead of you has reached solid ground." He paused for a moment, then added pointedly, "And don't become complacent. There is nothing simple about this."

As Cassidy watched Click push off into the deeper water, she remembered her earlier moment of sheer panic as she'd followed the float. Maybe the Tinker didn't realize it, but complacency was the farthest thing from her mind.

With the gray mare impatiently shifting and snorting behind

her, Cassidy waited as first Click, then Rowena, and finally the warden swam across the open water to where Kevin stood. Only when she was certain that the warden was on solid ground, and had pulled the float close after him, did she lean forward and kick off into the tepid and vaguely unpleasant-smelling water. It was almost a pleasure to be able just to stretch out and swim, however, and she even pushed herself a little, the subtle ache in the muscles of her arms and legs a welcome contrast to the long periods of constant tension. The sweep of her arms and the kick of her feet propelled her briskly through the turbid water. It was too bad, she thought wistfully, that they couldn't just swim across the whole damned swamp.

Then something brushed her ankle.

At first Cassidy tried to tell herself that her legs must have somehow crossed up and she had bumped herself, even though she realized that was patently absurd. But then what were the alternatives? Nothing that bore close scrutiny, at least not as long as she was stuck out there, helplessly swimming above the treacherous muck of the marsh bottom.

Behind her, Dragonfly still swam steadily, almost leisurely, her larger body creating a small forward wake that seemed to propel Cassidy along, as well. Cassidy suddenly realized that the horse would have to touch bottom before she did, and she hoped that when the mare did, there would be solid footing beneath her. Distracted by that concern, she didn't even flinch when she felt something lightly nudge her leg again. She was nearly up to the others; she refused to panic. Moments later, her feet touched the bottom; and when she looked back over her shoulder, the mare was already sloshing up into the shallows, the greenish water sluicing off her broad back and streaming from her long tail.

Cassidy didn't realize that she had hesitated until she felt Click grasping her by the wrists, pulling her to her feet. "Are you all right?" he asked her. His tone was level, but there was a thinly veiled concern in his dark eyes.

Feeling a little stupid, Cassidy quickly nodded. She was alarmed to find that she had been on the verge of blurting out what had just happened to her. But she caught herself, just as she regained her balance, standing in the waist-deep water. All she could think of was Kevin's calm steadiness on point and Rowena's nagging fears. It seemed both cruel and dangerous to alarm them over such flimsy evidence. Maybe she had just bumped into a waterlogged branch, or even a water snake, she thought resolutely. Even as she watched Kevin knotting the rope around his waist again, she deliberately forced herself to ignore the blatant transparency of her own explanations.

What the hell could you do even if it is monsters? she reminded herself acerbically. *Tell everyone to run for it?*

So Cassidy did the only thing she could under the circumstances. She dutifully took her place at the end of the line as they all started forward again, wading in the hip-deep water.

For a time, as they proceeded steadily through relatively shallow water, and the dark-green backdrop of the island's trees slowly grew closer, Cassidy was convinced the worst was over. After all, they were over halfway across the marsh. And Kevin seemed increasingly adept at ferreting out the submerged course of the Spine, adroitly weaving and winding his way from one tuft of brush to another. The depth of the water fluctuated, from barely knee deep to almost up to her neck again. But as they drew nearer to the island, close enough to be able to clearly see the vast wall of trees and the details of its sumpy, reed-choked shores, Cassidy thought it unlikely that they would have to swim again.

Her glance kept going to the verdant land that lay ahead. The size and variety of the trees suggested age and permanence, filling her with the unexpected concern that the island's terrain might turn out to be just as rough and trackless as the rugged hill country they had already crossed. The Woodsman had not provided them with any details about where they would find this odd man whom he had heard tell of. If the island was as large and heavily forested as it appeared, they could conceivably have a long hunt ahead of them.

Preoccupied, Cassidy nearly bumped right into the little float. When her attention snapped back to the line of people ahead of her, she immediately realized that the reason she'd overtaken the little raft was that everyone else had stopped moving. Kevin stood motionless in the thigh-deep water, his arms held out slightly from his body so that just the tips of his fingers skimmed the surface, and his head cocked as if he were listening for something.

"What is it, Kevin?" Click said calmly.

Kevin's voice was even, but there was a peculiar frown on his face, an expression that seemed oddly familiar to Cassidy. "Something touched me," he said.

To Cassidy's bemusement, the expected spurt of adrenaline did not come. Or if it did come, she simply didn't feel its usual effects.

"Go on, Kevin," Click said. His voice was quiet, but the words were most definitely a command.

The blond boy took a few more cautious steps, his head still cocked, staring down at the opaque surface of the slough as if he actually expected to be able to see anything beneath the water. Then he came to another abrupt halt, his body swaying slightly, like an aerialist maintaining his balance on a high wire.

"It's underneath me," he said softly.

Still no numbing tingle, no energizing racing of her pulse: Cassidy was mildly disappointed at the prospect of having to face the unseen hazard without the benefit of adrenaline's familiar effects. As she watched with a certain glum fascination, Kevin's entire body shuddered gently, as if he'd inadvertently stepped onto some kind of vibrating platform instead of firm ground.

"It's like the thing in the river," Kevin said, his tone a dull monotone. Only his odd-colored eyes betrayed his reaction, widening in recognition.

Without turning to look back at her, Click said, "Cassidy?" But in the uttering of that single word, the Tinker managed to convey to her exactly what he was asking of her.

Stepping around the quiescent float, Cassidy edged past the warden, Rowena, and finally Click himself. Midway between Click and where Kevin still stood, she paused, her feet stumbling over some minor unevenness in the submerged ground.

Cassidy tried to project into her voice some of the strangely detached calm that she still felt. "Kev?" she said. "Just go on. Walk right over it. I'll be right behind you."

Kevin's gaze lifted then, looking directly at her. His expression was not exactly one of fear, but more one of indecision. "How will I know where the ridge is?" he asked with surprising pragmatism. "It keeps moving under me."

Cassidy looked across at Kevin's face, rather than down at the dully reflective skin of green scum that floated over the marsh. She moved forward again, stepping slowly and deliberately. When she was almost to Kevin's side, she felt the light, spiraling caress of something winding its way between her calves; she had to stumble before she regained her balance. Then one of her feet came down on a surface that definitely was not the flooded earth of the Spine. The next thing she knew, she and Kevin both were being flung sideways, tumbling into the brackish water with a great sloppy splash.

Kevin's hands grasped Cassidy by the upper arms, immediately helping her right herself as the two of them staggered to their feet like a pair of drunken dancers. Once more the ground was reassuringly solid beneath them. As Kevin steadied her, Cassidy coughed out a mouthful of scummy water, mildly embarrassed that she had forgotten to hold her breath as her head had been dunked into the swamp.

"Cassidy?" Click said, again the single word.

"We're okay," she said, her voice still raspy from the large gulp of algae-laden water.

"Is it the same kind of creature you encountered in the Deadfall River?" Click asked.

"I think it's the same thing," Kevin said uncertainly. "We never actually saw anything then, so—"

The blond boy broke off abruptly as something—some formless mass that moved with amazing speed and an uncanny sinuous accuracy—slid between Cassidy and himself, its rapid passage not even stirring a ripple on the stagnant surface of the marsh. Cassidy rocked back slightly in surprise, but she was steadied by the grip of Kevin's hands on her arms.

The damned things were *toying* with them, she thought in wonder, just as earlier something had been toying with the float. She met Kevin's eyes, relieved to find that although he looked decidedly uneasy, he was a long way from panic.

"What are we going to do, Cassidy?" he asked quietly. "How are we going to get past them?"

Cassidy temporized by making a minor show of looking all around them, studying the motionless plane of algae as if some necessary clue might be found there. "I don't think they'll hurt us, Kev," she said. It was a major piece of whistling past a graveyard, especially considering what the water monsters had done to Kevin. "If they'd wanted to harm us, they could have come after us right away, as soon as we'd stepped into the swamp."

Duplicating Cassidy's scan of the surrounding water, Kevin retained a hint of skepticism. "Then what *are* they doing?" he asked.

"Damned if I know," Cassidy confessed readily. "Maybe they're just trying to annoy us; you know, make it harder for us to reach land."

"It's hard enough already," Kevin murmured heartily.

Cassidy reached down and began to tug free the hitching knot from the rope tied around Kevin's waist. As his hands dropped from her arms to prevent her from doing so, she stepped back, pulling the rope loose.

"Cassidy, what are you doing?" Rowena demanded anxiously.

"It's okay," she said. The nice thing about her inexplicable sense of calm was that her hands were deft and unshaking as she secured the end of the rope around her own waist. "I'm going to go first now. I think I'm the one they're really interested in."

"What do you mean, 'interested in'?" the brunette echoed unhappily. But Cassidy didn't even try to explain.

Click beckoned to Kevin. "Come back here, Kevin," he said. "Let Cassidy go first."

Cassidy didn't turn back because she didn't want to see the expressions on the faces behind her. She just gave Kevin a gentle shove in their direction. She waited a few moments, idly scanning the surface of the marsh, until she was certain the blond boy had safely reached the others. Then she began to move forward through the murky hip-deep water.

The one thing Cassidy found she really missed about the adrenaline high was its edge, the buzzy sort of rush that heightened her perceptions and stropped her senses to a finely honed acuity. Without it, even the basic task of seeking out the path of the Spine seemed so large that it occupied nearly all of her attention, at a time when she wanted to be able to concentrate on other matters, as well. Like just what the hell those things were, she thought, as she slowly waded forward, and just what the hell they were up to.

When she glanced ahead across the increasingly reed- and sedge-dotted marsh, Cassidy estimated that they were only a couple of hundred feet from the boggy shore of the island. It was close enough to see the details of the half-rotted snags and piles of waterlogged wood that clotted the sumpy holes at the water's edge. It was even close enough to imagine finally crawling up out of that sodden swamp, close enough to believe that not much more could possibly happen in so short a space. She could even see the ragged trail of the mostly submerged brush that marked the Spine, curving in an elongated S toward that rough point of land.

Cassidy was looking down at the marsh again, studying the location of the next cluster of bush tops, when a subtle, languid current stirred the bright layer of algae cloaking the surface of the water. Like some vague thermal current rising from a heating liquid, the flat plane of the water bulged slightly, as if buckling from some unseen pressure below. Then something huge and flat and darkly gleaming began to break the surface of the swamp directly ahead of Cassidy.

Blinking in surprise, she almost forgot to stop moving forward. Then the rope between her and Click tightened, biting into her waist. A *thing*—a monster, she guessed she would have had to concede—covered the entire surface of the water before her, its vast, more or less circular shape delicately fluttering to some secret rhythm of its own making. The velvety sheen of its mass reminded Cassidy of the soft, coal-colored bodies of the big black leeches they had discovered when they had crossed the Bracken River. But from its size and shape it resembled nothing so much as a giant floating floor mat. It looked as if someone had taken a glob of black rubber the size of a cow and then steamrolled it out into a flat circle about an inch thick. No wonder stepping onto it had felt like stepping onto a trampoline, Cassidy thought.

Because she couldn't quite see just walking right into the damned thing, Cassidy was forced to stand there, watching the creature as its quivering rhythm pulsated along its blunt edges, sending little waves of ripples racing over the surface of the marsh. She didn't see how anything that size could have slipped between her and Kevin earlier; or even how it could have frolicked about in the shallow water around the float without her having seen something. Were there other things in the swamp, as well, then; things smaller and more agile?

While Cassidy stood there deliberating her next move, the vast matlike creature suddenly moved. Barely disturbing the surface of the water, the huge black circle rolled itself up like a giant crepe and just . . . *melted together* was the only comparison that came to mind, as Cassidy watched in astonishment. What seconds earlier had been a thin, flat, circular expanse was then instantly transformed into something long and cylindrical, like a black snake. That sinuous shape coiled over on itself and disappeared beneath the turbid surface of the marsh, only the faintest of ripples even marking where it had been.

"Cassidy?" Click said. It was both a question and an expression of concern. For the first time the Tinker's voice had lost its seamless veneer of calm control; and that development surprised Cassidy nearly as much as anything she had just seen.

"It's gone," she said. "Let's go."

Boldly edging forward with one foot, Cassidy took a step, encountering nothing but solid ground. She began to walk again. She knew that Click was following, because she was not checked by the pull of the rope around her waist.

So close to their goal, Cassidy fiercely narrowed her focus to nothing but the gentle curve of the underwater ridge, thinking only from one scummy nest of bush tips to the next, refusing to anticipate anything else. The sedge-choked point of the rising wedge of dry land drew incrementally nearer, step by sloshing step. The water still came to midthigh, but refuge was less than fifty feet away.

Cassidy never even sensed it coming. The hidden force that jerked her legs out from beneath her and pulled her under the surface of the murky water caught her entirely by surprise. She involuntarily swallowed a large gasp of the bilious liquid as she went under. For a few seconds she found herself caught in an almost comic tug-of-war. The rope that was knotted around her waist pulled her one way, and something much stronger and yet oddly formless drew her feet and lower body in the opposite direction. She tried to struggle, but her burning lungs demanded most of her energy; her only thought was how badly she wanted to get some air.

But what might have turned into panic, had her brain been given sufficient oxygen for rational thought, became instead simple outrage. Doubling over under the water, Cassidy reached down toward her ankles and dug both of her hands into the powerful coils that ensnared her. A dull sprinkling of erratic light exploded behind her eyes, presaging the loss of consciousness. Her groping fingers sunk into the soft rubbery flesh of the snakelike black creature, and then—

—*And then everything simply stopped.*

Chapter 15 ◄▉▉

Later, Cassidy would remember thinking at that moment that she must have lost consciousness, and then realizing that couldn't be what had happened.

She couldn't have lost consciousness, because she hadn't ceased being aware of what was going on around her. Rather, *nothing* was going on around her. She could feel the vague pressure of the tepid swamp water pressing in around her body, suspending her, but nothing was moving. There was no pull on the rope around her waist and no tension on her legs from the creature that had coiled around her ankles. There was no aching sting in her lungs, no sharp throbbing in her head, no blood pounding in her veins. There was no sense of any movement anywhere. For some perfectly discrete but indeterminate space of time, it was as if everything in the world just stood still.

Then everything moved again.

And when the world started up again, it was with a lurch. The sinuous coils that had been holding her under the water suddenly released their grip, sending Cassidy shooting to the surface of the marsh, aided by the added propulsion of the rope. Coughing and gasping, she tried to stagger to her feet. She was only about ten feet away from Click, but as she slewed sideways she felt her feet sink into the soft sucking bottom of the swamp. She thought she heard someone shout her name, but her only immediate concern was trying to expel enough of the foul water from her trachea so that she could draw one deep breath before the treacherous mud dragged her beneath the water again.

As her feet plunged deeper into the grasping muck, the swamp water closing over her like the dropping of a coffin lid, Cassidy found herself fervently wishing that the world would just *stop* again. She had discovered that she harbored an impressive desire to live—in that world, in any damn world at all—and the prospect of imminent drowning finally tripped in her that long-delayed gush of adrenaline, a bolus of pure fire exploding through her veins. The rope was cutting painfully into her waist; she grappled futilely for the wet hemp, trying to pull herself free. Then suddenly another set of hands was on her body, arms locking around her torso, the fabric of her loose shirt ripping as ruthless fingers locked together beneath her breasts.

Oh, Click—no! Cassidy thought in despair, horrified to think that he had violated his own first rule of safety and had abandoned the firm footing of the ridge to join her in the deathtrap of the sinkhole, damning himself to share her fate.

But the tension on the rope around her waist never slackened, even as Click's body swung around hers in the water. With a sharp little stab of relief, she realized that Click was *swimming* beside her. The others still provided traction on the rope, as she and the Tinker rocked and bumped into each other. But for all of their combined efforts, Cassidy knew that she was still sinking; just as she knew that very soon, entirely without volition, she was going to have to take a deep breath. The fact that she would be filling her lungs with swamp water rather than air was not a matter of choice.

Hands trembling from the adrenaline, Cassidy released her hold on the rope and reached out to touch Click. Her fingers closed on the slippery wet leather of his vest, and then the two of them bumped heads. Even in her blindness, she realized that her lips were lightly brushing his ear. In that moment, the fleeting touch was the most intimate thing she could imagine.

And then beneath her the earth *moved*.

Something under her feet, something buried deeply in the cloying mud, heaved upward, violently propelling her out of the muck. The rolling wave of propulsion continued, carrying both her and Click to the surface of the water and beyond, and then catching hold of them in a backwash like that of one of the Gray Sea's big breakers. Riding on the frothing green crest of water, their bodies tumbled together across the remaining stretch of marsh. And before Cassidy could even catch her breath, she and Click were being deposited like bits of castoff driftwood on the boggy banks of the wedge-shaped point of land that marked the leading edge of the island.

Drenched, filthy, gasping for air, Cassidy was at first just stunned to be alive. She was unwilling and unable to do anything more than just lie there in an awkward jumble, tangled up with

Click and the rope. She suspected that he probably could have moved, but he didn't try to just then. She was lying supine beneath him, his larger body crossing hers like the off-center bar of an X, with one leg hooked between hers. Against her aching chest she felt the thudding of a pulse, rocking them both; but she wasn't certain if it was his racing heart, or her own, that she felt.

A large shadowy shape loomed over them then, startling Cassidy, until she was prodded by the gray mare's soft wet muzzle. Other shapes moved in around them, speaking past the buzzing in her head. She felt Click's body pulling away from hers as he carefully lifted himself off her. Then other hands were lifting her.

"Geez, Cassidy!" Rowena said anxiously. "Are you all right?" The warden assisted the brunette in pulling Cassidy up into a sitting position in the coarse sedge grass.

When Cassidy tried to reply, she found that all she could force out was a spasm of retching coughs. Rowena thumped her on the back, which only hurt like hell. Cassidy waved her off, trying to convey that all she needed was a few moments to catch her breath. Her lungs still ached as if she had inhaled fire, and the rest of her body was an amazing symphony of bruising pain.

"She'll be all right," Cassidy heard Click say; but was there just the slightest quaver of unsteadiness in that usually level voice? Shaking her dripping hair back out of her face, she turned her head until she could see the Tinker. He stood slightly hunched over beside Kevin, the blond boy supporting the larger man by one arm. Click looked almost as bad as Cassidy felt, covered with muck and algae, his dirty hair slicked back alongside his head like the pelt of a drowned rat.

"I'm okay," Cassidy croaked hoarsely. "What about everyone else?"

"What the hell happened out there?" Rowena said, glancing uneasily over her shoulder. "You were underwater for so long . . . for a minute there, I thought we were never going to see you again."

Beyond them, the swamp was again completely placid. If it hadn't been for the way that the disturbed layer of soft muck and decayed vegetation had been stirred up, coloring the scummy water the color of weak coffee, there would have been no evidence that anything untoward had happened in that quiet slough.

Making a deliberate decision about just how much she was going to reveal about what had really happened to her, Cassidy ran the tip of her tongue over her lower lip, skimming off a rime of slime. Then she spat down between her spread knees. "My little buddies," she said, protecting herself with sarcasm. She made an ineffectual effort to flick the algae off her soaked trousers and an only slightly more successful attempt to fling her wet hair back off her muddy face.

Click had straightened himself, easily pulling away from Kevin's support. The blond boy briefly glanced sideways at him and then looked anxiously to Cassidy.

"I thought you said they wouldn't hurt us," Kevin said. "They almost killed you!"

Seized by a fit of coughing, Cassidy had to lower her head between her knees momentarily. But even as she was hacking, she was shaking her head. "No," she said, "not deliberately."

"Come on!" Rowena protested indignantly. "They pulled you under! Are you saying that wasn't deliberate?"

The warden squatted down beside Cassidy, gently pushing back an errant swag of her sopping hair. "They forced you into the sinkhole, Cassidy," he reminded her quietly.

"And they pushed me back out again," Cassidy pointed out. In some small, sensible part of her mind, she had to wonder why the hell she was sitting there, half drowned, actually defending the damned monsters. But in the larger part of her mind, it seemed somehow important that the others not misunderstand. She could not tell them the rest, the odd void she had entered when she had seized hold of the rubbery creature; but she was convinced that her connection to the monsters was responsible. Then when Click spoke, Cassidy realized that at least he had some innate sense of what she meant.

"Cassidy is right," he said evenly, absently brushing a decaying stem of sedge grass off of his chin. "They could easily have killed us at any time, if that had been their intention."

Rowena alternated her baleful looks between Cassidy and Click, her expression still radiating skepticism. "Then what exactly *is* their intention?" she grumbled, unsatisfied. "That's what I'd like to know."

Click just shrugged, spreading his hands. "What is the intention of the rain, Rowena?" he asked her, his tone wry but not mocking. "For that matter, what is the intention of the swamp itself?"

Rowena scowled at him, but it was easy to see that he was not the real target of her frustration. "In other words, who the hell knows, right?" she muttered, starting to turn away. "Come on, then; let's find a halfway clear spot in this damned jungle, so we can build a fire and get out of these wet clothes."

"No," Cassidy said quietly.

Rowena spun around again in surprise, but it was Click who Cassidy was looking at as she went on. "I don't want to stop now; I want to keep going on until we find the Alchemist."

But when Click didn't respond immediately, and it looked as if Rowena might, the warden intervened. "Cassidy, this appears to be a rather large body of land," he said reasonably. "It might take us days to find one man in it. Let's rest now, and then—"

"No," Cassidy interrupted him, doggedly shaking her head. "I think we'll find him very close to this point of land."

The warden's brows rose quizzically, yet he seemed more intrigued than dubious about her conviction. He looked down speculatively at her. "What makes you believe that?" he asked.

Cassidy pulled her knees together, locking her arms around them. The gesture may have appeared casual, but it was actually done to steady herself. "Listen," she said, "if he got here the same way we just did, across this miserable swamp, do you really think he'd spend a couple of days hacking his way through the forest before he picked a place to settle? I doubt it. I think he'd just plunk himself down and stay in the first good spot he found." She tilted her head, indicating the broad green backdrop of trees behind them. "And if he somehow came from the west, what do you think he'd do when he got to this point? Strike out across this stinking slough? No, I think he'd just hunker down and stay right here." Cassidy shrugged. "Either way," she said, "he wouldn't have settled far from here."

Cassidy paused for a moment, looking down briefly at the tops of her muddy boots. "Besides," she added, looking up again, "don't you smell it? Woodsmoke."

The warden actually laughed, a sound so welcome that Cassidy had to look up directly into that weary, handsome face. He reached down and stroked the top of her head, a spontaneous gesture of fondness and delight. "Your nose is as keen as your mind, Cassidy," he said.

Click took a few strides across the tuffeted, uneven ground and stood looking toward the trees. His chin lifted as he slowly tested the air. "Woodsmoke," he echoed. "We're downwind, but it still can't be very far." He cocked his dark head expectantly. "Well, Cassidy," he said, "do you think if we untie you, you can walk?"

Cassidy realized that she was still sitting on her butt in the soggy grass, with the rope still knotted around her waist. She gave a self-deprecating grunt as she accepted the warden's hand up. Once she had gained her feet, she shook off the loose muck and algae from her clothing while he untied the line and began to re-coil it.

Rowena was regarding Cassidy with a mixture of concern and disapproval, and even Kevin seemed uncertain about the idea of going on immediately. Cassidy glanced around to locate her mare. The horse was already at the edge of the trees, daintily sampling a selection of twigs, as if nothing unusual had happened.

"Let's unpack the float then," Click said evenly, "and get under way again. We still have several hours of good light." He looked directly at Cassidy, and she could have sworn that he winked. "And it seems we're due for a piece of good luck."

Cassidy was not a big believer in luck, either good or bad, although she certainly had found fate to play fast and loose with the universe. Picking herself up again, wet and dirty and exhausted, and forcing herself to take up the trek into the forest's thick and tangled vegetation was one of the most physically difficult things she had ever had to do in that world. But even if her body ached and her feet stumbled, there was no doubt in her mind about the importance of going on. She had not felt such a single-minded determination since that first night when she had stood on the wharf in the Iron City, implacably insisting on being taken at once to the warden. And look what she had found then.

Beyond the first ranks of thick brush and saplings that crowded down to the sumpy banks of the broad marsh, the terrain grew measurably more passable. Once they had gotten past the younger growth that bordered the swamp, the wooded land was covered with more mature trees, forming a dense enough canopy to ensure reasonably clear ground beneath them. The ridge of land that formed the Snake's Spine rose again, becoming part of a topography similar to the hilly country they had crossed earlier in their journey, creating shallow wooded slopes and small rocky ravines. Following the smell of the woodsmoke, they trekked along one of the shaley ridges of land, beneath groves of big beech and oak and cypress trees.

Cassidy was content to let Click assume the lead. She walked with Rowena, behind Kevin and the warden. The brunette didn't say anything more about stopping and resting, but Cassidy was well aware of the concerned looks Rowena kept darting in her direction.

Dragonfly trailed along behind them, curious but calm. Any Horseman should have been appalled to have her horse look that scruffy, but at least the damage was only cosmetic. Even the claw wounds from the swamp cat were already beginning to fade. All things considered, the mare probably had fared better and was far less fatigued than any of her human companions.

They had been hiking along the narrow ridge for only fifteen or twenty minutes when Click signaled a halt. He pointed to the bottom of the shallow ravine at their left. The lower part of the little glen was brushy and littered with several shelflike projections of crumbling rock. It took Cassidy a moment to pick out what Click had seen, a small creek, nearly lost amid the rocks and bushes.

"That stream must be spring-fed," the warden said, looking down at the bright sparkle of water. "Runoff would never be that pure."

Nodding, Click studied the surrounding trees and the gradual but rugged incline that led down to the bottom of the ravine. "If our friend frequents this area," he said, "then perhaps he also frequents this creek."

"Do you think we might find a trail?" Cassidy asked, wary of hoping for that much.

Click's half-dry hair had been shaken back like a dark, shaggy cap, and his clothing was nearly as disheveled as Cassidy's. Yet there was still the presence of the old grace and composure about him as he shrugged lightly and replied, "It's possible."

Anything was possible, Cassidy thought; but she said nothing, and only returned Rowena's hopeful look with a noncommittal little lift of her brows. As they started forward again beneath the trees, Cassidy realized that the Alchemist had been her goal for so long that in many ways her quest had transformed him from a man into some sort of ethereal being. Mundane matters, such as his need for food and water, were things she had simply forgotten.

About a hundred feet from where Click had stopped to point out the creek, he halted again. He had found evidence that someone was using the little freshet on a regular basis. A narrow path, rough and winding like a goat track, but clearly manmade, dog-legged its way from the top of the ridge, around the brush and jutting slabs of rock, down to the bottom of the ravine.

"The trail keeps going along this ridge," Kevin said, pointing ahead of them.

Cassidy had often witnessed Kevin's tracking skills, but the trail was so obvious that even a rank greenhorn could have followed it. Someone came that way often enough to have worn a slight scoop in the leaf-covered ground and to have taken the trouble to move aside the occasional inconveniently placed stone and keep pruned back any encroaching branches. If the same kind of maintenance had been extended a few feet higher, the path would easily have been wide and clear enough for Cassidy to have ridden her mare along it.

Click let Kevin step into the lead, the younger man curiously scanning the path ahead of them. The smell of woodsmoke was lightly pervasive by then, distributed so widely in the air that it was no longer possible to discern the direction of its source. The warden gave Click a quizzical look, but the Tinker gestured him on ahead, as well. Rowena followed, but Cassidy hung back, eyeing Click. She had seen his hand briefly touch the edge of his vest, the inner pocket where she knew he carried his pistol.

Cassidy was experiencing a small tug of caution, the first real hesitation she had felt since they'd left the swamp. Pitching her voice so low that only Click could hear it, she said reluctantly, "Maybe just sneaking up on this guy isn't such a good idea. I get the feeling he doesn't get much company out here."

Click gave her a wry look. "If he's been able to survive by himself out here," he said, "I doubt that we could sneak up on him even if we tried."

Only partially mollified, Cassidy scanned the forest around them. "All the worse then," she muttered, "since he'll probably see us coming long before we can see him."

They continued to follow Kevin's lead along the ridge-top trail. Cassidy kept studying the surrounding trees and both slopes, but saw nothing more alarming than a few startled birds, disturbed from their roosts in the brush. About another hundred feet along the ridge from where the path had cut down to the creek, the trail veered off to the opposite side. The right slope was slightly steeper than the left, but the incline wasn't covered with brush. Mature cypress trees dominated the forest there, and the slope was punctuated with slanting outcrops of stratified shale, thrust out from the earth like rocky embattlements. The path became a narrow rut, smoothly worn by years of use, winding down around the shale ledges and the crisscrossing trunks of long-downed cypresses, which had over the years succumbed to age and gravity, their roots torn from the thin soil to fall among their fellows.

Kevin paused for a moment at the top of the ridge, waiting for the others to catch up before beginning his descent down the twisting trail. Cassidy noted that the mare had abandoned them in favor of finding her own way down the slope. The reason soon became obvious, for in one place the path passed right beneath the huge bole of a toppled tree, which had hung up on one of the rock outcrops, only four or five feet above the ground. Ducking beneath the bridgelike structure, Cassidy concentrated on keeping her footing on the packed and worn earth. Behind her, Click padded along with the casual stealth of a Woodsman.

At the bottom of the slope was a narrow valley, alternatingly filled with big cypress trees and rocky open patches, covered with slab shale and scree. Kevin, the warden, and Rowena had all come to a halt ahead of her, but Cassidy's view was still blocked by the thick horizontal trunk of a giant downed cypress. The scent of woodsmoke was definitely stronger there, fresh and oddly sweet in the cool, still air beneath the trees. Cassidy stepped around another crumbling cairn of shale and came up behind them. But the moment she could see what the three were staring at, she stumbled to a halt.

The fallen cypress whose massive trunk paralleled the end of the path had at one time stood at the bottom of the ravine on a relatively level stretch of ground. But the passage of time, probably aided by disease or some fierce storm, had uprooted the giant tree many years before, sending it toppling down to lie against the slope. Its ruptured roots had torn a hole in the earth beneath a ledge of shale, an aperture that had, over time, been artificially enlarged and enhanced to form a sort of cavern. The smoke they had been smelling since they had left the swamp came from a small, burned-down fire set in a pit in front of that cavern. And sitting cross-legged in front of that bed of embers was a man.

Rendered speechless, Cassidy took a few more steps forward, moving past the others until she was no more than a dozen feet from the seated man. It seemed impossible that anything merely human could have astonished her more than some of the creatures she had already encountered in that world; but for a few moments she simply didn't know how to respond.

The man was a young black, the skin on his face and bare arms the color of well-creamed coffee. His long, dark hair streamed back far past his shoulders, framing features that were both finely drawn and yet somehow exotic. He sat utterly motionless, his slim body slumped slightly forward, his eyes closed. And in his lap, resting against one leather-clad thigh and cradled in his limp brown hands, was an apparatus Cassidy immediately recognized—but that she had never in her wildest imagining thought she would ever see in that world.

Someone padded up almost silently behind her, and Kevin asked in a hushed voice, "He—he's not *dead*, is he?"

Cassidy gave a deprecating snort. "No, Kev, he's not dead," she said.

"He's not conscious," the warden said from her other side, "yet he hardly looks like he's sleeping." He gave Cassidy a puzzled sidelong glance. "Do you think he could be . . . ill?"

Cassidy struggled to keep the incipient sarcasm from her voice. "If you want to call it that," she said.

As if in response, Dragonfly gave a loud snort from behind them.

Curious, and emboldened by the black man's obvious lack of response, the others all began to move in even closer, studying him with puzzlement and concern. Only Rowena seemed to share Cassidy's odd mixture of surprised recognition and disgust.

The brunette leaned in across the low embers, staring with widened eyes at the young black. Then she looked back at Cassidy, her expression vacillating between righteous indignation and helpless laughter. "*This* is the Alchemist?" she said incredulously. "He's *drunk*!"

But Cassidy just shook her head, not bothering any longer to try to conceal her disappointment and contempt. "No, he's not drunk," she corrected. She gestured toward the crudely made but perfectly functional water pipe nestled in the unconscious man's lap. "The son of a bitch is *stoned*."

PART TWO ◀▮▮▮

Chapter 16 ◀▥

Consumed with the sharp and bitter pain of her own dashed hopes, for a few moments Cassidy just stood there, staring at the insensate black man. It was not until Kevin made a small sound right behind her that she realized how baffled he and the warden and Click must have been. When she turned and looked back at them, their expressions were nearly identical.

"What do you mean, 'stoned'?" Kevin asked her uncertainly, peering past Cassidy toward the seated man. "Has he had some sort of ... fit?"

Cassidy briskly shook her head. She was not impatient with Kevin's question, just sorely disappointed with the circumstances. "No, it's not a fit," she said. How the hell was she going to explain a drug-induced stupor to people who didn't even use intoxicants like alcohol? She threw Rowena a sidelong glance, but the brunette was occupied studying the young black. It might have been easier to have explained sex, Cassidy thought glumly; at least one of the three men already understood that.

"He's used some kind of a drug," Cassidy said, "probably from a plant. That's why he's unconscious. It's called being stoned."

Click stepped forward then, deftly rounding the edge of the small firepit. The man was seated just outside the uneven overhang that formed the roof of the dug-out cavern. The overhang was low enough that Click would have had to duck to get under it; but he stopped a few feet short of that, directly beside the unresponsive black. There the Tinker dropped down into an easy squat, frankly scrutinizing the man.

Once Cassidy had taken the time to look more closely, she could see that the stranger was not about Kevin's age, as she had originally thought, but a little older, probably in his late twenties. It was his slack lack of expression that had at first made him appear much younger. He wore a loose leather vest with no shirt beneath it and soft-soled shoes like moccasins. And what Cassidy had taken to be leather trousers, similar to those the Troopers wore, were actually some kind of leggings. They were laced on like stovepipe chaps over the remains of an extremely weathered pair of jeans.

Click's brows knotted as he studied the foreign object the black man had in his lap. Glancing back at Cassidy, he asked her bluntly, "This is the device he used to consume the drug?"

Disconcerted suddenly to find herself chief spokesperson for the drug culture, Cassidy threw Rowena another hasty look. But the brunette deliberately ignored her. "Yeah, it's what they call a water pipe," Cassidy explained. "They're also called hookahs." As Click reached out and lightly ran a fingertip along the rounded side of the pipe's bowl, she elaborated further. "You put the drug—the dried plant, or whatever—into the bowl, and then you ignite it. Then when you suck on the mouthpiece, you draw the smoke through the water chamber, and inhale it."

The Warden stepped up alongside Cassidy, his head cocked quizzically. "And inhaling the smoke from this burning plant causes a faint?" he asked.

What a way to put it! Cassidy thought. The Warden certainly had the knack for taking the glamour out of drug use. She threw Rowena another plaintive look, but the buxom woman not only seemed gleefully content to stay out of the discussion entirely, she also appeared visibly amused by Cassidy's discomfort. "Uh, yeah," Cassidy hedged. "That's more or less it."

Click gave her another incisive look, his dark brows canted in query. "What's the purpose of this loss of consciousness?" he asked.

Cassidy had become convinced it would have been easier to have explained almost anything else, even quantum physics, to them. She had given up looking to Rowena for any help; she had the distinct impression the brunette was on the verge of bursting into laughter at Cassidy's less-than-scholarly discourse on the recreational use of drugs.

"Well, that's not exactly the purpose," Cassidy temporized awkwardly. "Actually, when you first inhale the smoke there's a rush—a feeling of . . ." She winced at her own lame explanation. ". . . of euphoria—a really pleasant feeling. That's the reason for smoking the drug. The unconsciousness is sometimes just a kind of bad . . . side effect."

Cassidy glanced back and forth between Click and the warden, futilely trying to gauge if what she had said had made any sense to them. She had almost forgotten about Kevin until he spoke again. Too wary to move as close as Click had to the man slumped beside the fire, the blond boy had nevertheless been avidly studying the water pipe in his lap. He looked to Cassidy with an expression of open fascination.

"Is this hookah a found thing then?" he asked her.

Suddenly Cassidy locked eyes with Rowena, both women startled and stunned by the implication of Kevin's innocent question. In Rowena's widened hazel eyes, Cassidy could see the mirror image of her own shocked recognition. In what was almost a duel reflex, both of them darted a quick glance at the water pipe before their gazes met again.

Of course!

Cassidy was dismayed to find that she could have been so stupid, so obtuse. Only then did she realize how completely her initial impression of the young black, with its crushing disappointment and automatic disapproval, had diverted her mind and kept her from grasping the true significance of exactly what they had found there, sitting in the deepening shadows of the ancient cypress trees. Whether found or made, by the very fact of its *use* the water pipe should have stopped her dead in her tracks. And yet until Kevin's simple question, the enormity of what the crude hookah said about that unimpressive-looking man had completely eluded her. Alchemist or not, the long-haired black in the ragged clothing definitely retained at least one Memory of the real world: He understood and willingly employed the use of at least one psychoactive drug.

"Cassidy?" the Warden asked tentatively, apparently growing concerned by her sudden silence.

Cassidy held up one hand in a gesture meant to reassure him. Then her words were tumbling out, fueled by a growing excitement. "He may have found it, Kev," she said, "but I think he probably made it. The important thing is that he *uses* it." She looked eagerly from each of the men to the next. "Don't you see? Using drugs like this is something from the Slow World!"

The Warden's face brightened then with shared enthusiasm. "Then he must have at least some Memory, Cassidy," he said. "Perhaps this is the man we seek after all."

But Click was still studying the unconscious man with some reservation. "If this is your Alchemist," he said, "then he won't be of much use to us like this."

Sobering slightly, the Warden had to agree. "I'm afraid you've got a point there." He gave Cassidy a more hopeful look. "How long will this unconsciousness last?"

Frowning, Cassidy helplessly shook her head. "It's hard to say," she admitted, reluctantly looking back to the slumped figure in the ragged clothes. "I don't even know what it was that he smoked in that thing."

Click bent even closer over the black man, who could then be heard softly snoring. He reached out and gently peeled back one of the man's eyelids; then he made a small dubious sound. "Dead man's eyes," he said, inviting Cassidy's inspection of the same.

Cassidy took another step closer, peering through the increasingly deepening shadows at the man's partially averted face. The sweet smoky scent was much stronger at that proximity, and she knew it was not woodsmoke she was smelling. For the first time she noticed that his long hair was not just a very glossy black, but that it also had a fine natural crimp to it. A thin braid fell from both sides at his temples, with a narrow leather thong woven into each plait, holding back the wealth of his dark mane from his high forehead. Above a small, almost delicately shaped mouth and a strong straight nose, his eyes were set wide beneath symmetrically arched brows. And although he was obviously black, or at least mulatto, his features didn't suggest an African heritage. The eye that Click had pried open for her perusal was all of one shade, the thin iris as black as the dilated pupil.

"I thought you said he was just unconscious," Kevin said somewhat anxiously from behind Cassidy.

"He is," Cassidy replied, looking deeper into that exotic black eye. "But he's also stoned; it's the drug that's made his eyes look so funny."

Click released the young man's lid then, letting it drop closed again. His tanned fingers skimmed lower, across the smooth brown skin of the man's neck. The Tinker's long index finger hooked around a thin leather thong that hung there, and he lifted it. But there was nothing suspended from the knotted bit of leather; it was simply an empty thong.

Click looked across at Cassidy and met her eyes, his brow quirking. "You think this is your Alchemist?" he asked her, a faint tone of bemusement in his low voice.

Although for the life of her, just then Cassidy couldn't have even begun adequately to explain why, she was utterly convinced of it. The shabbily dressed black man, the doper, had ironically by his very stupor raised the truest flag of citizenship in the real world that Cassidy could have imagined: Without even saying a word, he had already demonstrated an overweening desire to *escape* reality, by whatever means available to him. Nothing could have more firmly convinced her that he had come from her own world.

Cassidy was aware that all of the others, not just Click, were waiting on her answer. She gave the unconscious man one last long, flat look. "Yeah," she said. "I don't know how much help he's going to be to us, but I'm certain that he's the man we've heard about—the man they call the Alchemist."

Lithely straightening up again, Click stepped back from the firepit. "Well, he's certainly strange enough to fit the Woodsman's description," he surmised wryly. "But until he rejoins us, there isn't any way to tell how useful he may be. I suggest we make ourselves a camp and prepare to wait."

Nodding absently, Cassidy took one last close look at the young black man's slack face. But if she hoped to find some trace of his real knowledge imprinted there, indelibly stamped onto the aristocratic fineness of his exotic features, she was doomed to disappointment. That smooth face betrayed nothing.

They set up camp on a level spot of the small valley's floor, perhaps a hundred feet from the black man's cavern beneath the fallen cypress's roots. There was almost no palatable forage there for the gray mare, but Cassidy was reluctant to let the horse stray from her sight. When Kevin and the Warden retraced the path back to the spring-fed creek to fill the water bags, they cut a couple of armsful of browse from the opposite side of the ridge, and the big gray was content.

Hot food and a chance to rest were simple luxuries that even Cassidy, in her preoccupied state of mind, could appreciate that night. Halfway through the meal, she found to her surprise that she was growing exceedingly sleepy. Despite the serious and bizarre nature of the day's events, conversation around their fire was confined to more trivial matters. Whether it was just the accumulated weight of fatigue, or the unanswerable questions that had seen the day brought to a close, Cassidy was grateful for the moratorium on any further discussion of the young man who still sat slumped, barely a stone's throw from their camp.

Another thing for which Cassidy was grateful was that despite the fouling they had all suffered in the swamp, no one initiated stripping to bathe. With the exception of the warden's and Kevin's leathers, most of their clothing was already dry. And the dirt had become so ingrained in the fabric that another rinsing out probably wouldn't have had much effect. Cassidy joined the others in a quick and desultory washing up of any exposed skin, but that was enough to suit her. As she practically nodded off over her second cup of coffee, her appearance, or even the way she smelled, was no longer particularly important to her.

When Rowena had to ask her the same question twice, Cassidy realized that she had almost fallen asleep sitting up. She was a little chagrined to find that Click had been watching her closely during the last part of their meal, silently amused even if he hadn't said anything.

"I'm sorry, what did you say?" she had to ask.

Smiling indulgently from across the fire, Rowena teased, "I asked you if you were finished with that plate—or if you were just going to plop facedown in it and fall asleep!"

Embarrassed, Cassidy passed the plate as she tried to stifle a yawn. "I'm not that sleepy," she lied, not very convincingly. "I want to stay awake, in case he starts to come around."

The Warden just shook his head. "You'd better get some sleep, Cassidy," he admonished. "Right now you don't look much better than he does."

"I'll take the first watch," Kevin volunteered.

Cassidy was on the verge of protesting when she felt Click's hand lightly clap her on the shoulder. "Get some sleep, Cassidy," he agreed. "Don't worry about him. No man whose eyes look like that is likely to be going anywhere soon."

"They're right," Rowena chimed in. "Unless you want to stay up and help me with the dishes?"

Holding up her hands in mock self-defense, Cassidy said, "Okay, okay—I'll get some sleep. But first I want to check on my horse."

"Click or I can do that," the Warden pointed out.

But Cassidy had already pushed herself stiffly to her feet, managing to conceal the effort it had taken, but feeling every aching muscle and joint emphatically object. "I'll sleep better if I do it myself," she argued, secretly glad that the mare was not far from the campfire.

"Then perhaps I can help you," Click said, falling into step beside her, guiding her with one hand lightly cupped around her elbow. "That way you'll get back to your blanket a little sooner."

Cassidy told herself that she was merely too tired to protest having Click come with her, even as her little voice smugly pointed out that she was actually enjoying the prospect of his company. *Sure,* she thought dourly, *this is so romantic. We both smell like swamp rats!* But as they padded quietly together across the smooth slabs of rock and mossy ground that formed the valley floor, their mutual odor was hardly the most important thing on Cassidy's mind. For the first time since she'd been forced to leave him behind in the Iron City the night of the rioting, she found herself seriously troubled by the realization that there might soon come a day when she would again be parted from the Tinker.

A deep nicker rumbled up from the mare's throat as Cassidy and Click approached her. The horse stood in a pool of nearly total darkness beneath a pair of huge cypress trees, motionless except for the slow and methodical grinding of her jaws as she worked on the pile of cut brush. If not for the horse's light color, she would have been invisible in the deep shadow.

"Hi, pig," Cassidy said fondly, reaching out to meet the lowered head that gently bunted against her chest. As she cradled the mare's head for a few moments, rubbing along the angle of her jaw and softly tugging on her curved ears, Cassidy was acutely aware of how closely Click stood beside her. Then the horse turned her head, sniffing solemnly at the damp leather of the Tinker's vest. Murmuring something wordless, he cupped the whiskery bottom of the mare's muzzle in his hand.

"She looks like shit," Cassidy said glumly, stepping back alongside the mare to run her hands over the scum that had dried on the pale swell of the horse's barrel.

"It'll brush out," Click said amiably, straightening the coarse hair of a crooked swag of the long silvery mane.

Moving farther away from him in the darkness, Cassidy bent to run her hands carefully down the horse's rear leg. The tendons and joints were so familiar to her that she could easily examine them by touch alone. For a time she lost herself in the comforting routine of checking each of the horse's limbs and feet, concentrating on the feel of the mare's smooth hide and the curves and contours of her body. The gray smelled faintly swampy, but mostly she just smelled like a horse, warm and sweet and vaguely herbal.

It was not until Cassidy had come all the way around the horse and was back at her head that she realized Click had been standing there the whole time, silently stroking the mare. Cassidy tried, a bit uneasily, to interpret his silence. She was less than two feet from him, yet she could not see his expression in the darkness.

"You're not convinced this man is the Alchemist, are you?" she said. "You're afraid we've all just risked our lives for nothing."

But when Click responded, Cassidy was surprised by the soft irony in the tone of his voice. "No, Cassidy," he said. "What I'm afraid of is that you may have found exactly what it is that you've been searching for."

Deliberately misunderstanding, Cassidy assumed the armor of puzzlement. "What do you mean?" she asked him. "If we've found the Alchemist, then we haven't gone through all of this for nothing."

But Cassidy knew that Click didn't need to be able to see her face to read her, any more than he needed to ponder over the shading in her voice. The most she could hope for was that he would still honor their truce and would continue to be willing to leave her heart its secrets, just as he still guarded those of his own. In the silence that greeted her last assertion, Cassidy was aware of Click moving closer to her, to stand beside the mare's shoulder. At that proximity, he actually did smell pretty much the way she did, she realized. It was a not entirely unpleasant melange of swamp, damp clothing, and perspiration. For some reason it even seemed to smell a little better on him, she decided, just as she felt the edge of his leather vest brush against her bare forearm.

It would have been so easy then to just reach out for him, Cassidy found herself thinking, with a dim edge of shock at the strength of the impulse. Lulled by her weariness and the comforting familiarity of his nearness, so much like the reassuring presence of the gray mare, Cassidy momentarily entertained the very specific desire just to press herself against Click and let him wrap his strength around her, to embrace the inevitable. And if the choice had only been hers to make, she might very well have done precisely that.

But before Cassidy could move, Click took a step sideways, draping his arm over her shoulders in a comradely fashion as he guided her away from the horse. "And now you'll be able to sleep," he said smoothly, turning to face them both back toward the campfire.

Although she said nothing on that short walk back in the darkness, Cassidy seriously doubted the likelihood of Click's calm assurance. Her nerves were adance, her formless hopes astir; she had the odd and anxious sensation that her skin was somehow a half size too small for her.

But in the end the Tinker was proven right after all. Once she had dutifully rolled herself in her blanket and settled down onto the yielding ground of the valley floor, Cassidy had no time to think about what had almost happened, what she had *wanted* to happen. Within moments, she had fallen into a dreamless sleep.

* * *

When she abruptly awoke to the gentle but insistent prodding of someone's hand on her shoulder, Cassidy had two immediate thoughts. One was that she could hardly have been asleep for more than five minutes; and the other was the blind assumption that the person waking her must be Andy Greene.

"Cassidy?" Rowena whispered, neatly torpedoing both presumptions.

Blinking into the near darkness of their quiet camp, Cassidy realized that the only way Rowena would have been awake, without some major fracas having roused her, was if she had already been up and on watch. And if Rowena was on watch, then Cassidy had slept at least through Kevin's watch.

"What is it?" she murmured, propping herself up on one elbow to squint up into the featureless oval of Rowena's face. Then sudden apprehension prickled through her, and she quickly asked, "Has he woken up?"

Cassidy didn't have to explain who she meant by "he." But Rowena hastily shook her head. "No, not yet." The brunette glanced around them to be sure that no one else had awakened before she went on. "It's just about time for your watch. But before you started, I wanted you to come over there with me for a minute and take a look at him."

Sitting up, Cassidy looked toward the big uprooted cypress tree and then peered curiously at her friend. "Why?" she asked. "He's still just crashed, isn't he?"

Cassidy couldn't clearly see Rowena's expression, but the brunette's manner seemed a little nonplussed. "Yeah," she said, "but he looks . . ." She shrugged helplessly. "He just looks so uncomfortable, the way he's all scrunched up."

Cassidy hoped that Rowena hadn't seen the small, quick smile that had pulled at her mouth. "Geez, Rowena," she hissed, "he's stoned out of his skull!" She got to her feet, adding "I doubt if he's feeling any pain."

Rowena moved back out of her way, stepping in the direction of the cavern. "I know," she conceded, "but what about when he does wake up?" She acknowledged Cassidy's continued and obvious amusement by giving the smaller woman a poke in the arm, even as she was cajoling Cassidy to follow her. "It just seems to me that he'll be a lot more agreeable to deal with tomorrow if he doesn't wake up with the world's worst stiff neck."

"Yeah? Well, what do you suggest we do about it?" Cassidy asked. The question was largely cosmetic, since she was already walking with Rowena across the floor of the ravine, toward where the young black was slumped.

Relieved to have gained Cassidy's tacit cooperation, Rowena's tone grew more assured. "I figure the least we can do is move him away from that dead fire and get him lying down so he can sleep normally."

"You want to put on his jammies and tuck him in, too?" Cassidy responded with mock sarcasm. But by then they had reached the base of the uprooted tree, and Rowena could easily ignore the comment.

The small fire had nearly burned itself out, only the faintest glow coming from the very center of its gray bed of ash. Because her eyes were adapted to the darkness, Cassidy could see the vague outline of the man's body. As the night had worn on, he had tilted slightly to one side, so that his right elbow almost touched the ground. His head was dropped so far forward onto his chest that his long hair hung over his shoulders like a black curtain. Rowena had certainly been right about one thing; it couldn't have been a very comfortable position.

"See?" Rowena said needlessly.

Studying the dim shape of the unconscious man for a few moments, Cassidy considered a course of action. Then she gestured to Rowena. "Okay, go look in that cave of his, and see if he's got some kind of bedroll or something in there where we could put him if we do move him."

Rowena peered cautiously into the darkened mouth of the dugout shelter. "It's dark in there," she announced. "How am I supposed to look for anything?"

Cassidy had squatted down a couple of feet to one side of the slumped man. She didn't even glance up as she replied, "Well, grope around then. There's no point in dragging him in there and then just dumping him on the ground. We could do that much right here where he is."

"Okay, okay," Rowena quickly acquiesced, ducking slightly as she stepped in under the overhang. "I just hope he doesn't have this place boobytrapped or anything . . ."

"Yeah," Cassidy muttered under her breath, "no good deed goes unpunished." She carefully leaned closer to the young man. His face was averted, but she could hear the faint whistle of his somnolent breathing. Even though he appeared to be about the same height as her or Rowena, he looked lean and wiry, and she was fairly confident that the two of them could lift him if they tried.

"Hey," Rowena called softly from inside the cavern, "guess what I found?" Before Cassidy could even shoot back with some flip response, the answer became obvious. A sharp little burst of light flared within the blackness of the shelter, followed by the immediate faint scent of sulfur. Then the light steadied and grew, bobbing slightly as Rowena lifted the lantern she had just lit. The brunette's rounded face appeared, clearly defined, floating in a yellow pool of light. "He's got a whole box of matches in there," she said, sounding impressed.

"Just see if he's got a blanket or something," Cassidy reminded her dryly.

She relaxed a bit when she determined that the unconscious man was in no condition to react to their presence. Cassidy reached out and grasped the water pipe, which still sat nestled in his lap. His slim brown hand, which had been curled limply along the pipe's curved side, simply slid off as she lifted the device away from him and set it at arm's length.

"You should see this" came Rowena's eager voice from inside the cavern. "It's really neat. He's got all kinds of stuff in here."

"We can take the guided tour some other time," Cassidy said impatiently. "What about a blanket?"

"There's a regular bed in here," the brunette said, still sounding impressed, "not just a blanket."

"Then get out here with that lantern, will you?" Cassidy said. "Give me a hand."

Rowena returned to the overhang, lantern in hand. The soft quavering light threw a warm glow over the slumped man's honey-brown skin and made his long crinky hair gleam with the inky iridescence of a crow's feathers. Rowena looked at him, her expression slightly dubious. "You think we can carry him?" she asked Cassidy.

"Yeah," Cassidy said, "he doesn't look that heavy." She gestured at the lantern. "Set that down just inside the edge, and let's give it a try."

As Rowena complied, Cassidy stepped over so that she was standing right behind the man's bent back. "I'll take him under the arms," she said, "and you get between his leg and lift him under the knees."

In order for Rowena to be able to get into position, Cassidy had to first turn the man slightly to the side and drag him backward a few feet from the firepit. He was heavier than he had looked, especially when he hung like dead weight, but at least the maneuver didn't provoke any sign of response from him. He remained as limp as a sack of sand.

"You should see all the stuff he's got in there," Rowena reiterated as she nudged the man's legs apart and stepped between them. "All kinds of bundles and packages and—"

"You can look at his packages some other time," Cassidy said. She effectively cut off Rowena's enthusiastic description by locking her hands under the young man's arms and tugging his rump up off the ground. His bare skin was warm and surprisingly soft against her own. Rowena had to scramble to get a grip under his knees, so that she could keep up her end of the carry. When the two women lifted in unison, he was not too heavy for them to move, although they had to proceed slowly and carefully. With his slack weight hanging between them, his lean rump was only inches from the ground. Grateful for the lantern's light, Cassidy edged her way into the shelter, immediately spotting the bed Rowena had seen. It was more like some kind of crude futon than a regular bed, with a framework of cut logs containing a mound of dried grass and leaves, and a tanned hide spread across it. She saw two blankets rolled up at the end of the low mattress.

The arched roof of the cavern, which was formed by the overturned stump and sundered roots of the huge downed cypress, was too low for Cassidy to be able to stand upright. She had to shuffle the last few steps, partially crouched over, staggering under the weight of their shared burden. Finally she was able to drop the man's head and shoulders, rather gracelessly but at least dead center, onto the springy surface of his bed.

Equally bent over, Rowena carefully disengaged herself from between the young man's legs. She knelt on the frame of the mattress to gently heft his lower body over into a straight line. "Oops!" she whispered; then she began to laugh softly.

Cassidy shot her a sharp look. "What?" she asked, puzzled by the brunette's sudden ribald chuckling.

Rowena jerked her chin toward the supine man's crotch, where her fumbling hands fussed with rearranging his ragged clothing. "These darn jeans are full of holes," she explained with a grin. "Talk about taking a look at his package!"

Cassidy scowled at her, but the expression was not especially convincing, and Rowena kept chuckling as she tried to tug the leather leggings back into place over the torn portion of his pants. "He's not even circumcised," she said, adding jokingly, "I wonder if he remembers sex?" Cassidy shot her another disapproving glare, but Rowena just grinned amiably. "Oh, come on, Cassidy.

You can't tell me that since you've remembered sex, you've never even thought once about doing it."

Rowena was hitting entirely too close to the target, and Cassidy countered by muttering "Not with some druggie, that's for sure."

Rowena's gaze dropped speculatively to the unconscious man sprawled languidly on his primitive bed. Lying there so quiescently, he looked harmless enough; more than harmless, he looked almost innocent. "Oh, I don't know," Rowena mused. "Don't you think he's kind of cute?"

Cassidy promptly fixed Rowena with what she meant to be an effectively withering stare, one adequate to prevent any further candid discussion of sex and just who might be suitable material for it. "I think he's a spaced-out doper, that's what I think," she said.

Taking Rowena's amused silence as the most concession she was likely to get, Cassidy retrieved the lantern from the ground and held it up, scanning the confines of the little shelter that had been hollowed and hewn out beneath the fallen cypress. Rowena hadn't been exaggerating when she'd said there was all kinds of stuff inside the cavern. The sides of the structure were almost completely covered with shelves, niches, and hooks, all crammed with bundles and packets and containers of every size and construction. Even more amazing to Cassidy, at the back of the shelter there was a low bench piled nearly to the top of the roof with articles of clothing, most of it neatly folded.

"Jesus, look at this," she hissed to Rowena. "Look at all the clothes he's got!"

Rowena looked up from spreading one of the blankets over the recumbent man. Her eyes widened perceptibly at the wildly varied collection of garments. "Wow!" she breathed reverently. "I haven't seen that many clothes since they kicked me out of the factory at Green Lake!" She glanced back down at the figure on the bed, then looked back to Cassidy's lantern-lit face. "You don't think he's a—a *Woodsman*, do you?"

Then it was Cassidy's turn to chuckle, although there was very little humor in the sound. "Are you kidding?" she said with a deprecating snort. "He's too well dressed for a Woodsman." She panned the lantern's light over the back recesses of the cavern again. "He's probably the guy who steals the clothes from *them*," she added with a note of grim satisfaction.

Rowena gazed down at the sleeping man, oblivious beneath the blanket that she had spread so conscientiously over his sprawled body. "I don't think he's a thief," she said as she watched the slow and rhythmic rise and fall of his chest. "Why would a thief live way out here in the middle of nowhere?"

Cassidy had moved the lantern again, to study the other wall of the shelter. "The Woodsmen live out in the middle of nowhere, too," she reminded Rowena acerbically, "and they're thieves. Come on, let's take a look at this stuff."

But Rowena, for all of her previous enthusiasm for the young black's possessions, suddenly seemed oddly hesitant about actually touching any of them. "Do you think that's such a good idea, Cassidy?" she said uneasily. She absently tugged a fold out of the hem of the blanket where it crossed the man's bare shoulder. "I mean, it's kind of like . . . robbing the dead."

Cassidy made a grunting sound of skepticism. "He's stoned, Rowena, not dead," she pointed out, "so if anything, it's more like rolling drunks. And besides," she added, turning away to get a closer look at something hanging from the wall, "who said anything about robbing him? I just want to make sure he doesn't have anything dangerous in here." She shot Rowena a grim little smile over her shoulder. "In case he wakes up in a bad mood tomorrow, in spite of your touching concern."

The brunette reluctantly came over to join Cassidy in her perfunctory search. "What exactly are we looking for?" Rowena asked uncertainly.

"Drugs, a gun, anything like that," Cassidy replied, giving her another thin and humorless smile. "Just pretend you're a narc with a righteous search warrant—and by the way, thanks for all your help explaining drug addiction to these people."

But Rowena absorbed Cassidy's testy sarcasm with equanimity, pointing out to her "Hey, you were doing a fine job on your own. Besides, I'm not as well versed in all that drug terminology as you seem to be!" Then Rowena deflected any riposte from Cassidy by suddenly stepping forward and reaching for something on the wall. "Look at this," she said, slipping an object off a peg and holding it up to the light for Cassidy's inspection. "Do you think he's a Finder?"

Cassidy had to step closer to clearly see what it was that dangled from Rowena's fingers. A silver St. Christopher's medal hung on a fine-linked chain, its polished surface gleaming softly in the lantern's gentle light. "Maybe," she said with a shrug, "or maybe he just stole it." She made an impatient gesture. "Come on, forget that stuff. We don't have time to inventory this whole place right now. Just look for anything that could be a hazard to our health."

"What do you suppose this is?' Rowena asked a moment later. She held up a flat wooden bowl, piled with a couple of dozen little folded oilpaper packets, each no more than a few inches square.

Cassidy snagged one of the packets and lifted it to her nose, sniffing suspiciously. The packet smelled vaguely like oregano. She unfolded one of its corners to find it was filled with a finely powdered greenish substance, like particles of tea. "I think we've just found his drug stash," she told Rowena. "Hang onto that bowl; we're taking that with us." Seeing Rowena's dubious frown, Cassidy added, "Come on; it might be the only way we can get this guy to straighten out long enough ever to talk to us."

Rowena's brows arched skeptically. "Yeah? Well, now if he does speak to us," she pointed out, "the first thing he's probably going to say is Where the hell is my stuff?"

"I'll take that chance," Cassidy retorted, thrusting the packet back into the bowl. She continued her cursory search of the cavern's contents, until she had poked at least superficially through the entire collection of various oddities, some of which she didn't even try to identify. Other than a few knives, most of which looked more like eating utensils than weapons, she hadn't found anything dangerous. "I guess he doesn't have a gun," she conceded, not meeting Rowena's eyes. "Come on, let's get out of here."

Outside the cavern, by the firepit, Cassidy bent to retrieve the water pipe. She held it out to Rowena, who was forced to take it from her. Then Cassidy damped the wick on the lantern, extinguishing it, before returning it to the mouth of the shelter.

As they started away from the ancient cypress, Rowena threw Cassidy a sidelong look. "What am I supposed to do with this stuff?" she asked, holding up the water pipe and the wooden bowl.

"Put them with my things," Cassidy said, "under my blanket." As sleepy as she had been earlier in the evening, Cassidy now felt completely rested and alert, quite ready to take up her watch.

When they parted company, Rowena turning toward their campsite as Cassidy headed out to begin her patrol, the brunette said, "Thanks for helping me move him inside."

"I had to," Cassidy teased her. "Hell, you never would have been able to sleep if you thought that poor bastard was going to sit there all night getting a stiff neck!"

Cassidy took up the methodical surveillance of her watch,

thankful that Rowena's friendship, at least, was one thing she would not have to question no matter what else might happen.

Cassidy gave Dragonfly a dismissive slap, turning away from the big gray as she resumed what would be her last turn across the narrow floor of the ravine before her watch ended and the warden's began. Other than the horse's occasional restless roamings, things had been quiet. But Cassidy had not been bored. It wasn't too difficult to remain alert when patrolling a strange area, and the valley with its numerous huge old trees and the shadowy outcroppings of rock was sufficiently challenging to keep her occupied. It had been easy to keep her mind occupied, as well, although she had found herself rejecting one potential line of thought after another during the hours she prowled the ravine. She didn't want to think about old conundrums, like Click or Andy Greene; and she refused to be trapped into fruitlessly speculating about her newest problem, the drugged young black man who slept nearby. By the end of her watch, Cassidy still wasn't really sleepy; but she was looking forward nevertheless to getting back to her bedroll for the few remaining hours of darkness. She wanted the oblivion of sleep, a break from the relentless cycle of her thoughts before she had to face the actualities of the new day.

Pausing to scan the uneven slope ahead of her, a mottled landscape of black on near black, Cassidy shivered slightly in the predawn chill. It was dead calm beneath the big cypresses, the faint rime of dew forming undisturbed upon every irregularity of every horizontal surface. The paths she had taken in her patrols showed up in barest relief, narrow strips of darkness on the humus and rock where the scuffle of her boots had swept away the fine beads of moisture. The valley was so silent that even the night insects and birds seemed to have fallen still. The loudest sound Cassidy could hear was the soft thump of Dragonfly's hooves as the horse wandered back to see what she could salvage from her picked-over pile of forage.

Because of the almost preternatural quiet, Cassidy actually could hear the light tread of his footsteps before she could clearly identify the man who approached her in the near darkness. She wasn't especially surprised when she recognized the warden, since he had the next watch, and he had always been notoriously punctual. She was surprised when he drew close enough for her to make out the basic features of his face, because she could see that he was smiling. Only as he walked right up to her, just seconds before he put his arms around her, did Cassidy realize that it was not the Warden after all, but rather Andy Greene.

"Cathy!" he exclaimed happily, embracing her in an enthusiastic bear hug. "I found you! You were right—I found you!"

Cassidy was pressed so tightly against his chest that for a few moments she couldn't speak; so she just surrendered to his obvious joy and hugged him back. A strobelike brilliance of light had washed through her at his touch, seeming to flush her from the inside out. Although nothing in that searing incandescence could have been described as subdued, there was a distinctly different feel to it that time. Perhaps because Andy seemed so happy instead of distressed and agitated, the light was bright without being harsh, penetrating without being disconcerting. Its fiery course was both familiar and profoundly intimate, with far more warmth than she had experienced before. For the brief course of its illumination, she almost felt as if she had somehow fused with Andy, as if their hearty embrace had literally united them—blood and bone, nerve and flesh—in a way that even conjugal joining could not have.

By the time the overpowering brightness had faded, Cassidy was able to push back a little in his arms. "God, Andy—am I glad to see you!" she told him with utter sincerity.

He was willing to step back then, too, so that he could see her face as he spoke, even if he wasn't willing to release his hold on her arms. "I did it, Cathy!" he said excitedly. "I *made* them take me to you!"

His pride in that accomplishment was so plain, lighting his youthful face with a gleam nearly as shining as the odd incandescence, that Cassidy could not keep from asking him the question he so obviously wanted to answer. "How did you make them, Andy?" she said. "How did you find me?"

"I banged, Cathy," he confided, a touch of giddy insouciance in his voice. "I know I'm not supposed to, but it worked! I banged until they gave in and took me to you!"

Cassidy was a little startled to find that she understood exactly what Andy was talking about. "Banging" was what the workers at Reiners Center called it when one of the patients repeatedly struck his head against something, usually the wall or the floor. It was frustrating behavior, most often without any discernible cause, and Cassidy remembered that Andy's therapists had been especially pleased when he seemed to have progressed beyond it after he had started in the riding program at Joel's farm. Equally startling to her was how Andy had been able to employ the behavior deliberately as leverage to get the center employees to give in to his demand—a demand he had no other way to articulate. They may have believed Andy to be noncommunicative and cut off from reality; but when he had shown such an obviously regressive sign of agitation, someone must have taken the chance that letting him see Cathy Delaney again just might calm him down. No wonder Andy was so triumphantly jubilant. Just as she had seen when he had worked with Dragonfly, Andy had made some small connection with the real world in which he lived.

"That's great, Andy," she said, her praise and enthusiasm genuine. "I knew you could do it!" As she looked across into his boyish face, she wished that she could see his features more clearly, because she had not seen him so buoyantly happy since the first time he had found her in that world. It would have been nice to be able to see some of the years and the stress erased from that handsome face, to see on Andy's lips the amazing smile that had so often disarmed her when she had seen it upon the Warden's. But for the moment she had to settle for the animation in his voice and the eager grip of his warm hands on her bare arms.

"And this is a better place, Cathy," he confided earnestly. "Better than the white place."

Rapidly trying to collect her thoughts and compose her questions, Cassidy let her hands drop down to rest lightly on his waist. She squeezed him gently. "Where did you find me, Andy?" she asked quietly. "Where am I now?"

Although some of his initial ebullience had moderated, Andy still seemed in good spirits as he considered her question. "It's nicer," he said confidently. "Not all those white coats and white walls and bright lights and noise. They have ladies here, real nice ladies." He paused, then announced, "One of them looks like Moms."

For a moment Cassidy was simply too surprised to respond. "Moms" was everyone's nickname for Joel's mother, a most unmatronly woman in her sixties whose gray hair was her only concession to her age. She even rode a big Harley motorcycle in all but the coldest weather. And Cassidy was stunned to discover that not only did Andy know what she was called, he had just compared someone else's appearance to hers. Just how much was he really aware of—and how much might he be able to tell her?

"Andy," Cassidy said with a quiet urgency, "what do they call the place where I am now? What's its name?"

But Andy seemed perplexed by her question. In her surprise over his comment about Moms, Cassidy had overanticipated. She had forgotten that Andy had a very limited ability to identify proper names. And like the people of the Warden's world, he had absolutely no concept of reading or writing.

Cassidy tried to redeem the situation by asking him something simpler. "Am I in a room now, Andy?" she asked. "What does it look like?"

Relaxing then, Andy's voice grew calm and confident. "A blue room," he said. "Blue walls, blue bed. You're just lying there, Cathy, but I know now that you're just sleeping."

Cassidy automatically leaned in slightly closer to him, her fingers tightening fractionally on his leather tunic. From the warmth of his body there rose a faint and familiar scent, smoke and horses and perspiration. "Is there anything in the room with me, Andy?" she asked. "Anything that might be . . . keeping me there?"

But Andy seemed blithely unconcerned. "There's a thing on your arm," he said. "But this is a much nicer place. It's not so noisy, and there's no white men."

White men: *"not all those white coats"* he had said before. Sudden comprehension spurred Cassidy on. She had to throttle down her impatience. She desperately needed to have Andy let the Warden take over, as he had on a previous lapse, the episode right before Andy's last brief and disturbing contact with her. But she kept remembering how that lapse had ended, how letting the Warden's consciousness intrude into Andy's world seemed to have flung Andy back abruptly to the real world, precipitously ending the whole interaction.

But Cassidy also could not forget that for those few moments when he'd been allowed to look through Andy Greene's eyes, the Warden had seen into the Slow World. And for at least a short time afterward, he had been able to recount what he'd seen there. If Andy would allow the Warden to do that again, perhaps he could tell Cassidy where Cathy Delaney was trapped back in the real world.

"Andy," Cassidy said, slowly and softly, "you and I both know that you're also the Warden of Horses. The Warden is who you are here, just like I'm Cassidy here." Andy was listening to her with quiet interest, as if waiting for her to make her point. He still gripped her arms, but his hold was light and easy. "Can you let the Warden see where you are now, Andy?" she asked. "Can you let him see me and my new room?"

Just as the last time it had happened, Andy's initial reaction threw Cassidy off. His face recomposed itself in a thoughtful frown, much as if he were seriously considering her request. Once again it took her a few moments to realize that the expression belonged not to Andy, but to the Warden, and that he was reacting not to her request, but to something in a world that was separated from their own by some minute but inestimable gulf of time.

Within less than a minute, a change came over him again. The frown became a grimace, and he shook his head, murmuring "That hurts!"

It was not the Warden again, but still Andy; the flash had not yet ended. Elated, Cassidy gave his waist a reassuring squeeze. "It's okay, Andy," she said quickly. "You did real good. Does your head hurt? I'm sorry, but—"

Cassidy broke off when she realized that Andy was no longer paying any attention to her. Rather, he was looking off over her left shoulder with an oddly quizzical expression on his face. But Andy had never before reacted to anything in that world except Cassidy herself. Had she been mistaken when she thought that he was still Andy Greene?

"Andy?" she asked tentatively.

He glanced down at her when she spoke his name, but then his gaze immediately returned to where he had been looking before. She watched his boyish features transform from puzzlement to a sort of friendly curiosity. Dropping one hand from his waist, Cassidy slowly turned her head far enough to follow his line of sight. Even in the near darkness, she could easily see what had attracted his attention.

Scarcely a dozen feet from them, standing in silence with his bare arms folded across his open vest, stood the young black man.

Astonishment rendered Cassidy speechless. Andy had never shown any sign that he had ever noticed anyone else during one of his flashes; he hadn't so much as recognized their names, even Kevin. How could he see the black man, an utter stranger?

Andy was still looking directly at the long-haired man. Then, with the blunt charm of an inquisitive child, he said, "Hi, who are you?"

Chapter 17 ◄IIII

Cassidy spun around, tearing free from Andy's grasp, just as the black man spoke.

"I was just about to ask you the same thing," he said. His voice was soft, just loud enough to carry across the small distance that still separated them, but something in the very mildness of his tone alarmed Cassidy. Perhaps what so unnerved her was just seeing him standing there so calmly and steadily, when she had left him only a few hours earlier, thinking that he would be totally wasted well into the next day.

Certainly she was disconcerted by the amazing discovery that Andy could not only see the man but had also reacted appropriately to his presence. "He can see you!" she blurted out.

The stranger's head cocked slightly, his bemusement plain. "I may be black," he said wryly, "but I'm not *that* dark."

Cassidy was still just staring at the man in surprise when she felt a hand land on her shoulder. "Cassidy?" the warden said expectantly.

Cassidy quickly turned back to him, impressed not only by the speed with which he had been transformed from Andy back to the warden, but also by how swiftly he seemed to have oriented himself again. He had become cognizant of the situation with the stranger almost instantly.

"You—Andy—*saw* him," she repeated stupidly.

One of the warden's brows climbed, and his head cocked quizzically toward the motionless man. "Him?" he asked Cassidy, obviously perplexed. "But how?"

Cassidy just shook her head, equally confused. But there was something more important there, a crucial moment that had almost been lost by the long-haired man's untimely intrusion. She seized the warden by both arms, causing him to look down into her face.

"What do you remember?" she asked him urgently. "What did you see?"

The warden threw a brief, automatic glance in the black man's direction before devoting himself to Cassidy's question. When he frowned in concentration, his expression was disarmingly like that of Andy Greene surrendering his consciousness to the warden. "You're in a different place," he said then. "It must be the place Andy said that they'd taken you." He paused, his brow furrowing as if the details were already fast eluding him. "You're still lying in a room, either sleeping or unconscious; but this is a bigger bed, a nicer room. The walls are blue, and there's a blue blanket covering you."

"What else?" Cassidy prompted, her fingers tightening on his arms. "Is there anyone else there with me? What else is in the room?"

The warden's frown intensified. "There's no one else there, just you. There are some things by the bed; some kind of machines, I think." He hesitated, as if grasping for something fleeing. "One of them keeps making a funny noise. There's a window in the room, but I couldn't see what was outside." He shook his head in frustration. "I'm sorry, Cassidy, but that's all I remember," he said. "I'm sorry it's not more helpful."

But Cassidy gave his arms an affirming squeeze. "That's the best yet," she assured him. "You remembered a lot. And what's more important is that Andy found me again. Not only that, but he let you see into his world again; and that isn't what ended the contact this time."

The warden gave her a small smile and pulled Cassidy into a quick and friendly embrace, a gesture of hope and comradeship that she was honestly enjoying until the stranger's voice calmly spoke again from the nearby darkness.

"Now that you two are done with your tripping," the black man drawled, "maybe you can answer my question. Who are you, and what are you doing camped here in my valley?"

Cassidy stiffened. The warden kept a restraining hand on her arm as she pulled back and turned toward the stranger. "Well, we've got a few questions of our own," she said. "That is, if you've still got a few brain cells left that haven't been completely fried."

"Cassidy," the warden said quietly, counseling some moderation with that single word.

But the black man took a few steps closer, his gait casual but sure, with none of the elaborate deliberation of the recently intoxicated. "It appears to me that you're the ones behaving irrationally," he said in that same infuriatingly even tone. "After all, I'm not the one standing out here in the middle of the night, spouting nonsense."

"Nonsense?" Cassidy snorted. She tried to take a step forward, but her attempt was truncated by the warden's grip on her arm. "And just what would you call that little performance of yours? Chemical therapy?"

Although her sarcasm did not provoke any visible reaction from the stranger, he still persisted in his matter-of-fact inquisition. "You still haven't told me who you are," he reminded them, "and what you're doing here."

It would have been a bit of a toss-up as to who would have gotten in the first reply: Cassidy, with a continuation of her prickly confrontational tactics, or the warden, trying to inject a note of civility. But Cassidy wasn't surprised when she heard another, very familiar voice intervene from behind them. Between the warden's lapse and the exchange that had followed it, they had been speaking loudly enough to have awakened a far heavier sleeper than Click. And the Tinker always had shown a propensity for inserting his own particular brand of even-handed logic into the small tempests that seemed to form wherever Cassidy went.

"We've come here from the Iron City," Click said. Out of the darkness, he stepped up alongside Cassidy and the warden. "From across the Great Swamp."

Glancing back, Cassidy could see that Kevin and Rowena had followed at a short distance. Both of them appeared somewhat confused about just what was going on and surprised to see the black man.

The stranger gave his head a little toss, sending his long hair back over his shoulders. He looked at Click in silence for a long moment. Cassidy couldn't tell if he was considering what the Tinker had said or merely considering the tall dark-haired man himself. But when he spoke again, the black's reply was not what Cassidy had expected. "I don't know anything about this Iron City," he said quietly, "but you've laid your fire in my valley. By sunup, I'll expect to see you gone."

Cassidy bridled at his calm presumption, but she felt the warden's fingers tighten on her arm, wordlessly urging her silence. Click stepped past them and smoothly approached the young black man. The Tinker kept his hands out, dangling at his sides and empty, almost like a reformed gunslinger displaying his harmless intent. He stopped a scant couple of feet short of the stranger, almost too close to be considered polite, and Cassidy grudgingly had to admire Click's polished audacity. At that proximity, he was clearly a good four or five inches taller than the younger man, a difference he used to casual advantage as he looked down mildly at him.

"We've come down the eastern coast, from the sea," Click said, "some weeks' journey from here. We're seeking a man who's said to live here."

It was difficult for Cassidy to read the expression on that dark, finely featured face, but the relaxed posture of the young man's slim body didn't change. "If you've come all the way across the swamp," he said, "and from the smell of you, I'd believe you have, then you've gone through a lot of trouble for nothing. Nobody lives here, except for a few spooks."

Click cocked his head. "By 'spooks' you mean the wild ones?" he asked, his overt curiosity effectively disarming.

The black man nodded. "If that's what you want to call them," he said. "And they move around enough, no one can say they live in any one place."

Click glanced over the other man's shoulder, toward the toppled cypress that formed his dug-out shelter. "You, on the other hand, appear to be an established resident," he said casually. "You even call this your valley."

"Yeah, that's why I expect to find you gone from it by dawn," the younger man repeated with unruffled certainty.

With the heat of her initial irritation fading, Cassidy had become fascinated by the soft-spoken duel of wills being performed by the two very different and yet oddly similar men. She wasn't worried that Click had finally met his match; but she had to concede that the black was a disconcertingly unknown factor. And she wasn't sure just where Click was going with his oblique line of conversation.

Click cocked one hip slightly, his posture seeming to suggest that his inquisitiveness was merely harmless curiosity. "Don't you even want to know," he said, "who it is that we've come all this way to seek?"

"It doesn't matter to me," the other man said, "because there isn't anyone here but me."

"Exactly," Click said.

It took a moment for Click's implication to sink in. When it did, for the first time the black man seemed to tense, his shoulders tightening slightly as he gazed at Click with a less than casual scrutiny. "If you're telling me that you've come all that way looking for me," he said then, his voice still soft but oddly without inflection, "then you've gone through a hell of a lot of hardship for the privilege of an overnight camp."

Click didn't flinch under the increasingly critical surveillance. He gently spread his hands, palms up. "Are you saying then," he said, "that you're not the man they call the Alchemist?"

The smaller man remained motionless, but his response was immediate. "That's not my name," he said flatly.

The black man's response didn't surprise Cassidy, but Click's sudden acquiescence did. The Tinker merely gave a thoughtful nod and said, "In that case, perhaps we've troubled you for nothing."

Ready with tart words of disbelief, Cassidy was prepared to step forward to confront the stranger herself. But the warden continued to hold her back firmly. She turned and glared at him, but he didn't release her. The black man was obviously lying—he had *Memory*! Maybe he didn't answer to the name of Alchemist, but Cassidy seriously doubted that he had never heard the term before. And Click was just letting him put them off with his flimsy evasions.

But Click's abrupt capitulation had momentarily disarmed the black man. The lines of his body were still warily tensed, but he studied the Tinker with fresh curiosity, apparently as surprised as Cassidy had been that he had been let off the hook so easily.

"Well," the stranger finally said in that quiet voice, "it'll be considerably less trouble to me if I find you all gone come morning."

Click spread his hands again, less in apology than by way of explanation. "As you can see," he said reasonably, "we've come a long way through some very rough country, and with a horse, as well. Before we can continue our search, we'll need some time to recoup. The mare will need rest and fodder." He paused briefly, as if he were reluctant to make a request of the stranger. It would have been a very convincing performance to anyone who didn't know the Tinker; but Cassidy knew that Click had never hesitated to ask anyone for anything, and his shameless exaggeration of the gray mare's needs left her impressed. "We are very eager to find this man," Click concluded. "Perhaps you have information that could help us."

Realizing that Click had actually conceded him nothing, the younger man stiffened again, directly meeting Click's umber eyes with his own even darker ones. "Stay a day then, if you need to," he said. "Feed your horse. Clean up those stinking clothes. But then I want you out of my valley."

The stranger turned sharply on his heel and began walking away into the darkness, toward his shelter. Cassidy glared after him, thinking that Click had made a major tactical error by letting him just walk away like that, when the black man suddenly stopped. From some twenty feet away, and without even looking back, he fired back at them, "And bring back what you've stolen from me, or you'll find that this country can get even rougher than you expected."

Cassidy saw that Rowena was studiously avoiding meeting her eyes. But for the moment Click did not address the black's last comment. Instead he turned back to the warden and Cassidy and asked without preface, "He had another one of those spells?"

Relieved by the sudden change in topics, Cassidy quickly nodded. Even though the warden had finally released her arm, she was then willing to remain standing right beside him. "I was just going to wake him for his watch," she said, "when he came to me as Andy." She shot the warden a quick glance. "He was so excited and happy because he had found me again. Even though Cathy had been moved, he'd made enough of a fuss that the people who take care of him finally took him to see her in the new place."

"And he was able to let me see this new place," the warden interjected, "so that I could describe it to Cassidy." His tone turned rueful. "Although I don't know how helpful that's been, since being able to describe the inside of one room has hardly narrowed down her location very much."

Cassidy could have said more then, something about her newly kindled suspicions about just what kind of place in which she feared she was being held, and why; but she didn't. She kept her silence.

"And is she still in danger there?" Click asked evenly.

The warden frowned. "I don't quite get that sense of urgency from Andy any more," he admitted. "Although he was so excited about just finding her again, it's hard to say." He shrugged unhappily. "I don't know how this change in location has affected her situation; but I think that to be safe, we should continue to assume she's still in danger."

Click gave the warden a friendly clap on the arm and said, "We can talk of this further tomorrow. Why don't you go back to your bedroll? I'll take the last watch."

The warden put up a mild protest. "There's no need of that," he said. "I feel fine."

Kevin came up to him and tugged on his sleeve. "Let Click," he cajoled.

"Go on," Click said, gesturing toward their campsite. "If you stand watch now, we'll have Kevin awake the rest of the night, as well."

Amiably giving in, the warden allowed Kevin to pull him along. On the way back to their bedrolls, Cassidy dropped back and walked beside Rowena. The brunette didn't say anything, but she didn't need to. And Cassidy could guess what was troubling her.

Their campfire had burned down to nothing but a bed of warm gray ash, shedding little heat and even less light. But Cassidy didn't need to see the expression on the warden's face as he stopped at his blanket and looked to her. "What did you take from the black man?" he asked her, his tone nonjudgmental but quite implacable.

In light of their relationship, much less that tone of voice, Cassidy never even considered dissembling. "I just took his drugs and that damned water pipe," she said defensively.

Kevin had dropped down beside their bedrolls and was straightening the blankets. But the warden continued to look directly at Cassidy. "Then in the morning you must return them to him," he said quietly but firmly.

Cassidy felt an irritating little stab of indignation. "Return them?" she repeated. "What if he goes and gets stoned again? How are we ever going to find out anything useful from him if he keeps—"

Gently interrupting her, the warden said, "From what we've just seen, I suspect no one will ever force or coerce cooperation out of this man. And stealing from him hardly seems likely to improve the situation."

"But with the drugs—"

The warden held up his hand, suddenly reminding Cassidy without having to even speak a word to her that the position he'd earned was not just some meaningless title. "Return them in the morning, Cassidy," he commanded her evenly.

Biting back another retort, she dropped down onto her bedroll and deliberately occupied herself with the rearrangement of her blanket. Unfortunately, in doing so she unwittingly uncovered the water pipe and the wooden bowl that she had told Rowena to stow there. She threw the brunette a scowl, as if daring her to comment; but Rowena just shrugged apologetically and crawled under her own blanket.

With the warden beside him once more, Kevin quickly slept, and the warden surrendered soon after. Beside Cassidy, Rowena was again emitting the soft snores of the innocent. Only Cassidy still lay awake, staring up at the black canopy of the cypress trees. She had seldom felt less like sleeping.

Cassidy's mind wanted to gnaw at the problem of the strange black man, to go over and over the details of Click's odd little duel of words with him, to chafe uselessly at the injustice of having to return his drug paraphernalia to him. But she kept ruthlessly turning her thoughts away from those things, things she was powerless to change, and instead forced herself to concentrate on what had happened earlier with the warden's lapse. Because the more she thought about it, the more certain she became that she had finally discovered the secret of how she had come to that world.

When Andy was describing the new place where Cathy was being held, his mention of "white coats" had caused something finally to click into place in Cassidy's mind. It was something that pulled together all of the previous details of Cathy's confinement, and everything that both Andy and the warden, looking through Andy's eyes, had seen in both of the places where she had been kept. Andy's "white men," the men in white coats, were doctors. Or, perhaps more likely, some kind of medical technicians. Cassidy still liked to think that no one who had ever taken the Hippocratic Oath would be capable of doing to another human being what she now suspected had been done to her.

Both of the places where Andy had seen Cathy, lying unconscious, had all the attributes of some kind of hospital. Andy had said that Cathy had been hit by a truck, but Cassidy had no idea what actually happened to her. Somehow her subconscious mind had stripped its gears and catapulted her conscious mind forward some fraction of a second in time, into that shadow world that existed just beyond the fringes of normal perception. And now her useless and still-unconscious body was still being kept alive by machines.

It was the one explanation that jibed with nearly everything she had found so puzzling about her situation. It explained the miracle of Andy Greene as the warden of Horses, a phenomenon that initially had come as such a shock to Cassidy that its very impossibility had long blocked any of her attempts to rationalize it. She had done extensive research on the subject of autism after Andy

had become her pupil in the riding therapy program, and one unanswered question had appeared again and again in the literature:
Where did the real consciousness of the profoundly autistic person
reside? If not in the real world, then where? Some of the articles
she'd read, as well as some of the workers from Reiners Center
with whom she'd spoken, had espoused a theory of temporal mis-
alignment. They postulated that the reason the profoundly autistic
couldn't seem to relate to reality was because their brains were
somehow out of sync with real time; that they perceived everything either a fraction of a second before or after it actually happened. The phrase "living in their own little world" was
frequently cited.

By her own experience, Cassidy had inadvertently found that
world: the place where the autistic's awareness resided—a literal
second world, separated from the real one by only some flicker of
time, populated by the cognizant and rational consciousnesses of
people like Andy Greene. But Cassidy never could have imagined
that it would be such a totally realized world; a bit primitive, perhaps, a bit oversimplified and emotionally stunted, but still as-
toundingly full.

And if Cassidy was right about what had happened to her, then
Andy had good reason to fear for her life so vehemently. If she
were comatose, she might very well be in danger of being "termi-
nated." The only thing about her precarious fate that still seemed
uncertain was why she had been moved to a different, apparently
more lavish facility. Was it some sort of reprieve? And what did
it have to do with Andy Greene?

Because Cassidy knew then that she had been right from the
very beginning: The answer to her dilemma lay with the warden
of Horses. She not only shared Andy's world, she shared his fate.
And through the lapses the two men became one. If the warden
could go back to the real world, was there some way he could
influence her destiny?

Long before the first faint hint of light began to pearl the eastern sky, the forest birds became active. Lying there in the darkness, staring up at the overhanging boughs of the ancient cypress
trees, Cassidy felt curiously detached from the enormity of what
she had just formulated, almost weightless in a sea of momentous
possibilities. How could she even begin to explain what she suspected to anyone, even to the warden? For if what she suspected
was true, what did she have to return to?

What was more, Cassidy was no longer certain if they still
needed the Alchemist's help so desperately. If that was indeed

who they had found there in the valley, there probably was no
point in even seeking his assistance after all.

At the first blush of dawn, before Rowena or the others had begun to stir, Cassidy slipped from her blanket and gathered up the
water pipe and wooden bowl filled with paper packets. She started
across the dew-spackled ground toward the uprooted cypress.
Dragonfly stood casually hip-shot near a large outcropping of
rock, watching Cassidy with lazy interest. She saw no sign of
Click, but that was hardly unexpected. She was sure that from
wherever the Tinker maintained his watch, he could see her and
everything else in the valley quite easily.

Cassidy realized that she was taking a chance on unpleasantly
surprising the black man by invading his shelter so early in the
morning, but she was eager to get the odious task behind her.
From a few dozen feet away, she could see that the ashes in his
small firepit had been raked together, forming the base for a new
fire to be laid. Glancing toward the dim mouth of the cavern, she
cautiously approached the overhang of sundered roots, holding out
the purloined articles ahead of her like warding talismans. But the
cavern appeared to be empty.

"An attack of conscience?"

The soft voice from a scant few feet behind her caused Cassidy
to start so violently that she almost dropped the pipe and bowl.
She spun around to see the long-haired black man padding up behind her, silent on his soft-soled shoes. His arms were filled with
dead branches and old dried knots of cypress root. She realized
that she must have been staring rather stupidly at him when he
jerked his chin toward the items she held and said, "Or were you
planning on sharing a toke over breakfast?"

Damning the incriminating heat that bloomed up from her neck
and around her ears, Cassidy awkwardly thrust out the pipe and
bowl toward him, realizing almost immediately after she'd done
so that he already had his hands full and could hardly have taken
them from her. He gave her an odd look as he detoured around
her to drop down onto his knees beside the firepit. After dumping
the armload of wood, he began to build his fire, not giving her so
much as a backward glance.

Cassidy edged uncomfortably closer, again proffering the objects she'd taken from his cavern the night before. "I, uh, brought
back your stuff," she said uneasily, trying to complete her obligation and get away from there as quickly as possible.

"So I see," he said evenly, still not even looking up at her.

Cassidy found herself watching with fascination as his slim brown hands deftly arranged the collection of sticks and knots into a neat pyramid in the firepit. Crouched there, he looked both serene and capable, so utterly unlike the man they had first discovered. She had trouble recapturing the sense of righteous indignation that he had aroused in her so easily only a few hours earlier, when he had been verbally sparring with Click. Feeling increasingly foolish, Cassidy was on the verge of just leaning over and setting down the stolen articles, so she could beat a hasty retreat, when he suddenly looked up at her.

"I can see you taking the pipe," he said mildly, "but you mind telling me what the hell you were going to do with a bunch of dried herbs?"

"H-herbs?" Cassidy stammered, staring down into the wooden bowl with its neatly folded little packets as if she had suddenly discovered something exotic living in it.

Although he concealed it well, Cassidy could tell that the black man was enjoying her discomfort and embarrassed surprise. Had the situation been reversed, she would have done the same. There was just the finest of flaring around his nostrils, and his black eyes glinted beneath the arch of his brows. "Yeah," he said with deliberate patience, "herbs. You know, for cooking? Oregano, basil—stuff like that?"

Because she knew that she was blushing again, Cassidy looked down determinedly into the bowl, rather than meet those eyes. "We didn't know it was herbs," she said in a small voice.

To her surprise, he seemed satisfied with her humiliation and didn't continue to press his advantage. In his place, she thought that she might have. Gracefully and without visible effort, he stood and reached out finally to relieve her of the pipe and bowl. "Where's your friend?" he asked her as she eagerly passed them over to him.

Cassidy thought that he must have meant either the warden or Click; but before she could respond, he elaborated. "The other woman who was here with you last night," he said.

Freshly surprised, Cassidy almost took an involuntary step backward. Being that close to him, she suddenly was acutely aware of just how ragged and dirty she was; and by contrast and for all of his well-worn clothing, just how clean and fastidious-looking he was. She couldn't keep from gaping at him. "You—you weren't awake," she said, almost accusingly.

He made a small sound of amusement, not quite a laugh. He ducked under the overhang to enter the opening of his shelter, his long gleaming hair swinging forward on either side of his head like the twin sweep of two black wings. "I wasn't sleeping," he reminded her without turning.

Cassidy's mind roiled, churning up both embarrassment and alarm. He had been unconscious—she would have sworn to it. How could he have known that she and Rowena had . . . ? Her thoughts caught abruptly on the way Rowena had touched him, and the brunette's joking comments about his genitalia, and sex, and Cassidy cringed inwardly. For the first time she found herself fervently hoping that the young black didn't have any Memory other than the use of drugs.

Cassidy's gaze jerked up again as he reemerged from the cavern, carrying a small metal box and a metal pan. Exactly as if he could read on her face precisely what Cassidy had been thinking during his brief absence, his expression remained wryly ironic. "I was stoned," he continued, as if there had been no break in his statement. "There's a difference."

Cassidy's shame gave her voice an edge of defensiveness that was rather inappropriate to the situation. After all, he was the one who had been wronged. "If you knew we were there," she challenged, "then why didn't you stop us from taking your stuff?"

"I was stoned," he repeated; apparently it was the only explanation he felt was necessary. Dropping down beside the firepit again, he set aside the pan. Then he popped open the lid on the metal box, withdrew a match, and, nimbly and one-handed, struck it on the abrasive strip on the box's side. When he touched the flame to the tinder he had arranged at the base of the stack of wood, the fire quickly caught. He no longer seemed to be paying Cassidy the slightest attention.

Relieved to consider herself effectively dismissed by him, Cassidy took a step backward and then turned to walk away. She had only gone a few yards when that soft voice halted her in her tracks.

"If you'd just come out and say why you're really here, Cassidy," he said to her back, "maybe we could work something out."

Initially, Cassidy was more surprised by his use of her name than by what he had said. Then she remembered that the warden had addressed her by name the night before. She hesitated a moment before turning back, because she didn't want him to detect just how easily he had caught her off guard again. When she did turn back, both her expression and her voice were studiously neutral. "I like to know who I'm dealing with," she said.

He was squatting before his prospering fire, the shallow metal pan held balanced lightly like a disc between his honey-colored palms. That finely symmetrical face was utterly calm. "Shad," he said, introducing himself.

"Well, Shad," she replied, "what did you have in mind?"

He shrugged casually. "Maybe a trade," he said. "Some of your shit for some of mine."

Cassidy's brain experienced momentary gridlock. It was not enough just to discover that she had absolutely no idea what he was talking about, when she had been so certain that she knew the kind of knowledge he had been concealing from them. It was also hearing a word like "shit" coming so trippingly from the lips of a man whose youthful face held the arch refinement of a prince, and whose dulcet voice was like that of an angel. Cassidy realized that she was staring stupidly at him, but she couldn't seem to do anything to redeem the situation. "What are you talking about?" she said.

The magnitude of her bewilderment must have rendered it credible to Shad, even if he might still have found her motives suspect. His dark eyes narrowed as he studied her in silence for a moment. "I'm talking about why you really came here," he said then, although without quite the same self-assurance he had evinced only minutes earlier. Even though Cassidy didn't respond, he seemed to regain a modicum of his previous equilibrium as he continued. "Come on, it's the only reason anyone's ever bothered to come here," he said matter-of-factly. "Unless you count the spooks, which I don't, because they don't even wear clothes, much less do shit."

Lulled by the soft rhythm of his speech, Cassidy's brain had finally begun to pull random bits of coherent thought from what he had said. It was mostly a matter of starting to think like Cathy Delaney rather than thinking like Cassidy, a talent for which she'd had so little use lately that she might be forgiven for having grown painfully rusty at it. But once she'd put the definition of the word "shit" into context, the rest of it started to fall into place as well.

"You—you're talking about *drugs*," Cassidy said, still staring at him.

"Yeah," Shad said patiently. He cocked his head slightly as he took in her sustained surprise. "I'm not making you any guarantees, though," he added, "because this shit doesn't seem to have much effect on most people. But I'd sure like to try whatever your pal in leather was traveling on last night."

Cassidy's brain raced, more hyped than any mere drug could have made it. Once she had realized what Shad was talking about, her surprise remained, replenished by the vastness of the misunderstanding that so obviously lay between them. He thought they had come all that way and sought him out to get drugs. When he had seen her with Andy last night, he'd thought the warden had been stoned. Cassidy didn't know whether to laugh or cry.

"Well," Shad prompted mildly, "what about it?"

How could she even begin to explain? Cassidy was almost tempted just to let his erroneous impression stand, to let him find out at his leisure just how wrong he had been. But she could see no use in that, beyond the perverse satisfaction she might derive from seeing him be the one to play the fool. And so in the end, pragmatism won out, and she decided just to tell him the truth. Or at least a portion of the truth.

"We didn't come here looking for drugs," she said, "we came here looking for the Alchemist." She made a small gesture toward him. "In fact, in the whole time I've been here, you're the first person I've found who's used drugs, or even known what the hell they are."

The expression on that fine and facile face swiftly changed from one of expectation to another look, one that was much more difficult for Cassidy to interpret. There was an element of surprise in it, quickly suppressed, and more than a little cool wariness. He gave her a long, skeptical look before he responded. "What about your buddy in leather?" he said. "You trying to tell me that he was perfectly straight last night?"

Cassidy tried to imagine how one of Andy's lapses must have looked to the totally uninitiated, especially someone well versed in drug use. Unless Shad believed in multiple personalities, she could easily see why he had assumed that the warden had been stoned. She wasn't especially concerned about convincing him, but she was silently debating just how much she should reveal.

"My buddy in leather is named Andy," she said. "He's one of the reasons we're looking for the Alchemist."

Shad had been absently rolling the rim of the pan gently back and forth in his hands. His appraising look was still cynical. "You telling me he did that without drugs?" he persisted.

Cassidy nodded, determined to maintain her casual composure. It was difficult to do, when she was squirming to *ask* questions rather than have to answer them. But the warden's words kept coming back to calm her, reminding her that neither force nor coercion was likely to be effective with this maddeningly enigmatic man.

Shad's curved brows arched even more sharply. "And you didn't come here looking for drugs?" he reiterated.

"No," Cassidy said, "just the Alchemist. Just information."

She deliberately did not explain any further, and she was rewarded by a subtle glint of curiosity in those darkly exotic eyes. Shad didn't ask her anything, but she was certain she had captured his interest.

"Well," Cassidy said after a moment, "I guess I'd better get back to camp. And don't worry; as soon as we've had a chance to clean up and make a decision about our next move, we'll be on our way again."

Shad set down the cooking pan, nudging it forward onto one of the flat rocks that edged his firepit. "Good," he said without looking up. But Cassidy was secretly satisfied to note the new lack of conviction in his tone.

Back at their camp, there was a healthy cook fire burning, and the alluring smell of fresh coffee filled the morning air. The Warden, Kevin, and Rowena all looked up at Cassidy's return with frank inquiry on their faces. Only Click, who sat with his face wreathed in steam from his coffee mug, betrayed no overt curiosity. Cassidy just dropped down and sat by the edge of the fire, nonchalantly reaching for the mug Rowena passed to her.

After Cassidy had taken several slow, delicate sips of the hot brew, Rowena couldn't stand it any longer. "Well?" she said impatiently. "What happened over there?"

Cassidy shrugged indifferently. "I brought back his stuff," she said, "and he took it."

Rowena looked ready to strangle her cheerfully. Luckily for Cassidy, the warden spoke up first. "You just seemed to have been gone a fairly long time, Cassidy," he pointed out, his tone one of wry amusement. "We were beginning to worry—about *his* welfare, that is; not yours."

That even evoked a soft grunt from Click. Glancing back over her shoulder at the uprooted cypress on the other end of the valley floor, Cassidy gave up her pretense of nonchalance and briefly explained her bizarre conversation with Shad. They listened without interruption, although Rowena appeared visibly relieved when Cassidy did not elaborate on Shad's possible awareness of their presence in his shelter the night before. The most important matter, Shad's misinterpretation of the warden's spell, was greeted with thoughtful speculation all around.

"Why didn't you just tell him why we're looking for the Alchemist?" Rowena asked.

But Cassidy firmly shook her head. "No," she said. "If I'm wrong and he's not the Alchemist, then there's no reason for him to know."

"Cassidy's correct," Click said. "And if this man is the one we seek, we want him to admit that and reveal something of what he already knows before we tell him everything *we* already know."

"And Cassidy has just done an excellent job of piquing his curiosity," the warden said. "I have the feeling this Shad is going to want to talk to us now; and when he does, I suspect he'll also find himself looking for answers."

"Well, if nothing else," Cassidy said pragmatically, "I may have bought us a little more time here, before he boots us out." She took another swallow of coffee. "As soon as we finish eating, I'm going to go back over the ridge and cut my mare some more fodder."

"Take someone with you," Click said mildly. "Except for the obvious necessity, I don't want anyone to go out of the sight of at least one other person as long as we're here."

Kevin shot a quick, automatic glance in the direction of Shad's shelter. "You don't think he's dangerous, do you?" he asked dubiously.

Click gave a small shrug. "I don't think we can assume that these woods are safe" was all he would say.

"I'll go with you, Cassidy," Rowena offered. "I need to refill the water bags anyway. And I'd really like a chance to get cleaned up."

"Yeah, good idea," Cassidy teased her.

"You should talk!" Rowena grumbled good-naturedly. Then her expression grew wistful. "I wonder if he'd be willing to part with some of those extra clothes he's got stashed in that dugout?"

"Gee, too bad we don't have any drugs to trade," Cassidy said, dodging a playful swat from the brunette.

But Click's face had taken on a thoughtful look. "Perhaps we might have something that is just as useful to him," he mused. "I suspect it's been a long time since this man has had anything to eat that he hasn't caught or gathered in this forest."

Rowena's eyes immediately widened in comprehension. "You mean like rice and beans and coffee?" she said.

"We may be getting tired of them," the warden remarked, "but our staples would probably be a luxury to him, the way he's living out here."

But before Rowena's enthusiasm could get completely out of hand, Click pointed out, "That kind of exchange should wait until we've had a chance to talk further with him. We wouldn't want him to think that we were trying to bribe or cheat him in any way."

Rowena sighed. "I guess I can wash these clothes one more time," she conceded.

When they had finished eating, and Cassidy and Rowena were preparing to go over the ridge, Kevin said, "I'll come along with you. I want to get cleaned up, too."

Cassidy pointedly ignored the leering wink Rowena surreptitiously threw her. "Sure, Kev," she said. "Come on."

Kevin looked across the waning cook fire to where the warden squatted, methodically rolling up blankets. "Maybe we all should go?" the blond boy suggested.

That only broadened Rowena's grin; but Cassidy's uneasy glance went not to the warden, but to Click. The Tinker was at that moment the picture of harmless domesticity, sitting on a large rock as he rinsed eating utensils in a pan of water.

"We don't want to leave our camp unattended, Kev," the Warden reminded him. "Click and I can bathe later."

Click looked up from his homey task, a faint glimmer of humor in his dark eyes. "When they come back smelling as fresh as flowers," he said wryly, "they'll probably chase us from the camp."

Kevin insisted on carrying the water bags as the three of them scrambled back up the winding path that led to the top of the ridge. The trail seemed much less intimidating once Cassidy had become a little more familiar with it, although it still would have been a difficult route for the mare. She could see why the horse was willing to go out of her way to find another path.

Once they reached the ridge, warm morning sunlight poured down in the gaps between the big trees. Down in the valley in the grove of cypresses, the weather achieved an almost artificial consistency, and Cassidy found her spirits unexpectedly lifted by the random and friendly dappling of sunshine as they hiked the short distance to where the trail cut off.

The path down to the creek was more uneven and eroded, but weeks of travel had given Cassidy the sure-footed confidence of one of Rowena's goats. When they reached the bottom of the ravine, where the clear, shallow creek glistened among the stones, Cassidy gestured to Kevin and Rowena.

"You two go ahead," she said. "I'm going to cut some brush for my horse first."

"You sure you don't want any help?" Kevin offered immediately. His generosity was so automatic and typical that Cassidy realized she had come to take it for granted, which made her feel a little rueful.

"No thanks, Kev," she said. "You did it for me last night. Besides, I only brought one knife." She gave Rowena a sardonic little wink. "Enjoy yourselves."

All feigned innocence, the brunette clapped Kevin on the arm. "I think we'd better fill the water bags first," Rowena said as she and Kevin turned away, "before we pollute the entire creek!"

Cassidy hiked a short distance along the bottom of the ravine, bypassing some of the coarser vegetation until she found the sort of succulent brush favored by her horse. She saw a stubble of severed stumps marking where the warden and Kevin had been cutting fodder the evening before. As she set to work, methodically grasping and slicing through the lush branches, Cassidy had to give Rowena the leniency of a private smile. After all, who had been the voyeur only a few nights before, with no compunctions about watching Click strip and bathe? And Kevin didn't even remember sex.

Cassidy was doing such a good job of avoiding obsessing over Shad that she was a little nonplussed to find her mind taking off and running with images of the Tinker instead. It had taken her until breakfast to realize just exactly what Click had been able to accomplish during his little verbal standoff with Shad in the predawn hours. Not only had he managed to keep Cassidy from hopelessly antagonizing Shad, but he had also set the stage for her own early-morning discussion with the black man. And Click had never even considered pointing out or taking credit for everything he had so deftly accomplished.

"Slick" doesn't even begin to describe it, Cassidy mused, setting aside another handful of cut branches. Unwillingly, her thoughts returned to her conversation with Click the night before beside the gray mare, when he had said that what he feared was not that they had failed, but that Cassidy had indeed found exactly what she had been seeking. She had had to pretend that she didn't understand what he meant; but she couldn't keep up that pretense within the secrecy of her own heart. How could Click say something like that—*and mean it*—and still so calmly and adroitly engineer for her the best chance to obtain the very kind of help she sought?

Or was the real question, she realized with a sudden knife-sharp stab of pain, how could Click *not* do it?

For that demonstrated a degree of love—*Yes, love,* her little voice commanded indefeasibly, even as the rest of her mind still shied away from the word like a spooky colt—against which Cassidy no longer knew how to defend herself.

Reluctantly forsaking her little patch of sunlight on the warmed surface of a huge slab of tilted rock, Cassidy stood up, stretched luxuriantly, and began to pull on her damp cotton clothing. Spread out on their backs nearby, both Kevin and Rowena squinted up at her when they saw she was dressing.

"Are you going back already?" Kevin asked.

"I'd better," Cassidy said almost apologetically as she bent to tug on her boots. "My horse will be chewing down the trees, waiting for this fodder."

It had been so pleasant just to lie there in the sun, with her eyes closed against its cheery brilliance upon her face and the smooth surface of the rock cool against her back. When she had finished cutting branches and returned to the creek to find Kevin and Rowena stripped and vigorously washing their dirty clothes, she hadn't hesitated to join them. And when they spread their clothing out to dry and then stretched out naked on the sunny rocks, it had felt so relaxing finally to be clean again. So if she had spent a little extra time surreptitiously eyeing Kevin, his lean young body a study in shades and gradations of gold, then Cassidy considered it time harmlessly spent. His friendly smile and cheerful banter were dispensed as freely as the sunshine, and she knew she was taking nothing from him with her secret appreciation of his appealing body.

"Our clothes aren't even dry yet," Rowena protested mildly.

"You two don't have to come back with me," Cassidy pointed out. "Why don't you stay awhile yet?"

But Kevin was already on his feet, shaking out his trousers. "I'd better get back, too," he said. "The warden and Click were talking about working on a signal flag for down by the swamp."

Outnumbered, Rowena sat up with a sigh and reached for her shirt. "What do you mean, a signal flag?" she asked as she tugged the still-damp garment on over her head.

There was a brief delay while Kevin pulled his leather tunic on. Then he said, "Some kind of a sign for Valerie and the others, when they've reached the end of the Spine. Something that's high enough that they can see it all the way across the swamp, so they'll know where to cross."

"It would have to be something pretty big," Cassidy remarked. She remembered how they had barely been able to see land from where they had stood on that last dry spit of the Snake's Spine.

Kevin had automatically bent to pick up more than half of the small mountain of branches Cassidy had cut. "I guess they're thinking of putting something up high," he said, straightening up with the armload of fodder. "Up in the big trees, so it can be seen from that far away."

"Sounds like a fun project," Rowena said without enthusiasm. She had just noticed that she was going to be the one stuck carrying back both of the water bags. "Maybe our buddy Shad's got some kind of flag stowed away along with all that other stuff he's got."

"I wouldn't count on too much help from him yet," Cassidy reminded her dryly. "Remember, he still thinks we'll be leaving soon."

For a few minutes none of them spoke then, as they carefully made their way back up the steep and narrow trail to the top of the ridge. With the burdens each of them carried, they had to devote a certain amount of attention to where they placed their feet. By the time they had reached the top, Cassidy found that the lingering dampness in her cotton shirt and pants felt pleasantly cooling.

Kevin took the lead along the path. "We aren't really going to leave, are we?" he asked Cassidy.

"Not until we get what we came here for, Kev," Cassidy assured him.

"But what if we . . . ?"

Because Cassidy had been trying simultaneously to balance the load of branches and watch her footing without really being able to see her feet, she nearly walked right into Kevin before she realized that he had abruptly halted. Behind her, Rowena almost bumped into Cassidy. Looking ahead, past Kevin's shoulder, Cassidy almost dropped her bundle of fodder.

Less than a dozen feet ahead of them, idly suspended just inches above the packed earth of the pathway, hovered a *thing*. With that odd acuity of vision familiar to her from an adrenaline rush, Cassidy noted with a certain clinically detached precision that what the creature most closely resembled was a giant black loop of bowel. It was perhaps ten or fifteen feet long, and about as big around as her thigh. Its inky surface gleamed dully without actually appearing to be smooth or moist, and rippled minutely, as if with hundreds of tiny muscular fasciculations. And even though it wasn't hanging from anything or touching the ground, it maintained its position in midair with no visible effort.

Kevin's eyes were enormous with alarm; Cassidy was surprised that he hadn't dropped his bundle of branches. "W-what *is* that?" he stammered hoarsely.

The creature was remarkably similar to the giant smokelike coils of the air monsters; only the miniature version hovering before them appeared to have more substance to it. Then again, Cassidy realized that she'd never seen the greasy-looking air creatures in the daylight, or when they were not in motion, so perhaps that accounted for the difference. Or perhaps like the small carrion eaters they had seen by the bog where they'd rescued the Woodsman, the creature may have been a variation on the huge flying ones.

"Cassidy?" Rowena whispered from behind her, the brunette's voice dry with fear.

Cassidy turned to reassure Rowena; but as she did so, she froze with the calming words stuck in her throat. A scant six feet behind Rowena, its ebony coils gently bobbing as if to some silent rhythm, was another of the hovering serpentine creatures.

Kevin's face was blanched with dread. "They—they won't hurt us, will they?" he murmured anxiously, his eyes darting from one of the lightly undulating creatures to the other.

Cassidy would have liked to be able to assure him that they wouldn't. But not only had she never before seen this particular kind of monster, she also had seen the creatures to which they seemed to be most closely related slaughter hundreds of people in the Iron City. So instead of wasting her time on speculation, she tried to formulate a plan of action.

"Both of you, set down what you're carrying," Cassidy hissed softly. "Do it slowly, but do it right now."

Cassidy didn't even bend over to drop her own armload of brush; she just loosened her grip enough for the fodder to slide right down the front of her thighs and pile at her feet. A quick glance assured her that neither of the creatures had reacted in any way to the movement. They both just continued casually to hover there, with little peristaltic shivers flickering along their coiled lengths. Cassidy crossed her empty arms over her midsection, her right hand feeling along the waistband of her trousers for the knife she had used to cut the branches. As her fingers closed over its haft, she gripped it tightly.

"I want you both to go over the edge," she whispered slowly, "off the ridge and down the slope into the valley. Don't try to stay together and don't look back; just keep your feet under you and run like hell for camp."

"B-but what are you . . . ?" Kevin began, typically concerned about abandoning Cassidy.

But Cassidy cut him off with a necessary ruthlessness, her voice low but harshly commanding. "Just *go*, Kev; don't worry about me." Her knuckles whitened around the handle of the knife. "They won't hurt me."

For another few seconds, Kevin and Rowena hesitated, as if by some mutual silent consent gathering themselves for the flight ahead. Then, without a word, they both leapt off the trail and began to slide and scramble down the steep, trackless slope.

The moment they were clear of the path, Cassidy spun around, her arm extended with the knife held like a sword. She made a complete, dizzying 360-degree circle, the blade passing within inches of the nearer of the two creatures. But neither of the two monsters recoiled; in fact, they didn't betray even the slightest interest in her. Cassidy was just beginning to consider what to do next when the creatures moved.

As quickly as a blink, almost more swiftly than her eyes could follow, the black, looplike creatures rolled over on themselves and were off, streaking like flying serpents down the slope where Kevin and Rowena had gone.

Cursing her own stupidity, Cassidy plunged over the edge of the trail. She landed roughly, skidding on the loose humus, nearly ten feet down the steep incline. Her bare arm glanced off the trunk of a tree, nearly causing her to drop the knife as tingling pain harped from her elbow to her fingertips. But she ignored the blow and flung herself onward, crashing through small saplings and nearly tripping over a half-buried slab of crumbling rock while her heart kicked frantically in her chest.

She had been an idiot; she never should have let Kevin and Rowena become separated from her. Cassidy berated herself mercilessly as she plummeted blindly down the side of the ravine. If she had been right about the creatures not harming her, then the other two would have been far safer with her. She had been a fool to think that she could control the monsters in any way, or keep them at bay while the others escaped. Images of the carnage she had witnessed that night in the Iron City came back to torment her then, searing memories of the giant air monsters dropping down from the dark sky like loops of oily black smoke and lingering visions of what they had left behind.

But these are smaller! she pleaded with those memories. *Maybe they aren't even the same things.*

But at the bottom of the slope, Cassidy saw the first signs of destruction along the path the creatures had taken. Several trees, one with a diameter greater than that of her own torso, were completely stripped of bark from the ground up to a height that was well over her head. The bark, or what was left of it, was freshly strewn all over the forest floor like a finely ground and pungent-smelling mulch. The lower portions of the trees were completely denuded.

Ahead of her along the valley floor, Cassidy could hear the thrashing sound of something moving rapidly and without caution through the trees. Rowena and Kevin? Or the creatures? Or both? Cassidy's heart was thudding painfully as she followed the path of willful mutilation through the woods. There were more tree trunks stripped, and pulverized fragments of bark were strewn around like confetti. Her breath was coming in short, stabbing gasps as she attempted to hurl herself over the partially rotted trunk of a long-downed cypress. She came up short on momentum, as she slid to the ground, the knife flew from her hand. Frantically groping for it in the leafy debris, Cassidy tried to orient herself in the valley. She couldn't be far from Shad's shelter and their campsite; the trail to the creek just wasn't that long, so they had never been very far away. But coming up the valley floor from its long axis instead of via the path was confusing. Nothing looked familiar to her.

Grappling hold of her knife again, Cassidy lurched to her feet and began to crawl over the top of the huge log. As she scrabbled across the curve of its spongy crest, she finally recognized where she was. She was approaching Shad's tree from the back side; the upthrust medusa shape of its giant cluster of uptorn roots was less than a dozen yards away. And approximately halfway across that space, among the gnarled trunks of the big cypress trees, Cassidy saw three people locked in a grim struggle with the two hideous creatures she had been pursuing.

Boa constrictors—that's what the damned things really were like, Cassidy thought as she leapt down off the rotting log and raced across the remaining distance. Or what boa constrictors would be like if snakes could fly. One of the creatures had slung a coil of its dark and sinuous body around Rowena's lower legs and brought her to the ground. The brunette was pounding on its gleaming and unyielding surface with her fists, her face contorted with anger and desperation. And Kevin was down on his back, with his head and the upper half of his body completely entrapped within a series of spiraling rolls of the second creature's undulating flesh. And braced between Kevin's uselessly flailing legs, with both of his hands locked onto the smooth and snakelike free end of the monster's body, was Shad.

Cassidy made an immediate priority judgment. As she sped toward the two men, her mouth was so dry with fear that she couldn't have formed a single word, even if she had known what to say. As she approached them, she realized that Shad wasn't just trying to pull the creature off Kevin. A couple of feet away, where Shad had obviously dropped them in his haste, lay the carcasses of two rabbits. In one sinewy brown hand, Shad clenched the blunt haft of a skinning knife, its long blade buried to the hilt in the all-too-substantial tissue of the monster's coiled body.

Cassidy flung herself to her knees on the ground beside Kevin, her own knife poised to plunge. She reached out with her other hand, both to brace herself and to secure the creature's winding thickness before she stabbed it. But the instant her fingers closed around the tough, gleaming surface, *the world simply stopped*.

Too startled at first to realize what had happened, Cassidy thought that she had suffered some kind of seizure or brief loss of consciousness. Until she discovered that she *was* still conscious. She was staring down at the monster's sinuous body, still coiled around Kevin; but neither was moving. At the periphery of her vision, she could still see Shad, frozen in time with his skinning knife embedded in the creature's flesh. She was alive and she could see; she could even feel the odd cool texture of the creature's smooth leathery skin. She just couldn't move. *Nothing moved.*

It was like the creature in the sinkhole, Cassidy realized then, her mind amazingly clear and rational in that little oasis of timelessness. Something about the monster, or her interaction with it, had caused everything in that world to come to a halt. Or at least everything but her mind, since that was obviously still functioning.

The sensation was disturbingly seductive. There was a sense of safety, of *freedom*, in the floating void where nothing moved. But Cassidy willfully resisted the siren's call of that timeless zone. Before her eyes she could still see the thick coils of the monster's body tightened around Kevin's limp form; and she could still see

Shad, his long black hair suspended in a flung-back fan as he bent to attack the creature.

A bolt of anger shot through Cassidy then, burning along her quiescent nerves and muscles like a jolt of electricity. It galvanized something in her, white-hot and almost maniacal. With a concerted effort of mind, she *willed* herself to move. And when she did, *the world moved on*.

Cassidy didn't know if Shad was even aware of her presence, so single-minded was his assault on the monster. As he pulled back with one hand, he tried to twist and saw his knife deeper into the creature's flesh with the other. And yet all of his efforts seemed fruitless. It appeared as if he were cutting into mud; the dark, oily mass flowed around the blade, parting and then closing again with no discernible damage.

Kevin's legs were jerking weakly, almost spasmodically, his heels thumping against the ground. With another flush of rage, Cassidy realized that the creature was going to kill him. Throwing herself forward, she plunged the blade of her knife into one of the coils tightening around Kevin's chest. And as she did so, the solid roll of flesh beneath her hand just *melted*.

As the creature's substance suddenly gave way, Cassidy fell forward so abruptly that she almost sank her blade into Kevin's belly. The serpentlike monster didn't simply vanish. It took several discrete seconds for the solidity to leach from its sinuous black coils, its form collapsing like a deflated bladder from which all of the water had emptied.

Then nothing remained of the creature, not even the faintest shred of its gleaming skin or any rime of grease. It was as if whatever had given the monster life had just bled from it; and when the last of that malignant life was gone, the creature had ceased to exist.

Chapter 18 ◀▥

Several things shook Cassidy from her stunned daze. One was Kevin moving beneath her, his chest heaving to pull in air with a deep groan. Someone's hands gripped her shoulders, gently but surely pulling her back off the young man. Unresisting, Cassidy allowed herself to be lifted to unsteady feet. Her eyes quickly darted to where Rowena had been struggling only moments earlier. Click was squatting beside the brunette, his arm around her, murmuring something too softly for Cassidy to hear. And of the second creature, there was no trace.

The warden said something to Cassidy, but she didn't immediately understand his words. She was staring down at Kevin, who was blinking and wheezing a little, but who otherwise looked remarkably well. There was an odd mottling on the bare skin of his face and arms, but he was not bleeding. Kevin seemed considerably perplexed to find Shad crouched between his legs; possibly he was just as surprised by that fact as by the discovery that the coiled monster was utterly gone.

As for Shad himself, amazement was not too strong a word for the expression on that exotic-featured face. But to Cassidy it did not seem precisely the astonishment of disbelief; it was more like the shock of recognition.

While Rowena had been badly shaken by her ordeal, Cassidy could see that the brunette had not actually been harmed. However, Click made no effort to coax her into trying to move.

Once the warden made certain that Cassidy could stand unassisted, he swiftly dropped down beside Kevin, helping the blond boy as he struggled to sit up. The strange mottled markings were already fading from Kevin's skin. When Kevin sat up, Shad finally moved.

The black man dropped back onto his rump beside Kevin's

legs. His dark eyes moved in an uneven triangle: from Kevin's flushed and breathless face, to Rowena's, and then to Cassidy's. Shad's gaze lingered there, the shaken look on his face slowly transforming into an expression that was a shifting mixture of reluctance, wariness, and resignation. He didn't even seem to realize that he still held the skinning knife clutched in one hand. He let out his breath in a soundless sigh, and when he spoke, his soft voice was just audible.

"I think," Shad said, "that we need to talk."

Back at their campsite, Click added tinder to the coals from their breakfast fire, kindling a fresh blaze as he wordlessly set up the coffeepot to brew. Cassidy had been so insistent about retrieving the abandoned fodder for her horse that the only way to make her stay put was for the warden to go back to the ridge to get it. And he had to promise to do so immediately, before Cassidy would acquiesce to stay in the camp. Rowena and Kevin seemed content to sit side by side before the flames, with their blankets wrapped around their shoulders. When Click first tried to drape Cassidy's blanket over her shoulders, she resisted him, even though her damp cotton clothing then felt distinctly clammy. But when he squatted down behind her and briefly put his arm around her, she relented and allowed him to cover her back with the blanket.

As the fire settled down into the radiance of a steady heat, and the heady aroma of fresh coffee permeated the calm morning air, Shad still stood a short distance away from the others, silently leaning against the trunk of a nearby tree. He had been studying her for some minutes, Cassidy realized; but although the scrutiny was frank, it was not offensive. If anything, Shad had a slightly abstracted air about him, as if even when he was looking right at her, his thoughts were on something else entirely.

When the warden reappeared on the valley floor, the gray mare greeted him with an impatient nicker and followed along behind him, until he finally dumped the cut branches a few yards from their campsite. It was perfectly clear where the horse's priorities lay; monsters had never frightened her, but the possibility of missing breakfast had made her anxious.

As if taking that sardonic observation directly from Cassidy's thoughts, Shad met her eyes. He didn't appear frightened, either, but there was something in his expression that Cassidy hadn't seen there earlier. He was regarding her in a new light.

As the warden rejoined them at the fire, he lightly touched both

Cassidy and Rowena on the back before passing them to reach his customary place beside Kevin. When he had gone back for the fodder, he also had retrieved one of the water bags, which he handed over to Click before settling down beside Kevin. He murmured something encouraging to the blond boy, just as Click lifted the coffeepot from the fire and began to pour.

Click held out the first steaming mug to Shad, a gesture plainly intended to prompt him to join them around the fire. Shad hesitated a moment, although Cassidy wasn't sure if it was the offer of coffee specifically or just the idea of sitting down with them in general that he seemed to be deliberating. But then, in much the same way as the gray mare was drawn to her fodder, Shad pushed himself off the tree and came around the edge of the firepit. He dropped down and sat cross-legged between Cassidy and Click, and took the hot mug in both hands.

While Click finished pouring coffee, Cassidy watched Shad with an unapologetic directness. And even though the coffee must still have been almost scaldingly hot, the black man drained his first mugful in one long steady draft. Before all the other mugs had even been passed around, he was already holding out his empty cup to Click again. Either he really craved the caffeine, Cassidy thought, or else the coffee was as much a luxury to him as the warden had suspected.

As Shad proceeded summarily to empty his second mugful, Cassidy cradled her own cup in her hands, relishing its warmth and aroma as much as she anticipated its taste. She continued to study Shad overtly as Click passed him yet another refill. But when he showed some sign of more slowly savoring the third mugful, Cassidy decided it was time to voice the question that had been foremost on her mind since immediately after the monsters' attack. Perhaps it wasn't even a question anymore.

"You've seen those things before, haven't you?" Cassidy said quietly, looking directly at Shad.

Peering over the rim of his coffee mug, Shad's black eyes were muted by a rising veil of steam; but he returned her look without evasion. In the nearby trees, a single bird's cry rose like a counterpoint to his silence. "Never any quite like those," he said then, his voice even, "and not for a long time."

The warden had been sitting with his shoulder leaning companionably into Kevin's, but at Shad's words, he immediately straightened, his brown eyes widening perceptibly. "You're saying that you've seen monsters before?" he asked.

Shad lowered his mug from his lips, slowly and with a studied deliberation. "Is that what you call them?" he said. "Monsters? We used to call them bogeys."

The other men may have been puzzled, but Rowena suddenly stirred. "Oh, you mean like the bogeyman," she said.

"Yeah," Shad said, the smallest flicker of a smile crossing his lips. "Bogeys."

The warden set down his mug, his interest obvious as he leaned forward slightly. "When and where did you see these creatures before?" he asked. It was more than mere curiosity for him. In the time they'd been away from the Iron City, Cassidy had almost forgotten the problems the monsters had wreaked in the warden's Territories; but it was plain the warden had not been able to.

Shad took a small sip from his mug. "It's been a few years," he replied, "back when I was still with Henry. But the ones I've seen didn't look anything like this. And they never attacked anybody."

Cassidy wanted to ask who Henry was, but instead she tried to keep the focus of the conversation on the creatures. "Do you know what they are?" she asked Shad.

His arched brows tented. "These?" he said. "Or the ones I saw? Henry said they were just mental garbage, like hangovers from bad dreams." He gave an evocative little shrug. "Obviously, Henry was never attacked by one of them."

"But you haven't seen any of them in this area for years?" the warden persisted, perplexed.

"Not since Henry left," Shad repeated. His gaze suddenly went to Cassidy. "You must be the one they're following."

In spite of herself, Cassidy was startled by his perspicacity. Before she could stammer out an answer, and before anyone else intervened, Shad added, "I guess that must be why you're here then."

His statement only left Cassidy more nonplussed. "I thought you thought we were here for drugs," she blurted out.

Shad took another slow, deliberate sip of coffee. "Same thing, isn't it?" he said sardonically.

Into the brief moment of confused silence that followed Shad's response, Click moved with quiet assurance. "I think the simplest way to explain why we're here," he said evenly, "is to begin by explaining who we are." Click kept his introductions succinct and to the point. He merely deemed himself a Tinker, but he casually named the warden of Horses. After introducing Rowena and Kevin, he turned to Cassidy and said, "I think Cassidy herself can best explain what has happened to her to bring her here. You may find you share a great deal in common."

For a few moments Cassidy felt unexpectantly tongue-tied, as if a college professor had just called her up in front of the entire class and asked her to explain the creation of the universe in fifty words or less. Explaining everything that had happened to her suddenly seemed an overwhelming task. As she stared uneasily at Shad, she found she didn't even know just how much of it she wanted to share with him. And so in preface, she blurted out another question.

"Just how much do you remember?" she said bluntly.

Shad didn't seem surprised, confused, or offended by her query. In fact, Cassidy swore she saw the glint of some bit of dry humor spark in those dark eyes. "You mean like who won the World Series in 1988?" he responded wryly.

Relief, almost euphoric in its intensity, poured through her. "Then you remember *everything*," she said in wonderment.

Shad shrugged. "Everything worth remembering, I guess. I've tried to forget the Reagan years."

Excitement made Cassidy stumble over her words, piling up questions like a haphazard stack of firewood. "Then what—when did you—how—" She broke off, helplessly shaking her head, as if to somehow rearrange everything that was inside it.

"Let me ask *you* something," Shad interrupted, his even tone winning him her willing cooperation. "How long have you been here?"

And Cassidy knew that Shad didn't mean "here" as in there in his valley, or in the swamp. He meant *here* exactly the same way Cassidy had always meant it, there in that world as opposed to the real world from which they'd come. She automatically leaned forward toward him, eagerness driving her voice an octave higher. "Weeks now—maybe a couple of months altogether, I guess."

Shad sat so calmly, so still, that his amazing questions only seemed all the more incredible for his lack of emphasis. "Did you remember everything from the very beginning?"

Cassidy didn't even care that Shad had taken over the direction of the exchange. She quickly shook her head. "No, at first I didn't remember anything. I just knew that I didn't belong here."

Cassidy went on to give the most abbreviated version possible of her experiences in that world and of the piecemeal return of her memory. Even as she was speaking, she realized that it was the first time she had ever revealed all of those things to anyone except Rowena; but she felt amazingly little reticence about it then.

During the lengthy narrative, Shad barely moved. He just sat there cross-legged, the coffee mug cradled between his slim brown hands, in much the same posture as they had found him the night before. It wasn't until nearly the end of her story that she saw him react. As she explained the events in the Iron City that had forced them to flee, she related how they had come to seek the mythical figure they knew only as the Alchemist. She could see the question in Shad's unblinking black eyes then. But to her surprise, he didn't ask her anything further when she finally finished speaking. Instead he shifted slightly, slowly rolling the mug between his palms, and began to tell them his own story.

Shad had been there for several years, but he knew nothing of the Eastern Territories and had never even heard of the warden or the Iron City. He had come from the west, a different kind of terrain that sounded even more primitive and less settled than the Territories. It was not farming country, but there were vast herds of cattle and sheep; and to Cassidy his description of the social organization of herdsmen sounded much like the parallel of Villagers and Horsemen in the east.

Shad had come from the mountains, and traveled steadily eastward for months. Although he didn't specifically say so, it became obvious his reason for the long journey was to avoid the trouble he kept having with the herdsmen. Because he had, like Cassidy and Rowena, been different from the other people around him, he seemed incapable of ever satisfactorily "adjusting."

Initially he had remembered nothing; he only had been haunted by the certainty that he didn't belong there. Like Cassidy, he'd had to struggle to turn that vague feeling into concrete memories of the real world. What he did remember came back to him in uneven fragments, often in his dreams, which were frequently violent and frightening. But little of what he remembered from them made sense to him, because he lacked any unifying vision of the real world.

Listening to the young black man describe a past so disconcertingly similar to her own, Cassidy was struck by how dispassionately he spoke of it. She realized that the passage of time and subsequent events may have helped to blunt the old pain of that formless longing for the life that he had lost; but she still found Shad's matter-of-fact delivery disquieting. Yet she certainly understood what he meant when he explained what his early months in that world had been like.

"Sometimes I felt like I was right on the edge, you know?" he said. "It was like having the theme song from some old movie

stuck in your head—and still not being able even to remember
what the hell a movie was."

But when Shad had reached what he called the Big River,
something happened that changed his whole life. He met up with
a kindred spirit, another man who was on the same kind of aim-
less journey of evasion. A subtle shift occurred in Shad's expression then, and in it Cassidy could detect an emotion that she had
not seen before on his face. He looked faintly sad, and his voice
seemed touched with regret.

The man he had met was Henry, another misfit wanderer who
apparently was only one step away from becoming one of the
wild ones. Henry had very little memory of the real world; but
what he did remember, he had utilized with relish. Henry remembered drugs.

"Is Henry the one who made your pipe?" Cassidy asked him
quietly.

Shad seemed to find some fond amusement in that idea. "No,
he was useless at making things. He found it." He shrugged.
"Henry was amazing at finding things. Lots of that junk I have
was stuff of his."

"And the monsters followed this man?" the warden interjected.

"Yeah, Henry had his own personal little bogeys," Shad replied.
"They were hideous little shits, but they were harmless. And
when he left, they all disappeared, too."

There was a moment of silence. When Shad didn't go on,
Cassidy ventured gently, "What happened to Henry?"

Shad's slender brown hands abandoned his mug, spreading
vaguely. "Damned if I know. One morning when I woke up, he
was just . . . gone."

Cassidy saw Click and the warden exchange a glance, but neither of them spoke. It was so quiet around the campfire that when
the gray mare exhaled loudly, the sudden sound made Cassidy
start.

"Do you think something happened to him?" she asked softly.

Again Shad made another vague gesture. "I don't know. I
didn't find any signs of a struggle. I suppose he could have just
moved on without me, but I don't know why he would have; and
he left all of his stuff behind—even his clothes."

"So you went on alone," the warden prompted.

Shad had continued his journey east, until he ultimately reached
that blunt wedge of forested land that jutted out into the Great
Swamp. So the "island" was actually just what they suspected, the
leading edge of a much vaster body of land. When he had arrived

there, the Snake's Spine had been partially submerged. He had obviously left the western herdsmen far behind; he hadn't seen another person in weeks. There really wasn't any reason for him to go on. In the valley he discovered the long-abandoned and partially collapsed cavern beneath the roots of the toppled cypress, where some other solitary soul had once lived. He repaired the shelter, moved in his collection of belongings, and stayed.

Having had Henry's experience to guide him, Shad's habit of using psychotropically active plants as drugs had already become well entrenched. In the swamp he discovered new and different substances, fungi and plants unlike anything he'd tried before. Shad discussed his drug use as casually as he had described his early days in that world, or his travel route. But of course only Cassidy and Rowena had any basis upon which to judge him for it, and suddenly disapproval seemed irrelevant to Cassidy.

During an experiment with one of those new substances, Shad had regained his full memory in the most direct and compelling way possible: His mind had unexpectedly stumbled into the real world.

Pausing, that surprising revelation left hanging without any further elaboration, Shad turned to Click and held out his coffee mug. His voice was almost jarring in the very banality of his request. "How about a refill?" he asked the Tinker.

As Click lifted the coffeepot from the fire, Cassidy prodded Shad to continue. "You're saying you actually traveled to the Slow World," she asked him incredulously, "by using *drugs*?"

Accepting his mug back from Click, Shad gave Cassidy a mildly bemused look. "The Slow World?" he queried with a little shake of his head. "That's what you call the real world? As if *this* place isn't slow enough!" He took a small sip of coffee before he answered her question. "Yeah, I went there," he said, "and it scared the shit out of me. Talk about an out-of-body experience; try an out-of-body-*and-mind* experience. I was actually *there*—I could see and hear what was happening around me, but I couldn't *do* anything." He took another sip of coffee, this one deeper and more rapid. His tone had grown rueful as he concluded, "But when I came down off that stuff, I finally remembered everything: who I really was, where I'd really come from—everything about the real world."

Intrigued despite her ingrained contempt for the use of drugs, Cassidy prompted him. "What did you do then?"

The black man gave her a long and dryly appraising stare.

"Threw that shit away," he said, "and didn't touch it again for almost two years."

Cassidy was stunned. She didn't understand how Shad could have abandoned the miraculous ability to reach into his real life, no matter how repugnant the means he'd used seemed to her. But before she could put her reaction into words, Shad had turned to the warden and was questioning him instead.

"So that's what you were doing last night, right?" he asked the warden. "Only you weren't using drugs to do it."

Even without a practical knowledge of the use and effect of mind-altering drugs, the warden understood the thrust of Shad's question, and nodded. "We think it's possible for me to connect with Andy Greene," he said, "because Cassidy knows me as him from the Slow World. I have absolutely no Memory of my own. And this didn't begin happening to me until Cassidy found me and remembered who she really is." The warden made a small self-effacing gesture. "I have these episodes—I guess you would call them 'trips,' but we call them lapses—where I assume the identity of Andy. And when that happens, I see Cassidy as Cathy, the person she is in the Slow World."

"But can you *do* anything?" Shad asked him.

The warden seemed mildly perplexed by the question, and he automatically glanced to Cassidy for assistance. She addressed Shad's question, reasonably certain that she finally had found someone who would understand what she meant when she explained Andy Greene's condition.

"The warden's limited by Andy's abilities in the real world," she said. "You know what autism is? Well, Andy is profoundly autistic. But we've discovered that during the lapses Andy is able to let the warden take over his consciousness; which means that at least for a few seconds, it's not just Andy back in the Slow World, it's also the warden. That's what we were doing last night."

"But he still can't *do* anything there, right?" Shad persisted.

Growing both puzzled and irritated by the question, Cassidy said, "He can see where I am, what's happening to me. If he can go back during a lapse, why not anytime? And if he can go back, then there must be a way for me to go back, too."

Shad was shaking his head, his raven-black hair swinging. But Cassidy was surprised to find that the expression on that fine-boned face was neither one of impatience nor annoyance; if anything, it was an expression of disappointment or even regret.

"And that's what you've come here looking for?" he asked her. "A way to go back there?"

With the implicit understanding that they had just reached the crux of the exchange of knowledge which had brought them together, and the uneasy sense that their purposes were still painfully far from being joined, Cassidy stared at Shad, a budding defiance lifting her chin. "It's not impossible," she maintained stiffly. "The warden's done it—hell, *you've* done it. There has to be a way to go back for good."

Shad quickly glanced around the fire at the other faces, his expression oddly taut. Meeting Cassidy's gaze again, he said in that deceptively soft voice, "You just don't get it, do you? Maybe you *could* go back; but why would you want to? I'll grant you, this place is no paradise; but going back, that would be like limbo."

The obvious confusion on Cassidy's face betrayed her, causing her dogmatic insistence to falter. "What do you mean?" she asked.

Shad leaned slightly forward, his bare elbows almost resting on his leather-clad knees. "Why do you think you're here?" he asked her intently. "Just what do you think happened to you back there?"

A modicum of Cassidy's confidence returned, bolstered by the conclusions she'd drawn from the warden's last lapse. "I know where I am back there," she asserted, "even if I'm not sure exactly why, or how they took me." She looked steadily into Shad's dark eyes, deliberately waiting for him to blink. But he didn't blink. "And I know if I don't go back there," Cassidy concluded emphatically, "I'll never get away from them."

Cassidy's declaration didn't impress Shad. "Listen, I don't know what you think happened to you," he said with a little toss of his head, "but I can tell you that you've got nothing there to go back to. Not unless you feel like lying around like a corpse for the rest of your life."

Cassidy hesitated, her self-assurance faltering again. What the hell was Shad talking about? Whatever had been done to her mind to separate her from her consciousness, it would be undone by her return to her own world—she was certain of it. It was just a matter of—

Shad's voice was so soft that its very tone snatched Cassidy from the tumult of her thoughts. The dry irony of his humor was gone, replaced by an acerbic bitterness that confounded her. "Let me tell you," he said, "what your buddy's seen when he's gone back: You're laid out, unconscious, on some kind of bed, surrounded by a bunch of monitors and other equipment, right? You don't move, you don't speak—maybe you aren't even breathing on your own, eh? Maybe you're on total life support."

"No!" Cassidy whispered harshly, her stricken eyes locking helplessly on Shad's as he inexorably went on.

"Why do you think you're here?" Shad repeated, quietly but implacably. "Maybe your head's been cracked like an eggshell; maybe someone blew away half your fucking skull with a hollow-point bullet." Those black eyes drilled into hers. "You're in a god-damned *coma*—probably brain-dead. Persistent vegetative state, that's what they call it. How do you think any of us got here?"

Images and phrases whirled through Cassidy's unwilling mind then, brutal substantiation of what Shad had just told her. From the very beginning, Andy had said he'd seen Cathy get hit by a truck; and he'd thought she was dead because she couldn't move or speak. The hospital: men in white coats, a white room, white walls, bright lights, a narrow bed surrounded by machines, the sound that never stopped . . .

The sudden horrific comprehension had a visceral effect on Cassidy, making her feel vaguely queasy and her limbs go numb and useless. Beside her, Rowena reached out to support her arm, the brunette's rounded face a blur of concern. Shad had begun to speak again, but his words were like latent percussives to Cassidy then, their impact perceived only distantly and belatedly.

"You really didn't know?" he persisted, but softly. "I thought you had figured it out." He seemed torn between compassion and the pain of his own long-buried rage; his dark eyes dropped to stare into his empty coffee mug. "Why do you think I didn't even try doing that shit again for two years?" he said. "Even now, go-ing back to that is like lying in my own coffin, even when I know I don't have to stay . . ." His voice trailed off, some unspoken memory tightening the muscles around that small, perfectly formed mouth. When he began to speak again, he was looking down steadily into the glowing bed of coals that filled the firepit, his manner once more calm and almost clinically detached.

"There was a time," he said, "not long after I got here, that I was convinced that I must have been dead. It certainly would have explained everything, wouldn't it?" His eyes narrowed sar-donically. "Well, for all practical purposes, everyone here *is* dead—at least in the real world. We'll all totally vegged out, ei-ther in comas or else so mentally scrambled that our minds don't have any lives left back there. That's why we're here."

In one single lithe movement, so smooth that it was almost eth-ereal, Shad suddenly stood. "If there is such a thing as a cosmic lost-and-found department for people's consciousnesses," he said, "then I guess this is it. And you can take a look at what you left behind, you can remember it and mourn it, but there's no way in hell that you're ever really going to go back to it."

Shad stepped deftly around Cassidy and started away, walking silently and steadily back toward his cavern beneath the cypress tree.

So stunned and wobbly that she could hardly sit up straight, much less walk, Cassidy nevertheless was prepared to lurch to her feet and go after the black man, propelled by a desperate sense of anger and disbelief. But Rowena was still clutching her by the arm, and when Cassidy tried to stand up, the brunette restrained her.

"No, Cassidy, don't," Rowena murmured, her fingers locked around Cassidy's elbow. "Just let him go."

The three men were looking at the two of them with a mixture of confusion and concern, but she was immediately drawn by the expression on Rowena's face. The brunette looked stricken, nearly as devastated as Cassidy herself felt. Then Cassidy realized that she was not the only one who remembered the real world. Just because Rowena didn't remember who she was there, she had still shared Cassidy's determination to return to it. They had, in fact, made a pact to return together.

The warden sat nearly motionless in the sudden silence. He didn't seem to know how to begin to ask the questions that beset him from all sides. It was left to Click finally to break the impasse. When he looked at Cassidy, his lean face was thoughtfully composed, his tone deliberately neutral.

"Do you believe that what this man says could be the truth?" he asked simply.

Cassidy hesitated a moment, not able to meet those deep and perceptive eyes. "Yes," she finally said, bitterly and reluctantly, her voice sounding low and hoarse even to her own ears. "I think that it's possible."

Cassidy didn't know exactly what she had expected Click's response to be. Her mind was too numbed by disappointment even to have considered his likely reactions. But she certainly hadn't anticipated the easy equanimity of his reply. "Well, there seems to be a great deal here that we still don't understand," he said calmly. He got to his feet and actually began to gather up the empty coffee mugs. "And I suspect that once he's had a chance to think about this," he went on, "Shad will have a good many questions, as well."

Cassidy could only look up mutely at Click, staring stupidly, incredulous at his response. It was an equally surprised Rowena who first found her voice.

"You mean we aren't leaving?" she asked Click in disbelief.

Click had his hand held out for Rowena to pass him her mug. He merely gave both women a mild look. "You have somewhere else you were supposed to be?" he asked her, with such perfect deadpan delivery that it took the brunette a few seconds to realize that the question was wryly rhetorical. Then Click shook his head. "No, unless there are any objections, I would suggest that we still give this some more time. We've come too long a way at far too great a hardship to give up so easily."

Sitting there before the waning fire, Cassidy had been prepared to wrap herself in despair and self-pity as surely as she had wrapped herself in her blanket. She was utterly perplexed and disarmed to see Click set about the banal task of washing up all the coffee mugs, much as if the entire incredible discussion that had just taken place had concerned nothing more daunting than some spell of foul weather or a particularly difficult stretch of terrain to be negotiated.

Cassidy realized something then about Click's reaction, even if she could not have put it into words. The Tinker didn't really understand the situation Shad had outlined, not entirely at least. He had long since lost the memory necessary to have put the grim revelation into context. But the thing Click did understand and had reacted to was Cassidy's feelings about it. It was also the only aspect he felt capable of affecting.

Cassidy exchanged a helpless glance with Rowena then, and the brunette shrugged.

"Maybe we should walk back and get the other water bag," Rowena suggested.

As she often did, Cassidy attempted to find solace in Dragonfly's company. The horse had long since polished off the choicest bits of the fodder that the warden had brought back to their camp, but the big gray was still busily sorting through the pile of cut branches when Cassidy returned with the rest of what she had cut early that morning. The leaves were a little wilted, but Dragonfly didn't seem to mind. She greeted the additional feed with an enthusiastic nicker, nearly tearing the branches from Cassidy's arms in her eagerness.

It never ceased to amaze Cassidy how simple life could be for a horse. She idly arranged a few errant swags of the thick iron-colored mane as the mare cropped at the new fodder. The last couple of hours may have seen Cassidy's long-borne hopes dashed and all of her carefully constructed theories demolished, leaving her dream of returning to the real world broken upon the treacherous shoals of Shad's brutal honesty. But for the mare, if she was comfortable and had enough to eat, then the world was all that it needed to be.

Joel had once laughed at Cathy when she announced that all of life's really important lessons could be learned from working around horses. Of course, perhaps the fact that she had been wielding a manure fork at the time had somewhat undermined the profundity of her observation.

Cassidy leaned against the mare's sleek shoulder, absently finger-combing the snarls out of the long coarse hair of her mane. She was completely absorbed when a familiar voice startled her out of her reverie.

"If you think you can get her nose out of that fodder for a while," Click said, walking around from the other side of the horse, "I have something I want to show you both."

In spite of herself, Cassidy found her interest piqued. Glancing over at Click, she said, "You mean me and the horse?"

Casually taking her by the arm, Click nodded. "Yes, you and the horse." As if anticipating her hesitation, he added, "It's not far from here."

But Cassidy needed little convincing. Even though she suspected Click was just trying to perk up her spirits, she was more than willing to quit the little valley for a while. That way her gaze wouldn't keep drifting over to the big toppled cypress, and she wouldn't have to keep thinking about the enigmatic man who was once again holed up under the shelter of its stump. At Click's gentle tug, she started forward, Calling the mare to follow.

The horse also seemed perfectly happy to venture out across the floor of the valley, even if it meant abandoning her feed. She tagged along a few yards behind them as Click led Cassidy past their campsite and toward the slope that formed the opposite side of the shallow valley. Click kept his hand on Cassidy's arm until they reached the incline; then he released her so that they could each climb unhindered.

Cassidy noticed that some time during the course of the morning, besides doing the dishes and tidying up around the camp, Click also had taken the time to clean himself up again. There wasn't much that could be done with his torn and stained clothing, any more than Cassidy could have worked miracles with her own ragged seaman's cottons. But Click had washed up, even his hair, and trimmed his mustache again. The makeshift toilet had erased years from that lean and tanned face.

The northern slope of land wasn't quite as steep as the southern one, and there were fewer downed trees to block their way. Apparently Shad seldom saw the need to travel in that direction, for there also were no established trails. But even without a path, it was a fairly easy climb. The day was sunny and had grown considerably warmer since dawn, but it was still cool enough there in the shade. The mare picked her own route, of necessity having to detour around a few places where the tree limbs were too low for her to pass, but she had no trouble keeping up with them. For the most part Cassidy and Click walked side by side; but whenever an obstacle made it more practical, he urged her to go first, even though he never used the occasions to offer her any assistance.

At the top of the ridge they paused, and Cassidy looked back down into the valley. From that vantage point, no one could have guessed what lay below them, blocked by the deep green of the cypress trees. And for the moment it was as if they were simply alone there, and nothing of the pain and disappointment Cassidy had experienced in that valley even existed. Glancing sideways at Click, she wondered if that had been the whole point of the excursion. But as Dragonfly came lurching up the last few feet of the incline, her long tail swishing as she attained the crest, Click led her on again.

They hiked along the high spine of land for a while, edging around the irregularly spaced trunks of the mature trees and the occasional outcroppings of shale. Cassidy grew increasingly curious. As unexpectedly pleasant as it was proving to be to get out of the valley, Click had said he had something to show her. Cassidy was happily surprised to find that rather than dreading such a proposal, as she once might have, she was actually looking forward to it. But just when she was about to question him, Click suddenly veered from the top of the ridge and started down its opposite slope.

Forced to watch her footing again, Cassidy momentarily forgot about asking Click anything. The incline wasn't particularly steep, but unlike the slopes facing Shad's valley, it was choked with brush and saplings. She had to dodge and weave behind Click to keep up with his longer strides. They were nearly to the bottom of the slope when he came to an abrupt halt.

For a long moment, he just stood there, looking at something he could see but Cassidy, behind him, couldn't. A tiny prickle of unease unfurled in her then, and she suddenly wondered just exactly what he'd brought her out there to see. If it was some kind of weird Woodsman thing, or something equally disgusting— But then Click silently stepped aside, taking her by the shoulders wordlessly to urge her forward; and Cassidy could finally see what he had been watching.

Along the bottom of the slope, winding among the scattered brush and trees of the valley floor, was a crude trail, narrow but well trampled. A deer path, Cassidy realized instantly, because there were five casually browsing deer along it, not a dozen yards from where they stood. The deer were much larger than the whitetails Cassidy had grown accustomed to seeing, with coarse ruddy-colored coats and big mulish ears. The buck and four does seemed oblivious to their presence until the mare made an impatient movement on the slope behind Cassidy and Click. Even then the deer didn't bound off. They looked back toward the horse and the two humans, their big ears and tails flipping and flicking uncertainly. Then, with an easy nonchalance, they broke as a group into a trot. Within seconds they had vanished up the trail.

"I came across this last night," Click explained then. As he started down the slope to the deer path, Cassidy followed, speechless with surprise at how far the Tinker had ranged in the darkness. "It's rather rough," he went on, "and I don't know how far it goes, but at least it should be passable." Turning to see the mystified look on Cassidy's face, he elaborated. "I thought you might like the chance to ride your horse again. Even if it's not the best of trails, it's more than we've had in a long time."

As comprehension flooded her, Cassidy felt a disarming mixture of gratitude and happiness overwhelm her, bringing her alarmingly close to tears. She fully realized Click's intention had been simply to make her feel good, to give her pleasure. She was afraid to look up into his face. Instead she stared at the crude little path, pocked by the tracks of the cloven hooves of the big deer, and tried to dispel the sudden thickening in her throat so that she would be able to speak normally.

"Thanks," she finally managed, her voice inescapably husky. "It's been so long . . ."

Click deliberately overlooked her surfeit of emotion and gave her an encouraging clap on the back. "Go ahead, then," he said. "I doubt you'll be able to get very far, but you never know."

Cassidy took a sudden and involuntary stumbling step forward; without being Called, the mare had come up behind her and given Cassidy an impatient shove with her head. Turning to push away the intrusive muzzle, Cassidy looked up at Click and blurted out, "Aren't you coming with us?"

Click just eyed her levelly for a moment; Cassidy knew what he must have been thinking. He had assumed that she had wanted to be alone. And if someone had asked her, she might even have said that she had wanted to be. But no one had asked her, and so Cassidy could admit to herself that she actually would rather continue to be with Click.

Imitating Click's deadpan remark, right down to his ironic drawl, she said, "You have somewhere else you were supposed to be?"

If she had thought that washing up had erased several years from Click's face, she should have remembered what a smile could do for it, especially when that smile was echoed in the glint of self-effacing humor in those umber eyes. "Nowhere that won't keep," he replied.

Click took a step back out of Cassidy's way so that she could mount. She felt most of the muscles in her body protest indignantly as she vaulted up onto the mare's broad back, but she managed to make it without any major embarrassments. Settling her legs over the mare's sides, she leaned forward slightly over the gray's withers as Click hopped astride. But he didn't bump into her; in fact, he barely seemed even to touch the horse until he was seated upon her back behind Cassidy. He was, after all, a Horseman, Cassidy reminded herself ruefully. More than a common Horseman, he had been the captain of the Troopers. She realized with a certain unsettling poignancy that this was not just a man who was competent around horses; this was a man who truly loved them.

As Cassidy urged the mare forward, she felt Click's hands settle lightly on her hips. Through the rumpled cotton of her baggy seaman's clothing, the touch should have been barely perceptible; and yet she could hardly have been more aware of it had he gripped her with hot iron tongs. The deer path was well traveled, but its surface was still littered with the sort of obstacles that animals merely circumvented, so any gait faster than a walk would have been imprudent. The mare still moved along smartly at that gait, as if happy finally to be fulfilling her usual role in Cassidy's life. Dragonfly didn't seem at all inconvenienced by having to step over rocks and bypass exposed tree roots and other debris. Cassidy found that she had to keep an eye on both the horizontal and vertical clearances, however; a moment's careless inattention could have led to being swept summarily off the horse's back by a tree limb.

Cassidy was content with the pace. As Click had pointed out, the trail probably wasn't very long, and so the slower they went, the longer the rare ride would last. Birds rocketed out of the surrounding brush, scolding loudly if uselessly at the odd three-headed creature that passed. Cassidy found herself becoming absorbed with the familiar sensation of the smooth glide of the horse's muscles beneath her thighs and the warm and unfamiliar apposition of the lower part of Click's body against her own. There was a soothing quality to the lulling repetition of the mare's steps and the rhythmic sway of her broad body, just as there was something oddly satisfying about the gentle contact between herself and the Tinker. It reminded Cassidy of the day she had ridden with him on the mule path along the Long River, a time of innocence that then seemed as if it must have happened to someone else in some lifetime far removed from that one.

It had been the first time she had seen Click naked, Cassidy thought with a little flush of heat, glad that he couldn't see her face. But she permitted herself to enjoy the memory, just as she was enjoying his company on the ride.

Once when they both had to duck to avoid being unhorsed by a low bough, Cassidy straightened back up a bit too abruptly, and the back of her head collided with Click's chin. "Oops, sorry," she murmured contritely, glancing back over her shoulder. But Click seemed amused by their ill-timed maneuver, and merely gave her hips a playful squeeze.

"Perhaps next time I should ride in front," he remarked teasingly.

They had ridden only for ten or fifteen minutes when the terrain surrounding the path began to change. The ridge that it had paralleled rapidly diminished, dropping off into the earth; and there were fewer mature trees and much more unruly brush. They were headed east, so it was easy to predict what was happening. They were nearing the end of the wedge of forest, and the higher ground was running down into the Great Swamp.

A short distance farther, the path itself began to deteriorate. Several rutted courses broke off from the main trail as it was reduced to little more than a thin spot in the brush. Cassidy finally had to signal the mare to halt, and when she did so, she felt Click hop down from behind her.

He pushed ahead through the growing thicket of branches for a few yards, studying the lay of the land. "We're not far from the marsh here," he said. He turned back to her, bouncing experimentally on his boot heels. "The ground is a bit peaty even here."

"Then I guess we can't ride any farther," Cassidy said, feeling keen disappointment. She realized that she really didn't want to return to their camp yet.

"Not safely," Click agreed, coming back to the horse. But then, as if he had read the thought directly from Cassidy's mind, he added, "But that doesn't mean that we have to go back just yet, either."

For the first time during their little adventure, Cassidy found herself acutely aware of the possible ramifications of being out there alone with Click. Looking down at him from atop the mare, she tried to keep any of that feeling from leaking onto her face. *You're the one with the dirty mind!* she chastised herself. Click hadn't given her any reason to feel uneasy in that regard.

He was looking up at her with a calmly speculative look on his face. "Come on," he said then, "let's walk a ways. Perhaps one of these side trails becomes passable."

Cassidy thought that was extremely unlikely, since the trails probably all just subdivided further until they petered out entirely. But she quickly hopped down off the mare's back anyway. As soon as she had dismounted, the horse fell to greedily cropping the surrounding brush. The action was so transparently self-serving and yet so utterly typical of Dragonfly's usual mind-set that Cassidy had to laugh.

"I guess we won't be inconveniencing her then," Click remarked drolly as he held out his hand to beckon Cassidy forward.

As they slowly moved away from the horse along one of the crude little pathways, Cassidy almost had to laugh again, this time at their unconventional attempt at taking a stroll. They couldn't even walk side by side, and Click, assuming the lead, often had to stop and jerk back some of the brush out of the way to keep it from whipping Cassidy across the face. Their every move dislodged whining clouds of insects, some of which would no doubt find them quite edible. If anyone else had seen what they were doing, Cassidy thought, the two of them would have looked like idiots. And yet she didn't complain or even consider turning back.

At some point about a hundred feet from where they had left the mare, the path, such as it was, just seemed to vanish entirely, and they were left standing in the middle of a tangle of bushes and saplings. They were near enough to the marsh that once they had stopped moving, Cassidy could hear the distant song of the peeper frogs above the soft rustle of the leaves in the light breeze.

She tilted her head back and looked straight up at a brilliantly blue patch of sky, edged all around by the deep green of the trees. The sense of isolation there was almost overwhelming, and yet Cassidy did not feel a sense of desolation. For some reason she found the remoteness comforting.

She had become so absorbed in her thoughts that she started slightly when she felt Click's hand land lightly on her shoulder. But when she looked over into his face, his expression revealed little beyond a pleasant sort of camaraderie. "Are you ready to go back?" he asked her.

Cassidy wanted to say no, that she wasn't ready to return yet. But those weren't the words that came from her mouth. Suddenly all she could see was the grim enormity of her situation, and she felt overcome with a clarity of feeling that she might normally have repressed. Looking directly into that calm and familiar face, she felt oddly emboldened, as if there in that strange isolation it was suddenly safe to say almost anything.

"Can I ask you something?" she said.

One of Click's brows climbed quizzically. "Of course," he said.

There still would have been ample time for Cassidy to have backed down or reconsidered, but something made her refuse to give in to her customary caution. Click's equanimity, his thinly veiled curiosity, his very nearness, all lobbied against such equivocation. He stood so close that she could see the faint pulse beating at his throat and the fine sun-bleached hairs that covered his tanned forearms and the backs of his hands. And so she just went ahead and asked him the question that she had asked herself a hundred times, but had never imagined she would be capable of asking him.

"How could you just give it all up?" she asked. "Being a Horseman, I mean." She also meant being a Trooper, the captain of the Troopers, and very likely the next warden, as well; but she didn't have to say that part, for it all was implicit in her query.

After a few long moments of silence, Cassidy thought that she must have overstepped the unspoken understanding that had long lay between them, and that by doing so she had offended Click. But as she continued to study his face, she realized that his expression, while a bit rueful, was merely pensive and not angry. She also realized that his hand still rested on her shoulder, and that in spite of the disheveled condition of his once-fastidious clothing, at that proximity the thing he smelled most like was Tinkers' soap. And when he finally did speak, his tone was actually wry and self-deprecating.

"I was expecting you to ask me about something simple," he
said, "like the fact that I remember sex." Seeing that Cassidy had
begun to color faintly, he went on. "You know that not every decision is a matter of choice. Or at least that if it is a matter of
choice, sometimes it comes down to a bad choice or worse ones."
His hand traveled from her shoulder to the curve of her neck,
where his long fingers spread to lightly frame the angle of her
jaw. "A successful leader must have two things, Cassidy: the respect of those who would follow him and respect for himself."
His gaze slipped from her face then, not evasively but almost con-
templatively, fixing on some place beyond her. "I once reached a
point in my life where I had neither of those things. And so I took
the best of those bad choices."

Once Cassidy had thought that she wanted to know about everything that had happened to Click in those dark days, to ferret
out the truth that lay behind all of Valerie's innuendoes and the
contempt of Justin and his fellow Troopers. But standing alone
with Click there, in that remote stretch of brush beneath that brilliantly blue sky, she suddenly realized that she no longer really
wanted to know the details. She not only felt no need to know,
she instead felt every need to protect his privacy in this deepest
and most personal pain. Cassidy almost blurted out that she didn't
want to hear any more, when Click looked back to her and continued.

"And so I went to the Tinkers," he explained, "because we
each had something the other one needed. They needed my leadership, and I needed their fellowship." He cupped her chin, the caress more whimsical than sensual. "Not a bad trade. And if you're
asking me if I miss what I had to leave behind, then the answer
is yes, of course. But I have salved that pain by doing the best job
that I could in leading the Tinkers." He gently ran the callused
edge of his thumb over her lower lip, a glint of irony in his dark
eyes. "Just as you have salved your pain in this world by exerci-
sing your compassion toward others."

For a few moments Cassidy was too perplexed to speak:
perplexed by everything—Click's touch, his words, his serene acceptance of the cruelty of his fate. She wanted, she admitted to
herself, to kiss him, and more. She wanted to touch him, stroke
him, stoke in him that heat which she sensed lay right beneath his
surface calm, even then. Or maybe most especially then. And so
to prevent that from happening, she hastily flung out another blunt
question, like a line of defense against her own impulses ever being realized.

"What about sex, then?" she asked. "How long have you remembered?"

Click's head dropped back with a quick laugh, his hand slipping again to her shoulder. "I guess I asked for that one, didn't I?" he said with resignation. "Let's just say that it was long enough ago for me to have made a fool out of myself several times before I realized that this was not a natural trait in this world."

Cassidy's eyes narrowed, peering at him with a speculative frown. Then her eyes widened again. "Not Valerie . . . ?" she began, shocked.

Click laughed again, quite heartily and with a certain delight. "Oh, no!" he assured Cassidy. "It was long before the captain and I ever crossed paths. I'm afraid she has other, far better reasons for her contempt for me." He tried to sober, but another rogue chuckle broke from him, undoubtedly at the mental image that had been supplied by Cassidy's assumption. "No, I learned quickly enough to conceal what was unacceptable that I have managed not to leave a trail of irate women in my wake," he concluded candidly.

Cassidy knew that she probably should quit while she was ahead, but something about Click's demeanor, perhaps his spontaneous laughter, made her go on now that she finally had the opportunity. If she had indeed ruptured their truce, then it seemed only fair to try to eliminate the conflict between them that had necessitated that truce in the first place.

"Why didn't you tell me?" she asked him, with more curiosity than accusation in her tone.

Click shrugged slightly; the silvered tips of his mustache rose even as his shoulders did. "At first I had no way of knowing what you knew," he said. Then he added with a raffish smile, "Although after our first meeting, I certainly could have suspected that something about you was . . . different."

Cassidy was dismayed to find herself blushing at the memory of that first encounter with the Tinkers' leader, when she and Rowena had ridden right into his camp, stark naked. As if to ameliorate her embarrassment, he quickly went on.

"And later, when I did suspect the truth . . ." He paused, studying Cassidy's flushed face with an almost disconcerting frankness. "Well, you would have to be the first to agree that this has been a complicated situation from the start, Cassidy. I didn't feel that I had the right to complicate it further, just because we both shared the capacity for a certain emotion."

Click's phrasing may have been deliberately formal, almost

clinical; but there was nothing detached about the quiet fire held banked in those deep-set eyes. Something in both his words and his calm expression provoked a response from Cassidy.

"Until that night in the city," she reminded him.

"Yes," he agreed, "until that night in the city." He was looking into her eyes so steadily, so unblinkingly, that Cassidy felt as if he were capable of looking right beyond them and into her mind. And as if he had discovered what secrets were kept captive there, Click concluded, "If I owe you an apology for my actions that night, or at any time since, then you most certainly have it from me, Cassidy. It was never my desire to offend you, and I have tried to do all that I could to keep you from harm."

Cassidy knew that the harm of which he spoke had little to do with monsters or sinkholes or swamp cats, for what they shared was far more dangerous than any of that. Her chest felt painfully tight, and the dense brush surrounding them suddenly blurred into a watercolor landscape in shades of green as her eyes filled with unshed tears. She was caught in a world where she could not stay, haunted by a world where her life as she recognized it probably no longer existed. And supporting her there, at the wrenching intersection of those two worlds, was Click, the man she loved but could not have.

Cassidy reached up clumsily with both hands and took hold of Click's hand where it still rested upon her shoulder. She meshed her fingers with his and squeezed them, but that was all that she would do. Because Click owed her nothing more, least of all an apology; but there was something that she owed him. He had always tried to protect her, and so she would force herself to protect him, as well.

The sun was just past midpoint in the sky when Cassidy and Click returned to their campsite. As they picked their way down the southern face of the slope, sometimes sliding a few steps in the steepest spots, Cassidy could see Kevin and Rowena working near the firepit, stacking firewood. As her gaze swept farther across the valley floor, she nearly stumbled.

Midway between their campsite and the big uprooted cypress, two men walked slowly side by side, their heads inclined toward each other as if they were immersed in conversation. The two men were the warden and Shad.

When Cassidy and Click had reached the bottom of the slope, Shad looked up, staring at them for a few moments. Then, casually clapping the warden on the arm, he turned around and began walking briskly back toward his shelter. The warden continued approaching them; by the time their paths intersected, they were nearly at the campsite.

Click's brows lifted quizzically, but he said nothing. Cassidy, however, was unable to keep her curiosity to herself.

"What happened?" she asked immediately.

The warden shrugged slightly and glanced back in the direction Shad had gone. "I went to ask him about trading for some of the extra clothing he has."

Just like that? Cassidy thought incredulously. The man had just lobbed a live grenade into the middle of all of her hopes and plans and then walked away—and then all the warden could think to ask him about were *clothes*? Exasperated with the warden's seeming nonchalance, Cassidy prompted, "Well? What did he say?"

As the warden fell into step beside them, Cassidy noted that much like Click, the younger man had done the best he could in cleaning up. He had washed and shaved, but he still smelled faintly of wet leather and swamp muck. "He said that he'd look through what he has," he reported, "and see what he was willing to part with."

Cassidy scowled. "Generous of him," she muttered.

"There's something else," the warden said. When Cassidy threw him a sidelong glance, she could see an oddly satisfied expression on that boyish face. "He asked that someone come and get him the next time I have a lapse."

Cassidy's scowl disappeared as her mouth rounded in surprise. "Why?" she asked.

The warden made a small gesture with his hands. "Since I—or rather, Andy—could see him, he wonders if perhaps he can contact Andy during a lapse." Shrugging at Cassidy's dubious expression, he concluded, "It's certainly worth a try."

"Yeah," Cassidy said. "I wonder how much he'll want for that?"

Ignoring Cassidy's ill-humored cynicism, Click addressed the warden about the particulars of his dealings with Shad. "In the matter of the clothing," he said, "what is he asking for in trade? Coffee?"

But the warden seemed mildly amused by that subject. "No," he explained, "actually he seemed more interested in rice and beans." He shrugged. "He said that caffeine was bad for his nerves."

Chapter 19 ◀▥

For the next two days things were quiet in the small valley. The weather remained fair and calm, and nothing unexpected happened. The warden, Kevin, and Click spent much of that first afternoon down at the point of land that led out into the marsh, constructing their signal flag. They cut and spliced together several saplings, forming a long pole. They lashed the pole to the upper limbs of one of the largest trees at the forest's edge, high enough to be seen from all the way across the swamp. Atop the crude mast they fastened a slightly faded red shirt and a black pair of trousers that they'd gotten from Shad. Kevin told Cassidy that the color combination was a Troopers' signal to proceed with caution.

Shad's cache of extra clothing easily yielded a wide enough selection of sizes and styles that none of them had any problem finding something new to wear. And while Cassidy had formed a certain sentimental attachment to her seaman's cottons, the bond was quickly broken when she discovered a handsome blue shirt and a pair of tailored khaki pants that actually fit. In much the same way, the warden and Kevin were reluctant to part with their traditional leathers; but when Rowena offered to spend the time needed to clean and patch the garments thoroughly, both men were willing to pick out temporary replacements of more conventional clothes.

When Cassidy had first met Click, she had taken him for a bit of a dandy. Since then she had come to realize that it wasn't so much what Click wore as the way he wore it. And on him, even the plain and unembellished ecru shirt and tan trousers he'd selected took on an entirely different quality, especially when topped by his silver conchaed vest.

Rowena, of course, was like a hen in a corn crib, so excited by

364

her wealth of choices that she could hardly make a decision. But she finally picked out a loosely cut shirt and matching pants in some kind of green knit material.

"You look like the Queen of the Forest in that outfit," Cassidy teased her as she sat on one of the big flat rocks beside the creek, watching Rowena industriously scrubbing at Kevin's leather tunic with a lump of soap.

"This outfit happens to be very comfortable," Rowena said, unperturbed, as she bent to her labors. "It's also very well made; I think it must have been sewn by some Tinker."

It was the afternoon of their second full day in the valley, and Cassidy and Rowena had gone to the creek in the adjacent ravine so the brunette could begin her planned renovation of the warden's and Kevin's leathers. Cassidy wasn't offering any assistance, but Rowena seemed content to just have her companionship. And Cassidy had a particular reason for wanting to spend some time alone with her friend.

It was warm on the rocks, even though the sun had traveled far enough across the sky that the shadows of the trees blocked its light from their slanted surfaces. Cassidy chewed idly on a twig as she watched the other woman work. "What did Kevin do with our old clothes?" she mused. "Burn them, or bury them?"

Rowena looked up with an impish grin. "First he burned them, then he buried them," she replied. Setting aside the soapy tunic, she reached for the matching trousers and began immersing them in the water. As she loosely wrung out the garment and spread it across a rock, she said, "I guess you weren't too far off with that crack about Shad stealing all those clothes from the Woodsmen. The warden told me that is where Shad got them. Only he doesn't have to steal them."

Her curiosity piqued, much as Rowena had intended, Cassidy cocked her head expectantly. When the brunette feigned being totally absorbed in her scrubbing, Cassidy loudly cleared her throat and prompted, "So then how does he get them?"

"The Woodsmen give them to him," Rowena said. "Actually, they *leave* them for him, all around the edges of the valley."

Cassidy's expression was skeptical. "You mean like sacred offerings?" she asked cynically.

The buxom woman shrugged blithely. "I guess so." She shot Cassidy a quick grin. "Looks like being a mythical figure has its perks after all."

Cassidy just grunted noncommittally. Back when they had still been searching for the Alchemist, he had taken on something of the qualities of a mythical figure to her. But once they had actually met Shad, Cassidy's crushing disappointment had quickly destroyed those illusions. She was no longer certain exactly what the young black man represented to her; certainly not a savior, but perhaps no longer a nemesis, either. Somewhere between hope and disillusionment lay the uneasy truth.

Someone far less perceptive than Rowena still would have had little trouble surmising what Cassidy was thinking about then. Without even looking up from her laundering, Rowena said, "I know this hasn't turned out the way we'd expected, Cassidy, but that still doesn't mean it's over yet."

Cassidy looked up sharply. "I'm not giving up," she said a bit defensively.

"I know," Rowena said, her plump fingers slowly and rhythmically rubbing the lump of soap into the wet leather. "I just don't want you to think that because we might not be able to get what we'd hoped for, you shouldn't try to take whatever you can get."

Rolling her eyes at the brunette's mangled syntax, Cassidy deliberately misunderstood Rowena's point. "I wouldn't worry about settling for whatever we can get yet," she pointed out. "Right now we've got nothing!"

Rowena's hands went still, and she looked over directly at Cassidy, patiently waiting for the smaller woman to meet her gaze. "You know what I'm talking about," she said, her tone mildly chastising. "If what Shad said is true, I'm not sure I'd want to try to go back, even if I could."

Cassidy stiffened. "*If* what Shad says is true," she repeated, her emphasis vehement. "He may be wrong about the real condition of a lot of the people here." She made an abrupt gesture. "Look at Andy," she reminded Rowena. "He's certainly not brain-dead. When he's connected with his consciousness here, he's perfectly normal. What makes you think we couldn't do the same thing?"

"I'm not saying it isn't possible," Rowena said mildly. "I'm just saying that if it turns out that you can go back and I can't, I'd understand. Besides," she added, "Andy is a special case. How many people do you think there are like him?"

Distracted from Rowena's original point by her subsequent comment, Cassidy shrugged and conceded, "I don't know. Maybe not many exactly like him. But if the rest of us are all in some kind of—" She balked at the term, but could summon no other. "—vegetative state, that doesn't necessarily mean that we're all permanently damaged physically. People have woken up from comas, you know."

"I know that," Rowena said gently but firmly, "and I'm not giving up. But we don't know what it's like for me back there. I just wanted you to know that if it turns out that I can't go back, too, I'm going to make the best of whatever does happen."

A vague sense of guilt had kept Cassidy defensive about Rowena's pragmatic tone. But when she looked into the brunette's calm and guileless hazel eyes, she felt nothing but a rush of gratitude, affection, and admiration for that remarkably resilient woman who had stood beside her from the very beginning. Cassidy's throat closed, thickening her voice as she leaned forward and gave Rowena a poke on the arm. "I think maybe you just want to stay here," she teased. "I think you've got the hots for this guy with the endless wardrobe and the well-packaged assets."

Rowena reached out and gave Cassidy a playful punch on the shoulder in return. "Yeah, well, there is that," she replied with a comical leer. "After all, if I do get stuck here, at least I'd like to get stuck with a guy who looks like he could be reminded about sex!"

After supper that night, a meal that had been considerably enhanced by the addition of a couple of fresh rabbits from the trapline Shad maintained, Cassidy approached the warden. "Would you take a little walk with me?" she asked. Even though they still stood near the fire, both Click and Rowena studiously ignored them. But Cassidy couldn't help but notice that Kevin was eyeing her oddly, so she bluntly added, "Alone."

"Of course," the warden said. He gestured her to go ahead of him as they walked away from the fire. "I think we have a lot to talk about," he told her with a small smile.

At least she would not have to explain her purpose to him, Cassidy realized gratefully. The warden might have another lapse at any time; or conceivably he might never have another one. Before they brought Shad, an unknown variable, into their bizarrely intimate relationship, Cassidy wanted to be able to fully and frankly discuss with the warden everything that had already happened.

They casually strolled away from the campsite, headed on a course that would not take them too near Shad's domain. As they walked side by side, Cassidy threw him surreptitious glances. She still hadn't gotten used to seeing him dressed in anything but his leathers; although she had to admit that the tan V-necked shirt and dark, fitted trousers he wore were almost equally flattering and had the effect of making him appear even more boyish than his years. The evening air was temperate, and the floor of the valley was purpled with deep shadow as the light beneath the big cypress trees slowly dimmed. As they ambled on, the warden reached out and lightly took Cassidy by the hand.

Coming from any other man, the gesture would have embarrassed Cassidy and made her feel uncomfortable. But with the warden she felt the easy affection behind the touch. Hell, she had even seen him hold hands with Kevin upon occasion; and while in her world that might have signified something sexual, in his world she didn't need to make anything of it. In a way the innocent action made the warden even more approachable, perhaps because it seemed to make him more childlike, more like Andy Greene.

So much had happened in that world to alter Cassidy's relationship with the autistic young man that she found herself no longer able to re-create their original relationship in the real world. In the real world he had never been able to understand her, to speak to her, to laugh and cry with her. And yet for all of the frustrating opacity of their communication, there had definitely been some sort of connection between her and Andy, something that had made her care deeply for him . . . even to want him.

It was somewhat embarrassing to Cassidy to remember that facet of their relationship, since she had discovered that for all of the love and devotion Andy obviously felt toward Cathy, he had been and would always be incapable of feeling anything sexual. Trying to seduce Andy would have been like trying to seduce the warden in his world, mistaking affection for desire.

Cassidy hadn't even realized that her ruminations had brought a touch of high color to her face until she glanced sideways again and saw that the warden was giving her an oddly appraising look. "Cassidy?" he asked, gently squeezing her fingers. "Do you feel all right? You look flushed."

Ruefully looking into that handsome face, its clean and youthful lines befitting the prince that the man had become in that world, Cassidy merely nodded. She felt like a fool sometimes, but she felt all right.

The warden slowed their already sedate pace to a near halt, less out of concern for Cassidy's peculiar behavior than out of simple expedience. The negotiable portion of the valley floor was limited, and they had nearly reached the boundary. Stepping ahead of her, he stopped. Cassidy felt a bit overwhelmed by everything she wanted to say. But he made things simpler for her by speaking first.

"I know how difficult it's been for you since we spoke with Shad yesterday morning," the warden said, still holding her hand. "But you mustn't give up hope, Cassidy." He smiled gently at her. "You refused to give up when I thought you were crazy, and you ended up proving to me that you were right. Of course," he added, "I still think that an argument could be made for me being right, as well!"

Cassidy couldn't help herself; his smile was too infectious not to respond in kind. He couldn't possibly realize how devastating the combination of his looks and the boyish charm of his self-effacing humor could be. It was not surprising, she thought, that he was the warden of Horses. In the real world, he probably could have been a movie star, a pop hero—hell, the president—anything he wanted to be. All he would have had to do is smile. "Don't worry," she assured him, "I'm not giving up. It's just that—"

She was groping for a relatively tactful way to phrase her reservations, when the warden interrupted her. "It's just that you don't trust Shad," he said.

Despite her earlier rationalization of how platonic her relationship with both the warden and, by extension, Andy Greene had become, Cassidy still found his nearness affecting. There was still just enough light that she could appreciate the disarming attractiveness of his earnest attentiveness to her. But even more than his mere good looks, it was the effect of his good nature, his automatic kindness, that she found so thoroughly disconcerting. Even just holding his hand made her feel lucky, like holding a winning lottery ticket.

"I'm not trying to criticize him as a person," she said, lowering her gaze. "And he's certainly not obligated to help us in any way. I'm sure that he honestly believes everything that he's told us. It's just that—"

"The drugs," the warden supplied.

Cassidy's gaze jerked back up to his face, surprised that he had anticipated what troubled her most about the black man.

The warden merely shrugged slightly. "He and I discussed that briefly the other day," he explained. "I must confess, I still don't understand the purpose of using such substances. It seems to me that real pleasure can come only from experiencing the world, not in avoiding it or insulating yourself from it. But there's no denying that these drugs have helped Shad discover things about the

Slow World. I think that we must be willing to consider that they might be of some use to us, as well."

Cassidy's shock clearly showed on her face, for the warden quickly held up his free hand in a restraining gesture and said, "We mustn't be too hasty in condemning Shad's use of these drugs, Cassidy. He may have discovered something that will also help us."

Cassidy doggedly shook her head. "Drugs do things to people," she said, "that sometimes make it a little difficult to take everything that they say at face value." She tried to be diplomatic. "The whole purpose of drugs is to alter perceptions, to distort reality. Maybe Shad hasn't really seen what he thinks he has."

The warden cocked his head quizzically. "Do you think that he hasn't actually seen into the Slow World, then?"

But Cassidy wasn't willing to go quite that far. "I don't know," she admitted. "He certainly regained his memory somehow, so maybe the drugs did work in his case. It's just that in the real world . . ." Cassidy hesitated, unwilling to sound too judgmental about a man with whom she sensed the warden was already forming a certain feeling of kinship. "Drugs have caused a lot of trouble in the Slow World," she finally said. "I find it hard to rely on the judgment of anyone who's used them over any period of time, no matter what his reason."

The warden seemed to accept her reservation with equanimity, making a small sound of agreement as he lightly swung their joined hands in the space between them. "Then I understand your caution, Cassidy," he said. "All I ask is that you also be willing to consider Shad's point of view. I think you may have more in common with him than you realize." At the skeptical arch of her brows, he elaborated. "Both of you have memories of things that no one else here could share. Think of how isolated his life here must have been."

When Cassidy did not respond, the warden continued to study her face. "Something more is troubling you," he surmised. "Are you still concerned about Andy being kept from you?"

Cassidy looked down at their clasped hands, bemused to note that her skin had become nearly as tanned as his. "It's hard not to worry about that," she confessed. "If you don't have another lapse, we may have reached a dead end."

But the warden simply smiled confidently at her. "Remember that Andy is not a quitter, either, Cassidy," he said. "They haven't succeeded yet in keeping him from you for long."

Even though she couldn't share his stolid faith, Cassidy looked up steadily at his face. "There's something else I wanted to ask you about," she said. "Something about the flashes of light."

The warden shifted his weight, easily and casually, giving her fingers another encouraging little squeeze. "What flashes, Cassidy?"

Did nothing daunt him? she wondered. It was not so much that she felt uneasy about what they were about to discuss; her real discomfort came from the fact that she had waited so long to bring it up. "What do you remember afterward," she asked him, "about what happens when Andy first takes over?"

The dusk had faded further, making it more difficult to see the expression on his face clearly. But his puzzlement was telegraphed plainly enough in the cant of his head and the tone of his voice. "With the first few episodes, I didn't remember anything afterward," he reminded her. "I'm not sure what you mean. Other than impressions of Andy's emotional state, the only things I've remembered afterward are what Andy's let me see as the Warden." He paused, studying her face in the gathering dimness. "What exactly are you asking me about, Cassidy?"

She should have told him from the very beginning, Cassidy realized then. Only she had never been quite sure what to make of the phenomenon of the all-consuming wash of brilliant light, or to figure out just how it related to anything that may have happened afterward, during the lapse itself. *And it's embarrassed you,* her little voice prodded ruthlessly, *because it's always seemed so intimate, so ... sexual.* But since she'd brought up the subject, she could hardly back down then, and the warden's patent interest urged her on.

"Each time Andy's come to me," Cassidy said, "something really weird has happened when we first touch." She tried to make a one-handed gesture, something to evoke the nature of the light. "I see a brilliant light all around us; only I don't just *see* it, I *feel* it, too. It's bright like a flare, but there's no heat. It only lasts a few seconds, but while it does, I feel like—" She broke off awkwardly, then forced herself to go on. "I feel like we're *connected* somehow, like I can feel everything that's inside you." She shook her head, eyes lowering. "I know that must sound really stupid, but—"

To her dismay, the warden captured her other hand, as well, holding them both gently but firmly, tugging at her until she had to look up into his face again. "It doesn't sound stupid at all, Cassidy," he chastised. "It sounds intriguing. And perhaps it's something important, too. Has this happened every time I've had a lapse?"

Her initial discomfort effectively replaced by the unwitting intimacy of his grasp on her hands, Cassidy quickly nodded. "The first time, it was just a split-second kind of thing. I didn't really see any light. The second time, on Webb's boat, I was so startled by it that I actually jumped back from you when it happened. But since then, I've come to expect it, and it seems to have become stronger each time it's happened."

His fingers twined warmly with hers. "And this light isn't visible to anyone else?" he persisted.

Cassidy shrugged. "No one's ever mentioned it," she said. Then suddenly she remembered Click. "But there was something else, something that happened that night after the swamp cat attacked us. When you first had the lapse, Andy came through so agitated that Kevin and Click had to hold onto you to restrain you. And Click was still holding you when I first touched you." She felt the heat rise in her face and hoped that the darkness would conceal the color from the warden. "That time I felt like the light was linking all three of us, at least for an instant, until he released you."

If the warden noticed her embarrassment, he didn't comment on it; his voice revealed only avid interest. "But you've never noticed that effect with anyone else who was touching me?"

Cassidy had to think for a moment. "I don't think there ever *was* anyone else touching you when I first touched you," she said then.

"And this light doesn't persist during the lapse?"

"No," she said, "it just lasts the first few seconds that I touch you." She paused, distracted by the warm pressure of his hands around hers. "What do you think it could be?" she finally asked, relieved to have told him about it and genuinely curious about his reaction.

"Might it have something to do with our relationship in the Slow World?" the warden mused softly, almost to himself. "But then why would it extend to include Click? Unless . . ." He shrugged, the movement causing a gentle tugging on Cassidy's hands. "This sense of connection—is it anything like the bond you feel for your mare?"

That comparison had, quite simply, never occurred to Cassidy before, and she had to consider it for a moment. "In a way," she said. With Dragonfly there had been moments of true unity, when she had felt as if she were inside her horse's body as well as inside her mind. Because the warden was a man and not an animal, perhaps Cassidy had unwittingly assigned a sexual component to the sensation.

"Maybe that would explain why you felt connected to Click, as well, that one time," the warden offered, "since he is a Horseman, too." He paused for a moment, seemingly to explore the implications of what Cassidy had described further. "Now that this sensation no longer surprises you," he said, "you don't find it alarming or unpleasant?"

Fresh warmth suffused Cassidy's cheeks, and she had to fight to keep from calling the warden's attention to her reaction by automatically turning her face away. She was certain it was finally too dark out for him to see the blush. "No, it's not unpleasant," she said truthfully. "It's just a little . . . intense. I wish I knew what it meant."

"We could say that about a good many things we've experienced lately, couldn't we," he said. "At least this seems like a harmless occurrence, which these days is virtue enough in itself." He squeezed her hands again, his touch both playful and encouraging. "Why don't we tell the others about this, Cassidy? Even if none of them has noticed anything before, perhaps they could detect something if they were aware of what you're experiencing."

Cassidy thought immediately of the way Click had questioned her in the middle of the night, after one of the warden's lapses, the night after they'd found the Woodsman's body. The Tinker had detected something then; he had seen her body contort, as if in pain, when Andy had awakened her with his touch. She'd put Click off by blaming the reaction on the nightmare from which she'd just awakened, but she knew that wasn't what Click had noticed. Perhaps the warden was right about telling the others.

"Okay," she agreed reluctantly, "if you think it'll help."

The warden lifted both of her hands up between them, giving her an ironic little bow. "Cassidy, I have no idea if it will help," he confessed. "I just don't see how it can hurt."

Dropping one of her hands, he turned, gently tugging her along after him with the other as he started back for their camp. "Just don't give up," he repeated as they walked. "I can't believe that our fates have brought us all this way for nothing."

Cassidy didn't believe in fate, but she didn't say that because, regardless, she had no intention of giving up. There was only one thing of which she was still certain: Something would happen. It was the truest law of the universe. Something always happened.

* * *

Cassidy's corollary to the truest law of the universe was that something always happened in the middle of the night when you were trying to sleep.

Despite their de facto truce with Shad, the valley was still far from a harmless place, and they had continued to stand their nightly watches. Cassidy had come off her stint in the small hours after midnight; and she would have been willing to swear that she had barely closed her eyes when she was rudely awakened by Rowena shaking her.

"Wake up!" Rowena hissed in her ear. "It's happening."

Even in her semisoporific state, Cassidy knew precisely what "it" was. As she struggled to kick free of her blanket and got to her feet, she was relieved to find that Andy didn't appear to be agitated, or at least not agitated enough to be crying out or calling loudly for her. Their cook fire was long dead, and there was almost no ambient light beneath the thick canopy of the cypress trees, but as she stumbled around the edge of the firepit to where the warden had been sleeping, she could dimly make out the outline of two seated figures. She recognized the soft murmur of Kevin's voice, but Andy was not responding to the blond boy's reassurances in any way. He was just sitting there, as if calmly waiting for her.

Turning to Rowena, Cassidy started to say, "Go get—"

But the brunette quickly interrupted her. "Click already went to get him."

As Cassidy dropped down in front of Kevin and Andy, she could see that even if Andy hadn't been paying any attention to the younger man's quiet words of reassurance, Kevin had insured that Andy hadn't gone anywhere by gripping him tightly by both wrists. Looking up in relief as Cassidy knelt down before them, Kevin was about to release his warden and move aside when she stopped him with a soft command.

"No, keep holding him for a minute, Kev," she whispered, "until I've touched him, too."

Immediately understanding, Kevin released one of Andy's wrists so that he could reach out for Cassidy. Andy looked at her with at least as much relief as Kevin had, and far more emotion. "Cathy!" he exclaimed happily, reaching out with his free hand to clutch her arm.

Cassidy had unconsciously tried to brace herself, not to diminish what would happen next, but to try to define it, to somehow separate and delineate the stunning flood of light. But the all-encompassing glow simply overwhelmed her, burning past her retinas and pouring through her body like electricity. She felt the flow join her to Andy, so utterly that the mere touch of his hand on her arm seemed coincidental to the real connection that existed between them. She was vaguely aware that Kevin still held Andy by one wrist, but she had only the faintest sense of Kevin as a person in the light. It was nothing like the moment with Click had been, when she had for a split second felt the amazing essence of who Click was. The illumination united her with Andy, but it barely suggested Kevin's presence there beside them. And once Andy continued to speak, Cassidy saw that Kevin had released him and moved back away from them.

"They brought me back, Cathy!" Andy said excitedly. He used both hands to grip her arms then, and as he rose to his feet he brought her along with him. "All I had to do is bang, and they brought me back!"

"That's good, Andy," Cassidy said, trying to calm him without sounding as if she were encouraging his behavior. Frankly, the method he'd been using to get his way had her quite concerned. She knew that the patients at Reiners were sometimes restrained or sedated for head banging. Rather than earning himself the desired trip to see Cathy, Andy's actions might yet win him a large dose of some kind of tranquilizer. She took hold of his forearms and gently pulled his hands down. "You've got to be careful," she said. "I don't want to see you get in trouble."

He just looked steadily into her face. "Nobody's going to hurt me," he said, sounding mildly puzzled by her concern.

There was no simple way to explain what she feared, and Cassidy didn't want to confuse or upset Andy, so she just dropped that topic and moved on to something more safe and familiar. "Where am I, Andy? Am I still in the nice place, in the blue room?"

How could anyone, she wondered, much less Andy Greene, pack so much animation into those mercurial shifts in mood? Cassidy was freshly amazed by that sparkling version of the young man who stood before her. "Yes, it's a good place," he pronounced with conviction. "I like going to see you here." But then, just as suddenly, his tone grew more anxious. "But I want you to wake up, Cathy, so you can do things again. So everyone will smile, and not be crying. Cathy," he concluded plaintively, "when are you going to come back?"

Cassidy felt her throat thicken and she had to fight back tears. Andy was incredibly sensitive to her emotional state, and she didn't want him to realize how close she was to crying, so she didn't respond to his question immediately. And while she hesitated, composing herself, she saw Andy's eyes open and focus on a point just over her shoulder. She didn't have to turn around to know what had caught his attention.

"Hi," Andy said, brightly but with just a touch of shyness. "You came back."

From the corner of her eye, Cassidy could see Shad's slim silhouette materialize on the periphery of her vision. "Yeah," the black man said quietly, "and you came back, too, didn't you, Andy." Shad stopped just a few feet away from them, a bit tentatively, as if he half expected his appearance might abruptly terminate Andy's. But when nothing happened after a moment's wait, Shad stepped closer.

Andy was looking at him with frank curiosity. "Who are you?" he asked. "How do you know my name?"

With an odd formality, Shad offered Andy his hand. "My name is Shad," he said. "Cathy's told me a lot about you."

Andy's reaction was a childlike vacillation between friendliness and suspicion. "Are you a friend of Cathy's, too?" he asked, making no move to shake Shad's outstretched hand.

The black man threw Cassidy a brief wry glance. "You could say that, Andy," he replied, dropping his hand. "We've just kind of met since she's been here."

Andy pulled away from Cassidy to face Shad then, and she let go of him to allow him to move. "You're in the blue place, too?" Andy probed further.

Shad cocked his dark head. "It's starting to look that way," he said enigmatically. "That's where you are now, isn't it? The big place with the blue rooms and blue blankets and lots of ladies in blue clothes?"

Andy nodded eagerly, adding "The ladies are nice, too."

"Yeah," Shad agreed, "I've always thought they were nice."

Cassidy was studying Shad, trying to discern the expression on his face even as she puzzled over just where he was trying to go with Andy. She didn't want to confuse Andy by starting to question Shad, as well, so she kept silent.

Shad was looking at Andy with what appeared to be a rather impolite intensity, but Andy seemed equally blunt in his scrutiny of the black man. Something about the long-haired man interested Andy. Maybe it was just that Shad was the only other person Andy had even seen on his visits with Cassidy. But she almost had the impression that Andy recognized him somehow.

After a long moment of silent appraisal, Shad said calmly,

"There's something in Cathy's room I'd like you to look for, Andy. Do you think you could do that for me?"

Cassidy had to interrupt then. She averted her face from Andy's, but not before she noted the quizzical way the young man was cocking his head. "You're going to confuse him," she hissed softly at Shad. "Remember, in the real world his perceptions aren't like other people's. He can't—"

"Cathy?" Andy said anxiously, reaching out to grasp her shirt sleeve.

"It's okay, Andy," she soothed him easily. "Shad and I were just wondering if you could let the warden do something for us?"

"Okay," Andy said immediately, but he still clung to her shirt-sleeve, and his eyes stayed on Cassidy rather than returning to Shad.

Cassidy threw Shad a quick look, hoping the black man understood her intentions. She realized that asking Andy to allow the warden to enter the Slow World would most likely cut short his lapse, but whatever it was that Shad was fishing for, she knew that Andy would be of no help to him. She also had to admit that there didn't seem to be much more that Andy himself could tell them that would be of any use. Nevertheless, she found herself thinking grimly that whatever it was Shad wanted to know, it had better have been worth the risk of breaking off the increasingly unpredictable contact with Andy.

"Andy," she said, "we need you to let the warden see where you and I are again." She threw Shad another weighted look, urging some further clue.

"There should be stuff all around your bed," Shad said in a low voice. "He'll never make any sense of all the monitors, but see what he can find in your chart. It should be hanging at the foot of the bed."

Andy was regarding Shad with a hesitant mixture of puzzlement and wariness, but Cassidy quickly reclaimed his attention. She tugged his hand free of her sleeve and held it lightly sandwiched between both of hers. "There's something by my bed, Andy," she said, "that I want the warden to look at. Not a machine," she added hastily, but then she was at something of a loss as to how to describe a medical chart. The warden would have no idea what a book was; even comparing it to a notepad or a sign would have been useless, since those things didn't exist in his world. Andy was waiting expectantly, so Cassidy just fumbled onward, resorting to a purely literal description. "It's probably hanging at the foot of my bed, Andy, and it's got two parts that are hinged together so that you can open it up—like a door. I want the warden to look inside it and—" *And what?* she thought. *Read it all back to me? This is crazy!* "And try to remember the designs that are inside it," she finished lamely, afraid that she'd probably just set up an impossible task for the earnest young man before her.

But Andy simply nodded agreeably and said, "Okay, Cathy."

Shad's body posture radiated overt skepticism, but as Andy's boyish face rapidly assumed that particular stillness of intense concentration that Cassidy had come to associate with the warden's forays into the real world, she just glared back at the black man. "What did you expect me to do?" she hissed at him. "Neither one of them can read or write. Maybe this way at least we can get some idea of where the hell I am."

But Shad responded, "I think I already know where you are."

Cassidy looked sharply at him, but before she could say anything, Andy's hand was twisting in hers, and his whole body went taut with alarm.

"I wasn't supposed to touch it, Cathy!" he said unhappily. "They're going to make me go away again!" He reached for her with both arms, embracing her as if to somehow anchor himself there in that world. But Cassidy was helpless to affect whatever was happening some split second and another world away. Even as Andy moaned out her name, she felt the tension suddenly ebb from his body. For a moment he hung limply against her, incredibly warm and solid. Then he was straightening up again, stepping back from her with only his hands resting on her shoulders. When he spoke, it was once more with the warden's calm voice.

"Cassidy?" he asked. He glanced over at Shad and then back again. "Did it work? Could I see Shad again?"

Cassidy nodded, but she knew that was far from the most important thing. They had to move quickly if they were to retrieve anything the warden might have seen in the real world. "Andy let you see into the Slow World again," she told him intently. "You were looking for my medical chart. It looks like two—"

"Two pieces of flat metal hinged together," the warden interrupted, excitement in his voice. He pulled his hands back from her shoulders to hold them out, describing a rectangle about the size of a legal pad in the air between them. "There were sheets of paper inside it," he went on, "all different colors and with designs."

Cassidy tried to keep her voice even. "Do you remember the designs?"

The warden's head cocked, a gesture so much like Andy's, and yet when the warden did it he seemed less boyishly quizzical and more just plainly puzzled. He frowned. "They didn't make any sense to me."

Cassidy knew an anxious edge was starting to creep into her tone. "Can you remember what any of them looked like?"

"The top of the paper," the warden said, still frowning. "The marks there were larger, darker."

Cassidy reached out and snatched one of his hands, grasping him by the wrist. "Show me," she urged. "Trace the shapes of the designs on my palm—anything you can remember from the top of the paper."

The warden seemed greatly perplexed, but willing. But then he had become accustomed to coming out of his lapses in much the same state. And he trusted Cassidy implicitly. Slowly, hesitantly, he tried to duplicate with his forefinger on her palm the strange shapes of the designs he had seen when Andy had opened Cathy's chart for him.

Cassidy stared down at the juncture of their hands, tonelessly whispering the letters as he drew them. "S T A N N S..."

Shaking his head in frustration, the warden gently folded her fingers over and wrapped his hand around hers. "I'm sorry, Cassidy," he said softly. "There was much more than that, but that's all that I can remember now."

For the first time since the lapse had ended, Shad spoke up. But he didn't address Cassidy, or comment on the sequence of letters she had just recited. She couldn't read his expression in the darkness, but there was an oddly taut posture to his slender body. "Was there something stuck on the outside of her chart?" he asked the warden. "On the front cover of it?"

The warden's head canted sharply, as if he were surprised to find some unexpected fragment of memory being tugged from him. He turned to Shad. "Yes," he said, with a softly speculative tone in his voice, "there was. There was a small patch of something stuck to the metal." He hesitated. "But what was it?" he asked, plainly puzzled.

Shad stood motionless, as strangely motionless as Andy had stood when he had given over his consciousness to the warden. "Did this patch have letters—designs—on it?" he asked the warden.

"I don't remember," the warden admitted. He darted a glance to Cassidy before looking back to Shad again. "Would that have been important?" he asked him, obviously regretting his frustrating loss of detail.

But Shad appeared to ignore the question. The black man was so tensely poised that Cassidy thought, with some surprise, that he looked about ready to either flee or punch somebody out.

"What color was the patch?" Shad asked the warden.

"Gold," the warden replied promptly.

"Shit," the black man said, so softly that his dulcet pronunciation made the word sound less like an expletive and more like a benediction.

Cassidy spun toward Shad, automatically reaching out to grasp him by one smooth bare forearm. His muscles were rigidly corded beneath her fingers. "What the hell are you talking about?" she demanded, an edge of fear in her voice.

The warden lightly touched Cassidy on the elbow, as if trying to placate her. From the surrounding darkness, Cassidy could see the dim shapes of Click, Rowena, and Kevin drawing nearer then. She wasn't certain if their approach was due to their concern for her welfare or their concern for Shad's. The combination of their presence and the warden's silent bid for restraint kept Cassidy from doing what she felt sorely tempted to do, which was to grab Shad by the shoulders and just shake him until she knocked loose something that made some sense.

The warden was looking directly at Shad, his manner civil, but firm. "What is the meaning of what I saw on Cassidy's chart?" he asked.

Shad deliberately jerked his arm free of her hold. Cassidy half expected him to turn and just walk away, in much the same manner as he had ended their last such discussion. But he held his ground, his body still tautly erect. "The thing on her chart is a status sticker," he said, his voice low but rough. "It shows the staff what kind of care a patient's supposed to get."

Appearing to respond to the odd tension inherent in Shad's entire demeanor, the warden's tone moderated, his next query softer. "And what is the significance of the sticker's color?"

Shad shot Cassidy a brief glance before he answered. When he spoke, his voice was flat and without inflection, almost as if his vocal cords were as rigid as the rest of his body. "Amber means there's a legal ruling pending."

From the way the warden cocked his head, he appeared no less puzzled than he had been before Shad had replied. But Cassidy felt a numbingly cool kind of comprehension sluice through her, filling her veins like ice water. Unmindful of the warden's restraining hand—which was really no longer necessary, since the fleeting urge to do violence to Shad had long since passed—Cassidy looked across into the dark outline of that ascetic, emotionless face.

"You said you know where I am," she said to Shad.

For the first time, Shad deliberately looked away from both Cassidy and the warden, his gaze dropping to some vague point on the darkened ground between them. "When he talked about all the blue stuff—blue rooms, blue blankets, blue uniforms—I thought I knew," he said quietly. "And then when he spelled it out for you . . ." His voice trailed off for a moment, but he finally looked up again. His slim shoulders jerked slightly, whether in a shrug or a shudder, Cassidy couldn't tell. "You're in St. Ann's," he said. "It's a long-term care facility outside of Albany."

As she studied him more intently, Cassidy realized that Shad's body was so tense he was nearly shaking. Was it anger, or fear; or both? Adopting some of the warden's moderation, Cassidy managed to keep her voice low and even as she asked him, "Have you ever been there?"

Shad gave a grim laugh, a harsh barking little burst, entirely devoid of humor. "Been there?" he echoed. "Lady, I *am* there! It looks like you're stuck in the same vegetable bin that I am."

Shad's shoulders were still hunched like those of an angry cat. He swung around and was about to stalk away when Cassidy's hand shot out and reached for his arm. The warden was still holding her by one elbow, so her grasp probably would have come up short if Shad's movement hadn't been so stiffly exaggerated and if she hadn't anticipated that he was about to flee. As it was, her fingers missed his arm but caught the loose edge of his leather vest, tethering him. Shad rounded on her, wound up and edgy, and she was prepared for anything. Or at least for anything but what she found.

Even in the dimness, Cassidy could see the glint of the twin wet trails on the dark planes of Shad's high cheekbones. "What do you want me to say?" he demanded of her, his voice thick. "You want me to draw you a picture? That sticker means that the only reason they haven't pulled the plug on you yet is that someone—probably your doctors—have dragged the whole thing into court."

Cassidy's nerveless fingers slipped from Shad's vest. She stared at him. "You mean they might . . . kill me?" she whispered thinly.

Shad's voice dropped then, softening, yet without a hint of comfort in it. "What I mean is that some poor son of a bitch in your family is trying to carry out what are probably your own orders," he said, "and they've gone to court to give you the right to die."

Cassidy couldn't seem to look away from him. "If they let me die . . . ?" she rasped.

"If you die in the real world," Shad said flatly, "you'll die here, too." He paused, and once again Cassidy had some sense of just how profoundly upset he was. He exhaled in a long, ragged breath. "There're some things you're just better off not knowing, aren't there?" Shad concluded. And that time when he turned and started to stride away, Cassidy did not try to stop him.

Cassidy felt an arm slide over her shoulders, and she turned her face into the warm fabric of the warden's shirt. He may not have understood the exact significance of everything Shad had said, but—like Click—he certainly could recognize her shock and dismay. Tightening his arm, the warden pulled her unresisting body against himself, his chin resting lightly on the top of her head.

"Don't give up hope, Cassidy," the warden whispered, his embrace closing reassuringly. "Just remember that I am your friend in both worlds. Together we'll find a way through this—I swear it on my blood."

Chapter 20 ◄▦

Looking at him with unveiled reproof across their morning cook fire, Cassidy found herself wishing that she was still dealing with Andy Greene, rather than his completely lucid and politely stubborn counterpart, the warden of Horses. How could anyone who had become the nominal leader of all the Eastern Territories be so obstinately stupid?

"No," Cassidy reiterated, for at least the sixth time, her own expression steeled in indefeasible obdurance. "It's too dangerous—and it's *crazy!*"

Cassidy would have thought that anyone like herself, who had had the opportunity on more than a few occasions to watch the way the warden handled Valerie, would have been better prepared to cope with his method of argument. He was never loud or imperious; he just had ways of circumventing all logic with his own coercive brand of reasoning.

Sitting cross-legged across the fire from her, the warden set aside his coffee mug and spread his hands in the space between his knees. "It would be less dangerous with your cooperation, Cassidy," he pointed out, "which is just one of the reasons I would hope you'd offer your help. Shad's experience will be useful, but you're still the only person who can really prepare me for what I might face if we succeed."

It was another fair, sunny morning, but Cassidy's mood hardly matched the weather. "This is nuts!" she muttered. She ran a quick glance over the other faces around the fire; but no one was willing to interfere in the ongoing argument between herself and the warden—just as Cassidy had never been willing to interject herself into that same free-fire zone whenever a dispute had erupted between the warden and his captain. She couldn't blame any of them for staying out of it, but she was still irritated.

Couldn't they see that what the warden was proposing was lunacy?

Refocusing her ire on the young man in question, she ran down her list of objections once more. "First of all," Cassidy said, "we've got no idea what the hell these drugs are that he's using, or how safe they are. Even if they haven't harmed him yet, you've never used drugs, so there's no way to predict how they might affect you." Warming to her argument, Cassidy's voice grew more vehement. "Assuming the damned stuff doesn't just kill you outright, what makes you think it'd even work? And if by some fluke it actually does send you back into Andy's body, what the hell are you going to do then? What if you're trapped in the same state of consciousness that Andy is? If you're autistic, you're going to be helpless there." She paused for breath, staring hard and deliberately at the warden. "And what if you go there and get trapped like Andy, and we can't get you back? Then what?"

With infuriating calm, the warden merely acknowledged her fears with reason and equanimity. "I understand the risks, Cassidy—" he began. But she cut him off, ruthlessly blunt.

"No—you may think that you're *aware* of the risks, but I can tell you one thing for certain: There's no way you *understand* them." She glowered at him, her knuckles white around the handle of her mug. "You have no idea, really, what Andy's life is like in the Slow World." Her voice dropped to a harsh near whisper. "There's no way I could be a part of condemning anyone, least of all you, to that kind of limbo."

The warden didn't move. In fact, the most striking thing about him in the silence that followed was the utter stillness of his body, as he appeared to consider what she had said. He was not a dispassionate man, and Cassidy had seen him react on numerous occasions with vivid outbursts of intense emotion. But not then. The fire in him was contained, like lightning in a bottle; and the only place where the true heat of his response was revealed was in the gleam of those chocolate-brown eyes.

Looking directly into her face, the warden said softly, "You seem to forget, Cassidy, that I already *am* Andy Greene. I have lived his life for all of my own. And all you know of his life is what it seems like to you, comparing it with your own, which makes your pity for him rather presumptuous."

Cassidy felt a flush of shame color her face then. The warden's quiet remarks were an embarrassingly accurate indictment of her own prejudices. But before she could stammer out any words of apology, he went on, his tone a little more sympathetic if no less earnest.

"What if I could return to Andy's body—and by doing so, make him normal? Would you deny him that chance?" He leaned slightly forward toward her from the opposite side of the fire. "And even if I can change nothing for Andy, would you condemn him to live the rest of his life knowing that he didn't even try to help his only friend?" His voice was a soft entreaty, as he appealed to her with the real crux of the situation. "Because you're not just facing limbo in the Slow World, Cassidy. How can you deny Andy—how can you deny *me*—the chance to try to save your life?"

Cassidy's face tightened in a grimace of dismay, her coffee mug still clenched mercilessly in her hands. "But don't you see?" she said. "We don't even know if it's possible for you to enter Andy's body. And if you can, we don't know what would happen to you and to Andy. We don't know if there's anything you could do to help me. We don't even know what the hell we're doing!"

"Since when has that ever stopped you?" Click drawled.

Of all the times for the Tinker to break his neutrality, Cassidy thought that was certainly the worst. She turned to Click, primed to tell him just that. But he went on before she had a chance, not only preventing her from chastising him, but also effectively disarming her by adroitly altering the entire course of the dispute.

"Cassidy," Click said, "explain to me what Shad discovered about your condition in the Slow World. What is the precise significance of what the warden saw in the room where you're being confined?"

She should have realized that the others would need some better sort of explanation. Click had succeeded where the warden had failed by deftly leaving Cassidy at least temporarily at a total loss for words. She glanced from one man to the other, weighing her reply. Her hesitation wasn't because she didn't understand Click's question, or even because she didn't know its answer. She had been able to think of little else since Shad's chilling revelation the night before. She couldn't even convincingly dispute the validity of what the black man had told them then. She hesitated only because to acknowledge what Shad had learned would automatically force her to admit that what the warden was proposing was actually her only hope of surviving in either world.

To Cassidy's chagrin, Rowena also broke the neutrality of her silence and ventured another question into the uncomfortable pause. "What was the thing about your chart and the sticker on it?" the brunette prompted.

Her genuine concern was echoed on the faces of all her friends around the fire. Sitting there in that quiet valley, with the birds flitting through the trees, Cassidy finally realized the absurd futility of continuing to try to avoid or deny the situation. By whatever means they had become involved in her quest, each of the people there ultimately had come to help her. And unless she was totally honest with them, they had all risked their lives for nothing. She took a deep breath and fixed her gaze on the glowing embers of the fire. Then she began to try to explain.

"From what Shad says," she said, "I'm in this medical facility where they keep people who've been injured so badly that they haven't regained consciousness. I think that must be the way I first came here, when I lost consciousness in the Slow World." Cassidy deliberately avoided looking at any of their faces because she didn't want the distraction of their expressions to prevent her from going on. "From the things that Andy said the first few times he came to me," she said, "I think I was involved in some kind of accident that must have caused the injury. He apparently witnessed what happened to me . . ."

Fresh consternation at how traumatic that must have been for Andy caused Cassidy to lose her resolve momentarily, and she almost looked over to the warden. But she quickly recovered and went on.

"I think I was probably in a regular hospital at first. They must have moved me when it became obvious that I wasn't just going to wake up again. The place where they moved me to is called St. Ann's. From what Shad has seen on his own, it's the same facility where he is in the Slow World."

Cassidy paused for breath. About fifty feet from their campsite, Dragonfly stood placidly sorting through a large pile of cut fodder. The sight made Cassidy feel so tethered in that world that she hardly knew how to go on, until Rowena repeated her initial question.

"What about the chart?" the brunette asked.

"Shad wanted the warden to look at my medical chart," Cassidy said, "because he thought it might tell us exactly what my condition was. In places like St. Ann's, they put colored stickers on the covers of the charts so that the people who work there know what a patient's status is." She realized that what she'd just said was uselessly euphemistic, but she hesitated at a more blunt explanation. "If a person who's been unconscious for so long were to just stop breathing, or if their heart would stop beating, or if anything would happen to them where they could die, the people who work there have to know if they should try to revive them."

"Or if they should simply allow them to die," Click said.

"Yeah," Cassidy said, staring into the fire, "or if they should just let them die."

"And the gold sticker on Cathy's chart?" the warden asked. "What did Shad mean by 'legal ruling pending'?"

Her eyes fixed on the slowly waning radiance of the embers, Cassidy wet her lips and went on. "Before any of this ever happened to me, I'd always made it known to my doctor and to my friends that if I was ever injured beyond reasonable hope—like becoming unconscious without the likelihood of ever waking up again—that I didn't want to continue to be kept alive by artificial means. It's called a living will; it gives the people who care about me the right to stop all medical treatment . . . and to let me die."

Reduced to its simplest terms, especially in the light of what Cassidy had discovered in the past couple of months, the decision sounded both cruel and ghoulish. But she shouldn't have been too quick to judge the capacity of her friends' understanding.

"That would only seem sensible," Click said, "and certainly would be an act of kindness for those who would otherwise be left with an impossibly difficult decision."

"Yeah," Cassidy murmured, "that's what I always thought; at least before I found myself *here*."

"Do you think that's what happened to all of us then?" Kevin asked, his voice hushed with wonder. "That all of us are unconscious in the Slow World?"

Momentarily distracted from her previous line of thought, Cassidy realized that the whole concept was still something of a revelation to most of them. She looked up, meeting the blond boy's wide-eyed expression of surprise. "Yeah, Kev, more or less," she replied. "Not that everyone here was necessarily injured in the Slow World. There are probably a lot of people like the warden who were born with some condition that keeps them from being mentally capable there. But I think that the basic reason all of us are here is the same for everyone: When we lost our conscious lives in the Slow World, we began to live in this one."

Kevin's odd-colored eyes were turbulent, and he seemed deeply troubled. "But Shad said that if you—if you die in the Slow World, you'll die here, too," he said anxiously.

The warden reached over and took hold of Kevin's hand, gently squeezing it. "Which is at the heart of Cassidy's problem," he reminded them all. His words prompted her to try to complete her explanation while she still could.

"Long before I was ever injured," she said, "I gave the people who were important to me there the permission to not take any extraordinary steps to keep me alive. If what Shad says about the colored sticker on my chart is true, then there must be some kind of dispute going on over whether or not to follow my wishes." That was a bit of an oversimplification, but there was no way in hell that Cassidy was going to try to explain the American legal system to people who'd had the singular good fortune to not even know what a lawyer was. Instead, she tried to condense the possible ramifications of legal battle over her condition. "What it means," she said, "is that depending on the outcome of that dispute, my life could be in danger."

"If the dispute is decided against you," the warden said, "they'll let you die."

But Cassidy obstinately shook her head. "No, we don't know that for sure. First of all," she reminded them all with a certain grim irony, "the living will was *my* wish; so if they decide to follow it, they're actually deciding in my *favor*." She shrugged then, acutely aware of the black humor inherent in the situation. "Of course, I made that decision before I knew about any of this," she pointed out. "And second, even if they do follow my wishes, I still might just continue to live."

"And yet that hardly seems likely, does it?" Click interjected. "After all, if it was not likely to make a difference, why would anyone be disputing your wishes now?"

Click's matter-of-fact conclusion was dishearteningly logical, and Cassidy knew of no reasonable argument against it. All she could do was doggedly repeat "We don't know that for sure."

Still holding Kevin's hand, the warden entreated her from across the firepit's coals, "Which is the very reason we have to do this, Cassidy. If I could go back, I could find out more about your condition and in how much danger you might still be." He paused for a moment, then concluded earnestly, "I could find out if it would be safe for you to try to go back yourself."

Or if I'd be trying to pour my consciousness back into a crushed skull . . . Cassidy could not help thinking, the possibility filled with bitter irony.

Cassidy did not reply immediately. She just sat there openly studying the young man who was so indefatigably committed to risking his life for hers. Was that commitment built upon the warden's implacable sense of duty or upon Andy Greene's pure and childlike devotion? Or was it built upon something else entirely, some hybrid sort of dedication and attachment that was as much a mixture of the two motives as the warden had become to her a mixture of the two men? And regardless of its source or motivation, could Cassidy allow herself to trade upon it?

"You still can go back again," she finally said, as calmly and rationally as she was able. "The next time you have a lapse, we can—"

"No!" the warden said, startling Kevin by releasing the younger man's hand, and startling Cassidy by the alacrity with which he gained his feet and came around the firepit to drop down in front of her. The intensity of his expression could have backed down Valerie, she thought, perhaps even Click. "No," he repeated more quietly, his hands reaching for Cassidy's shoulders. "We don't know how long it might take before I have another lapse, we don't even know *if* I'll have another one." His voice grew low and compelling. "We don't have the luxury of that time, Cassidy. We can't wait for Andy to come to us. I have to go to him."

Cassidy just shook her head, trying without success to evade the piercing hold of those deep brown eyes. "No, I should be the one to go back," she said. "Even if you do reach Andy, you've got no idea how to—"

"No!" the warden reiterated, actually giving her shoulders a sharp little shake. "Look at this rationally, Cassidy. We know that it's possible for me to go back; I've already done it."

"But only during a lapse," Cassidy reminded him. "Only when Andy was already here."

But the warden remained implacable. "And that proved it can be done," he said firmly. "And if I go back, we know that I have someone whole to go back to; I have Andy. We don't know what you have. With Andy's body, at least I have a chance of being effective."

Cassidy just glared at him. That was his idea of looking at the situation "rationally"? Her shoulders were rigid beneath the grip of his hands. "It's too dangerous," she repeated.

Cassidy didn't know if their dispute was hopelessly deadlocked, or even if the situation was on the verge of disintegrating into some kind of a shoving match. She was so upset and indignant about the warden's obstinance that almost anything seemed possible to her at that point. And so she was almost grateful for Click's intervention when the older man again quietly interposed his opinion into the tense silence that lay between her and the warden.

"Yes, it's dangerous," the Tinker told her. "And if you're truly concerned about the warden's safety, then you'll do everything you can to minimize that danger by helping him."

Cassidy's head snapped around, and she stared at Click with unconcealed dismay. She recognized the devastating efficacy of his argument because it was the exact same line of reasoning she had used a couple of times herself, both with Click and the warden. The first time had been when she had wanted the Tinker to help her procure a boat to go south, and the second had been when she had convinced the warden to accompany her on that same journey. For a moment Cassidy was so stunned by both Click's audacity and his adroitness that she couldn't speak.

The warden's face softened then, his tone gently cajoling. "At least go with me to talk to Shad about it," he urged her, lightly squeezing her shoulders until she finally looked up at him. "If he agrees with you that it's too dangerous, then we'll do as you wish, and wait."

Still stung by Click's defection, Cassidy looked at the warden's determined face with open skepticism. "And if he agrees with you?" she said tersely.

Ever gracious in victory, the warden released her shoulders. "The sooner we can proceed," he said, "the sooner we'll learn what we need to know."

Neither of them spoke on the short walk over to Shad's shelter. Cassidy knew that the others must have been concerned, but they remained behind. And she also knew that it was a pleasant summer morning, but she scarcely noticed it. Her mind was still filled with reservations about the warden's proposed scheme and irritation at the indefeasible truth behind Click's observation regarding it. If the warden was determined to proceed with his plan, he would do it with or without Cassidy's help. Her cooperation might prove to be inconsequential, but that was not a risk she was willing to take—any more than Click or the warden had been, when she had gone to them for help.

On the packed earth in front of Shad's dugout, the ashes in his firepit had long since gone cold. As the two of them came to a halt, the warden gave her a quizzical look.

"Shad?" the warden called out. But there was no reply from within or around the shelter. Then to Cassidy, he said, "Where do you suppose he's gone?"

Cassidy merely shrugged. Shad's time was certainly his own; she just considered it fortuitous that he wasn't there to encourage the warden's plan. Perhaps she would get another chance at trying to talk him out of the idea of using drugs to return to the Slow World. Cassidy was about to say something when the warden suddenly turned expectantly toward the bottom of the huge toppled tree.

Cassidy's spirits plunged as she saw Shad coming around the upturned mass of old broken roots. But immediately upon the heels of that disappointment came surprise and alarm, for the black man was approaching at a businesslike clip, and in one bloodstained hand he gripped a grisly object that made her stare in fascinated revulsion.

Shad slowed when he saw the two of them standing beside his firepit. "Good—just the people I was looking for," he said bluntly. He swung the object he held, bringing it up in front of him and brandishing it. "Seems like your little pals are at it again."

Shad was holding a long bone of some kind, probably a femur, nearly stripped of all flesh and tendons. He used a blood-soaked scrap of cloth with which to grip its slippery surface. For a few queasy seconds Cassidy thought the bone must be human and that the scrap had been part of someone's clothing. But then she recognized the cloth from the pair of black pants they'd used to fashion their signal flag. Almost simultaneously, she realized that the nearly denuded bone was far too slender in comparison to its length to have been human.

"The monsters?" the warden asked. It was, Cassidy thought, a rather needless question, since the creatures were the only things that could have been linked to both her and wanton carnage of any sort.

Shad used the disarticulated bone like a gruesome pointer, indicating the direction from which he'd come. "Take a look for yourselves," he invited them.

The warden exchanged a look with Cassidy. "I think we'd better call the others," he said.

Twenty minutes later they all were standing at the wooded wedge of land that protruded out into the vast marsh, witnesses to the latest act of inexplicable mayhem caused by the hideous creatures. Not only had their signal flag been torn down, so had the upper half of the tree to which it had been affixed. Numerous other large trees around it also had been heavily damaged, and all of the smaller trees and brush had been completely shredded in an orgy of destruction. Of the red shirt and black trousers, no scrap remained any larger than the swatch that Shad had used to wrap around the bloody bone.

Even more striking than the damage wrought upon the trees

and their makeshift flag were the gory remnants that festooned the newly created clearing. The shattered trunks of the trees and the sundered ground around them were splattered with blood and macerated bits of unidentifiable flesh and other animal matter. Cassidy could see nothing else that was even remotely the size of the intact leg bone Shad had salvaged.

Click squatted down beside the pulverized remains of some bushes. With one forefinger he reached out and lightly touched a small tuft of reddish-brown hair, which had become plastered to the shredded vegetation with a gobbet of blood. "Marsh deer," he said matter-of-factly, glancing around the ruined piece of forest. "Several, from the looks of this."

Kevin had stayed right at the warden's side during the grimly silent hike out to the far spur of land. His odd-colored eyes took in the scene of the rampage with open dismay. "Monsters," he said, his voice hardly louder than a whisper.

Rowena stood with both arms locked across her chest, hugging herself. She gave the entire area a wary survey. "Why would the monsters do this?" she asked, plainly puzzled.

"Good question," Shad replied, finally tossing aside the long bone he had been carrying. It hit end-on against the gore-strewn ground, bounced, and then landed amid the pulverized bits of leaves and branches. His sculpted brows lifted. "Maybe they didn't like your flag."

"Maybe they don't like Andy letting me see back into the Slow World," the warden said.

Cassidy had been morosely studying the devastated landscape, but at the warden's soft-spoken observation she spun around to face him, frankly surprised. "What do you mean?" she demanded, even as some part of her already understood to what he was alluding.

The warden calmly spread his hands. "We know that the creatures are somehow connected to you, Cassidy," he said. "They're following you. And we suspect that they might somehow be associated with you remembering your past, possibly even with my lapses." He shrugged. "What if they're also related to the way we've been using my lapses to cross the gap between our two worlds?"

Cassidy glanced around again at the bloodied, demolished stretch of forest. "Then anything connected with my knowledge of the Slow World might be influencing them," she said, locking eyes with the warden. "In a way, everything that I've been able to remember about the real world has been a kind of breach between the two worlds, too. And the more I've remembered, the more widespread the monsters seem to have become." She frowned. "Then if anything that narrows that space—or time—between this world and the Slow World affects the monsters, what we've been doing during your lapses might be related to this."

Shad had methodically folded up the ragged little swatch of bloody cloth that he had used to hold the deer's bone. "Now that's a cheery thought," he said, flipping the stained scrap aside.

Kevin's anxiety had been increasing noticeably as Cassidy and the warden had discussed the monsters. He looked uneasily at the warden, the object of his unmitigated devotion. "If the monsters come from the gap between the two worlds," he said plaintively, "what will happen if you try to go back into Andy Greene? Won't the monsters attack you?"

Shad's head abruptly lifted, his interest immediately piqued. "What do you mean, 'go back into Andy Greene'?" he asked sharply.

"We were just coming to discuss it with you," the warden said, "when you came back to your shelter. I wanted to ask you if you'd be willing to help us. I want to try to use drugs, like you have, to return to the Slow World."

For all of the mercurial diversity of moods that she had witnessed in Shad in the short time she had known him, Cassidy still found that she couldn't read him accurately enough to be able to interpret the particular look which crossed that eloquently expressive face just then. It was not surprise, she decided; certainly not anger. Shad's dark eyes moved from her to the warden and then back again, filled with an odd intensity. Then, abruptly and almost explosively, he laughed.

"Let me get this straight," he said with a little shake of his glossy mane. "You're going to try to go back to the Slow World and get inside Andy's body—and you want me to give you the drugs to do it?"

"It's not my idea," Cassidy snapped. "I told him—"

But the warden gently interrupted Cassidy, the very calmness of his voice cutting past her objection. "If what I saw on Cathy's medical chart is accurate, time may be crucial to her survival there," he told Shad with simple candor. "And we can't be certain when, or even if, I'll have another episode. If there's another way that I can unite myself with Andy in the Slow World—"

"And you want me to help you?" Shad repeated, interrupting him. There was little mystery about the expression on that smooth brown face then, where scorn and amusement vied for supremacy.

"I had hoped that you would, yes," the warden said.

Shad made a contemptuous sound, a little grunt of disgust. "Look at this mess," he said, waving at the demolished forest around them. "What the hell do you think you're getting involved with here? And I should *help* you?"

Astonishingly—for she actually agreed with Shad—Cassidy found herself vigorously attacking the black man's attitude. "Yeah, I think you should help us," she shot back at him, "and be damned glad to do it!" She mimicked his gesture, waving theatrically at the gore-splattered stretch of ruined land. "Take a really good look at this. You think that if we just try to ignore what's happening here, these creatures will disappear?" Her tone of scorn was even more convincing than Shad's had been. "Well, good luck, pal! You know as well as I do that these things followed me here. As long as I stay here, they'll just keep getting worse. They already destroyed the Iron City." She stared directly at Shad, bluntly meeting the cynicism that clung so stubbornly to those elegant features. "You'll help us because it's the only way you're ever going to get rid of us!"

One of Shad's neatly drawn brows rose in a tented arch; he quickly demonstrated that he had lost none of his edge. "What if he tries to go back and it kills him?" he asked with an almost casual brutality.

But Cassidy was too wound up by then to be deflected effectively by any displays of ersatz logic. "It never killed you," she reminded Shad.

"Yeah," Shad said, "but I'm not autistic."

"Just a vegetable," Cassidy replied.

Quickly intervening before Cassidy's temper could undo all of the ground she had just gained for them, the warden told Shad, "No matter what you think the risks might be, I'm willing to accept them."

Shad laughed, a short and essentially mirthless little bark. "I can't even *imagine* what the hell the risks are!" he pointed out.

"But that never stopped you," the warden said, reprising Cassidy's blunt tactic.

Shad stared hard at the two of them again, his scornful amusement replaced by a genuine incredulity. "You're really serious about this," he said.

Still disconcerted by how neatly she had been channeled into adopting the warden's position, Cassidy nodded grimly. "Absolutely serious."

Shad eyed the warden, his dark head cocked, his expression a marriage of bemusement and skepticism. "She talked you into this?" he persisted.

Cassidy knew then that they had Shad. His very cynicism had betrayed him. He did not want to believe that a man would willingly risk his life in an act of altruism. Apparently the warden realized it, as well, for he allowed most of the stiff determination to ease from his stance as, stepping forward, he surprised Shad by clapping the black man on the shoulder. "Actually," the warden confessed with an effective display of that incredible smile, "she thought it was a terrible idea. I had to talk *her* into it."

"Yeah?" Shad muttered, pulling back from the warden with an uneasy sort of self-consciousness. "Well, you know what? She was fucking right."

But the warden merely gave Shad another, more tempered smile. "I would say that remains to be seen," he said, obviously confident that he was going to be given that chance.

"What is that stuff?" Cassidy asked Shad. In the uneven, quavering light from Shad's fire, she stared at the small dark lumps that the black man held cupped in one palm. She was unhappy about nearly every aspect of their intended course of action, including the fact that Shad had insisted that they wait until nightfall to proceed.

"I don't know—some kind of fungus or lichen or something," Shad replied. He ignored Cassidy's persistent scrutiny as he edged past her to drop down into a squat beside the warden, who was sitting before the fire. As he offered the other man a few of the shriveled-looking bits of vegetable matter, he instructed, "Just chew them and swallow."

"No, wait," Cassidy interrupted. She reached down between the two men and grasped the warden's wrist. "What exactly is this?" she repeated.

"How the hell should I know?" Shad said, his tone mildly exasperated. "What do I look like to you, a botanist?"

Unfortunately, what Shad still looked like to Cassidy was a dangerously unknown factor; but she bit her lip to keep from saying as much. Throughout the whole of that sunny day, while the warden, Click, and Kevin had occupied themselves with erecting another signal flag amid the wreckage on the far point of land, and Rowena busied herself repairing the warden's and Kevin's leathers, Cassidy had had more than enough time to brood. All day she had hoped that either the warden would come to his senses or Shad would change his mind about helping them. But there in front of Shad's fire, with the night well gathered around them and her perfunctory supper nothing more than a vague fullness riding uneasily in her stomach, Cassidy realized that there was not going to be any last-minute reprieve from their crazy plan. The warden was convinced that his consciousness could be united with Andy's in the real world by the use of one of Shad's psychoactive drugs. And unfortunately Shad, while not necessarily ascribing to that belief, was willing to be a partner to testing it.

The warden reached up with his free hand and gently extracted his wrist from Cassidy's grip. "It's all right, Cassidy," he told her. "Shad has used this substance before."

"He doesn't even know what it is," Cassidy said doggedly, though in her heart she knew she had long since lost the argument.

To her surprise, Shad did not make any smart retort. He just shot her an unexpectedly tolerant look and said, "Listen, this is real tame shit. It'll barely give him a buzz; maybe it won't even do anything. The spooks think it's useless." He made a small shrugging movement. "But let's give it a try and see what happens, huh?"

"We're just trying something very mild," the warden reassured Cassidy, giving her hand a light squeeze before he released it.

"Okay, just chew and swallow," Shad repeated to the warden.

Cassidy turned and paced a few anxious steps away from the two men, practically past the edge of Shad's shelter. When she looked back toward the fire, the warden was just sitting there. Shad had dropped down onto the packed earth, sitting cross-legged with his elbows resting on his knees. From that position he addressed Cassidy without even looking in her direction.

"Might as well make yourself comfortable," he suggested. "This is probably going to take awhile."

Cassidy's first reaction was to defy Shad's suggestion. But she knew if she stayed on her feet, she probably would begin to pace back and forth, and she realized the warden would find that distracting. So she reluctantly returned to the fireside and sat down on the warden's other side, trying to be surreptitious about the sidelong glances she kept giving him.

It was a warm, clear evening, and the night air smelled like cypress and woodsmoke. From where she sat, their own campfire was a small smudge of orange light. In that camp the others waited just as she did, filled with concern and perhaps the same doubts. Cassidy knew that even Click, who had taken the warden's side against her in this bizarre matter, genuinely cared about the younger man's welfare. The problem was that the Tinker, just like the warden himself, cared about Cassidy's welfare even more.

Wrenching her thoughts away from Click and all the attendant memories, Cassidy glanced at the warden again. She began to wonder if Shad was just having them on. The warden continued to sit silently before the fire, his posture comfortably casual but essentially motionless, his eyes gazing steadily ahead into the flames. How long did it take for the drug to take effect anyway? After nearly twenty minutes, Cassidy was close to fidgeting, her threadbare patience with the whole idea stretched almost to the point of rupture.

Cassidy would have sworn that the warden hadn't moved in the whole time since he had taken the drug, other than the inevitable slow rhythm of breathing that rocked his body. Was the drug some sort of tranquilizer? She shot a sharp glance past him toward Shad. The black man also looked as if he were posing as the poster boy for Valium. He just sat there, seemingly totally self-contained and unconcerned about anything. Had he taken some of the drug, as well? Cassidy really hadn't been paying close enough attention at the time to have noticed if Shad had given all of the dark lumpish matter to the warden, or if he had consumed part of it himself.

Cassidy's anxiety and impatience were further inflamed by the anger she felt at that possibility. In defiance of Shad's almost stuporous stillness, she leaned in closer to the warden. Stopping just short of actually touching him, she asked, "Are you all right?"

Cassidy had been falsely lulled by Shad's seeming languor, and she was startled by the speed with which the young man attained his feet. In an instant he was behind her, bending down to chastise her in a harsh whisper. "Shh! Don't try to distract him!"

A brief glance at the warden revealed no response either to her question or to Shad's admonishment. Cassidy glared up balefully at Shad. "I just wanted to—"

Not only was he capable of surprising swiftness, Shad was also unexpectedly strong for someone so lithe. Hooking Cassidy under the arms, he had her up on her feet and stumbling backward after him so quickly that she never even had time to resist. By the time they had come to a halt inside his dugout, the abruptness with which he released her made Cassidy have to struggle to keep her balance. But before she could protest, Shad spun her around to face him, his voice soft but commanding.

"Do you want this to work," he demanded, "or not?"

Of course! she wanted to retort, but the words wouldn't leave her lips. Because although in the larger sense she did want the warden to succeed, to be able to intervene in the Slow World and save her life, she still had deep reservations about the means he had chosen to go about it. She wanted it to work; she just didn't want the warden to take that kind of risk. She didn't want him to save her by endangering himself experimenting with Shad's frightening pharmacopoeia.

Reading the painful ambivalence in her grim expression, Shad dropped his hands from Cassidy's forearms and gave a little shake of his head. "What did you think was going to happen?" he asked. "He's just stoned."

Unconsciously rubbing her arms where Shad's fingers had gripped her, Cassidy said defensively, "He doesn't know anything about drugs."

Shad pushed back a gleaming swag of his crinky black hair over his shoulder. His slim brown hand lingered at his throat, his forefinger crooking absently to touch the empty thong that was knotted there. Watching the faint play of firelight over the creamy coffee color of his bare arms, Cassidy was freshly cognizant of the wiry strength in that lean body. In the moments that followed, she also became aware of something else, something she had never before attributed to that unpredictable young man. Shad was slowly and deliberately marshaling his patience with her, and he was doing it because he could see the honesty of her concern for the warden.

"Listen," he said, "if he's going to loosen his control enough to be able to project his consciousness, he's got to give in to the shit." He gestured back toward the firepit, where the warden still sat quiescently. "He's not going to look or act normal."

Oddly embarrassed by Shad's unexpected solicitude, Cassidy quickly asked him, "How long before we know if this is going to work?"

Shad shrugged. "Too soon to say. This shit can be kind of funny that way."

Bolstered by a more familiar feeling, that of suspicion, Cassidy immediately said, "I thought you said this stuff was mild?"

"It is," Shad said. "That's why it sometimes takes a little while before it kicks in." He glanced back toward the warden again. "He mellowed out real quick, so at least we're headed in the right direction. Now we've just got to wait and see."

Cassidy's gaze panned around the dimly lit confines of Shad's dugout, its numerous storage niches and crannies thrown into an abstract pattern of shadows by the reflected light of the fire. The only other illumination inside the shelter was the oil lantern, its wick trimmed low, hung near the futonlike bed. Although it was anything but a social situation, Cassidy found herself distinctly ill at ease waiting there with Shad. Technically she wasn't alone with him, but considering the warden's condition she might just as well have been, and it made her feel uncomfortable.

Interpreting her discomfort, Shad gestured toward the opening overhang of the shelter. "Let's go back by the fire," he said. "Just don't try to distract him again."

Abashed by how transparent she had been, Cassidy quickly stepped back outside. She moved around the periphery of the firepit, so that when she sat down again on the packed earth, she was almost directly across the fire from the warden. He still hadn't moved, and from that vantage point she could see that his eyes were closed. She wondered if she pried open the warden's lids if she would find his pupils as dilated as Shad's had been when they had first found him, slumped beside his fire. But she really didn't want to know the answer to that question.

Shad followed her out of the shelter a minute or two later. He also came around to the other side of the fire; Cassidy was a bit surprised, considering the tenor of their relationship thus far, when the black man dropped down with an artless grace, practically at her side. She was also a little unsettled by Shad's seeming nonchalance. As he settled himself in, cross-legged, she could see that he was chewing on something. Catching her eye, he proffered something with one hand extended.

"Jerky?" he asked, cocking his head expectantly. At her nonplussed silence, he elaborated, "It's venison, but it's pretty good."

Food was the farthest thing from Cassidy's mind. She was already regretting the small meal she'd eaten earlier that evening at her own campfire. But she was caught off guard by the odd, offhanded hospitality, and so she automatically reached for the ragged strip of dried meat he was holding out to her.

"First time I ever got the munchies just *watching* somebody do shit," Shad remarked, tearing off another bite from his own stick of jerky.

The venison jerky was pungently smoky and almost as tough as a chunk of rawhide; but once Cassidy managed to bite off a piece of it, she found it was actually rather bland tasting. She also suspected that one piece might last her all night, since it was also impossible to chew.

"So," Shad said, inclining his head toward the warden, "what was this Andy Greene to you back in the real world?"

Cassidy swallowed the half-chewed hunk of jerky with an involuntary gulp. She wasn't sure what surprised her more, Shad's perceptiveness concerning her complicated relationship with the man who sat in a blissful stupor across the fire from them, or just hearing someone refer so casually to the real world. She had to cough before she could speak without choking. And then she had to deliberately misunderstand Shad's question.

"He was my pupil," Cassidy said.

Shad bit off another piece of the dried meat with his even white teeth. His chewing was methodically effective. "No," he said, "I mean what was he to you personally?"

Cassidy shook her head. "I was just his riding instructor. The farm where I worked took part in a program of riding therapy for patients from the center where he lived."

"Oh yeah, the horse thing," Shad said, temporarily diverted. He made a vague but surprisingly evocative gesture. "With the herdsmen it was those damned cows and sheep; here, it must be horses. Before I got here, the closest I'd ever been to a horse was on the merry-go-round. And cows were just something out in the fields that you drove by on the freeway." He paused just long enough to rip off another hunk of jerky. Then he gave Cassidy a sidelong speculative look. "So that's how you got into this whole Horseman thing, huh?"

Cassidy hesitated a moment, unsure if Shad was honestly interested in that aspect of her life, or if he was merely making small talk. Either way, she could see no harm in discussing it with him, and the subject was considerably less volatile than that of Andy Greene.

"Dragonfly came here with me," she said. "I was a Horseman before I even knew what the hell one was."

Whatever Shad's initial motivation, Cassidy had definitely piqued his curiosity. His dark head cocked, those neatly drawn brows tenting. "You mean you had the same horse in the real world?" he asked her.

Cassidy nodded. "She was the horse that I taught Andy how to ride on. He was one of my disabled students."

Shad made a soft snorting sound, which seemed more of an acknowledgment of the irony of the situation than an expression of amusement. "And here he's the warden of Horses," he said. He gave her another long look, disquieting in its astuteness. "It must have really thrown you for a loop when he didn't even recognize you then."

Cassidy deliberately avoided meeting the steady stare of those wide-set dark eyes. Shad was advancing into some intensely personal territory, an area that she had explored only with the warden himself. She shrugged, feigning nonchalance. "He doesn't have any primary memory of his own," she pointed out. "Even now, the only things he knows about Andy and the real world are whatever he's discovered during his lapses, and the things I've told him."

But Shad's gaze didn't drop. "Then he must have developed one hell of an attachment for you in this world," he said bluntly, "to be willing to risk going back there for you."

Cassidy felt herself flush, both from the acuity of Shad's observation and from his audacity in voicing it. "He's the warden," she said, clumsily trying to cover her reaction. "He feels that he has a duty to—"

But Shad cut her off in that soft but compelling voice. "This is no duty to him," he said flatly. "All he cares about is saving your life."

Cassidy couldn't argue with Shad's assessment; she didn't even try to. Anything she might have said would only have deepened Shad's impression of the true nature of her relationship with both Andy and the warden. And although Cassidy was not ashamed of that relationship, she was hardly about to discuss it with an enigmatic young man who was a near stranger to her.

As Shad continued, his tone was an incongruous mixture of casual speculation and sober contemplation. "It's hard to say how this autism thing will affect what he's trying to do," he said. "There's another consciousness back there, some kind of awareness anyway, controlling Andy Greene."

Blindsided by the seeming swerve in the direction of the conversation, Cassidy had to scramble mentally to follow Shad's line of thought. "What do you mean?" she asked, feeling a disconcerting echo of her earlier anxiety about what the warden was attempting to do.

Shad popped the last fragment of his jerky into his mouth; for a few moments he was occupied with chewing on it. "I mean that it's not like what I did when I went back," he said then. "Back there, I'm nothing but a well-maintained corpse. But with his autism, even if Andy's awareness isn't in sync with the real world, there must be *something* there—call it what you want." He gave an evocative shrug. "Otherwise Andy never would have been capable of learning something as complicated as riding a horse. And during the lapses into this world, he sure as hell wouldn't have been capable of recognizing and caring about you."

Conceding Shad's point, Cassidy instead returned to his original speculation about the effect of Andy's autism. "You don't think it's possible for the warden's consciousness to coexist with Andy's?" she asked anxiously. "Then why are we . . . ?"

But Shad simply shook his head, his glossy black hair shimmering in the firelight. Cassidy was struck once again by the canny intelligence in his face. "Of course it's possible," he said. "What do you think he's done every time he's had one of those lapses? Andy's consciousness has come to this world and coexisted with the warden's in this body. And the warden's already gone back into Andy's body a couple of times." He shrugged again, his shoulders quirking limberly beneath his loose leather vest. "I'm just wondering where Andy's consciousness was when the warden took over his body. Was it back here in the warden's body? Or were both of them in Andy's body?"

Almost without volition, Cassidy leaned in closer to Shad, searching his composed face. "If Andy did go back to the Slow World with the warden during the lapses," she said, "then do you think it's more likely that what the warden's trying to do now will work?"

Shad didn't even have to respond; Cassidy's very question had neatly summarized his hypothesis. But Cassidy's study of the black man's expression only intensified, her own face tightening with a frown of concentration.

"But if both of their consciousnesses went back to Andy's body in the Slow World during the connection," she said uneasily, "who, or what, was controlling the warden's body here?"

Shad made a little sound of reprover, like a gruff but kindly professor indulgently correcting a misguided pupil. "Nothing," he said succinctly. At Cassidy's look of patent disbelief, he pointed out, "What do you think is controlling me and you back there in the real world right now?"

As blunt and surprising as Shad's conclusion was, had she been given a moment to consider it, Cassidy would have had to concede that it was also dead-center accurate. She probably would have ended up agreeing with the sharp-witted young black. But before she could reply, the warden suddenly stirred.

Actually, "stir" was perhaps too extreme a term, for initially the warden barely moved. He groaned, a deep guttural sound that was almost eerie in its tone and disturbing in its volume. He probably could have been heard all the way over to their campsite. Even before the sound faded, Cassidy was on her feet, scrambling around the fire to him.

"Wait!" Shad hissed at her; but his command went without effect. For by then Cassidy was already dropping to her knees at the warden's side.

As she lifted her hands to touch him, his slack posture abruptly straightened. His spine stiffened and his head lifted with a jerk. The instant Cassidy's fingers closed around his shoulders, she reeled backward, nearly losing her grip on him. Then she would have gladly released him, but she *couldn't*.

In a perverted parody of the flood of light that engulfed her whenever she first touched the warden during one of his lapses, Cassidy found herself suddenly frozen in the icy hold of a roaring tide of blackness. She tried to close her eyes against it, but the invading darkness seemed to penetrate right through her lids, right through her skull, overwhelming her. Her numb fingers curled like claws, helplessly digging even deeper into the warden's shoulders, while all around them rose a gagging miasma of rotting stench.

Except for the absence of actual slime, it was like being enfolded in the caullike embrace of one of the huge carrion eaters' fetid bodies. But the all-permeating void was not a solid thing, like the monsters' flesh; it was air, it was like a foul cyclone of—

And then suddenly everything just *stopped*.

From out of the chill and whirling maelstrom, Cassidy was abruptly suspended in a motionless, unfeeling state of *nothing*. Just as before, in the swamp and when the snakelike monster had attacked Kevin, Cassidy was conscious only of *being*. She could not move, she could not feel—she could only *be*.

And yet in that odd and airless suspension, there was something that called to her, a siren's call seducing her. Until she wrenched herself free.

And then, unexpectedly, the world *moved* again.

Cassidy's limbs jerked spasmodically, causing her to topple backward helplessly, pulling the warden with her. As she fell beneath him, her eyes flew open again and she saw a mass of *things*—a writhing nest of roiling black coils—blossom between her body and the warden's, like a nest of mutinous serpents. Except that the things weren't just springing out from between them, they were rising up from *inside* him, boiling out from the warden's body like twisting streamers of cold black smoke. And Cassidy saw them unfurling not only up and around her, but *through* her—

Sinewy fingers bit into the shivering flesh of Cassidy's upper arms, forcibly tearing her and the warden apart. She felt herself being lifted and pulled backward, so abruptly that her teeth snapped together with an audible click, nearly trapping her tongue between them. Then Shad released her and scrambled forward again, reaching the warden just in time to prevent his slumping body from tumbling right into the firepit. Shad dragged the dazed man backward, as well, almost to the mouth of his shelter.

Numbly, Cassidy gaped up into the still night air. The scream that she was certain she must have given voice to remained frozen in her aching throat. And the malignant rush of black air and the coiling creatures that had sprang from it were gone.

"Cassidy, are you all right?"

Shad had already repeated the question before it even registered with her. The black man was still holding the warden by the shoulders to keep him sitting upright. The warden looked as stupefied as if he'd just been struck by lightning.

"Did you see them?" Cassidy blurted out, her voice an alarming croak.

Shad's face was garishly limned by the firelight, his black eyes wide pools of bright reflection. "You bet your sweet ass I saw them!" he shot back at her. "Damn it, are you all right?"

Cassidy was violently shaken by a huge involuntary shudder. But she determinedly pushed herself forward onto her hands and knees and crawled toward the two men. "Is he okay?" she demanded anxiously.

Dark shadows moved in from behind her, surrounding them. Cassidy started reflexively before she recognized Click, Rowena, and Kevin converging upon them. Certainly they'd created enough fuss, beginning with the warden's loud groan, to have alerted anyone in the entire valley. With Click taking her one arm and Rowena the other, Cassidy could no longer reach for the warden; but by then she was close enough to him to see that at least physically he appeared unharmed.

Kevin immediately attached himself to the warden with such proprietary ferocity that Shad could hardly get himself free of the ensuing tangle of arms and legs. "Hey, take it easy," Shad advised Kevin, even as he scrambled clear. His hands spread placatingly. "He'll be all right. Just give him a chance to get his head on straight again."

Rowena reached out to smooth back an errant lock of Cassidy's hair, as if seeking to defuse with the maternal gesture some of the charged alarm she felt. "Geez!" she exclaimed. "Where the hell did those things come from?"

Cassidy's head snapped around. "You saw them, too?" she demanded of the brunette.

"*Saw* them?" Rowena echoed incredulously. "They were shooting out of you guys like fireworks!"

At Cassidy's other side, Click scanned the empty night sky. But not a trace of the noxious creatures remained.

With Kevin's help, or in spite of it, the warden finally had managed to sit upright again. When Cassidy looked across at him, he was blinking muzzily, his handsome face unfocused and creased by a confused frown. "Cassidy?" he asked, his voice hoarse. "Are you all right?"

With Click and Rowena's reluctant leave, and under Kevin's warily protective watch, Cassidy leaned forward and clasped one of the warden's hands. To her relief, she felt only his warm dry skin. "I'm fine," she assured him. "But what about you? What the hell just happened?"

The warden's reaction was not what Cassidy or anyone else could have expected. Even though his response left no doubt that he was fully aware of everything that had just happened in those explosive moments following Cassidy touching him, he appeared only passingly disgusted, and not at all frightened, by the loathsome creatures that had so swiftly fumed up between them.

In us, Cassidy reminded herself sharply. *Through us!*

"They were waiting for me," he said, "there in between." His tone was almost dismissive, as if he had been discussing nothing more alarming than an annoying cloud of mosquitoes that had ambushed him from the brush. He made a vague shooing motion, so casually that it would have been comedic under less dramatic circumstances. "They don't matter," he said.

Cassidy just stared at him, too surprised to speak. She watched as both the focus and the keen incisiveness returned to that familiar face. The warden leaned forward, tightly squeezing her hand between both of his, as excitement kindled in those warm brown eyes.

"It worked, Cassidy," he said. "I did it—I went back to the Slow World!"

Chapter 21 ◀▥

For nearly the entire time she'd been in that world, even before she had regained any clear memory of the time or place from which she'd come, Cassidy had set for herself one immutable goal: to return to the world in which she belonged. The warden's stunning declaration should have both thrilled and amazed her, representing as it did the first concrete validation of everything she had striven toward for so long. And yet, oddly enough, Cassidy did not automatically feel any sense of exhilaration or jubilation. Rather, as she knelt there in front of Shad's shelter, confronting the eager excitement on the warden's face, her only immediate reaction was that of concern for his condition. The gleam in those brown eyes was almost fever bright, his spark of enthusiasm too uncomfortably close to a pharmaceutical euphoria.

Interpreting her concern as disbelief, the warden gripped Cassidy's hand even tighter. He tried to pull himself up onto his knees to more closely approximate her. In the process, he nearly lurched over sideways. Kevin's hold on him kept the warden from falling flat on his face, but even his obvious unsteadiness failed to diminish his zeal.

"It was amazing!" he exclaimed. "Cassidy, I was *there*!"

"Whoa," Cassidy counseled, "take it easy." She found herself facilitating Kevin's efforts to get the warden to sit back down again, using his hold on her hand as a lever. "Are you sure you're all right? You still look pretty shaky."

Shad emerged from the dimness of his shelter, carrying a tin mug. Cassidy hadn't even noticed when the black man had slipped away from beside the fire. Shad dropped down beside them, reinforcing her admonition to the warden.

"Here, take this," Shad said, proffering the mug. "And I'd plan on just sitting for a while yet."

Cassidy had no idea what was in the mug, and she really didn't much care, as long as it got the warden to sit back down and catch his breath. As the warden sank back, Cassidy slipped her hand from between his so that he could take the cup. She watched approvingly as he lifted it and sipped at the contents. Click and Rowena had settled in behind her, and Cassidy was distinctly grateful for her friends' presence as she prepared to face the specifics of the warden's momentous revelation.

After several long swallows from the mug, the warden seemed to have regained both his breath and some of his composure. Lowering the cup, he looked across at Cassidy, concern evident in his expression. "Are you sure you're all right?" he asked her.

"I'm fine," she said. "Now tell us what happened."

Settling the tin mug against his thigh, the warden permitted himself to lean back slightly into the support of Kevin's side, as his gaze quickly traveled over the faces of those who had gathered around Shad's fire. "At first, I didn't think anything was going to happen," he admitted, with just the trace of one of those self-effacing smiles pulling at his mouth. "After I swallowed the drug, I didn't feel any different. I know it couldn't possibly have been that long, but it seemed like I just sat there staring at the fire for hours." He shot Shad a brief look of inquiry. "I suppose it was only a few minutes."

Shad made a small equivocating motion with one slim brown hand. "Maybe ten or fifteen minutes," he said. "But after that, you were gone."

Cassidy shifted uneasily on the packed earth. "Could you hear us . . . talking?" she asked. She had almost said arguing, which would have been far more accurate; but she was hoping that the warden hadn't heard her and Shad at all.

But the warden merely shook his head. "I don't remember hearing anyone say anything," he replied. "I was just sitting there staring into the fire, actually starting to feel a little sleepy, when I finally noticed that the fire wasn't there anymore."

His words had been delivered calmly enough, almost casually, and yet Cassidy felt the hairs on the nape of her neck and on the backs of her forearms rise. While the warden paused, seemingly searching for words, she had to fight to keep herself from beginning to question him.

"What seems most remarkable to me now," the warden said, "was just how unremarkable the transition was. A moment after I noticed that the fire wasn't there any longer, I realized that everything around me had changed. I was—*Andy* was—sitting in a big room with at least a dozen other people." His head canted slightly, as if to summon up the image more clearly. "It was a very pleasant, open room, much like a large parlor. It was raining outside, and the rain was washing down the glass panes of the tall windows . . ."

As the warden's voice trailed off, he suddenly looked directly at Cassidy. "I saw the most amazing things!" he said, gazing at her with an almost childlike effervescence. "The lamps on the ceiling and on the tables had no wicks or flames. And there was this large crate or box, with a glass window—and there were images moving inside of it! It was incredible!"

Under other circumstances, Cassidy would have been better able to appreciate the humor inherent in the warden's reaction. Here the man had literally crossed the plane between two realms of time, and he seemed less impressed by that feat than he had been by electric lights and television.

"What about Andy," she prompted him. "Were you aware of his . . . presence? Was he aware of you?"

The warden frowned, his ebullience waning. "I'm not sure how to explain this," he said, "but even though I know I was *in* him, I had no real feeling of connection with him."

"In other words," Shad said simply, "you were there, but you weren't able to *do* anything."

The warden's frown deepened. "No, I couldn't," he admitted. "It was as if I existed where Andy was, but he was there, as well, and still separate from me. It wasn't like during the other episodes. I don't think he was even aware of my presence."

Feeling disappointed in spite of her initial skepticism, Cassidy asked the warden, "But you could see everything that Andy saw and hear everything that he heard?"

Cassidy could tell that the warden was struggling to strike a balance between optimism and reality with his response. "Well," he said, "that was another odd thing. I could see our surroundings clearly enough—the room, its fixtures, the other people, the image box—but I couldn't understand what anyone was saying." His expression had grown troubled. "There was a man there in blue trousers and a white shirt who spoke several times to Andy; and yet I couldn't understand a single word he said. It was all gibberish. And the sounds coming from the box—there was some kind of awful music, but everything spoken was unintelligible to me."

Cassidy's mind raced with the implication of what the warden had discovered on his journey to the Slow World. *AFB—autistic from birth*, she thought numbly. Coexisting in the real world with his alternate self, the warden had graphically experienced one of the painful parameters of Andy's daily existence. If Andy's perceptions truly were out of sync with real time, then normal human speech would sound like nothing but meaningless babble to him. No wonder Andy had never developed language; that he seemed to understand anything at all was a miracle in itself.

Interpreting Cassidy's silence as the same sort of bafflement he himself felt, the warden continued. "I don't know how long I was there. Subjectively, it only seemed like a few minutes; but it must have been longer."

"Less than an hour," Shad offered.

"Then everything I could see there in the big room began to grow dim," the warden said, "like the light was failing, or night was falling. But it happened too rapidly for it to have been nightfall." His shoulders rounded slightly, as if he were unconsciously drawing into himself. He leaned again into the supporting warmth of Kevin's body. "And when it grew dark, it suddenly became colder. I could hear a harsh roaring sound, and then—"

As the warden's voice broke off, Cassidy realized that her own body also had tightened automatically, her muscles braced against the reliving of that bizarre moment when she had touched him and the monsters had bloomed up out of the blackness between them. "And that was when you came back," she said hoarsely.

The warden's eyes sought hers again, steadying them both with the abrupt comprehension behind his gaze. "The monsters, Cassidy," he said intently. "That's where they've come from. They were waiting there for me as I came back, crossing the gap between the two worlds."

Beside the warden, Kevin released a shaky breath. "You mean the monsters followed you from the Slow World?" he said.

"No, not from the Slow World, Kev," the warden corrected him in an oddly gentle voice. "From whatever lies between that world and this one."

From that smothering blackness, Cassidy thought immediately. From that freezing void where there was no time . . .

"Then those things aren't just following Cassidy here," Shad said. "They must have come here when she did."

"That seems most likely," the warden said. "We know for certain now that at least one form of the creatures was there between the two worlds when I returned. And this current problem with the monsters began around the time Cassidy came here."

"And the longer I've been here," Cassidy said, "and the more

I've regained of my memory, the more widespread and vicious those things have become."

"From where have Cassidy's memories come?" Click asked.

"You mean what triggered them?" Cassidy said. Then she abruptly understood what he was implying. She turned to look at that calm, lean face, its weathered features thrown into sharp relief by the firelight. "You mean my memories have come from the real world," she said, "so they've come across the same gap."

"Wait a minute," Rowena protested. "Are you saying that Cassidy remembering stuff has been what's been causing all the problems with the monsters?"

"She suspected a correlation almost from the beginning," Click pointed out.

"But if that's the case," Rowena persisted, "then why hasn't everybody who's ever had the Memories done the same thing?"

It was the warden who responded, his expression speculative. "Maybe they have, Rowena," he said. "There've always been reports of monsters—nothing like this, of course," he added wryly, "but then again, who else who has come here has ever had the Memories like Cassidy does?"

"Shad," the brunette said immediately. "Shad remembers everything, too, and there aren't any monsters following him."

A bit nonplussed suddenly to find himself the object of conversation, Shad had to agree with Rowena. "I haven't even seen a bogey since Henry left," he said, adding needlessly, "at least not until you guys got here. And why were they following Henry? He didn't remember hardly anything."

The warden nodded, conceding the point as taken, but he still was warming to his theory. His eyes were unnaturally bright, his voice animated. "Then maybe it has something to do with Cassidy being a Horseman, as well," he said. "Maybe the monsters—"

"Maybe all this can just wait until tomorrow," Shad interrupted him, holding up both hands in a warding gesture. "No offense, warden, but you're starting to sound like a guy who's about to crash, and when you do, I'd rather it was in your own bedroll and not here on my doorstep."

The warden probably still would have tried to go on, further expanding on his idea, had not his friends all quickly sided with Shad. "He's right," Kevin insisted, tugging on the warden's arm. "You should go to bed; you can hardly even sit up straight."

The warden threw Kevin an indulgent look, but then Click added his own counsel. "The questions will still be there in the morning," the Tinker remarked. He gained his feet with an artless sort of grace and then held out his hand to Cassidy. "We can discuss all of this further then."

As Cassidy accepted Click's hand up and stood, she thought the warden looked as if he still might protest. But then a huge yawn, apparently unexpected and far too broad to conceal, overtook him; and he yielded to Kevin's urging with a sheepish nod.

When they were only a few yards from Shad's firepit, the warden turned around, as if he had just thought of some last comment or question. But he would have been talking to thin air, because the young black man had already disappeared into his shelter, and the hard-packed earth at its threshold was deserted.

Cassidy didn't feel in the least bit sleepy, but she at least made the pretense of rolling herself in her blanket beside the cooling ashes of their campfire. She didn't know if it qualified as "crashing," but the warden quickly had settled down beside Kevin, and both men were soon asleep. From the space between them and her own bedroll, Cassidy could hear the soft rasp of Rowena's nasal breathing. Click was taking the first watch, despite Cassidy's offer to do so. She thought that she might just as well stand guard, since she knew that she wasn't going to sleep.

It wasn't the questions that had been raised about the monsters which so occupied her mind, or even the bizarre experience she had shared with the warden the moment he had come back from the Slow World. Click had been right; those matters could wait until morning. It was a deeper quandary that had captured her thoughts and kept her from sleep. She found herself troubled by a vague anxiety so vast that it was essentially formless and that encompassed issues far more chronic than the evening's dramatic events.

After nearly an hour of failed attempts at slumber, Cassidy sought out the most basic and reliable comfort she knew in that world. Stepping soundlessly across the dewy ground, she made her way across the valley floor. The night air was still warm enough that she was quite comfortable without her blanket. The sounds of night birds and insects formed a faint backdrop for her foray.

Contentedly ensconced with another generous pile of cut brush, Dragonfly stood like a tall silver shadow against the blackness of the cypress-covered slope. The horse watched her approach in silence, only the twin curve of her pricked ears betraying any interest. When Cassidy took the long head in her arms, the horse tolerated the interruption in her meal. She exhaled a gust of sweet-smelling breath across Cassidy's chest, her nostrils flaring as she solemnly examined the front of Cassidy's shirt. Then Dragonfly began to chew again, the powerful muscles of her jaws rippling beneath Cassidy's cradling fingers.

Moving back alongside the mare's body, Cassidy leaned against the sleek warmth of the gray's shoulder for a moment. There Cassidy finally found a focus for her free-floating anxiety, as she was torn by a sudden thought. If she did succeed in going back to the real world, what would happen to Dragonfly?

The chilling reality behind the reason for her own presence in that alternate world was something Cassidy was finally being forced to accept as fact, but what about the mare? The horse had definitely come there with her, but how and why? She'd never heard of a horse surviving in a vegetative state, so that only left two possibilities: Back in the real world, Dragonfly must either be still unaffected—or she must be dead.

As she felt the hot press of tears welling up in her burning eyes, Cassidy turned her face into the mare's silky hide. *Oh, this is just great!* she chastised herself. She had come to the horse seeking solace, not to twist the cruel blade of her nameless, formless pain any deeper.

Recognizing Cassidy's distress, the mare swung her head around, nickering softly. The velvety prod of her soft, prehensile upper lip ruffled the sleeve of Cassidy's shirt. Cassidy hopped up onto the gray's broad back. She leaned forward over the horse's withers, her arms bracketing the lowered neck as the mare calmly resumed her feeding. With her face safely buried in the thick, iron-colored mane, Cassidy allowed herself a luxury that before had always seemed too dangerously self-indulgent for the constant adversity of that world. Hugging the horse's wide shoulders, Cassidy softly wept.

Cassidy had no idea how long she lay there astride the horse, giving near-silent vent to her pain. Even after she had stopped weeping, her swollen eyes burned and her throat felt raw and dry. The warm solid bulk of the mare's body beneath hers lulled her with the gentle rocking of the horse's breathing and the minute little shifts in Dragonfly's weight as she methodically attacked the pile of fodder. At some point Cassidy knew that she had begun to drowse, because she remembered fleetingly considering the possibility that she might fall off the horse if she actually fell asleep.

When she felt the strong but careful hands gently pulling her arms from around the mare's neck, Cassidy was not surprised. It was almost as if she had expected him to find her. Bonelessly, she allowed herself to be drawn down and held against Click's chest. She burrowed her face into the smooth angle between his shoulder and his neck, inhaling the comforting scent of him, as familiar to her then as the mare's sweet smell. Cassidy felt as small as a child in his arms.

Click murmured something interrogative—her name, she thought. But she was too sleepy to respond. She was vaguely aware of being carried by him, his stride shorter but less swaying than the mare's. But that was the last thing she remembered.

When Cassidy awoke the next morning, it was out of a dream. But oddly enough, she could recall nothing of what she had been dreaming. Feeling somehow cheated, she blinked up into the hazy half-light of dawn to find herself rolled in her blanket beside their campfire. Across the firepit from her, the warden and Kevin still slept, twin mounds beneath a tangle of blankets. Alongside her, Rowena was patiently feeding kindling into her fledgling fire, coaxing the small flame to catch hold.

Seeing Cassidy stir, Rowena gave her an apologetic look. "Did I wake you?" she asked in a near whisper. "I know it's still early, but I thought I'd get some coffee on and start on breakfast."

In the shadows of the cypress trees, the first weak sunlight had not yet penetrated; yet the morning was comfortably warm. Across the floor of the valley, birds darted like small squadrons of aircraft. There was a heavy dew, and it promised to be a muggy day.

Cassidy sat up, yawning and rubbing her eyes. "Where's Click?" she asked, surprised by how sore her throat still felt and how hoarse the words sounded.

"Out there somewhere, I guess," Rowena said, shooting a glance toward the warden's and Kevin's sprawled forms. "Nobody even woke me up last night for watch," she added, sounding mildly mystified.

Cassidy suspected that no one had been awakened for their watch last night, but she didn't say that. Click, like the Woodsmen—like the moon and the planets and all the stars in their place—moved to his own rhythm, she thought wryly. Rather than comment, Cassidy just got slowly and carefully to her feet, feeling several decades older. She gave Rowena a reassuringly casual look. "I'll be back in a bit," she said.

Cassidy knew that Rowena would assume she was just going out to relieve herself; and that idea actually was somewhere on her agenda. But another need compelled her more, and the early-morning solitude would just make her mission far simpler. Glancing back across the shadowy valley to make sure that Rowena wasn't paying any particular attention to her, Cassidy angled north, where the trunks of the larger cypresses would conceal her. Then she started toward Shad's dugout.

Twittering sharply, small birds shot out from around the base of one of the large tilted slabs of shale that protruded near the huge toppled tree. As Cassidy crossed the rock, she was surprised to see what had occupied the birds. Someone had spread a thin scattering of the coarsely ground wheat on the smooth surface of the slab. Some of the grain had been included with the supplies they had traded Shad for the clothing, but Cassidy still was puzzled. She just couldn't picture the black man feeding the birds. *Unless he's planning on fattening them up to eat!* she thought.

Much as Cassidy had hoped, Shad was up but still at his shelter. She doubted that he'd needed the noisy flurry of the birds' departure to alert him to her approach, since he had pretty much an unobstructed view of the entire valley floor from anywhere around his dugout. He was crouched over something he had spread out on the ground, and he didn't even bother to glance up at Cassidy until she was practically alongside him.

Shad saved her from the inanity of some casual greeting by simply asking her without preface, "He still sleeping?"

"Yeah," she said, "him and Kevin both."

"The Hardy boys," Shad said, not looking up.

Looking down over Shad's shoulder, Cassidy was a little disconcerted to notice suddenly that he had changed his clothes. She didn't know why that should surprise her; heaven knew, Shad had enough clothing crammed into his shelter that he could have worn a new outfit every day for weeks. Perhaps it was just that his leather vest and leggings and the disintegrating jeans had looked so much like he lived twenty-four hours a day in them that she hadn't expected to see him wearing anything else. He wore another leather vest, one made of tan suede, over fitted brown trousers. Both of the garments looked virtually new.

After a moment, Cassidy noticed what Shad had spread out on the ground in front of him. It was a long strip of canvas, fitted with various loops and slots to hold an impressive array of knives. While she was staring at the cutlery, she realized that he had said something to her and that she had missed it completely.

"What?" she had to ask.

"I said," Shad repeated without looking up, "he'll probably be pretty wiped out for a few hours yet." He had selected one knife from the group and seemed to be considering a second. "That shit's mild, but it's got kind of a long afterkick to it." He finally threw Cassidy a quick glance, just as he reached for another knife. "I'm still surprised that it even worked for him."

Shad deftly rolled up the long strip of canvas and then smoothly gained his feet, holding the bundle in one hand and the two knives in the other. As he turned toward her, Cassidy was a little chagrined to realize that he might well be expecting some sort of explanation for her early-morning visit. With equal alacrity, she realized that she didn't have one—at least not one that would have made any sense. She simply blurted out the first thing that came to mind. "You feed the birds," she said.

Shad gave a vague shrug. "They don't eat much," he pointed out. Stepping part way into his shelter, he stowed the roll of canvas in one of the ubiquitous niches. As he reemerged, he was tucking the two knives under the waistband of his pants. He cocked his head expectantly at Cassidy. "You know how to gut rabbits?"

"I've had some experience," she said, recalling all the time she had spent living off the land.

"I'm going to go check my trapline," he said. "You want to come along and help, we'll go halves on the rabbits."

Somewhat surprised by the invitation, Cassidy fell into step behind Shad as he started across the valley floor toward the slope. They had already enjoyed the largesse of his trapline. Unlike the crude system she and Rowena had employed when they were on the run from Double Creek, Shad's snares were quite sophisticated, and made of copper wire. In the brushy ravines surrounding the valley there were many rabbit runs, and as a permanent resident, Shad had the luxury of moving his trapline whenever one area became depleted.

It was full daylight when they reached the site of his current trapline. They had hiked in silence up and down the slopes of several ridges, into an area entirely unfamiliar to Cassidy. And yet she felt curiously calm following the black man through the brush. Shad seemed a creature entirely in his own element there, padding quietly along in his soft-soled shoes. Watching his leather-clad back slip through some bushes ahead of her, Cassidy found that even though she still didn't understand why she had sought out Shad that morning, she felt quite comfortable with him.

When Shad halted at the bottom of a narrow ravine, Cassidy's shirt was already lightly dampened with perspiration, and stray tendrils of her hair hung across her shining forehead. For the first time since they left his shelter, Shad turned to face her.

"You can wait here if you want," he said, "while I check the line." Before she could offer to help, he added, "It's kind of cramped crawling around in the bushes, and I'd just as soon not have you tripping all of my snares."

"I'll just wait here," she said. She had spent enough time wriggling through rabbit runs already.

Within moments Shad had disappeared into the tangled brush that covered the bottom of the ravine. The random bobbing of a few branches was all that marked his route. After a minute or two, the birds resumed singing in the bushes as normalcy returned to the forest.

Lifting her damp hair up off the back of her neck, Cassidy relished the cool kiss of air on her perspiring skin. Glancing around, she selected a low shelf of jutting shale as a seat and dropped down to wait for Shad's return. When she thought about it, she had to admit that his practical skills came as a surprise to her. Not that they should have, she admonished herself; the man had obviously lived essentially on his own for years there in the forest. Just because he didn't fit her mental image of a frontier kind of guy didn't mean that he wasn't experienced and capable. In fact, considering how far Shad had traveled just to get there, and how long he had survived in solitude, self-sufficiency was more of a necessity than an affectation.

Shifting slightly, Cassidy gazed at the nearly solid wall of brush where Shad had disappeared. For the first time giving it some thought, she found herself wondering just what made the young man remain out there alone in the middle of nowhere. From his brief description of his early life in that world, Cassidy could easily empathize with Shad's feelings of alienation and uneasiness. But unless the western herdsmen were substantially different from the Villagers Cassidy had encountered, Shad should have easily been able to feign a certain attitude of "adjustment," especially before his true memory had begun to return. He could have found at least some temporary comfort among the people of that world; yet he had kept on the move until he had reached the valley at the edge of the Great Swamp.

Idly chipping away at a bit of crumbling shale with one fingernail, Cassidy scanned the high canopy of trees overhead. The forest was beautiful, even if its unsuitability for horseback travel was a drawback in her mind. It just seemed strange to her that someone like Shad—that anyone, for that matter—would journey all that way, and then just stop when he'd reached that particular valley, and stay there living alone in a cavern under the roots of a dead tree.

But it really wasn't that different from what she had done, Cassidy realized ruefully as she flipped a chip of rock into the bushes. She, too, had spent nearly her whole time in that world traveling. And at any given point during her journey, no matter what she thought her ultimate goal would be, that valley had turned out to be her final destination, as well.

Cassidy was still sitting there musing over the irony of that realization when Shad returned. He caught her by surprise, because he didn't retrace his original route. He also moved through the forest with such casual stealth that no matter which direction he'd come from, Cassidy probably wouldn't have seen him until he was right in front of her. Four plump rabbits were slung by bits of leather tether over his shoulders as he stepped out of the bushes.

Cassidy got to her feet, giving his catch an appreciative look. "You must be pretty good at this," she said.

But as Shad shrugged the rabbits off his shoulders, he simply said, "Lucky for us, rabbits are pretty stupid." After dropping the carcasses to the ground, he slipped the knives out of his waistband and offered one to Cassidy, haft first.

"Just gut them," he said, dropping down onto his knees in the leafy humus. "You don't have to skin them. I don't save the hides, so I'd just as soon leave them on until I use the meat."

As Cassidy knelt down beside him, she couldn't help but think of her and Rowena's disastrous attempts at curing rabbit hides when they were on the lam. She'd managed to become fairly adept at gutting and skinning rabbits, but one thing she'd definitely learned was not to bother saving the damned hides.

Both of them worked in silence for a couple of minutes, eviscerating the rabbits and severing and discarding the heads, tails, and feet. From the methodical, economical way Shad worked, Cassidy could see that he had butchered more than his share of the animals over the years.

Looking over at Shad, Cassidy asked, "Do you save the liver?"

Shad made a face, an expression of distaste that was disarmingly childlike. "You can have them all if you want," he offered. "I hate the stuff."

Thinking of Webb, Cassidy remarked, "I've eaten worse."

Shad paused, one of his gracefully arched brows tenting skeptically. "I'd still take a Quarter Pounder with cheese anytime," he said.

His nonchalant reference to something so utterly mundane and rooted in the real world caught Cassidy totally by surprise. She realized that she was gaping rather stupidly at Shad, but she couldn't help herself.

But Shad merely stared back at her, his other brow climbing, as well. "What?" he said then. "I suppose you're more of a chicken salad person, huh?"

The limp carcass of the rabbit lay beneath her bloody fingers, completely forgotten. Cassidy tried to stop gaping and make some intelligent response. She had a momentary vision of that fey, leather-clad figure in the drive-through at McDonald's and had to suppress an unexpected smile. "Is that the first thing you think of," she asked him somewhat incredulously, "when you remember the real world?"

Pausing again in his task, Shad gave her a wry look. "What am I supposed to say?" he responded. "That what I really miss is Sartre and Mozart?" Further amused by the obvious surprise on Cassidy's face, he turned her question right back on her. "Okay then; what do *you* miss most about the real world?"

Cassidy was fully aware that her hesitation was overly long, and awkwardly obvious. She hoped that Shad would just assume that she was giving serious consideration to her answer. But the real reason for her continuing silence was because she was stunned to suddenly realize something about herself and her situation there: She wasn't even certain anymore that there even *was* anything she still missed about the real world.

Still dazed, Cassidy mentally grappled for what she at least *should* say, what she would have said had he asked the question even a week or two ago. Her family? She was an only child, and both of her parents were dead. She wasn't particularly close to any of her more distant relatives. Her friends then? Other than Joel and Joel's wife, Cindy, Cassidy really didn't have many other people she could have described as good friends. Certainly there was no one in the real world whose friendship she valued as much as she'd come to treasure that of the friends she'd made in her short tenure in that world. No one like Rowena, the warden, Kevin, Allen. And certainly no one like Click.

Staggered afresh by that realization, Cassidy finally began to recognize the source of much of the formless anxiety that had dogged her for the last twenty-four hours. She felt a deep and disturbing ambivalence about something that she had grown accustomed to holding as an absolute tenet: She was no longer certain that she even wanted to return to her own world anymore.

The admission was so disconcerting that Cassidy almost blurted it aloud. *What on earth has happened to me?* she thought in amazement and dismay. But even as one part of her mind was displaying appropriately convincing shock, another more intuitive part of her mind was already reminding her of the reason, the truth she had long tried to bury in her heart.

I was a damned Tinker long before I ever met Click and his band, she admitted to herself, *long before I even came here.* For Cassidy realized then that for most of her adult life, she had been an emotional itinerant, a heart without a home. In every relationship that she had attempted, she had ultimately ended up bartering away her own identity in exchange for someone else's approval. And the deals had never stuck. It had taken coming to this world, and losing the whole of her past, for Cassidy to discover who she really was and who she was capable of becoming.

Shad's head was lowered again as he nonchalantly resumed dressing his second rabbit. Studying his face in profile, Cassidy also had to admit to herself that it had taken that man—a cynical black doper, with the same memories she had—to have completed her journey of discovery. What an ultimate irony it would be, she thought, if he really was the Alchemist; if he actually could help her return, now that she knew she no longer really wanted to go back.

Either Shad had intended his question to be rhetorical, or he at least assumed Cassidy to have taken it that way. For when he spoke, without even looking up, he answered the query himself.

"Pizza," he said matter-of-factly. "Either deep-dish pizza, or really good ice cream. Not that soft-serve crap, either; I mean the kind you have to hack out of the carton if you've just taken it out of the freezer."

When Cassidy didn't respond, Shad looked over at her. At her dumbfounded look, he gave a little shrug and offered without a trace of defensiveness, "You thought I was going to say my mama's sweet smile?"

Actually, Cassidy hadn't had any idea what Shad was going to say. She hadn't even realized that he was going to answer the question at all. And the thought of him even having had a mother, smiling or otherwise, was so far out of left field that it practically sailed right past her without even registering. Her mind still churning, she stared down at the partially butchered carcass of her own second rabbit, the bloody knife clutched motionless in her hand.

"You know the last thing I remember seeing?" Shad went on, canny and yet completely casual in his perceptiveness. "The muzzle flash from the gun of the son of a bitch who shot me." His dark head canted slightly, almost thoughtfully, his long hair a gleaming raven curtain. His knife dangled from those slender fingers by its wooden haft. His face was turned in Cassidy's direction, but he wasn't really looking at her. "It was like something happening in slow motion. I swear I could actually see the bullet coming at me. Only I just couldn't move." His fingers tightened, his knuckles whitening on the knife. "The only good thing was, I never even felt it hit me."

Cassidy found that her own body had tensed helplessly, as well. She was gripping the knife so hard that her nails were digging into her palm.

Interpreting her taut expression, Shad sat back onto his heels, the rabbit forgotten. "I know what you're thinking," he said. "You figure it was a fucked-up drug deal, right? Maybe even a shootout with the cops?"

Cassidy had to glance away, her face flushed with embarrassment for how transparent she had been. But Shad went on as if he had been discussing something as neutral as the weather.

"Yeah, it was a fuckup all right," he said flatly. "I was working undercover with a couple of hotdog Feds from DEA. One of the dealers made me." Shad formed the crude representation of a gun with the fingers of one hand and, pointing to his temple, simulated squeezing the imaginary trigger. "Pow," he concluded softly.

Cassidy knew that she was gaping dumbly at him, but she was simply too astounded to speak, even had she known what to say. Shad had been a *cop*? Nothing she could have learned about him would have surprised her more. As she studied him, she tried to imagine the man even existing in the real world, much less existing in such a role. But her imagination failed her.

When Shad continued, his voice was level and conversational. "After the first time I went back," he said, "I used to fantasize about nailing the bastard who'd taken me out. But once I realized what had really happened to me—how I really existed back there—things like revenge seemed pretty inconsequential." Shad toyed with the bloodied knife for a moment, as if ruminating over something he had not thought of in a long time. Then he shot Cassidy a disarmingly wry smile, an expression that utterly transformed his face. "Something about having the whole back of your head blown off," he said, "tends to alter your perspective about things like that."

Still shocked, Cassidy fumbled clumsily for an intelligent response. "You—you said that after you went back the first time," she stammered, "and realized what had happened to you, that you didn't try it again for two years?"

Shad nodded. "Yeah, more or less."

Cassidy didn't have to ask him why he hadn't; what she couldn't understand is why he ever did go back again. "But you did go back again?" she asked him uncertainly, studying the subtle play of emotion across that honey-brown face.

Shad shrugged. "A couple of times." Almost as if it were an afterthought, he added, "My wife—ex-wife now—had been six months' pregnant when I was shot. I guess maybe I thought I'd at least get to see my kid . . ." His voice trailed off, but to Cassidy's amazement there was no trace of acrimony in his tone as he concluded by surmising, "Guess I should have figured out that by then it was probably too hard for her even to come to see me by herself anymore, much less bring a baby." Under the circumstances, his equanimity seemed astonishing. "I'm just glad she found someone else, you know?"

Fighting a wave of both incredulity and sympathy, Cassidy blurted out, "How long has it been since you last went back there?"

"A long time," Shad said simply. "Mostly I stopped going because it was too painful." He quickly spread his hands, the gesture explanatory. "Not just seeing what I'd become, but knowing how much it must hurt my wife, my folks." He made another small motion, vague yet evocative. "And I stopped partly because I was afraid that sometime I might go back and then not be able to get away again—that I might get trapped there in that useless lump of meat."

As difficult as it was for her to discuss the subject, Cassidy couldn't help but ask the next question. "How do you know," she said, "that they won't—that you won't be . . . ?"

"Unplugged?" Shad suggested. He laughed then, a real laugh, a soft sound entirely free of bitterness. "Lawyers," he said, and laughed again at Cassidy's bewildered expression. "The guy who shot me is doing an open-ended stint at one of our finer federal facilities for attempted murder. If they unplugged me, they could drop the 'attempted' part, and the bastard would fry." Shad actually smiled again, his face suddenly becoming as guilelessly happy as a child's. "Believe me, he's got a regular tag team of

ACLU humps filing enough motions to keep me safely hooked up until I wither away from old age."

Cassidy could only stare speechlessly at Shad. He calmly started wiping the bloody blade of his knife on the dry leafy humus to clean it. The things that he had just told her were incredible enough; that he could relay them in such a dispassionate and ironic manner only made their impact all the more disabling to Cassidy. Worst of all, she could see that in her own smug self-righteousness, she had not only misjudged him, she had gravely wronged him. What she had taken for self-indulgence and cynicism had blinded her to the true strength that lay beneath that facile exterior. For the first time, she looked at Shad and saw him for what he actually was: a man who had lost everything and yet had somehow given himself a reason to go on. And Cassidy thought that she was finally just beginning to get the barest glimpse of what that reason might be.

"You finished?" Shad asked, glancing sideways at her. With a single deft movement of his hand, he gathered up the two butchered rabbits by the truncated stumps of their hind legs and then smoothly stood.

Cassidy had to fumble to catch up with him, hastily wiping off her knife and grappling for her rabbits. When she looked up at him, she saw that Shad had his free hand extended to her, and for one confusing moment she thought that he meant to help her to her feet. Then she realized that he was just waiting for her to hand him back his knife.

As she stood, Cassidy felt the long muscles in her thighs and calves cramp in protest. While she adjusted her grip on the rabbits, Shad tucked both knives back into the waistband of his pants. But when Cassidy looked at him again, she saw that he was simply standing there, watching her.

Cassidy hesitated a moment, then said, "He wants to try again."

"I know," Shad said.

"He wants to use the drug that you used."

"I know," Shad repeated.

She paused briefly again. "You aren't going to try to stop him?"

Shad cocked his head, one of his arched brows quirking. "Are you?" He started forward, the rabbits swinging in his hand as he stepped past Cassidy. "He knows what he has to do."

The remark, delivered so calmly, and literally in passing, defined the black man in a way Cassidy would not have thought possible even a half hour earlier. There might have been many reasons for the odd kinship that Cassidy had recognized developing between the warden and Shad, but she was certain then what at least one of those reasons was. And it was at the crux of why Shad was helping them. The warden had something that Shad needed, something that drew the soft-spoken black man to him like a moth to a flame. The warden had exhibited tremendous courage and altruism. And Shad wanted, Shad *needed*, to believe in something again. Among the tangled skein of the warden's relationship with Cassidy, he had found the crucial elements of what it took to sustain belief.

Cassidy had followed Shad through the woods in silence for almost five minutes before she suddenly spoke. "Books," she said.

Shad not only looked back at her, he actually stopped dead in his tracks to do so. The glossy mane of his crimped black hair framed a face askew with puzzlement. "What?"

"You wanted to know what I missed most about the real world," she said with a small shrug. "Books: That's what I miss the most."

Shad's features softened, an entirely uncalculated change of expression that gave his face an indulgently amused cast. "Well," he said, starting forward again, "if you ever get back, you can write a book of your own. And I can tell you one thing: It'd sure be the damnedest book anyone's ever read."

The warden and Kevin were alone at their camp when Cassidy returned. The two men appeared to be lingering over the last of their late breakfast coffee; yet even though they were only sitting a few feet apart, there was an odd and unfamiliar tension to their postures that made Cassidy suspect she had just interrupted some kind of disagreement. Both looked up at her in interest as she approached, but Cassidy sensed a certain element of relief.

The warden greeted her with his usual warmth, but she couldn't conceal her concern. "Are you feeling all right?" she asked him.

"A little sleepy," he said easily.

Kevin had been eyeing the rabbits she was carrying. "Were you out hunting?" he asked.

"I went with Shad out to his trapline," Cassidy explained, casually dropping the rabbits onto one of the canvas wraps from their supplies. She glanced around the immediate area. Dragonfly stood a few dozen yards away, engrossed in a large pile of freshly cut brush. "Where're Click and Rowena?" she asked.

Cassidy had not missed the way the warden's expression had changed when she had mentioned Shad; but he had adroitly concealed his surprise. "Rowena wanted to go to the creek to get fresh water," he said, still studying Cassidy somewhat expectantly. "And Click said he wanted to bathe, so he offered to go along with her."

Cassidy rummaged around looking for her coffee mug, and then she calmly bent over the nearly empty coffeepot and poured herself half a cup of the dark brew.

A somewhat awkward lag occurred in the conversation then. Surreptitiously watching the warden and Kevin over the rim of her mug, Cassidy was certain that her initial impression had been correct. They had been arguing about something before she had come back. And she didn't have to guess to know what the disagreement had been about. Although Kevin's loyalty to the warden was absolute, his obedience had already been proven a more flexible concept. Cassidy couldn't fault Kevin for his concern. She just hoped that his opposition to what the warden was determined to attempt hadn't caused any irreparable strain to the mutual trust and affection that bound the two men.

As she sat silently sipping her coffee, Cassidy was perfectly aware of the warden's covert glances in her direction. Fresh from his dispute with Kevin, the young man was probably resigning himself to the prospect of another pitched battle with Cassidy over his plans to continue using Shad's drugs. His stolid anticipation of what he must have considered to be an inevitable confrontation filled Cassidy with so much sympathy that she almost made an outright declaration of her newfound understanding of what he had set himself to do. But she wasn't quite ready yet for that kind of candor, especially in front of Kevin.

As she sat there watching the warden watch her, Cassidy allowed herself the indulgence of appreciating exactly how extraordinary a man he truly was. And she made herself a promise then that sometime later, when she had the opportunity, she would tell the warden just how much his belief and determination meant to her.

Kevin got to his feet, drawing Cassidy from her introspection. Wordlessly, and with a most atypical lassitude, the boy carried his dishes over to the wash pot. The sudden surge of sympathy she felt for Kevin succeeded in making Cassidy feel guilty. And while she wasn't about to delude him with any meaningless reassurances regarding his very legitimate concern for his warden, she also realized that there was something she could do to make Kevin's anxiety more bearable.

"Have you got time to help me with something, Kev?" she asked casually.

With characteristic promptness and affability, Kevin looked up from rinsing his plate and immediately offered, "Sure," even before he had any idea what she wanted of him.

Cassidy lowered his mug. "My mare really looks like hell," she said, exaggerating a bit for effect. "In fact, she doesn't even look good enough to be pulling some Villager's plow right now, much less to be a Horseman's horse." That elicited the desired smile from Kevin. "What I'd like to do," she continued, "is give her a really good working over, from forelock to hooves. And I sure could use some help."

There was nothing forced or feigned in Kevin's eager response. "Sure, Cassidy," he said, "I'd be glad to help."

Studiously ignoring the appreciative glance that the warden shot her, Cassidy got to her feet. "Well, let's get at it then," she said, "or we may not get finished before dark."

The warden's face contorted in a paroxysm of coughing, the involuntary jerking of his hands nearly overturning the water pipe, which rested on the ground in the small space formed by the juncture of his crossed legs. "I'm sorry," he wheezed, tears streaming from his reddened eyes as he gasped to get his breath. "I don't think I've quite gotten the hang of this yet!"

Seated beside him in front of the small campfire, Shad merely steadied the bowl of the hookah until the warden was able to get himself under control again. "That's okay," Shad said. "Just don't try to take such a big hit your first time out."

Cassidy sat a few feet away, on the other side of the warden. She leaned forward slightly and hugged her tented legs, her chin nearly resting on her knees. Only the warden, she thought wryly, would find it necessary to apologize for not knowing how to smoke dope. Sitting there in silence, she watched the play of firelight over both his and Shad's faces, the contrast between the light and the night painting the two of them in sharp relief. It had been a hot and humid day, and the evening air was still warm and muggy. Shad's fire was partially burned down, but the warmth that still radiated from it was something less than welcome.

The warden had not objected when Shad had said they would wait until after nightfall to begin. First of all, Shad had said, he wanted to wait twenty-four hours to be sure the other drug was out of the warden's system. And the other thing was that he hoped it would be a little cooler after sundown.

The warden had, however, put up a mild protest when he found he was going to have to smoke the drug. He had been plainly nonplussed by the hookah. "You want me to inhale the smoke?" he had asked reluctantly. "Why can't I just eat this substance?"

But Shad had shaken his head. "That's not the way this shit works," he'd explained. "You've got to smoke it."

The pipe's small reservoir had been filled with something that resembled lumpy black lint. Shad had patiently demonstrated the workings of the hookah and then prompted the warden to try it. With all of the feckless zeal of the uninitiated, the warden had immediately tried to draw in a huge breath of the filtered smoke, with the predictable results. It took several minutes for normal color to return to his face and for his hacking spasms to subside. Considerably chastened, the warden heeded Shad's counsel as he took another, far more cautious pull off the pipe's mouthpiece.

Cassidy realized that her lack of opposition to his continued experimentation with Shad's drugs had kept the warden noticeably perplexed all day. But Cassidy had moved through the main part of the day in something of a perplexed state herself. The unexpected gestalt she had experienced that morning in the woods with Shad had paradoxically filled Cassidy with both a calm resignation and a strong feeling of restlessness. Once she had accepted the ineffable logic of what the warden had set out to accomplish, she found herself anxious if not eager to just get on with it. She could only imagine that the warden had spent the long sultry day suffering from the same sense of edgy anticipation. And his bafflement over the argument that they had never had probably had only exacerbated his uneasiness.

When his small and shallow inhalation off the pipe did not bring the same disastrous results, the warden took several more almost comically delicate pulls of smoke off the stem of the hookah's tubing. An aroma, sweet and yet biting, like the scent of scorched flowers, began to permeate the humid air around the little campfire. The warden's face looked faintly flushed and his eyes were still watering slightly, but Cassidy wasn't sure if that was still an aftereffect of his near-choking experience, or if it was in response to the drug itself. But when the warden spoke, she started to suspect that the changes were being caused by whatever he was smoking.

"This isn't too bad," he announced. His voice was slow and deliberately distinct, as if he were purposely trying not to slur his words. He gave Cassidy a loopy little salute with the pipe's mouthpiece. "Not bad," he repeated gravely.

The look that Shad threw Cassidy across the fire confirmed her supposition. The black man made a swift, surprisingly evocative gesture with one hand, his fingers waggling like the sweep of imaginary wings. Cassidy easily translated: The warden was starting to fly.

With all of the solemn precision of a serious drunk measuring out his next drink, the warden slowly and methodically took another pull from the pipe. Caught between fascination and dismay, Cassidy watched the busy burble of the air bubbles in the water chamber as he drew the smoke deeply into his lungs. It certainly hadn't taken him long to master the mechanics of smoking dope, she thought ruefully.

The odor of the burning drug was becoming cloying, almost sickeningly sweet the way it hung in the calm and humid night air. Cassidy wondered if she would be affected by breathing it in secondhand. She glanced over at Shad, but even though he was sitting there as motionless as a stump, he looked entirely sober. And when he noticed Cassidy's look of uncertainty, he gave her a small "okay" sign with joined thumb and forefinger.

Shifting slightly on the bare earth in front of the firepit, Cassidy tried to make herself more comfortable. She was still sticky with perspiration from the day's efforts. She found the sweetish smoke irritating, but her uneasiness had far less to do with her physical discomfort than it did with her anxiety about what the warden was attempting to do. There had once been a time, she realized without pride, when she wouldn't have had a second thought about trading on the knowledge, willingness, and allegiance of anyone necessary to discover a way to return to the Slow World. And yet once fate had finally handed her that opportunity, she would have passed on it eagerly, had the choice still been hers alone.

The warden made a small sound, drawing Cassidy out of her reverie. There was an alarmingly unfocused look on that serenely handsome young face. Staring with a fixed sort of bliss at the pipestem that he held loosely in his hand, the warden slowly and deliberately took another deep draw of smoke. Then his arm dropped back limply into his lap, the mouthpiece slipping from his unfurling fingers.

Cassidy felt a strong compulsion to lean forward and lift the water pipe out of the warden's lap, out of his reach. But she caught Shad's eye again and resisted the impulse. *He's all right,* she told herself, wanting desperately to believe it. She realized that to Shad, the warden's reaction was neither unfamiliar nor alarming. It was just that she was not accustomed to seeing anyone, much less someone for which she cared so much, in that condition.

Something disturbed the roosting birds in the cypress trees behind them, and there was a burst of sleepy chittering. Probably an owl, Cassidy thought, starting out on its nightly hunt. She felt her damp hair pull stickily against the back of her neck as she craned her head to look. But the unrest in the blackness of the branches overhead had already subsided, and she could see nothing amiss.

The warden's seated posture had slumped further, his chin nearly touching his chest. Cassidy was just thinking that he looked very much like a drowsy little boy who had stayed up way past his bedtime, when a faint waver, the slightest glimmer of distortion, quivered through his image.

And then, right before Cassidy's stunned and uncomprehending eyes, the warden of Horses simply vanished.

Chapter 22 ◀▥

For one long moment Cassidy was simply too astounded to do anything more than just sit there and stare at the neatly collapsed little pile of empty clothing that marked the place where the warden had been. Like the shed skin of a snake or the fragile chrysalis of a butterfly, the suddenly abandoned garments were all that remained of the man who had been wearing them. Then Cassidy lurched to her feet and spun toward Shad.

"What the hell happened to him?" she demanded. "Where did he go?"

Certainly no less astonished, but somewhat more composed, Shad leaned forward and gingerly poked at the discarded clothing. The tubing from the hookah was visible beneath the limp sleeve of the shirt, the mouthpiece peeking out like the snout of a small curious animal.

"I don't know," Shad admitted, looking up. He glanced around the periphery of the firepit, from the threshold of his shelter to the border of the darkness beyond the firelight. His head was cocked in an oddly expectant manner, much as if he anticipated finding the warden was just playing some sort of joke on them both.

Dropping down onto her knees before the pile of clothes, Cassidy actually had to touch the garments to convince herself that what she was seeing was real. The warden was undeniably gone. Down on the same level as Shad then, she glared directly into his face. "It was your damned drug!" she accused. "Did this ever happen to *you*?"

Even as the words left her mouth, Cassidy realized how inane her question was. To his considerable credit, Shad managed not to raise his voice when he responded. "How should I know?" he pointed out, calmly and needlessly. "I could hardly watch myself disappear, could I?"

For a few moments the two of them just stared at each other, until their mutual amazement and dismay gave way to an unwilling comprehension. Then Cassidy whispered hoarsely, "He—he *went back*, didn't he?"

Before Shad could reply, they were interrupted by the arrival of Click, Rowena, and Kevin. Cassidy realized that even if none of them had seen what had happened, her raised voice would have been enough to alert them to trouble, and past experience would have been enough to bring them running. She also realized, only belatedly, that the way she and Shad were kneeling confronting each other over the warden's pile of clothing, they must have looked like two combative tomcats.

"What happened?" Rowena asked breathlessly, her expression more one of confusion than alarm as she took in the little tableau in front of the firepit.

But Kevin's plaintive query was only seconds behind Rowena's. "Where's the warden?" the blond boy asked, looking around the site of the toppled cypress as if his friend and mentor certainly couldn't have gotten very far yet. "Where did he go?"

Rapidly assessing the situation, Click had seen fit to interpose himself between Cassidy and Shad. His knee almost clipped her chin as he bent down, offering Cassidy a hand. "Are you all right?" he asked with his usual calm.

Despite the gravity of the situation, Cassidy felt a twinge of embarrassment when she realized that Click had assumed she and Shad had been on the verge of coming to blows. Given their past exchanges, it was a reasonable assumption, so Cassidy couldn't fault Click for his concern. She allowed him to assist her to her feet. Then she took a step back from both men and said, "We're fine, but the warden's disappeared."

"What do you mean, *disappeared*?" Kevin exclaimed. Once Cassidy had stood, the pile of clothing became clearly visible. "Where would he go without his clothes?"

Shad also got to his feet, reflexively glancing around the small arc of light thrown by the fire. "I don't know," he said, gently nudging the exposed portion of the water pipe with the toe of one moccasin. "But if I had to venture a guess, I'd say he went back."

"Back where?" Kevin demanded, his voice steadily rising in both volume and pitch.

But Click silenced Kevin by holding up one hand, a warding gesture that was meant more to calm the boy than to restrain him. "Start from the beginning," he told Shad and Cassidy, "and tell us exactly what happened here."

Cassidy exchanged a swift glance with the black man. "All three of us were just sitting here around the fire," she said. "The warden was using the water pipe to inhale the smoke from the drug Shad had given him." She hesitated, debating how much detail about the drug's effect was necessary. "It took a little while for it to have much effect on him, but then he started to get real ... relaxed. He was just sitting there, sort of slumping and looking real drowsy, when all of a sudden—" Cassidy broke off, shrugging helplessly. She found herself directly addressing Kevin, as if to somehow apologize to him. "All of a sudden he just *vanished*."

"Yeah," Shad echoed, "he went from real mellow to just *gone*. All that was left behind was the pipe and his clothes."

"And you think that he returned to the Slow World?" Click asked, his neutral tone betraying neither skepticism nor agreement.

Then it was Shad's turn to shrug. "I don't know where the hell else he could have gone," he said.

It wasn't that Rowena was any less concerned about what had happened to the warden, but sometimes the brunette had a tendency to fixate on the quirkier aspects of a situation. She bent to inspect the discarded clothing, her fingers lightly touching the hem of the crumpled shirt. "But why would he go back without his clothes?" she asked.

Despite the rational tone of the conversation, Kevin's odd-colored eyes had grown even wider with dismay. "What if he's *dead*?"

"He's not dead, Kevin!" Cassidy asserted immediately, startling the young man with her vehemence.

"If he were dead," Click pointed out, "we'd have his body, Kevin. No, I think that at least for the time being, we'll have to assume that Shad and Cassidy are right, and that the warden has somehow returned to the other world."

Rowena looked up from her study of the abandoned clothing. "I still don't understand why his clothes didn't go with him then," she said. "When we came here, we all had clothes, right?"

Cassidy cocked her head, suddenly struck by something Rowena had said. "Yeah," she replied, "we had clothes—but they were *our* clothes, the ones we'd been wearing in the real world." She looked down pensively at the warden's clothing. "All of this stuff he was wearing was made here, in this world. Maybe it *couldn't* go back. Maybe nothing created in this world can."

Comprehension altered Rowena's expression, erasing the incipient frown lines around her full mouth. "Right," she agreed, "and if he's really gone back into Andy, then Andy's got his own clothes."

Kevin was still shifting uneasily, glancing from Cassidy's face to the place before the firepit where the warden had last been seated. "But what about *him*?" he said. "What about his body?" Kevin was obviously distressed by the thought of the warden not only disappearing, but also ceasing to exist. "How can he just not . . . be here any more?"

Cassidy reached out and gently touched the boy's arm. "How long have you been here, Kev?" she asked.

Puzzled, Kevin looked down at her hand where it rested on his bare upper arm. "I don't know," he said.

"A year, maybe two?" she suggested. At his bewildered shrug, Cassidy continued, "I know that I've only been here a couple of months." Using her free hand, she tapped her own chest, just above her breasts. "So where was this body three months ago? For that matter, where was it the split second before I came here?"

Kevin still looked baffled, so Click expanded on Cassidy's point. "Just as no one has a body in this world until they actually come here, Kevin, if the warden has truly gone back to his other existence in the Slow World, then he would no longer have a body here."

Cassidy squeezed Kevin's arm until his eyes raised to meet hers. "He's *not* dead, Kevin," she repeated. "He's just gone."

Kevin still looked far from convinced or comforted, but before Cassidy could say anything more, Rowena spoke up again. She spoke directly to Shad, and on her rounded face was a particular expression that Cassidy had long since come to recognize.

"You remember your friend, Henry?" she asked the black man.

Shad just nodded, his expression both puzzled and mildly curious about where Rowena was leading.

"That night he disappeared," Rowena went on. "Could he have *literally* disappeared—like the warden just did?"

Recognition and doubt chased each other across Shad's expressive face. "You mean could he have gone back?" he asked her a bit skeptically.

But Rowena had already turned to Cassidy. "Remember that guy I told you about from when I was in Green Lake—Jeff?" she asked, mounting excitement creeping into her voice.

Cassidy was confused. "You mean the guy you thought they'd gotten rid of because he was a troublemaker?"

Rowena's eyes were shining. "What if nobody got rid of Jeff?" she said. "What if he just went back?" She looked back to Shad, earnest in her newfound conviction. "The monsters—you said you didn't see bogeys any more once Henry was gone, right? Well, what if that was because he went back to the real world?"

Cassidy was tracking Rowena then, but she was considerably more cautious in her enthusiasm for embracing the brunette's theory. "You think Jeff and Henry went back to the Slow World?"

"Why not? It would explain a lot, wouldn't it?"

But Shad also remained dubious. "But how did they do it?" he asked, frowning.

"Henry used drugs," Rowena pointed out.

"Yeah," Shad said, "but even when he did, he never was even able to see back into the real world, much less go there."

"Unless he didn't tell you he did," Rowena pointed out.

Shad's frown only deepened. But before he and Rowena could wrangle over his brief relationship with Henry, Cassidy intervened.

"Maybe Henry and Jeff didn't *do* anything," she said. "Maybe they didn't have to. Maybe neither of them was really supposed to have come here in the first place."

Too filled with anxiety to continue listening to their esoterical debate, Kevin blurted out, "But what are we going to *do*? We have to find him!"

"Once the effects of the drug wear off," Shad said, "he might just come back on his own."

Personally, Cassidy thought that was a rather slim hope, especially considering that the body which had inhaled that drug had become nonexistent. But it would have been cruel to have pointed that out, and besides, crazier things had happened there. But Kevin seemed equally unconvinced.

"What if he *doesn't*?" the blond boy persisted.

Cassidy reached up with her free hand and took hold of Kevin's other arm, looking steadily into those vulnerably wide eyes. "Then I'll go after him, Kev," she declared. "I'll go back to the Slow World myself and get him back."

Shad and Click both gave Cassidy a sidelong look, but she deliberately ignored them, concentrating instead on assuring Kevin that she was entirely sincere. That wasn't much of a stretch for her, because Cassidy was utterly serious; she no longer had any choice. Her life might very well be in imminent danger in the real world. Without the warden's report, she would have no way of knowing for certain, and therefore no choice but to try to return herself.

Into the depths of that gloomy rumination, Click spoke, so softly that Cassidy almost missed his first words. "How long will it take for the effects of this drug to dissipate?" he asked Shad.

Shad spread his hands. "It depends," he admitted. "It's not easy to quantitate something you inhale like that."

"An hour? A day?"

"A few hours, maybe. A day would really be the outside limit."

The Tinker took them all in with a long, solemn look. "Then I would suggest that the best thing we can do, as unsatisfying as it may seem, would be to just wait and see if the warden returns on his own."

Cassidy couldn't look Kevin in the eye then, because she didn't want him to see how little credence she gave to that hope. But she also knew that, at least for the moment, Click was right. All they could do was wait.

One thing that the world had taught Cassidy was that time was relative. And she was certain that she had never spent a longer night than the one that followed the warden's disappearance.

Another thing that had disappeared from the valley that night was the demarcation between the two camps. Cassidy didn't even consider returning to their own campsite, and when she settled down again in front of Shad's firepit to wait, Rowena moved in companionably beside her. Kevin, of course, could not be moved. And for some reason, no one wanted to pick up or move the warden's clothing. It was almost as if to alter that last trace of his presence among them would have been to somehow deny his very existence. So Kevin hunkered down right beside the little pile of clothes and sat there, his arms folded across his lap, his young face blank with grief.

Shad wordlessly brought them blankets from inside his shelter. For a time he sat with them; but eventually, as the night wore on, he went back into the dugout and stayed.

Rowena remained awake with Cassidy for as long as she could, but long before Shad had moved back inside, the brunette was leaning against Cassidy's shoulder, softly snoring. For a long time Cassidy couldn't tell if Kevin was awake or asleep, his face was so expressionless. But at length the young man's weary body betrayed him and she saw him slumping forward, his chin bobbing slightly with each breath.

Cassidy saw very little of Click throughout the night, but that was not to say she wasn't aware of his presence. The Tinker kept his usual patrol, silently prowling the darkened valley and the slopes around it, returning from time to time to check on them from a small distance.

Although she felt heavily weighted by fatigue, Cassidy was unable to sleep. The muggy night was warm enough that the blankets had been unnecessary, but she appreciated Shad's thoughtfulness, and their faint smoky smell proved strangely soothing as the endless hours passed. After Rowena and Kevin had fallen asleep, and Shad had finally retired to his own bed, Cassidy felt utterly alone there by the fire. Her thoughts drifted back to another humid summer night not that long ago, when she had sat sleeplessly in the darkness of the front room of the warden's big brick house, also waiting for his return. Then she had been discouraged and resigned to moving on, waiting only to confront him about whatever knowledge he might have that would help her in her search. Ironically enough, that was also the night Cassidy had given up hope that the way back to the Slow World had anything to do with the warden of Horses.

Brushing absently at a mosquito that hovered, whining thinly, around her forehead, Cassidy gave a small grim smile at the unexpected twists fate had taken since that night. Not only had the warden proved to be her link with the Slow World; unless all of their assumptions were in error, he also ultimately had turned out to be the one who had actually returned to it. And so once again Cassidy was being forced to make a decision about moving on, with the real choice already out of her hands. She would have given anything to have been able to see the warden one last time first.

He still might come back, she tried to tell herself; but it was a flimsy and contrived hope, without substance enough to stand up to the ruddy light of dawn. If the warden had reached the real world, then he was caught there, trapped in Andy Greene's body in much the same way as Cathy Delaney initially had found herself trapped in the familiar body of a woman who had called herself Cassidy because she hadn't even known her own name.

You know he's not coming back, her little inner voice told her ruthlessly. *Not unless you go back and get him.*

The first faint light of morning had barely penetrated the thick gray clouds when Shad reemerged from his shelter. The day was heavily overcast, the promise of rain in the near-oppressive humidity, and even the birds' early activity seemed oddly muted.

At some point during the night, Kevin had finally succumbed to gravity. He still lay sleeping across the empty husks of the warden's clothes. Rowena had similarly slid down into a more comfortable position hours earlier, and Cassidy had used their common blanket to cover her slumbering friend. Neither Kevin nor Rowena stirred as Shad padded soundlessly around the periphery of the dead campfire. As Cassidy looked up at him, she felt the muscles in her neck and back cramp in protest.

Shad proffered a tin cup and she automatically reached for it. "You hungry?" he asked quietly.

Cassidy shook her head. She took a sip from the cup, happy to find that it contained only water. She was thirsty enough to drain it in a couple of gulps. When she set the cup aside and began to gather herself to rise, Shad extended his hand. His slender fingers were warm, dry, and surprisingly strong, and Cassidy had the feeling that he could have easily lifted her right to her feet even if she had been nothing but dead weight.

Standing beside him, Cassidy felt a small riot of aches and pains shoot up and down her legs and spine. No matter how mild the weather had been, sitting in front of the fire all night had hardly done wonders for her joints and tendons.

Shad gave her a sympathetic look. "Better stretch your legs," he suggested.

Cassidy glanced at Rowena and Kevin, two blanket-covered mounds still sprawled around the firepit. Then she looked back hesitantly at Shad.

Interpreting her concern, he said, "Go on. I'll stay here until you get back."

Grateful that he realized she didn't want to have either of her friends wake up and find both her and Shad gone, Cassidy began to walk away from the shelter. At the rear of the toppled cypress, the gnarled mass of weathered and broken roots thrust up like black tentacles against the dull gray of the early-dawn sky. She was so stiff from sitting that she had to hobble the first few yards. But by the time she had rounded the eroded mound of earth that had been heaved up by the giant tree's fall, she began to limber up again.

Despite the humidity, there was no dew. Just another harbinger of rain, Cassidy thought, as she found a secluded spot to relieve herself. As she came back along the floor of the valley, she looked back toward their campsite. The gray mare still stood in her usual bedding spot, her body a large shadow in the murkiness of the half-light. Cassidy was surprised to see that there was already a sizable pile of freshly cut fodder in front of the horse, evidence of Click's industry in those early hours.

Coming back around the roots of the fallen cypress, Cassidy hesitated. She didn't want to make enough noise to wake up Kevin and Rowena, but on the other hand, she also didn't want to surprise Shad with his pants down. Circumstance and shared memory had forged a totally unexpected friendship between herself and the young black man, but one of the memories they shared was that of a common sensibility from the real world. She wouldn't have felt comfortable violating that sensibility, even if it had no strong counterpart in that world.

When Cassidy reached the front of Shad's shelter, he was merely crouched in front of the firepit, slowly and patiently rekindling his fire, and attempting not to awaken Kevin or Rowena in the process. Cassidy waited for him to finish feeding broken branches onto the little blaze he had ignited. When he stood again, she caught his eye and he turned to her with a mildly quizzical look on his face.

"You know he's not coming back again," Cassidy said, her voice low and nearly without inflection.

Shad's dark eyes narrowed slightly. His expression suggested he was waiting for her to make her point. "I wouldn't hold my breath," he said.

Cassidy looked steadily at him, her gaze unblinking. "I want to use the drug he took," she said. "I have to go after him."

Cassidy's declaration hardly came as a surprise to Shad, and he didn't entertain any illusions about dissuading her. She hadn't expected him to; in fact, she would have been hard-pressed to have come up with any reason why he might even want to try. He just said, "Tonight."

Cassidy had actually opened her mouth to object, but before she could say a word, Shad had one hand held up in front of her face. "First," he said, "I've got to gather some more of that shit. He used up the last that I had. And besides," he added, "the night is better."

Cassidy threw a morose glance at the gloomy, pewter-gray sky. "It'll probably be raining by tonight," she said.

Shad merely shrugged. "I'll let you sit inside," he said wryly. Then acknowledging the restlessness and frustration that hung about Cassidy, as palpable as the thick air of the coming storm, he offered, "As soon as these two wake up, you can come along with me if you want. We'll go on a little fungus-hunting expedition."

Cassidy's stance and expression softened slightly in unwilling concession. She watched curiously as Shad wormed one hand into the hip pocket of his tight trousers and then held out his closed hand to her.

"Here," he said, "I've got a little something for you."

She reached out tentatively then with an open palm, half expecting with a disorienting rush of déjà vu that he was about to present her with a metal key. But the small metal object Shad dropped into her hand was a silver medal. Her eyes gone wide with wonder, Cassidy slipped her fingers through the loop of fine chain and held it up to study it further. She recognized it as the silver St. Christopher's medal that she and Rowena had seen in his shelter the first night they had come to his valley, when the two of them had moved the insensate young man inside and onto his bed.

"It's beautiful," she said. Her eyes suddenly lifted from the silver disc to Shad's face. "But where . . . ?"

"It's just something Henry found once," Shad said, cutting her off with a negligent wave of his hand. "Think of it as a good luck charm," he added, "although it obviously wasn't lucky for whoever lost it."

Cassidy looked up from the medal again. "You know about the found things then," she said.

"Sure," Shad replied with another vaguely dismissive wave of his hand. "It's all crap that people've lost in the real world. I don't know how the hell it ends up here, but I know there're people like Henry who seem to have a knack for finding it."

Cassidy quickly slipped the silver chain over her head and dropped the medal down inside the collar of her shirt, where her last talisman, the Ford key Click had given her beside the Long River, had once rested. "Thanks," she said sincerely.

But Shad just turned back toward his threshold. "Don't bother to thank me yet," he pointed out. "You may not be going anywhere."

But Cassidy found his blunt cynicism considerably less convincing than it would have sounded only a day earlier. "You know who St. Christopher was, don't you?" she said to Shad's back. She had the satisfaction of seeing him come to a halt before she continued, "He's supposed to be the patron saint of travelers."

Shad was muttering something about a patron saint for idiots as Cassidy followed him into the shelter to start preparations for breakfast.

* * *

On Dragonfly's back again, Cassidy felt both comforted and oddly energized. The frustrating languor of the long and anxious wait for the day to pass had been pressing down upon her like the rising humidity and dropping barometric pressure of the coming storm. Seeking a temporary escape, by midafternoon she had finally Called the gray mare and slipped off over the ridge toward the deer path that Click had showed her. Mounted on the horse and riding at a steady walk down the narrow trail, Cassidy had at last found a brief respite from the unbearable wait for nightfall.

Easily synchronizing the shifting of her body to the movement of the big horse's swaying walk, Cassidy reveled in the feel of the broad sleek barrel beneath her. Even the stickiness of the mare's light sweat, a response to the weather and certainly not to the mild exercise, was a pleasant bond between them as the moisture soaked the inseams of Cassidy's trousers. There along the deer path, it was almost possible to forget about everything else but the beauty of the forest and the reassuring familiarity of the horse's warm bulk between her knees.

It had fleetingly occurred to Cassidy that going off alone like that might not be the most sensible thing to do. But then she had been struck by the ironic insignificance of all of her previous precautions. What did she really have to be afraid of? Woodsmen? Monsters? She was on the verge of attempting to make her way back across an entire plane of time, to force her consciousness back into a vessel that might well prove to be too fragile to contain it. What could there possibly be there in that cypress forest on the edge of the Great Swamp that could be of any greater danger to her than that?

When the mare slowed her pace, Cassidy was disappointed to find that they were already at the end of the main portion of the trail. Beyond that point, the deer path subdivided into numerous side branches, most of which quickly became too overgrown and rutted to be negotiated by a rider on a horse. She allowed the mare to continue along the winding course, but within a few dozen yards the path finally disappeared into the brush and saplings.

Dragonfly came to a halt, blowing loudly through her nostrils. For a few moments Cassidy just sat there, feeling the heat of the afternoon soak through her shirt even as the heat of the mare's body soaked through her pants. It was oddly silent in that stretch of woods. Cassidy had seen only a few birds during the entire ride, and there had been no fresh signs of deer along the path. Then again, she thought as she slipped down off the horse's back, birds usually holed up before a storm. She glanced around at the vivid green of the thick vegetation, the myriad of leaves hanging limply in the utterly calm air. And as for the deer, well, considering what had happened out on the point by the marsh just a couple of days earlier, Cassidy was not surprised that the animals seemed to have fled the area.

She walked a few yards through the brush, just far enough to find a convenient seat on the upthrust brow of a large slab of rock. As she sat down, she looked back at the mare, amused to see that the horse quickly had fallen to cropping at the lush greenery. Idly plucking a leafy tip from an overhanging branch, Cassidy began to shred it, slowly and absently, her mind drifting.

It was only natural that she would think of the last time she had come that way along the deer path on the mare, on the ride she had taken with Click. The Tinker was one person that Cassidy had found consistently impossible to keep from her thoughts. Admitting to herself the depth and strength of her feelings for Click had in one way given her a certain measure of peace. And yet in another, far more insistent way, that admission was making it all the more painful and difficult for her to do what she knew she must. *You're in love with him,* her little voice said, and for once it got no argument from her. Cassidy was in love with him, but she was about to leave him forever.

Just as the time Cassidy had spent beside Shad's firepit the night before had seemed to lengthen to the point of infinity, the time she spent sitting there on that small prominence of rock in the near silence of the muggy forest seemed curiously open-ended, without parameters. The subtle rustling and occasional snort of the foraging horse were the only sounds that connected her with the mundane reality of time passing. And had it not been for the frequent necessity of taking a swat at some annoying insect, Cassidy might very well have appeared to have slipped into some trancelike state as she sat alone with her thoughts. She wasn't even sure how long she sat there. It must have been at least half an hour; it could have been several times that long. While she sat there, time—which had assumed such portent in her life of late—simply ceased to matter.

Before she had even heard anything to alert her, Cassidy noticed that the mare had lifted her head and pricked her ears. The horse seemed singularly unalarmed, however, and never even stopped chewing. Then Cassidy picked up the slight sounds of someone approaching along the trail, someone who moved with a natural grace but who was deliberately making just enough noise to herald his arrival, so that she would not be caught by surprise. As Cassidy watched, Click came into view, moving past the horse and giving her wide rump a gentle thump as he went.

Click stopped a few feet away from the rock where Cassidy had perched and spent a long moment giving her a candid looking over. "When no one knew where you'd gone to," he said then, "and your horse was missing, as well, I thought that I might find you here."

Although there was no hint of reproach in his tone, Cassidy felt a pang of conscience for any worry that she may have caused her friends. "I'm sorry," she said immediately. "I guess I shouldn't have gone off like that without telling anyone. I just wanted to be alone for a while."

Cassidy realized only belatedly how ungracious her last comment might have sounded, especially considering that Click had just hiked all that way out there in the humid heat to check on her. But before she could blurt out some further apology, Click gave an evocative shrug, his hands spread. Neither the gesture nor his expression suggested that her careless behavior had been of no importance; merely that it had been perfectly understandable under the circumstances. Taking another step closer, Click offered, "Sometimes solitude can be the best companion."

Studying him, Cassidy noticed that in the pervasive humidity even the relatively easy trek to the end of the deer path had raised a fine sheen of perspiration on Click's tanned skin. At his temples his hair was dampened, as well, causing it to curl in loose ringlets; and the fabric of his shirt was darkened at the neckline and armpits.

Cassidy became a little nonplussed when she realized that Click was standing there watching her watch him. Glancing down at her feet for a moment, she feigned a brief interest in the toes of her boots. She supposed that he had come out there to fetch her back; but she found herself reluctant to give up the illusion of peace that she had found there along the deer path. And when she looked back up and met his eyes again, she saw that Click's expression was calm and yet somehow expectant.

"Can I ask you something?" she said. Then, interpreting the sudden shift in expression on his face, she hastily elaborated, "I mean ask you to *do* something for me, not ask you *about* something."

The silvered tips of Click's mustache quirked as he closed that last step's worth of space which had remained between them. "I'm relieved to hear that," he told her, his umber eyes holding a precious glint of that old amusement. "As we've already discussed both sex and my ignominious past, I was trembling to think what else you might want to know about me."

As much as Cassidy appreciated the intent of Click's easy and affable manner with her, it caused her to hesitate a moment. During that pause, Click dropped down into a squat before her, so that they were essentially eye to eye. Reading her uneasiness, his expression gently sobered then. "You know that you can ask me anything, Cassidy," he said.

Forcing herself to continue, Cassidy cleared her throat and somehow managed to look at Click without actually meeting his eyes. "If something happens to me," she said in a small voice, "and I don't come back, would you take care of my mare for me?"

Click didn't insult her intelligence by denying the obvious or offering her some meaningless platitude. He would not give her the empty promise that nothing would happen to her. He merely nodded. "I would consider it an honor as well as a duty."

Cassidy tried not to look into those dark, unsettlingly astute eyes then, but just as she could not keep the words from leaving her mouth, she could not seem to keep from meeting that deeply compelling gaze. "I don't want to go back any more—you know that, don't you?" she blurted out.

Click made a soft shushing sound, lifting his hand to place his index finger lightly against her lower lip. "I know," he soothed.

But Cassidy had to keep on, talking right past his gentle attempt to silence her. "If it was just me," she said, "I'd be willing to let it go and just take my chances here." Her voice grew more breathless as the words tumbled out faster. "But he may be trapped there forever otherwise—trapped the way Andy is trapped. I have to—"

Since the application of his single digit had done nothing to halt Cassidy's anxious flow of words, Click then laid the tips of all four fingers across her mouth. "Shh," he said softly. "I know."

His face was so close to hers that Cassidy could see in detail each discrete hair that made up his mustache, from the glossy dark ones that spread from the center right below his nose, to the graying ones on either side that formed the silvery tips. All of them were coarser and straighter than the deep-brown hair on his head, which curled damply around his lean and weathered face. She stared at Click in momentary fascination, amazed afresh at what this man had come to mean to her in the span of just a few short weeks. Almost without volition, Cassidy found her hand reaching out for him then, the pad of her forefinger gently tracing the sweeping wing of one half of that graying mustache. Even as she felt the crisp texture of his hair pass beneath her fingertip, tears began to well up in her eyes, and her throat spasmed painfully. She dipped her head, evading his hand, evading his eyes.

"What—what if I don't even *remember* you?" she whispered hoarsely, the pain of that thought like a blow to her chest.

Both of Click's hands rose to frame her face then, the callused warmth of his palms lifting her head. He touched his mouth to hers, so briefly and tenderly that it could have been the kiss of a caring father or brother. But when he pulled back again, his eyes had narrowed, focusing on hers with a fiercesome intensity. "That will never happen," he told her. And his certainty left no room for her doubts.

When Click moved closer again, the movement was so slow and deliberate that Cassidy easily could have avoided his approaching mouth if that had been her desire. But her desire was for something else entirely. She leaned forward, meeting him more than halfway as her lips fastened on his. Only his arms closing around her kept her from sliding right off the rock. As they embraced, Cassidy felt the warm, damp solidity of his body against hers. And even in the torpor of that muggy afternoon, the heat of his mouth was shockingly distinct, his tongue like a flash of fire as it met her own.

Digging her trembling fingers into the soft leather of his worn vest, Cassidy clung to him, her breasts pressed to his chest. The kiss's clumsy passion caught and ignited. She greedily explored his mouth, probing the velvety softness of his palate and the slick clean edge of his teeth. Then she captured his tongue, coaxing it into her own mouth, sucking it gently but with an eagerness that promised much more.

Cassidy's heart was racing by the time they parted for air. Pulling back for a moment, Click's gaze swept over her face, his eyes gone dusky and dilated. His fingertips skimmed along her cheek and then dipped lower, lightly touching the skin of her throat.

Cassidy remembered the time during one of the warden's lapses, when she had reached for Andy and Click had still been touching him. For that fleeting second, it was as if the essence of who Click was had also become a part of her. Cassidy had that same feeling again; and she could make it happen. She leaned in closer, kissing the edge of his mustache. Then her mouth moved lower, tasting the salty dampness of his chin and neck. She tugged open the top buttons of his shirt, nibbling the hollow between his collarbones, scraping her tongue over the coarse hairs on his chest.

Click made a low sound and pulled back from her. Unwilling to relinquish him, his chest hairs had to be forcibly drawn from between her teeth. But Click was only trying to remove his shirt. As he jerked down the rest of the buttons and wriggled free of the sleeves, Cassidy's head moved in again. She caught one of his nipples between her lips and held it there, swabbing the soft skin with her tongue as the little bud became erect in her mouth.

Cassidy's hands measured the breadth of Click's bare shoulders, and her fingers stroked down the long lean line of his spine. Everywhere she touched him, his skin was warm, damp from perspiration, and incredibly evocative. She remembered the night he had stripped and bathed just a few feet away from her, and summoning up those images with his body actually beneath her hands filled Cassidy with a further flush of desire for him. She wanted to touch him everywhere, taste him everywhere, memorize his body forever.

Cassidy's mouth followed the line of dark hair down Click's belly until she reached the waistband of his trousers. But as her shaky fingers fumbled for the fastening there, Click groaned her name and gently pushed her back. Prepared to resist his intervention, Cassidy once again found that Click was only trying to be helpful. Dropping down onto the ground, he swiftly yanked off his boots, artlessly tossing them aside into the brush. Then, rather than remove his pants, he reached up and grasped the bottom of Cassidy's shirt and drew it off over her head.

Cassidy's excitement was far too advanced to be easily derailed, but the sudden glint of amusement in Click's dark eyes did give her a moment's pause. She was not very generously endowed, but it wasn't as if he had never seen her breasts before. Her brows rose quizzically until Click's hand reached out and hooked the delicate silver chain that hung from her neck. Then she almost laughed aloud.

Cradling the St. Christopher's medal in his palm, Click smiled and then touched it to his lips. "I see you have a new talisman," he teased her, his voice low and husky.

But before Cassidy could make any reply, Click's mouth moved from the medal to one of her nipples, and explanations seemed superfluous. The touch of his lips and tongue seemed to shoot an electric spark directly from her breast to her aching center, and her urgency for him flooded her again. Ironically, in all of her fervid fantasies Cassidy had imagined what it would be like to touch

Click, and not what it could be like to have Click touch her. She cupped one hand behind his head, her fingers carding into his thick, curling hair.

The ground was spongy but damp, littered with leafy humus. A small cloud of insects had been disturbed by their movements amid the bushes, and nearby branches intruded. But Cassidy didn't care. Click's hands spread across her bare back, caressing her even as his lips and tongue and teeth attended first one nipple and then the other. She endured the stimulation as long as possible, until she was so close to the edge of climax that she could hardly force herself to stop him. Then she closed her fingers around his hair, slowly but firmly drawing his head back. Her nipple popped from his mouth with an audible smack.

Click's expression was heavy-lidded, heated, vaguely puzzled. But as Cassidy pushed him down onto his back, he went without resistance. And when her fingers skimmed over the buttons on his trousers, opening them, he lifted his hips so that she could tug off his pants. At the same time Cassidy's head lowered toward him, Click's hands reached for her, gently digging into her hair.

Sprawled amid the brush, a detritus of dry twigs and pebbles beneath them and dead leaves sticking to their perspiring skin, the minor inconveniences of their surroundings never even entered Cassidy's mind. When she touched him, she heard the sharp intake of Click's breath. When he tried to pull her face away, she fought him for a moment. Then, dazed with desire, she relented, even though she lacked the coherency to be of much assistance in Click's hastily graceless effort to strip down her trousers.

Their skins slick with perspiration and saliva, his larger body rode easily over hers. His mouth seeking hers again, he held himself back until she was capable of guiding him in. Even then, he would have been careful and gentle, at least at first, had not Cassidy bucked demandingly beneath him, impatiently overwhelming his control. They both had been brought too close to consummation for the act to be prolonged; but there was another sort of satisfaction, deep and fiery, in the sheer ferocity of their release.

And afterward, locked with him, tightly embracing him to hold him deep even after he was spent, Cassidy came to believe indelibly what Click had assured her.

Whatever might happen, she would never forget this man.

Cassidy was still lying with her head resting on Click's chest when the first drizzle began to fall. Like everything else beyond the immediate boundaries of their bodies, the gathering greenish gloom and the distant grumble of thunder had faded from their awareness during what had happened between them. And so it was a bit of a surprise to Cassidy when she felt the warm mist sprinkle over her bare, sticky skin.

Click didn't give any immediate indication of stirring; his only movements remained the gradually easing rise and fall of his chest and the gentle carding of his fingers through the damp hair at the nape of Cassidy's neck. And if there had truly been such a thing as an alchemist of time, she thought, her mind still pleasantly muzzy and her body still utterly sated, she would have put in her request to freeze that moment forever, so they wouldn't have to go on and would never have to part.

A random rise of breeze blew over them then, spilling the accumulating droplets of water from the brush overhead and carrying a spatter of heavier rain. Click reluctantly lifted his head, one hand shielding his eyes from the increasing drizzle. The sky had become the malignant color of an old bruise, and the tops of the cypress trees dipped spasmodically in another sudden gust of air.

Cassidy unwillingly raised her face from the solid warmth of Click's chest and met his eyes. He was about to speak, and she knew what he was going to say. What was worse, she would have had to agree with him, even though she had no desire to move so much as an arm or a leg from the lush intimacy of their mutual sprawl. But before Click could speak, a sharp booming sound reverberated through the humid air.

Not thunder, Cassidy recognized immediately, even as she and Click both jerked up into sitting positions. Her head was cocked, casting for the direction of the sound's origin, when the second crack of gunfire broke the thick sultriness of the coming storm.

Click swiftly gained his feet, turning as unerringly as a hunting dog toward the unmistakable sound. "It's coming from the swamp," he said, reaching down to give her a hand up.

The sudden disturbance had left Cassidy somewhat disoriented, and as Click lifted her to her feet, her first thought was of Shad. But she was almost positive that Shad didn't have a gun, and Click's weapon was still secure in the inside pocket of his vest. And that vest was still laying on the ground, along with all the rest of their scattered clothing.

The third shot made Cassidy flinch involuntarily. She looked up at Click, her brow furrowing. "Who the hell could be shooting in the swamp?" she asked him. But even as the words left her mouth, Cassidy could have provided for herself the only possible answer.

"Valerie," Click said.

Chapter 23 ◀▥

The clumsy urgency with which Cassidy's clothing had been removed had nothing on the frantic haste with which she then fumbled to get it back on. The hammering of her heart and the sudden sour dryness in her mouth served as graphic evidence of the adrenaline push that rushed through her at the significance of the gunshots. Struggling to tug on her pants over her sticky thighs, Cassidy threw Click an anxious glance.

"It can't be Val," she objected, wrestling with the buttons on the fly. "Those shots were much too close to have come from the end of the Spine."

Click was either slightly more limber or more composed than Cassidy, for he had already donned his clothing and was jerking on his boots. Without pausing, he said, "At least halfway across the marsh would be my estimate." One sharp stamp of his foot forced on his second boot, and he abruptly stooped to scoop up Cassidy's. Thrusting them at her, he added, "The captain still seems to have a predilection for disobeying orders."

Confusion only made Cassidy's movements more awkward; she hopped about, trying to pull her damp boots onto her feet without benefit of socks. "What orders?" she asked, just as she staggered sideways, hard enough to have fallen had Click not been there to grab her arm.

"Last night after the warden disappeared," Click said, "I changed the signal flag." He steadied Cassidy as she tackled her second boot. "Valerie wasn't supposed to enter the swamp at all without our signal to go ahead."

Cassidy's head jerked up. "Then what the hell is she doing in the marsh?" she demanded. "And why is she shooting?"

Seeing that Cassidy had gotten the second boot at least nominally onto her foot, Click began to tow her after him. "I would hate to guess," he tossed off over his shoulder as he started to plow forward through the brush.

"Wait a minute!" Cassidy protested, tripping as she tried to keep up with his prodigious pace. "Shouldn't we go back to . . . ?"

Responding to both the plaintive tone of Cassidy's voice and the obvious difficulty she was having in trying to match his haste, Click first slowed and then came to a complete halt on the narrow rut of the deer track. There was apology in his eyes, even if he didn't speak it. "The deer paths lead right down to the north side of the point of the forest," he quickly explained. "It's rough going, but it still will be much faster than going all the way back to the valley and taking the other trail." He paused, easing his firm grip on Cassidy's bare forearm and slipping his hand down to mesh with hers. He squeezed it gently. "Stay right behind me," he said. Then he swiftly bent forward, briefly catching her by the nape of the neck and emphatically joining his mouth with hers.

When Click released her, it was so abruptly that Cassidy almost stumbled forward into him. He gave her one last look, a fleeting flash of fire from those umber eyes, an echo of the fervid union that they had shared. Then he was thrusting forward again through the brush. Forcing her protesting legs into action, Cassidy plunged after him. Less than a minute later, the rapid retort of two more gunshots goaded her on to even greater effort.

Tripping over the uneven ground as she dodged the whipping branches swept aside by Click's precipitous passage, Cassidy vainly tried to make some sense of what was happening. She had no problem understanding why Click had changed the signal flag at the edge of the swamp. Considering what had happened to the warden, Cassidy didn't exactly relish the thought of unexpectedly confronting the captain of his Troopers. But despite Click's somewhat jaundiced assessment of Valerie's obedience, Cassidy still had difficulty understanding why the woman had so summarily disobeyed a clear order to hold her position. And if she and Becky and Allen were already in the middle of the swamp, then what the hell were they shooting at?

What the hell do you think? her inner voice mocked sarcastically.

Momentarily distracted by that chilling realization, Cassidy was almost blinded by the backlash of a slapping branch. *Monsters*— and Valerie was trying to *shoot* them.

Click had not been exaggerating when he'd said that the path to the swamp would be rough going. Cassidy wasn't even sure if they were still on a trail, or if Click had just plunged willy-nilly right into the undergrowth. It was all she could do to keep his back in sight, and she quickly found it hopeless to try to match his furious pace. Her hair and clothing were so drenched with perspiration that she hardly even noticed when the fine drizzle, which had been falling sporadically since they had heard the first shots, changed into a fitful spattering of harder drops of rain. The thunder and lightning, which had been faint and distant when they had been lying amid the bushes, was rapidly drawing nearer.

Cassidy and Click had dodged and swerved so much along the way that by the time they reached the boggy swath of reeds marking the deer's watering place at the edge of the swamp, she was no longer certain exactly how they'd gotten there. As the dripping waist-high reeds slapped against their legs, and their boots began to sink into the soft wet muck, Click turned back to Cassidy and grasped her arm again.

"Be careful," he cautioned her. "The ground can be treacherous here." Click pulled her along after himself, as gently as his haste would permit. Cassidy was impressed to find that he didn't even sound out of breath as he continued, "You see that topped-off pine there, just across this bog? Just beyond that is the point and the area the monsters demolished."

Shaking her saturated hair back out of her eyes, Cassidy was able to pick out the pine tree. Click kept hustling her along over the spongy ground, the thick growth of rushes and sedge grass forming a tangled barrier that kept tripping them up. But at least where the reeds and sedge grew, the underlying footing was firm enough to support their weight. Cassidy recalled all of the times the mare had carried her over ground just that boggy without even checking her pace. The horse . . .

Cassidy stumbled, her arm almost jerked from Click's grasp as she tried to spin around. *Dragonfly!* But to Cassidy's mingled sense of relief and dismay, she realized that the horse was nowhere near. Either she had remained where they had left her, at the end of the deer path, or she had returned to their camp. In either case, she probably had been smart enough to get out of the rain, which was beginning to drive heavily. And the powerful grip of Click's hand kept Cassidy slogging steadily after him, with no time to fret about the horse as her soaked boots sucked across the wind-whipped reeds at the edge of the slough.

When they reached the topped-off pine tree and rounded the point of land, the full brunt of the thunderstorm hit them. For a moment Cassidy had to squeeze her eyes shut against the sudden hard pelting of the gusting rain. As she stumbled up behind Click, she used his body as a crude windbreak. She had to blink furiously just to clear her vision. But when she tried to go forward, she was stymied by Click's immobility.

He had stopped there on the very edge of the little peninsula, the northernmost border of the site of the monsters' destruction. But it was not the soggy, tuffeted ground beneath their feet that made him pause, nor was it the rucked-up and littered stretch of higher land that lay ahead. As Cassidy took an unsteady step around Click, past the shelter of his shoulders, she saw what had brought him to such an abrupt halt.

Squinting into the pouring rain, Cassidy's panning gaze froze. No more than a hundred yards out into the swamp, Valerie, Becky, and Allen stood waist deep in the turbulent water of the vast marsh. They obviously were still on the relatively firm ground of the submerged Snake's Spine, but that was the only certainty in their position. The captain held her pistol in both hands, lifted high over her head. And around the three of them, in an uneven ring, their gleaming black bodies fluttering like a carousel of huge animated rubber mats, were at least a dozen of the bizarre swamp creatures.

For a few moments, Cassidy was too stupefied to even move. She watched as one of the big disclike creatures abruptly reformed itself, swiftly rolling into its cylindrical shape and then disappearing beneath the surface of the water. Valerie drew back, lowering the weapon she had held over her head. The captain had barely aimed before the sharp cracks of two more gunshots, squeezed off in rapid succession, reverberated across the swamp.

The surface of the marsh erupted in a tremendous spray of fouled water, dark liquid the color and consistency of old motor oil. Valerie, Becky, and Allen all staggered backward, nearly knocked off their feet by the impact of the explosive gout of fluid.

Cassidy lurched forward without thought. Only Click calling out her name, in a tone commanding enough to make her hesitate momentarily, caused her to look back.

"Cassidy, wait!" he insisted. "We'll get the others and—"

"No!" she countermanded immediately. "Stay here—stay out of the water! Those things won't hurt me."

Cassidy no longer had any reason to believe that was true, but she would have said anything to convince Click not to enter the swamp with her. She could hear other voices calling then, still distant but approaching. She didn't need to turn and look to know that the gunshots had drawn Shad, Rowena, and Kevin, as well. But it was imperative that they not have any more people in the water. And while Cassidy had no idea whether the weird matlike monsters would attack her, she was reasonably certain of one thing: If she went out into the marsh, at least she would be able to deflect them from her besieged friends.

The stretch of ground that the monsters' previous rampage had savaged was like an obstacle course, littered with shattered wood and leaves, the footing rutted and slick from the rain. Cassidy scrambled across it with desperate urgency, nearly falling several times. By the time she reached the bank of the marsh, her soggy trouser legs were torn and filthy and she was bleeding from several cuts on her hands and arms. She staggered out into the knee-deep water, her eyes still locked on the trio trapped by the circling creatures.

"Don't move!" Cassidy shouted to them, her voice breaking hoarsely. "And *don't shoot!*"

Cassidy couldn't even be certain if they had heard her over the rumble of the thunder and the rising sough of the wind. As she plunged out into the swamp, the sky appeared nearly the same bilious dark-green color as the opaque surface of the rain-pocked water, and the drumming downpour fell like a waterfall from the low swollen bellies of the gray clouds.

From that distance, Valerie, Becky, and Allen all appeared uninjured, if somewhat the worse for wear. Their bodies were blackened with the liquid remnants of the creatures the captain had succeeded in shooting. Glistening gobbets of something thick, black, and tenacious covered their heads, arms, and torsos. But in spite of a renewed spate of flapping and wet fluttering from the monsters that still surrounded them, all three of them stood still, Valerie again bracing her pistol in a two-handed grip over her head.

Glancing back over her shoulder as she waded deeper, Cassidy saw Shad, Rowena, and Kevin emerging from the woods to join Click on the rucked-up stretch of land. But she deliberately turned back toward the swamp. And when she turned back, she saw *them.*

Cassidy was oddly relieved that Valerie, Becky, and Allen were looking in her direction, toward the peninsula, and had not yet seen what had appeared behind them. Across the rain-swept surface of the marsh, so vast that they seemed to fill the entire breadth of the storm-torn sky, streamed a roiling squadron of the huge coillike air monsters. How could anything that massive have just materialized out of nowhere? She wondered in a daze as she sloshed to a halt in the murky, thigh-deep water. It was as if they had just dropped out of . . .

Not out of nowhere, Cassidy realized then, dizzy with the sudden comprehension: Out of *no-when* . . .

She swayed unsteadily in the driving rain, squinting up against the deluge at the gathering mass of the giant apparitions that were assembling overhead. The boom of thunder rolled again across the water, a thick, percussive sound that seemed to be trapped between the bulk of the creatures above and the surface of the marsh below. Lightning sparked fitfully between the gigantic bodies.

They've followed me from the very beginning, she thought in amazement, *from that place between the two worlds where time had slipped just so slightly out of joint* . . . She stretched out her arms, her fingertips just brushing the rain-stippled surface of the greenish water. *And when they disappear* . . .

A harsh shout from Allen jerked Cassidy from the maelstrom of her thoughts. At first she thought he had cried out because he had seen the monstrous creatures rolling overhead. Then she realized Allen wasn't even looking up; he was looking in her direction, and he was gesturing vehemently. The cry had been meant as a warning to her.

The flotilla of flattened monsters that had been circling Valerie and the others like renegade Indians circling a hapless wagon train had vanished. Or rather, they had moved. A broad tracery of surging wakes marked the progress of the sleekly reconstructed creatures across the turbid water of the swamp, directly toward Cassidy. Torn from her study of the enormous looping coils in the air, she staggered sideways when she felt the sinuous caress of something very swift and winding against her lower legs.

Cassidy's feet were suddenly jerked out from beneath her, tumbling her backward into the marsh's tepid embrace. The last thing she heard before the water closed over her head was someone shouting her name. But she couldn't tell who it had been.

Like the formless envelopment of some gelatinous mass, the inky flaps of one of the swamp monsters enfolded Cassidy. She felt her lungs burn in protest. Trying to kick free of its suffocating darkness was like trying to escape from a living sinkhole, and the more she struggled, the more dizzily desperate grew her need for air. *I can't die like this!* she thought indignantly. *I have to go back and save the warden!*

And then, as if in ironic counterpoint to that declaration, the world just *stopped.*

Freed at least temporarily of the painful imperative of having to breathe, Cassidy floated in the gellid darkness of the nontime. All around her in that frozen stillness, she sensed a vague myriad of presences, great masses of *something*, trapped in the unfathomable vastness of the *nothing* that comprised that incredible interzone. And as before, everything that was in her raged to pull free of that smothering void, to tear herself away from that terrifying emptiness and to reemerge, struggling and choking, back into the real world again.

Except that world was not the *real* world . . . and the Slow World, the world that was real, lay on its opposite side.

The insight was so staggering that it did not take much effort for Cassidy suddenly to cease her resistance. Here was the path she had sought for so long—not dreams, not drugs, but *this*. Could it have been what the creatures had been trying to accomplish all along?

Cassidy no longer tried to pull away from the numbing untime. Instead, with all that she could summon of her will, she went forth to embrace it. And as she did so, she felt the most curious sense of completion. Then, with a disorienting lurch, the world began to *move* again.

When it moved, everything began to spin, twirling in a frenzy, like a huge whirlpool that was sucking her down, down, down— and all around her roiled the coiling black shapes of the monsters, no longer fearsome things, spinning with her, faster and faster until—

Cathy glanced both ways before she stepped out onto the pavement. She led the gray mare across the road to where her truck and horse trailer were parked along the shoulder on the opposite side. The horse's shod hooves clattered hollowly on the wet asphalt.

One of the things Cathy had always hated about shows at Templar's farm was the woefully inadequate space for the entrants to park their rigs. They had a great ring, but having to park up on the roadway was a pain in the ass. And the fine drizzle that had been falling all day hadn't helped matters any, miring several cars and trucks in the narrow muddy field behind the show ring. But Templar's had always been good about including the special noncompetitive classes for the riding therapy students in their program of events, and Cathy found it difficult to say no whenever Joel asked her to haul Dragonfly to one of their horse shows.

Working with the special students from Reiners Center had made Cathy quite dogmatic about the use of safety hard hats for any of her riding pupils. So when she discovered that they were going to come up one helmet short for the upcoming exhibition class, she immediately offered to make a quick trip back to where her battered Ford Ranger pickup and horse trailer were parked, to fetch the extra hard hat she always carried along with the rest of the clutter on the floor of the seldom-used passenger side of the cab.

With the mare's reins slung over her arm, Cathy struggled to locate the elusive truck key in the snug confines of her wet, skin-tight jeans. Behind her, Dragonfly snorted in either boredom or impatience. Finally snagging the key between her fingertips, Cathy glanced up over her shoulder—and froze.

Barreling over the crest of the low hill a hundred feet up the road from where she stood, plowing through the gray mist like a runaway locomotive, hurtled a huge black shape. A split second later, the hapless driver of the speeding semi truck and trailer apparently saw Cathy and the gray mare, partially out in the lane of traffic.

Even in that moment of high panic, Cathy was fully cognizant that only the slightest deviation in the huge truck's course would easily have caused it to bypass her and the horse. But for some reason she would never know, the driver of the semi made a horrendous misjudgment. Perhaps he thought the mare would shy in fear and leap into the path of his rig. Perhaps he merely overestimated either the capacity of his vehicle or his own skill in handling it. Whatever his reason, the semi's driver hit both his wheel and his brakes, belatedly attempting to temper his imprudent speed as he swerved to give the woman and her horse a wider berth.

Moving at the elongated pace of a nightmare, Cathy began to swing around. Before her horrified eyes, the massive black bullet shape of the jackknifing semi spun toward her across the slick pavement, and she instinctively braced herself for the impact.

But Cathy never felt that crushing blow; nor could she even remember it ever having happened. The bulk of the gray mare's body swung against her, flattening her against the cab of the Ranger. The last thing she saw as her head cracked back against the pickup's window, crazing the glass into a million glittering fragments, was the upflung wave of the horse's mane, like a spray of silver against the dark looming mass of the skidding semi.

As she swam back toward the surface of that black pool of nothingness that had engulfed her, it was as if the long-deferred pain of every injury she had ever sustained was suddenly being visited upon her at once. She found herself recumbent, but when she tried to stir, she couldn't even move her limbs. Her head pounded blindingly, and even with the fiercest of efforts she couldn't force open her eyelids. Her first aborted attempt at speech ended with a dry, raw swallow.

Gritting her teeth, she swallowed again, the pain like a gulp of acid. She still was unable to open her eyes, but she could finally move one of her arms, slightly and clumsily.

"Dragonfly . . ." she whispered, her voice a husky croak.

From the darkness there was a wordless cry of astonishment, and almost simultaneous with it, the tinny cacophony of several hollow metal objects hitting a hard surface and then bouncing and skittering across it.

"Oh, my *God*!" a woman's voice exclaimed. Then she heard the same voice shouting, breathless as it rapidly receded, "She's awake! Call Dr. Hunt—*she's awake*!"

Chapter 24 ◀||||

"You are one incredibly lucky young woman," the doctor said as he bent over her, the focused brilliance of his ophthalmoscope's light boring into her defenseless eyes.

Luck was not an attribute either Cathy Delaney or Cassidy would have connected with her current situation. She blinked rebelliously against the glare of the light. It was an act that had become simple enough once they had removed the adhesive strips which had held her lids closed to protect her corneas from dehydration when she'd been unconscious.

"Please, look straight ahead," the doctor cajoled. "We're almost done."

"We" may have been almost done, but she was just getting started. Literally squirming with impatience, she tested the fettering encumbrance of the heavy plaster casts that encased both of her legs from hip to toe and the splint that covered her left arm from elbow to wrist. Multiple long bone fractures, two crushed spinal discs, a ruptured spleen, and a cracked skull that had put her in a coma for over two months: *Yeah, how in-fucking-credibly lucky can you get?* she thought.

"Did you call Reiners?" she demanded impatiently. Her voice was still a grating croak, unfamiliar even to her own ears.

Dr. Hunt, St. Ann's head neurologist, and at that moment still one genuinely amazed man, moved the ophthalmoscope to her other eye. "We've notified the Benders," he said reassuringly. "They're probably here already, waiting out in reception."

Cathy realized that even though Joel and Cindy Bender weren't actually related to her in any way, they must have been listed as her next of kin on her medical records. In the major upheaval created by her unexpected emergence from her coma, and the flurry of medical activity that had attended it, Cathy was dismayed to discover that she had barely even given Joel and Cindy a thought. She'd been concentrating on focusing all of her fragile physical energy, and all of her considerable stubbornness, on her demands regarding Andy Greene.

Dr. Hunt had proven surprisingly tolerant of his newly wakened patient's irritability. Fiftyish, with his neatly groomed silver hair and carefully manicured hands, the neurologist looked like a man who paid a lot of attention to details. But he had seemed willing to overlook a few in this case, such as the inexplicable streaks of black slime that he had discovered on her body, and the silver medal around her neck that all of the nurses swore they had never seen before. Most of all he had been willing to overlook her intractable attitude.

"What did they say at Reiners?" Cathy persisted the moment Hunt straightened up. "Did anyone reach Marty Terrell?"

Lowering the ophthalmoscope, the doctor just stared at the woman lying before him, a woman who had, up until about forty-five minutes earlier, spent almost eighty days in what could only have been medically and legally classified as a persistent vegetative state. That she was conscious at all, much less lucid and in fact downright gratingly determined about a course of action, still astonished him. He had the distinct feeling that, if not for the bulky casts that physically anchored her to the bed, she would have already been up and on her way, on her odd crusade to reach Reiners Center. Even at that, Hunt half expected her to try to heave herself off the bed at any moment, if she didn't get the answers she was demanding.

"Listen, Cathy," Hunt said reasoningly, holding up his free hand in a placating gesture, "we still need to run an EEG and some other—"

Cathy's head and shoulders literally did come up off the bed then, requiring Hunt to restrain her physically as he hastily tried to reassure her.

"But I'm going to let the Benders in to see you first," he said, "if—*if*—you promise me that I'm not going to have to sedate you to keep you from irreparably damaging about fifty thousand dollars' worth of orthopedic surgery!"

Subsiding slightly, Cathy settled back down onto her pillow. She glared up at Hunt, only mildly perplexed by the fact that although the man had been caring for her for months, she had for all practical purposes just met him. "What about Reiners?" she reiterated doggedly.

Returning her stare with an expression that only imperfectly managed to conceal his growing ambivalence over her newly regained consciousness, Hunt said, "I'll check."

She let out a loud, impatient sigh as he turned and, grabbing up her chart from the foot of the bed, made good his escape from the room.

Less than a minute later, the door swung open again. Cathy was totally disarmed by her reaction to the man and woman who swept into her room. She knew that what Joel uttered was her name; but the sound that she made as she reached out to him with her one good arm was inchoate, and as he engulfed her in an awkward embrace, her throat thickened and closed as emotion overcame her.

God, how could I have ever forgotten him? she thought in amazement and dismay. As her face pressed into the rough wool of his shirt, the smell of him—horses and fabric softener and the faint hint of auto exhaust—filled her nostrils. And even when she had remembered him, how could she have failed to recognize how much he reminded her of Allen? A big cheerful bear of a man, Joel could have been the sheriff's brother, even if his hair and beard were darker and he wore round steel-rimmed glasses.

When they finally separated, Joel made an embarrassed swipe at his wet cheeks as he pulled back. Cindy joined him, crowding alongside Cathy's bed. A girlishly slim redhead barely half her husband's size, she made no attempt to check the tears that freely streamed from her own eyes. Cindy clutched at Cathy's one unemcumbered hand, shaking her head in mute and joyful amazement.

"Cathy, I still can't believe it!" she finally exclaimed. "And to think that we—" Her expression suddenly crumpled, alarm and horror transforming her delicate heart-shaped face. "Oh my God, Cathy—we've been trying to—"

Sharply squeezing Cindy's fingers, Cathy cut her off with a vehement shake of her head. "No! No, you did exactly what I'd asked you to do," she said firmly.

As he also comprehended how close they had unwittingly come to terminating Cathy's life, Joel looked positively stricken. "Christ—the hearing is scheduled for the day after tomorrow!" he rasped in a shocked whisper.

But Cathy seemed utterly unconcerned with how close she'd come to death. "Forget that," she said, jerking on Cindy's hand to get the woman's total attention. "I need to talk to Marty or someone else from Reiners about Andy, and all I'm getting from these people here is a runaround." She fixed Joel with an imperative look. "I've got to see him, Joel—*now*. It's a matter of life and death."

Under any other circumstances, her pronouncement might have sounded hopelessly melodramatic; but given the high drama of her own situation, neither Joel nor Cindy seemed inclined to take Cathy's statement with anything less than complete seriousness. And yet they both seemed oddly uncomfortable with her demand, as if she'd just mentioned a particularly sensitive subject.

Joel leaned in closer over Cathy, laying his hand on top of Cindy's and over Cathy's. "Something's happened with Andy," he began, softly but uneasily. "Ever since your accident, he's been affected by . . . losing you. They tried bringing him in to see you a few times, but that only seemed to make it worse. He started regressing . . ." Shifting slightly, his reluctance palpable, Joel concluded, "Just yesterday he completely flipped out. Terrell said Andy—"

"I *know* that!" Cathy interrupted him, startling both Joel and Cindy more by her vehemence than by the incongruity of what she had just said. Seeing the worry and alarm on their faces, Cathy tried to throttle down her monumental anxiety and impatience. "That's why I have to see him," she explained in a quiet but intense voice.

Joel and Cindy exchanged a dubious glance. "I don't know, Cath," he said, trying to be reasonable. "They've got him pretty heavily sedated; I guess there wasn't anything they could do with him."

Struggling to draw a breath past the painful constriction that seized her chest at those words, Cathy fought to remain calm. "It's a matter of life and death, Joel," she repeated in a soft, implacable whisper, her hand tightening into a cramped knot beneath theirs. "I don't care how you get him here, just do it. Or I swear *I'll* go to *him*—even if I have to check myself out of here right now and hire Federal Express to haul me over to Reiners."

Joel stared down glumly at her, caught somewhere between dismay and resignation. Then he exhaled loudly, his capitulation obvious. "Try UPS," he said wryly, looking into the face of the most stubborn woman he had ever known. "Their bulk rate is cheaper."

Cathy ultimately ended up getting her way by ruthlessly and shamelessly trading upon every bit of leverage she could exert over both Dr. Hunt and the director of Patient Outreach Programs at Reiners Center, Martin Terrell. First of all, her miraculous recovery had caught Marty so completely by surprise that he was predisposed to listen to her impassioned telephone plea. He was also quick to admit that, autistic or not, Andy Greene had definitely been emotionally traumatized by witnessing Cathy's accident, and that the young man's condition had deteriorated since that fateful day. He didn't even dispute the likelihood that seeing how Cathy had so amazingly recovered could prove therapeutically beneficial for Andy. But he balked at her insistence that she be allowed to see Andy immediately, forcing Cathy to resort to blatant coercion.

"Maybe another day won't make any difference to Andy," Cathy said, awkwardly cradling the phone's receiver with her good hand. "But it makes a difference to *me*. I need this, Marty—I need to see Andy *now*."

Dr. Hunt might have been deluded into thinking that he held the final authority over his patient's activities, but he was even more lopsidedly outgunned than Terrell by Cathy's feckless determination. All of Hunt's threats to sedate her, to prohibit all visitors, to put her under guard, were just empty noise. Cathy knew damned well that short of checking herself out of St. Ann's— something that she actually declared herself ready to do at one point in the heated debate—there was nothing she could have requested of him that would have compelled the neurologist to endanger her physical or mental health at that stage in her stunning resurrection.

"At least wait until tomorrow morning, then," Hunt argued wearily. "Let us finish the basic—"

"This can't wait until tomorrow," Cathy said with finality. Valerie and Click would probably have killed each other by tomorrow. "You get Andy in here now, or I swear to God I'm out of here."

Cindy Bender just spread her hands placatingly, trying to cinch Hunt's acquiescence. "I told you," Cathy heard Joel mutter under his breath as he and the neurologist were leaving the room. "Why do you think Terrell gave up?"

As the door clicked softly shut behind them, Cathy slumped back onto her pillow, her eyes squeezing shut. *God, let this work*, she silently prayed. *Let me give both of them their lives back again.*

Still unexpectedly moved by how overcome with emotion the normally laconic Marty Terrell had become when he had actually seen her conscious again, Cathy gripped his hand and looked up into the tall black man's angular face. "I need to see him *alone*, Marty," she said emphatically.

"You know I can't do that, Cath," Marty said, visibly uncomfortable with having to refuse her anything at that point. "He's on Thorazine; it's against center policy for me to—"

She cut him off with an urgent tightening of her fingers around his. "It was against center policy just bringing him over here," she reminded him. "Please, Marty—just for a few minutes. After everything that's happened, I just need a few minutes alone with him."

Obviously torn, Terrell glanced back toward the closed door of her room. Cathy knew that just beyond that door waited the one man in that world who she most desperately needed to see, the man to whom she owed the debt of her freedom.

"Please, Marty," she whispered.

Although Marty Terrell looked more like a veteran of pro basketball, he had actually spent a dozen years in the Marine Corps before he had gone back to college and earned degrees in psychology and business management. His volunteer work with the mentally handicapped had ultimately led him to join the staff at Reiners. None of his previous experience, however, had prepared him to deny Cathy Delaney's request. He looked down at their joined hands, his as dark and rawboned as hers was pale and slender. Finally he just shook his head in utter capitulation.

"You've got five minutes," he muttered, pulling free of her grasp and turning toward the door. "And I'm going to be right outside the whole damned time," he warned.

In those few moments Cathy was alone, waiting, she gave fleeting thought to how bad she must look lying there in bed, immobilized, pale-faced, her hair lank across the pillow. At least the blanket covered the casts on her legs, and the splint on her arm was—

"And there's a thing on your arm"—

She suddenly realized the laughable irony of her reflexive self-consciousness about her appearance. Both Andy and the warden had already seen the way she looked; there was no need for vanity.

Then the door to her room swung open again, and Marty was pushing a wheelchair in ahead of him across the threshold, and Cathy could only think of one thing.

Pausing to close the door behind him, the lanky black man looked up and saw Cathy's face. Interpreting her stunned expression, he said immediately, "It's not as bad as it looks, Cath." He moved forward again, slowly maneuvering the wheelchair along-side her bed. "I'm sorry that we've had to use the Thorazine, but he—"

Cathy interrupted Marty's apologetic explanation with a brisk, dismissive wave of her hand. Her visible shock had not come from any alarm about the condition of the young man who was slumped so lifelessly in the wheelchair. Rather, she had been caught completely off guard by how utterly Andy Greene's appearance mimicked the state in which she'd last seen the warden of Horses, just before his precipitous disappearance from his own world. In almost every detail, right down to the lax hang of his arms, the vagrant sweep of his forelock of hair, and the way his chin nearly rested upon his chest, Andy's sedation appeared identical to the warden's drug-induced stupor.

"It's okay," she told Terrell. "Just leave us, huh?"

Marty hesitated, looking uneasily from the insensate man sitting strapped in the wheelchair, to Cathy's calm and determined face. His expression was still dubious.

"For Christ's sake, Marty, just *leave* us, will you?" Cathy suddenly snapped at him. "Just give me a few minutes—*I* did this to him!"

Accepting her urgent remorse without knowing the full truth behind it, Marty took a reluctant step backward. "I'll be right outside the door," he reminded her. Cathy made one more sharp gesture of dismissal before he finally backed out of the room.

Although time, as always, was of the essence, Cathy spared a few moments simply to look at the young man who sat so vacantly beside her bed. Part of the reason for her delay was simply to marvel over how exact a replica of the warden Andy really was. But another part of the reason was to gather her courage; because if what she was about to try didn't work, she had absolutely no idea what else to do. When at last she marshaled her resolve and leaned forward in bed to touch him, she was surprised and dismayed to find that she *couldn't*—Marty had left the wheelchair parked a little too far from the bed.

Not knowing if she should laugh or cry, Cathy pushed herself forward against the immobile bulk of her leg casts and stretched out her one good arm to reach as far as she could. Several major muscle groups throbbed in protest, but with an added grunt of effort she was able to snag the free end of the wide web belt that bound Andy's limp body upright. Much to her relief, Marty had been too preoccupied before he had left to have locked the wheels on the chair; and once she grasped the strap, she was able to use it to tow the wheelchair closer. Slowly and carefully, she drew back until the chrome footrests bumped against the metal frame of her bed, putting Andy within her reach. Exhaling shakily, Cathy dropped the strap. Then she lifted her hand and rested it gently upon Andy's motionless forearm.

Even though she was expecting it, the effect was so stunning, so galvanizing, that Cathy almost cried out in sheer relief and joy. Cool brilliance, a veritable explosion of light, washed over her, *through* her, bathing every cell and synapse in the familiar yet amazing flood of luminescence. For a few frozen seconds of time, she was joined with Andy Greene—she *was* Andy Greene. But for the first time there was another presence in the union of light. For the first time she also felt the separate and distinct essence of the warden of Horses. Then, as abruptly as it had erupted, the cascade of illumination was gone, and the man before her suddenly stirred to life.

Cathy leaned forward even farther, her fingers digging into the warm skin of his bare forearm as he lifted his head. Incredibly enough, even though he was blinking and looking about in momentary confusion, he did not appear in the least bit sedated. Then those chocolate-brown eyes settled on her face, and his expression swiftly changed to a heartening compilation of recognition, surprise, and unadulterated elation.

"Cassidy," the warden of Horses said happily, "you did it! You came back!"

It was more than she had dared to hope for. Like the flip side of a lapse, Andy Greene had assumed the persona of the warden. And not only had she been able to reach the warden, he appeared to be entirely cognizant, in spite of the drugging that Andy had endured. He was trying to rise out of the wheelchair and come to her, but he was stymied by the wide web belt that secured him. He had to settle for grasping the rail of her bed and yanking himself closer, close enough for the two of them to mesh in a clumsy but fierce embrace. Burying her face against the sweet-smelling skin of his neck, Cathy clung desperately to him, choking back the sobs that threatened to overcome her. Murmuring some wordless sound of reassurance, the warden held her tightly, gently stroking her hair.

Only one thing could have made her pull away from him again, and that was their old mutual nemesis, time. To her dismay, Cathy realized that they had so little of it then. Lifting her head from his shoulder, she made a futile swipe at her wet eyes and tried to clear the thickness from her throat.

The warden still held her by both upper arms. When he looked across at her, the expression on his face was simply radiant; and when he glanced around the room, it was obvious that he could hardly believe what they had done.

"The blue room!" he said with happy incredulity. "Cassidy, it's exactly as I saw it!" Then he looked directly into her eyes, his voice dropping intently. "And you've really come back."

Loath to destroy the moment, Cathy nevertheless had no choice. "Listen," she said, her voice low but urgent, "you can go back again—you *have* to go back again."

The warden swiftly sobered then, frown lines crossing that smooth, oddly pale face. But to her relief, he understood the exact nature of her concern. "When I came here," he said quietly, "everything was chaos." He hesitated, then admitted, "I wasn't even certain what had happened until just now, until you drew me out."

Cathy's hand grasped his wrist, gripping him even as he hung onto her. "You and Andy can't exist in the same time," she told him earnestly. "It would destroy you both." Her fingers tightened. "But you can go back—and when you do, you'll give him back his life, too."

She could see from the look on the warden's face that he comprehended completely. But there was also a distinct reluctance there, as he realized that by going back without her, he would surely lose his link to the Slow World. He studied her face in silence for a moment, interpreting the particular pain that could be read so easily there. Then he nodded in acquiescence.

"If I let go of Andy," he said softly, "I'll cross back again."

Gripping his wrist even more tightly, Cathy nodded helplessly. "Yes, I think so," she whispered. "If you separate yourself from him, he'll return to his original condition. And when he does, you should exist again in your own world."

The sober scrutiny of those thoughtful brown eyes did not surprise her, but his question did. "Will I ever see you again?" the warden asked her.

Cathy had to drop both her gaze and the grip she had on his wrist to be able to retain her composure then. But her answer surprised her as much as his question had. "I—I don't know," she said.

The slightest curl of a rueful smile shaped the margins of that voluble mouth. "Then I will have to make certain," the warden said quietly, "that I remember you, Cassidy."

The intrusion of a distant sound from outside the room jerked Cathy back to the precariousness of their situation there. Marty might walk in at any moment, and if he saw the man who was then sitting before Cathy's bed, there was no way in hell she would ever be able to explain what was going on. Her arm trembled as she reached for the silver chain that hung around her neck. Clumsily, because the warden still had hold of her, she lifted the St. Christopher's medal over her head and held it out to him. His brows arched quizzically, but he automatically leaned in toward her, like an acolyte seeking her benediction, and she dropped the loop of chain around his neck.

"For luck," she whispered, her voice hoarse with long-pent tears.

He smiled at her then, one last flash of that devastating expression that transformed even Andy's pale face into the countenance of a young king. One of his slender hands lifted from her arm, his fingers gently framing her cheek. "Cassidy," he said, "you have been all the luck a man would ever need."

There was a muffled exchange of voices immediately outside the door, and Cathy tore her eyes away from him for just a moment to glance apprehensively in that direction. Their time was gone then. And when she looked back at him, his hands had already dropped back into his lap, and he was slowly settling into the confines of the wheelchair. He sat calmly but motionlessly, his hands resting limply on his thighs. He held his head up, but his face was an almost perfect mask of utter blankness.

And right before Cathy's eyes, the silver St. Christopher's medal that had been lying on his chest flickered, winked, and then vanished. The warden of Horses had gone, leaving only Andy Greene behind.

And when she looked into his eyes, she thought that perhaps there might still have been something there, some faintest glint of light. But she could not be sure.

Epilogue ⬅||||

The November wind was more than merely bracing, it was biting, and it took most of Cathy Delaney's concentration to steady herself as she crossed the small stretch of sidewalk between the medical complex and the street curb. The casts had been off for only three weeks, and she was still supposed to be using crutches, but she hated the damned things and was stubbornly relying on the less offensive support of a footed aluminum cane. Joel had gone out ahead of her to bring his van around, and as reluctant as she was to have to admit it, she was relieved to see that the vehicle was already pulling up. Although her therapists found her progress remarkable, Cathy was still frustrated daily by how weak and unstable she still was on her feet, and the trips to the rehab center always seemed to wear her out for the whole damned day.

They'd shit bricks—sideways—if they knew I've been getting up on a horse, Cathy thought, with a certain perverse sense of satisfaction, as the dark-blue van drew up alongside the curb in front of her. Joel, her coconspirator in that little bit of unauthorized physical therapy, came trotting around the front of the vehicle, a habitual look of concern etched on his broad bearded face.

"Jeez, Cath, you could have waited inside," he chided as he reached for her arm to assist her.

Cathy thrust the cane at him instead and reached for the door handle herself. "Did you see that Marty and Dr. Hunt both got their copies of my last wishes?" she asked him as she slid the door open.

Joel frowned, visibly struggling to prevent himself from automatically reaching out to give her a boost up. "I did that two days ago," he reminded her, wincing as he watched her propel herself up onto the van's running board, and from there onto the front seat. "I can certainly understand why you wanted to revise your will," he added, a trifle uncomfortably, "but do you really think it's necessary to give a copy of the new one to everyone you know?"

From her perch on the van's high seat, Cathy flashed him a wry look. "Better safe than sorry," she said.

Sliding the door shut, Joel came around to the driver's side and climbed in. He was still frowning, an expression Cathy realized that she had been responsible for keeping more or less permanently planted on that usually genial face. Relenting, she reached across the center well and gave him a gentle poke on the arm.

"Listen, you asshole," she said firmly, "I already told you: You did exactly what I asked you to do. But for obvious reasons, I've changed my mind now. And if anything like this would ever happen to me again, I just want to make it as easy as possible for everyone to know exactly what I'd want done now."

Looking back over his shoulder, Joel edged the van out into a break in the traffic on the busy street. His expression was still entirely too somber for Cathy's liking. "Dr. Hunt said you don't have to worry about any kind of relapse," he said after a moment, obviously ill at ease with the whole subject.

Rather than continue to try to reassure Joel, Cathy abruptly changed topics. "Did you hear anything yet from that guy you know at the University at Charleston?" she asked. "You know, the botanist?"

Equally puzzled by both the shift in the conversation and Cathy's inexplicable interest in his old college buddy from South Carolina, Joel just shrugged. "I talked to his wife," he said. "She said Terry's still down there on that rain forest thing. But he should be back before Christmas."

As they pulled up to a stoplight, Cathy looked through the windshield at the dull gray pall of the wintery sky. "I guess that'll be soon enough," she muttered, rubbing absently at her aching thigh.

Glancing over at her, Joel could not conceal his perplexity at the odd set of priorities that his best friend had adopted since her remarkable return from the near dead. "I still don't understand this sudden interest in botany, Cath," he said. "And those other patients you've been trying to trace down; Dr. Hung told me that you—"

Cathy interrupted him with a gentle punch in the arm. "Light's changed," she pointed out, a split second before the driver behind them leaned on his horn. It was an amazingly *noisy* world, she thought as Joel accelerated again. She had not remembered just how little real silence there was. As Joel drove, she contented herself with watching the impressive array of buildings they passed, strangely fascinated by all the glitzy trappings of modern life that she'd always taken for granted, or even considered a nuisance. Just being able to flick on the lights as she entered a room still continued to strike her afresh as nothing less than a miracle.

Cathy hadn't realized how long she had remained silent, or how deeply she'd been immersed in thought, until Joel cautiously intruded upon her ruminations. "Cindy was talking with her boss again yesterday," he said. "He still thinks that you should seriously reconsider bringing a suit against St. Ann's."

Cindy Bender worked for a firm of lawyers; her boss thought that everyone should reach out and sue someone. Cathy almost said as much, but Joel had been such a brick about everything; she didn't want him to think that she was mocking his and Cindy's honest concern. Toying with the head of her cane, she merely said, "I just don't see the point."

Joel startled Cathy with his sudden vehemence. "The point?" he exclaimed, nearly cutting over into another lane of traffic when he jerked around to stare at her. A car horn blared alongside them, and the irate driver gave Joel the finger. Joel sheepishly flashed the peace sign in return and redevoted himself to his driving for a long moment, composing himself. When he spoke again, his voice was deliberately calm, and he kept his eyes on the road. "The point is that you were in that place for over three weeks after you regained consciousness," he said. "And the day you get out, your doctor tells you that you're *four* weeks' pregnant. That doesn't suggest a lawsuit to you?"

Unconsciously folding one arm over her still-flat abdomen, Cathy reached over and placed the other hand placatingly on Joel's thigh. "What do you want me to do," she said, "demand child support from every man in the place?"

Cathy could almost hear Joel gritting his teeth, and she regretted her flip tone. "Cath," he said, "someone in that place took advantage of you—when you were unconscious! I just don't understand how you can—"

"I'll think about it, okay?" she said, not adding that she had absolutely no intention of suing anyone, least of all St. Ann's. As she felt Joel relax fractionally, the tensed muscles of his leg easing beneath her hand, she gave his thigh a playful squeeze. "You still going to that horse auction this weekend?" she asked him.

Effectively distracted, at least for the moment, he gave her a quick hopeful glance. "Why? You want to come along?"

"I might," she said. "If I want to have a horse ready to use in the riding therapy program by the time those quacks tell me that I can ride again, I guess I'd better start looking."

The almost palpable relief that exuded from the big bearded man beside her convinced Cathy that she had said exactly the right thing at just the right time. And as he drove on, the miles rolling by as they left the city behind and traded the six-lane freeway for winding blacktopped rural roads, Joel talked eagerly and at great length about possible prospects for her, horses he had heard about or had already even looked at, all in readiness for the day when Cathy Delaney would be ready to begin again.

Sitting across the seat from him, contentedly quiescent for the time being, Cathy merely listened with half an ear as she watched the empty fields and dark leafless trees flash by. She had been serious about going to the auction, but she was not especially concerned about training a new schooling horse. Her thoughts were on a particular mare, and there was not room in her heart for another. Her thoughts were also on a particular man and on the nascent scrap of life within her that bound her to him. That bond had spanned the temporal gap between two worlds, and the child's very existence had imbued her with proof of the possibility of one day crossing that breach again and regaining the world that lay beyond it.

KAREN RIPLEY

Published by Del Rey Books.
Available in your local bookstore.